CROWN
IMPERIAL

by

J. Delves-Broughton

FABER AND FABER LTD
24 Russell Square
London

First published in mcmxlix
by Faber and Faber Limited
24 Russell Square London W.C.1
Second impression August mcmxlix
Printed in Great Britain by
Latimer Trend & Co Ltd Plymouth

Susan Stewart. Menzies

CROWN IMPERIAL

To

Judith Listowel

"The Love I dedickate to yr Ladyeshippe
is without ende; whereof this Booke is but a
superfluous Moietie. Yr honourable Disposition not the Worthe of my untutor'd
Lynes makes it assur'd of acceptance. What
I have done is yrs; what I have to doe is yrs,
being parte in al I have, devoted yrs. Were
my Worthe greater my Dutye wolde show
greater, meantime as it is, it is bounde to yr
Ladyeshippe, to whom I wish long Lyfe still
lengthen'd with Happienesse."

Author's Note

Shakespeare's England   *Clarendon Press*
English Social History (the two chapters
    on Shakespeare's England)   *Prof. G. M. Trevelyan*
Elizabethan Journals   *G. B. Harrison*

Extracts from: *The Calendar of State Papers, Calendar of Spanish State Papers, Camden's Annales, Stow's Annales, Nugæ Antiquæ* (Harington) *Fragmenta Regalia,* (Naunton) *Sidney Papers,* biographies of many famous men of the Elizabethan Age, together with much prose, verse and drama of the age, too numerous to be listed.

Author's Note

Shakespeare's England — Clarendon Press
English Social History (the two chapters
on Shakespeare's England) — Prof. G. M. Trevelyan
Elizabethan Journals — G. B. Harrison

Extracts from: *The Calendar of State Papers; Calendar of Spanish State Papers; Camden's Annales; Stow's Annales; Nugae Antiquae (Harington) Progresses Regalia (Nauton) Sidney Papers,* biographies of many famous men of the Elizabethan Age together with much prose, verse and drama of the age, too numerous to be listed.

"The glory of the name of a King may deceive those princes who know not how to rule, as gilded pills may deceive a sick patient, but I am none of those princes, for I know that the Commonwealth is to be governed to the good and advantage of them that are entrusted to me, who will have to give an account one day to a Higher Prince of my Stewardship. . . .

. . . And though you have had, and may have, many mightier and wiser princes sitting in this seat, yet you never had, nor shall have any that will love you better."

Queen Elizabeth's last speech to the House of Commons

"She was the wisest woman that ever was, for she understood the interests and dispositions of all the princes in her time, and was so perfect in the knowledge of her own realm, that no Councillor she had could tell her anything she did not know before."

Her principal Minister, Lord Burghley

"She was more than a man, and, in troth, sometimes less than a woman."

His son and successor, Sir Robert Cecil

"—what a pretty business it is to have to treat with this woman, who I think must have a hundred thousand devils in her body—"

Alvarez de Quadra, Ambassador of Spain

Chapter One

Sir William Cecil rode towards Hatfield in a steady drizzle of rain. The sky hung low over the bare, black branches of the trees, as opaque and grey as pewter; nearly all the leaves lay sodden underfoot, quietening the passage of wayfarers. Only a faint creaking of the saddle leather and a faint jingle from the bits, marked the movement of the two riders, the solitary servant half a length behind his master. Sir William, tightly wrapped in his cloak, had hardly spoken six words to his man since they had left London; his whole being was consumed in thought, and he seemed to follow the now familiar route with a sort of automatic instinct. Only once he looked up, frowning. Some two hundred yards ahead of him, a troop of horse swept into the main road, scabbards clanking against spurs, hoofs pounding up the flying mud, gay colour flaunting against the grey November landscape. He knew well enough where they were going and their object. Certainly it was the same as his, but his careful passionless nature deplored the swagger and ostentation. After all, the Queen was not yet dead.

Death was in the very air at St. James's, and yet Mary Tudor still lived. The Spanish Tudor they had called her, and it seemed that she had brought the dark Spanish pride and passion to the tremendous Tudor obstinacy, a darkness lit most luridly by Bonner's fires consuming the flesh of wilful heretics. Insatiable, too, were the fires consuming the heart of that unhappy woman for the Spanish bridegroom who had so quickly wearied of her. The tragedy of Catherine of Aragon was not buried in her grave, it still overshadowed her daughter, and its bitterness came not from frustrated hate but frustrated love. For the mother from whom she had been so harshly separated, for the cousin-bridegroom who could not conceal the distaste he felt for her, for her Church—the church of mother and bridegroom alike—

19

which had been denied and persecuted for so long. These three she had loved with all the strength of her nature, and there was nothing which she would not sacrifice for them. And so she had dragged her country into the hated war against France, as ally of Spain, a war which was draining England of treasure and blood, and had raised a sullen enduring hatred against her Church by those very heresy laws with which she sought to strengthen it. All this she did; yet Philip her husband had now left her forever. He had hastened to go from her the moment the tragic farce of her false pregnancy had been played out. His second visit had been as brief as he could make it, and though afterwards a sick fancy had made her believe she was pregnant again, it was whispered in the court where the shadows were coming on so fast, that if she had conceived, it was with Death and not Life. The Queen's Grace was quick with death and dissolution. The unseen fires had burned her to ashes.

Still she lived and not yet were the heralds to cry: "The Queen is dead! Long live the Queen!" Sir William reflected upon the strange adaptation of the immemorial proclamation. A Queen to follow a Queen! In all history, England had had but one Queen Regnant, before Mary came to the throne, Matilda whose unhappy reign had proved a byword. Mary had done little to lift the prejudice against a woman as the supreme power. What would her sister do?

Sir William had been studying that same sister very closely for the past two months and more, and his chief conclusion was that her potentialities were unbounded.

The Lady Elizabeth was clever. She was a product of that new learning, which had flowered so amazingly at Cambridge, to which he too belonged. It had been a tremendous burgeoning of the High Renaissance, the new school at Cambridge which had based its learning on the Greek, contrary to the latinists of the older university of Oxford. The young King, Edward VI, the unfortunate Lady Jane Grey, and Elizabeth herself, had been taught by three of Cambridge's brightest jewels, Cheke, Grindal and Ascham. But Sir William—himself an intensely scholarly man—was well aware that scholarship had only polished the brains which the good God had already given her. She could vary from a subtlety which plumbed the very depths of cunning, to an openness as keen and disconcerting as a sword thrust. If it had not been for that great adroitness of hers, she would have been swallowed up by peril long ago.

Sunrise

Adroitness, yes, that was the word, he reflected. How coolly and lightly she had slid between dangers which had seemed likely to crush her. First in her brother's reign, the plot of the Lord Admiral, Thomas Seymour, seeking to wed her, and so gain power to overthrow his brother, Lord Protector Somerset. How far had she really been implicated, Cecil wondered? Her reputation had been somewhat tarnished, but he was not so concerned with that as by the amazing skill with which that child (she was hardly more) had parried the fierce interrogations of those sworn to entrap her. Yet again she had fenced most adroitly and desperately with death in her sister's reign, to emerge unscathed after two months' imprisonment in the Tower. She *must* have been implicated in some part in Wyatt's conspiracy, he thought, but they had not been able to wring one damaging admission from her. She had taken a diamond ring and scratched upon a window pane:

"Much suspected of me,
Nothing proved can be."

"And I," he thought, "*I* too suspect much and wonder more, and can prove nothing!" How she would shape as Queen, only the future could prove. His thoughts went swiftly ahead of him, to her manor at Hatfield. She must account as good the news that he was bringing her. Would her reaction reveal anything of the real woman? It had been dangerous in the past for her to give herself away, but now when the danger was swiftly passing, what had she to give?

In the courtyard at Hatfield, he found every groom of the establishment attending to the lathered horses of the cavalcade which had just ridden in. They were coming rapidly now, noblemen and gentlemen with their retainers, pledging their support, hoping to ride in triumph with the new Queen to London when that happy day came. But even in the crowd he was known at once; there was a horse-boy at his stirrup, as soon as he reined in.

The great hall was filled with many men, and the roar of voices rose to the raftered ceiling. By the great chimneypiece, he saw a tall swaggering figure, bravely attired in crimson and cloth of silver beside a dignified greybeard, whose jackboots steamed in the warmth of the blazing logs, and who seemed likely to be the leader of the party which had just ridden in. Cecil remarked the magnificent young man by his side, before the notice was mutual. But as he rapidly crossed

21

the hall, he saw that the fine dark eyes were regarding him with a sudden curiosity. But he did not wish then to wait and be questioned. Making a hasty salutation, he caught at the shoulder of a passing serving-man and told him to conduct him instantly to her Grace.

The sound of voices died away, as the door closed, and only their feet on the paving flags of the corridor broke the stillness. The fellow rapped on a door—"Sir William Cecil desires immediate speech with her Grace"—and then across the slower elderly woman's voice, came another, a younger one, with a sudden eagerness. ("She has a beautiful voice," he thought, "and she knows it well. . . .")

"Bring him in instantly!"

He hardly crossed the threshold, when he was aware of her moving towards him with the swiftness of thought. The light of the windows was behind her, so he could not see the expression on her face, but he could see the tense expectancy of that sudden flowing movement.

"Sir William, you have news for me?"

"News of great moment, your Grace." He had gone down on his knee, and raised one of those long slender Italianate hands, of which she was inordinately—and justly—vain, to his lips. The hand was cool, but he could feel its tenseness.

"Come!" she said. "Sit down. You must be weary after your ride. . . ." ("For one so self-centred", he thought, "she can be astonishingly considerate. . . .") It was with a quick impatient movement, that she gestured to him to sit beside her on the cushions of the window-seat, but there she composed herself to stillness, with her hands lying quiet against the brocade of her full skirts. She must have been in a fever of curiosity, but she waited in silence for him to speak. She was so near to him, that he caught a slight waft of her perfume, and it made him aware of another side of her nature, than cold brain power. As he spoke, he looked keenly at her, his eyes travelling from the pointed tip of her chin, up that pale oval face, past the lips which were well shaped if rather thin and firm for a woman, past the aquiline nose, which would curve like a hawk's beak in old age, to those eyes, wide open under the high arching brows, eyes dark and vivid. ("Her mother's eyes," he thought, but as his glance travelled on over the high brow to the hair rippling under a jewelled coif: "A lover or a poet might call it golden, but it is as red as old King Harry's.")

"The Queen's Grace", he said with deliberation, "having been

Sunrise

brought this morning to recognize the grievous and mortal nature of her sickness, acceded to her councillors' wishes, and formally appointed Your Grace her Successor"—he could hear the sigh as she drew in her breath—"with the most fervent request that you would uphold and maintain the Catholic religion."

She was silent for a moment, the tenseness seeming to relax, and the long fingers unclenching. Then she actually made a sound like the beginning of a laugh.

"As to the last," she said, "naturally!"

Cecil stared at her. She was regarded as the hope of the Protestants, but she had conformed outwardly to the Catholic faith when at her sister's court. To take either side was fraught with danger, there was a pitfall on each hand. And which did she truly favour?

"Naturally, your Grace?" he queried.

"Naturally that should be my sister's dying wish!"

He had a feeling that a keen blade had come up and deftly parried his thrust. She would not give herself away. Then she surprised him.

"My sister is a good woman," she said.

"Her Grace's piety is well known," replied Cecil, stiffly. Inwardly he inclined towards the severe doctrines of extreme Protestantism which came from Geneva, but there was also in him a spirit of toleration foreign to the age.

"I was not referring to her piety!" said Elizabeth with a sudden flash. Then she was calm again. "Else", she continued, "I might not be here now."

"But——" he began hesitating. She helped him out.

"I did not give her a peg to hang her conscience upon. It is only natural that she should hate me, or rather all that for which I stand."

"It is understandable," he agreed. Hate the daughter of Anne Boleyn who had displaced her own mother, and who might turn against her beloved Church, it was the most natural thing in the world. Perhaps Mary *was* a good woman else her sister had not come alive from the Tower. . . . Was this one a good woman? He listened to her.

"I do not really know", she continued, "whether she hated *me*. Sometimes, of course! She never trusted me. . . ."

"I think her Grace was jealous."

He remembered Mary's ceremonial entry into London at the beginning of her reign. She was small and dumpy, without much presence, although she had a certain natural dignity. And at thirty-eight she

23

had been a prematurely old woman, aged by sickness and sorrow. Behind her, reining her horse respectfully back, had come her half-sister, her coppery hair radiant in the sunlight, her smile radiant. How the crowds had shouted while the bells jangled! The people had turned readily against that upstart Northumberland with his attempt at putting his son and Lady Jane Grey on the throne, and had shouted themselves hoarse for King Harry's own daughters. But it had been obvious for which daughter they had shouted louder. Mary had thrown away her popularity quickly enough.

"Yes," said Elizabeth as if the matter was unimportant. "She was jealous of me. But she was most bitter against me because I would not love her. She did not know how to gain anyone's love, though she chose a hard subject in me."

"Your Grace speaks somewhat in riddles."

"Why!" she said. "Look at her childhood and mine! She at the commencement, was the beloved daughter of her parents. So it was harder for her later on. . . . I learned to steel myself young." ("Truly," he thought. "Her mother executed before she was three years old, her father indifferent and neglectful, lonely, lonely and enmeshed in intrigues and plots as soon as she could begin to reason. . . .")

"So she turned bitter", she continued, "and filled herself with hate and misery so that she did many foolish things." Her voice seemed to gather strength and solemnity till it pealed. "She did so much folly and so many grievous things against this land and its people, that I think her memory will not be forgiven in all time."

Feet were echoing on the flagstones of the corridor. Elizabeth made one of her swift movements towards the middle-aged waiting-woman who had been placidly embroidering at her frame while they talked. Her eyes had the plaintive affection of a spaniel for the princess.

"See who it is, Ashley. Don't let anyone in except——"

But a figure in red and silver was towering in the doorway, and Ashley was saying with a delighted, sentimental unction: "Lord Robert, your Grace!"

"Talk of the devil," thought Cecil. He had been thinking of "that upstart Northumberland" who had come to the scaffold for his ambition like his father before him, and here was "that upstart's" son, the third generation, Lord Robert Dudley. Certainly he was a splendid young man, with regular, delicately carved features, fine

24

Sunrise

dark eyes, hands as long and slender as Elizabeth's own, and a graceful swagger in those virile fripperies of crimson velvet slashed with cloth of silver, a jewelled rapier swinging by his long crimson legs.

He came in with unconcealed eagerness.

"Oh, My Lady! Are these joyful tidings true?"

"Joyful tidings?"

She was looking at him with unconcealed appreciation.

"The Queen's death?" he pressed.

The rebuke came as unexpectedly as a clap of thunder from a clear sky.

"God's precious soul! My sister's death—joyful?"

Thought Cecil: "She's too quick for him! One moment, she looks at him as if for two pins she would throw her arms around his neck, and then she rolls out an oath like old King Harry and rebukes him like King Harry's self."

Dudley's jaw had dropped. He stood staring, foolishly. Then a ghost of a smile flickered across her face, and both her voice and her eyes held a caress which must have been soothing to his vanity.

"But Sir William has brought the most excellent tidings, Robin."

"My Lady?"

"My sister, realizing the mortal nature of her sickness, has this morning, formally appointed me as her Successor to her councillors."

He was on his knees before her, pressing her hand to his lips.

"This is indeed happy news. But whatever or whomsoever the Queen's Grace might appoint, there are those who would proclaim you with their hearts and their swords!"

"I want their hearts, Robin. But I hope there will be no need for their swords. . . ."

He remained on his knees and did not relinquish her hand. He had turned it over, and was devouring the palm with kisses which ventured up her wrist. She permitted it and did not draw her hand away, but her eyes seemed remote from the man at her feet. Cecil wondered what she was thinking about. How much of the Throne and how much of Lord Robert? Suddenly she flashed a glance downwards.

"Robin, who were they that rode in now?"

"Sir Henry Reedham, three of his sons, his son-in-law and a party of horse. He had heard that the Queen was dead, and he hoped for the honour of escorting your Grace to London."

Sunrise

"Give my best thanks to Sir Henry, Robin. I will come presently. You must see to them. Let them sup of the best."

"Do you sup with us?"

"No. You attend to all this, Rob. It is difficult for a woman alone."

"Alone? I am here!"

"Ah, what should I do without you, Robin?" But she drew her hand away at last, so that he rose to his feet.

("You would do as well as you do now," thought Cecil, "and find some other pretty fellow. . . .")

"I have much to ask Sir William, so he will stay and sup with me in private. Then I will come and give my thanks to Sir Henry."

Dudley gave a comical, disconcerted glance and withdrew.

"Lord Robert is very faithful to my cause," said she demurely.

"It is easy to be faithful to the rising sun!"

"I was not always the rising sun. There were days when to favour me was to bring ill luck and danger. He sold lands for me when I had need of money. I am faithful to my friends, Sir William."

Sir William cast a glance at the plump Mistress Ashley. When she and the Princess's cofferer had been arrested at the time of the Seymour plot, their terrors had led to indiscretions which had nearly ruined their young mistress. But she had borne no malice, and had fought back, not only for herself but for them. She, too, had been faithful in adversity. Then he noticed that her keen glance was following his. She missed nothing!

"It will be good", she said, "to reward my friends. My poor good Ashley. . . . And Lord Robert!"

"Lord Robert is a pretty man!"

"I like pretty men!" Adding with that flashing quickness: "To look at! I think my Lord Robert would be very well in such a position as Master of Horse."

"Very well."

"Ah—Sir William! What good fortune it is for me to have you at my elbow at such a time."

She had the air of turning towards him with relief and confidence, as if she had put away thought of less important things. That air, and something in her smile, awoke a warmth in him which surprised him. She would never wholly give herself away, he thought, and she would always have that fencer's cold calculation, and yet there was

26

Sunrise

something warm and glowing in the inmost heart of her. A good woman? He did not know, but he believed she would be a good Sovereign.

something warm and glowing in the inmost heart of her. A good woman! He did not know, but he believed she would be a good Sovereign.

Chapter Two

At the supper table, she did not talk much at first, and only toyed with her food, while pressing him to eat. By the light of the candles in the November dusk, he could see her eyes shining.

"I would not have you go to London again," she said. "You have brought me the most fateful piece of news while my sister still lives. Now I need you here. Sir Nicholas Throckmorton is in London, and writes me daily. But you must not budge from my side. And send for your good brother-in-law, Nicholas Bacon."

"He comes to-morrow."

She made a sign to the serving-man to refill his goblet with wine, refused it for herself, and then seemed lost in meditation, her chin resting on her hands, her eyelids half down. Then she looked up suddenly, and he saw that her eyes were alight.

"How long now?" she said. "Weeks? Hours?"

"Days, I think," he answered her. She took a deep breath, and then smiled in open exultation. "So long and such a difficult way. . . ."

"Not so very long now before the happy day when the heralds proclaim that high and mighty princess, our Sovereign Lady, Elizabeth!"

"Ah, that sounds sweet. . . . Happy indeed. . . . But it was necessary to check Lord Robert." She raised her eyebrows. "One can rejoice too soon."

"Certainly."

"And I will rejoice! Yet. . . . I pity my sister, as a woman. Whatever I think her as a queen. But we princes are like players, set on a stage for all the world to see. Our private lives may not be flaunted. . . . In private I will pity her. In my public character I must condemn her."

"She has done much harm."

28

"Too much!" Then her mood seemed to swing back. "She suffers now in her sickness?"

"Grievously, I understand."

"She has suffered so much too. And this faith of hers, does it help her now?"

Cecil stared.

"I could not know that, your Grace."

"Nor I!" She made a gesture with her hands. "Peace be with her! But I think there will be little peace of her handiwork. . . ."

"Little indeed. Calais has fallen. But it was doomed, and it is well that it fell in her reign, not yours."

"Very well!" she said and then appeared to think. "I am in two minds about it. I would not have the arms of England defeated, England which once was overlord of more French land than the King of France, and now Calais is the only poor remnant left. And yet. . . . I think so long as England held Calais, it was a thorn in the flesh of the King of France, to resent and strive against. Well! Tell me what you think."

"I agree", he said, "with the last. Though being a town of the Staple, it may be a sore loss to the wool and cloth trade."

He was surprised at the gaiety of her laughter.

"I regret the ancient glories, and you the cloth trade! No, no, you are right. . . . But perhaps the French will be disposed to good will by the regaining of Calais, so to good trade."

"I hope so."

"And does she know, my sister, that Calais has fallen? How did she take it?"

"I heard a rumour at court. Your Grace must credit it as you please. It was supposed to be started by a Woman of the Bedchamber. And by her retailed to a Gentleman Pensioner enamoured of her and so on. . . ."

"Well, out with it, man!"

"When the Queen heard the news, she gave such a cry of lamentation that all were amazed. Then she burst forth: "When I die—and I die soon—take out my heart! You will find 'Calais' written upon it. . . ." I do not know if it is a truth or an invention. There are many strange stories whispered in the court."

He heard her draw in her breath and saw her clench her hands.

"I believe it. She is my father's daughter—not all Spaniard. But these wars! What lasting good ever came of war? Blood spilt, treasure spilt. Only a little windy fame for unthrifty braggarts!"

"I do agree," said Cecil from the bottom of his heart.

"And yet I will be unreasonable, and unsay part. . . . I would wish that in my reign there should be some great victory that would resound down all the ages! But it will not come in this unhappy campaign. We have trouble before us and long negotiation."

"Spain does well," said Cecil, "but neglects her ally. A new envoy has come from the King but her Grace was too ill to see him. The Count de Feria."

"*I* have seen him!"

"But, your Grace! When?"

"Yesterday. He rode down with many protestations of Philip's goodwill and more admonitions. I did not answer him as I might regarding the last as I have need of the former. . . ."

"You have, indeed. The King of Spain's influence will be needed to offset that of the King of France with the Pope. I have told you before, we must proceed very carefully. We dare not risk a Papal Bull of Excommunication now. The King of France will urge for a holy war against England so that his daughter-in-law's claim to the throne can be pressed."

"Yes and Philip would not have England a possession of France. . . . This young Queen of Scots—Madame la Dauphine—she's sixteen. I have heard she is a very lovely girl. . . ."

Cecil passed this by as unimportant.

"Her claim can make trouble. . . . The best of it is, King Philip must oppose it."

"My poor good brother!" she said with what he considered much levity. "I must tell you what I *did* say to the Count de Feria. It is a very haughty overbearing man. . . . He told me to keep in mind the goodness of the King's favour to me, and how I could not possibly hold the throne without it. So I replied—as to the throne that depended rather on the goodwill of God—and of the English people! He was prepared to dispute the last—but he could not dispute the first!" Her laugh rang out gaily.

("Will she, one day, be too clever?" Cecil reflected.)

She leaned forward with eagerness.

"Now, tell me everything else and what you think of it. You are my good and faithful spirit. . . ."

Sunrise

"Cardinal Pole is so sorely ill that no one knows if he or the Queen will die first, so there can be no question of his filling those five vacant bishoprics, which is great good fortune for us."

She broke in suddenly: "Can there never be a spirit of toleration amongst men? They are most bitter and evilly disposed when in the name of God! Can there not be a church broad enough to shelter all?"

"I doubt it, your Grace," said Cecil, once again staring at her with some surprise.

"Why," she said, "the ordinary humble man desires to worship after the manner of his ancestors. He would not thank the extreme reformers of Geneva who would tear the crucifix and candles from the altar. . . . He craves for the familiar things. But to him, the Bishop of Rome is a foreign prince against whom he prefers his own sovereign. And such persecutions as my sister has caused, are abominable to everyone! I told her that such burnings would light a fire of hatred against the Catholic Church which would be of her doing. Whereon she fell into so great a fury with me that my life was in peril." To this she added quietly: "And all to no purpose. . . ."

The quick, smooth fencing had been laid aside. It sounded, he thought, as if she had spoken from her heart. He had met this mood in her once or twice before, and believed it sincere. Then her mood swung again. She lifted one of her finely pencilled brows.

"Travellers' tales tell us of the vultures which gather about a dead body. It is the human sort of vulture which forsakes the dead and the dying, for the living. 'Where the treasure is, there will the heart be also. . . .'"

"I do not understand."

"You will. I have been hearing horsemen riding in ever since you came. I must greet them. Robin has his hands full."

As she swept through the door which Cecil held open for her, she said: "He is an excellent creature. Lord Robert, I mean. I wish that you realized his goodness of heart."

"It is a pity", said Cecil dryly, "that so fine a man is bound to an unloved and unwanted wife. Has he presented his lady to you?"

He saw her hands clench before she could restrain herself.

"God's death, no! Nor spoke of her!" The voice came with an almost hissing fierceness. Then her control returned. "I know she exists, and lives on his property in Oxfordshire. Cumnor Hall. She has long grown out of his love."

31

Sunrise

"It was a marriage made in his extreme youth," Cecil told her. "And entered into in youthful folly. Marriage is best made by the head and not by the heart. It should be of the intellects and not the passions." Both his own marriages had been arranged on this principle.

"I daresay!" she said with scorn. What she scorned, he did not know. She turned to regard him over her shoulder, and he could see the glint of her teeth on her lip.

"Marriage is an abyss!" she declared. "In which many are swallowed. As my sister!"

But as she went forward to greet the company in the hall, she was all radiance again, with the firelight dancing on her billowing brocade skirts, picking out the threads of gold and silver, and striking a copper gleam from her hair. Lord Robert had hastened to her side and now towered protectively over her, while Cecil followed her like her shadow. He started a little at the many faces to be seen. Not only Sir Henry Reedham and his family troop. There was my Lord Robert's elder brother, Ambrose Dudley, Earl of Warwick. And there were faces which he had seen that very morning at the court of the dying Mary. The Earls of Arundel and Pembroke, that fine, swaggering gallant, Sir William Pickering, and many in attendance on them—Mary must be on the very threshold of death!

Elizabeth's voice rang out melodiously: "My lords and gentlemen! I am very sensible of your goodness and loyalty in coming thus, to me. . . ."

She found the right thing to say to all of them, Cecil noticed, in the days to come, as more and more rode in to offer her their support and service. She sparkled with life; already she felt it were safe to rejoice and her supporters rejoiced with her. Sometimes she seemed only young and gay and dazzled by the prospect of the throne—or dazzled by the swaggering beauty of Lord Robert. Then she would roll out one of her pungent oaths, and crush the young man—always hitherto a conqueror with women—to gaping, indignant silence. Neither he, nor Cecil, nor anyone else could gauge how much she fancied him. With Cecil and his brother-in-law, the equally learned, infinitely painstaking but surly Nicholas Bacon, she worked tirelessly. There, Cecil saw only the diamond hardness and brightness of her brain. One could reason with her as if she were a man—sometimes. At others, her capriciousness drove him desperate. She delighted in showing her cleverness, in wrapping up her meaning in a hundred misty veils, in gliding adroitly from one situation to another so that her right hand never knew what her left hand did—so how then her councillors? Sometimes her speech was only that verbal fencing which made him think of two Toledo blades ringing upon each other. Then at her smoothest and most cynical, she would drop her delight in her own quick, cruel cleverness, and speak simply, quietly from the bottom of her heart, in those plain but glowing words which the High Renaissance was to make flower from the English tongue till they reached their apotheosis in the poems and plays of Shakespeare and the English Bible. And Cecil found himself developing warmer, more human feelings towards her. He did not only marvel at her verbal cleverness, or guess at her motives. He began to feel the stirrings of affection—and at times he wanted to box her ears for very exasperation at her wilfulness!

So they waited and worked and planned while Mary Tudor went out into the darkness, alone and unloved, knowing that her life work was tumbling into ruin. Others beside Cecil wondered as to the Lady Elizabeth's favour towards Lord Robert. On the morning of 17th November, heavy with damp grey mist, his own brother, Ambrose of Warwick, pressed him for information as they sat over their breakfast ale. Many lords and gentlemen were living at the princess's expense; the fat cofferer, Thomas Parry, raised his hands to heaven and declared that the Queen would soon be too long a-dying for the Lady Elizabeth's credit!

Warwick had neither the presence nor beauty of his brother, Robert. He was simpler and blunter, but had managed to make something of a name for himself as a soldier even in the late disastrous campaign, so that he was supposed to have inherited part of the military genius of his father who had done so well against the Scots and French.

"Two days ago", he said to his brother, "you told me you were sure of her Grace. Are you so sure now?"

Robert swore a great oath. "As sure as of the devil! Why, she lifts me up one moment and throws me down the next."

"And all the more rejoice when she throws you down," quoth Ambrose. "You've made so many jealous, that if you are once down they'll all be on to you. You had better step carefully till you are more sure."

"Sure! Shall I ever be sure?"

"It's a pity you're married. . . ."

"The devil's pity! Not that there's much health in Amy. She ails and frets! Always sick and complaining, nothing does her any good. . . ." He looked at his brother with an injured air. "Why did I marry her?"

"I never knew," declared his brother bluntly. Robert swore again and got up abruptly, to walk off indignation in the grounds. He was surprised when he found Elizabeth sauntering in a yew-bordered walk, and making a face at the grey sky. The faithful Ashley waddled along at her side. She beamed at the sight of Lord Robert, and then discreetly withdrew; she could not resist a sentimental admiration for a bold and pretty fellow, and was all for helping her young mistress to a suitable gallant.

"I wanted some fresh air," Elizabeth told Robert. "I've been cooped up so long with Sir William, Sir Nicholas and parchments, parchments, parchments! I haven't been abroad for days."

"Let me order horses!" he said. "And squire you through the woods. Gallop away from musty parchments!"

"I wish I could, Rob. But I must remain in call."

"Yes," he said, and their thoughts ran together.

"Give me your arm," she said at last. "We'll stroll. The air is sweet and fresh even if the sun will not shine."

They strolled, her arm resting lightly on his, and Robert was baffled and intrigued by her. She had blown hot and cold, held him off and coaxed him on—how in the devil's name was a man to know what she meant? Women usually did not resist Lord Robert. But he did not know how to handle this one.

It was not long before he heard a faint far-off drumming sound. She heard it too, and he felt the arm within his stiffen.

"A galloping horse," he declared and gently pressed her arm.

"It could be," she said, hesitating.

"Relays have been posted," he told her eagerly, "so a man riding from St. James's could spur all the way. He could do it in three hours if he galloped——"

"Yes," she said breathlessly. "Yes. We had better go back to the house."

"Very well. But I feel in my bones what news that horseman brings."

Sunrise

"I too. . . ."

"So I can be the first to tell you my joy. Joy for you. In moments, you will be so far above me——"

"Will I?" she interrupted him. She was looking straight at him now. With another woman he would have read an invitation. He hesitated.

"So long my Queen," he began, "and now—England's."

"So long your Queen?"

He could not mistake that glance. Courage came to him with his old assurance in love-making. He caught her suddenly to him with a practised ease and yet his hands were not too steady. She was still— neither resisting nor responding—and her eyes were closed. Then she sighed and he felt her arms go round him too, and her hands—those beautiful hands—pass lightly and caressingly over the back of his head and neck, and her lips were responding with a warmth he had never believed.

There was a breathless surprise in his voice when at last he spoke. "Could you love me—a little?"

He could only just catch her whispered answer. "Not a little. . . ."

"*I* love you!" He believed himself as he said it. He had said it often before to other women. There were other times too when he had believed it, but he had forgotten them all now.

"Say it," she murmured. "Say it again, Rob. Say all the foolish things lovers do. I'm not Queen yet. I can believe you. . . . I want to hear you saying them. . . ."

So he said them, and gave all the tenderness he knew of word and touch, till the faint sounds of bustle from the house reached them. She put up her hands again and took his face between them.

"Now, I can always hear you saying those things. I have a good memory! I'll remember them. When I am alone. When I am old."

"You'll never be old. Nor alone as long as I am here."

"Oh, Rob! I wonder. There's one thing more lonely than a throne. A coffin. Now I must walk towards the first. They'll be seeking me."

Then she was apart from him as if those last moments had never been, walking swiftly but with great dignity. He could not touch her again. He followed her advancing towards her destiny.

They were clustering in the great hall about a man, booted to the thigh, splashed with mud and his spur rowels red. Cecil was there,

thinking of the proclamation which he had spent the morning draft-
ing, his brother-in-law beside him. The portly figure of Thomas
Parry, the cofferer, had pushed forward in perspiring eagerness.
With him was Mistress Kate Ashley, sinking in a low curtsy, her eyes
like an adoring spaniel's as they turned towards Elizabeth. These two
had served her and loved her longer than any others, had failed her
with fear and foolishness, and been forgiven and saved by her resolution. They pushed in front of the nobles and gentlemen, knowing their
privileges.

It was the messenger's moment, and he took it. Falling stiffly on his
knees, in his jackboots, he cried out: "God save your Grace! I have
come straight away from St. James's Palace. The Queen died at
seven o'clock this morning."

As Robert Dudley slipped quietly in behind her and took his place
at his brother's side, he was aware that he had passed beyond her
thoughts for that moment.

Chapter Three

The Queen and her train lay at the Charterhouse, my Lord North's house, the old Carthusian monastery close by the horse-market on the outskirts of the city of London. Attended by a thousand lords and gentlemen with their followers, she had ridden from Hatfield on 23rd November. Not even the English climate, the rain and mud which belonged to the season, could damp the enthusiasm of the people who had clustered about the route, shouting and cheering, which had grown into a roaring crescendo of exultation as they came in sight of London, still enfolded in its ancient walls, reflected in its wide river tangled in the lower reaches with the spars of many ships, the sky above it beginning to be dimmed by the smoke of its thousands of chimneys, now that sea coal—brought in barges from Newcastle—was commencing to replace wood for fuel. The Queen and her attendants were not yet to enter the walls; they rested at the Charterhouse just without. They could hear the cheers and joyful singing of the citizens of London as they danced about bonfires lighted in the streets, which reddened the evening's murky gloom, while the bells jangling ecstatically from the city's hundred steeples vied with the booming salvoes of artillery from the Tower.

Cecil hearing the joyful clamour, reflected with some cynicism how the unmourned woman, lying in state at St. James's, had once been loudly acclaimed, and it had taken less than five years to bring acclamation to hatred. None knew better than he, the parlous state to which she had brought the kingdom, the war against France on behalf of Spain being its crowning folly. Three days ago, Elizabeth had had him sworn in as a member of her Council, and had made him Principal Secretary. As he stood by the casement window, from whence came the confused roar of happy voices and the red glow of bonfires, he could still hear her firm, clear, young voice as she had said: "This judgment I have of you, that you will not be corrupted with any manner of gift, and that you will be faithful to the State, and without respect of my private will, you will give me the counsel that you think best."

The Queen, too, was gazing from her windows across the dignified quadrangle of the ancient monastery. She could hear the voices and see the glow in the skies, and her spirits leapt. Behind her, in the great bedchamber, Mistress Ashley warmed her hands by the flickering flames burning brightly in the big chimney, no sea coal here, but fragrant smelling logs. She had ordered and scolded the serving-men bearing in trunks and the serving-women unpacking them, to her heart's content. Now she was waiting till Elizabeth would settle from walking about, and leaning from the window.

"Dear heart, my Lady!" she besought her. "Close the windows! The evil humours of the night air are rising thick...."

Elizabeth turned.

"I want to hear the people," she said. "They're happy."

"Well, they may be! But I beg of you, close the windows...."

Elizabeth withdrew her head reluctantly, and put the casement to. She had not yet changed from her grey riding-dress slashed with silver, and her hat with its high crown and plume, her tasselled and fringed gauntlets and her riding switch, were all spread about the room in the different places where she had thrown them down. Her riding-boots had been pulled off and as she kneeled on a settle by the window, she had wriggled her toes in freedom from the stiff leather. Now she came over to the fire, pacing on them with a dancer's step.

"I'm happy!" she declared, settling in a fireside seat.

"Happy!" cried Mistress Ashley. She embraced the knees of her young mistress. "Oh, this blessed, happy day! If I'd seen it in those bad years which have gone.... My dearest child—what am I saying? And you the Queen's Grace!"

"No, call me 'my dearest child'. No one else but you says it." Elizabeth leaned forward and rested her cheek a moment, rather awkwardly, against Mistress Ashley's head. A few minutes later, she added, a smile which was faintly bitter, curling her lips:

"You won't say it much longer...."

"Now we must think of attiring you!"

"Yes! I must look beautiful.... It's the first reception of my reign!

38

Sunrise

They're all coming from London, from the court to look at me. The lords and gentlemen, the bishops, the foreign ambassadors. They want to see what sort I am. I *will* impress them!"

"You'll look beautiful!" Ashley told her, and added (but already it sounded strange to her): "My dearest child. . . . You decided, did you not, on the dress with the black velvet body, faced with cloth of gold and sewn with seed pearls, and the sleeves of brocade figured in gold and likewise sewn in seed pearls?"

"Yes, I'll wear that."

"Mercy on me, and your hair going out of curl with this horrid damp! I must do it again."

"Yes. And I'll have a bath, I think. To wash off my hours in the saddle."

Mistress Ashley threw up her plump hands.

"A bath? On a cold damp winter's night like this, and the air full of the most evil and melancholy humours! Do you want to catch a chill and fever and die before you're crowned?"

"I won't catch a chill. I never get ill when I'm happy! How can I take cold in front of this great fire? And we'll pour into the water some of that rare French essence which Lord Robert gave me, so I shall be perfumed like all the flowers of Araby. . . ."

"A bath in winter!" wailed Mistress Ashley.

Elizabeth leaned forward, took Ashley's double chin in her long thin fingers, and said with mock ferocity: "God's precious soul! One more word of argument and you go to the Tower for defying the Queen!"

"How you swear!" complained Mistress Ashley. "Two months ago, you never did."

"I'm going to do many a thing I never did before! You wait and see! Now go and do what I tell you. It is a mighty unruly subject. . . ."

Mistress Ashley went, and hustled the serving-maids till they were almost desperate. But she had an infinite patience and her plump hands a great skill, as she waited on the Queen. Elizabeth was dressed in the robe of heavy, lustrous, black velvet, yards and yards draping the farthingale. The neck was cut low and square, and from it, to the hem of the skirts, stretched the facing of cloth of gold, embroidered in elaborate designs with seed pearls, garnets and other semi-precious stones, while a gold chain girdle, encrusted with gems, encircled her narrow waist. The great sleeves billowed out like brocade balloons, stiff with gold thread and gems, till they were caught in tightly at her slender wrists. Mistress Ashley, smoothing the pile of the velvet, stepped back to contemplate with rapture; she might have been said to purr. She was like a plump cat or spaniel with the same love of comfort and easy uncritical affection, Elizabeth thought. The affection was there, however much foolishness and self-seeking was mixed up in it. But where was the sovereign who could look for disinterested love? Ashley had been with her from childhood, and was even distantly connected with the Boleyns; if she were sick or afraid, she would want Ashley with her. A bitter little smile flickered on her lips. She could never show fear to anyone, not even Ashley. Never since earliest childhood had she dared show fear. Only once in those hard years had her steely control cracked for a few minutes, when the barge had set her down at the Traitor's Gate, to begin her captivity in the Tower. She could hear now the suck of the turbid water against those slimy stone steps and the grating of the rowlocks of the shipped oars, as she could smell the dank river air. Far worse still, she could remember her own thoughts, of the many who had come here, never to leave again; Thomas Seymour, who had used her in his ambition, that lusty, vigorous man; her cousin Jane Grey, the meek and studious, freshly dead, and that figure who had lain at the back of her mind so long, shrouded in the darkness of doom and mystery, her own mother. She had cried out in an agony of despair, as she had stepped ashore: "Oh, Lord! I never thought to have come in here as a prisoner!" But at once she had caught hold of herself, adding: "And I pray you all, good friends and fellows, bear me witness that I come in no traitor, but as true a woman to the Queen's Majesty as any now living: and thereon will I take my death." She could remember that first sleepless night in the Bell Tower, while the clock clanged away the slow hours, and she argued silently in the darkness, planning and marshalling her arguments and wits against the cross-examination which would soon follow, trying not to think of those things which she had heard whispered of her mother, how she had clasped her throat with her fingers, and with a laugh which might have been hysteria or bravado or a mixture of both, had cried out: "They won't have much difficulty. . . . I have such a little neck!"

Now her own eyes in the mirror before her seemed to be staring with a dark intensity in the candlelight. Mistress Ashley was staring, too, in surprise.

"What troubles you?" she asked anxiously. "What are you thinking about?"

Elizabeth collected herself and the dark flame died down in her eyes.

"Nothing", she said, "that matters now," as Mistress Ashley put a wrapper about her shoulders, preparatory to dressing her hair and setting it within a jewelled coif like a small crown. Contemplating her face in the mirror, now with calmness, Elizabeth called for rouge.

"I must make a good appearance to-night," she said, "and spare no pomp or gaud. It is a long time since Edward"—her voice touched her brother's name with gentleness—"called me Sweet Sister Temperance. I will not be so temperate now. I would be magnificent. . . ." She painted her lips skilfully, firmly outlining the cupid's bow.

"You will be!" cried Kate Ashley. "You'll set them all agape. And break Lord Robert's heart!"

"I wonder! Would Lord Robert fancy me if I were not Queen?"

"Look in your mirror!" said Kate Ashley confidently. Elizabeth looked and then smiled.

"Perhaps. . . ."

She took jewels from a casket, setting them on her fingers and to dangle from her ears. Kate Ashley hung a long rope of softly lustrous pearls about her neck, reaching almost to her girdle. A great blood-red ruby pendant glowed against her pale skin, above the low-cut bosom of her dress. Her neck was encircled by a starched and fluted ruff which accentuated the fine point of her chin. Now she was ready, adorned to take part in the first ceremonial of her reign, and her ladies came, a rustling, curtsying group.

She acknowledged their reverence coolly, and ran her eyes over them, discovering to her satisfaction that in a group they looked well enough to support her but there was no figure sufficiently lovely or radiant to steal attention from the Queen. So she gave them a smile. She had no woman friends, for where was the woman she could trust? There was only that fondness of old association for Kate Ashley, a fondness which was disillusioned. She knew the limits of her good Kate, but it was all she had. In the great world all were seeking and scheming and plotting to gain advantage from her. How could she know whether any man desired her for herself or for her throne? Had not Thomas Seymour shown her the greed of man's desire? If she were to have anything approaching a friendship, it might be with such a one as Secretary Cecil, a dry and unemotional relationship for their interests ran together and their intellects were harmonious.

But the ladies knew what was expected of them, praising her, and using the new title which her father had taken and which was to replace the older "your Grace"—"your Majesty".

Her Majesty swept down the great carved oak staircase of the Charterhouse, with them all rustling behind her, to be received by the Lord High Treasurer of England, the aged Marquess of Winchester, and her host, Lord North, and led to her place on the dais, above the brilliant crowd which packed the greatest apartment. There was Cecil, attired in black velvet, keenly eyeing the throng, here Lord Robert, in Lincoln green, newly appointed Master of Horse, swaggering consciously. There was the stout Thomas Parry, the erstwhile Cofferer, a massive golden chain about his neck, now knighted and made Comptroller of the Royal Household, as joyful as Mistress Ashley at the outcome. And the great world had put off its formal mourning and had crowded to the Charterhouse to see the new Queen.

A profound silence fell as she entered. She was aware of every eye upon her, of every head turned in that vast company. She drew herself up with a dignity which seemed to spring from the new realization of the pomp belonging to her, and moved across the polished oaken floor with a proud grace. She could hear the drawn breath of those about her, as if they had been impressed. From the dais, she smiled on them, suddenly and radiantly, "like the sun in his splendour breaking from a cloud", with all the warmth of her own exultation shining. Robert Dudley met that smile and took it for himself, but she was not thinking of him then. When, one of the first to kneel at her feet, he pressed his lips passionately to her hand, the hand received his homage with as little response as for any other noble.

But she was wooing them all, remembering that which she had known or heard of each promising man, so as to address him a few suitable words, and as she felt them respond, a delight in her own powers filled her. All the while Cecil stood watching in silent approbation. She could play the regal part with dignity and charm, he confessed. She could look impressive and it was necessary for a Sovereign to have presence, and although he was by nature a cold and unemotional man who had chosen his wives for their learning, piety and sobriety (the first, sister to Cheke, Edward VI's tutor, and his second, the sister of Sir Anthony Cooke, acclaimed as one of the most learned women in England) he admitted that Elizabeth was a handsome young creature and knew how to adorn herself to the best advantage. Underneath this balanced summing-up, he felt a warmer, almost parental, appreciation of her skill and dexterity.

She was soon to have need of all her adroit wits. There was a stir at the entrance, and the retainers announced loudly: "Way there for the Count de Feria, Ambassador of his most Catholic Majesty, the King of Spain!" Elizabeth turned, still smiling sweetly, to observe the tall, imposing figure in black velvet, the Golden Fleece about his neck, as he strode through the crowd with as much arrogance as if he had been a sovereign prince. He bowed low and then raised his eyes with a haughty keenness. She met them unruffled, her smile a little more dazzling.

"How happy I am", she murmured, "to receive the Envoy of my dear brother, Philip!"

"I bear his most loving greetings, your Grace," Feria assured her.

"And pray give him mine. I think of him constantly. . . ."

"He will be most happy. . . . I have the honour to bear certain gifts as a token of his goodwill"—here he proffered a silver-bound casket—"and to assure you of his constant interest in your welfare and that of your realm."

"I am all too sensible of my dear brother's goodness. . . ."

"If your Grace desires to give pleasure to King Philip, you will be very careful of religious affairs. . . ."

Cecil stiffened. It seemed—even to his unfanciful mind—that a cold wind had blown through the great chamber, fluttering the arras on the walls, and making the flambeaux dance and dip. Could it only be the sigh which he heard from the onlookers? So many were turning towards the dais, the supporters of the two religious factions, waiting breathless for the Queen's decision. Dare she oppose King Philip when she so bitterly needed his support? Dare she oppose the religious wishes of the bulk of her subjects, driven desperate by the Marian persecutions? What a dilemma! thought Cecil, forced upon her so soon. . . . He gazed at her, realizing that he could not help her out. Could those diamond-bright, diamond-hard brains of hers help?

Elizabeth looked down at her feet with demureness and modesty. Then she raised her head, and regarded Feria serenely and levelly. In

43

a calm voice she replied: "It would indeed be wicked of me to forget God, who has shown me such great goodness. . . ."

Cecil saw the flush come on Feria's swarthy cheek, as he bowed in silence to the Queen. In silence, Cecil gave thanks for that fencer's skill which she possessed in debate. The tension eased in all but Feria, and the sound of voices again rose vigorously.

The guests had gone and the Queen was withdrawing to her private apartments; already the torches were burning low and their guttering was being extinguished by yawning retainers. At the foot of the stairs, Cecil bowed low to the Queen.

"Well, Sir Spirit?" she said interrogatively, raising her eyebrows.

"It was well done, your Grace," he told her.

She tossed her head, and laughed, a sound which had more mockery than mirth.

"He gave me better diamonds than ever he gave my sister. . . ."

"Indeed?"

She leaned forward, her eyes provocative.

"My good brother-in-law," she said, "he admired me."

"I have heard it said, your Grace." Cecil was imperturbable.

"And it surprises you?"

"To the contrary!"

She clapped his cheek, and went up the stairs laughing. Cecil permitted himself a smile.

Upstairs the ladies dutifully complimented the Queen on how her appearance had struck beholders, and began to retail gossip of this one and that. Elizabeth let them run on, wanting knowledge, even if it were only court tittle-tattle, and laughing at a jest or two which did not strike her as particularly humorous but which showed the way the wind blew. Then she gave them her hand to kiss, let a Maid of Honour take off her shoes, and dismissed them. She wanted no one but Ashley to put her to bed, now she was tired she only wished for those plump, competent hands.

Kate Ashley exclaimed upon King Philip's diamonds, holding them up to sparkle in the candlelight.

"Everyone said that the King of Spain was wild for you," she told her young mistress. "They say how he lamented he was married to the elder sister."

But Elizabeth had stopped smiling.

44

Sunrise

"After all," she said, "I was nearly eighteen years younger. . . . My sister was fair in her youth."

"Nothing to you!" declared the fond Ashley.

"Tell me, why did my sister love him so desperately?"

Mistress Ashley sneered. "An old maid of nearly forty? She would be wild for any man!"

"It seems to me that love has nothing to do with reason."

"Why, it is reasonable to love some proper handsome fellow!"

"Rather natural than reasonable. . . ."

Kate Ashley made a clucking sound with her tongue, as she arranged the many-coloured woven blankets over Elizabeth when she lay in the great bed, the coverlet and hangings worked with Tudor roses. Let the Queen marry some fine fellow and she would understand a lot of things! Kneeling she kissed that beautiful hand, which patted her cheek with a murmur of "Good Kate!"

In the darkness, lighted dimly by the red glow of the fire, Elizabeth saw a pageant of faces passing before her. The arrogant appraisal of Feria, summing her up, trying to dominate her; the swarthy flush of anger which had succeeded his immense self-possession; the cooler, considered calculation of Cecil, missing nothing; the hungry gaze of Robert Dudley which brought keenly the memory of his strong arms around her in the garden at Hatfield, and his lips on hers. She sighed and then his face, too, passed on in the procession which became a dream.

Chapter Four

The court had moved to Whitehall for Christmas, while the preparations were being made for the pomp and solemnity of the coronation, in January. In the bright, keen winter air, London's one hundred thousand inhabitants rejoiced in their new Queen, and designed pageants for her as she rode amongst them, at the head of a magnificent retinue, or else proceeded down the Thames in her barge "to the sound of trumpets". They were glad to forget the miseries brought on them in Mary's reign, and to celebrate the hopes springing in their hearts. These had been kindled by the handsome young woman with the red-gold hair, sitting easily on her fine horse, reining in to talk to this person and that, to jest and laugh merrily with one, and to give shrewd sympathy to another. She belonged to them, they felt. She declared that she was "mere English", no proud brat of Spain to fasten a cruel, arrogant and alien rule upon them. London was the heart of the kingdom, beating strongly, and Elizabeth kept her hand upon that mighty pulse.

Every day she felt an increase in that strange emotional satisfaction brought by the evidences of the people's affection. About her—as for so long—were intriguing and scheming, she could look for no uninterested devotion. Except from the ordinary people who pressed, shouting and cheering, to her. Her vein of cynicism at first made her say that they, too, hoped much from her, but another feeling rose and drowned this bitterness. There was something simple even in their expectation of benefits from her; so might children expect good gifts from a loving mother. To her, it seemed as if she had come in from a winter's night to warm herself at a great fire. It alone was safe.

Nothing could quench her instinctive delight in Robert Dudley, but her reason would not allow her to build upon it. She knew she was happy merely when he was near to her. When he swaggered into her presence and bowed low over the hand he kissed so passionately, the sudden desire came to her to press that black head to her heart, a desire which was like a pain. In the tiltyard, it seemed that her whole being followed his figure in its damascened armour, as the hoofs thundered down to that savage clash of steel. Then as the swirl of dust parted, she would see his great war horse plunging and rearing, as he waved his splintered lance butt in exultant salutation. Sometimes his very open-handed reckless generosity which outraged her careful reasoning, irrationally delighted her. He would throw money head-long to anything which caught his fancy. She had rebuked him for giving a heavy purse to a needy poet, and he had answered: "Ah, my sweet lady! He's such a rare fellow and his verses sing like the trumpets when you go out in your barge, with everyone cheering you from their hearts. . . . He shouldn't have to think of the dingy reckonings of every day!"

"God's soul, Robin! Where should we all be if someone did not think of the dingy reckonings of every day? You would go dancing down the gay road to ruin!"

"As long as you smile at me how can I be ruined?"

"I feel more inclined to box your ears. . . ." But she smiled in spite of herself.

"There's a sparkle in the air to-day," he told her. "When do you wish to ride out?"

"It is not when I wish but when I can. *I* have to think of the dingy reckonings of every day! My sister Mary's debts. . . . I cannot sleep for them!"

"Ah, sweet! If I could pay them with my blood. . . ."

"And what would the Antwerp usurers do with your blood?" But she touched his cheek in a moment's caress before she turned away to meet her councillors.

The cost of the war against France was a mill-stone round the neck of the nation. Abruptly she had refused to pay one more penny in subsidies to the greedy ally, Spain. She must even risk Philip's anger for that. The debasing of the coinage started by her father had now reached perilous proportions. Cecil had brought to her Sir Thomas Gresham, the great merchant already famous for his knowledge of financial matters, and he had taken a sombre view of the English currency.

"No one will take English money at its face value. It destroys our credit. Bad money drives out good, your Grace. Such weakness corrupts strength."

She leaned forward, her eyes bright and intent on his face.

"Might it be possible to call in and replace this debased coinage, Sir Thomas?"

Gresham looked at Cecil for a moment, before replying.

"It would be possible, your Grace. It would not be easy. . . ."

"Then if it is possible, it must be done! My gentlemen, you must draw up a plan. Sir William has perhaps told you that I am cutting expenditure to the bone. There are too many greedy graspers living at the court's expense in duty-less offices, too many tax collectors with limed fingers and holes in their pockets. . . .There is a wind coming which will sweep them out of their shelters!"

"I have all the details here," said Cecil prosaically, "wishing that Sir Thomas might peruse them."

He did peruse them. Cecil and he then fell into a long financial debate, while Elizabeth listened, her pointed chin resting on her beautiful hands, her eyes narrowed to bright slits, weighing their arguments, keeping her mind to their discourse, like a sword's edge to the grindstone. It suited her better to receive one or two councillors at a time, and let her wishes filter through Cecil to the bulk of her council. United, she felt the disapproval of many middle-aged men for the views of a girl of twenty-five. Individually she could handle them. She said little till the financial discussion was ended. Gresham was going as her agent to Antwerp, then one of the chief money markets of the Continent. She had issued a proclamation that she would pay her sister's debts; by these acute economies, she hoped that in some six months she could fulfil part of her promises. She had mocked at Dudley when he had told her that he wished he might pay her debts with his blood, but sometimes she felt that her own blood was draining away with the flow of gold. Extravagance and folly aroused in her a burning exasperation. "Let them call me parsimonious!" she thought. "A spendthrift's popularity is quick come, quick go!"

Gresham took his leave and Cecil gathered up the papers.

"With your Majesty's leave I will present these memoranda to the Council. Is there anything further?"

"For your ear alone. Not for the Council as yet. This reply from King Henry of France."

Sunrise

"Reply from King Henry of France?" Cecil was aghast. So she was writing to negotiate with the enemy behind the back not only of her whole Council, but without his so much as dreaming of it! A young woman of twenty-five who would be better occupied with a husband and babies—to pit her wits (remarkable though these were) with hardened statesmen!

"Your Grace wrote to him?"

"My Grace did. I have some ease in the French language. . . . It is a very gallant, chivalrous gentleman. . . ." She laughed gaily, and tilted her head provocatively sideways at him. "What do you think of my earrings?"

"This is not a time to discuss your Grace's earrings!"

"Oh, but it is! They are a gift from the King of France and came with his letter. You should observe the beauty of these matching pear-shaped pearls. They are as good as any he ever gave to Madame de Poitiers. . . ."

"But what did he *say*?"

"Oh, most interesting! He suggested that he holds Calais in trust till my grandson is of age to wed with Mary Stuart's granddaughter by his son, Monsieur le Dauphin. . . ."

"Your Grace?"

"I am thinking of replying, after many compliments and thanks, that *I* should act as trustee till these two interesting infants should have emerged from the womb of time and become of marriageable age!"

"Will your Grace enlighten me as to the point of these exchanges?" asked Cecil in a cold and bitter voice.

"Oh, my Spirit, don't you see for yourself? My good brother Philip will learn that I am negotiating with Henry—in fact I shall see to it that he does. He will imagine my making a treaty with the Valois at *his* expense, instead of Spain making a treaty with France at England's expense! That is one of the reasons he has already proposed marriage to me. I won't deny he has some personal inclination towards me. There were love passages in my sister's lifetime." She cast her eyes demurely on the ground. "Wasn't it shameful?"

This was one of the occasions when Cecil desired to slap her.

"I would be grateful if your Grace were serious."

"I am serious enough." Her short laugh was bitter. "I fight with my own weapons. I want this business, this miserable war brought about by my sister's folly, settled! I must make the best I can out of this sorry matter of Calais. It must be ended as satisfactorily as possible, before the religious settlement and the financial settlement can be brought into being. Till then I need Philip."

Cecil looked at her for a long time.

"I understand, your Grace," he said at last. "But the very idea of another Spanish marriage is repugnant to all Englishmen!"

"And what do you think it is to me?" She was suddenly fierce. "That cold greedy bigot. . . . But I count no subterfuge too crooked if it saves English blood and English money. Of both, my sister was too prodigal. I have to clear up the confusion and dirt she left behind. Very likely my hands will not be clean. As for marrying Philip—I'd rather die. And I enjoy life! Still, I have sent Feria a reply which will tickle his vanity. . . . To tell you the truth, between our two selves, I have no mind to marry at all!"

"Many women say that, your Grace."

"I didn't credit my sex with so much sense!"

She went out impatiently, feeling suddenly wearied and sickened. Even her own acuteness seemed stale. It would be good to get away from it all for a couple of hours or so, to canter in the fields beyond Westminster, past Ebury Farm, across the West Bourne brook to the Thames-side village of Chelsea. . . . Robert had suggested a ride before she had gone to interview Cecil and Gresham. He and she were much of an age, but there were times when she felt a whole generation older.

Then a warm flow of happiness filled her. There he was, standing in a deep window embrasure in the wide corridor. Had he waited all this time for her—faithful Robin? She was about to call his name when she saw he was not alone, saw the soft sheen of a lilac-coloured silk farthingale, so close to him that they were almost touching, as he leaned tenderly over his companion. Didn't she know too well that protective gesture of his? It struck her like a searing whiplash.

"Well, my Lord!" she said and was surprised by the harshness of her own voice. He stepped back smartly and she found herself staring at a piquant heart-shaped face under tawny hair; dark, sullen yet glowing eyes above slanting cheekbones; moist red lips just apart as if breathless. It was one of her Maids of Honour, her own young cousin, Lettice Knollys.

She was fond of those relatives. When her cousin Catherine

50

Sunrise

(daughter of her mother's elder sister, Mary Boleyn) and her husband, Francis Knollys, being staunch Protestants, had fled abroad at the beginning of the Marian persecutions, she had written an affectionate letter to them, and had welcomed them back with genuine pleasure. Feeling that there was none she could trust so well, she had made Sir Francis Captain of her own Bodyguard. The daughter had been admitted amongst her Maids of Honour. Previously, Elizabeth had hardly noticed her. She must be about sixteen or seventeen.

"Lettice!" she exclaimed. "I' God's name! Who gave you leave to dilly-dally so?"

The girl had sunk almost to the floor in a deep curtsy. Now she raised her head and the dark eyes looked levelly back at Elizabeth, and the young voice answered with a coolness which was insolent.

"I crave your Grace's pardon! I did not know that I were forbid to walk in these corridors or speak with my lord Robert!"

Elizabeth's palm came in tingling contact with a cheek which felt as smooth as a ripe peach. She was surprised at the vehemence of her own anger, and the feeling in her hand.

"Don't bandy words with me! Get to your proper place!"

For a moment she was surprised by the glint of naked hatred in those dark eyes, and then Lettice humbly bowed her head, hiding the one cheek which was scarlet and the other deadly white. In silence, and with another obeisance, she withdrew swiftly. Elizabeth turned on Robert Dudley.

"I'll not have you trifling with my Maids of Honour. They're under my care. . . . That child is my own cousin!" As she spoke, she thought how singularly unchildlike had been that glance of fury in Lettice Knollys's eyes.

"I only passed a word or two with her, while I was wearying for you to come forth!"

"Did you indeed? She's a pretty girl. . . ."

"I suppose so," he conceded. "If one admires that type. . . ."

"Isn't my Lord condescending? What type do you deign to admire?"

"If there were a mirror here, you would see!"

"It's easy to flatter."

"Unlucky, you mean. If you take truth for flattery."

"I think no woman's safe from you!"

He said with a sulky indignation: "You talk like my wife!"

Elizabeth's hand came again into furious contact with a harder cheek.

"God's death! This is too much! So I'm to be reproved in one breath with your wife? What do you think you are?"

"A man who loves you more than his own soul."

"If I could be sure of that——" the anger had died out of her voice. She put her hand up to the slapped cheek. "Did I hurt you, Rob?"

"No, strike me again, if it pleases you."

"It doesn't please me. Oh, I've got a headache, Robin! From listening to Sir Thomas Gresham talking about the ruinous state of our finances, and showing William Cecil that I'm cleverer than he thinks. . . . And one plots and twists, and makes one's course between Scylla and Charybdis every day. . . . As for the religious settlement—I smell gunpowder, Rob!"

"You've done well. Bonner's prisoners are all set free and the exiles are flocking back."

"Yes, and the Bishop of Winchester thundering against the wolves of heresy! I gave the world a sign didn't I, on Christmas Day? I told the Bishop not to elevate the Host, and when he disobeyed—I walked out!"

"You did indeed. . . ."

"And then I have Feria storming at me as if I merely governed England in the name of the King of Spain, so I told him that I had issued a ban on preaching for the time being. He thought to silence the heretics as he calls them. I think I silenced the extremists of both sides. . . . Can there be no peace and toleration? I told Cecil I wanted a church which might shelter all. . . . But I think I would needs first change mankind!"

"I wish I could deliver you from all your troubles!"

"Why, Robin, I enjoy them sometimes! I like to pit my wits against an adversary. . . ." She looked at him, sideways but keenly. "Such as my brother-in-law who now seeks to marry me!"

Dudley struck his hand against the wall in a silent fury.

"So that angers you, Robin?"

"I'm flesh and blood!"

He was looking down at her, with his eyes burning.

"So am I!" she murmured.

His arms were round her again as they had been in the garden in Hatfield, and the heat in her blood was answering his. In that hard, lonely and dangerous road which she must tread, could she not comfort herself with a human love? Why should she not take the strength, passion and tenderness of this tall Robin and love him in secret till it were safe—if ever—to love him in public? And yet she knew, now when his lips were on hers, that even if she gave him the whole of herself as she so much wanted, one part of her would always be separate from him. It seemed that there was a sealed chamber in the recesses of her brain, where lived that being who had listened so keenly and calculated so sharply when Sir Thomas Gresham discoursed on financial matters, who dealt with the Kings of Spain and France, balancing this and that in scales which might be tipped by a hair, who twisted and double-laid her own path so none might follow her directly. Robin could never gain entrance to that chamber; there she must always be alone.

Would that have comforted Lettice Knollys, as she cautiously peeped round a bend in the corridor, and saw the Queen in the arms of Lord Robert? Her other cheek flamed to the colour of the one the Queen had slapped, as she turned swiftly away, the pointed teeth resting for a moment on her full red lip, making her look like a young wolf. She drove her nails into her palms in an access of fury as she moved away. "I hate her! I hate her! I hate her!" It seemed that she drew hatred instead of breath.

Elizabeth stepped out of his arms, sighed, laughed a little and said: "Now take me back in a seemly manner, sir! I wonder we have not been interrupted."

"One cannot be alone for more than a few minutes!" he complained.

"Better for me, Rob! Else I might be cast away utterly. . . . Who can trust men? And you would turn my little cousin's head!"

"Indeed I would not. She has a score of gallants already! Why, Essex is dangling after her!"

"My Lord Essex! Why, Robin, it would be an excellent match for her! Good Kate and Frank would be delighted. I'll sponsor it! Devereux—it is a fine and ancient name, and he's a fine enough fellow. . . . I'll help it on."

That evening there was dancing in Whitehall. The richly dressed figures moved like animated chessmen over the great black and white marble squares of the floor, to those airs throbbing from a consort of viols, or fluting clear and cool from a consort of recorders, airs which lilt as they might, or carry the greenwood freshness of country songs, were yet shot through and through with a strange melancholy. The sadness and the springlike freshness of sixteenth-century music can still come through, even on the instruments of another day, untouched by the sophistication of later music. It was an age when death was always near and often sudden. War came rolling over the land in the smoke of burning houses and the angry clash of steel; in shadowed corners daggers whipped their cruel brightness into defiant flesh; from the narrow stinking alleys where rats ran eagerly about the garbage, foul plagues rose with the stench of decay. And yet life was joyful, and new horizons, in enchanted spaces beyond the immemorial seas, new faiths and new learning, all promised untold riches, material and spiritual. So men and women danced and sang with an unquenchable hope.

Elizabeth loved dancing and knew that she danced gracefully. This evening, she let another than Robert lead her out in the first galliard. She dare not show him too much favour as yet, even in her love, she must balance those delicate scales. So she chose one reputed the handsomest man in all the court, the greatest lady-killer, although he was now over forty, Sir William Pickering. She smiled sweetly on him, as he handed her elegantly through the formal movements, and watched the other dancers sidelong, or rather two of them. Robert did not dance with Lettice Knollys. Either he did not care—or he was being wise. He danced with a court lady whom he had never noticed especially before, and his eyes followed the Queen, rashly but gratifyingly. Lettice danced with the Earl of Essex, her heart-shaped face a mask, though sometimes she raised her eyes to his face, those dark, sullen and yet glowing eyes which had come to her from the Boleyns—once spelled "Bullen" in those days before their ill-fated grandeur came upon them. Their women were said to be enchantresses, witches who stole a man's heart out of his breast by spells of the devil. Had not Mary once flashed out madly at the child, Elizabeth: "Your mother was a wicked witch!" The child, quaking inwardly, had answered with a sturdy defiance: "Then perhaps I'm a witch too and will turn you into a—a toad or a rabbit——" But then Mary, who, for all her fanaticism born of misery, for all her hysteria which drove her to unbalanced cruelty, was at heart a good woman, had been overcome with compunction, and had picked up her little sister and squeezed her painfully against her flat bosom

54

Sunrise

(which Elizabeth did not particularly enjoy) and then had given her some trifle which pleased her better.

The dance ended, and Elizabeth, contrary to her usual practice, went back to her dais, waving the musicians to play on. No, she was not tired, but for a change she would like to watch this figure. She beckoned to the upright soldierly cousin who commanded her Bodyguard—"Frank, a word in your ear!" He came, bowed abruptly and stood before her.

"Sit down, Frank! I want to speak of family matters to you."

"Family matters?"

"Yes! You have a very pretty daughter, Frank."

"Your Grace is very good. The wench is—none so bad. . . ."

"Oh, come, modest Frank! She's turning all the gallants' heads. Now look at Essex." The father looked. "You see?" Elizabeth laid light fingers on his arm. "I thought to-day, he would do very well for her. Would you have her Countess of Essex? It is a great name, Devereux. An ancient Norman name. And he's a likely fellow in himself."

"Devereux, yes. . . ." said Francis Knollys, thoughtfully. The Wars of the Roses had bled the ancient *noblesse* white, and the cold, clever Henry VII, to ensure the safety of his new dynasty, had driven most of the survivors into obscurity. Where was Bohun, Mowbray, de Clare, and Mortimer? On the Northern Marches, that kingdom within a kingdom, Percy still ruled in Northumberland, and Neville in Westmorland, but for the rest of the country, few remained. Howard of Norfolk was still premier Duke of England, and here was Devereux, Earl of Essex. But the Court was filled with the new gentry, faithful civil servants of the powerful Tudor crown, enriched by monastery lands, gift of those same Tudors, the Cecils, Bacons, Throckmortons, Dudleys, Careys, Haringtons—and Bullens.

"I will sponsor it," said Elizabeth. "It will please you and Kate? Ah—good. An' if there is any trouble about a dowry"—she winced slightly, for it was a pain to pour out that gold which was so thirstily needed—"remember I am your loving kinswoman."

"Indeed you are, God bless you!" said Knollys, pressing her hand to his lips. She tapped a page on his shoulder. "Bid my Lord of Essex come here!"

When the three-cornered interview had ended to her entire satisfaction, the musicians were playing a lively coranto. She looked across and caught Robert's eye. He came swiftly, and stood before her.

"If your Grace will do me the honour?"

"I will, Rob."

As he led her on to the floor, looking down at her (as he had looked down at Lettice Knollys this very morning), he murmured: "I've been waiting for this. . . ."

"So have I, Rob!"

"You look happy?"

"I am happy!" Her smile was dazzling.

But Sir Francis and his wife were somewhat displeased with their daughter's reaction to the great match arranged for her. She had stamped her foot on the ground when told how thankful she should be for her royal cousin's kindness, and had darted a black glance from those burning eyes of hers.

"Essex is a fool!" she cried.

Her parents, very properly, paid no attention to her.

Chapter Five

The bells of London clashed and jangled, rocking the city's one hundred steeples. Their shouting exultant music had disturbed Elizabeth's dreams, penetrating the warm, secret depths of the great bed, where she was snugly curled against the cold of the January night. Merrily they seemed to ring out the old nursery jingle:

> "Upon Paul's steeple stands a tree
> As full of apples as may be,
> The little boys of London town,
> They run with hooks to pull them down.
> And then they run from hedge to hedge
> Until they come to London Bridge."

The grim walls of the Tower encircled her, as following the immemorial custom of England's sovereigns, she and her court lay there, before her Coronation. To-day was Saturday, the 14th of January 1559, when she was to move in grand procession through the city to Westminster, where she would be crowned the following day.

She lay awake, happy in the dark, hearing the rocking, brazen music of the bells, which matched the song her heart sang. Twenty years of lonely danger, with pitfalls opening under her feet, plots, schemes and intrigues coiling about her like serpents, not one safe place where she could shelter, or one safe friend on whom she might lean, had now ended in this full and glorious consummation. She had waited with a strange, almost inhuman patience, armouring herself with her wits against the perpetual strokes of danger. Here, in this sinister fortress, had she not argued and debated, while hourly expecting a grim death? She had held her hand when many had begged her to precipitate fate, trusting Time to bear her on like a flowing river. One day she was to write:

"I have let time pass, which I generally find helps more than reasoning."

There was another happiness in her heart. To-day, her subjects in her greatest city (and many, she had heard, coming in from the countryside around) would greet her, with that warmth which seemed to increase with her craving for it. She had likened it to a great fire on a winter's night, but now it seemed that it was food and drink as well as firing, and that she drew most of her strength from it. For here, she felt, was safety. She could—and did—glow with a return of love for these people who greeted her so fervently, and she believed she might trust them. Because of that, she, who had before trusted no one, felt a passion of gratitude. She would fight and work and struggle for them, lie and plot and scheme, if needs be. They were her children. The time was to come when she would cry passionately to her "faithful Commons": "And do not upbraid me with a miserable lack of children: for every one of you, and as many as are Englishmen, are children and kinsmen to me: of whom if God deprive me not—which God forbid—I cannot without injury be accounted barren." This was the one rock on which she might build, for where is the soul which can stand alone utterly, without God or man, though she was more lonely than most?

So the bells triumphed on and she triumphed with them. To-day she might be happy, might keep her mind off the religious settlement, the financial settlement, the peace settlement (but a better prospect was dawning there as the French were now talking of paying a subsidy for Calais) and worst of all the problem of her future marriage, for a Queen *must* marry—and every day she realized more strongly with what a passion she loved her Robin, a passion which tumultuously argued with her cold and wary brain.

Yesterday, when creating Knights of the Bath, according to ancient custom, she had thought: "Robin must have the Garter. . . ."

"Presently," said that cold and wary brain.

"Am I not Queen?" her heart had burst out.

"Give him this honour in company with others, and later on . . ." warned the brain.

She remembered her imprisonment, when sick and weary in body, her mind strained to unbearable tension, she had been at last allowed

Sunrise

to walk in a little paved garden where bushes of red and white roses grew. She remembered his dark head stooping over those bushes, when she had come into the garden, thinking: "It's the Dudley boy —Robert. . . ." and how he had turned to her with an eager smile, his hands full of roses: "When I saw you coming, I thought, that at least here is something I can give you, in this abominable place. . . ." His father, his brother, Guildford, and his sister-in-law, Jane Grey, had just gone to the block; he himself was under a commuted death sentence, and yet had he not put his own fears and sorrows aside, to try and lighten her captivity? Now, the evening before, when the ceremonies had been concluded, and she was withdrawing to her own apartments, he had come swiftly to her side, and had suddenly offered her, lying on his palm, a small, tight, frost-withered rosebud.

"Do you remember?" he whispered. "The rose garden here? I found only this one bud, and the frost has got at it. Yet if you put it to your heart, it will flower. . . ."

She had raised the bud to her lips. "Dear Robin. . . ."

Footsteps were echoing nearer than the clamour of the bells, and a bright light sparkled painfully in her eyes. Behind the double candlestick came the ample form of Kate Ashley.

"Just listen to those bells!" she declared. "They'll give those saucy bishops cause to think. . . . A fine lot they are, and I know how I would handle them!"

"Sit down on my bed and gossip," said Elizabeth, smiling. "I confess I would like to hear how you would handle them!"

"Your Grace is teasing me. . . ." But she settled herself comfortably almost on the royal feet.

"Come, now!" Elizabeth urged her. "If you were Queen Kate, how would you deal with these same bishops?"

"I'd duck them in the River Thames!" declared Mistress Ashley. "In midsummer when it stinks so mightily. . . ."

"So hot against the bishops? I don't care which one crowns me— so long as one is found. If Oglethorpe of Carlisle will do it, he will serve."

"And he's borrowing vestments from Bonner!" declared Kate Ashley, who always knew every piece of gossip.

"With Bonner's will?"

"I can't say! Your Grace should burn Bonner at the stake!"

"God forbid," said Elizabeth quietly.

59

Sunrise

"But your Grace, you are not angry!"

"I have no need to waste my anger."

"I can't get over the insolence of Bishop White when he preached the funeral sermon over your Grace's sister. Calling you a live dog and she a dead lion! Why, if I'd known the Latin—but there wasn't such education for gentlewomen in my day!—I'd have thrown something at him and bid him hush his ugly mouth."

"You'll know again, my Kate, the meaning of the words—'melior est canis vivus leone mortuo'?"

"And your Grace sat through it?"

"Would you have me brawl at my sister's funeral? Besides the man had some spirit. I believe he had a real regard for my sister."

"More fool or knave he!" complained Ashley. "You should show them that you are your father's daughter!"

Elizabeth stretched out her arm and took Mistress Ashley's wrist in a strong grip of her long thin fingers.

"Don't fear, Kate. I'll show them that I'm my father's daughter. Sooner than they expect, perhaps. . . . But I'll show them when I want! Now make my people bring me something to eat, and then you and Blanche Parry and the maids must set things ready. How is the weather? Does it snow?"

"A little. But they say it's clearing."

They spent hours of that morning dressing and adorning her in a robe of cloth of gold, as stiff as mail. Jewels blazed upon her, and set on her coppery hair was that princess's crown which she had worn at the coronation of her sister, Mary. She gazed for a short while at a mirror which showed her a gorgeous image strangely removed from everyday life. But in that pale oval face with the pointed chin resting on the stiffly wired ruff, the dark eyes burned with an intense life of their own. She called for rouge and wondered what Lord Robert and the citizens of London would think of her, not knowing which she wanted to impress the more.

In the afternoon, the whole court was assembled, crowding about the central keep, the oblong block of the White Tower, with its pepper-box turrets at the corners. From the greenish leaden sky a few snowflakes drifted on to the already whitened ground, but the gold collars and sparkling jewels of that brilliant assembly seemed to burn like torches, clearing the air. Hitherto, in all State processions, Elizabeth had ridden on horseback, but now she was to be carried in an open litter, hung to the ground with cloth of gold, and borne by two white mules, covered with the same material. Over her head a canopy was upheld by four knights. Behind her rode Robert Dudley, Master of Horse, on a black charger, his red velvet cloak thrown back to show a gilded cuirass, leading her white horse, caparisoned in cloth of gold. On each side of the litter walked Gentlemen Pensioners, that part of her Bodyguard formed by young men of good birth (as distinct from the professional soldiers called Yeomen), wearing for this occasion crimson damask and carrying gilt-headed battle-axes. The foot soldiers were in crimson velvet jerkins adorned with the Tudor Rose set about with silver-gilt studs and the royal cipher. Beyond these, the court made an escort of at least a thousand horsemen, moving slowly and with dignity, from the great fortress, through the city to Westminster. For a country so near bankruptcy, it was a brave show; Elizabeth looked at it with satisfaction. She might have to pledge her jewels later at Antwerp, but she would make a display now to impress the world.

The bells soared to their exultant climax as if they would shake down the steeples on the heads of the devoted ringers. And with their music, came the roaring of thousands of throats, from the packed roadway. They had been waiting for hours in the cold, beating their numbed fingers, stamping their numbed feet, their faces blue and pinched. Many had collapsed from cold and weariness and had been carried away. Fortunate were those near the triumphal bonfires. But they could shout, pressing into the roadway, thrusting through the ranks of the Yeomen and Gentleman Pensioners, trying to touch the Queen, or her litter, to press upon her small nosegays lovingly gathered. Here and there she checked her litter, smiled or spoke to the excited people; an old woman had pushed through to give her a supplication with a branch of rosemary and she kept them, an old man in the front row of spectators broke down and wept. She bade a Gentleman Pensioner question him. "Your Grace, he weeps for joy to see the true Queen——" A voice rang out: "Remember old King Harry!"

In the city itself banners and streamers waved in the keen air, the streets between Fenchurch Street and Cheapside had railed galleries hung with tapestries, silks and velvets, erected by the great city companies who stood behind them in their famous liveries. The city had prepared pageants, each with its musicians and trumpeters joining and drowning the cheers and the endless brazen song of the bells. At

Sunrise

Gracechurch was a stage of three tiers, representing the House of Tudor. On the lowest was Henry VII, founder of the dynasty, seated upon the Red Rose of Lancaster, his hand joined with that of his bride, Elizabeth (for whom she had been named), upon the White Rose of York. Above them came Henry VIII and Anne Boleyn. For twenty-two years no one had dared to mention her name—the witch-queen who had driven men mad for love of her, the enchantress for whom the King had defied the very powers of heaven, only to turn savagely from her in less than three years. But here was her effigy, robed and diademed as a Queen by her grim husband's side, as her daughter rode past in triumph, and on the top tier was a resplendent effigy of that same daughter, the whole stage garlanded with the red and white roses. There were other pageants, one representing Elizabeth as "Deborah, judge and restorer of the House of Israel"; in another Old Father Time and his daughter, Truth, presented her with an English Bible, which she first kissed and then held up for all to see. In Cheapside, the City Trumpeters and the City Waits strove against each other in sound when the City Recorder presented the Queen with a crimson purse containing a thousand marks in gold. Her eyes were wet with a sudden emotion when she ended her speech of thanks: "And persuade yourselves that for the safety and quietness of you all, I will not spare, if need be, to spend my blood. . . . ." On and on, past the huge gothic mass of St. Paul's, whose bells had clanged louder than any, to hear a tribute to her scholarship in the cool treble voice of a boy from Dean Colet's School, likening her to Plato's philosopher king. So at last she left the city by Temple Bar, adorned with more banners and streamers and the great mythical shapes of Gog and Magog, where her voice came ringing out: "Be ye well assured I will stand your good Queen!"

The next day she came to Westminster Abbey to be crowned, met by Oglethorpe, the solitary bishop, in the borrowed mitre and vestments of Bonner, three crosses borne before him, the choristers of the Queen's Chapel singing "Salve feste dies" as they led the procession, whose way was spread with blue cloth. The solemn ritual of the coronation proceeded, fanfares of trumpets pealing to the high vaulted roof between every proclamation. When she was presented to the people in the Abbey as their Queen, the sound of trumpets and other instruments seemed to split the air, so that a witness was to declare that it sounded like the end of the world.

Sunrise

Behind the High Altar, behind the traverse which had been set for a tiring room, Kate Ashley waited with Blanche Parry and some serving-maids. Mistress Ashley's plump face was creased with emotion, her lips quivered and tears began to run down, disturbing the rouge on her cheeks.

"When I think of this day! My dear blessed child crowned at the High Altar in the face of the whole nobility—in spite of all the plots and scheming of people like the roaring lion in the Scriptures—and her own sister as unnatural as a—what is that wicked pagan Roman Emperor my Lady told me about? Nero. The Queen Mary was no better than a Nero or any other pagan monster, and the dear child like a blessed martyr——" She broke off her confused words to blow her nose and dab at her streaming eyes. Blanche Parry, the principal waiting-woman, raised her eyes with a sort of demure mockery.

"Her Grace is too clever to be a martyr!" she observed.

"Well, she nearly was a martyr, and you know that as well as I do!" retorted Mistress Ashley. "Not that I'd deny her cleverness. All those years of reading Latin and Greek with Master Grindal and Master Ascham till no wonder her pretty head ached and ached. . . . Quick she is, and as sharp as any needle, and she needed it with those lawyers. You pray you never get in the hands of those advocates, Blanche! They toss you and twist you worse than the rack! I tell you you'd find you'd said your own parents were highway robbers before you'd know how you came at it. . . . But she! Even those devils—and devils they were—could hold her to nothing. Sharp she may be, sometimes I don't know what she means after all these years with her, and a temper she's got I don't deny! But I tell you she's better at heart than anyone suspects. I should know how good she is. . . ." Mistress Ashley wiped away a few more tears and sadly disarranged her make-up, as she thought how her voluble tongue and unrestrained terrors had once so grievously harmed her beloved mistress. "Do you know she's never said one word of reproach to me, Blanche, nor to your father, though he was more to blame than I? But never a hard word have I had—and if that isn't Christian forgiveness!"

"She's been a good mistress to us all," said Blanche Parry. She was aware of her father's damaging statements, but wasn't he now Sir Thomas Parry, Comptroller of the Royal Household, and she, Blanche, second only to Mistress Ashley in attendance on the Queen's person? Elizabeth had forgiven royally.

"Yes, you'd think she would only be in mind of her own danger, but off she writes at once for me and for your father—unworthy creatures we are, though we love her dearly—to my Lord Protector Somerset and doesn't rest till she has us out of prison. . . . Ah! He came to a bad end, the Lord Protector! They were served right for their arrogance, those Seymours. . . . Though I must confess the Lord Admiral was as pretty a man as I ever saw except my Lord Robert. . . ." she added incorrigibly.

"It's a pity Lord Robert's a married man. . . ."

"Well, they say his wife has a malady in one of her breasts and won't live long! I had it from Lady Sidney's principal gentlewoman, and if Lady Sidney doesn't know the health of her own brother's wife!"

"Creaking doors hang longest," quoted Blanche Parry.

They looked up suddenly. Elizabeth was coming towards them with a strange sleepwalker's step. They were ready to change her swiftly, so that her robes might be offered with the rest of the regalia at the altar, but Kate Ashley put down the articles of attire she had ready. In her golden robe and jewels, her red hair bright above her pale face, Elizabeth looked like a flame against the cold grey stone, but Mistress Ashley was frightened by the unnatural pallor of her face, the dazed unseeing stare in her dark eyes, and the uncertainty of her step, as if she scarcely knew where she was going. Kate ran to her mistress, guiding her into a carved oak chair, rubbing her icy cold hands and telling Blanche to get out the cordial wine—"and it's a blessing I thought to bring it! The poor lamb's ready to faint!" —fussing over her till a realization seemed to come to Elizabeth.

"Don't be frightened, Kate. I—I'm a little tired perhaps. That's all. From the feelings in my heart and the things I seemed to see. . . ." She sipped a little of the cordial wine and then put it from her. "Do you see this ring on my finger? With it, I have just been wedded to this realm. It's a most solemn thought, more solemn than any ordinary marriage. England is my husband now. . . ."

"Bless you, my love!" said Kate Ashley, chafing the cold hands and wishing she might lay that red head on her ample bosom—but could she now a crown had been placed on it? "Bless you! I hope I'll soon see you wedded to something warmer and closer than a country! To some proper tall man who'll take all these burdens off you, and deal with your Councillors and——"

"But that", said Elizabeth firmly, "is just what no one shall ever do!" She was quite collected now. "These burdens are mine, and this country is mine, and no one can share with me! And the burdens are my pride. . . ." She could not explain to her faithful Kate, she could not explain to anyone, the feelings she had had as she had knelt on her golden brocade cushions before the High Altar. The Bishop had laid the Sword of State—her sword—upon the altar as an offering. She had felt that the whole of herself, all those strange and complex qualities were laid there. All that polished adroit cleverness, all that hair-scale balancing, all the dark subtle planning, all the lies even —besides that sudden deep passion of love and dedication and service. . . . Before her eyes, in the light of the many wax candles on the altar, the golden plate had shone and quivered, and she had seemed to see those other things like smoke of sacrifice. Soundlessly she had prayed: "Oh God, who made me and know what I am and what is in me—You know I offer it all. . . ." That keen relentless brain of hers, the devotion of her heart, and the blood which she had promised to shed if need be for her subjects, she had promised them all. A vision of Robert's dark handsome face seemed to pass before her eyeballs, but she put it from her. All private happiness and chance of happiness must be offered too, must be laid on the altar besides those symbols which could be seen, the sword and the sceptre, the crown and the ring. She would hold nothing back. But she had risen from her knees in a daze, and only now with the cordial burning in her throat and Kate Ashley's warm hands rubbing hers, was she noticing the everyday world.

"Come, change me into my purple velvet! Faugh!" She wrinkled up her high nose. "The consecrating oil wasn't oil at all, but grease, and it smells! Wipe it off, I beg of you. . . ."

She did not need any such rancid symbol. She felt that an unseen flame had touched and consecrated her whole being. So they changed her into a robe of purple velvet, and then with the State Crown upon her head, and the sceptre and the orb in her hands, she led the brilliant procession to the long and ceremonial banquet in Westminster, "her smile like sunshine on the beholders" as she heard the Garter King at Arms proclaim in a sonorous voice: "The most high and mighty princess, our dread sovereign lady, Elizabeth by the Grace of God Queen of England, France, Ireland, Defender of the True, Ancient and Catholic Faith, most worthy Empress from the Orcade Isles to the mountains Pyrenée!"

Chapter Six

The Queen sat at chess with Lord Robert, at a table in a deep window embrasure of one of her withdrawing chambers. The long slender fingers hardly hesitated as they moved the white knight, but they continued to rest on the carved mane of the ivory piece. The red king was finally encompassed; menaced by the diademed white queen and a satellite bishop, his last square of escape was now closed.

"I have you, Rob!" she said.

His dark eyes flickered over the board and then came to rest on her face.

"For the third time. . . ."

"And yet you are a good player. I've watched you. Are you letting me win?"

"No," he answered her. "I wouldn't so mock at your intelligence. It is—when I am so close to you, my wits wander——"

"And why?"

He leaned across the table, and lightly took hold of her hand, turning it this way and that.

"You have the most beautiful hands in the whole world. . . . When I am so near to you, I can't polish my wits, and plot and fight. I only think of you. . . ."

The hand withdrew from his, came up, and took his chin between thumb and forefinger, so she might look steadily at him.

"If you tell lies, Robin, you tell them more prettily than any other man."

"They aren't lies. . . ."

"Yet when you joust, your wits don't wander. Yesterday you bore down three men."

"I would be a poor knight if I could not strike down all adversaries

Sunrise

for my Lady. . . . But I tell you it enrages me that every young pup of a Gentleman Pensioner considers himself to be breaking a lance for the Queen's most excellent Majesty! That booby yesterday proclaiming that he would hold the lists against all comers in honour of Gloriana, queen and goddess!" He frowned. "I served him out for his presumption!"

"So you did—over his horse's tail with a clang of steel that startled the birds from the trees! And he was a gallant lad too."

"A gallant idiot!"

"To give his vows to Gloriana?"

"To presume so far! I won't share——"

"*You* won't share? My Lord, I think the Queen's Majesty belongs in equal part to all her loyal subjects. But the woman, Elizabeth——"

"Ah! She's the one that matters to me."

"I wonder? I thought she had been rather kind to you. . . ."

"Sometimes she gives me heaven—for about five minutes."

"Perhaps that's too long. . . ."

"It's not long enough!"

Their eyes met steadily without swerving, and they saw nothing else. But the Queen's ladies working at their embroideries or talking in low voices, looked up and saw them. If they talked the less, they thought the more, and not for the first time.

Robert was baffled. Since his boyhood, women had fallen too easily to his handsome face and his strong graceful body. The wife he had married at seventeen—who wearied him unutterably now— had adored him in a way he found cloying and wearisome. So many others had succumbed to the briefest of sieges. But this one played with him as coolly as she played the game of politics. He could not tell how much he mattered to her and it maddened him. Last night in the famous gardens of Hampton Court, a still July night which yet held all the warmth of the vanished sun, she had come into his arms, in a secluded arbour, and for that brief moment had seemed to return all his passion. It was always so—they would cling to each other madly and then she would break away from him, and be the Queen, remote and untouchable. He was consumed with ambition; he snatched at every glittering prize she gave him and lorded it perilously over other courtiers; if she had not been Queen his courtship might have followed another and rougher course. Yet the woman Elizabeth was driving him to desperation with her waywardness, with her

67

blowing from hot to cold with a swiftness which left him gasping. He did not know how much of it came from the nature of the woman, or from her sovereignty. If he might sweep her off her feet, he would not only subdue and possess that wayward but enchanting creature, he would possess all the power and the glory in the realm. But. . . .

He might not be sure enough of the woman to assay the perils which surrounded the Queen. Those lips which he had kissed so violently the evening before, seemed to have a little lilt of mockery.

"Robin!" she said. "You are a sad rascal! I think I am not safe to be alone with you!"

"Do you want to be safe?" he challenged her.

"Life is very seldom what one wants," she countered.

They were so leaning across the chessboard, gazing at each other, when Mr. Secretary Cecil was announced, and he saw them before they saw him. He frowned; this business of Lord Robert was getting too much. People were talking freely. It was unwise for any young woman—let alone a Queen—to look at a young man in such a fashion. And Elizabeth was a Queen, and Robert was a married man. Even if he were not married, reflected the Secretary, he came of a family of arrogant upstarts whose ambition was too well known and too dangerous. What were people already whispering? That Lord Robert's great-grandfather was a carpenter; his grandfather, Henry VII's clever, shady lawyer; his father, the notorious second Lord Protector who had tried to place his son on the throne beside the unlucky Lady Jane Grey—and of these three, the only one to die in his bed was the carpenter—who was the only honest man of the lot. . . ."

"Despatches from Scotland, your Grace!" he said in a voice icy with disapproval. Elizabeth shrugged.

"I must be serious, Robin. . . ." she said, in a voice which held a note of mockery. Neither man was certain for whom. But she was moving towards her secretary, her attention obviously switching to him.

"Come, Sir Spirit!"

Robert was forgotten. She beckoned Cecil to an inner chamber, and seated herself behind a table on which were spread some writing materials and a pile of beautifully bound books. He knew it was her daily custom to spend an hour or so reading Greek and Latin with her former tutor, Roger Ascham. It kept (she said) her brain bright and whetted. Her knowledge of modern languages also, he admitted, was as remarkable as that of the classics.

"Sit down," she said. "What is the latest news from Scotland?"

"Your Grace will forgive me if I speak of something else?"

"Proceed."

"If your Grace will forgive me, your very marked favour to Lord Robert is causing too much talk."

"In other words, people are jealous of him?"

"You can put it that way."

She burst out with a sudden heat: "Of course they are jealous of him! I know his devotion and his loyalty. I know how it was tested. And of course all the miserable curs yap at his heels! There isn't a man in this court to touch him in look or manner. He's—he's princely——"

"Even if I agree with your Grace as regards his appearance, is there any need to make him a prince?"

"God's death! Who talks of making him a prince?"

"Too many people whisper it, in corners, already, your Grace."

"Too many rats. . . . I'll have no princes here. Do you know he wants an earldom? And that I am not at present disposed to give it to him?"

"Your Grace has given him much."

"Master of Horse and who should fill the post better? I made him a Knight of the Garter in company with other noble and worthy gentlemen."

"Your Grace has just given him a fair house and land at Kew."

"If I can't reward my loyal friends, it is a pretty pass!"

"Your Grace, you know I speak for your good weal. People have not forgotten his father. John Dudley was a very dangerous man. His ambition was boundless. You should remember Lord Robert's father, your Grace!"

He saw her bosom rise and her long fingers clench. Her eyes were black with passion.

"God's soul, Mr. Secretary! You should remember mine. . . ."

But a minute later she was smiling.

"Sir Spirit, never think that I underestimate what *you* have done for me or this country. . . . Believe that. . . . Now! Let us deal with those plaguey people, the Scots."

Cecil agreed with the last. It seemed obvious that the Good God, in His often inexplicable wisdom, had created those same Scots only to be a thorn in England's side. But the present situation seemed to promise hopeful if intricate possibilities. It was a situation curiously adapted to the Queen's talents.

It was surprising how well they had emerged from the appalling difficulties which had confronted them at the beginning of the reign. The war was concluded and not so badly as he had feared. Calais was gone, but the French were to pay a subsidy of 500,000 crowns if they did not restore it in eight years. ("I am thinking, my Spirit, that the money may be more use to us!") She had played cunningly on King Philip's fears of her making a separate peace, and had extracted everything she could get from his proposal of marriage till she was to reject it with a sudden fury, saying how might she marry her sister's former husband, when her father had dissolved *his* first marriage because it had been with his brother's widow? That brother's widow being Philip's great-aunt, the reminder must have been peculiarly mortifying. There was private revenge in it. She had said to Cecil, her teeth on her lip and her eyes hot: "That will repay my good brother-in-law for being scarcely able to keep his hands off me, at Greenwich Palace, under my sister's very nose. . . ." But she had used his proposal to the full. The thunders of the Vatican had not fallen on her head while they were drawing up the National Church, a church which seemed to promise a great deal to a great many people. Her delight in being ambiguous had been used to the full, and yet at the same time it seemed an honest attempt at what he believed she really wanted with that queer sincerity which she sometimes showed —"a Church broad enough to shelter all". . . . The Marian bishops had naturally enough opposed her, but they had been quietly and firmly placed in the Tower, nor were they given the extravagant martyrdom for which the extremists clamoured. Elizabeth was always opposing the extremists and saving as much as she could of the old ritual. She had spoken to Cecil with what he believed was that same sincerity: "Have you ever reflected on one of the things which religion should be to people?"

"Please enlighten me, your Grace."

"Why," she said. "Religion should be a comfort, I believe. And is the new or the familiar the greatest comfort? Surely the familiar! That is why I like the use of the old Latin prayers translated into English so all can understand them. . . ."

Sunrise

Cecil had never considered that religion was to be a comfort to people. He had had to contemplate it too long as a department of politics.

"I trust your Grace finds it a comfort," he had said dryly.

"I? A comfort?" A naked bitterness had flashed into her voice. "Since I was born—no—before I was born—I was the puppet of one religious faction to be played off against the other! Much comfort of any kind I've had in my life!"

Finally the finances of the kingdom were coming slowly round. They had been skilfully and relentlessly reorganized. Six months after her accession, Sir Thomas Gresham had been able to pay a substantial amount of her sister's debts abroad which, he had jubilantly announced, sent Elizabeth's credit soaring in the international money markets. Next year the great reform of the coinage could be achieved. Yes, when they had done so much out of so very little, was she—she with that cold, wary, brilliant brain of hers—to kick down those foundations so painstakingly laid, because of desire for an attractive but impossible young man? Surely that brain of hers would warn her? And yet. . . . She was not all brain and if heredity counted for anything (and hadn't he been arguing Dudley's heredity?) wasn't she the child of "Old Harry" by the most devastating of all his six unlucky queens? She had been born of a passion as violent and destructive as a stroke of summer lightning. Supposing she were capable of it too?

He shook his head as he turned to the business of the Scots. Their country had been for a long time a virtual province of France, garrisoned and held down by French soldiers, and ruled by the Queen Regent, Mary of Guise, for her young daughter who was now Queen consort of France. But the Scots were wearying of foreign rule and at the same time embracing the most extreme form of Protestantism available, speeded thereto by the prophetic thunders of that "Apostle of the Reformation", that right-hand man of Calvin, Master John Knox. They were now beginning to rise against the Queen Regent and her Frenchmen. Such troubled waters promised good fishing. There was a sparkle in Elizabeth's eye.

"After all," said she, "if we assist the 'Lords of the Congregation' and their godly followers to throw out a foreign domination—assist them by all means short of war—we are only being neighbourly to the Scots. The one country with which we have a land frontier."

"We should have their eternal gratitude."

"Should we? Gratitude is such a rare virtue. . . . I'll believe in gratitude when I see it! But if they get rid of the French and Catholicism at the same time, we will be the only friends they'll have. I believe in expediency before gratitude which is an excellent maxim for a child's copybook but bears no fruit in this grown-up world."

Cecil was driven by pure curiosity to ask: "Does your Grace then believe in no genuine virtues in the human heart?"

"Oh, yes. Because there are even a few in my own heart. . . . But believing in them is not the same thing as building upon them."

"The Earl of Arran has gone safely north."

"That half-wit? I hope he may encourage them. . . . Still, it was the neatest thing in the world the way we smuggled him out of France under the nose of the Guises and concealed him here. I hope he gets safely into Scotland before the French Ambassador asks me if he is in this country. M. de Noailles never believes a word I say and it would be delicious to tell him the truth for once, when, of course, he would be convinced that it is a lie as usual."

Cecil had now got used to this levity and ignored it.

"Your Grace has no opinion of Arran's abilities?"

"None whatsoever. But he has a certain value as a token. After all he has a fairly good claim to the Scottish throne should the Scots decide to remove its present occupant. As long as the pro-French party think I may marry him, they are going to be greatly discouraged. And the Protestant party equally well encouraged. So I must pretend that he is a most favoured suitor a little longer. . . . It's distressing"— here she made a gesture skilfully showing a wistful mockery—"that all my Protestant suitors are inclined to insanity. Now Eric of Sweden who is so rich, so eligible, and so persistent!—Lord Robert tells me he is quite an imbecile."

"I fail to see what concern it is of Lord Robert's. . . ."

"He has his sovereign's welfare very close to his heart."

"The Archduke Charles is not insane."

"No, but he's a Catholic and that would upset so many people in this country."

"Your Grace, I do beg of you to consider the Archduke Charles most seriously. There could not be a better match——"

"My Spirit, don't be so dull! Haven't I just told you that it is essential for us to encourage our adherents in Scotland—and discourage their enemies—with the belief that I am all ready to fall into Arran's arms like a ripe plum? So long as it is necessary for them to believe that, I dare not seem to take interest in another suitor."

("She'll always find some excuse not to marry. . . ." he thought gloomily.)

"For my own inclinations," she said, "I don't want to marry. It is quite true what I said to the House of Commons, that I hope one day it should be engraved upon my tomb: 'Here lieth Elizabeth, who reigned a virgin and died a virgin'. . . ."

("Only the Lord God and the Lord Robert know if she is one!" thought her exasperated minister.) But he had an awkward feeling that she had read his thoughts. She rested her chin on her interlaced fingers and made a grimace at him.

"Now as to these excellent Scots. . . . Who is the trusty man to take my three thousand pounds in gold to cheer their hearts?"

"Sir Ralph Sadler. He *is* a trusty man."

"And I hope Master Knox has promised a pithy exhortation?"

"Presumably. It is said that he heartens them more than a hundred trumpets blowing."

She made a mouth. "If it's their taste!" she said. "When he preached here at court in my brother's reign, I heard that remarkable—instrument!"

"Very forceful, your Grace."

"*Very.* Since we are told that the blood of the martyrs is the seed of the Church, we must regret he left this realm so swiftly when my sister ascended the throne. . . ."

"Your Grace must realize he is useful!"

"I do! If he does—I expect it mortifies him. However—— They say any stick does to beat a dog with. . . . We find each other mutually useful against Mary of Guise, though I still think it is a pity that such a vessel of the Lord should have been denied a martyr's crown! If Bonner had found him a stake, *my* tears would never have put out the flames. . . . And though he encourages his followers to take my money, he continues to blow the trumpet against what he is pleased to call 'the Monstrous Regiment of Women'. . . ."

("She'll never forgive him that," thought Cecil." Certainly the 'Blast was blown out of Season'. . . .")

But Robert Dudley walked by the edge of the river and thought about Amy, that pretty, dull and stupid girl to whom he had been married in boyhood. Sweetness had turned to insipidity, varied only by plaintive tears and bewailing of her real or imagined ill health. Certainly she spent her time dosing herself with medicine and, considering what medicine was like at that time, it was not remarkable if she were ill. Some months ago she had made a great outcry about a swelling in her breast which she had declared was cancer and she was likely to die. He had posted off at once to her, but she had gone on a visit to the Hyde family at Denchworth and seemed better for company. Also she had a new physician of whom she thought highly and who was treating her with a popular but expensive remedy, dissolved pearls. Robert, being a dutiful husband, bought plenty of pearls for her to take, and a string to hang round her neck. One could always silence a woman's plaints with a present. Except Elizabeth, of course—but then she was not an ordinary woman. . . .

Amy liked being at the Hydes'. There was plenty of company, card playing, and endless trivial chatter (so he found it) to keep her occupied. She could hardly read or write and was bored with the ordering of her own household. He could not have found a greater contrast to Elizabeth if he had sought for ten years. He had stayed there as short a time with her as decency permitted, lost a lot of money at card play which pleased everyone and he felt was expected of him. But he was too irritated and troubled to concentrate on primero, gleek and trump. Amy being fretfully affectionate and asking to be taken to court, Amy dosing herself with endless potions, Amy babbling like a brook with the females of the Hyde family, Amy frightened and plaintive over her ailments—he did not know which annoyed him most. So he had given her a very large sum of money, told her to stay at the Hydes' as long as she pleased or if she returned to Cumnor Hall, to ask as many guests as she liked. She had got weary of Cumnor, she said, and she had taken a dislike to Anthony Forster who managed the property for him. . . . He had not told her of his new house at Kew lest she should wish to live there. He had gone back to court thankfully, and Elizabeth had lost her temper savagely with him for staying away.

He looked at his own image, distorted by the dark, sluggish waters of the river. If Amy *had* been seriously ill, if she had died—he didn't want her to die of course, least of all to suffer, poor foolish creature, but. . . . But if he were free of her! If he had no wife round his neck like a mill-stone. . . .

74

Sunrise

Elizabeth was so damned jealous, she must care about him! When he had her in his arms, he never doubted it. Yet ambition might drive her into some great match, such as the King of Sweden or the Archduke Charles. She was as proud as the devil. And anyway he was tied to Amy. But whether she did marry, the Archduke or another, and whether he remained tied to Amy, was it possible for him to become the Queen's lover, and in secret gain the power that he might not have openly? He scowled at the river and the water distorted his features hideously.

Supposing he was free! The thought was filling his mind with a clamour. What might not come to him? If the devil had then risen from the waters, and made him such an offer as he made to Dr. Faustus, for what would he ask?

Chapter Seven

Lord Robert Dudley stretched his long legs in their crimson hose and moodily contemplated his slashed toe caps. His sister watched these signs of unease as she had watched others ever since he had burst into her house with an urgency which did not seem able yet to express itself in words. Rob would tell her in time why he had come to her in this urgent distraught manner, she would not hurry him. Mary, Lady Sidney of Penshurst, had love and pride for her handsome brother. He was the finest and best beloved of all her five brothers, out of whom only he and Ambrose now survived. As she watched his mounting success, she thought of her parents, especially her mother, who, after husband's violent downfall and death on the scaffold, had worn herself out in her struggle to get her boys out of imprisonment in that most terrible of all prisons, the Tower. "If Mother could have seen Rob now!" she thought and sighed. She knew too well the dangers of greatness.

But Rob was looking at her and no longer at his stylish shoes.

"It's the devil, Mary!" he said simply. "I thought I understood women rather well too. . . ."

Mary Sidney smiled.

"Women have always spoilt you, you mean!" she said with gentle amusement. "Mother and I started it, I know! And then all your loves kept it up. . . . Now you've met a woman who says 'no' to you for the first time!"

He leaned forward and she could see that his brow was damp.

"But listen, Mary! If I were in a position to ask her for a definite answer, would she say 'no'?"

"But you aren't in a position, Robin!"

"Don't you use that damnation fencing that she does!"

Sunrise

Mary Sidney got to her feet, and passed her hand gently over his black head.

"Poor old Rob. . . . Yes, I know you are in a wretched way! I understand. . . ."

"Listen," he said. "I've heard again from Amy. At least I have a message from my fellow, Blount, whom I sent down there. She's ill again—or says she is. The old trouble. Swears it's cancer and she'll die. . . ."

"Are you going down there?"

"No, I am not! I went down—and found her giggling with the Hyde girls and saying she was better—that's what happened before! And the Queen in a hellish fury. . . . No! I'm sending Amy more money and telling her to spare nothing as regards physicians. She wants to come to court. And how could I bring her here? She's such a stupid little rustic!"

"She's the last wife for you, Robin."

"Don't I know it! But supposing she is ill? I can't make her better, can I? I can only tell her to spare no stint as regards doctors and medicines. I've done that. But, Mary, if she were to die. . . . I've got to face that. Or rather the situation which would come out of it."

"Yes. . . ."

His voice was afraid, almost as if he were aghast at the temerity of his own words. "If I were a widower and I asked Elizabeth to marry me. . . . What would *she* say?" He turned to his sister almost in despair. "Mary, she talks to you. She hasn't many women friends but she seems to like you. Or talk to you more than to anyone else."

"Oh, yes, she talks to me. About you."

"What does she say about me?"

"She doesn't say much. She's the most wary creature alive. I never before met anyone so terrified of giving herself away. What she likes is for me to tell her things about you."

"Well, then——!" he made a gesture of despair.

"She's in love with you, Rob," said his sister calmly. "I am as certain of that as I am certain of anything. But I haven't the least idea what she intends to do about it. Perhaps she doesn't know, herself— yet. Tell me this, Robin. Naturally, she's one of the world's most glittering prizes, and you are ambitious. As ambitious as Father was. . . . What man of ambition wouldn't struggle to be King Consort? But apart from all that. Are you in love with her as a woman?"

"Yes. I think so. . . . I want her damnably. She's played such a game with me, leading me on, holding me off——"

"Do you want her chiefly because you can't get her?"

"It adds a spice. . . . No, I honestly want her. She's a handsome creature with a good streak of the devil in her, and I like women to have some devil in them. It's the same with horses!"

"She'll not disappoint you that way. . . ." said Lady Sidney dryly. "But apart from her position as Queen, she has a difficult character. And I don't believe one can think of her apart from being Queen. She'll always be Queen first—and woman a long way after. I can't imagine her as a wife."

"Nor can I. . . . There's nothing soft and domestic in her. Yet, you mayn't believe it, Mary, but she's very fond of children."

"Of course I believe it. She's utterly charming with Philip and he adores her." She smiled as she spoke the name of her little son who was, one day, to be so famous. "She talks to him as if he were a man not a little boy, teaches him to play chess and he says he's her knight and will fight all her battles for her."

"I'll be replaced by my nephew, I think. But young Philip's a lovely lad! Everyone takes to him. I was thinking of the time when we were both in the Tower and she used to play with the gaoler's children."

"People are now whispering, Rob, that you had an affair with her in the Tower."

"I'd like them to see how that could have been contrived! We only met three or four times in that little garden with yeomen and halberdiers within earshot, and it took some managing as naturally I wasn't supposed to be there the same time as the Princess."

"But you managed it?"

"The first time it was a chance. It was when Jack began to sicken of the fever and craved sweet-smelling herbs to drown the stench from the river." Mary sighed, thinking of her eldest brother, John, Earl of Warwick, who had been struck down by one of the dangerous fevers so prevalent by the crowded Thames-side in summer. Only three days after he and the others (except the luckless Guildford) had been released by a general pardon, he had died in her husband's castle, Penshurst.

"So I prevailed on one of the yeomen to let me into the garden. I thought there might be lavender, rosemary or something of the kind, but there wasn't. Only a few bushes of red and white roses.

Then I looked up and saw her coming. I picked those poor roses and said that I was glad that I could offer her something. . . ."

"Always the gallant, Rob!"

"Well, Mary, I stopped thinking about my own troubles and I tried to do what I could to please her. She looked so ill, as white as a sheet, with only those dark eyes of hers alight. I know she was sick to her very soul with fear—and well she might be—but she'd rather die than show it! I've seen a man look like that the first time under fire. . . . I tell you she has a rare soul! I never thought she'd come alive from the Tower any more than her mother. Every time I parted with her, I thought I was seeing her for the last time."

"I expect the thought was mutual, and romantic!"

"It was romantic, I don't deny, but we were too close to the edge to think of romance. We tried, I think, to comfort ourselves as much as we could with each other's company."

"You were both twenty," said Mary Sidney, "good looking and apparently doomed. Yes, Rob, it was a romantic foundation for a future attachment. Did you meet her often after that?"

"Only a few times. She used to send one of the children to me sometimes with a message. She liked to have the gaoler's two to play with. She said their prattle was such a relief after the lawyers' questions. I dare swear it was! They used to bring her nosegays of herbs against the fever, and she gave one to me that first morning for Jack. She gave me other things for him too—a vinaigrette and her own kerchief. She said: "I am very sorry for your brother. I was grievously ill when I came in here, and no tending have I had, except lawyers' wolf traps!"

"Yes, she was very ill at the time of Wyatt's conspiracy. I have heard it said that the doctors declared her too ill to be moved, but the Queen insisted. People saw her carried in an open litter past the gibbets with Wyatt's men hanging on them, and said she looked at the point of death, as white as wax with her face dreadfully swollen."

"Yes, and her sister threw her into the Tower! By God, no wonder they call her 'Bloody' now! Elizabeth was better though, when I saw her. It was an odd time, Mary. . . . We used to walk in that little garden, and talk and try to laugh. We used to play with the children, and one day I brought my lute and we tried to teach them to sing catches. 'Greensleeves' and 'As ye came from the Holy Land of Walsinghame'. But what they liked, those two babes, was the new political song that everyone was singing then, even the very warders.

Sunrise

"Mary, Mary, quite contrary!
How does your garden grow?
With silver bells and cockle shells
And pretty maids in a row!

"It meant she would set the Abbey bells a-ringing again, and the Palmers, with their cockle shells, off on their pilgrimages, and the pretty maids into the nunneries.... Elizabeth hadn't heard it before, and she said: 'Mary is *so* contrary. . . .' and she laughed. A brave effort, I think. But she told me to stop it, for she said: 'That's a dangerous song, and just the sort of jingle to stay in children's minds. Harm may come of it.' "

"Did it?"

"I don't know. But harm did come of our games with the children. Or at least it prevented us meeting again. We were romping, and I had the little girl on my back, the way I do with Philip, and somehow I bounced her off, and she cut her hands and knees and started yelling the way brats do. Elizabeth had her up in a moment and quietened her down very well, but unluckily one of the senior warders was passing by, and in he came with two halberdiers, and they haled me out. . . . Elizabeth said to me—so softly that only I might hear as the fellows burst in—'For God's pity, don't endanger yourself for me. . . .' and I answered that I would very gladly endanger myself if it were for her good, before they dragged me out. I can remember the look in her eyes now. . . ." How alive and tense they had been in her pale face above the flaxen head of the child clinging to her, one of her slender hands in a quick, nervous caress on the child's neck.

"The warder", he continued, "told me if I wanted to go courting I'd find myself courting without a head and my Lady also. So for her sake I never tried to see her again. I sent her a message by one of those poor little brats explaining why, and she sent me back another—all by word of mouth—that she understood and I had done right."

"So that's how it all began!" said Mary Sidney.

"And how will it end? Can anyone tell me that? Dee, the astrologer, says her stars and mine are linked. . . ."

He got to his feet and began to walk nervously and impatiently up and down. His sister waited in silence till his next stormy outbreak of words came.

"And how can she care anything for me? Look at the way she made

80

use of me—made use of the very rumours and scandals coupling my name to hers! You know, Mary, you were in it, too. She feels she needs Philip of Spain's goodwill because of her schemes in Scotland being likely to go ill. What does she do? She sends us both to the Spanish ambassador—I who am reputed to be her lover; you, my sister, and one of her few women friends—to tell him that she really wants to marry King Philip's cousin, the Archduke Charles. Coming from *us*, he must believe it. Off he writes to Philip, who is delighted to think that England's to be kept in the family—so he's all smiles for Elizabeth again, and menacing frowns for France lest they should think of actively intervening on the side of Mary of Guise."

"A large French army in Scotland would be very dangerous for England, Rob. And when the Queen's bribes to the Protestant Lords were captured on the border by the Earl of Bothwell, it was very fortunate that Mary of Guise's kinsmen should be prevented from coming to her assistance."

"Bothwell!" said Robert. "Throckmorton calls him a 'rash, glorious and hazardous young man'. Elizabeth said that she hoped that these qualities would bring him to a speedy end. But d'you know what she said after Mary of Guise had told her in diplomatic language that she was a liar? (She having denied all aid to the Protestant Lords.) 'Alas, I must do better next time. . . . I hate to be found out in a clumsy lie. Not that I often am. . . . But a good lie for a good purpose, I'm as proud of that as you would be of a good sword thrust in a duello.' Who's to know what to believe of her?"

"She doesn't intend anyone to know her motives."

Robert reverted to the early part of the subject. "I can't get over our mission to the ambassador! Then when it's served her turn, she coolly denies we ever went with her authority, and says that she has no intention of marrying the Archduke—and I'm forced into the position of sponsor to an unpopular foreign marriage for the Queen —who happens to be the woman I want to marry myself!"

"So you nearly fight Norfolk in the Queen's presence."

Robert's eyes were black with anger.

"He may be the only duke in England but I won't have him or any man say the things he did! And she—she who's the cause of it all— when we are next alone together, she puts up one of those lovely hands of hers, strokes my cheek and says: 'Poor Rob. . . . But you helped me nicely!' What can I say? But what am I to think? Can she love me after that?"

"She loves you," said Mary Sidney with assurance. "But the Queen comes first. And always will."

"But if I married her?"

"Robin, you have a wife!"

"But if she dies?"

"That's dangerous. . . ."

Their eyes met, and then he dropped his with a sort of sulky despair.

"Amy's the least of it," he said at last. "Poor creature, I wish her no harm. Only to be free from her. . . . But it's Elizabeth. I can never be sure of Elizabeth!"

Chapter Eight

The wind blew with a whistle from a cold grey sky, and the bare black branches of the little copse whipped up and down. The voice of the Commanding Officer struggled raucously against that high, shrill note, and then as it dropped, had the field to itself. The mass of men wheeled raggedly, the earth quivering slightly under them, and then as they charged forward, a wet gleam from that winter sky touched their steel caps and pike heads. The party of horsemen on the high ground by their flank wheeled too, to watch their progress. The chestnut horse pricked his quivering ears and side-stepped with a sudden impatience. His rider gentled him and then turned eagerly to her right-hand neighbour.

"Robin, I commend your taste in horses! This is a splendid beast."

"To find a horse worthy to carry you, took some striving. But it was happy labour if you are pleased."

He looked at her with appreciation. The wind had flicked a splash of colour into her usually pale face and played mockingly with a lock of coppery hair which had broken free from the close-fitting cap adorned with a heron's plume set with a large pearl clasp. Then she turned impatiently to her left-hand neighbour, who was staring after the pikemen, a squat, powerful man, looking doubly massive by being encased in steel from neck to knee, and enormous jackboots nearly as heavy.

"Where are my brave cousin's wits wandering? Harry, why don't you admire my Neapolitan courser?"

Henry Carey, brother of Catherine Knollys, whose barony of Hunsdon had been one of the first peerages created in her reign, turned.

"It's a mettlesome and pretty chestnut!" he declared in a deep, rough voice. "For another mettlesome and pretty chestnut to ride!"

She laughed headlong, striking her hip with her gauntleted hand.

"God's precious soul, have I got a compliment out of Harry at last?"

"You can take it as you please, young Bess! Your Grace—pardon me!"

"You know you don't need pardon. But why do you glare and scowl so at the gallant trained bands?"

"God damme, gallant fiddlesticks! They run about like maids at a fair. There's no drive in those plaguey fellows! What d'you think, Dudley? You were at St. Quentin. I warrant the pikemen there weren't such mincing fellows. . . ."

"That was a battle!" admitted Robert. "And I don't know how these fellows would shape in such. At St. Quentin the whole trained and armoured might of France was struck by the trained and armoured might of Spain."

"And there was an English contingent, Rob! I seem to have heard of a gallant youth who distinguished himself so much that King Philip sent him with the despatches to my sister, at Greenwich."

"I did no more than any man there, no more than my two brothers. But it was a lucky chance which sent me with the despatches, getting me the Queen's favour, so finally the Act of Attainder was lifted from our family. Though too late for my brother, Henry, who fell on that day."

"I know," she said gently. "And all say, none did better on that day than the three brothers Dudley."

Hunsdon was looking shrewdly at her and at the magnificent young man in the heavily damascened armour.

"Yes, young Bess, your knight isn't only of the tiltyard!"

The colour came and went quickly in her cheeks.

"My knight. . . ."

"There isn't a prouder title!" Robert told her. Hunsdon, either from tact or because he was interested, was staring keenly after the pikemen, now re-forming. She leaned forward and said so softly that only Robert could hear : "Then I award it to you, freely!"

Hunsdon swung his horse round, resting his big hand on his armoured thigh.

"Will you go down and order those fellows? Perhaps their Queen's command will put some drive into them."

Sunrise

"I will! I'd like to command my soldiers. Robin, give me your sword!"

He had it out, proffering the jewelled hilt.

"How do I hold it? So?" His hand guided hers. "You must teach me the guards. . . ."

"Gladly. I'll get you a lad's sword which will not be so long and you'll find it easier to balance."

"For fighting on horseback", muttered Hunsdon, "you don't want a pinking rapier. You want a good cut-and-thrust. Still—you handle it prettily. . . ."

"I fancy if I were a man, I'd play the soldier well enough."

"D'you want to be a man?" her cousin asked her.

"Sometimes, yes. Sometimes—no! If I were a king. Not otherwise. If a private citizen, a woman."

"If you were nothing but a woman," said Hunsdon bluntly, "you'd be a most confounded flirt!"

Her laugh had a high-pitched ring of delight.

"And an't I one now?"

"If it's not treason to say so—yes!"

She lunged forward and tapped his breastplate with the tip of Robert's rapier. She seemed more at her ease, always, with these cousins, Hunsdon and the Knollys.

"I'll order my men into battle!" she said, and cracked her horse on the flank with the flat of Dudley's sword, so he bounded forward into a headlong canter which soon became a gallop, Dudley and Hunsdon riding level with her stirrup, and a band of Gentlemen Pensioners, armed cap-a-pie, clanking behind. On the open ground the pikemen had formed up, with a company of arquebusiers on their flank. Their mounted officer rode forward and saluted.

"Give you good day, Captain. I would propose to take the command now, and order your company forward, across the stream to take that piece of rising ground."

The men were cheering wildly and waving their steel morions. Their acclamation brought a quick flush of delight into Elizabeth's cheeks. ("How", thought Robert Dudley, "she loves her popularity. . . . That's the one thing of which I'm sure. The devotion of such fellows matters to her as much as anything.") She saluted them with his sword, saying in a low voice to him: "Robin. The ordering of the troops. What do I do with the arquebusiers?"

85

Sunrise

"Let them advance to the stream, fire a volley and then wheel back so that the horse can go through with the pikes following." And hold your beast when they fire!"

When the unwieldy weapons broke into an uneven fire, the acrid smoke coiling upwards from their chased barrels, the hot little Neapolitan horse plunged wildly, rearing up, but Elizabeth sat him easily. Then she was waving the sword and shouting: "Forward! To me, men-at-arms!" putting her horse resolutely at the stream, to gallop hell-for-leather for the rising ground, the cavalry clanking and clattering after her, followed by the yelling, running pikemen. At the top of the rise, she reined in, looking (thought Robert) every inch a queen.

"Well, Harry!" she demanded. "Can I lead my soldiers?"

"You can. And you put some spirit into them!"

"Who'll wonder at it?" said Robert.

But on the way back, some of her exultation went. Hunsdon and Robert were discussing the command of the army (now the war with Scotland—or rather with the forces of the Queen Regent—was imminent) which was to be given to the Duke of Norfolk.

"He's a proud, windy fellow!" said Robert, who had not forgotten Norfolk's insults, at the time when he had found himself in the hated position of sponsoring the Queen's marriage to the Archduke Charles.

"Aye! They're proud, our great kinsmen the Howards," said Hunsdon. "There've been times when they were too mighty to acknowledge Bullens and Careys. . . ."

"And Tudors, too!" said Elizabeth. She laughed. "Never mind. He'll do well enough. If war must come."

"Must? And you've been playing the soldier so boldly!"

"Ah! But I'd never have a war if I could. . . . The expense is enough to turn the brain!"

"But look how different to a year ago!" said Robert eagerly. "Gresham has raised two hundred thousand pounds in Antwerp, your credit is so strong now."

"My credit won't continue strong with wars! Ah! Money, money, money. . . . Getting it from my loving faithful Commons, is like getting blood from a stone! But I must. As a man said, the King of France bestrides the seas with one foot in Scotland, and England's not safe till those French garrisons are out. There must be a Regency since the Queen of Scots is Queen consort of France, so let it be of the

86

Protestant nobles with Arran or the Queen's bastard brother, Lord James Stuart, at their head. Cecil fancies the last. He can't be a bigger fool than Arran. . . . But even then if an accommodation could be found, I'd not fight. That's why I ordered Winter as I did."

Robert reflected. Christmas had seen a mighty French fleet under the command of the Marquis d'Elboeuf, brother of Mary of Guise, Queen Regent of Scotland, sailing to her aid with reinforcements. Elizabeth had ordered Sir William Winter with the fourteen best ships of that Tudor navy which her father had so greatly built but which had fallen into weakness in the reigns of her brother and sister, to intercept him. A tempest had burst on those winter seas; d'Elboeuf's surviving ships had limped back to French ports. Winter, with magnificent seamanship, had finally come to the Firth of Forth, which he proceeded to blockade, but not in the name of the Queen of England. He had his orders. "We will that ye shall of your own courage attempt these things."

"But the man risks universal condemnation as a pirate!" Robert had expostulated with her when hearing of the order. "If anyone believes him! Your honour!"

The bitterness in her voice had been all the deeper for its quietness. The words seemed to fall like drops of acid biting into wood.

"My honour?" she continued. "It's cheap. My pride in the face of the world? Cheaper still. There is but one thing of value. The goodweal of this country, which I have sworn to maintain. If I have honour—it's there. If I have pride—it's there. If I can prevent a war with the entire might of France, my good name is a very little thing."

He had been silent in the face of an emotion he could not plumb.

"You think me cynical, Rob? Ah! I know these fine knight-errants who ride to the scaffold and bring down so many that trusted them, for their pride in their very selves. Is that honour? Then I don't wish for honour. Let any honour or glory in this matter go to William Winter. I ask none. I ask this country's safety."

They had been sitting side by side, as they talked in a deep window-seat which overlooked the busy waters of the Thames. Elizabeth had been gazing out. Now she turned to him, leaning slightly forward.

"Would you understand me, Rob? Could you? Could any living soul? My conception of honour is to this my country."

"I would never doubt your honour to your country. . . ."

"Yet you do not understand. You look for glory. And glory is paid for in blood. In blood and in tears. And the country aches for peace and safety. Peace to build up. Peace to gain strength. And my own honour to set in the scales against that! Listen, Robin! Before the High Altar at Westminster, I vowed the whole of myself, and that comprised both my happiness and my honour! I seemed to see myself laid on the altar beside Crown and Sceptre, Sword and Ring. . . .

"And I owe something to three others. To *their* honour. . . . First to the ordinary people in England who looked to me, and thought not of their own danger to demonstrate for me against a Government which hated me. Secondly to Mary my sister. Although she must have held me in detestation, she would not condemn me to death without proof of my complicity in Wyatt's rising. She had a weapon in her hand which can strike down the innocent—an Act of Attainder. But she would not use it. . . . And then Sir Thomas Wyatt was told if he implicated me, if he could give direct proof that his rising had been at my orders, he would be granted his life. But he died steadfast, proclaiming my innocence. I do not forget it." With a sudden fierceness she added: "I forget nothing! I will never forget. . . .

"Without these three I should be dead. My clever brain, my clever tongue—yes, they helped! But without the honour of Thomas Wyatt's loyalty, without the honour of my sister's conscience—she longed for my death but beneath her bitter fanaticism and warped nature, she had a true conscience—without the honour of the ordinary people of England who made such an outcry for me, I were dead. I owe to all three that I am alive. And this is how I shall repay. To uphold my solemn trust to this country, I will if necessary sacrifice all personal things. My private happiness if needs be. My good name if needs be. What the world calls honour. What I call honour is upholding that trust."

He had not spoken. He raised first one of her hands and then the other to his lips, not with his usual passion, but for the first time with reverence. He did not see that inmost Elizabeth again for a long time. The woman who now rode home between him and the Lord Hunsdon from watching the trained bands exercise, talked keenly and cynically of the preparations for war.

She was easier for Robert's comprehension, as was the resolute, soberly valiant woman who faced the reverses which came speedily after the open declaration of war and the joining of her army with that of the Lords of the Congregation. William Winter and his ships

Sunrise

now acting openly might prevent any further succour from France, but that professional, highly trained French infantry was too much for the Lords of the Congregation and the English alike. Elizabeth did not fall into vain recriminations when her Council panicked and even Cecil prepared agitated memoranda which were to be abruptly ruled off with the words: "Not allowed by the Queen's Majesty." She preferred to wage war by committee, to leave the striving to the Scots Lords, urging them with bribes, and ordering her admiral to take the role of a pirate; but if war came, she was courageous and steady. She sent a message to hearten her troops, and her cousin to investigate the complaints of corruption and inefficiency, at the same time ordering reinforcement of men and material.

"We must make an end," she said.

"If it were not for the sorrow of leaving you," Robert told her, "I would crave permission to go to this war and strike a blow for you."

"I can't spare my Master of Horse. You'll get no glory, Robin. This won't be a glorious war. But I hope it will bring solid achievement."

"You are not romantic," he complained.

"I like romance well enough in a tale or a ballad."

"And in your own life?" he pressed.

"So little of my life is my own. . . ."

"If you were to marry——" he began. He was surprised at the anger with which she answered.

"God's death! Will you leave the subject of my marriage to my faithful Commons and to William Cecil who nearly drive me to desperation? I don't *want* to marry!"

"Never?" he pressed her.

"I did not say 'never'. . . ." she admitted. He had possessed himself of both her hands now, so she might not interpose her plumed fan between them.

"I love you!" he said.

"You say so. . . ."

"Elizabeth—if I were free——"

"But you aren't free!"

"If I were!"

Her eyes met his steadily and with a strangely intense glance.

"If you were," she repeated. "Then you might speak of this again."

89

Sunrise

Such a feeling of triumph rose in him, that he could scarcely breathe. He lowered his head to kiss those hands which he found he had been holding so tightly that his fingers had left imprints. He might do no more, the eternal group of ladies were gathered at the other end of the tapestry-hung apartment. But one looked up. It was Mistress Ashley. Her needle was stilled and the embroidery's bright threads trailed down to the floor. She had seen that handsome young man lean forward, clasping her mistress's hands, the colour come swiftly into Elizabeth's cheeks to leave them paler than before, and then most telling of all, the expression on her face as she looked at the head bent over her hands to kiss them. Kate Ashley's mouth opened with dismay, and her double chin creased in several folds on her well-starched ruff. Slowly and nervously, she took up her embroidery again. Heaven have mercy! And the things people were saying already! She knew all the women around her were aware too and she seemed to feel the excited pressure of their thoughts. Lord Robert was getting up, but it was only to fetch his lute. On a brocade-covered stool at the Queen's feet, he began to sing in a pleasing baritone voice, his eyes intent on hers, and the intensity of passion in his singing.

> "As ye came from the holy land
>   of Walsinghame,
> Met you not with my true love
>   By the way as you came?
>
> How should I know your true love,
>   That have met many a one
> As I came from the holy land,
>   That have come, that have gone?"

Elizabeth had put up her plumed fan with its jewelled handle, as if to hide his eyes from her with its soft feathers. ("But", thought Kate Ashley, "how she displays her hands—which he above all praises!") His voice rang out with a fervour of conviction.

> "She is neither white nor brown,
>   But as the heavens fair;
> There is none hath her form divine
>   In the earth or the air."

With fear in her eyes, Mistress Ashley watched those swaying

90

plumes as if she were hypnotized. She seemed to remember another such fan swaying idly in another long, slender hand. (But it had had a strange malformation like the beginning of a sixth finger.) And in the pale face above that fan, the lids had dropped demurely over those great slanting black eyes, and the scarlet lips had curled into a little secret smile, while the powerful bulk of the man beside her had turned irresistibly towards her, the small glittering eyes in his square face, devouring her. And now, there was another such secret smile playing on the lips of her daughter as Robert sang.

That evening, when the Queen was preparing for bed, she could keep her fears to herself no longer. Blanche Parry had taken off the Queen's ruff and had handed it to a maid; now she had gone to fetch the caskets for the Queen's jewels. Elizabeth was standing by her dressing-table, gently rubbing the slight mark made on her throat by the ruff. No one was near her, Blanche and the maids being at the other end of the chamber. Kate Ashley took her courage into her hands. She was on her knees before her mistress, her fat hands anxiously clasping Elizabeth's full brocade skirts.

"Kate—what's this?"

"Oh, your Grace!" murmured Mistress Ashley.

"What ails you, Kate? What's wrong? Tell me!"

"Oh, my Lady, you'll be so angry!"

"Not with you, Kate, if you will tell me openly what it is."

"Oh, my dear Lady! If I didn't love you so much—like my own child if you'll forgive the presumption—but they are saying such things——"

"Who? What?" Elizabeth's queries were abrupt.

"About your Grace and Lord Robert. . . . Your Grace, forgive me, but you show such marked favour to him, that everyone's talking. . . ."

She could feel Elizabeth stiffen. But when she spoke it was in a voice of unexpected calm.

"Kate," she said. "I only deal with Lord Robert as he deserves. I know better than anyone his honourable nature and his devoted loyalty to me."

(Thought Kate Ashley: "She loves him. . . .")

"My dear Lady, it wounds me to the heart to hear what so many say because you smile on him so much."

"You must tell me what they say, Kate. I will not be angry with you. I give my word."

Sunrise

Kate Ashley gulped and then plunged on. "They say your Grace loves him beyond all reason, that you give him everything he asks for. Even yourself. . . ."

"Even myself?"

"The French Ambassador has been telling everyone that Lord Robert, on New Year's Eve, lay all night with you. . . ."

"New Year's Eve?" Elizabeth's voice was cold and flat, as if she had deliberately purged it of all emotion. "On that night, you slept in my bedchamber as you nearly always do. And there were two, if not three, of my ladies in the ante-chamber, and Yeomen of the Guard without. Did any see Lord Robert come to me? Did any see him go? Am I not always surrounded by my ladies and maids of honour? Am I alone ever for more than ten minutes? Am I not watched constantly by all my attendants and guards?" The flatness was cracking, and a defiant note was beginning to ring through: "But if ever I had the will or found pleasure in such a dishonourable life—from which may God preserve me!—I know of none to forbid me!"

("There her father speaks," thought Kate Ashley.)

Reassured by a pat on the cheek, she rose awkwardly from her knees. Elizabeth had seated herself in her chair before the mirror and was staring into it as if she expected to see something strange. Then she aroused herself from her abstracted mood, and with a slow, deliberate care, unfastened her earrings and her other jewellery, taking off all her rings except the Coronation ring, which day and night she kept upon her finger, with a superstitious dread of removal.

Chapter Nine

S ir William Cecil had cause for discontent after his labours. The hot summer of 1560 had seen an English army enter Edinburgh in triumph with their allies, the Lords of the Congregation. After long and hard haggling, during which he had been principal English plenipotentiary in Scotland, a treaty had been hammered out which was all that he and his country might desire. Mary of Guise, that valiant and resolute woman, had died in Edinburgh Castle, and it seemed that the shadow of France was removed. "The postern gate" at England's rear was secured, and there was such goodwill towards their ancient enemy from the Protestant Lords and such expressions of devotion to Cecil's own sovereign, that his heart was delighted. That sovereign of his had urged the hardest bargaining upon him, though once or twice she showed signs of caprice which had disconcerted him. She had seemed particularly annoyed that the young Queen of Scots, and her husband the boy King of France, quartered the Arms of England with theirs, as if Mary were the rightful Queen of England, which she boasted to be. The matter of the Arms had been settled in the new treaty, though only the future would show if the haughty young couple in France would carry out these provisions. Still, reflected the sagacious Secretary, the quartering of the Arms and Mary's boast to be rightful Queen of England, were only the shadow, not the substance. Possession was, after all, nine-tenths of the law. The real danger, the substance, was Mary's claim to be Elizabeth's successor, and the very strong chance that she might be, while Elizabeth wilfully remained unwed. But to pester him over the Arms question while he was dealing with matters of real importance, was provoking.

Of course, the unguarded tongue of the young Queen of Scots had something to do with it. Elizabeth herself had, earlier, repeated to him those words which, unfortunately, she had learned. "She says 'I am the rightful and legitimate Queen of England. After all, *she's* only Elizabeth Bullen the Alderman's grand-daughter —the old king's bastard. . . .' God's death, Mr. Secretary! I am Henry Tudor's daughter too, and one day I'll make her learn it!"

"It is a very foolish young woman, your Grace. Badly brought up and very spoilt. Reflect, she is no more than eighteen."

"Yes, and I am an old hag of seven and twenty! And she is so beautiful that she turns everyone's head. . . ."

"She is a foolish young woman," repeated Cecil in what he hoped was a mollifying voice. "And makes the most tactless remarks. I have heard on good authority what she said of her mother-in-law, the Queen-Dowager of France. It would translate thus : 'Fat old Catherine, the pawnbroker's daughter. . . .' A *most* unfortunate reference to the origins of the House of Medici. . . ."

Elizabeth gave a short harsh laugh, but when she spoke, the anger was out of her voice. He thought it had that strange note of sincerity.

"The silly child! Is there no one to warn her, to guide her? Hasn't she enough wits in her lovely head to realize the appalling danger of making such enemies? Has she been so spoilt and pampered all her life, or has she been so loved and guarded, that she feels safe whatever she says?" She added with deep bitterness : "My Spirit, I think as soon as I was old enough to realize anything, I realized that I was not—safe. . . ."

The memory of that conversation must have caused her present anger. Another letter from her had demanded an indemnity from France suggesting the seizure of a French port for security. It sounded just the sort of idea which might have come from that vainglorious and ambitious young man, Lord Robert Dudley. Cecil shook his head. It was more disconcerting than the royal rage over the heraldic question. Was Elizabeth losing her cold, hard reasoning power, and becoming only what Master John Knox had declared all women to be—"painted forth by nature to be weak, frail, impatient, feeble and foolish"?

His brief stay in London after the wearisome journey from Scotland gave him no comfort. One of his intelligence agents reported that a foreign ambassador had written home describing Robert as the "King that is to be". The court was not in London, the heat as usual breeding plague from its steaming alleys. Cecil went on to Hampton

Sunrise

Court, its rosemary-covered walls surrounded by a soothing greenery. He had expected to find the Queen in the gardens, but after waiting longer than ever before, he was informed that—"her Grace has a bad headache, but will receive you in her bedchamber".

This room was so darkened against the sunshine that at first he could hardly see anything. Then he gradually made out the tall, fantastically carved posts of the great bed, and the indistinct figures on the tapestry hangings, appearing like persons in a dream. Kate Ashley sat in a low chair at the bed's foot, almost motionless, her fat body in an attitude of resignation.

"What's that?" said Elizabeth's voice, sounding peevish. "Mr. Secretary?" He noticed she did not use her nickname for him of "Spirit". Kneeling down by the edge of the bed, he said: "I am here at your pleasure, your Grace."

"Much pleasure I have!" she said sulkily, giving him her hand to kiss. "My head's nigh to bursting."

He could see that she lay on top of her many quilts, with cushions around her, wrapped only in a silk chamber gown, and her hair unbound. The hand he kissed felt hot, dry and nervous.

"I am very sorry, your Grace. Perhaps your Grace has a touch of fever and should have blood let."

"Indeed, I'll do nothing of the sort. To-morrow is the great Tournament when my Lord Robert and my cousin Hunsdon are to hold the lists against all comers. I'll not be laid up for that."

"I have the copy of the Treaty here, your Grace——"

"Leave it, leave it! I can't read through miles of parchment now." Turning over, she thumped a pillow with the air of a petulant schoolgirl.

"I thought it best to come straight to your Grace!"

"Poor Spirit. . . ." her voice was more conciliatory. She sat up with a jerk, pushing back the loose hair, and clasping her temples with both hands. "I feel most wretched now. 'Twill pass. . . ."

A little light fell on her face, making it seem a curious waxen white, as white as the fleur-de-lis which the angel in the tapestry was handing to the stiffly kneeling figure of King Clovis. Cecil took his eyes from the formal and yet dreamlike tapestry figures with an effort. They seemed to blend as in a fantasy with that other figure with the pale face, its heavy eyelids closed, framed with the tumbled tawny hair. The thin silk showed up the sharp outline of the bones of

95

shoulder and knee, giving her a fragile brittleness which he had never seen in her stiffly gorgeous robes. He thought her sick and distraught.

"I will only trouble your Grace with one further matter. The Scottish nobles are so full of violent protestations of loyalty to your Grace's person, that it might be well to secure their perpetual adherence by means of judicious payments——"

"Payments!" her voice cut across his with fury. Her eyes were wide open now, and as ever when in any passion, they looked black. "Money, money, money! Everyone grasping at it! Where am I to find it? It's my brother-in-law who has the gold mines of the New World, not I! I merely have my faithful Commons who haggle over every penny, and not enough ordinary revenue to run this realm. . . . I know those Scots will take bribes. If it's necessary—I'll bribe them again. Not unless!" She pressed her hands to her throbbing head. "Now leave me, Mr. Secretary. We'll discuss the Treaty later."

It was, reflected Cecil indignantly, small thanks for all his striving and trouble. Yet on the next day, she seemed to be completely recovered, ablaze with jewels and stiff brocades, an enormous wired ruff about her slender throat, as she sat under her canopy in the gallery high above the tan-strewn lists. A flourish of trumpets heralded the entry of a retinue of pages and esquires in crimson and silver, blazoned with the Bear and Ragged Staff, which had once been the cognizance of the mighty Earl of Warwick in the Wars of the Roses. (When that arrogant Dudley had been created Earl of Warwick, reflected Cecil gloomily, he had taken the Kingmaker's badge with his ancient title. Viewing the record of the father and the prospects of the son, it was ominous. . . .) After his followers, on a powerful black charger tossing its head sideways to jingle its curb chain, came Lord Robert in black armour inlaid with gilt, his visor open. Beneath the Queen's gallery, he reined in to salute her with his lance. Leaning forward, her eyes bright and her lips just apart, she unfastened a scarf of purple silk, and threw it down to him. He caught it gracefully, saluted her again, and then bound it about his arm.

Cecil turned away with exasperation. But it seemed that he could not escape Lord Robert and his relationship to the Queen. When he left the dusty, clanging lists, he could not help overhearing a conversation, carried on behind one of the barriers, in lowered, but eager voices.

"—My Lord Robert was shooting for this wager, and all were pressing forward to look at him——"

"Yes, and he looks as brave in a doublet of Kendal-green as in his tilting armour!"

"And there was one woman in a blue cloak, rather muffled, a serving-wench by her dress, who pressed right into the staked enclosure, so that all said: 'Here's a forward piece!' And when my Lord had shot, she went up to him, and touched him on the sleeve, throwing back her cloak. And it was the Queen! Making eyes at him as bold as you please. 'M'Lord,' said she, 'you are beholden to me for I have passed the pikes for your sake!' "

"Ah, she's Nan Bullen's daughter!"

"*And* Old Harry's. . . ."

The Secretary was thrown into such despair and anger that not long after this he found himself confiding his woes to the ready ears of one whom he knew was ordinarily opposed to him in everything —and referred to him in dispatches as a "pestilent heretic"—the new Spanish Ambassador who had recently replaced the haughty Feria, Alvarez de Quadra, Bishop of Aquila, in the Kingdom of Naples. Bitterly, Cecil declared that he did not know what the Queen thought she was doing, and added, after imploring the ambassador to keep secrecy: "I am too bad a sailor not to make for port when I see a storm coming. . . . I will retire from public affairs!" For once this imperturbable man's nerve was shattered. "Lord Robert", he declared, "were better in Paradise."

The mournful Latin eyes in the heavy solemn face summed him up.

"You have my sympathy, Sir William," said the Ambassador-Bishop suavely. But he could hardly wait for his distracted visitor to go before he was at his desk, writing swiftly of all that Cecil had said, not actually to his master, the all-powerful King of Spain, but to that King's half-sister, Margaret of Parma, Regent of the Netherlands. How many letters of his had been devoted to this very subject? At the time when the Queen had appeared to be toying with the project of marrying the Archduke Charles, he had written to King Philip:

"*I have heard from a person who is accustomed to giving me veracious news, that Lord Robert has sent to poison his wife. Certainly all that the Queen will do with us in the matter of her marriage is only keeping the country engaged with words until this wicked deed is consummated."*

He had described Lord Robert succinctly thus: *"He is the worst young fellow I have ever encountered."*

Of the Queen he bitterly declared: *"She is very difficult to negotiate with, having learnt shifty speech from the heretics who brought her up. For with her all is falsehood and vanity. She is a Jezebel!"*

His busy pen ran swiftly on, describing all the rumours of how "the worst young fellow in the world" was proposing to murder his wife so that he could marry his "Jezebel".

Those two characters were riding side by side, on a woodland path, at the head of a hunting party. Through the high green foliage, the sunlight penetrated, dappling the riders with gold. The Master of Horse had drawn level with his Sovereign; he leaned forward and placed one hand on the pommel of her saddle.

"I am asking you for permission to do the thing I hate most," he said. "Go away from you for a short while."

"Where to?"

"Cumnor. My wife has returned there. I believe her sickness is such that she cannot recover."

That pale face regarded him steadily, the thin lips deliberately still, the eyes intent on his as if they would read his very soul. He would always remember that long look. At last she spoke.

"If you must—then go." She put her hand over the one on her pommel. "But Rob—don't stay away from me longer than you must. . . ."

"I won't stay an hour longer!"

That afternoon he broke suddenly in on the Sidneys, nor did he leave them long wondering the reason of his visit.

"Well, Mary! Well, Henry! I've come for a brief farewell. I start at once on my way to Cumnor."

"To Cumnor!" repeated his sister, and her husband added: "Why?"

"Amy has returned there." His face had grown strangely hard and stiff as he spoke his wife's name. "It seems that her illness really is cancer and she cannot live long. I must go there."

"The Queen knows of it?" asked his brother-in-law.

"She gave me her gracious permission to go immediately."

"But is Amy alone at Cumnor?" inquired Mary Sidney.

"Lord, no! There's that fellow of mine, my treasurer and man of affairs, Anthony Forster, he always lives there. And Amy has two gentlewomen with her. The sister of Hyde, whose house she visited so long, a Mrs. Odingsells, whom she brought back with her. And a Mrs. Owen. She has every care!" He added the last sentence with irritation.

"The poor creature," said Mary Sidney. "I am sorry for her, Rob, but she has been no wife to you for a long time, and because of her you have been caught into such difficulties, that one must hope for a release both for her and you."

"You have gone so far, Robert," said his brother-in-law, "in one direction, that it would be dangerous for you if you had to withdraw now."

"I have my enemies!" declared Robert. "But they won't dare for much longer. . . . Come, Mary, give me a kiss and wish me Godspeed. I'm for the road now." They could see he was booted and spurred and with a riding-cloak over his arm. "Where's Philip?" he continued.

"Riding the new pony his uncle gave him. That's a splendid pony, Rob."

"He deserves one worthy of him, and after all, as Master of Horse, the best bloodstock in the country passes through my hands. Ah! Philip's a rare lad! I envy you both of him."

"My dear brother," said Mary, "I hope one day you will have a son like him."

"It would be hard to get him a cousin to match him. But perhaps one day I will. A cousin who will be called—Henry, Prince of Wales!"

"Robert, have a care!" cried his brother-in-law.

"The day will soon come when I'll no longer have to care!"

He stooped, kissed his sister's cheek, clapped Henry Sidney on the shoulder and was gone. They heard his running feet clattering away.

The news ran like wildfire through the court that Lord Robert's wife was at the point of death. . . .

He returned in a few days and it was noticed that his face had that hard stiff look which his sister had observed, as if features and muscles were carved in wood. He gave terse answers to those who asked him for his Lady's health. Yes, undoubtedly she had cancer. How long she might live, the physicians did not know, but her days must be numbered. Cecil, in despair, confided again in the Spanish Ambassador. It is the only known time when he lost his nerve and became indiscreet. Perhaps he found Quadra's manner soothing. At any rate he told him that he did not believe in the illness of Lord Robert's wife, but he did believe that her husband would posion her. The Queen seemed to have withdrawn from public affairs. She left the business of State to her uneasy ministers, appearing strangely distracted and her masterful will laid aside.

The end of August had seen the court's removal to Windsor Castle. Rumour travelled with it. The hot, close air seemed full of whispers, like the small, dry wind which murmurs before the onslaught of a thunderstorm. Robert's tall figure, arrogant in crimson silk, strode across the crowded Presence Chamber, with an air of violent determination which was not missed by all those eyes which followed him wherever he went. Any day now, the world would hear of the death of his unwanted and inconvenient wife, and the world was quite sure how it would come about. Officially it would be called cancer, but in reality it would be some subtle poison. There seemed no possible alternative.

It was on one of these still, hot summer evenings, that the Queen sat at the keyboard of the virginals, letting her long fingers stray idly as she struck notes and chords, as if she were seeking for a tune. Silently she watched the tall figure leaning against the wall, his crimson a harsh, brilliant splash of colour against the soft ancient blues, greens and fawns of the tapestry. Silently she saw the gems flash in the hilt of his dagger as he thrust it into the staples of the door. All she said was: "Do you know this motet?" and began to play with a nervous precision. The music ended.

"My father wrote it," she said. Dudley crossed over to stand beside her.

"He was a fine musician, the old King. And he knew what he wanted!"

"Yes," she repeated. "He knew what he wanted. But did he want it when he had it?"

To Robert there was only one way to deal with this. He put his arms round her and drew her against him. She did not resist and her head went naturally back on his shoulder. But she said: "Rob, why did you bolt the door with your dagger?"

"Because there isn't a bolt! I am weary of never having you alone! Always your ladies about you, day and night. . . . Now I will secure us against interruption."

"But never against scandal."

She had got up, out of his arms, and was walking up and down.

"Hell fly away with scandal!" he said impatiently. "Do you care about it?"

"I should be inured," she said bitterly. "It started when I was fifteen. I think it will live after I am dead."

He applied his earlier remedy for this, but she set her forearms against his chest and held him away from her, even while in his embrace. Unable to stop her mouth with kisses, he murmured: "Well, I don't know if it's so much!"

"Don't you?" she said. "The Brentford Magistrates have just had up before them an old woman, Annie Dowe, 'Mother' Dowe to her gossips, who has been telling all who will listen to her that 'Lord Robert has gotten the Queen's Grace with child'."

"The old witch!" he said. But an enormous confidence filled him. He caught her hands and drew those resisting arms round his neck. "She's premature, that's all! We'll have lovely children, Elizabeth! And then that spoilt little beauty in France, the Greys and the rest of the ragtag and bobtail who fancy they've a claim to the Succession —they'll have a headache instead of a crown!"

"I—wonder——"

But he could kiss her now and did. He thought he might sweep her off her feet, but at last she resisted him, pushing him from her. "No— Rob!"

"But why?"

He had an immense belief in himself and his magnificent virility. Once let him possess her and she would have no will but his. Already in the past few weeks the Tudor arrogance was falling away to show only a woman in love.

"Listen to me, Robin!"

"Yes, sweeting, but——" He had more tenderness of manner than tenderness of thought.

"Always," she said, "I have had to pursue devious ways. To work in the dark like a mole. Always in the depths. Never in the sunlight. I have scarcely ever dared to speak openly of what is in my heart. First to save my own life. Now it seems to save my country. But I don't want to love you in secret. I don't want a stolen love, a midnight love. I want to acknowledge my love for you before the whole world."

Sunrise

He was touched, inevitably, but he continued to coax her. He was wild with love for her, he told her, and this delay was a torture. But she did not yield. The flaming headlong arrogance had gone but underneath he found a resistance as strong as a rock. He might have read that her reason would always conquer her emotions, but he was not so given to analysis. Women were capricious and nervous, he had no need to doubt her love for him.

She drew out his dagger and he went down on his knees to take it back from her. Then she ran her fingers in a light caress over his black head, moving the heavy silky hair. She loved that head—perhaps since she had seen it stooping over the rose bushes in her prison garden—and wanted to hold it against her heart. It could appease that ache of loneliness. But now she must call in the brain which so rarely failed her. It demanded occupation, even of a trivial kind. She went back to her ladies and declared that she wished to play a hand of primero. A page brought the cards and they played, she concentrating with deliberation. Afterwards she demanded her winnings to the last penny.

Lord Robert went to his own chambers, and told his body-servant to fetch Thomas Blount immediately. This was one of his most confidential followers, a very distant kinsman in fact. Poor relations made themselves into useful hangers-on, in those days. Most grand ladies, in imitation of the Queen's Grace, had several gentlewomen in attendance on them.

"Tom," he said, "I want you to take the best horse in the stables and ride straight away for Cumnor."

"Yes, m'lord."

"My lady is very ill. I want someone at the place that I can trust, who will keep me posted with all news. Be ready for anything, Tom, and keep your ears and eyes open. I want you to study everything down there."

"Keep an eye on Anthony Forster, my lord? He's a deep one."

"Aye! You'll need to be deeper than a well, yourself, Tom, if he is not to realize it. And realize it, he must not. . . . You must use your wits in all things. If anything untoward happens, you must get the news to me as speedily as you can, even if it means foundering half a dozen horses. Do you understand?"

"I understand, m'lord."

Chapter Ten

The afternoon sun was casting long slanting shadows between the tree trunks on the dusty road to Abingdon. Thomas Blount had eased his horse to a walk, having made good going from Windsor, and would arrive at Cumnor Hall (which lay some three or four miles to the north of Abingdon) with several hours in hand before sunset. Suddenly the urgent beat of hoofs fell upon his ears. In a cloud of dust, a horseman came racing round the bend of the road, using his whip and spurs with generosity. Blount drew into the side of the road to let the hastener by, but he was hailed with a shout of "God save you, Master Blount!" and the galloping horse was jerked almost on to its haunches.

"Why, Bowes!" said Thomas Blount, recognizing one of the senior servants at Cumnor Hall. "What ails you?"

He could see the red face, wet with sweat, goggling at him.

"My lady's dead, Master Blount!"

Hardly any emotion passed over the thin, tanned features of Thomas Blount, though under the shade of his hat brim, his eyes narrowed with a shrewd gleam.

"My lady dead?" he repeated. "So soon of her sickness?"

" 'Twas no sickness. She was found dead at the foot of the stairs with her neck broken!"

"Her neck broken!" Blount pursed his lips. Of all deaths which the unfortunate woman might die, this was the most unexpected. "How did it happen?"

"I don't know. Neither does anyone. We were at Abingdon Fair. My lady would have us all go. Why, she even fell into a passion with her gentlewoman, Mrs. Odingsells, who did not wish to go, saying that Sunday was not the day for the quality to be at the fair. But my lady would have everyone out of the house."

"My lady was usually fond of company and liked many around her," suggested Blount.

"She'd have no one in the house to-day. And we came back and found her dead!"

"Who found her? Master Forster?"

"That I can't say, Master Blount. As soon as I came back from the fair, Master Forster told me to take Brown Bayard, who as you know is the best beast in the stables, and spur all the way to my lord at Windsor. Shall I go on, Master Blount?"

"Yes. Your horse is fresh and mine is not. As fast as you can, and if you founder Bayard, you'll find that my lord will make it right for you and for Master Forster. One moment! Tell my lord that you encountered me and gave me the news, and tell him that I will write him as soon as I have further news."

Bowes kicked his horse into a gallop and was off again as fast as possible. Blount looked after him for a few moments.

"Heigh-ho!" he said, and touched his horse with his heel so that it broke into a steady jog trot, which finally brought him to Abingdon, the hoofbeats ringing hollow in the almost deserted streets. The reason for this emptiness was not far to seek. It came from the dull roar of sound which eddied from the vast, dusty concourse beyond the town, where the fair was held. Abingdon made high holiday. Blount hesitated a moment, and then turned into a hostelry on the main street, where he gave a good tip to the sulky ostler who came to his horse's head, obviously longing to join his fellows at the fair.

The inn seemed cool and dark after the dusty glare of the streets outside. The host himself came bustling up to Blount who bespoke a room for the night.

"Would you eat, sir? Say the word and I'll have something on a spit for you, but to tell the truth, we are supping later to-night as so many will be long at the fair, and on the fair nights, this place and every other hostelry will be filled."

"I am not so hungry that I cannot wait. But my throat is dry with the long ride. I could do with a cup of your best sack. Come, join me, host!"

When they were settled with a flagon between them to refill their pewter tankards, Blount encouraged the host in conversation. Like most men of his calling, he was nothing loth. He had been at the fair himself in the morning, but had returned at noon, not trusting the

serving-men and wenches to see to things properly without his eye
upon them. Would the gentleman himself look in at the fair?

"Why, no," said Blount. "I am tired. I've come from Windsor and
must set out to-morrow on my way for Gloucester."

"Gloucester? That's a long journey! Still, you'll hear the news of
the fair to-night. Though there's a piece of news in this neighbour-
hood which will set all tongues a-going like mill wheels after a cloud-
burst!"

"And what might that be?"

"If you come from Windsor where the court now lies, I don't have
to ask you if you have seen my Lord Robert Dudley, the Queen's
Master of Horse?"

"I have seen him," said Blount truthfully, "many times."

"His lady dwelt here, or rather some miles distant at Cumnor Hall
which is the dwelling of one Master Anthony Forster, man of affairs
for his lordship. Very secluded was the lady for the wife of so great
a man. . . . But it was said that she was grievously sick. And many
other things were said too. . . . But what do you think has happened
this very day?"

Blount gave a man-of-the-world shrug.

"The lady's eloped with some pretty fellow in my lord's absence?"
he suggested.

"God rest her soul, no! When her household came back from the
fair this morning, they found the poor lady lying dead at the bottom
of the stairs with her neck broken!"

"How did that come about?" demanded Blount with every show of
appalled surprise. The landlord spread out his fat hands with a gesture of dismay.

"No man knows!"

"What is your judgment and that of the people?"[1]

The host hesitated.

"Some were disposed to say well, and some evil. . . ." he said
cautiously.

"What is your own judgment?" pressed Blount.

"By my troth, I judge it a very misfortune because it chanced in
that honest gentleman's house."

"Master Forster?" Blount's eyes were narrowing.

"His great honesty does much curb the thoughts of the people."

[1] This part of the conversation is practically verbatim.

But the host put a curious emphasis on Forster's "great honesty".

In the evening, the crowded taproom could talk of nothing else. Blount sat in a corner, his ears acute, missing nothing, and when he heard any of a promising garrulity, helped them forward with a drink which he mixed himself most cunningly of old ale, liberally laced with brandy and spices. He had a head like a rock, and drank steadily without any change. But tongues around him wagged more and more furiously.

". . . i' God's name, they'll need to plumb Tony Forster, but that's a bottomless well!"

"Ah—when the last trump sounds and as the preacher says, the secrets of all hearts will be shown, then mayhap we'll know what Master Forster could tell!"

"Have a guard to your tongue!"

" 'Tis only reason that Master Forster must know somewhat?"

"How can he? He was at the fair!"

"All the day? Did you see him?"

Blount filled his neighbours' tankards to the brim.

"It's to my mind that the poor lady made away with herself. . . ."

"And would a gentlewoman of her standing do such a thing? And put herself beyond all hope of Christian mercy? She would have to be desperate beyond her reason to do such a thing. . . ."

"Well, they said she drove all out of the house——"

"And Tony Forster went willingly enough! He did nothing to prevent a distracted female——"

"They say she's only died just soon enough!"

"That tongue of yours will be slit, Jack, an' you don't rule it!"

"D'you think that Tony Forster would lose a chance to make the greatest in the land beholden to him?" cried the incorrigible.

The next morning, Blount rode over to Cumnor. Under the clear sky, so pale a blue it seemed almost white, the downs quivered in a heat haze, behind the solid rectangle of the Hall. Light sparkled on the leaves of the massive trees in the park and gardens which surrounded it. The monks of Abingdon (to which it had belonged before the Dissolution) had laid out formal gardens with terraces, paved walks and darkly sleeping fish-ponds. Master Anthony Forster, whose epitaph was to describe him as: "Very learned, a great musician, builder and planter," added to and maintained them. Blount found him walking in front of the house, dressed in black velvet, a man in early middle age with a quiet, grave manner, which revealed nothing of his thoughts. He did not appear surprised in the least to see Blount, but offered no information till it was demanded. When Blount asked for his opinion, he only answered: "Who can say? My Lady Dudley was in a strange state of mind. Yesterday she would have none by her, and urged all to leave her."

"Which was not customary for her?"

"Which", repeated Forster, "was not customary for her."

"And when will the Crowner's Quest sit?"

"Very soon. Many of the jury are chosen and some are in the house already according to custom."

"What sort are they?"

"Such country fellows as we have around here."

"Good Master Forster, my Lord will desire all information. Can you advise me?"

"You might question her maid, Pirto. She perhaps knew my lady more intimately than any."

Blount entered the house, talked with "some of the country fellows" and thought them reliable and honest. He also gained the impression, slight but definite, that they mistrusted Anthony Forster. Afterwards he wandered to the foot of the fatal staircase, gauged the height from top to bottom with his eye, and shrewdly scanned posts and banisters. But all he said after pursing up his lips, was: "Heigh-ho!" Then he sent for the deceased lady's maid, who had the odd name of Pirto.

The woman, her face swollen and puffy with long weeping, but with an odd sense of her own consequence in these tragic events, was ready enough to talk. Blount commenced gently, leading her on.

"What d'you make of it all?" he asked her in a casual tone. "Chance or villainy?"

"By my faith! I do judge very chance, and neither done by man nor by herself. . . ."[1]

She broke off short, casting panic-stricken glances about her. Had she actually voiced the dreadful thought which lay in her mind? The slight narrowing of Blount's eyes, the only feature to change in that hard, sunburnt face, warned her. Was she to declare that her beloved lady had committed the terrible sin of self-destruction? She began to sob, pouring out her words amid tears.

[1] Mostly verbatim.

"My lady was as good and virtuous a gentlewoman as ever was seen. . . . Didn't she daily pray to God on her knees? The last person to commit so sinful an act! Why, haven't I myself heard her praying aloud to God to deliver her from desperation?"

"Then perhaps she might have had some evil toy in her mind?"

"No, good Master Blount! Do not judge so of my words! If you should so gather, I am sorry I said so much. . . ." Whereupon she proceeded to have noisy hysterics. Blount left her, but the idea had taken root. He wrote to his master: *Truly the tales I do hear of her maketh me to think she had a strange mind in her; as I will tell you at my coming. . . .*"

But while he wrote, a letter was being carried to him by a messenger "riding for his life". On the paper, Robert's handwriting sprawled with a strange urgency.

"The greatness and suddenness of the misfortune doth so perplex me, until I hear from you how the matter standeth, or how this evil should light upon me, considering what the malicious world will say, as I can take no rest.

"And, because I have no way to purge myself of the malicious talk but one which is the very plain truth to be known, I pray you . . . that you will use all devices and means that you can possible for the learning of the truth. . . ."

There was much more, bidding him to tell the Coroner to do his utmost, and choose "discreet and substantial" men for jurors who would search thoroughly till they got to the bottom of the matter. He had written off at once after seeing Bowes; if there was one thing which reassured him, it was the thought of the shrewd and reliable Blount, already at the scene.

While Blount was encouraging the taproom gossips to spill the contents of their minds, Robert was with the Queen, having heard Bowes and dashed off the first letter to Blount. Elizabeth had taken one glance at his face and then had led him to the inner cabinet where she conferred with Cecil or read the classics with Ascham, closing the door with her own hands. It was not a time to consider trivial scandalmaking; she had lived so long on the edge of desperation that she knew desperation when she saw it in another's eyes.

"Rob," she said. "What has happened?"

"My wife is dead. . . . And in such a manner I do not know what to think!"

Sunrise

She swallowed to moisten her dry mouth.

"Then you mean she did not die of her sickness?"

"She died from a fall which broke her neck."

"How did it happen?"

"No one seems to know. I have just had a messenger from Cumnor with the news. Amy was found dead at the foot of the stairs this morning."

"Was no one with her?"

"That is the strangest part. She drove everyone out of the house to go to the fair. She would have no one with her, and she was a woman who ordinarily craved for company and would not be alone day or night."

"Then", said Elizabeth slowly, "it was a plot to make away with her or she made away with herself, or else it was an accident which will overtax all men's credulity."

"I know that! I know what they will say. That I had her done away with. . . ."

"And I was privy to it," she said.

"You? But——!"

"Oh, yes, Robin. Here is a queen who has a favourite. She is freely believed to be his mistress and with child by him. His unwanted wife is found strangely dead. What else *can* anyone think?" She paused and then went on in a voice of such quiet bitterness as he had never heard before: "I think through all eternity we will be held guilty."

"Not you, Elizabeth!"

"Oh, yes, my dear! That's what comes of open honesty. . . . They call me the arch-dissembler, Robin. They say I delight in not letting my right hand know what my left hand does. But now I have been open. I have not concealed my love for you. I have let the whole court see—and through them the outside world—the joy I have in you. And now—this happens! If I had dissembled and cloaked my feelings, and been your mistress in secret as they say, I am clever enough to have deceived them all! But I want to be your wife, Robin, before the whole world. What have I had of human love? I did want this, and now, I think it can never be. . . ."

For the first time he ventured to touch her, taking her hands and drawing her tightly against him.

"But, Elizabeth! It must be found, the cause. If someone has done her to death, he will be convicted and swing for it! They must find the culprit—then the suspicion will be cleared from me—from us. . . . Though surely no one could be so wicked as to accuse you. . . ."

"I wonder! No, Robin, don't touch me. I must think and I can't think clearly in your arms. . . ."

She sat down, leaning back in a great chair, clasping the carved lions' heads on the arms. He could see her knuckles shining like polished ivory with the tightness of her grasp.

"You must go, Robin," she said at last, "to your house at Kew, and stay there. Consider yourself as under arrest till some verdict is arrived at. By the inquest I mean. Until then, all must suspect you. And if I keep you by me, I will be held privy to it."

"But, Elizabeth——"

"I am the Queen of England as well as your Elizabeth. . . . What touches the throne, touches the whole country. I know what would happen if I were to be overturned from the throne. The country would be torn to pieces, like a deer torn by wolves. . . . And I must put the country first. . . . It is my heart which must be torn to pieces. Do you think I *want* to do it?"

"God knows!" he said, staring at her.

"Listen to me. If we were ordinary man and woman. If I were no more than your Elizabeth—I would go to you now, my love, and put my hand in yours, and stay with you even if it meant standing by your side in the dock."

He was on his knees with his head in her lap, and she put one hand on his neck, adding in a voice so low that he could only just hear: "Even if it meant standing beside you at the gallows' foot. . . ." A bitter little smile twisted her lips. "Though perhaps my clever tongue which has saved my neck twice, might save us both. Who knows? But I would dare it for you, Robin, if I could. But I cannot! For I know what would happen if this country were thrown to the factions which would dispute the succession."

"But. . . ." he said, raising his head. "They must find the culprit. Unless she did it herself. . . . Surely she would not do such a thing—to be damned through eternity! All the churches teach that——"

"The churches!" she said with that same bitterness. "Well, they may, since man persists in making God in his own image. Man and his different creeds raise such a clamour that God is lost, and who can find Him?

Sunrise

"Now, listen to me, Robin. You must go to Kew. Have you sent anyone to Cumnor?"

"The best of all my fellows, Tom Blount. A most shrewd and reliable man. . . ."

"So may he prove! You must be very careful. Do nothing rash. I will send to you. But go now. Go, I beseech you. . . ."

Chapter Eleven

T he storm burst, its clamour ringing out further and further
each day and each succeeding week, till the echoes began
to ring back again. De Quadra, that smooth, suave,
malicious ambassador-bishop, being at Windsor, was one
of the first to send his pen swiftly over sheets of parchment, while his
heart sang "Laus Deo!" "Jezebel" had overreached herself, and surely
now her outraged subjects would hurl her from the throne which she
had so wrongfully occupied. Even those abominable ultra-Protes-
tants—those followers of Calvin—would be side-by-side with the
most zealous Catholics. De Quadra settled himself happily to writing,
remembering the white, tense face of the young Queen, as she came
in from hunting, and told him briefly that Lord Robert's wife was
dead. It was a *little* surprising, the Bishop reflected, that she should
have died by violence—Elizabeth had said definitely in her fluent
Italian: "Si ha rotto il collo"[1]—when it would have been so much
simpler and safer to have poisoned the unhappy woman. But one must
reflect that the English were clumsy fools. Of course "Jezebel" had
planned the whole thing, she had better brains than her paramour,
though again one felt she would have preferred poison. He must have
forced the pace at the last moment, through impatience. But it was
imperative to impress on King Philip that his sister-in-law was virtually a murderess. De Quadra never doubted his master's fervour for
the true faith or for the advancement of the Spanish Empire, but he
could not help realizing that the King had once found his sister-in-
law a very desirable young woman. It was therefore his bounden
duty, both as a Churchman and a Spaniard, to blacken Elizabeth's
character as much as possible.

If only he might have definite proof that "Jezebel" had known

[1] "She has broken her neck."

beforehand of this atrocious crime? De Quadra never doubted for one moment that she was guilty. He honestly felt that he was advancing the truth, when he wrote his dispatch relating to the death of Lady Robert Dudley, by carefully omitting certain dates, so it would seem that the Queen had informed him of the death *before* she could possibly have known of the occurrence. . . . Later, observing the growing clamour, he was to write with unction that the nuptials of the Queen and Lord Robert were expected hourly, but in his opinion she would go to bed the Queen of England and arise the next morning plain Mistress Elizabeth Dudley. The thought filled de Quadra's heart with rapture.

When William Cecil was bidden to the Queen's presence, he did not know what he might find. She was sitting very still in the great chair whose arms were carved lions, wearing a dress of white tissue, worked with stiff silver and light green, a long lustrous rope of pearls hanging almost to the girdle which was set with emeralds. Above this gorgeous attire, her face had that waxen look, cheeks and eyepits hollow, the tightly strained skin showing the sharp point of her chin below the long jaw and the curving ridge of her high nose. Her eyes had that dry steady glance which held beyond exhaustion, but he could feel that she was strained—and had been strained long—to the utmost.

"Good," she said tersely. "I am glad you have come, Sir Spirit."

Inevitably he felt sorry for her.

"Your Grace looks tired."

"I have not slept since this dreadful thing occurred."

"Yes, your Grace, it is a dreadful thing and not only for Lord Robert."

"Not only for Lord Robert. . . ." she repeated.

"The consequences, your Grace, may be incalculable."

"I know that. . . . They have been going round and round in my head like a wheel. I've had my cousins, Frank Knollys and Harry Hunsdon with me, and they have admonished me as kinsmen, rather than subjects to their sovereign."

Cecil, who himself had spoken at length with Knollys, inclined his head.

"Frank has rebuked me for my levity and ill-judged favour," she said with deliberation, "being very firm in his righteousness. Nor do I doubt he sincerely desires my good. He told me of a certain preacher of Coventry, Master Lever, who has been thundering from his pulpit."

"I have the report on Lever, your Grace. You must realize that there is a very dangerous spirit in the country as a result of this happening."

"I realize it very well, without good Frank dotting the i's and crossing the t's. . . . As for honest Harry, he came with his usual volley of oaths, clapping his hand on his hilt and declaring that he wished he could run through all that defamed me. But he added, and I could tell that it came from the bottom of his heart, that he implored me to guard my actions. There has—he said—been enough evil talk of the Bullen women. . . ." Nothing could describe the bitterness with which she repeated: "The Bullen women!"

It was not, thought Cecil, a way to speak to a sovereign—nor even a wise way to speak to a high-spirited young woman.

She added with a sudden flash of temper: "Sweet cousin Catherine was married young to such a godly man as Frank—so she had no chance for levity or wantonness. But they should both be grateful that I settled their vixen of a daughter!" When she continued she was calm. "Perhaps I have merited some of their reproaches so I suffered them. But whatever they may think I do not forget that I am their sovereign." She leaned forward, her eyes intent. "I never forget! Nor ever will."

"If I might advise your Grace——?"

"That is what I want."

"It is imperative for your Grace to behave with the utmost discretion. There cannot now be talk—of a certain marriage."

"It will not come from me," she said. "I sent Lord Robert from court, at least till the verdict upon his wife's death is arrived at."

"Your Grace was very wise."

"If I were foolish before," she said, "I will not be foolish now. Rest assured." Her words were firm, but as her voice died away, she closed her eyes and her lips quivered. Cecil, moved more than he thought possible, put his hand on hers which rested on the carved lion's head. She opened her eyes again.

"I know what they say. That I am Lord Robert's mistress. That I am even with child by him, so that he and I had to contrive his wife's death. . . . I love him—I love him dearly—but as God is my witness, nothing improper has ever passed between us. . . ."

Sunrise

He was surprised by the strength in those thin fingers which suddenly clutched his sympathetic hand as she leaned forward, pressing her forehead against his arm. Her body was convulsed as if by a spasm of pain. He thought: "If she could weep, it would ease her. But afterwards she would not like to remember it. . . ." For the moment he was seeing her without that enormous arrogant regality with which the Tudors had fenced themselves off from the rest of mankind as no medieval king had ever done, taking upon themselves semi-divine loftiness. He put his hand on her shoulder. "There," he said, "there!" as if she had been one of his children. Under the rich material of her dress, he could feel the brittle sharpness of the bones of her shoulder. Beneath those imposing and gorgeous trappings she was fragile to face her daily battle; only the wayward vigour of her mother had saved her from the curses of disease and degeneracy from Henry VIII's tainted blood. And for the first time he saw into the abyss of her loneliness.

"There. . . ." he repeated. This would pass, and neither he nor she might ever allude to it. But they would both remember it.

The tenseness went out of her and her grasp on him relaxed. She raised her head and though her eyes were wet, she had forced back the tears.

"I'm not weak any longer. . . . But, Spirit! Do something for me."

"Anything your Grace commands."

"Go to Rob—to Lord Robert at Kew for me. You are the wisest man in England. Counsel him. He'll need good advice. And tell him that I think of him without ceasing. . . . But he must, for both our sakes, use wisdom and prudence."

"I will go, your Grace."

He went and his visit was acknowledged afterwards with a letter of almost frantic gratitude from Robert, who waited feverishly for Blount's repeated bulletins from Cumnor. Messengers galloped headlong with their exchange of letters. In his anxiety, Robert was even so foolish as to write to the foreman of the jury "one Smith" to try and anticipate the verdict. Blount rebuked his lord for this, and Robert took it meekly. But neither Blount's lynx eyes nor the deliberations of Smith and the other "good men and true", could find a murderer. Only a felon swinging on the gallows after a fair and open trial could have eternally lifted the weight of suspicion from Robert's shoulders.

Sunrise

But none was forthcoming. Nor in spite of the evidence for it, did the jury bring in a verdict of suicide. Perhaps they could not believe that a lady of quality could commit such a deed. Perhaps they wished to be merciful to the unhappy creature's memory. Finally they returned a verdict of death by misadventure. In spite of local gossip, Anthony Forster's name seemed to have been kept out of the proceedings. Amy Dudley, born Robsart, was given a solemn and dignified funeral, which to those Renaissance minds who craved a heady melodrama, must have seemed a curious anti-climax.

For no climax came—at least outwardly. The reverberations were terrible, most of the foreign countries sharing the opinion of the Spanish Ambassador. Cecil had unpalatable dispatches from the English Ambassadors abroad. First came one from Randolph in Scotland declaring that the news "so passioneth my heart that no grief I ever felt was like unto it". He also added it was likely to undo the good work of the successful campaign and treaty. The brilliant Throckmorton, Ambassador in Paris, wished to crawl away into a corner and die, such things were said about his Queen. Not only did they gleefully call her harlot and murderess like her mother before her (it was a good time to repeat the ancient rumour that Anne Boleyn—saucy Nan Bullen—had tried to poison the unhappy Queen Catherine) but they attacked Elizabeth's new Church. "What sort of religion is this, that a subject shall kill his wife, and the Prince not only bear withal but marry him?"

Cecil did not show his sovereign the most scurrilous, but he repeated to her a few of the accusations. He knew that she had the courage to take such blows without flinching, and he must strengthen her resolve against future foolishness. He had a queer pride in her these days, the way she faced life. He knew—and she knew he knew—how near she had come to breaking point, but she had set her jaw and gone on, outwardly unmoved. Before the catastrophe he had despaired of her and had thought seriously of resigning; now he was delighted by the way she took again her grasp of affairs. If the woman had once nearly wrecked the queen, it was now the queen who supported the woman. And so the loud noise of gossip and conjecture gradually faded into an inquisitive murmur. Lord Robert, cleared in the eyes of the law, came back to court to resume his position as Master of Horse.

At last they found themselves alone together in that little cabinet which had held so much human emotion. She was sitting in her lion chair, leaning back, her hands limp in her lap.

"It's been a nightmare," he said.

"It's been a nightmare . . ." she repeated slowly. He thought how exhausted she looked.

"But it's over now!"

"Over? Will it ever be over in our two lifetimes?"

"Dear heart, how long must we wait? Would six months satisfy decorum? It seems very long, but I'll do whatever you wish. Could we shorten it to three months before we marry?"

"We can never marry. . . ."

"Elizabeth!"

"Perhaps years and years afterwards when men have forgotten this. But I do not think they ever will forget or we can ever marry."

He was aghast. Throwing himself down on his knees, he caught hold of the cold hands.

"Elizabeth—you cannot use me so! I am desperate—wild for you —am I nothing to you?"

"I love you," she said. She repeated it twice on a strange note which seemed to have the cadence of a funeral knell. "I love you. I love you!"

"You sound like the passing bell!"

"It is the passing bell. . . . The passing bell of all our hopes."

"But——"

"They are gone, those hopes. That the whole world might say: 'No woman has such joy of her husband as the Queen has of Lord Robert.' . . . They'll never say that now. I don't think the Queen will ever marry. If she had to, for reasons of State, I think it might kill her. . . . There's no pride or joy or open happiness left. We can only do that of which we are already accused. We can love—but we can't marry. Stolen love, hole-and-corner love, midnight love which can never face the sun. That's all that's left to us. . . ."

He would not accept this. Catching her up, he made stormy, violent love to her, but she was cold, limp and unresponsive. Baffled, he let her go.

"I think", he said with anger, "that you mean to drive me mad!"

"Robin, let's try not to hurt each other. There are things we must say."

"Are there? I think you care for nothing but your crown!"

Her dry little laugh was drained of all pretence at mirth.

"A crowned head has such rest. . . . I believe I have a task which only I can fulfil. And I shall not be allowed to, if we marry. So we cannot marry."

"I'm banished from the court, am I? I'll best go as a soldier of fortune!"

"No, Robin. We can have a little. If you want to. . . . We need not separate. I said we can love though we can never marry."

"*Can* you love?" His voice was sharp with derision.

"You will see. . . . But there are two questions I must ask you and you must answer me with the whole truth. Do not swear, either by God or by His Cross. For men have been forsworn of both those. Neither swear by the love you say you have for me, because men have been forsworn of that also. But tell me the truth because I shall know if you lie. Robin, is it the woman or the throne that you want?"

He looked into her eyes and knew he must tell the truth.

"I want both!"

She made a strange little sound, a laugh, a sigh and a sob all in one.

"Robin, you are greedy. . . . The woman is yours, but the Queen you can never have. I can separate them. I must—to live. And this other thing you must answer me. No one shall know your answer but you and I. If they were to have me on the rack, they would not get it from me. Had you any hand in your wife's death?"

"No! But——"

"Ah! 'But.' . . . Tell me, Robin. Was she really ill? Was it cancer?"

"She was ill or thought she was. . . . As to cancer, I cannot say! One moment she swore to it. The next moment she was giggling foolishly with her companions. I'll never know." He raised his head and began to speak with vehemence. "I didn't want her harmed, but I wanted to be rid of her. I'll not deny it. . . ."

"I, too," she said. "I never thought of her as a person at all, only as a block in my way, an impediment. I am my father's daughter and you know how he dealt with impediments! We both wanted to be rid of her, Robin, and so we will pay for it, all our lives. . . . When you went down to Cumnor yourself, how was she?"

"She had sent to me saying that she was desperately ill. So I went and she was not more ill than ordinarily. But she was in such a hysterical state as I have never seen before. She cried and unbraided me and said she had heard that I loved the Queen and the Queen would marry me, so that I was going to poison her. But she would not live to be poisoned, she said. She would make an end of herself. She was on her knees holding on to me, and I pushed her away, and swore that I did not care what she did. . . . Then I went away so quickly that I saw Forster disappearing down the corridor. I am certain he had overheard all.

"I believe that she killed herself and I drove her to it. . . . Unless Forster—— He is a very strange man. But the inquest cleared him. He was nowhere near the house at the time. And yet I wonder. I shall always wonder. I don't believe in the accident. Either she killed herself or Forster did it, believing then that he should have a king beholden to him."

"Can he hold anything against you?"

"No. Not on the bare facts. Yet when he told me that he wished to purchase the freehold of Cumnor, I gave him the money, though I was hard put to find it. But I will take no risk."

"I will give you the money."

"You have given me so much money and I have repaid none of it."

"Robin, we must share the cost and the blame. If she killed herself, you drove her to it, and I drove you. If Forster killed her, it was from hearing your words, and I drove you to them."

"No. You honestly believed she was ill. You believed she might die soon naturally."

"No, Robin, I will not lay down any part of the blame. I will pay for it, with you. I have already begun to pay."

"There is a third alternative. Forster did not actually harm her, but he knew she was going to take her own life, and he made things easier for her, by persuading all the others to leave the house."

"That amounts to the same. It was your words saying that you did not care if she killed herself which caused it. And *I* caused those words. . . . It doesn't matter now what actually happened. We will never know the exact figures which were added up, but we know the total. As I have said, we cannot escape it in all eternity."

She was lying back in her chair, with her eyes closed. Her face looked drawn and bloodless. He could only just hear her whisper: "And we could have been so happy. . . ."

"We will be!" he cried eagerly. "This is a horrible thing. Poor luckless Amy! But she's dead. It's finished. There's nothing more I can

do for her now. And in time, people will forget. In a year—in two at
the most! We can marry!"

"No. Never."

He swore a great oath.

"You care for nothing but your throne!"

She heard him go violently from her and did not speak or try to
hold him back. Presently she got up and went to the keyboard of her
instrument. Afterwards it was to be said of her that an air on the
virginals meant more to her than a prayer. She played till her hands
were steady again, and her eyes inscrutable.

That evening there was music in the great hall. The torches flickered and cast their light on shining silks and satins and on the dull
sheen of velvet on the many figures grouped around the pillars.
Sweetly, sadly, the music rang out, dying away amongst the shadows.
A boy sang in a voice higher and purer than any woman's. On her
dais, the Queen swayed her jewelled and plumed fan to and fro in
time with the music's beat. In purple and cloth of silver, she had a
glittering unreality, and her face, carefully painted, was a mask. In
the shadows, Lord Robert Dudley lounged against a pillar, his eyes
sullen. Cecil had noted him and thought: "The Dudley ambition is
set down." Beside him, the young Countess of Essex raised her pansy-
black eyes to him, as she sat in her cushioned chair.

"You used to sing as well as any," she told him. "And now you are
silent!"

"I have no lady to sing to!"

"You could choose one. . . . Perhaps you chose badly before."

"Perhaps I did." He looked at her with a hard appraisal. She was
a delectable baggage, and he dared say, no more faithless than any
other, Queen, countess or kitchenmaid, they were much of a much-
ness. "I could choose again," he said.

He was torn with frustration, thwarted ambition and thwarted
desire. Sleep did not come to him quickly that night. He lay awake
revolving different plans. He would leave the country as a foreign
mercenary. The King of Spain had praised him on the field of St.
Quentin. . . . . He would be killed gloriously in some far-off battle,
and Elizabeth would be sorry when it was too late. . . . He would
court Lettice Essex openly in defiance of her husband, and the whole
court—and the Queen—would see. Both the woman and the throne
had been so near to him, within his grasp, and then had suddenly

been snatched from him. Amy—poor foolish unwanted Amy—was as great a barrier dead as living. If she had killed herself on account of his cruel words, she had repaid them tenfold.

There was a sound in the ante-chamber where his body-servant slept on a pallet bed. Robert sat up abruptly, his ears straining. Then he was on his feet, muffling himself in his velvet bedgown. His thought was first of Lettice Essex. In return for his bold, angry appraisal, she had given him such a glance as her great-aunt, Anne Boleyn, might have given King Henry. She was a likely wench! he thought. I'll take what the gods send. . . .

His man was there, yawning, but his eyes bright. Something else was bright, the glint of a gold piece in his hand.

"M'lord! There's a lady. Says you expect her."

Robert was into the ante-chamber. She was wrapped in a green velvet cloak which hooded and hid her face. He paused for a moment, and then thought his heart would stop beating. He knew that hand holding the fold of velvet in front of her face. He put his arm round her, and felt her tenseness. In silence, he hurried her into his room and then turned back.

"Jem!"

"M'lord?"

"Bolt that door and put your dagger in as well. Then put your bed across it. Don't let anyone in—if they come in the Queen's name! An' if you ever speak of this, I'll cut your ears off!"

"M'lord, they can cut me to pieces before I'll let anyone in. Nor shall anyone know." He gave his master a saucy wink. "Least of all m'lord of Essex. . . ."

"Good lad. . . ."

He went in swiftly, bolting the inner door behind him. She was in a chair by the empty hearth, and had let the cloak fall from her head and face. In the candle light, her hair, falling loosely on her shoulders, was tawny bright, but her face was as white as a ghost. Her breath came unevenly.

"Elizabeth!" he said softly, his voice shaking with astonishment. "Elizabeth!"

"Your fellow thinks me my cousin, Lettice. . . ."

"Well," he murmured, "perhaps there is the slightest resemblance." There *was*, he reflected, dizzily. Only Lettice, rounded, voluptuous and as sleek as a contented cat, was already more ample than her elder cousin. There was a flame in Elizabeth which drove her and devoured her. "They both know what they want!" he thought.

She whispered bitterly: "So she comes here?"

"No, I swear it!"

He knelt down beside her but did not touch her.

"A family resemblance. . . ." she said in the same bitter voice. "The Bullen women! I've proved I'm one, haven't I, by coming so?"

"Dear heart!" He took her hands which were cold and shaking. "But how did you——?"

"Ashley sleeps like a log," she said. "She usually never stirs unless I call her. I put my face quite close to hers, and she never moved, snoring away comfortably into her pillows. And the women in the ante-chamber seemed sound asleep too. Just at the foot of the little stairway, I met a yeoman." He drew a deep breath, but she went on: "He had no idea—of course! I had my cloak over my face. He called out: 'Ho, my pretty sweeting! If the Queen knew—you'd smart for it!' So I put a gold piece into his hand. Like the one for your fellow. And then he said: 'I'm no tell-tale! God speed you and the lucky gentleman!' He didn't seem surprised. There must be a lot of what Ashley calls 'goings on'. . . . I know those wretched Maids of Honour of mine are forever running after the Gentlemen Pensioners!"

Her anger amused him. She was gloriously inconsistent!

"Well, sweet! These things happen. . . ."

"And I've happened!" she said lightheadedly. "You thought I couldn't care, Rob! You thought I was all ambition. My ambition is asleep with the Queen! All the cares of State—I've escaped them—just for this little hour."

He pressed her tightly to him, so that the only sound in the silence was their two hearts beating. At last she whispered again: "I couldn't go on, utterly alone, any longer, Rob. . . . To-night, when they sang the old ballads, they were only singing for me.

> "For in my mind, of all mankind
> I love but you alone. . . ."

He got lightly to his feet, drawing her up with him. Tenderness was there, but it was drowned with an immense exultation. "I've conquered!" he thought. "She can't do without me!" He heard her whisper against his shoulder: "Be kind to me, Robin. For I am utterly in your hands. . . ."

Sunrise

So at last she had his black head where she would have it, asleep on her heart. And the long pain of loneliness had stopped its aching. She had her hour in which she could set down her burdens, and as she lay awake in the darkness, while he slept, she knew it was all she would ever have. But the head resting on her heart, dreamed of itself wearing a crown.

So at last she laid his black head where she would have it, asleep on her breast. And the long pain of long lines had stopped its aching. She had these hours in which she could set down her burdens, and as she lay awake in the sleeping palace, she knew it was all she would ever have. But the head resting on her heart dreamed of itself wearing a crown.

Chapter Twelve

S o they reached their compromise with circumstance and fate; but Robert did not realize that it was a compromise. His self-confidence restored, his ambition began to hope again. He had one of those natures which could not live without hope, but being naturally buoyant, he could be optimistic on little. Since he was seventeen, women had spoilt, adored and given way to him. This was another woman like the rest, he thought. She loved him and she would give him everything he wanted. So he swaggered through the court, once more with the air of the King-to-be. Cecil regarded him thoughtfully. But he now had more reliance on his Queen's judgment.

"Your Grace does not intend eventually to marry Lord Robert?"

"Not", she said smoothly, "without the full approval of the people of this country."

But Robert had no such doubts. To a little group of his adherents, his brother-in-law, Sidney of Penshurst, his brother, Warwick, and his faithful friend, the Earl of Pembroke, he loudly declared that the marriage was only postponed owing to the unfortunate hubbub which had arisen over the death of his wife.

"But, Rob!" objected his brother, Ambrose. "You've been confident before. You've sworn a thousand times that you are sure of the Queen. And the next moment, you are cursing the very heavens, because you can never have any certainty of her."

Robert smiled a little and thrust out his long legs.

"I am as sure of her as any man can be of any woman."

"But", said Ambrose shrewdly, "she isn't any woman. She is the Queen."

Robert did not see it that way. She was his dear love, and only he knew how much she loved him. So he smiled again with some superiority. Ambrose was the best fellow alive, no man could ask for a more loyal and devoted brother, but Ambrose did not understand a lot of things. Women did not fall headlong in love with him, as they did with Robert.

That she could love him so much, and yet set it aside at the cold, hard dictates of reason, was beyond Robert, She thought sometimes, with a sad humour, that her brain would not be set aside. For so long it had been trained and prepared, burnished and sharpened into a formidable weapon which had first guarded her life and then her country. It was enchanting to think of being nothing but Robert's wife and the mother of Robert's children. Life could not give her anything sweeter, but it would not suffice her. Her brain with remorseless cruelty would permit her few illusions, about herself least of all. Some of her madder caprices, her frivolities, her very turnings and twistings were only her efforts to prevent its edge wounding her. It was painful to see everything so clearly. Love had nothing to do with reason, she could see her Robin's faults at the same time as she realized that she loved him more than he did her. His ambition was unbounded but she did not see it as a sinister menace as her Minister did. Robert was her beloved greedy child whom she would spoil as much as she could with safety. He had honestly admitted that he wanted the throne as well as the woman, and that she could never give him. The woman must face competition with other women, and she was twenty-seven, only a few months younger than he, and all the girls ten years younger were ready to snatch a disgruntled Robert from her.

But none of these things had anything to do with loving him. Her brain might persecute her but it could not answer why she loved him so much. It could only tell her that death alone would end her feelings. There would never be another man in Robert's place; there could never be again this happiness. She had not wanted it in secret; she had wanted to own him in the face of the world. History shows that in all her long life of adroit dissembling, she had been most open in those months when she had hoped to marry him. She did not want to be Nan Bullen's daughter stealing away to a secret lover. All normal family affections and relationships had been twisted and poisoned and perverted into hideous situations since her childhood. Every sentiment and emotion cried out for happy compensation. When she had realized that this was impossible it had almost broken her. She

125

had looked at the facts with the dry-eyed grim courage which had carried her so far. She could not have Robert without sacrificing all meaning in her life. She could not think of herself as other than the Queen. She knew she had a mission. But she knew she could not carry on utterly alone; she must have some solace. So she took it, and could quieten the arguments in her head, and dim the too bright mirror which reflected life in her mind, for a little while, because she was young and she was in love. And Robert, even if he did not know much of love's sacrifices, knew all its arts. He was as accomplished in love as he was in all things pleasing. She could understand now the song her musicians sang to their lutes.

> "How the birds sang,
>   How green was the tree.
> How the sun shone,
>   When my Love loved me."

He wanted some say in the things of State, asking as well as for his coveted earldom, to be made a Privy Councillor.

"Why not? Later. . . ."

"But why later? I could help you. . . ."

"Could you?" she said coolly. She knew she had an infinitely better brain than his. It caused her neither pleasure nor chagrin. It was simply an accepted fact. But he had abilities which were not fully brought out. He could be more than the valiant young soldier, the conquering jouster, the elegant gallant accomplished in all the courtly graces.

"Well, Rob!" She picked up a long scroll of parchment. "There is this State dispatch. Read it. Give me your opinion on it."

It was easy to pick his brains. She picked all the brains she might, leading them on skilfully and drawing them out to the utmost. Then before the tribunal of her own brain, she weighed and sifted the evidence. Yes, Rob had ability. She might make something of him. But he was so headlong! It was part of his fascination. She who understood the delicate art of procrastination, who hesitated and balanced, was thrilled by his adventurous spirit. Just as she—who had a horror of spendthriftness—gave him money with admiring dismay, she would not have him other than he was. And he might prove an admirable balance to the over-careful Cecil. But she must temper his fine steel, school her thoroughbred. It would not be easy but it would be worth doing. So unheard laughter pealed in her brain, when he put an arm round her and said: "Sweeting, if we were only married, think of the burdens I could take from you. Deal with all your Council!" She leaned her cheek against his. "You're so dear," she said. "Never, never!" said her brain.

But life was not always so easy. Robert gave himself airs. His swagger became immense. If he had been a prince of the blood he could have hardly lorded it more. Too many, especially amongst the older nobility, thirsted for his blood. There were plots cogitated against his life, and a foreign ambassador was to ask plaintively whether England contained a man of enough spirit to run a poniard into him?

It happened one afternoon that she kept him waiting, being, as so often, closeted with Cecil. Robert, slapping his perfumed and tas-selled gloves against his thigh, walked up and down with irritation. Now, he reflected, if only they were married, he could insist on instant admission, no matter who was with her. His anger was so profound that he did not notice at first that another was waiting, a pale-faced young man in a black velvet suit. Casting a brief glance at him, Robert recognized him as one John Hatherill, a newly admitted Gentleman Pensioner, who owed his position largely to the favour of the Earl of Arundel, cousin of the Duke of Norfolk. Norfolk and Arundel were leaders of the more conservative faction and abomin-ated Robert, who did not deign to throw a word to their follower. In due course an usher came to them, saying that her Majesty would graciously see Master Hatherill.

"Her Majesty doesn't know I'm here!" declared Robert. "*I* will go now."

"Her Majesty especially said Master Hatherill, m'lord," said the usher hesitantly.

"My Lord, I have been waiting upwards of two hours," began young Hatherill, his pale face going crimson. "And her Majesty was so good as to promise me an interview on my petition."

"Damme, pup! Who are you to push before your betters? You can wait another two hours if needs be. . . ."

He had raised his voice and it carried. The next thing he realized was another voice with a strident ring to it.

"God's death, my Lord!" She was in front of him, her face drained of blood, her eyes glowing. Her hand came up and struck him across the face as hard as she might. "My favour is not so locked up for you that others shall not partake thereof. . . . For I have many servants, to whom I have, and will at my pleasure, bequeath my favour! If you think to rule here I will take a course to see you forthcoming! I will have here but one mistress and no master. . . ."

The blood drummed giddily in Robert's temples and he could scarcely see. Besides rage and humiliation, perhaps even surpassing them, he was drowned in an enormous, all-embracing amazement. . . . In silence he bowed low and removed himself from the infuriated royal presence, to hasten to the Sidneys and pour out his woes, his natural indignation, and utter astonishment.

Evening had come and the lamp filled with perfumed oil was casting a mellow light on the panelled walls. Robert sat, in his usual position, his long legs thrust out, his hands tugging at his sword belt with nervous irritation, while the Sidneys watched him, with some apprehension. He had talked his indignation to a standstill and then, as if intoxicated with the sound of his own voice, was throwing forward a new and reckless idea, as a painter might rough out some brilliant but wild sketch, by hurling paint on to his canvas, while scarcely pausing to consider the effect.

". . . I know how troubled she is about this Council to be held at Trent. . . . It is the same danger as when she came to the throne. If she refuses the invitation to go, there's a chance of the Catholics rising. That fellow Quadra and the Frenchman are intriguing with them. . . . But if she accepts, the extreme Protestants will rise. She says she wishes she could go to lead an English delegation—there's nothing she likes as well as a detailed theological argument. She'll speak Latin and Greek, refer to the Early Fathers, to the Councils of the Roman Empire, the Epistles, the lives of the saints. . . . She has it all at her fingertips. Myself, I think a woman can have too much learning! Still, she can't go and argue at Trent. . . . And I know she's in the devil's quandary."

"Still, I don't see how this helps you."

"Listen, Henry! She would marry me if I had sufficiently strong backing. She *wants* to. . . . If I came forward, sponsored by the entire Catholic party and Philip of Spain—she'd take me."

"But, Rob!" cried his sister. "It is the Catholic party who are most hot against you!"

"Never mind! They'd not be hot if I as King-consort led an English delegation to Trent with the approval of Philip. Didn't he praise me on the field of St. Quentin? He hasn't forgotten me so soon. And I think Elizabeth is a Catholic at heart——"

"Nobody", said Henry Sidney, "can be sure what she is at heart."

"Man, look how she likes the ancient order and ritual of service! She was mightily annoyed when that lunatic fellow cast down the Crucifix and candles in her chapel. Some say her cousin Knollys arranged it. He's one of these puritan fellows. She is none so fond of the Knollys's as she was."

"It's on account of the daughter," Mary Sidney told him. "She asked me if you ever spoke of Lettice Essex."

"Lettice Essex!" said Robert contemptuously. "She's a likely girl enough, but I'm talking of serious matters. Listen, Henry! If you were to go to de Quadra—he'll scarcely trust Mary or me after the way we were involved in the negotiations over the Archduke Charles—but you're a sober fellow. . . . It need only be a nominal submission to Rome. Elizabeth's no Mary to have persecutions. She utterly abominates them. For all her temper, she's an uncommon merciful woman. . . . After all, would it make so much difference? The parish priests could give up their wives—and Elizabeth doesn't like the clergy marrying. . . ."

"They could give up their wives so you could get yours," said Mary. "Still, Rob, it is an odd new idea the clergy marrying. . . ."

"Now, Henry!" said Robert, turning eagerly to his brother-in-law.

The next afternoon a pair-oared wherry shot down the river in the direction of Westminster. It was hardly noticed on the broad waters, not yet fouled by the filth of the town which mostly piled up in the narrow, overhung streets. The Thames was the easiest thoroughfare in London, especially for people going to the stately palaces beyond the walls of the city, such as those of the Strand. Here John of Gaunt had built the Savoy, and from his age to that of the Tudors, the nobility had raised their huge buildings, of curiously carved and wrought timber and plaster, hewn stone from as far away as Caen in Normandy and the prevailing rose-red brick, with many a carefully laid out garden stretching to the river's edge. It was at the river stairs of the Spanish Embassy, that the wherry set down Sir Henry Sidney.

De Quadra reflected, not for the first time, what an odd race the English were. . . . How many of them had come and poured the most extraordinary communications into his ears? They appeared to have no reticence or regard. . . . But when he realized the consequences of this interview, he was to hold them the most deceitful race alive. For all their air of bluffness, their apparent clumsiness and stupidity, they were as guileful as the proverbial Italian. No Florentine could produce such cunning—"their Queen is worthy of them!"

But the offer was a wonderful one. He had no belief in either "Jezebel" or her paramour genuinely turning to the true faith, but if they were prepared to lead the country back to it, however unworthy their motive, he could not say nay. Further, as Henry Sidney had hastened to point out, the present claimant to the throne, supported by the Catholics, was Mary, Queen of Scotland and Queen-consort of France. And that would mean an England under the influence of France, enemy of Spain. De Quadra hastened to his writing-table so he could communicate immediately with his august master. Soon after Sir Henry Sidney had left the Embassy, one of the servants who had stood by the door of the Ambassador's chamber, also hastened away, to the nearby house of Sir William Cecil. . . .

Cecil brought his spy's evidence to Elizabeth. She drew a deep breath, but her voice was calm when she said : "We can make use of this."

"Yes, your Grace. Lord Robert is one of the most hated men in England, especially with the Catholic party."

"And they would never forgive King Philip if he tried to set Lord Robert up as King over them. They would even prefer that I should refuse the entrance of the Nuncio bidding me send to Trent."

Cecil looked at her with a sensation as close to delight as he could achieve. She was no longer capable of throwing her cap over the windmill for young Dudley. She was her original self, ready to seize and exploit every advantage.

"And I must and shall refuse to admit the Nuncio," she said. "This will soften the blow. If Quadra asks me for an interview—and he will—he must be granted one with all despatch."

But when Cecil had gone, she said : "Rob, Rob. . . ."

De Quadra got his interview with "Jezebel". He found her, gorgeously adorned, in a black velvet dress with the fullest skirts he had ever seen, banded with cloth of gold, King Philip's diamonds sparkling on her neck beneath the immense ruff. She looked at him boldly over the crimson plumes of her fan, as crimson as her painted lips.

Sunrise

A diplomatic remark on his part, designed to lead to the subject of matrimony, produced immediate results.

"Ah—if you were my Father confessor!" she said. "I am not an angel. I won't deny I have some affection for Lord Robert. . . ." She made eyes shamelessly at the Bishop over her crimson plumes, and then proceeded to give a remarkable imitation of the modest young girl scarcely daring to admit her love.

"It would please my people if I were to marry an Englishman. . . . That is—since I must marry. . . . But what do you think my dear brother Philip would say? I must confess his approval would strengme! If—well—I don't know if *he* has ever had in mind any English gentleman?"

"Of course your Grace must understand that until I have a communication from King Philip, I cannot say anything definite. But I know he has always held Lord Robert Dudley in great esteem for his gallantry on the field of St. Quentin."

"Lord Robert always remembers the King's favour!"

But when de Quadra had gone—to pen yet another dispatch—that smile, those brazen glances and posturings were suddenly wiped from the mask which had deceived him. When she received Cecil he found her white under her paint, and her mouth bitter.

"Your Grace," he said. "This foolish action of Lord Robert's has helped us greatly. My agents are busily spreading the story. The Catholic gentry will soon learn that King Philip proposed to set a Dudley as king over them!"

"We have done what is necessary."

"I have not seen Lord Robert lately, in attendance on your Grace." Her lips were tight. "Lord Robert is sick. Of a slight fever it is said."

It was de Quadra who felt sick when, like a thunderclap, the news burst on him. Elizabeth refused the admission of the Nuncio and refused to send a delegation to Trent, which filled the hearts of the Protestants with delight. As for the Catholic nobility and gentry whom Quadra had hoped to see start a rising against her, they heaped reproaches on the unhappy head of the Ambassador. Had his royal master and he proposed seriously to set over them that abominable, vainglorious young man, that badly born, ambitious upstart? There was no sign of a Catholic rising. . . .

Jem, body-servant to my Lord Robert, was waiting in a harassed manner in the ante-chamber to his master's room. Lord Robert was sick and he could not say how seriously. He had had a rheum (as colds and other catarrhal diseases were called then) for some days, and this very morning had come in, his teeth chattering as if in the cold fit of a fever. His face had been grey, and he had seemed to be shaking all over. With a burst of oaths, he had admitted to being ill, and had torn off his clothes with his man's anxious help. Yes, he would go to bed, and might he never rise from it! Jem timidly suggested summoning physicians. With a steeper oath, his lord consigned all physicians to an exceedingly warm place. Jem then suggested sending to my Lady Sidney. Robert answered this by a threat to despatch Jem to the same place as the physicians if he dared to meddle. Since then he had refused all food and attention, tossing feverishly amongst his bedclothes, and hurling blood-curdling threats at the wretched Jem who longed to seek assistance. Lord Robert was a generous master and he was truly troubled about him. If only he could send to my Lord Warwick or my Lady Sidney! How they would blame him afterwards for not so sending!

Nightfall brought the sound of a foot in the corridor. Jem, starting up, thought it sounded like the mysterious lady in the green cloak. At first he had thought her to be the Countess of Essex but now he was not sure. The Countess was not the only lady to make eyes at his master, he had only to lift his finger and half the court's proud beauties would come running. Didn't the Queen's Grace herself favour him so much that all knew she would marry him to-morrow if she had her way? It wouldn't go well with Green Cloak if the Queen knew of her secret visits. . . . He wondered who she might be, his master always seemed so agitated—she must have a very jealous and dangerous husband! But never had Jem seen her face or heard anything more than the whispered tones of her voice. This step at the door must be hers. He opened it. But it was no Green Cloak. Before the resplendent figure in black and gold he knelt, stricken to dumbness.

"Lord Robert is ill?"

"Yes—your Grace!" he gasped.

"Who is with him?"

"Oh, your Grace, I crave pardon, but I didn't dare, my lord was so hot against it, and truly I wanted to send for the Lady Sidney but—but pardon me, your Grace——"

"Stop babbling and explain clearly. You can have any pardon if you speak quickly and plainly."

Somehow he got out his explanation of his lord's state. She nodded her head in understanding.

"I'll attend to this. Be ready. I shall probably need you."

He stayed on his knees, in silence, watching her go in.

She stood for a moment looking down on the figure lying on the great bed, in the light of the one lamp. He had buried his face deep in the pillows as if he never wanted to see anything again, and his arms were sprawled out in an anguished manner across the bedclothes which were tossed and twisted into a nightmarish confusion. She put her hand on his neck. Yes, he was burning with fever. "Rob!" she said. "How long have you been sick?"

He turned and stared at her.

"The sooner I'm dead the better!" he muttered thickly.

"Ah—but people don't die so easily as that!" She lightly caressed the hot head.

"The only thing left for me is to die—after what you have done."

Sitting on the edge of the bed, she coaxed his head and shoulders on to her lap. She thought: "He says what *you* have done. . . . Never what *I* have done! Oh, Robin, you spoilt child!"

"You know I was desperate!" he complained. "Else I would not have made that plan. . . . After all, it need only have been a nominal submission. You're so clever, you could have found some way out of it!"

"I am so clever", she said bitterly, "that I can do everything except give myself true happiness!"

"And now", he went on, "you've made me a laughing stock, you've set everyone against me—just to keep the peace!"

"Just to keep the peace," she repeated softly.

"And we can never marry now. If they'd all backed me, we could have done—easily!"

"We cannot marry because of your wife's death."

"Oh, *that*! People are forgetting it!" She thought: "As *you* forget it. I must carry that, too, alone."

"Never mind, Robin. You are ill and we won't argue. In the morning I'll send my physicians. Now let me see if I can make you more comfortable!"

She soon had the anxious Jem running. A herb tea must be brewed at whose bitterness Robert made a grimace, but she spooned it down his throat with inexorable calm. She turned and re-arranged his pillows, smoothed and re-assembled his bedclothes into comfort. Finally she made Jem fill a silver basin with warm water and bring towels. Then to the goggling astonishment of the lackey she proceeded to bathe his master's feverish face. She noticed how serenely Robert accepted it all. As his sister had said, women had always spoilt him. She thought with a spurt of bitter amusement: "I suppose I can caress and cosset him as well as any! Better than my cousin, Lettice!" Much of Robert's illness must have been caused by mental stress; under her attentions he was obviously eased. When she had settled him, he kept one of her hands, pressing it against his cheek.

"You are an angel!"

"No, Robin, I am not in the least like an angel! You should tell that to de Quadra."

He chuckled weakly but added on a plaintive note: "What I mind is looking a fool in front of him. He will see me as a fool and a dupe!"

"No, dear heart," she said swiftly. "He will think you were hand-in-glove in the plot with me."

"He says that you would delight the heart of Machiavelli—you know, the crafty Italian knave who served Cesare Borgia."

"I know his *Il Principe* from cover to cover, and it's true, every word, Robin! Yes, they call me the Florentine. Needs must!"

As she sat by him, soothing him towards sleep, her mind echoed: "Needs must. . . ." She was slowly beginning to see that even if Amy Dudley's strange and dreadful death had not taken place, if that stumbling block could have been removed, a marriage between her and Robin would have fatal results. She could not give him any authority over her, she must be Queen and rule—him as well as the others. Her love must always be thrust away into some dark corner in her life.

He was sleeping now, peacefully. With great care she withdrew her cramped fingers, leaned forward and touched his hair with her lips. In the ante-chamber she gave a few swift instructions to Jem, and then was gone as silently as a dream.

By a window, she paused, pushing aside the curtains. The sky was still black, starless and impenetrable. There was not even a streak of grey in the east. She could get a few hours' rest perhaps, before the sun rose on another day. She began to reflect—for she did not want to think too long of Robert's sleeping face—on all the difficulties

Sunrise

through which she had passed, since that day nearly three years ago at Hatfield, when she had heard of her sister's death. Like a ship she had surmounted the waves which might have dashed her to pieces, and ridden smoothly on. Think of the sullen, divided, almost bankrupt England menaced by strong enemies abroad, which she had been called upon to rule in 1558! Think of the serenity which was just beginning to show in 1560, with the immediate dangers past and the careful foundations built. Think of these things, so as not to feel that tenderness, which was like a pain and was so utterly unreasonable, when she thought of Robert's face on his pillows and how long his eyelashes were. . . . Her sun had risen but it cast its shadows.

Book Two

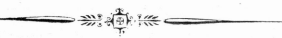

ZENITH

. . . "No, thou proud dream,
That play'd so subtly with a king's repose:
I am a king, that find thee; and I know
'Tis not the balm, the sceptre and the ball,
The sword, the mace, the crown imperial,
The inter-tissu'd robe of gold and pearl,
The farcèd title running 'fore the king,
The throne he sits on, nor the tide of pomp
That beats on the high shore of this world—
No, not all these, thrice gorgeous ceremony,
Not all these laid in bed majestical,
Can sleep so soundly as the wretched slave. . . ."

SHAKESPEARE: *Henry V, Act IV, Sc. 1*

Chapter One

The sunlight came through the tall rectangular windows in the Long Gallery and touched the Queen's dress of cloth of silver with a cold flame. She was reclining on the floor— a favourite position—with cushions under her and about her, scarlet cushions sewn with seed pearls and her monogram, E.R., worked in golden thread, golden brocade cushions stitched in scarlet. From the billowing silver skirts, a scarlet brocade shoe projected, and a couple of inches of ankle in a scarlet silk stocking. She was regal, even upon the floor, and still a handsome woman in spite of the smallpox which had struck her so suddenly the last year, causing terror in court and country. She seemed hardly marked but it had been noticed that afterwards she painted more heavily and perhaps the red and white of her long, oval face had something of a mask's formality; but it accorded well with the stiff richness of her apparel, with the jewels which lay on the ripples of her hair dependent from the coif, dangled from her neck or glittered on her long fingers. Those fingers were holding some sheets of paper which she was intently studying. No less intently was she watched by the boy, Philip Sidney, kneeling beside her on one of the many cushions.

She looked up, and her eyes rested affectionately on the graceful serious little boy in black velvet, his fair hair ruffled, his grey eyes looking at her with the adoration which belongs to some children and all dogs. This was good; she was used to adoration expressed in a thousand fanciful ways, to a perpetual incense of adulation; but this was as genuine and unforced as from the people in the streets who crowded to her stirrup.

"You have a remarkable knack for verse, Boy Philip," she said. "I could not write such verses when I was your age."

"Oh, your Grace!" he said, reddening.

"Give me another cushion—put it behind my shoulders—so! Now you may sit, Philip. Be comfortable."

He sat back on his heels. Ambassadors and great noblemen must kneel or stand in her presence; the immense ritual of the court had given her an almost Olympian elevation. To a romantic child who fed his imagination on all the legends of the ancients, she was scarcely less than a goddess. Yet, when he was alone with her thus, she was one of the most sympathetic and understanding of the grown-up world. The other evening she had called him suddenly to her.

"Young Philip! I hear you write verse. . . ."

That must have been Uncle Rob, he thought. That splendid uncle of his seemed to be her Majesty's very shadow, standing close behind her, ready to whisper into her jewelled ear some remark which would make her laugh suddenly and clap his cheek.

"Yes, your Grace," said Philip, looking at his shoes. "I do—write verse——" But then remembering that this great lady whom the world held in awe was always indulgent to him, he looked up at the dark eyes which were regarding him with humorous affection. "I wrote some for you, your Grace."

"Then I must see them. You told me you were my knight when you were five years old. Bring them to me, to-morrow."

So here he was in his best suit of black velvet with a gold chain round his neck, and the gold-hilted poniard which Uncle Rob had given him, in his girdle, and a newly frilled and starched ruff enclosing his neck almost to his ears. (But he had a feeling that his hair was standing up at the back in spite of all his efforts!)

"Philip," she said, "I am going to be proud of you some day. I will make a prophecy. That you will be a very bright star in this little firmament, my court."

"I will be your knight and fight your battles."

"No battles outside the tiltyard! Too much is lost in battles."

"But, your Grace! Think of the glory and the honour——"

"And think", she said, "of the empty saddles. . . . No, that's the difference between men and women. Though some women pretend. . . . I think you have read some of Malory's *Morte d'Arthur*."

"Oh yes, your Grace! I think it is the most wonderful book that ever was, though I don't understand all of it quite yet. But I shall!"

"You shall—my young Tristam—young Percivale! I think your father does well to let you read it."

Zenith

"My father lets me read his books, because he says, your Grace, that he knows I will handle them carefully, and have my fingers clean."

"You shall read some of my books, I promise you."

"May I really—your Grace?"

"You may. What are you reading now?"

"It is a new book my father bought. Master Gerard Legh's *Accedens of Armory*. It is on heraldry and blazonry, and tells of all the legends of the ancients about the beasts displayed and of all colours of the devices and what they mean. Now purple is called, in heraldry, purpure, and it is the most noble of all colours——"

"The colour for a king," she said softly. "Go on, boy."

"Plato, the ancient philosopher, said it was great wickedness to use the hue of majesty wantonly. It was the colour of Solomon's seal and under the influence of the planet Mercury, whose stone is the 'Amatist' which was in Aaron's breastplate."

"You remember very well what you have read. But I think nothing will equal Malory in your eyes."

"No, your Grace. I make games and plays from Malory for the others—my brother and sister—and we pretend to be the different knights. Some days ago, we went off, Mary, Rob and I, pretending we were seeking the Holy Graal and we followed the small stream behind the hill till it got lost in the marshes. *We* got lost in the marshes for a while, and my mother was displeased."

Elizabeth lifted one eyebrow but her lips curled into a smile.

"You were somewhat muddy?" she suggested.

"Well, yes, your Grace. You see I had Mary on the pillion behind me and when the ground got very boggy I dismounted and led the pony. Because of the weight. I made Rob dismount too. But Mary came to no harm. My mother knows I would never let harm come to Mary."

"Your sister is very dear to you?"

"Yes, your Grace. She—she understands. I make my verses and my plays for her and tell her my stories. She understands them better than Rob. He likes hearing of the tilts and battles in Malory, so long as lances are splintered and there's plenty of hacking and hewing, he's content."

"But you want more? Strange child. . . . I had a brother, who was very dear to me, and perhaps we were like your sister and you. We were never so happy as when together. Alas—we were not together very long. . . . Bring your sister with you to see me, Philip."

"If your Grace wishes." He added with a ten-year-old solemnity: "She is very young and so—rather bashful in company. . . ."

"Both are good faults and time remedies them! But I am sorry the quest for the Graal led you into a boggy marsh."

"We flushed a great heron, your Grace!" He spread his arms as if vainly trying to give the wing span. "I wished then I had Uncle Rob's new falcon. He has a haggard of the rock, newly trained and he was speaking of her to-day. I think he means to give her to your Grace—perhaps I should not have told as yet——"

"I will keep the secret," she promised him. "Your uncle likes a haggard[1] better than an eyass[2]."

"Yes, he does. Though they are more trouble. He said to Lord Pembroke that hawks are like women——" She threw back her head and laughed merrily at this.

"Phil—you delight me."

"But your Grace—I scarce see what he meant!"

"I do," she said. "When did this most sage conversation take place?"

"This morning, your Grace. I was down at the tiltyard to see Uncle Rob ride a course with Lord Pembroke. He was trying his new Great Horse—it's dapple-grey from Flanders. It's very strong, but needs more schooling in the manège, he said, because it did not answer the bit quickly enough. So Uncle Rob only rode two courses and then took the horse to the manège."

"Your uncle is a very accomplished cavalier."

"He's teaching me. To ride in the manège after the Italian manner, and to tilt at the ring."

"None could teach you better."

"He put me up on the horse while Jem and Will were unarming him to ride in the manège, and it was then he spoke of hawks. My Lord Pembroke laughed and said: "Rob, you fancy a wild hawk that can strike for herself, however hard she may be to train," and Uncle Robert said: "Yes, give me no hand-trained eyass as meek as milk, with no spirit to her. I like to see a hawk that can strike for herself however unruly she may be—for the wildest ramage[2] will strike better

---

[1] Haggard—a hawk fully grown on capture.
[2] Eyass—taken from the nest as a fledgling.
[8] Ramage—a hawk very wild and shy of man.

than any other. It's the same with women. They are like hawks, and the better spirit they have, the harder to handle," and Lord Pembroke laughed greatly. Then they talked no more of hawks or women for others came down to the tiltyard, several Gentlemen Pensioners and Lord Darnley. His brother, Charles, watched with me. I sometimes play with Charles."

"So Harry Darnley was there? What did he do?"

"He looked at Uncle Robert's Great Horse, and he talked about it, and about horses, with his thumbs in his belt—so! And his legs apart like this, and his cheeks get pink like a girl's when he is excited. He laughs and talks very loudly."

"What do *you* think of Harry Darnley, Boy Philip? Tell me exactly."
Philip creased his forehead with concentration.

"He is a good lance and a good horseman but I don't think he is a good knight, your Grace."

"Pray, why, Sir Oracle?"

"Well, he is cruel! I have seen him cut his horse over the head when it disobeyed him. And though he is very proud and high, sometimes he will make free and merry with his huntsmen and grooms as if he were one of them, and then he turns on them and calls them dogs and curs."

"Which is hard on the poor knaves. Does his young brother tell you this?"

"Some of it, your Grace. Some I have seen and heard from others. Charles Stuart is not high like Harry Darnley. I quite like Charles. . . . But he said that his mother told them never to forget that they were princes of the blood and related to two royal houses."

"So my cousin Margaret tells her sons that? Well—she and I share a grandfather, that's true enough. She is half Tudor and her mother was once Queen of Scotland."

"Oh, and another thing Harry Darnley said, your Grace. He asked Uncle Robert where he got his Great Horse, for he said he fancied one like it. He is buying horses, because he wants to travel north. He said: 'My sweet cousin of Scotland wishes to see me.' "

Elizabeth drew in her breath. "Philip, I call your Uncle Robert my eyes, and I think I will call you my ears. . . . So my young cockerel thinks his cousin the Queen of Scots would like to see him? Or his mother thinks it! She'll curse his free tongue. Tell me, what did he say of the Queen of Scots?"

"Only that she wished to see him."

"A treat for her, no doubt!"

"And he would like to see her."

"So would I, Philip! So would I!"

"When your Grace sent my father on an embassy to her last year he said that she wept because her meeting with you was put off."

"I might have wept if I were given that way. . . . Tell me now. What did your father say of her at home? Did he think her beautiful?"

She leaned forward, so her face was close to the boy's, and he could see that her eyes were narrowed and bright. Strange things moved the grown-ups, far away and foreign to his world of lessons and games and the golden dreams which came to him from the ringing prose of Malory. He took his troubled concentrated look.

"My father said it was hard to tell if she had true beauty."

"And why?"

"Because—so he said—she had such enchantment. . . ."

The figure in the glittering dress stiffened suddenly, the painted mouth hardening in a grimace half open. Then she whispered bitterly: "And she is only one and twenty. . . .'

Philip was worried. Then her eyes opened wider and saw him, and her lips relaxed into a smile.

"That's a monstrous age to you, isn't it? The same as thirty!"

"Well, your Grace—— When one is grown up—one is grown up. Till one is really old. With a long white beard!"

Her smile widened. "I know!" she said. "We are all of an age—till we grow long white beards!" And then suddenly he began to laugh and so did she. When they stopped, it was easier to speak on that upsetting subject, the Queen of Scots, and there was no more bitterness.

"Did your father describe her? I wonder so much what she looks like. And none of her portraits are the same!"

"Your Grace, my mother kept asking my father and he said he could not. He would tell us that her eyes were a very deep brown and she was tall and slender and her skin so rarely white that men said when she drank the red wine of Burgundy, one could see it running down her throat."

"A pretty conceit!" . . . .

Philip thought she was not pleased but then she smiled again, and his hair must be standing up at the back, for she began to smooth it down with her long fingers.

"I wonder, your Grace!" he ventured.

"What do you wonder?"

"If the Queen of Scots is a good lady!"

"Ah, Philip, if only I knew that too!"

But she began to study his verses again, correcting a fault in the syntax of a set in Latin—"then your master shall not beat you!"

"I should like well to learn of your Grace!" said Philip, comfortably resting his chin on the silver sleeve which smelt of musk and ambergris. She cuffed him lightly.

"I have a mighty temper, I promise you!" She chuckled. "I know well what your Uncle meant when he spoke of women and wild falcons! Did you know that your Uncle Rob loves a lady who deals most provokingly with him?"

Here was a grown-up joke beyond comprehension.

"I don't think Uncle Rob loves any lady. He always rides in all the tourneys with your Grace's colours!"

"And very gallantly! Come! I must deal with certain weighty matters."

He knelt on one knee, as he had been taught, to offer her his arm to rise. She came to her feet as lightly as a girl, and then walked down the long apartment, her hand resting on his shoulder. Amongst the group of ladies who rose to curtsy to her, was his mother.

"Mary," she said. "I would buy this boy from you if I possessed anything of equal value to give you in exchange!"

Smiling, she patted his cheek, and then swept on, to shout like a man for her usher to bid Sir William Cecil come to her, instantly!

Cecil found her keenly alert.

"Have you heard that my cousin Margaret Lennox's hopeful sprig is thinking of journeying to Scotland to delight the eye of its Queen?"

"Your Grace will remember that there was talk of the Earl of Lennox's forfeited estates in Scotland being restored to him, and he had applied for your Grace's permission to go to Scotland upon this matter."

"A good excuse! Lennox is an old fool—and my cousin Margaret is half Tudor and wholly ambitious. The boy is the child of both his parents—a fool and ambitious. And more too perhaps. What do you think of him, Sir Spirit?"

"He is very young, your Grace, and gives all his time to hunting and jousting. I suppose he is a handsome lad."

"Would women fancy him?"

"Your Grace should know that better than I!"

"If I had a fancy for babes, I know a better, I have been closeted with him the past hour. A very gallant little cavalier! No—I resemble my father when he said he liked to look upon a *man*. . . . Yet Harry Darnley is a pretty lad and might please some. But there's a bad streak in him. I think he's vicious. To-day I've had my judgment confirmed. Out of the mouths of babes and sucklings!"

"Your Grace is fearing that the Queen of Scots might consider the young Lord Darnley as a suitor?"

"She will consider him as a suitor. . . . I do not know whether it is to be feared or not. I wonder. How I wonder!"

"Anything would be better than her marriage to Don Carlos!" said Cecil with anxiety. "I know Maitland her Secretary is in touch with the court of Spain. Spain in Scotland would be a terrible danger for us!"

"I know. But Carlos is a boy—a sickly frenzied epileptic boy. Poor brother Philip is not lucky in his heir."

"Don Carlos may be all these things, your Grace, but he is still the son of the greatest monarch on earth. Royal marriages are of policy, not affection."

"Is that a thrust for me?"

"Your Grace is very nice upon these matters!" complained the secretary.

"Aye! I've watched my sister's marriage. . . . Too closely!"

"Then there is the young King of France, her brother-in-law."

"I do not fear that. Catherine de Medici wants no more of her sons to marry Mary Stuart. . . . And Scotland has given a headache to the wearer of the crown of France—I saw to it!"

"Then there is the Archduke Charles with whom your Grace has positively trifled!"

"I must resume trifling, I think. We must see if we can re-open marriage negotiations. From a worldly point of view I am the better match—even if she is nine years younger!"

"Your Grace, I beseech you to consider the Archduke seriously! He is not bigoted in his faith, I have even heard it said that he is interested in the reformed religion. Last year, when your Grace was sick almost to death, the country was in a desperate state with no rightful heir. The House of Commons, your Grace, will be utterly unmanageable if you do not soon marry. I have never before seen them in such a mood."

"You needn't talk of their moods. I told you—let us reopen negotiations with Vienna!"

"But does your Grace seriously intend to marry the Archduke?"

"I seriously intend to do whatever is best for this country. Ah! Why did you stop me meeting the Queen of Scots last year?" She drummed upon the table fiercely with her jewelled fingers.

"I am not aware that I ever stopped your Grace—I merely advised against it," said the secretary mildly. He added with some fervour: "Your Grace is not so easily—stopped!"

"God's wounds, I'm not!" she swore with a sudden fury. "I get what I want in the end, however long and crooked the road is! But you and the whole Council were so hot against it—then the very weather had to join you, and there were such storms and rain, that all said my retinue would never get so far as York—the roads were quagmires! The very stars in their courses fought against our meeting. Then the Guises had to stir up religious persecution in France and I must not meet their niece! Ah, the pity of it!"

"Really, your Grace, I cannot see what good the meeting would have done——"

"I should have seen her, and judged her for myself! Why—none agree on her. Her very portraits are all different! She has golden hair in one, black in another, red in a third."

"The French, your Grace, are very fanciful and much given to such conceits and toys as dyeing and colouring the hair."

"And no one will say if she is truly beautiful. Her features don't *look* beautiful, except perhaps her eyes, but even sober Henry Sidney says she is enchanting! She is like some enchanted princess in an ancient legend."

"Your Grace is not usually so fanciful!"

"I am strangely concerned about her. I feel trouble around her, trouble for her, trouble for me. Who knows? I am like a hound with his bristles rising in the dark. . . . Do you know what she said to Throckmorton?"

"I think he was baffled by her too, your Grace. Though he considered her attractive."

"She's more than attractive—confound her! She's dangerous. . . . Listen to this. She goes like a sleepwalker, hardly heeding where she

147

treads. She insults her mother-in-law, Catherine de Medici; she insults me. Does nothing tell her that we can be perilous enemies? She breaks her word and refuses to ratify the Treaty of Edinburgh which she promised to sign. So naturally, when she asks for a safe conduct on her return to Scotland, I refuse to answer till she ratifies the treaty. A prince's word must be kept. I was angry with her, I admit it. She calls me 'bastard', 'alderman's grand-daughter', she quarters my arms and declares she should be in my seat—and then demands favours as a right! So Throckmorton gives her my answer and she bursts out in temper, saying that she can return to her own realm without my permission! And then the temper goes, she looks dreamily at him, as if she were gazing beyond the clouds, and she says these strange words: 'If the winds cast me on the coast of England, then my cousin may make sacrifice of me if she will. Peradventure that casualty might be better for me than to live, but God's will be done'. I sent that safe conduct off at once, but it was too late, she had taken ship. I was afraid, Spirit, as I seldom have been afraid before. . . . Here was a girl with the world at her feet. Almost born a queen, crowns tossed into her lap, all the luxury, the culture, the adulation of France, the ability to turn men's heads when she smiles—didn't her mother-in-law who hates her, say that? And only nineteen too! And then she says it might be better for her to die! In her own country they would call her 'fey'. They say her grandfather was fey when he rode to Flodden Field. . . .

"I hated her before that, Spirit. Sometimes I hate her now. But then I felt that dreadful fear. I wanted to help her, to save her, to protect her from some vast unknown peril. . . . And I realized my mistake. I should have invited her to travel to Scotland by way of England. It is the shorter sea voyage, and she might have been my honoured guest and I could have talked to her. I must talk to her! England and Scotland must stand together. Perhaps I could reason with her, and by reasoning save untold bloodshed. But I fear sometimes that she will never listen to reason. Reason is not a thing which belongs to her."

"It is a great pity that she has replaced her bastard brother as actual ruler. The Lord James Stuart—she created him Earl of Moray —is a reasonable man. Your Grace, the safest thing for us would be for her to marry an English nobleman on whom we could rely."

The Queen seemed to have abandoned her fancies, he noticed with pleasure. Her reply was crisp. "Wise Spirit! Whom shall we find?"

"The Duke of Norfolk?"

"He's weak, my cousin Norfolk. She would turn him round her finger. And he is proud as premier peer—he would not heed *me* so well. It's a pity Lord Warwick has none of his brother's graces. He's a good fellow, Ambrose, but he has not the grace and gallantry of his brother."

Cecil thought that the Queen of Scots would hold a Dudley far beneath her but he was too wise to say so.

"We must consider the matter carefully," she continued.

"Yes, your Grace. And if Lord Lennox and his son ask for the permission to go to Scotland?"

"I can't well refuse them. Harry Darnley's long legs and sweet singing to the lute might distract her from thoughts of being daughter-in-law to Spain or Austria. . . . And yet I mistrust him. Perhaps for her good, I mistrust him."

When he had gone, she sat, resting her chin on her thin fingers, till the summer dusk began to darken the corners of the room. She thought of the strange girl who now reigned in Edinburgh, who one moment whipped her to a frenzy of jealous anger with a careless insult, and then with strange doomed words, awoke in her an agony of pity. No, Mary was not reasonable, one could not deal and bargain with her as with her Italian mother-in-law, Catherine de Medici. . . . Truly, she went like a sleepwalker towards an unknown destination, dangerous to others, dangerous to herself, at once enchantress and enchanted. What would she make of that tall lad, straddling his long legs, the high colour in his cheeks, the high, arrogant laugh ringing from his lips? Under his boyish swagger, there was that vicious streak, cruelty and unreliability, which might be driven on by unbounded ambition. She thought: "I play with strange chessmen. . . ."

Chapter Two

The quarrel began from so little—or so it seemed. Or was it the cloud the size of a man's hand in the Scriptures, was it the shadow of coming events, far off now but advancing as implacably as doom? A day's hunting in the Surrey woods around the royal palace of Nonesuch, and a quick burst through a tangled encumbered ride, a horse plunging and struggling in the undergrowth, a woman's nervous cry—"Oh, m'lord!"—and Robert Dudley swiftly dismounting to free the Countess of Essex's palfrey, and support its rider with a strong arm in her insecure saddle. Elizabeth had cast one glance at them, and then had laid her whip mercilessly on her impetuous barb so that he bounded forward headlong. She was one of the best mounted as usual, and that day she rode as if the devil possessed her. Her ladies fell back, a Gentleman Pensioner came over his horse's ears as it stumbled on a root, the company were dispersed here and there. Only the boy, Philip Sidney, on a pony, the gift of his uncle and crossed with barb blood, kept level with her, guiding her through gaps in the barriers of greenery, with a dexterity which took them swiftly away from the others. "Here, your Grace! I know this way!" And she answered, a quick colour whipped into her cheeks under their paint: "Go on, Boy Philip!"

He was like a champion in the *Morte d'Arthur* leading his Queen, and elation made him too bold. He set his spurs into his pony at an overgrown bank; the hot little beast went gallantly at it, but stumbled at the crest, somersaulting over, and throwing his young rider far away. Elizabeth reined in sharply. She saw the pony recover himself, and get up again, but she did not see his rider.

"Philip!" she said loudly, and then on a note of urgency: "Philip!!!" But nothing stirred in the leafy confusion beyond the bank. She looked about her; far off she could hear the sounds of horses blundering

150

about but there was no one near. With some difficulty, encumbered by the long skirts of her riding-dress, she dismounted, knotted her reins to a limb of hazel and climbed up the bank. He was lying on his face in the crushed bracken.

She was down on her knees beside him, turning him over. His face was drained and white except where a trickle of blood ran down from a graze on his forehead. Unfastening his collar and ruff, she thrust her hand inside his doublet. Yes—his heart was beating but slowly, slowly, while her own seemed to be thundering in her ears. For once she was alone, with none of the eternal hangers-on. In her mind twisted with anger and fear, anger against Robert setting his arm round her cousin Lettice, fear for the child whose limp head lay on her lap, she took malicious pleasure at the thought of her followers' anxiety seeking her. They would be in a pretty state at losing the Queen! She would make them smart for it! That she had wilfully lost them did not matter. But now she wished for someone to help her. If she could get water and bathe the cut on the boy's head! He might be only stunned, but he might be more hurt. She had a nagging little feeling of guilt that her reckless riding had harmed the child for whom she cared.

She tried to lift him, but he was almost too heavy for her; her strength lay mainly in nervous energy and will power, but finally she got him up. At this moment there was a pounding of hoofs and crunching of undergrowth, and a big black horse cleared the bank. Robert Dudley flung himself out of the saddle and came hurrying towards her.

"Dear heart, thank God, no harm's come to you——"

"Small thanks to you if it's not!"

"What's happened to the boy?"

"If he's killed it's your fault!"

"Killed . . . ? Give him to me! He's too heavy for you——"

"No—you might be rough with him. He's not Lettice Essex!"

"Damme——!"

But young Philip had opened his eyes. Elizabeth seated herself on the ground again to hold him comfortably.

"Get water!" she said. "There must be a stream or a pool. . . . Dip my kerchief in."

Philip came out of confusion and darkness to a dizzy realization of his surroundings. The Queen was bathing his head—which hurt—

151

and he could see her face and Uncle Rob's bent over him from a strange angle.

"Philip!" she said. "How do you feel?"

"Thank you, your Grace," he said gravely. "I feel better."

"Of course he's better!" declared his uncle. "What d'you mean frightening the Queen's Grace, you rascal?"

He tried to raise his head but everything swam round, the Queen, Uncle Rob, the tall bracken and the trees.

"But I feel mighty queer...."

"Lie still," she told him.

"Whitefoot fell, I think.... Is he hurt, your Grace?"

"He's cropping grass. You need not worry for him."

"But we outrode the whole hunt, your Grace!"

"We outrode them!"

"I can't think what possessed you!" cried his uncle. He was leaning forward, so his face was close to the Queen's, in the dizzy vision of the boy. Their voices rose and fell as part of the confusion he swam in; but they did not sound like Queen and courtier. They seemed to be quarrelling like man and woman.

"I didn't want to dally for your pleasure! If you had been in your proper place at my side, no harm would have come to the boy."

"No harm would have come to the boy—and it's only luck that *you* escaped harm—if you hadn't ridden like a mad creature!"

"Oh, so you blame me! God's death, am I to dismount and wait your lordship's pleasure while you toy with my cousin?"

"Will you listen to me? Her horse was caught up in the bushes, and I happened to be the nearest horseman to her."

"Surely! She took good care to fall into difficulties when you were close by."

"That's fantastic nonsense!"

"I know my cousin...."

The silence which fell was somehow as angry as the voices had been. But it was broken; horns shrilled, horses came crunching through bushes and bracken, voices exclaimed. A Gentleman Pensioner hastily brought up the Queen's horse, and the Earl of Pembroke mounted her. Her Master of Horse stood silent, a splash of red in his cheeks, carrying his nephew. She flung a sentence at him: "Have a care of that boy!" and then turned round to face her followers. Only the Countess of Essex faced those angry eyes

152

for more than a moment; Elizabeth caught her flicker of defiance.

"God's death! It seems my court has grown timorous. . . . I only found a ten-year-old boy to ride with me! I think my gentlemen had better get themselves fans and farthingales."

It was a silent party which rode back disconsolately to the Palace of Nonesuch. Young Philip, suffering from no more than mild concussion, was happy enough in bed, looking at the lurid woodcuts in a heavy volume of Foxe's *Book of Martyrs*, though his eyes swam too much for the printed text; his sister and brother came and sat on top of him, for the Sidneys were an affectionate family. Their mother was not a little surprised at the appearance of the Queen, as soon as she had time to change her clothes.

"Mary—how is the boy?" Her voice had a sort of hard anxiety.

"Your Grace is too good. Boys are always having such mishaps. I had five brothers and never a week passed but one or the other fell on his head, off his pony or out of a tree. They come to no lasting harm."

"I had one brother," said Elizabeth, "and if he had fallen as Philip did, he would have been ill for weeks."

"Philip is strong," said his mother. "Not like the little King, God rest him!"

"I blame myself!" said Elizabeth. "But I blame more your brother, Robert!" Mary Sidney looked at her with some surprise. There seemed to be some secret emotional crisis underlying the quite ordinary matter of Philip taking a toss out hunting. Robert carrying the boy in, had had a face like thunder.

The Queen swept in, so that Philip raised his head in its vinegar-soaked bandages, and the younger children scurried off the bed, to kneel dutifully, peeping with scared excitement at Elizabeth. They were not on such terms of happy familiarity with her as their elder brother.

"Well, my wounded knight! I am afraid I am the cause of your hurt. . . ."

Philip replied gravely, in such words as Sir Lancelot might have spoken from the page of Malory: "To be hurt in your Majesty's service is great honour."

"But I would not have you hurt!"

("She's strangely agitated," thought Philip's mother.) But Elizabeth pulled herself together, and told Philip he must write a ballad on their mad gallop when they had outdistanced the whole field.

"Oh yes, your Grace! Some ballads—you can hear the horses galloping in them!"

"You study Greek? Of course! Wait till you come to these lines of Homer"—she quoted the sonorous words—"Can't you hear the thunder of the Greek war chariots?"

The younger children were losing their shyness, and Philip was raising himself on one elbow to quote from the *Ballad of the Chevy Chase* for which he had a passion. "It has a sound like a trumpet!" Smiling, Elizabeth pushed him down again on his pillows. "Now! Don't heat your head with such fancies. I am glad to see you are less hurt than I feared!"

When she had gone, Lady Sidney sent for her brother.

"Robert," she said, "what have you done to upset the Queen? She blames you for Philip's fall—and the next moment she blames herself!"

"I think a devil possessed her!" declared Robert angrily. "I stopped to help the Countess of Essex, whose horse became entangled in the bushes, when the Queen suddenly flogs her own horse and gallops off hell-for-leather. Young Philip, like any boy, wanted to take his own way and she chose to follow him, regardless of the risk. It's a mercy she didn't come down!"

"Oh, Rob, be careful! Leave Lettice Essex alone. She's in love with you for one thing——"

"Nonsense, Mary! She's a mighty attractive young woman who is weary of her own husband, and is not averse to a bold glance at a likely fellow—but to say she fancies me more than any other——"

"She does, and the Queen knows it. There's the same blood in them."

"Bullen blood!"

"Yes, Bullen blood and it will stop at nothing! Leave her alone, Rob! And go now, and make your peace with the Queen."

But neither Robert nor Elizabeth were in the mood for peace. Their angry voices began to clash together like sword blades.

"What took you to ride off headlong like that! If the boy was hurt, it was your fault!"

"My fault, i' God's name! That gallant child took your proper place. He's a better man than you! Because you had to make a fool of yourself with Lettice Essex——"

"I did no more than any man should! Naturally when she got entangled with the greenery——"

154

"The greenest thing she got entangled with was you, my poor Robin! Anyone can see how she pursues you!"

"She does not!"

"I tell you she does!"

"So I am not even to look at another woman? While you——"

"While I?"

"While you flirt outrageously with any man who takes your fancy! Scattering smiles and soft glances on that puppy, Heneage! I told him I'd cane him for his presumption——"

"And he very properly told you he'd meet your cane with a cut-and-thrust! You're a pair of brawling puppies!"

"And now you fancy this prancing young lawyer, Christopher Hatton! You see him tripping in a masque given in your honour at the Inns of Court, and you have to have him for one of your Gentlemen Pensioners!"

"Christopher Hatton is a very handsome and graceful man, and I have never seen anyone step a galliard with more elegance. Naturally I wanted to have him to lead me out in the measures at court!" She looked at her lover's face, now red with anger, and chuckled. "And he is madly in love with me, Robin. Oh, but madly!"

"Is he, by God?"

"Oh, I dare swear you are weary of me. I'm thirty—I had the small-pox last year—but he adores me! Such letters as he writes! I like men to fall in love with me—and I shall flirt with anyone I please!"

" 'Tis a damnable situation! You could very well marry me—— You refuse so that you can insult and slight me! I'll not endure it!"

"*You'll* not endure it? Where are my insults and slights? You have the Garter, you are now a Privy Councillor, you are Lord Lieutenant of Windsor Castle and my Master of Horse. I've just given you Kenilworth, one of the most splendid properties in England!"

"Ah! So you remind me that everything comes from you, and I, myself, am nothing!"

Her headlong anger and mockery were now gone. Her voice had a weary bitterness. "I give you what I can, Robin. . . ."

"Do you? There is nothing now to prevent our marrying!"

Her brain then seemed to take a life of its own, apart from her feelings and emotions, it turned like a dagger in her hand and gashed her.

"You only want my throne—my crown! Else you would not say

that. You don't want *me*. . . . You have me! An' you know anything
at all about women—you must know that I love you. . . ."

"Do you? You think me not good enough for you—for a throne
—— If I could show you!"

"Well—show me then!" That weapon, her brain, was under control again. An idea flashed from her, as brilliant and as pitiless as
lightning.

"Wed the Queen of Scots!"

He stared blankly and at last found his breath.

"Have you run mad?"

"No, I have not run mad. . . ." Her voice was quite quiet, but the
blood had drained out of her cheeks. Her dignity had come back;
she was aloof from him, remote and cold.

"The only safety for England is for her to marry an Englishman
whom *I* can trust. Cecil was to put it to the Council and discuss likely
candidates. I can bribe her towards it by dangling the Succession
before her. Otherwise she will make a dangerous foreign marriage—
or take young Darnley. As he is my cousin, and has some claim in the
Succession, it might be dangerous to join him to her, and thereby
unite their claims." She drew her breath in and as she seemed to
strike him with her tongue, she truly struck herself. "I know your
greed for power—but I also know that you would put the interests of
your own country first." Then her temper flared up again: "By God's
soul! You shall have the crown, the throne, the power and the pomp
you crave!"

He said neither yes nor no. He was dazed. He continued dazed
during the long nightmare which followed. Her brain could carry her
through anything now, and even make her watch her own sufferings
dispassionately. She looked at Cecil's quickly schooled amazement,
and when at last he said doubtfully: "But Lord Robert is not even a
peer of the realm. . . ." She heard her own flat, calm voice as if it had
been someone else's: "I will create him an Earl." She even achieved
a little flicker of malicious satisfaction at the rumours of Mary's
reception of the news. That high pride had exploded at the incredible
insult. Was she, the daughter of a hundred kings, to take the leavings
of one she had branded as the "alderman's grand-daughter", as
"bastard" and "usurper"? Was she, whose forefathers had been
Kings of Scotland when the Tudors were unknown menials in Wales,
whose mother's descent went back to Charlemagne, she who was

Zenith

Queen of Scotland, Queen Dowager of France and rightful Queen of England, to marry and raise to the throne beside her, her cousin's kept man? But for all that pride and for all that strange streak of other-worldliness which made Mary Stuart such an enigma, she wanted fiercely that same despised cousin to promise her the English Succession. So she did not hurl the furious refusal for which she longed; she sent the most polished and astute of all her ministers, Maitland of Lethington, to treat with England, and at the same time secretly to approach the Spanish Ambassador to try and revive her flagging Spanish suit.

Elizabeth received the brilliantly clever and subtle Maitland, heard with a sort of appraisal, his riposte as merciless as any of hers— "Knowing the high value you set upon the Lord Robert, one would not think to deprive you of him. . . . Rather that your Majesty should wed him, and then should you unhappily die without issue, leave him in your will to your cousin together with your kingdom. . . ." Afterwards to Cecil she conceded that Maitland was the flower of the wits of Scotland. "He is the only cultured and civilized man they possess," agreed the secretary, who like all typical Englishmen, hated Scotland.

Robert was such a tardy wooer that the English Ambassador in Edinburgh, Thomas Randolph, bade him send a gift to the Queen of Scots, and he sent her some horses, for was he not one of the best judges of horseflesh in England? But he was still dazed, and wandered about the court in a sort of blank amazement. Elizabeth watched him with outward serenity, and inwardly wondered how there could be such pain in the whole world. Only Kate Ashley, who had suddenly got old and was failing, was one night disturbed by the sound of heartbroken sobs which seemed to be tearing their giver apart. She fumbled for tinder and lighting her candle, padded across the floor to the great four-poster bed, and began to use soothing endearments, not employed for years.

"There, there, my love! My lamb—my poor dear child!"

It was not the Queen who grasped her suddenly and fiercely and sobbed on her ample bosom, it was that strange child who had had a leaping flame in her, who had once loved handsome Tom Seymour, or rather, in him, had loved love and life and the dream of power. But even now, after she had choked out: "I wish I were dead, Kate!" she had added, with that dreadful steely control: "No—I don't wish that. My life is encircled by the crown. I *must* live."

157

So she went on, and flirted a little with the elegant Master Hatton who danced better than any man at court, and seemed genuinely and gratifyingly in love with her. He handed her through the graceful steps of the galliard, the solemn measure of the pavane, or the liveliness of a coranto or lavolta, so that all might applaud them, for she had learned to dance after the Florentine fashion, "very high and disposedly". Sometimes she was led out by her long-legged cousin, young Harry Darnley, and she watched him with narrowed gleaming eyes which he never heeded, as the pink colour flooded his smooth cheeks, and his high laugh rang out with as much arrogance as if he had been an emperor's heir. Cecil and her ministers found her almost unnaturally logical and very inclined to mock at human failings in others; sometimes her ladies-in-waiting winced under the caustic edge of her tongue. Young Philip Sidney was sent to school at Shrewsbury, and she seemed to take none close to her heart.

Mary despatched another ambassador, a courtly and attractive young man, James Melville, who showed that he found the Queen of England a handsome woman. He made an even better mirror than Messrs. Heneage and Hatton (who naturally looked for advancement at her hands) in which she might read that she was still a desirable woman even if Robert did not apparently think so. So she flirted in desperation with the Scottish envoy, thrusting shrewd questions as to his Queen, in between bouts of coquetry. She changed her dress three and four times a day, so that he might debate with grave appreciation on which style suited her best, and made searching queries between herself and Mary. His diplomatic finesse was admirable; he showed that he admired both her and Mary as women as well as Queens. The skill with which he balanced their contrasting claims to beauty and charm was remarkable. Elizabeth had been angry because Mary was taller than she. It was right for a Queen's dignity to have height, and she herself had sufficient to give her presence without making her awkward. But this Mary had to over-top her! She snapped: "Then she is over-high, for I am neither too high nor too low!" But Melville mollified her by extravagant praise of her playing on the virginals. Mary only played "reasonably well for a Queen". And in her inmost heart, she thought: "What does any of this foolery matter? Can I go on thus?"

But Robert Dudley went to his sister Mary, who for such years had taken the place of their devoted and indomitable mother, and burst out: "I cannot go through with this! If Elizabeth has no heart, I have!"

"So you really love her, Rob?"

"Yes, I do, though she drives me to desperation. Other women seem tame and cloying after her. She's got a flame in her——" he stopped short, thinking that Lettice Essex also had had that flame, that determination, that fierceness mixed with seduction, but at the moment he turned from Lettice Essex. She was in some sort the author of his troubles. He went on: "I don't see why she won't wed me. But for all that—I won't be used in such a heartless scheme. I will not marry the Queen of Scots. Whether Elizabeth casts me into the Tower or no!"

"Robin, you know very little about women really. If you tell Elizabeth that you cannot give her up even for a crown—I scarce think you'll find she'll cast you into the Tower!"

So he asked for a private interview with the Queen and got it. Like a gambler making his last fling, he declared furiously that even if she sent him to the block on Tower Hill for his obstinacy, he would not wed the Queen of Scots. He loved her alone and would not give her up for all the Crowns Matrimonial in Christendom. . . . He had always believed that his sister, Mary, was a wise woman, but he had hardly credited the good result of her advice.

It seemed with the quickness of thought that Elizabeth was in his arms, laughing and sobbing at the same time. "Robin, Robin, is that really true?"

"I swear it!" he cried. "I'd rather die than go from you!"

She could hardly believe the evidence of her ears. She had learned to distrust too young and had seen her lesson bitterly confirmed a hundred times over. She had loved Robert with her eyes wide open, taking what comfort and joy she might, but hardly permitting herself a single illusion. But here he was, giving up a crown—and none knew better than she the value of a crown—just so that he could hold her in his arms and tell her he loved her.

That evening it was not Master Hatton, the suave Melville or the swaggering young Lord Darnley who led out the Queen in the first galliard. It was Lord Robert Dudley, magnificent in crimson and silver, beside his sovereign resplendent in black and gold. They held the attention of the court, in the light of hundreds of candles, and their eyes and their hearts danced too. Night came, extinguishing those candles which had shone so brightly on the jewels and gold collars and the rich colours of gorgeous attire, silencing the throbbing of the viols. Its darkness brought an ecstatic reunion to those two who had been so long estranged and divided. They had never loved so much before, and they tried to put it into words, yet words were so inadequate.

But on the very edge of sleep, Robert murmured drowsily: "To-morrow you were to give me my earldom before the Ambassadors of Scotland and France—for the express purpose of marrying me to the Queen of Scots. . . ."

She thought: "Beloved Robin, if he does want his earldom, hasn't he given up a king's crown for me?"

She whispered: "Dear heart, to-morrow you shall be created Earl of Leicester. . . ."

"But *how* are we to escape from this marriage?"

"Leave it to me, dear heart!" She laughed softly in the darkness. "You will see. They all will see!"

The next day, she was a gorgeous and imposing figure in cloth of gold and silver, a demi-crown of pearls and diamonds set on her red hair, as she sat high on her dais, guarded by her Gentlemen Pensioners in crimson damask, bearing their gilt-headed battle axes, while the Yeomen of the Guard, in jerkins embroidered with the Tudor Rose and royal cipher, bore halberds as they lined the Presence Chamber and corridors. Amongst the former was her Majesty's favourite dancing partner, the elegant Christopher Hatton. Most of those young men of good birth were handsome fellows, and as well as guarding her Majesty's person in high ceremonial, had to show their prowess before her in the tiltyard, the hunting-field, and on the dancing-floor. Her nobles were gathered about her, headed by her cousin, the Duke of Norfolk, premier peer of England, the Marquesses of Northampton and Winchester, the Earls of Arundel, Sussex, Pembroke, Bedford, Oxford, Essex and Warwick, and many lords of lesser rank. Cecil was there, smiling his inscrutable smile, which made people think that he knew beforehand of many of his sovereign's caprices which actually took him as much by surprise as they did the rest of the world. Close to the throne were the Ambassadors of Scotland and France. Last—but in his own eyes, greatest—there was the young Lord Darnley, bearing the Sword of State, every one of his many inches aware that he was a Prince of the Blood, dressed in blue and gold which so well set off his corn-coloured hair and that fresh pink and white complexion which any girl might envy.

Kneeling before the throne, his long ceremonial fur-trimmed mantle trailing down its steps, was the new peer, Robert Dudley, just created Earl of Leicester and Baron Denbigh. With her own hands the Queen set his earl's coronet upon his head, and looked about her, a quick flashing glance which took in everything. Then those long, slender fingers, stiff with gems, stole down from the coronet, from the silky black hair to the strong sunburnt neck, and strayed about it, fondling, even tickling it. The French Ambassador raised his eyes to heaven at such outrageous behaviour in public. Young Melville thought when his royal mistress heard of it she would wildly refuse the offer of the new earl, even were he to bring with him the promised Succession she craved. Young Harry Darnley looked down his princely nose and thought: "S'death—my cousin Bess goes too far! She shows that infernal mercer's blood—the Bullen in her!" Certainly she showed the Bullen in her, thought all those old enough to remember that far-distant day when Nan Bullen, just created Marchioness of Pembroke, had appeared at court, a striking figure in unrelieved black satin against which Queen Katherine's diamonds sparkled— but they had not sparkled as the black eyes in the pale face had done. There had been a look of triumph in them, the triumph of the woman who knows that the man she wants, desires her above all things else. It was in her daughter's eyes as she faced her court and in particular the staggered Melville. But he was a diplomat by nature as well as by training and when she demanded of him what he thought of the new earl, he answered: "I am happy to see a worthy princess who can discern and reward good service. . . ." (She thought: "When Scotsmen have a wit, it has an edge!") But she would show him her own sharpness as she intercepted his glance straying to Harry Darnley.

"I think", she said swiftly, "you like better that long lad!" Melville gave an almost imperceptible start. Could she know of his secret meetings with that indefatigable schemer, the Countess of Lennox and her fatuously conceited husband? He had, at that very moment, been thinking that their son had a fine presence which would surely please his young Queen, pining as she was for the courtly gallants of France. But he expostulated with the Queen before him: "Your Grace, no woman of spirit would choose such a man—beardless and lady-faced!"

Zenith

Robert remained demurely on his knees before the throne. If his ambition for everything, except to be Elizabeth's husband, was now satisfied, he was not at this moment playing a triumphant role. She was in charge of the situation, not he. But those caressing fingers on his neck seemed to hold soothing and reassurance. He could still hear her whispered words: "Leave it to me, dear heart. Leave it to me!"

Chapter Three

Harry Darnley rode north to Scotland, with his Great Horses for battles and tourneys, his jennets and barbs for hunting and hacking, his gilded armour, those rich suits of apparel in brocade, velvet, satin and cloth of gold, the gold-hilted toledo rapiers, the silver-mounted dags and crossbows, and his lute inlaid with mother-of-pearl to which he could sing in a pleasing tenor voice. He was preparing to make a great show of himself, considering that he was only accompanying his father, the old Earl of Lennox, to receive their restored Scottish estates. Cecil and other councillors had implored the Queen to refuse father and son the permission to go, but she had shrugged. "I cannot well refuse them," said she, knowing that if she had wished, she might easily have done so, and knowing that Cecil knew it.

"Suppose the Queen of Scots should marry Lord Darnley, your Grace! Their claims to the Succession united——"

"A child of theirs would have a very good claim," she said in a voice he could not read, except that it was solemn.

"Then your Grace, if she weds him——"

"She won't wed Spain or France or Austria and I needn't press my courtship so hard with the Archduke Charles. What a useful man that is!"

Cecil shook his head.

"Your Grace, after we have offered the Queen of Scots Lord Leicester, and the matter is now hanging fire—she is not unlikely to take such offence that she might—do anything. Women when piqued in their vanity, are apt to allow their judgments to become unbalanced."

"My poor Spirit! Have I taught you so much about my abominable sex?"

There was a dry twinkle in the secretary's eyes as he replied: "I would not presume to judge all women by your Grace!"

She laughed in hearty appreciation.

"I should hope not!"

"But, your Grace, the Earl of Leicester is not proceeding in his courtship. It appears as if he had abandoned it."

"I think he has." She made a delicious assumption of demureness. "I have reason to believe that his affections are otherwise engaged."

"Indeed, your Grace?"

Later that day, when she was alone with the newly created earl, she asked him saucily: "Is that silly fellow, my Lord of Leicester, truly engaged elsewhere in his affections?"

"He is a silly fellow indeed," agreed Robert in the same bantering tone. "He is in love with a woman with red hair and a bad temper!"

"His taste is desperate bad. . . ." She pressed her cheek against his. "I'm glad you're not smooth and pink like a girl—as Harry Darnley! His skin is so soft——"

"How the devil do you know?"

"I had to test it—only with my fingers! Don't glare, Robin. . . . Those children, your nephew Rob Sidney in particular, were teasing that wretched whey-faced little Charles Stuart because his brother couldn't grow a beard! And poor little Charles stood up to them and declared that he mightn't be able to grow a beard, but hadn't he emptied three saddles that morning in the tournament? A good retort."

"The lad's a good lance, I admit. And has a very good seat in the saddle."

"I agree, he is at his best on horseback. But he has to dismount!" She giggled. "I like *you* on a horse, Robin. . . . And off it!" Robin kissed her.

But later, when Cecil came to her, wringing his hands over the sudden and violent favour which the Queen of Scots was showing Lord Darnley, he found her cool and collected.

"The next thing we'll hear, your Grace, is that she has wedded him!"

"Very likely!"

"But, your Grace!"

"We didn't want her to wed Spain—France—Austria! We didn't want the danger of foreign influence in Scotland. Why, I was almost prepared to promise her the Succession in return for her making a safe marriage. Though, as I told the House of Commons, I'd sooner wear my winding-sheet than appoint a Successor in my lifetime! Listen, Spirit!" She leaned forward, her eyes narrowed and glittering: "If she marries young Darnley, she cannot marry Spain or France. And she'll take him without any promise whatsoever from me of the Succession. . . ."

"Then did your Grace——?" he paused, aghast.

"Calculate, Spirit? Calculate that I would provoke her into marrying Harry Darnley?" A cold wintry smile flickered across her face. "Perhaps I did. . . ."

"There is danger in her marrying Lord Darnley!"

"There is. But more to her than to me. . . ."

"More to her, your Grace?"

"Have you ever seen two tall ships sailing the sea, with all their canvas crowded on, struck by a sudden squall, and too foolish or too proud to furl their sails?"

"I scarcely see, your Grace." He was staring at that strangely cruel smile on her face.

"You will. You will. I've watched my cousin Darnley. Under that ridiculous pride, he is a weathercock to sway this way or that, for whatever wind blows. And there is a vicious streak in him. Those are the only foundations for that soaring pride of his. And for hers—— There's something strange and unstable in her—it frightens me." She drew a deep breath. "But if anything is destroyed it won't be me. Or what is infinitely more important than I. My England!" She repeated with an extraordinary vehemence. "My England!"

Cecil seemed to feel the passion throbbing in her. She was like a tigress, guarding her cubs.

But later when she was alone, a vision crossed her mind of that unknown cousin in her northern kingdom, that tall, slender girl who seemed to be made of fragile white porcelain, who had appeared to be born with a golden spoon in her mouth, one of Fate's darlings, and yet had said in a voice cold with prophecy: "Peradventure that casualty might be better for me than to live. . . ." And at the same moment, she could remember herself landing at Traitor's Gate with the rain falling on her face like vain tears, and the suck of the dank water against the sodden stone. But Mary had never had the shadow of a scaffold lying upon her. . . .

Aloud she said to argue with herself: "But she turned Throck-morton's head like all the other fools of men. Else he had not re-membered. . . ." Yet she herself could not help remembering. Then she recollected that Sir Nicholas Throckmorton was on a visit to England from his post in France. First she sent for the Earl of Leicester.

"Robin, I want you to fetch here Throckmorton. If he's not at his house, ride after him and find him wherever he is. I must have him. It's urgent!"

At last he stood before her, that man whose brilliant letters to her at Hatfield while her sister lay dying, had prompted her to give him the Embassy in France. None could send important news so well from far off, she thought, and he was a skilled judge of men as well as being courtly and elegant. A good judge of women? Who knows? She was sure that Mary of Scotland had turned his head too.

"Sir Nicholas," she said, "I think you were on good terms with my cousin of Scotland?"

"Yes, your Grace," replied Throckmorton after a moment's hesi-tation. She laughed harshly.

"I think she turned you round her finger like many another. But you were friendly with her? You think she would listen to you?"

"Your Grace, she always showed me friendship. I think she would always consider what I might say, though it is very difficult to know how she would act."

"D'you think there is another Englishman in my service to whom she would listen—more than to you?" She paused, and he saw that her eyes were gleaming. Then her voice thundered at him: ("She's every inch King Hal's daughter," he thought)—like a lion demanding its prey: "God's soul, man! Speak up! Is there another one in my service she would heed more than you?"

"No, your Grace," said Throckmorton. "There is not."

"Good. Now I want you to get to Scotland with all the haste you can. I'll have the arrangements made forthwith. And you must stop her from marrying that unlicked cub, Henry Darnley. For her own good. Not for mine. It might be for my good that she did marry him. . . ."

Sir Nicholas Throckmorton gaped. So did the Earl of Leicester.

"If I had her here," said Elizabeth, "I'd be tempted to take hold of her and shake her—yes, shake her, as if she were my younger sister! And try to shake some sense into her. Doesn't she know that the world is a dangerous place?"

"Your Grace," said Throckmorton slowly. "I don't know if she yet realizes that. You see—she has always been greatly loved. . . ."

Into the heavy silence, Robert said with a chuckle: "Except by the godly Master Knox!"

Elizabeth found her voice again. "He's an abominable creature. But useful," she added bitterly. "Now, listen, Sir Nicholas. You must use all the means in your power. Threaten her. Tell her I'll consider it an unfriendly act—and take order with the Lennoxes and their cub! And promise her anything short of the Succession. But tell her we must meet. At York or Carlisle. York, I think. Never mind the weather—never mind the roads! If needs be, let us each take a small retinue. When I go on Progress, the court needs five hundred carts. But the matter's too important for frippery! She and I will have to forbear from dressing up in our bravest, to impress the other. Oh, yes, we would—ordinarily! God's death! I'd ride north with one tiring woman and a dozen Gentleman Pensioners commanded by my Lord Leicester here—and a few horsemen can always cover the roads! I *must* see her! Tell her, if I have private conversation with her, I can explain the matter of the Succession to her, in a way she'll understand. . . . Coax her, bully her, flatter her—whatever she'll heed! Only stop her from marrying Darnley. Or they'll gallop each other into the abyss!"

When Sir Nicholas Throckmorton had hurriedly departed to make preparations for his journey, she said suddenly to Robert: "But it's too late! Always too late between her and me! All my good impulses are too late!"

"Sweeting, you are quite distraught. . . . Why do you agitate yourself so over that Queen of Scots?"

"Because she is the bane of my life! Because she tears me into two parts. One wants to wipe her off the face of the earth! And the other wants to save her, to protect her from all her enemies. . . ." She put her hands to her head, pressing the palms against the wide, high brow, the long fingers lying on the crisply waved red hair, covering the great pearls suspended from her coif.

"It's too late!" she repeated. "Hell is paved with good intentions, they say. I wonder why my good impulses are too late always! Is it that cold Machiavellian little devil which sits here"—and she pressed her brow hard—"and knows nothing of pity or remorse or tenderness, but is made of steely reason, and won't let me give way to weak or foolish impulses? Or good ones for that matter—except for this country. That devil of reason and I—we work for England. That new religious order which was founded by the Spaniard, Loyola—the Society of Jesus—has been accused of saying 'the end justifies the means'. They deny saying it. *I* don't deny it! My end justifies any means. The safety, the prosperity, the glory of this country. . . ." She covered her face with her hands. Through her fingers, he could hear her voice: "If there's a Judgment Day, let them judge me as Queen of England—and nothing else! If I fail my people, then damn me eternally! I should damn myself!"

He hesitated a moment. She had gone far beyond him. The flame in her was burning her up. Those sudden tempestuous rages, those agonized nerve storms—her body was made to pay like an overridden horse. But he could help her in a way which did not belong to reason but rather to instinct, soothe her and gentle her with loving touch which could help so much more than words. She could do anything with words, they were her keen arrows.

He drew her close so that the tautness began to relax from her thin body.

"You're weary, sweet," he said. "You've been too long at night beside Mistress Ashley's sickbed."

"Poor old Kate. She's dying, Robin. And the last of my childhood is dying with her. Not that it was a happy one. . . . She likes me near her."

"I am sure. You're good at tending the sick." She was, oddly enough. "D'you remember when you moved me to the apartments next to yours, so that you could nurse me better through an illness—mighty convenient it's been since—and how you said: 'Quadra will write home a whole dispatch on this'? And he did!"

She smiled. "When the plague rid us of Quadra, it did us a good turn. De Silva is a very charming and intelligent man."

He could feel her relaxing in his arms. He whispered: 'The Queen of Scots would never have done for me! She's too tall by all accounts. Now your head comes on my shoulder—just so—just right! *We* fit each other."

He heard her sigh before she spoke.

"How hard it would be to go on without you, Rob. Nearly impossible."

"Nearly?"

"Oh, yes, I must go on. . . . But thank God for you, Robin!"

Kate Ashley was steadily sinking, that summer of 1565. However long she might work on affairs of State, Elizabeth was ready to give up to her her hours of leisure or sleep. Strangely enough for one neither tender nor sentimental by nature or circumstances, she had a gentle competence with the sick. Perhaps she had learnt it with the ailing little brother who had been separated from her so soon. The entire court might conjecture her exact relationship with Robert, but they all knew that were he to be ill, the Queen was sure to spend long vigils by his bedside, and tend him with devoted care. Now it was old Mistress Ashley.

She was glad, one late summer afternoon, to walk in the gardens by the river's edge. Most of the night had been given up to Kate, sitting in the close atmosphere of the sickroom—everyone knew the danger of the night air, especially to those ill—for the physicians had not believed that their patient could survive the night, rather those dangerous hours in the early morning when man's soul becomes loosened from his body and so glides easily away. But Kate Ashley had slept peacefully through them. As Elizabeth now settled herself on a bench surrounded by formal flowering shrubs and gazed across a smooth expanse of lawn, at whose far end a handful of brightly clad figures stooped over a game of bowls, she recollected vividly the night before and the very ideas which had crossed her mind.

The candles had burned with a flickering, feverish light. She could still hear the confused muttering of Kate Ashley, who had seemed to be begging forgiveness for those far-off days when her indiscreet tongue had revealed too much of Thomas Seymour's perilous courtship. Elizabeth had leaned forward, taking the limp hand, speaking with a quiet determination that pierced the mists which were clouding that failing brain.

"Kate, have you ever heard me utter one word of reproach?"

The bluish lips whispered: "No."

"Nor ever will you!"

She could only just catch: "But you will remember——"

"Your kindness to me. Only that."

It had evidently soothed Mistress Ashley for after that she had slept. But Elizabeth had remained beside her, watching the candles fluttering, now throwing into relief the figures on the hangings, now sweeping forward the soft shadows. Soon Kate would be gone, the only person who shared certain memories, the only person but one who knew of the rare nightmare, which awoke her, shrieking. Blanche Parry, who slept in her chamber since Kate Ashley's illness, and knew so much—especially when to withdraw in silence—did not know of that horror which sometimes curdled the hours of darkness. Elizabeth was back in the Tower, and her custodians had told her to prepare herself, as they had done years before in reality, for Sir Henry Bedingfield had come to fetch her. She had cried out then, before she could assert her self-control: "Is the Lady Jane's scaffold prepared?" And they had told her, no, that she was to be taken from the Tower. . . . But in the dream, the scaffold had been there and she had been slowly led to it, and beside her had been those shadowy figures which had sometimes actually seemed to *be* her. Thomas Seymour who had so harshly ended her childhood and made her a woman before her time, bringing terror and enchantment together, Thomas Seymour who had sprung up from the block and grappled with his executioner —and in such contrast, that pale, meek little cousin, Jane Grey, who (all said) had died with such docile courage. Those two she had seen clearly, but the figure of her mother had no face, for Elizabeth did not remember her mother or her face. . . . But she knew who it was because of the high, mad laugh (hearing about which had haunted her childhood) and the whisper: "I have such a little neck!" Oh, yes, she would then wake up, screaming, and clutch Kate and sob it all out, and finally be comforted. But lately this dream had come more rarely, and now (she thought) I will have to comfort myself. . . .

She had told Robert about it. After all, his father had died too, that way on the scaffold. But Robert, though he must have been an affectionate son because he was affectionate in all his family relationships, had a wonderful capacity for putting the past behind him and living only in the present. He seemed to do so easily what she forced herself to do with the discipline of long training. He had been tender and soothing and had wished that *he* might be the one to comfort her—"But I'd never get that dream in your arms. Instinctively I feel safe, I suppose," she had told him. He had said quickly: "If we were married, then you'd always feel safe! She had put her hand over his mouth. "Don't talk politics to me, now, Rob!" "Why politics?" "My marriage is entirely a matter of politics. . . ."

Zenith

In the day she was Queen. Only at night, it seemed, could she be wholly human. Then she gave way to instinctive terrors, loved Robert or sat by the bedside of sick friends. . . . . Evidently the Queen of Scots had taken a leaf out of her book, because the latest news to come was of her nursing the young Darnley through the measles. . . . "And perhaps he will prove more appealing even with that complaint, than tilting in his gilded armour or singing love songs to the lute!" Elizabeth thought, and then realized that she had dozed off, while one of her ladies fanned her, and the sun was sending a red glow through her closed eyelids.

She heard the sound of treble voices above the duller sound of older ones. Philip Sidney was passing, the leader as always of a small collection of children belonging to the court. On one side of him was his sister, Mary, his inseparable companion, on the other, Fulke Greville, who was to adore him so much all his life, that when he came to choose his own epitaph, he was to have added to his achievements and virtues, the phrase—"friend of Sir Philip Sidney". Those three were talking eagerly. After them came three little boys, scuffling as they went, and behind them another, very small for his age and deformed. The small boys were Rob Sidney and Jack Harington, plaguing Charles Stuart, the younger brother of Darnley. Jack was Elizabeth's godson, a pert and lively child for whom she had quite an affection though he could not compare with Philip. His parents had first served Thomas Seymour and then her, with equal faithful devotion. Mistress Harington had come to attend on her in the Tower, a time when few wished to show adherence to her. The last boy was Robert Cecil, the second son of the secretary. Sir William Cecil and his learned wife, Mildred, had been sadly disappointed in the heir. No amount of solemn admonishings, no amount of whippings had made Tom Cecil heed his books. He liked to eat vastly and brawl and play boisterous games. Now he was approaching manhood, he was beginning to drink as well and his horrified father could find no enthusiasm in him except for tennis. This second son, Robert, was all that his parents could wish as regards intelligence and studiousness, but he was small, peaky, delicate and worst of all—a hunchback.

Elizabeth looked at them. "The coming generation!" she thought. Philip will surely make a name for himself. And perhaps the boy, Cecil, too. . . ."

Philip and his two companions had now passed out of sight, but the others lingered. Rob and Jack were teasing the unfortunate little Charles, and Robert Cecil watched them dispassionately. Charles was an insignificant pallid little boy who had always been overshadowed by his swaggering elder brother. His ambitious mother, and his foolishly conceited father, had built everything on Harry, and Charles knew he was of no importance beside him. His only weapon was to brag of the triumphs of this godlike being—although a god who sometimes turned on him and cruelly twisted his arm or his ear—when assailed by the quips of the lively Jack Harington and others like him. Rob Sidney had to revive the old taunt: "Hoo! Your brother Harry can't grow a beard!" Their voices rose shrilly. They were not aware that the Queen and her ladies were so near.

Charles faced his persecutors.

"I tell you my brother's a *King!!!*"

"King!" snorted Jack. "King o' nothing. King in a card pack!"

"I tell you he's King of Scots!"

Elizabeth had risen to her feet and with one swift movement was amongst them, her long fingers clutching Charles's shoulder.

"What's that you say, boy?"

At the sudden appearance of angry majesty, Jack Harington and Rob Sidney simply vanished out of sight into the bushes. Jack explained tersely: "I know my godmother. [He was very proud of being her godchild.] She gets monstrous angry. But it's all over soon. . . ."

But Robert Cecil, after making a polite obeisance, stood watching with his head on one side. As for Charles he was stricken into dumbness, paralysed like a mouse in the paws of a cat. He was utterly terrified of the Queen. Elizabeth, looking at that white face, the open mouth and dilated eyes, suddenly remembered herself as a terrified and friendless child ringed around with implacable cross-examiners, trying to force a confession from her. Her more cynical reasoning half told her that the boy was too frightened even to speak.

She sat back on the ornamental bench, making him stand at her knees. Her voice was quiet: "I am not going to hurt you, Charles!"

She took a leaf from Robert's book, Robert who could fondle and soothe a frightened child, a nervous horse, a wild hawk, and something more difficult still—herself. She patted his cheek and found it clammy, put an arm round him and found his small body shaking.

"Has your brother Harry married the Queen of Scots?"

"Yes, your Grace!" he gasped.

172

She thought: "How the Tudor stock which once seemed to be so strong has run to weakness. . . . This is a poor little creature, and the other lad is weak even if he is showy. The Greys were poor, weak things and I am the only child of my father to remain alive!" Aloud she said: "Has she made him King then?"

"He is to be called King," said Charles reflecting miserably that his mother of whom he was also afraid (she didn't love him as she did Harry) had told him not to speak of this to anyone. From sheer nervousness he blurted out: "I heard Mother read from a letter that the Queen of Scots saw Harry riding on the sands of Leith and she said he was 'the properest long man she had ever seen'!"

This Queen laughed harshly and spoke incomprehensibly.

"I was a prophet! Let her wait till he dismounts. . . ." She rose abruptly to her feet and then became aware of the steady gaze of the boy, Cecil. The hunchback had quite a pleasant face, small regular features, mild blue-grey eyes and an amiable smile, but there was something almost inhuman in the detachment with which he had watched her and the frightened boy. He seemed to be weighing and judging them, and missing no word, or gesture, with a cold serenity which was not natural at his age. She shivered for a second. But she could not know that those blue-grey eyes and that glance of serene intelligent detachment were one day to watch her dying. . . .

She whirled into the palace again, with a tense rustle of silks and brocades, and summoned Sir William Cecil and a few other councillors. The Countess of Lennox was instantly to be committed to the Tower.

"Yes, your Grace," said Cecil, wishing he might dare to say: 'I told you that the Queen of Scots would marry Lord Darnley. . . .'" But one did not say that to Elizabeth, Queen of England. He added: 'Your Grace will propose a State trial?"

"I will not try my Cousin Margaret Lennox. But I will teach her not to meddle and plot! And I will keep her securely for the present. She is to be lodged as comfortably as possible, and take with her such of her servants and gentlewomen as she wishes. I don't have to tell you to watch all communications with the outer world! I don't think either France or Spain are behind this, but I should like to be certain."

"Of course, your Grace. And the younger son? Is he to be regarded as a hostage?"

"He is not. If his mother wishes to take him with her to the Tower, she may. If she wishes him to stay outside with friends, he can do that. The choice is allowed to her."

"Certainly, your Grace." Cecil and his royal mistress, in a cruel age, were surprisingly merciful.

The warrant for the committal of the Countess to the Tower was drawn up, and the Queen was writing her signature to it, the big ELIZABETH R. with the elaborate flourishes and loops, when the news came by the official messenger that the Queen of Scots had married Henry, Lord Darnley. Cecil, wringing his hands, came near to saying "I told you so" to majesty.

"Your Grace, I have long dreaded this. The Catholics in England will consider that Lord Darnley has an excellent claim to the English throne, and united to Queen Mary——"

"Spirit, I made a light-hearted prophecy to Lord Leicester that if the Queen of Scots saw Harry Darnley on horseback, she would fancy him! And it has come about! But I will make a far more serious prophecy. . . . That either he will destroy her, or she will destroy him. And she is the stronger."

Chapter Four

The Queen of Scots had called the dance; she had given her hand to the tall youth with the high colour in his cheeks and the high arrogant laugh, and they were stepping the measure together. Behind them, around them, the other faces and figures swung into the light or dipped back into the shadows, the gloomy disapproving face of her illegitimate brother, the Earl of Moray, the more subtle disapproving figure of Maitland of Lethington who seemed to turn aside with a shrug, then a little dark, monkeyish latin face with sharp sparkling eyes setting the tongues of the world wagging as fast as the music for this imagined Dance of Death, and close behind came those turbulent nobles of Scotland, steel clashing in the midst of courtly airs. But the music was playing so fast now that it might be for a witches' dance, as out of these turbulent men, stepped one into the lead, a man violent even amongst his violent fellows, a man filled with a dark ruthless passionate strength; and that tall slender girl whose long white throat was as fragile as porcelain, forgot her chosen partner, forgot the golden crown on her head, forgot her own uncanny words which had seemed to recognize the danger and doom hanging over her—forgot everything but this one man. The music of a devil's sabbath was mounting wildly as she gave him her hand and the torches were burning red; soon the darkness would come and Death sweep up his playthings.

So it seemed to pass before the eyes of Elizabeth, as she watched those two crowded furious doomed years. The Queen of Scots had called the dance; but have I called the tune? So she asked of herself. Could she have prevented that first fatal marriage? If she could—would she? When it was too late, she tried her hardest to avert calamity. There are parchments covered with faded ink, still pre-

175

served, which record the urgency with which she wrote, words of un-questioned good sense and shrewd understanding, and behind these is the note of desperation. Before it is too late! But all she did was too late, and she scarcely knew herself whether this were witting or no. Neither did she know whether the central figure in that Dance of Death was leader or led, enchantress or enchanted. For all her moods of piety, there was something strangely pagan about Mary; one would need to go to the myths of ancient Greece to find that wild defiance of the Fates; as soon say 'good' or 'bad' of her as of some demi-god or nymph of the magic grove.

So Elizabeth watched, and a variety of emotions seized her and hurt her. It seemed that Mary could hurt her more than anyone else, and yet do it casually and unintentionally, as if it did not matter very much one way or the other. She learned of Mary doting on that golden and pink youth, read the dispatches of her ambassador, Thomas Randolph: "All honour that may be attributed to any man by a wife, he hath it wholly and fully"—learned how this adoration infuriated the sullen, turbulent Scots lords, till finally Mary's ambi-tious, illegitimate brother, the Earl of Moray, rose in open rebellion against her. Cecil had wrung his hands again, over the "Good Lord James" being set aside by his royal sister and her new husband, and had made protestations of his loyalty to the Queen of England. "To my money, you mean!" she snapped at her minister. But when Moray appealed to her for some money and assistance, she gave him a little by roundabout channels. At least, let his rising be sufficient to rock Mary's throne and make her feel it insecure. But Mary rose to the occasion. With a sword by her side and pistols at her saddlebow, she rode gallantly at the head of her troops and sent Moray's forces flying headlong. His rising spluttered out like a damped torch. Mary was gay over her triumph and declared that she wished she were a man to go campaigning and know what it was "to lie all night in the fields and go abroad with sword and buckler". Young Harry Darnley —now known as "that high and mighty prince, King Henry of Scotland"—rode, it was said, on the campaign in his gilded armour and so many fripperies that he might have been going to tilt at White-hall, rather than to war, but no doubt his adoring wife thought him splendid.

Elizabeth was the more displeased that Moray fled to her. A nice business if the slight help she had given him was to come to the ears of Mary and the world in general! She stormed at Cecil who had a high opinion of the Earl of Moray, but finally said: "I'll not throw him away utterly. He's a useful tool and may come to hand again. . . . But he must learn not to embarrass me—or to fail! School him, Spirit!" So the Earl of Moray knelt at her feet in the presence of the French Ambassador, and she rated him furiously for his treachery to his sister, her "dear cousin", and he (duly schooled by Cecil) accepted it humbly and contritely. Her anger was genuine—at Moray for being a failure and at Mary for being a success. And above all at Mary for playing the heroic role in triumph, while she was forced into underhand ways and to the enactment of such a farce. Her reason told her that her end justified her means; in summer on one of the Progresses which she enjoyed so much, she could see her country green, prosperous and happy, spared the torments of civil war which ravaged Scotland and the Continent, and allowed to develop in peace. It was to this end that she the cynic, the disciple of Machiavelli, had dedicated herself before the high altar at Westminster, with a passion of sincerity which belonged to a knight in the romances of chivalry. But Mary made her want a personal triumph.

Crowns and glory and the homage of men's hearts came easily to Mary. She picked them as if they were ripe fruit, with a sort of heedless grace. And it awoke the fires of jealousy in Elizabeth, so that she envied and admired—and hated Mary all in one. Could she never play a heroic role herself? She was surely as brave as Mary, if her courage was of the cold, hard, enduring sort. It had been tried in a fiery crucible and tempered in bitterness. But to comfort that inner woman who sustained herself on Robert's love and sometimes cried out against the domination of the crown and the brain, she longed to do the high and heroic. But that wish must be stamped down. To have occasion for such heroism, her country must be in danger. For nothing, would she ask that!

So she watched her cousin, and saw the incredible occur. Mary ceased to dote on her young husband, he seemed to have slipped away from her, out of her interest, and new faces came forward. The Scots lords were momentarily quieted because the strongest, the fiercest and most ruthless of all, James Hepburn, Earl of Bothwell, Lieutenant of the Border, was serving her with apparent fidelity, although he had earlier declared that she and Elizabeth put together would not make one honest woman. "A paragon of honesty he

—to prate of honesty in others!" Elizabeth cried angrily. But she admitted that he had once shown an unbroken loyalty to Mary's mother. Had not he caused Elizabeth the first bad embarrassment of her reign by capturing her gold on its way to the "Lords of the Congregation"—that "glorious, rash and hazardous young man"? Elizabeth used other epithets for him.

But if *he* held the country quiet, Mary had chosen a strange confidant. A little Italian musician, once scarcely more than a servant in the train of the Marchese Moretta, the Savoyard Ambassador, from whom Mary had begged him, being taken with his excellent bass voice, his gifts as a composer and his ability to arrange masques and festivals. Then Darnley, one moment filled with high arrogance and the next roistering with grooms, had to have him as confidant and playfellow, "David le Chantre" who in the Palace Account Books was awarded a salary of sixty-five pounds. Next David Riccio —beginning to be known as Seigneur Davie—being a well-educated knave, was taken by the Queen as her private secretary. He knew most of the languages of Europe, it was said. But then more and more was said. . . .

David the Singer was the real Secretary of State and the deep and wise Maitland of Lethington was thrust aside for him. David was treated by the Queen as if he were a great noble, he sat in her presence wearing his cap, he was adorned and bejewelled, he and the Queen were closeted alone into the small hours, intriguing, plotting against the Reformed Religion, against her brother, against her husband, against the Queen of England—plotting and were they doing more than plotting? Smoke rolled over the scene, hiding all true facts, twisting into strange shapes impossible to grasp or hold, but griming everything it touched. And that weak but vicious boy to whom she had once given the empty title of king and of whom now she was wearied and sickened, cried out that David had had more company of her body than he these past two months. . . . So he turned to his former enemies, the Scots lords.

Elizabeth watched. She read Randolph's information and reflected. There came rumours of a plot to "dagger Seigneur Davie and the King privy to it". Elizabeth said nothing. She did not warn Mary. She was not Mary's keeper. Mary had now refused to meet her. Perhaps it was true what Cecil declared—that Mary and Riccio were plotting to establish the Counter-Reformation in Scotland and a return of the French dominance. The Scots lords had a habit of daggering—sometimes the inconvenient, as well as the innocent perished by it. Let them. She could not prevent it.

But she cried out at the horror of what was done. Mary, supping with Riccio and one or two other intimates at Holyrood Palace, the young King coming to join their meal, giving his wife a Judas-kiss, and then suddenly the armoured men bursting in, dragging the wretched David from his Queen, to whose skirts he clung screaming, falling upon him like wolves at a kill rather than human beings, stabbing and hacking at the writhing body in a lust of hatred so that the blood ran in pools on the floor. Nor had they failed to threaten their Queen, six months gone with child, thrusting a pistol into her side as her husband held her down forcibly in her chair.

Elizabeth swore a great oath that in the Queen of Scots' place, she would have snatched her husband's dagger and stabbed him to the heart. But seeing the gravely considering eyes of the Spanish Ambassador upon her, she had said swiftly: "You must not think that I would draw a knife on the Archduke Charles if he visited me!" For that long-tried man, her suitor of seven years, was being encouraged again to offset the anger of the House of Commons, who were urging their Queen towards marriage.

But, incredibly, Mary was to triumph again. A prisoner in the murderers' bloodstained hands, she yet managed to outwit them. Firstly she detached from them their fellow-conspirator, her weak and treacherous husband, a weathercock to blow this way and that in every gust; secondly, she managed to escape with him by night to her friends, and Bothwell raised an army for her. The conspirators' nerve gave; the most guilty fled and with them Master John Knox, who had egged them on from the pulpit; the others came humbly to beg for pardon. Mary rode back to Edinburgh in triumph, between her despicable husband and Bothwell, the man of iron, and she reconciled the latter to his mortal enemy, her brother Moray, who—canny man!—though he had stayed away till the murder was accomplished, had known of it long beforehand. . . . Now she had gone to the towering Castle of Edinburgh so that her child might be born in the security of its strong walls.

"But she can't give birth to a live child—not after that!" Elizabeth declared to Robert.

"Probably not," he said in a mollifying voice. He had noticed that

while the Queen of Scots could exasperate his dear love more than
any other mortal, Elizabeth, also, was always exasperated by marriage and maternity in other women. He could see her long hands
clench themselves in her lap, so that the knuckles gleamed like ivory
above the gems of her many rings.

"What a dance of death it is!" she cried. "You know that great
picture which Holbein painted for my father? Faster, faster, faster
and then, after Death into the abyss! What can come of it? The murderers cowed but not broken, those two mortal enemies, Bothwell
and Moray feigning friendship, and that man of straw, Harry Darnley, whom she must hate and despise from the bottom of her heart!"

But Mary had one more triumph over her cousin, her eternal and
lasting triumph. Midsummer found the English court at Greenwich,
the Palace of Placentia by the river's edge. From its windows could
be seen all the shipping of the port of London, bearing the city's
wealth to and fro, under those soaring masts. Everywhere a tangled
forest of spars met the eye. Tall galleons which might slip away to
waters undreamt of by the fathers of their crews, waters which the
King of Spain believed were sacrosanct to him, alongside sturdy
coasters or flat, grimy barges from Newcastle bringing down the sea-
coal, and whippy pinnaces towered over by great carracks, their hulls
bright with paint and leaf-gold, their sails emblazoned, banners flying from their mastheads. Elizabeth liked the palace which was her
birthplace, she liked to wave her hand to ships going by, and hear
the thunder of their salutes as they passed the Royal Standard. The
end of June 1566 saw her recovering from an illness there.

To-night she was well enough to dance. The music of recorders and
viols thrummed and lilted, bright clothes and jewels gleamed in the
candlelight. Light, colour and music had a special freshness for Elizabeth after the dreariness of days in a sick chamber, they all seemed to
have been created anew for her. She had never stepped so "high and
disposedly" through the formal and elegant measure of the dance,
her fingers lying lightly in those of a handsome and graceful young
Gentleman Pensioner, gazing at her with adoring eyes. She was just
reflecting on the fervour of that adoration, when she saw the dignified
figure of Secretary Cecil carefully picking his way over the floor between the dancing figures. Something important must have happened
or he would not interrupt the dance. He was coming up to her, his
rather small eyes intent upon her face. She stepped out of the figure,

casting a flashing smile at the disappointed youth as she withdrew her hand from his.

"Well, Sir Spirit?"

"Your Majesty must forgive the interruption, but I have just had news of great moment from Scotland." Scotland—that dark land of doom and bloodshed! Her smile stiffened.

"Sir James Melville has arrived in person, but he is scarcely attired to enter your Grace's presence, after riding with the fewest pauses possible from Edinburgh."

"From Edinburgh? What is it? Another insurrection? My poor cousin——"

"Oh no, your Grace, it is good news. On the nineteenth, the Queen of Scots was safely delivered of a fine and healthy son. . . ."

The music, the lights and the colours seemed to slide away from her. She was scarcely aware that she made a furious gesture so that the musicians abruptly stopped playing. She put her hand to her side as if a dagger had stabbed her. What steel blade could hurt like this? Through all her difficult life she had armoured herself with an iron control which hardly ever slipped. But now—any torturer, any rackmaster, would tell you that there came a point when the human body could bear no more. Did no one tell of the worse agony which the mind and the spirit could no longer endure? It had come on her now. She thrust out of the throng, hardly heeding the glances, the whispering, the rustling stir, and like a wounded beast, made for the privacy of her withdrawing chambers. They followed her of course, her ladies exclaiming and twittering with dismay, Cecil solemn in the rear, and on the very outskirts, James Melville—with whom she had once flirted as she cross-examined him on his Queen—now feeling too sweaty and dusty to come into the royal presence. But she did not heed them. She heard her own voice, almost as if it were someone else's, with that cry of agony wrenched out of her.

"The Queen of Scots is mother of a fair son, and I am but a barren stock!"

Cecil, with tact and foresight, withdrew, taking with him the Scottish envoy who was to write of the scene years later in his memoirs. She was left to her ladies, who supported her into her bedchamber, pressed vinaigrettes to her nose, took off her ruff and suggested undoing her stay laces. Yes, she was feeling ill again, she muttered, she would go to bed. . . . No, she did not want her physicians. . . . The ladies undressed her, taking away her heavy jewels and finery, and attiring her in a nightrail of the finest white cambric, profusely embroidered with black silk and silver threads, the fashion of the moment, and wrapped over it a loose silk bedgown. She did not want anyone to remain with her but Blanche Parry, she told them, glad for the rest to withdraw. Blanche was a strange daughter for the fat and garrulous Thomas Parry. Now he and Kate Ashley were both dead but Blanche remained, Blanche who was silent and deft, knew so much of herbs and simples and sometimes could be persuaded to tell the Maids of Honour's fortunes, Blanche who had originally introduced Dr. Dee, the famous astrologer, to Elizabeth. She did not have Kate Ashley's simple affection, but she knew so much without being told.

She knew now what to do for her distracted mistress, knew the only person who could calm and comfort her. She bade an usher at the door of the ante-chamber find the Earl of Leicester, and when he came, brought him in by the private way, and then swiftly and silently withdrew.

"Dear love," said Robert, "what's grieving you?"

Strange, she thought, what comfort there was just in being in his arms, what unreasonable security it gave her! But nothing could heal the wound she had received to-night. Yet now she could give way, she need dissimulate no more, as she had forced herself to do, after her first bitter outcry. She cried as if she were heartbroken, Robert had never seen her weep such stormy, helpless tears, he had never before seen her give way to such an abandonment of sorrow. He let the first gale of misery blow itself out. One could say nothing reasonable to help, he thought, pressing his cheek against her red head, murmuring: "Sweet. . . . Poor Love. . . . Poor Heart!" When she was at last quiet against his shoulder (from exhaustion, he thought), he asked her: "But what is it?"

She raised her head, and he thought that her tear-reddened eyes were so dark they might be caverns—hell mouths. But she spoke quietly and with control.

"The King of England was born", she said, "in Edinburgh Castle on the nineteenth of this month."

He stared for a moment, not at first understanding her. Only the words "Edinburgh Castle" brought some realization to him. He had expected her to be upset if the Queen of Scots had a son, expected some scathing comment, but not this frenzy.

"He? King of England? Why, he is not yet King of Scotland!"

"He will be!"

"By God's soul, he shall not!" He caught her roughly by the shoulders. "Listen to me! Now, with this Scots princeling born and the Commons already yelling for you to marry, no one will say 'no' to *our* marriage! Then we'll have a red-headed lad——"

"Robin—don't be a fool!" She had shaken off his gripping hands, and put up her own, to take his face between them so he could not evade her glance. "Robin—did you never think that we might have a child?"

"Well——" he temporized, trying to turn his head.

She gave a bitter little laugh with no amusement in it, and her lips curled into a more bitter smile.

"Tell me the truth, Robin! Didn't you expect it? Didn't you hope for it? Pray for it?" A grimace distorted her face for a second as she whispered: "So at heart, did I. . . ."

"Well," he said once more, "I did think of it."

The laugh came again. "Weren't you counting on it, Robin? Then you thought I'd come running, like any betrayed village maid, begging for a ring. . . . We'd have to be wed swiftly then, wouldn't we? My father and Cranmer only just got *me* born in wedlock!"

His face showed a transparent agreement. He *had* thought these things, and he had wondered, considering her in some ways an odd creature and unwomanly, if she would realize in time, for the birth not to provoke too appalling a scandal. She looked at him—and read him as if he were a book.

"Don't you realize why I don't marry? Think of my sister——"

"You can't compare yourself with her—that withered old hag!"

"But the same curse is on us! Some would say the Tudors were accursed. . . . My sister could not bear a child. Nor can I. . . . Huic, my physician, once warned me, years ago. He said: 'You will no more be able to bear children than the Queen.' And I cried out at him, for I was young then, and she withered before her time, and no man would want her, while men found me desirable—to no purpose! And I hoped and prayed that he might be proved wrong. You will never know how much!"

She jerked herself out of his arms and began to walk up and down, as he had seen captive beasts walk in cages. Her speech was jerky too, bitter and emphatic.

"The marriage of any Queen-Regnant is a danger which may become a disaster. Look at my sister. Look at this other Mary. Ah, yes! She has this moment of triumph, but I tell you she is caught up in a veritable dance of death! The Queen's husband who is not a king! He is an impossibility. . . . If he be a foreigner—look at my sister and King Philip! Look at the danger of foreign influence. Look at the natural hatred the people have for foreigners. Look at religious difficulties. Then consider marrying a nobleman of the realm—such as you! Think of the mad jealousy—of the factions which will rise and may blaze into civil war. There must be a Virgin Queen! She's an image on a platform, raised up high, bright with jewels, to whom the world must bow, to rule, rule, rule! Not to live. . . ."

"But the Succession——" he began.

"Oh, yes, the Succession! A healthy son is the one thing which can balance the danger of marriage. Only with the surety of an heir, could I face these perils. Now do you understand how I dared give myself to you?"

"We'll have a son yet!" he cried. He did not know whether he was trying to convince her or himself.

"Never! Oh, God, if I could! *She* can. . . . But I'm barren, barren!"

She threw her hands out in a wild gesture and he saw the rings flash. He got up swiftly, fearing she might injure herself with the hysterical fit on her again, caught her up in his arms, holding her close in protection as he sat on the low couch at the foot of her great bed. She was sobbing incoherently again, choking on the words "barren". Then once more, just when he thought in despair that he had better try to find Mistress Parry and get help, she began to quieten.

"Sweet, do you want your women?"

"No!!! Only you, Robin, only you. Oh, Robin, forgive me! But I can never forgive *her*. Does she realize how blessed she is? No, I don't suppose she does. Holy Writ says 'to him that hath it shall be given'. She takes everything for granted."

"Don't think of her."

"How can I fail to think of her? I can't escape her. And she can't escape me! If we could have been born at different times!"

"I tell you—don't think of her! If we marry, we may yet have a son. A curse on that fellow, Huic!"

"Ah, Robin! When was it easier to get lawful children than bastards? Poor Robin. . . . And you have no son. It's hard on you too. I have made your earldom to descend to Philip Sidney. You love the boy, don't you? So do I."

"Yes. Almost as if he were my own. . . . I've made him my heir."

"He is your earldom's heir. Oh, Robin, if we had such a child! Not that I should ever have anything so simple and chivalrous. He will be a knight *sans peur* and *sans reproche*—and a poet! Not such for me."

("But", she thought, "sometimes it's intolerable when Robin and I are together with the boy and I think he might be ours. . . . Or remembering the stolen hours in that poor garden of the Tower, and Robin tossing that other child up in play, or when it rode upon his back and he held its little legs with his strong brown hands. I used to comfort myself with fantasies—of a better garden with my own children beside me and my husband—a husband in his image. . . . But in those days I did not dare admit to myself that I loved him. Tom Seymour had taught me that man's love was as perilous as walking on too thin ice. . . .")

"Robin," she said aloud. "There are two things I have always wanted. The Crown of England. Yes! Even from childhood. That I have. And I wanted my love to love me, as I, him. To give him a son. To give a son to England. A son who would bridge my two worlds of desire. And that I cannot have! How long will you love me, Rob?" She was clutching him with those stiff, jewelled hands. "Rob—are you faithful to me?"

"Yes, I swear it!"

He had been, so far, oddly enough. His nature was not to be faithful to one woman. He had wearied so quickly of the wife of his boyhood. But apart from the danger of offending Elizabeth's savage jealousy—that furious regal Tudor jealousy which had made her father sacrifice her mother—there was a quality in the woman herself which he had often described as a flame. She had absorbed him if even sometimes his attention had strayed. Just as the words—"I swear it!"—sprang to his lips he recollected last year's Progress when they had halted at the castle of Lord Sheffield, whose young and lovely wife was a distant cousin of Elizabeth's, being born a Howard with the unusual Christian name of Douglass.

It had not taken him long to find that Douglass was a delectable creature, that she was not happy with her husband and that she looked on the Queen's Master of Horse with more than interest. . . . After all, what was a stolen kiss with Douglass, and a few afterthoughts of her? She did not resemble Lettice Essex, who was fiercely possessive and fiercely desirous; like Elizabeth, *she* demanded all or nothing. But Douglass was sweeter and milder, of the clinging, adoring kind who would have no other will but his. At this very time, his thoughts returned to Douglass with uncomfortable persistence.

But Elizabeth at the moment was neither Tudor lioness nor leaping flame. It was the woman, not the Queen, whom he held and comforted, and she was heartbroken, weeping for the children she could not have. Finally she sobbed herself to sleep in his arms from sheer exhaustion. Once he thought to rise and slip away, but she held on to him, whether in sleep or waking he could hardly judge. But at last, she lay still, and he withdrew his cramped arm and left her, in the cool darkness of the small hours. His thoughts were confused; they seemed to flow in two different channels. One was: "She will marry me after all! Even if she can't have a child, I don't believe that the marriage would be dangerous. . . . Now the Queen of Scots has a son, Parliament and the Council will force her into marrying. . . ." But the other was thoughts of a woman like Douglass who would be no more than the mistress of Kenilworth and that magnificent mansion he had just erected, Leicester House in the Strand—not the mistress of the court and country! Finally, before he too slept, his natural affection and tenderness (which showed so strongly with his family) predominated. Poor Love, how she suffered! He would think of something to distract her, besides an immediate present. Now he had been made Chancellor of the University of Oxford, he must arrange a State visit for her, on her summer's Progress, so that she could display her learning, her elegancies of scholarship, as well as those elegancies of appearance, and delight in the appreciation of learned scholars as well as the devotion of her adoring subjects. He would discuss it with her the next day. Of course, she would be exhausted. . . .

But she astonished him. She had lain in bed late that morning, making her ladies cover her face with icy-cold wet cloths so that the swelling and inflammation of her eyes abated and the throbbing of her brow ceased. Then carefully painted and gorgeously attired and jewelled, she received the Scottish envoy. The news had been such a welcome surprise, she told him, that it was all that was needed to complete her cure from her recent illness! Of course, she would be only too delighted to accede to her "dear sister and cousin's" request to become godmother to the little prince, James. . . .

When Robert came to her, sitting in one of the withdrawing chambers overlooking the shipping of London river, he found her discussing the preparations for the christening. She had ordered a font to the value of a thousand pounds to be made by her goldsmith. The Earl of Bedford was to represent her and lead the English delegation. She thought she would send Master Christopher Hatton with him, to gain diplomatic experience. William Cecil had told her that her elegant dancing partner was shaping as a good House of Commons man. She would make something useful of him. . . . The distraught, frenzied woman of the preceding night had vanished. He could only marvel.

But later she was to repeat to him: "That child will be King of England."

"You'll never proclaim him as your Successor?" he said, incredulous.

"On my death-bed!"

Chapter Five

P
hilip Sidney came to Oxford at the end of August 1566. It
was a sudden, wonderful and unexpected holiday. Only the
other day he had sat on one of the hard benches of Shrewsbury School, in the dim hours of morning, when the bare
classroom smelt of ink and snuffed candle wicks, so early were the
scholars required to rise. By the time the rising sun had reddened the
leaded panes of the windows he would have been long settled to his
Virgil, the inseparable Fulke Greville close beside him, and his other
friends not far off, James Harington, his cousin, Edward Onslow, son
of the Solicitor-General, and many others; for wherever Philip went
he seemed to gather a devoted band about him which acknowledged
him as leader. Now he was transported, after several days' riding,
away from the shadows of the blue hills of Wales, over the low,
rolling green hills of Cotswold till his party came at last to the ancient
university city, where the Queen was to pay her State visit.

They had stopped on the way at Kenilworth, that magnificent
castle and estate which belonged to Uncle Robert, for this holiday
was one of the splendid things Uncle Robert would toss down, with
a godlike carelessness. He had evidently paused, in the middle of his
busy and important life, to consider that Philip was lonely at Shrewsbury School since his father had been created Lord Deputy in Ireland,
and had sailed for Dublin in January, taking with him his wife and
the younger children. Uncle Rob was a paladin amongst uncles.

Philip had enjoyed staying at Kenilworth, and exploring the huge
place, climbing to the top of Caesar's Tower, and gazing out over
the great trees of the park. Uncle Robert had some wonderful possessions nowadays, huge paintings which covered the panelled walls,
tapestries on which the figures of allegory and myth gestured, soft,
deep carpets under foot, one especially magnificent, being in crimson

Zenith

velvet, embroidered in gold and silver with bears and ragged staves, Uncle Rob's cognisance, which appeared everywhere on the furniture together with his favourite colour, crimson. There was a "caborett" of crimson satin, richly embroidered in gold and silver with a "device of hunting the stag", having silver cups and glasses of flowers standing upon it; there were chairs of crimson velvet and cloth of gold, studded with gilt nails and blazoned with more bears and ragged staves in silver; there were organs, regals and virginals covered with crimson velvet. Most impressive of all was a gigantic bedstead painted crimson with silver Tudor roses, its four tall posts silver bears, each clasping his ragged staff, the curtains and hangings in crimson satin.

"When the Queen visited Kenilworth, she slept in that bed," Philip was informed by Master Thomas Blount, that humorously alert man with the thin, sunburnt face, who managed Uncle Rob's vast domain. "Did she really?" asked young Philip, putting his hand cautiously where the royal head had lain. "I hope she likes crimson! *I* do! It's a brave colour."

A smile just flickered over Blount's thin lips. He was thinking: "She would have liked it better if my lord had been at her side! Openly as her consort!" But that day seemed no nearer than on that hot summer afternoon when he had ridden on his lord's business to Cumnor. So far his lord had gone, and yet he did not take the final step. . . .

Master Blount was very good to Philip, showing him round and arranging fishing for him. Perhaps he knew of the remark Uncle Robert was to make lightly to Philip who had been praising Kenilworth: "You like it, Phil? It will be yours when I am dead."

Philip did not know which he enjoyed best, catching bream, whose scaled bodies had a silver gleam in the slight shade which the drooping trees cast on the water, or reading Uncle Rob's books in tooled red leather adorned with gilt, books he approached with eager but reverent fingers. He was quite glad to rest too, for long hours of riding in the hot weather had given him chafing sores called "meriegalles" by Marshall, that middle-aged serving-man who watched over Philip like a mother, and treated the "meriegalles" with ointment. Marshall had also been worried over Philip's clothes for this great occasion, doing the best he could with the little money at his disposal, buying lace and silk to renew the slashing in trunk hose and sleeves, and new silk points to tie hose and sleeves to the doublet. For the Sidneys were poor, and had recently suffered a great misfortune when the ship carrying their plate, Lady Mary's jewels, and much of their furnishings and apparel, had gone down on the way across to Ireland. They had never been rich before that, their Castle of Penshurst, with its high great hall, whose rafters were so strangely carved, seeming bare besides the splendours of Uncle Rob's Kenilworth. But Philip had one day heard Uncle Rob say with a shrug: "I must make a show! But my debt to the Queen is enormous!" And Philip's mother had answered with an unguarded bitterness: "You're lucky, Robin! We find it is as difficult to get moneys from her, rightly owed, as blood from a stone!"

Uncle Rob had reddened as he admitted: "Yes, she can be a hard paymaster.... Though truly she has not too much with the Commons fighting every subsidy. Still, to me, she is marvellously generous."

Uncle Rob had suddenly arrived at Kenilworth, made much of Philip, and condemned his patched-up wardrobe with a sweeping gesture, declaring: "I'll have my tailor, Whittell, make him suitable clothes. He's to be presented to the Queen's Majesty, and no one shall say my nephew does not make a brave show!" ("His lordship is very generous, Master Philip," said Marshall afterwards.) Whittell and his apprentices arrived, measured Philip with care and then commenced their rapid stitching upon doublets of satin, damask, taffeta and velvet, with slashed hose of the same, while silk stockings of many gorgeous hues such as "carnation", shoes of many coloured leathers, white cambric shirts worked with black silk and silver thread and starched and fluted ruffs were bought to go with them. Uncle Robert also ordered plainer clothes for Philip to wear at school, "canvas doublets streaked with red and blue" and leather jerkins and hose for riding. He had never had such a wardrobe in his life before. Everyone knew that Uncle Rob was the best-dressed man at court, which meant the best-dressed in England. . . .

So, now attired in a most princely way and his "meriegalles" almost healed, Philip rode over the green ridges of Cotswold into Oxford. All he could have asked for was to have Fulke Greville beside him, but he would do his best to make up by telling him about everything on his return to school. He must write about it, too, to his father and mother and ask them to read bits out to his sister, Mary. They were a remarkably loving and devoted family, the Sidneys, parents and children having the happiest confidence in each other. It had been a terrible thing when he had seen the ship sailing away with his family into the stormy waters of the Irish Channel, he had almost disgraced his eleven years by crying openly. He knew too that his father had not wanted his difficult and dangerous post in that savage, barbarous and unhappy country, and anticipated nothing but trouble in the fulfilling of his duty to the Queen. Was he not to write to her of Ireland: "Surely there was never people that lived in more misery than they do—such misery as in truth hardly any Christian with dry eyes could behold."

But in the middle of all his work and worries, Sir Henry Sidney had also found time to write to the little son at Shrewsbury, a long and careful letter telling him how to shape his conduct and life now his parents were far away from him, telling him to study diligently and heed the matter of which he read as well as the words, to let his first action always be prayer, and much other wise and thoughtful advice, amongst which was to refrain from swearing and ribaldry, which made Philip reflect on the oaths that rolled on occasion from the lips of the Queen. ("Yes, bless her, she can swear!" said Uncle Rob when this difficult point was put to him. "But all the Tudors did. You should have heard old King Harry! Nevertheless, your father's right—albeit rare.") Sir Henry had concluded with the words: "Well, my little Philip, this is enough for me, and too much I fear for you!" and Philip could so well imagine the gentle smile curling his father's lips. But if it were very hard for his family to be in another country, no other boy had a better uncle!

Oxford delighted him, with its ancient grey buildings set in smooth green turf, the grace of Magdalen Tower (which of course he climbed, for were not towers and trees meant to be climbed?) and the stir and bustle of town and gown. On every hand strolled and swaggered boys not much older than himself, for thirteen was quite a usual age to commence University studies, but they seemed to have a marvellously worldly air to Philip the schoolboy. He often escaped into the streets, then being furiously cleansed of the usual filth of sixteenth-century towns against her Majesty's coming; when Marshall was busy, attended only by the serving-lad of his own age, Randal Calcott, who gaped open-mouthed—"Ow, Master Philip!"—at the sights to be seen till Philip stopped his mouth with sugared comfits, for Uncle Rob had filled his pouch at the same time as covering his back. Philip knew that in two years he was to go to Christ Church for he had heard his father and Uncle Rob discussing it. Fulke was going to Oxford too. . . . He looked forward to the day.

After a brief halt at an inn, Philip and his two attendants were sent to Lincoln College to stay with Uncle Robert's chaplain, the Reverend Master Bridgewater, a kindly man who took Philip about and told him the histories of the different colleges. The undergraduates were being bundled into every possible corner and sleeping four and five in a bed as their usual quarters were needed for the court, but Philip was better lodged as befitted the nephew of Oxford's Chancellor. Christ Church itself was being prepared for her Majesty. Mr. Bridgewater told Philip that this college had been founded by the great Cardinal Wolsey and had been originally known as Cardinal College; on Wolsey's downfall it had been re-named King's, and now, said the Rev. Bridgewater: "It is dedicated to the Glory of God, being named College of Christ's Church." The preparations to make it ready for the Queen were little short of frantic. . . . The Queen's Progresses were already famous. In the summer months she delighted in travelling about, being received in the towns with elaborate loyal addresses, feastings and pageantry, and nearly as elaborate festivity in those country houses to which she gave the expensive honour of her presence. Philip had hoped that she would come on Progress to Penshurst but his father had shaken his head. "I can't afford it! We'll leave the costly honour of entertaining her Majesty to your Uncle Robin." Philip stopped to reflect that Uncle Robin was almost like her Majesty's shadow or her echo; he was never far away from her, and somehow one thought of them together.

Then Uncle Robin himself arrived amidst the clatter of hoofs and the whirl of crimson and silver liveries blazoned with the bear and ragged staff, and swept Philip up into his orbit once more. He had left his nephew at Kenilworth till his wardrobe was prepared, and ridden back to court; now he rode ahead of the court to see all the preparations were in hand, both as Chancellor of the University and one of her Majesty's greatest officials. And with him was another famous man, the Queen's chief minister, Sir William Cecil, who descended, wincing, from his sedate horse—a great contrast to Uncle Rob's champing black charger—for he was greatly troubled with the gout, and thankful to exchange his boot for a velvet slipper. He spoke with kindness to Philip, telling him of the affection and esteem he had for both his parents, and setting his hand on Philip's shoulder for support as he painfully ascended the winding stairs, said: "Pray, boy, that you never have the gout!" "Rest your foot now you have the chance!" declared Uncle Robin. "We shall be busy enough in a few days!" The painful foot reposed on a cushioned stool as Sir William and Uncle Robin checked the lists and the arrangements.

The University had wished to welcome its Chancellor with a long Latin oration in public, but this had to be delivered in the lodgings of the Commissary at Christ Church, because a summer storm had whipped the streets and buildings with sudden, furious rain. The indescribable, sweet, fresh scent of rain on the dry ground filled Philip's nostrils as he listened to the long oration and the few brief Latin sentences with which his uncle replied. For Uncle Robin, although he was cultured and spoke many foreign languages, was no great Latinist. Striding back to his lodgings with the adoring small boy trotting at his heels, he confessed with a grin: "To make a speech of great length in Latin is a heavy labour for me! An' I had to compose such an oration—I needs must ask the Queen to help me. She teases me because I prefer what she calls Euclid's pricks and lines, to the ancient languages. . . ."

"*Would* she help you?" asked Philip.

"Elizabeth?" (Philip gasped at this unguarded and familiar way of referring to the Queen.) "I tell you she'd write as good a Latin speech as any scholar here, and give it me, saying: "Rob, you idle fellow!" He chuckled tenderly.

"She once helped *me* with a Latin verse," recollected Philip.

"Oh, she's amazingly learned. She and William Cecil are a pair! I'll tell you what I'm going to do, young Philip! I'm going to give the University a printing press so it can print its own books."

Philip was to see other evidences of his uncle's generosity, that sudden, golden, careless bounty. Lads stammering with eager thanks would make their awkward way from his presence, and he would explain thus: "Why, 'tis a poor scholar who can't find his fees. His Chancellor has settled the matter for him!"

At last came the great day, when Philip was to watch the Queen's entry into Oxford by Bocardo, the northern gate. First came the Clarencieux-King-at-arms in his emblazoned medieval tabard, followed by three Esquire Bedells bearing golden staves. Then there was Uncle Robin looking princely on his black charger, with the scarlet-robed Mayor of Oxford riding on his right hand, and after them came many of the greatest nobles of the court, some of whom were Philip's relatives, and others well known to him by sight and hearsay. There was his Uncle Ambrose, Earl of Warwick, and another uncle, the Earl of Huntingdon who was married to his Aunt Kate, his mother's youngest sister Catherine, after them Sir William Cecil on his quiet horse beside the courtly Spanish Ambassador, Don Guzman de Silva, who was a personal friend of Philip's father, and here was one whom Philip had learned was a bitter enemy of his father and opposed his Irish policy savagely on the Council, the Earl of Ormonde, the head of the great house of Butler who owned such vast territories in Ireland, and at his side was a youth with a fiercely arrogant air as if he spurned the beholders, the young Earl of Oxford. These magnificently adorned, magnificently horsed noblemen were followed by royal lictors carrying gilded sceptres and finally came another uncle of Philip's, the Earl of Sussex, bearing the Sword of State. Sussex had married Philip's father's sister, but he himself was Uncle Robert's sworn enemy and leader of the court faction opposed to his. The Queen had shrewdly settled the claims of these rival potentates for this day's ceremony; the Earl of Leicester as Chancellor of the University leading the procession of nobles, but the Earl of Sussex bearing the Sword.

Then came such a roar from townsmen and scholars alike, thickly crowding the route, that the blood rose hotly in Philip's cheeks and he found that he himself was shouting, though he could hardly hear the sound in his excitement. For here was the Queen at last. Her open litter was drawn by white mules with ground-length trappings of scarlet and gold; scarlet woven with gold was the robe she wore and over it was flung a mantle of royal purple trimmed with ermine, while her head-dress was of the finest spun gold. She seemed to blaze like a great fiery jewel set against the cool grey stone of the ancient buildings. Around her the Gentlemen Pensioners, in coats of cloth of gold, pressed back the excited crowds with their ornamental battle-axes. Behind her came her ladies on horseback, many of them in white and silver to set off the scarlet and golden Queen, and to close the procession, came her palfreys, led riderless in rich trappings, and finally two hundred of her yeomen, scarlet and gold again, blazoned with the Tudor rose and the royal cipher, E. R., armed with longbows and heavy iron maces.

Philip was intoxicated with this pageantry and colour, as the procession swept along Northgate Street to the Carfax, gowned under-graduates lining the streets, falling on their knees with shouts of "Vivat Regina" to which the Queen replied "Gratias ago". At the Carfax, the procession was halted for the Queen to hear a long oration in Greek. A mule fidgeted and side-stepped, another tossed its head, attendants went to them. Then the Queen replied in another Greek speech nearly as long as the one she heard. Listening to the sonorous Greek words, her voice high-pitched to carry, Philip thought of Uncle Robert's remarks about her learning. How wonderful to be the Queen and know everything and *have* everything!

Within the great hall of Christ Church, she had to listen to another oration, this time in Latin. Learned Fellows and Doctors were presented to her; presently Philip found himself kneeling to kiss that really beautiful hand. It took him by the chin and its possessor said: "Well, Boy Philip! I'll have speech with you later." The ceremony of arrival ended in the Cathedral where Philip, close by his uncle's side, peeped through his fingers at the Queen kneeling under her golden canopy while the Dean gave thanks for her safe coming.

This gorgeous and solemn arrival was to epitomize that crowded week which followed. Imagination was always to hover near Philip, giving him those wings which she allows to creative artists and which can carry them to an infinitely more glorious world, though they pay for this with great suffering when their wings are withdrawn—"intense the agony" as Emily Brontë would write. But now the everyday world was clothed with the colour and pageantry of imagination. To the sound of sonorous Latin and Greek declamations, the brilliant spectacle unfolded. At night the great hall of Christ Church was ablaze with a thousand wax candles for the performance of plays. Especially, Philip was to remember *Palamon and Arcite*, written by Richard Edwardes, Master of the Children of the Chapel Royal. It was in English, a relief after concentrating so deeply on the Latin, and Philip was greatly interested to learn that the graceful little boy who played Emilia the heroine (after the custom of the time) was dressed in a purple velvet gown which had once belonged to the Queen's sister, Queen Mary! In the hunting scene when the undergraduates whooped and halloaed so lustily at the cry of the hounds and the winding of horns, Philip—sitting at his uncle's feet—heard the Queen's jolly laugh and her amused remark: "Excellent! These boys in very truth are ready to leap out of the windows to follow the hounds!"

Zenith

But a tragedy was to mar an otherwise successful performance. Townsfolk had crowded to this, the only play in English, and were sitting on walls, steps and windows to see. There came a rumble and a dull crash, followed by a subdued outcry. Philip saw the Queen's face grow tense, and her glance go sideways although she did not move her head. How alert she was! He had the feeling that all the time she was listening to and enjoying the play, she was watching the spectators as well, and missing nothing. The figure of an usher bobbed up at her side in swift response to her raised finger. He heard the whispered words: "A wall fell, your Grace, from the press." "Send my surgeons at once to attend to the injured." The play went on. Not until it was finished did the Queen and the rest of the audience learn that three people were killed. The contemporary chronicler observes with a certain smug satisfaction that "none of the court was hurt and only one scholar".

Through the formality of the ceremonies the Queen's personality flashed out. Philip saw the eminent divine, Dr. Laurence Humphrey, a leader of the Puritan party (as those who rigidly followed the tenets of Geneva were beginning to be called), presented to her Majesty. Her Majesty's keen eyes flickered over him with a sparkle of mockery; mockery too lilted in the tone of her voice as she spoke. "Mr. Doctor, that loose gown becomes you well! I wonder your notions should be so narrow. . . ." On another day, in St. Mary's Church when the Queen was delivering yet one more interminable oration in Latin, Philip's attention strayed to the figure of Sir William Cecil endeavouring to balance on one leg to rest his gouty foot. But other eyes were watching Sir William. The Latin oration stopped abruptly and the clear, forceful voice spoke in English: "Sir William must sit down and rest his leg immediately on a stool!" Sir William was settled as comfortably as possible before the oration was resumed.

Before that bright cavalcade was to wind its way through the streets once more, leaving the little city strangely quiet and empty, an usher of the Privy Chamber came to Lincoln College with the message that the Queen's Majesty desired to see Master Sidney. Marshall fell upon Philip, washing him, brushing him and dressing him in the best of his new finery, crimson damask doublet trimmed with velvet, crimson velvet trunk-hose slashed with damask and satin, long crimson silk stockings and crimson shoes with silver rosettes.

Zenith

"I wish my Lady could see you," said he.

As Philip entered Christ Church, following the usher, a man came running down the staircase with a heedless violence, colliding with Philip and knocking him against the wall. He stopped and Philip saw it was the young Earl of Oxford, his handsome but insolent face dark with the flush of temper. He, too, recognized the boy who had been at the Earl of Leicester's heels for most of the ceremonies.

"Godslife!" he swore. "The place is encumbered with the Dudleys and their spawn!"

Then he had gone and the stillness left by his furious passing was palpable. Philip found he was holding the hilt of his dagger and a cold sweat was starting out on his body. Everyone had been so kind to him since he came to Oxford that the Earl's brutal rudeness was the greater shock. His first impulse was to tell his Uncle Robert, but it only lasted a moment; this was *his* quarrel. "When I am a man", he thought, "I will fight him and kill him!"

"You had best keep out of his way, Master Sidney," said the usher. "He's very violent, bloody and deboshed, his lordship."

But Philip promised himself that a day should come when he would not keep out of the Earl of Oxford's way. At the top of the stairs they passed through a door guarded by a Yeoman halberdier into an ante-chamber where several Gentlemen Pensioners lounged, playing dice against each other, and one had his naked sword lying on the table before him, it being his duty to guard the Queen's person. He passed Philip into the next room which was full of the Queen's ladies, several of whom Philip knew quite well, his mother having formerly been in attendance on the Queen for many years, during which time he had often paid visits to court. Dame Harington, the mother of little Jack, came first to him and gave him an affectionate hug, exclaiming loudly: "Lord, Philip! How you have grown! And how is that sweet lady, your mother?" Over her shoulder, Philip could see a group of Maids of Honour, girls a few years older than himself, clustering round Mistress Parry in the window. So when he had answered Dame Harington's questions as to his family, he asked: "What are those girls doing?"

"Bless you, they've persuaded Mistress Blanche to read their hands! They want her to find them husbands in the lines of their palms— proper tall ones! When the Queen's done with you, perhaps Blanche will tell your fortune. Find you a wife!" and she laughed.

197

"I don't want a wife," said Philip. Girls, except his sister Mary, were inexpressibly silly. "You see I intend to travel with my friend, Fulke Greville, and see the world."

Dame Harington was chuckling. "Bless you!" she said again. "All men have wives! You wait!"

Philip reflected. Most men *did* have wives, except——

"My Uncle Robert hasn't!"

Dame Harington raised her eyes to the ceiling with a comical gesture.

"Your Uncle Robert", said she, "may not be married but he has his trouble—and his pleasure. . . . Now get along with you to the Queen's Grace!"

The Queen was in a little closet opening out of the long room. She was sitting on the floor on her cushions, as Philip remembered her before, and his Uncle Robert knelt beside her, so that she rested against his shoulder.

"Here's my Philip!" she said. Philip went down on his knees and kissed her hand.

"*Your* Philip?" inquired his uncle.

"I call him *my* Philip to distinguish him from the King of Spain! Who indeed did once want to be my Philip, but I wasn't having him! Well, my Philip! Are you enjoying this visit to Oxford?"

"Mightily, your Grace!"

"Good. So am I. Your uncle has arranged an excellent entertainment." Uncle Robert smiled over her head, and Philip noticed for the first time that he had his arm round the Queen's waist as if the better to support her.

"And do you follow the Latin of the speeches and plays?"

"Fairly well, your Grace."

"Your uncle tells me that your master, Aston, commends your study. I was sorry indeed not to come to Shrewsbury School this May when I was on Progress."

"Oh, your Grace, we were sorry!" Philip burst out eagerly. "We had a Latin play to act for you. *Julian the Apostate*, and I had a part. . . . So did Fulke and Ned Onslow," he added.

"My solicitor's son? Yes, Philip, I am sorry I did not see your play. But the plague broke out in Shrewsbury—so no play, no Queen! Were you sent away?"

"Yes, your Grace."

"But you didn't mind a holiday from your books? What are you studying now?"

"Virgil, your Grace. I like it! I mean there's a *story*——"

"Aha, my poet! There's a story if you dig for it. If your Latin is good enough, and it should be from what I hear of you. Sir William Cecil has spoken well of you, and that is rare commendation. For he is the wisest man in England."

"Sir William is very kind to me," murmured Philip. "I am sorry for his foot, your Grace."

"I have cushions carried around for that foot of his now."

"You fuss over him as if you were his daughter!" said Uncle Robert. "You should see her Grace, young Philip, arranging cushions for Mr. Secretary! The Maid of Honour couldn't do it to her satisfaction!"

"The little fool was clumsy and hurt him. So I fetched her a box on the ear and made him comfortable myself. These girls get more foolish every day! What was all that giggling going on just now?"

"I think they were having their fortunes told, your Grace."

"Who by?"

"Mistress Parry, Dame Harington said they wanted her to find husbands for them, your Grace. And she joked and said Mistress Parry might find me a wife, and I said I didn't want a wife, but she said: *All* men have wives. So I told her, not Uncle Robert."

"Ha! So you held me up as an example?"

The Queen's smile was dancing.

"And what did my dear good Harington say then? Come now!"

"I didn't quite understand, your Grace. She said something about him not being married but having his trouble and his pleasure."

The Queen laughed heartily. She laughed till she shook and the tears came into her eyes.

"Bless you—and my old Harington!" She put her hand up and took hold of Uncle Robert's little pointed black beard, pulling his face round so she could look into his eyes, a strange intent glance.

"Trouble, Rob?" she said. "Or pleasure?"

"Why, both," said he after a pause, and she cuffed his cheek. "But mostly the latter," he added.

"Would you like your fortune told, Philip?" she asked.

"Oh, yes, your Grace! But not a wife!" he said firmly.

"I agree with you there. Rob, I beg you go and fetch Blanche in from those cackling geese of girls!"

When Uncle Rob had gone, and Philip was still kneeling beside the Queen, he wondered suddenly if he ought to put his arm round her waist to support her. No one had ever told him to do so but perhaps one ought, when a lady sat on the floor. He raised his arm and then put it down, wondering if it were presumption. But the Queen saw, smiled, and taking hold of his arm, clapped it firmly round her waist.

"There's a proper cavalier! You must start some day, my Philip, and why not with the Queen of England?"

But Uncle Rob was coming in with the demure Blanche Parry, smiling her small, secret smile. "Your Grace wants me?"

"Yes, Blanche. Read the hand if you please of this hopeful youth!"

By the light from the one casement, Blanche Parry peered closely at his palms with her weak eyes. The silence was sudden and heavy. It was almost a relief when Uncle Rob demanded: "Find him a dozen wives like the Grand Turk!" But the Queen cried: "Monster!" and put her hand over his mouth. Philip heard his own tense voice: "Please, will I have glory in battle?"

A strange smile touched Blanche Parry's lips. "Yes," she said. "I can promise you all the glory in battle you can desire. . . . You shall have glory, and your name shall be remembered for a time without end. . . . You won't be rich or have great possessions except the hearts of your friends. You shall have the favour of princes. I can see journeys in your hand and sojourns in foreign lands. In one you shall be in great danger but it will pass you by. You will love twice. One love will bring you fame and sorrow. The other peace and happiness. Yes, you will get married!"

"I don't mind when I'm old," murmured Philip softly.

That night when Blanche Parry was about to draw the royal bed curtains, the Queen's hand came out to stay her.

"Blanche, you read a marvellous fortune for that child. With scarcely any shadows on it. Was there anything bad of which you did not speak?"

"Not bad, your Grace," said Blanche after a moment's pause. "It is a life on which the sun will shine."

"But, Blanche, there is something wrong! I sensed it. Tell me!"

"Your Grace," said Blanche Parry, after another pause. "In that

Zenith

hand there is sorrow but nothing evil. It is remarkable in many ways. But his life line is so short. So very short. . . ."

"Ah—croaker!" cried the Queen. "Just when I am happy and wish to think of pleasant things. No! I asked you! And I *felt* it. . . ."

Chapter Six

But life was not a holiday progress, passing over a green and smiling countryside, here shaded by forest, there yellowed by ripening corn, stopping in little towns of ruddy brick, or cool grey stone, to hear those unforced shouts of the excited eager crowds. Her work went on, unceasing, and winter came, bringing the court according to custom to Whitehall, greeted as they rode through the city of London by the Lord Mayor, the Aldermen and the wealthier citizens. Was not London the heart of the country? She would have it beat for her, as she leaned forward, flashing her smile at the Lord Mayor riding beside her, to speak of her great-grandfather, who had once been Lord Mayor himself, Sir Geoffrey Bullen, the wealthy mercer of Cheapside. Let foreign princes mock! She was proud of Sir Geoffrey. It was a good mixture of blood that came to her from her mother, the small, but solid landed gentry of Norfolk, the rich merchant of London and finally a dash of grandeur in the proud Howard blood—very typical of what she was pleased to call "mere English". But she turned for a moment from the smiling mayor to look swiftly at the sullen aspect of the fine profile of the man on the other side of her. Did Robert not like this talk of ancestors when he was aware of the malicious whisper that *his* great-grandfather had been a carpenter? "Sweet Robin," she thought. "And he looks every inch a king now. . . . Still, I am not my cousin of Scotland to rate kingliness in inches or looks!"

Her cousin of Scotland! She was a perpetual shadow, an eternal potential menace. When she had nearly died at Jedburgh, Cecil had shaken his head and said: "Your Grace, it would have been well for us if she *had* died!"

"How?"

"Her infant would have been crowned King, and who else would be regent but that wise and reliable man, the Earl of Moray?"

"Who else! I think the Lord Bothwell might have something to say to that. He is the strongest man in Scotland. And if the child's father is a man of straw, a rat!—his parents, the Lennoxes, could amount to something, if only a nuisance."

"I was assuming that the Earl of Bothwell would have died too. You will recollect, your Grace, that he was so seriously wounded in a border affray that his life was despaired of, and the Queen visited him at Hermitage Castle, in his sick bed. It was after that, your Grace, that she fell so desperately ill, and it is said that her recovery started from the day when the Earl was brought in a litter to *her* bedside. . . ."

"God's wounds! Are there rumours about her and him now, as there were about that fellow, David?"

"There might be said to be whispers, your Grace!"

"Bah!" she said. "There'll always be talk around that woman! And she even makes you, my mild and reasonable Spirit, become bloodthirsty!"

Her envoys came back from the christening of Mary's son at Stirling Castle. She received them, leaning back in her high carved chair, the Earl of Leicester standing close behind her, and Sir William Cecil at her elbow, his gouty foot carefully propped on cushions. There was the leader of the English delegation, the Earl of Bedford, small and stocky with a very large head, towered over by the handsome Hatton. But at first she could get little from them but indignation. In the masque acted before the guests at Stirling, Mary's saucy French servants had exploited the medieval belief that Englishmen had tails. They had danced before the English guests, wagging long tails, and it had taken all the efforts of the Queen of Scots, aided by the efforts of Lord Bedford, to prevent the furious Englishmen assaulting their mockers. Master Hatton was enraged. He swore his Queen's oath: "God's death! If I had not been representing my own sweet lady as a diplomatic delegate, I should have fallen on the knaves, sword in hand! As it was, I turned my chair round, so that I had not to behold them!"

"A plague on their tails!" said Elizabeth impatiently. "Come, my Lord Bedford, have you nothing else to tell me but tails? How was my cousin of Scotland?"

"She was very gracious, your Majesty. And I must say apologized most prettily for the affair of the tails——"

"The foul fiend fly away with the tails and you too! I forbid the mention of the word 'tail'. How did she seem?"

"She's very elegant in that French manner, your Majesty."

"Which you men all admire so exceedingly! Did she seem happy? At her ease?"

"She was gay, your Majesty. Perhaps there was a tenseness in her demeanour."

"I'll warrant! Come, Christopher, my good Mutton! You're a ladies' man. What did you think of her?"

"Your Grace, I am one lady's man. I hardly see others!"

"Then you're a fool! Bedford, what was my hopeful godson like?"

"I think he resembles his father, your Majesty."

"So his mother thinks. 'He is so much your son that it will prove the worse for him hereafter!' *I* never believed that part of the rumour about David Riccio!"

"Nor I, your Majesty," said Bedford. "The child has Darnley's round blue eyes and loose lips."

" 'Pon my soul, my Lord!" expostulated Hatton. "All infants look the same."

"Wait till you have some of your own!" retorted Bedford, and Cecil added blandly: "At the age of six months, infants vary considerably." The Queen laughed harshly.

"And what of Henry Darnley?"

"A very sore problem, your Majesty. We scarcely saw him. He sulked in his chamber most of the time and did not attend the christening. Some say from vanity for his suit of cloth-of-gold was not ready in time, some because he had heard that your Majesty had forbidden us to give him the title of King. Still others said that the Queen had affronted him so much that he would not come forth. And there is yet another version which I am inclined to believe. That he is in mortal fear of the Lord Bothwell."

"He has a guard day and night of Lennox men, your Grace," said Hatton. "Though they say he is plotting against the Queen and her advisers. He is a very low fellow! The French Ambassador, du Croc, said he would not stay in the same room with him!"

"What thought you of the Earl of Bothwell?"

"Why, he received the guests, your Majesty," said Bedford, "and I must say was more courteous and gracious than I had expected."

"That Border reiver's travelled and been Captain of the Scottish

Archers in France. I daresay he can assume a polish if he pleases."

"It is obvious, your Majesty, that the Queen of Scots depends greatly upon him."

"Would you say she had a tenderness for him?"

"I could not judge, your Majesty." Bedford hesitated. "But I must say, I think if it pleased her to turn any man's head, she could do it...."

The other Queen said bitterly: "I am well aware that men are as great fools as it pleases them to represent women!"

The tempo of that infernal dance was getting faster and faster. While Mary and the Scots lords debated the possibility of a divorce, Darnley fled to Glasgow, a stronghold of his father's and it was said that a ship waited in the Clyde to carry him out of the country. But the truth of this would never be known as almost immediately he fell sick of smallpox. Then the incredible occurred; the wife from whom he had been alienated so long, followed him to Glasgow, nursed him with apparent devotion and finally brought him back to Edinburgh with her. As he was still infectious, he was not taken to Holyrood Palace, but lodged in a house in a suburb called Kirk o' Field. . . .

When the sound of that explosion died away, the conviction seized Elizabeth that a nightmare had suddenly become real. . . . She had expected some unnamed terror, but not one as stark as this. She had prophesied in grim mockery to Cecil, that Darnley would destroy his wife or she him, but she had hardly anticipated literal destruction. She had imagined Mary reduced to impotence by the very emptiness, the idle vanity and the viciousness of the youth she had taken as consort. She had imagined a long, sordid matrimonial disagreement, but not this elemental violence. But Mary was an elemental creature and she appealed to the elemental in others. Reason and logic were only clothing which she might tear off; neither was part of her. She gave her emotions rein; each one, primitive hate or primitive love, whichever passion filled her, she gave herself utterly to it, in an ecstasy of intoxication.

"And *that*", thought Elizabeth, "is why she and I are eternally opposed. She is ruled by her emotions, I by my intellect. My blood is as hot as hers, but I rule it with an iron lack of mercy. I despise her— but I envy her! Because I can never let myself taste that bliss of abandonment. . . . I may want it too, but my brain forever holds up to me the consequences."

Zenith

Into that echoing silence crept rumour, speaking with such savage tongues, that the murder of David Riccio paled to nothingness. The very midnight streets of Edinburgh were filled with voices crying out like unappeased ghosts, and proclamations were pasted up, even on the gates of the Palace, indicting the murderers, and heading every list was one name—Bothwell! Elizabeth read the reports of her spies and agents, she conversed with her councillors and the ambassadors of France and Spain, she read the halting statement of Mary's Council containing these words: "The matter is so horrible and strange, as we believe the like was never heard in any country. . . ."

Cecil came to her one afternoon.

"More reports from Scotland, your Grace. I am beginning to think that the Queen of Scots is not only an exceptionally wicked woman! She is an amazingly foolish one. . . ."

"I will agree with the latter," said Elizabeth. "Foolish—yes! Wicked? I cannot tell."

"Will your Grace be pleased to listen to this? She has suddenly left Edinburgh for the house of Lord Seton, one of her principal supporters. Rumour says she immediately called for the musicians to play an air called 'Joy is me for I am free'!"

"My good Spirit, if you discounted one-half of the rumours you might arrive near the truth! Well, what else did she do?"

"This is the serious part, your Grace. The first visitor she received was the Earl of Bothwell, who is placarded in the streets of Edinburgh, as the murderer of her husband!"

"Yes, that was very foolish of her!"

"And what do you think she did next, your Grace? At a time when public decency would surely have constrained her—if nothing else did—to observe the usual mourning customs for her late husband. She went forth and played golf with Bothwell!"

"Golf!" said the Earl of Leicester, who had been lounging behind the Queen's chair, and had not hitherto appeared to pay much attention to the remarks of the secretary. "What *is* golf, Sir William?"

"It is a game, my lord, to which the Scots are immoderately addicted. I observed them playing it in '59 when I was at the conference which drew up the Treaty of Edinburgh," said the secretary, with marked coldness.

"How do they play it?" persisted Robert. "Did you join in?"

206

"I did not! I play no games. It seems to consist in hitting a small ball along the ground with a specially prepared stick or club with the apparent object of causing it to enter a hole in the ground."

"I don't quite see——" began Robert.

"Have done with your talk of play, Rob! Sir Spirit, has that unhappy young woman no loyal friend to advise her?"

"She would heed none, your Grace!"

"But she must heed me!" She was out of her chair, her hands clenched. "I must make her listen to me. Oh, I've spoken ill of her in the past and she of me—we've opposed each other! What does that matter? I must save her!"

She was thinking of that agonized time when Robert's wife had died with such mysterious violence, of the whispers and rumours, the denunciations from the pulpits, the clamour and gloating abroad. How could she ever forget? Had Robert—leaning carelessly against her chair and talking of games—had he forgotten? She could remember that afternoon at Windsor, his head on her lap as she told him to go to Kew to await the result of the inquiry into his wife's death, to go away from her at a moment when she longed, as she had longed for little else in life, to cling to him in the face of everything. Oh, remembered pain! He had not felt it as much as she. She had known that soon enough—not that she wanted him hurt, beloved, spoilt, heedless Rob—but it had made her loneliness more deep. Still, why dwell on that now? She had not had her heart's desire, and she knew she could never have it, but he had brought the only delight, the only human tenderness into her life. Now, let her use all her bitterly bought experience to help this younger woman, who was so strangely in the same position. Mary must listen to her for that reason alone. Had not she too jeered: "Now my cousin of England is free to marry her horse keeper!"

Words were echoing in her head, drowning even those cries which seemed to spring from Darnley's blood demanding the blood of his killers, words more terrible in the quietness with which they presaged unalterable disaster: "Peradventure that casualty might be better for me than to live. . . ." Thought Elizabeth: "It *would* have been better! If she had died before she ever came to those dark shores again, if she had died in the sunshine of France where the verse of Ronsard and du Bellay would have given her a safer immortality, where she would be remembered as one of those whom the gods loved—dying young to become a golden memory." But a more terrible quotation of the wishes of the gods, sprang to her lips.

"Quos deus perdere vult, prius dementat! I *must* write to her!"

She did not heed the expostulations of her minister or of Robert, but immediately ordered her writing materials to be brought to her. When the quill was in her hand, she wrote with a fierce but controlled determination. Gone was her delight in metaphor and ambiguity. She wrote from her heart in a white-hot sincerity.

"*Madam,*

"*My ears have been so astounded and my heart so frightened to hear of the horrible and abominable murder of your husband and my own cousin that I have scarcely spirit to write; yet I cannot conceal that I grieve more for you than for him. I should not do the office of a faithful cousin and friend, if I did not urge you to preserve your honour, rather than look through your fingers at revenge on those who have done you that pleasure as most people say.*

"*I counsel you so to take this matter to heart, that you may show the world what a noble princess and loyal woman you are. I write thus vehemently not that I doubt, but for affection. . . .*"

She laid down her pen with a feeling of fear that Mary was a sleep-walker, unseeing, unhearing, separated from the rest of humanity, as she approached the abyss.

"God grant", she said, "that she listens to me!"

But Mary listened to nothing but the voice in her heart which drove her along her road of destiny. There followed the brutal jest of Bothwell's "cleansing" where his judges, overawed by his armed followers who packed Edinburgh, hastily acquitted him, and the Queen herself waved to him from the palace window as he rode to this travesty of a trial. The next day, he triumphantly bore the Crown of Scotland before her as she opened Parliament.

The end was approaching swiftly. Scarcely a week after this, Mary, returning from a visit to her infant son at Stirling, was carried off by Bothwell at the head of a band of armed followers who bore her to Dunbar Castle. Rumour said that she went willingly. . . .

Robert came, laughing uproariously, to Elizabeth, his breath smelling of wine. He had been supping with Pembroke and a few others, and they had made merry over the amours of Bothwell. Had he not a newly wed wife, the Earl of Huntly's sister? And in addition

he was "handfasted" to two or three more, and there was that Nor-
wegian Admiral's daughter who had followed him for years, and in
every country he left behind him discarded mistresses and bastards.
Now—God's blood! he had added a Queen to his collection! What
a bold impudent blade! How did her Grace of Scotland like taking
her place in the procession?

"I suppose there are such guffaws in every tavern in the country!"
said Elizabeth bitterly.

"Come, sweet! You weren't wont to be so prim! You liked a merry
bawdy tale as well as any other."

"Merry! As merry as death!"

"Why!" said Robin, putting his arm round her waist. "I am sorry
England is so civilized a country! Else I might have tried Bothwell's
game, and carried off a Queen!"

She looked at him. For one moment she visualized a man who
would be her master in all things, who could compel her brain by his
own transcendent superiority, could force the surrender of her mind
and will, which was so much more important than the surrender of
her body, a man in whom she might drown herself as in deep, dark
waters. But there could not be such a man except in a moment's
imagination; yet that moment was enough to stop her breath.

"But, dear heart!" His voice sounded anxious. "You surely did not
think—that I did anything but jest?"

"No," she said. "Not even for a moment, Rob!"

But he was laughing again over Bothwell's taking Maitland of
Lethington, the Secretary of State, when he carried off the Queen
of Scots. Now they were safely on the level of a joke, he added: "I
tell you if I *did* carry you off, I'd not carry off William Cecil!"

She laughed too. "But you would have to, Rob! For unless he and
I are together, the affairs of State can hardly progress! My poor
Spirit! How monstrously indignant he would be. . . . Ah—Rob! For
that jest you may kiss me."

Robert kissed her—comprehensively. But afterwards he asked her:
"Don't you ever stop thinking of the affairs of State?"

"No," she said.

The dance of death was swirling to its climax. The world watched
the hasty farce of Bothwell's divorce from his young wife, and his
hurried marriage to the Queen at four o'clock in the morning in the
chapel of Holyrood Palace. For one month they held their uneasy

reign and then the country rose. The ghastly finale came at Carberry Hill with Bothwell fled and the Queen dragged a prisoner, with an angry mob cursing and reviling her terribly—"Burn the murderess! Burn the whore!" before she disappeared into the dark walls of Lochleven Castle.

Elizabeth swore a great oath that she would send her army across the frontier, and restore her outraged and insulted cousin to her throne. She hardly heeded the frantic expostulations of Cecil and her other councillors. The Protestant Anglophil "Lords of the Congregation", headed by Mary's half-brother, Moray, had deposed her and held the power. Was Elizabeth now to undo the work of ten years to make England's "postern gate" secure, and to drive the friendly party straight into the arms of France? Mary deserved death, Cecil argued. Elizabeth looked at him, checked her fury long enough to whip up her reason. This man understood logic, not emotion.

"Am I—an anointed Queen—to encourage the murder of another anointed Queen by her subjects?"

"I perceive your Grace's meaning," conceded the secretary.

But Elizabeth sent as her special envoy, Throckmorton, who both understood the situation in Scotland and had a tenderness for its Queen. She told him to threaten the Scots lords with war if they did not restore Mary until Throckmorton wrote hastily to tell her that he feared her threats would cause Mary's murder. "And then", said Elizabeth bitterly, "the rest of the world would say I had done it on purpose. . . ." She told Throckmorton to alter the threats. If Mary was harmed—*then* she would bring fire and sword till Flodden itself was forgotten! Mary's life hung by a thread and only the Queen of England strove on her behalf. The rest of the world watched till the deadlock ended with Mary's escape from Lochleven, to put herself at the head of a force which the Hamiltons—jealous of Moray's power and repression—had raised for her. Again Elizabeth wrote—to congratulate her on her escape, but Mary never received that letter. Silence was filled with rumours of a battle at Langside—the Regent, Moray, had gained the victory and then. . . .

A diamond ornament was brought to Elizabeth which she recognized with a start of foreboding. It was a gift she had sent to Mary, years ago. With it came a letter sent from Workington in Cumberland where Mary had landed, and this letter contained the poignant sentence:

Zenith

"I am now forced out of my kingdom, and driven to such straits that, next to God, I have no hope but in your goodness."

Elizabeth's first impulse was immediately to send for Mary to bring her to court, but here she encountered the greatest resistance which she had yet had in her reign. Cecil was beside himself. Mary was a peril beyond compass; to support her would drive Moray and the Lords of the Congregation irrevocably into the arms of France. Scotland would become a dangerous enemy and a base for yet more powerful enemies. . . . So he and the other councillors argued and Elizabeth's reason argued with them. What had reason to do with her pity for Mary, for her strange desire to obtain Mary's admiration if she were the one to succour and restore her? But she would not yield to Cecil's urging to hand Mary over to the Scots. John Knox was demanding that she be burnt at the stake—"for a Queen had no more licence to commit murder and adultery than any woman in her realm".

"By God's precious soul!" Elizabeth swore. "I will protect her from her foes!" But she thought: "I cannot protect her from the worst—herself!"

Nor dare she let Mary go to France where surely the influence of the powerful House of Guise would send her back to Scotland with a French Catholic army. Mary must be kept under guard in England now she had so unfortunately come there, but she must be given every comfort and honour. And, finally, Elizabeth agreed to arbitrate between her and her subjects who now claimed to have captured compromising letters.

The Conference opened at York in October, Elizabeth's representatives being her cousin, the Duke of Norfolk, the Earl of Sussex and Sir Ralph Sadler. Mary's representatives were Lesley, Bishop of Ross, and the Lord Herries. Moray came in person with a large delegation —having, amongst others, Maitland of Lethington. They produced a silver-gilt casket containing letters which they said that Mary had written to Bothwell; these letters were duly read by the English Commissioners with protestations of horror. But later Norfolk, after a long private meeting with Maitland, showed a complete change of face.

"The trial's going strangely now," said Robert to his Queen.

"It's not even a trial. Mary would never accept my jurisdiction and

what right have I to try a crime which occurred outside my country?
I am arbitrating between her and her rebellious subjects. Ah—Rob!
One does better without hard-drawn lines. Blur them and then one
is not rigidly confined. All my life I have been making compromises,
I think, I have balanced this against that so my country may survive.
I have built a Church which is a compromise between the dictates of
Rome and Geneva. I have even compromised with my love!" She
sighed and then continued: "A trial must have a verdict. And I think
we dare not have a verdict for either side."

"Why?"

"Listen to this. I told her own ambassador, Herries, that if I found
that Moray and his confederates had no proper case against her I
would restore her to her throne. And he said, if, which God forbid, I
found they had a case, what then? So I told him I would make the
best compromise I could between her and her subjects. I should never
hand her over to them."

"So her own ambassador thought she might be found guilty?"

"Apparently. . . . And I have my cousin Margaret Lennox on her
knees begging for vengeance on that wicked woman who murdered
her son, her lovely boy, her Harry! Old Lennox is with Moray. They'll
blacken her face to their utmost! And there is the cunning Maitland
of Lethington who serves two sides. He is Moray's principal delegate
but for certain he is intriguing with my cousin Norfolk, and there is a
whisper that his wife, who was Mary Fleming, one of the Queen's
four Marys, has copied out the Casket letters, and he has sent them to
the Queen of Scots."

"Do you think her guilty?"

"I am not God," she said wearily. "I have not even read the letters.
. . . I tell you, Rob, I think many are guilty! I do not trust those Scots
lords one inch. Be sure they will only let such evidence be shown as
will suit them. Cecil very wisely asked for the appearance, as a witness, of Bothwell's French valet, Hubert Paris, whose deposition
seems to be the chief evidence apart from the letters. What happens?
He is hanged as soon as they get our request! He knew too much. . . .
Stone dead hath no fellow, as the popular saying goes. . . . They
can amend his deposition, they can amend the letters—but I dare not
let there be a verdict against Moray and his party! Let them be overthrown and there is chaos in Scotland for which we shall pay! Sussex
thinks Mary has a case against them—he does not specifically say

she can clear herself but only accuse them—but Cecil declares that we dare not let her give evidence in public as she demands. She would pull down the pillars of the house upon us all like Samson!"

"But if you cannot have a verdict on either side, what can you do?"

"I have told you. I will make the best compromise I can for her which will safeguard this realm. But who knows what will come out of this witches' broth cooking at York? I'll have them moved down here, where I at least can keep an eye on the intrigues! I'd like my wise Spirit to be a delegate. But he knows nothing of the emotions. You must be a delegate too, Rob, and we must have some that are supposed to support Mary, such as Arundel."

So the Conference was moved to London and sat in the Great Hall at Westminster. The Queen was at Hampton Court and she summoned the Earl of Leicester from the Conference to consult with her. The December sun was touching the river with a brilliant icy light as his barge ran smoothly to the landing-stage at Hampton Court. Against the stabbing brightness of the sky, its red-brick façade and the rich, elaborate gardens were drained of colour; roof, gable, tree and shrub were harshly outlined and dark. The air was filled with the strange odour of frost, sharp, pure and inhuman; underfoot the ground was crisp. The last of the dying sun was gilding the tapestries and sparkling on the window panes when Robert knelt before the Queen in the Long Gallery where she sat amongst her ladies.

It was never her will to eat in solemn state in the Presence Chamber, surrounded by the court, and she avoided it, except upon occasions of high ceremonial. Supper was served in a small room hung with greenish tapestries, holding in their shadowed folds all the depth of a sunless wood in which wandered a hunting party with hounds and horses, pale, glittering figures. Only a few of the Queen's senior ladies, amongst them his sister-in-law, that quiet woman the Countess of Warwick, were at table with her and her guest; they were waited on by the Maids of Honour who received the burnished silver dishes from the grooms of the chamber. Their wine was served in fantastic, gold-fretted goblets of Venetian glass, shimmering like bubbles in the wax lights. Robert watched the Queen's long fingers crumbling and playing with a manchet of new bread; a little of it she ate, but most she wasted. She never had a big appetite, but to-night, she scarcely took anything beyond soup. Lady Warwick noticed her brother-in-law's glance, and said quietly: "Robert, I wish you would persuade her Grace to eat more. She has eaten so little these past days that we are all afraid."

"You need not be," said Elizabeth. "I take what suits me."

"Come!" Robert urged her. "Sweet lady, you'll waste away if this is a sample of your meals. Look at me!"

"You eat too much, Rob!"

"I have a mighty appetite!" he confessed cheerfully.

"My poor ladies will be complaining to you next that as I cannot sleep much either, I wake them up to play cards. And the poor creatures' eyes are so heavy, that I win all too easily, and there is no sport."

"This", said he, "will not do at all!" He smiled, confident and tender, but not exceeding the bounds of Queen and favoured nobleman. If they had been alone he would have taken her by the shoulders to give her a gentle shake to reinforce his argument. She smiled back at him, a quick, sidelong and yet humorous smile, as if she read his thoughts.

When the meal was concluded, she announced that she had weighty business of State to discuss with my Lord of Leicester; laying her hand on his proffered arm, she swept into her book-lined cabinet. As he closed the door behind them, the wax lights flickered in the movement of air. She was like those small flames, he suddenly thought, intense, vibrating, endangered by the sudden gusts.

"No," he repeated. "This will not do at all! You are making yourself ill."

She made a swift movement with one long slender hand.

"I have a capacity", she said drily, "for surviving all things." She paused and then added irrelevantly: "Your sister-in-law is a pleasant woman."

"So my brother finds," he answered smiling.

"She's restful. . . ."

He thought: "And she's childless!" He was beginning to understand many things now, after ten years of almost incessant companionship with Elizabeth. This resentment against marriage and maternity in other women was like an unhealed wound which incautious fingers might suddenly probe. In those early days before the death of his wife, when she had hoped and believed that she would one day marry him and bear his children, it had not been there. Those were the days when she had been friendly with his sister, Mary Sidney. Now she preferred the quiet, childless Countess of Warwick. Another thing he understood too ; her sudden fancies for this handsome fellow and that, her furious flirtations, her brazen coquetries. It was a guard against that searing feeling of inadequacy and incompleteness now that she believed, irrevocably, that she was barren ; a guard and a reassurance to prove that she was still a woman desirable to men. So, comprehending now, his anger at her new favourites had ceased, an anger which had once been compounded between the ambitious dread of losing her favour, and natural male jealousy. He knew also that she was capable of sacrificing their love or anything belonging to it, for any move of statecraft, but in spite of these things, he never doubted her ultimate devotion to him. Sometimes it awed him, for before she had taken possession of his life, he had loved lightly. Strange, too, he thought, that the daughter of Henry VIII and Anne Boleyn should be so faithful!

He took her gently by the shoulders.

"You must get rest," he said. "Now what can I do for you? Shall we play cards till the sun rises? Or have in your musicians?"

"You can comfort me in better ways, Robin. . . . But there is much to do or rather discuss before. Now, what I say to you, is not as the Queen to one of her Chief Commissioners. I will, perhaps, explain some points there too, but Cecil has his brief, he knows what is to be done. I want to talk to you, Rob, as to the human being closest to me. Sit down there. I have here the letters of the Casket."

"What? The actual letters? None of us in London have seen them, yet. That is to come. *Her* men have marched out because the letters are to be produced!"

"I demanded them. They have been brought down closely guarded for my private reading, and they must go back for to-morrow's conference. The French originals and the English copies."

"Sadler told me they were mighty spicy! Love poems and one letter in particular which seems proof—if it's genuine! Norfolk was horrified at first, but now he appears to doubt them. Lethington has put certain ideas in his head."

"My cousin Norfolk! All ideas have to be put into his head, he has so few of his own!" But her quick irritation went, and a shadow passed over her face. "Spicy! Merry pothouse jests on souls in hell!"

"Do you think they are genuine?" he asked. She was a long time answering, so long that he wondered where her thoughts were.

"Genuine?" she repeated at length. "By what assessment? Ah, Rob, here—as so often—there is no verdict. Or rather there are two. Let us come to the first, the legal, the definite—that which can be proved or disproved. Look at this page of writing! Now at this. . . . The second is a letter which she wrote to me with her own hand."

"They appear the same."

"They do. Yet she has a hand easy enough to counterfeit. It is undisciplined. She always looks as if she were writing in a hurry. Her pen gallops. So do her thoughts. I repeat, it would be easy to forge. Again, that casket has been so long in the hands of her enemies. They both take out and put in what they will. Be sure they can employ skilled forgers! They can present the evidence to suit themselves. . . . I am certain only of two things. There was more than one party engaged upon the death of Henry Darnley. Those who blew up the house with gunpowder, were not the ones who strangled him in the garden. Amongst the ruling faction headed by Moray—there is guilt. Perhaps Moray himself is guilty. Who knows?"

"So——?"

"So—this. On the evidence given, there can be no absolute proof whether the letters are forgeries or not. But it is also impossible to declare the Queen of Scots innocent. . . . We must have the verdict which is no verdict. We must try to silence the facts—to muffle them —to hush them! Moray will be only too glad to assist in this. . . . We *dare* not let her speak! She must be denied that right." Swiftly she put her hands to her head with gesture he knew so well, palms pressed to the high brow, long fingers digging into the roots of that jewel-adorned red hair.

"Now for the second verdict, Robin. Which cannot be proved or disproved by any tribunal. It is what one's own heart tells—strengthened and tempered by one's knowledge of humanity. *I* believe these letters and poems genuine. There is one letter which I think no forger could create. It—and above all one sentence therein—gives the answer. At least—to me." She took up the papers, but did not start reading them yet.

"When one lies awake at night, Robin, with fever, pain or distress of mind and the darkness is painted with remembered faces, and remembered sounds seem to echo! Faces that crowd close to the fluttering, sick, yellow light of the bedside candle—think of the strange ideas which come without reason or coherence, a weird and ghastly procession! Do you know what I mean?"

"Yes. . . ."

"Such is this letter. It rambles like a nightmare. She is sitting by the bedside of the wretched youth whom once she believed that she loved—but now she hates him! He has fallen into a feverish sleep but he has begged her not to leave him. As much as his petty nature can, he loves her—poor rat! And she knows what she has come to do, but her heart shrinks from it. Yet she must go on. In the whole of her life, she has but one object left. To appease her own agony, she writes to the man to whom she belongs—body and soul. She spills out her thoughts in confusion—the confusion of delirium. I will not read aloud all her ramblings. you shall read the letter for yourself, but I will first read out part."

"She comes to the bedside of Darnley and this is what she writes: '*He said he did dream, and that he was so glad to see me that he thought he should die. . . .*' And again he begs her: '*I am young. . . . You will say that you have also pardoned me many times and that I return to my fault. May not a man of my age, for want of counsel, fail twice or thrice and miss of promise, and at the last repent and rebuke himself by his experience? . . . And I ask nothing but we may be at bed and table together as husband and wife; and if you will not, I will never rise from this bed. God knoweth that I am punished to have made my god of you and had no other mind but of you. . . .*' "

"Ah—poor devil!" said Robert softly. "Poor devil!"

"Aye!" Elizabeth declared. "One must pity him. Further on she writes he says '*that he could not mistrust me for Hiegate's word, for he could not believe that his own flesh (which was myself) could do him any hurt——*' This strikes her. Listen to what *she* says. '*. . . if I had not proof of his heart to be of wax and that mine were not a diamond, no stroke but coming from your hand, could make me but to have pity of him. . . .*' and yet again: '*You make me dissemble so much that I am afraid thereof with horror, and you make me almost to play the part of a traitor. Remember that if it were not for obeying, I had rather be dead. My heart bleedeth for it.*' And here is the sentence which, to me, sums up all. '*Alas! and I never deceived anybody; but I remit myself wholly to your will. . . .*'

"Read it, Rob, read the whole. It is unbearably long. It wanders eternally. She says herself that she cannot forbear from scribbling.

She must write down her tormented thoughts as they come."

He read, with candles burning between them, and she watched him. At last he looked up and their eyes met. Elizabeth spoke first.

"She's guilty," she said quietly.

"So I think! And yet I pity her!"

"I pity her from the bottom of my heart. . . ."

"What are you going to do?" he asked at last.

"Cecil will find the formula which will blanket as much as possible. He will always find formulas! He has found one to prevent my meeting her. As I am yet unmarried, it might damage my reputation to meet a woman accused of murder and adultery! My reputation. . . . He is like a careful father. We must try to make an arrangement with Moray. In time she may go back and have the shadow of power and he the substance. For that I will work. But I will not give her up to them to be put to death. Never."

"In the meanwhile?"

"She must stay here. With every comfort and honour. But watched and guarded lest she do harm. That is what I dread. Wherever she goes, she brings trouble!"

"You will not meet her?"

"Not now! It is too late. . . . Once I refused the chance, once she, and once circumstance. It will not come again. I cannot face her, Rob, because she will not understand any of my reasons, and I have denied her the right to answer her accusers and condemn them. She thinks I have judged her, but as I said—I will not be judge! Who am I to judge her? What about your wife?"

He caught her wrists. "*You* had no part in her death!"

"No, but I wanted her dead!"

He was silent and she spoke again. "To me this tells everything. 'Alas! and I never deceived anybody; but I remit myself wholly to your will.' " He heard her sigh before she continued: "Alas! and *I* have deceived many; but I did none of it for myself."

Chapter Seven

※———◈———※

Night lay softly on the great mass of Leicester House. Around the windows' edges, in the void of a suddenly outflung door, a warmer, yellower, closer light challenged the cold remote glitter of the stars. There was a stillness in the great stables, except for an occasional drowsy hoof-beat; the hawks slept on their perches, the hounds in their kennels. In the daytime, it was a centre of pulsating earthy energy, sleek flanks glossy in the sunlight from vigorous strapping, shod hoofs clinking on the cobblestones, rich pungent smells rising from the steaming straw tossed in heaps by busy forks. Always bustle, men and horses coming and going in the greatest stables in the country except her Majesty's own, as befitted those which belonged to her Majesty's Master of Horse; full of gallants and grooms serving the Bear and Ragged Staff, of barbs and jennets from Naples and Andalusia, Great Horses from Flanders and Almain massive to carry a man in steel, of swift deerhounds, stubborn boarhounds and savage, tenacious mastiffs to bait a bear, of ger-falcons, goshawks and peregrines, the wild, free haggards (which his lordship preferred) and the more manageable eyasses; all for the service and pleasure of his lordship, and his lordship's Gentlemen of the Horse, occupation for his stable-men and falconers, and provision of a perpetual spectacle for the onlookers who came to gape. Now night's dark blanket lay on the huge yard and its buildings, driving the life, light and warmth indoors. Only a handful of stablemen in their crimson liveries came forward in the torch light, to take the horses of the small band which had ridden to the main door.

The usher welcoming them had a swift: "Good even, m'lord!" for the Earl of Pembroke; a constant and trusted guest. But he paused for a moment, blinking his eyes a trifle at the tall man, now throwing back

his cloak of heavy black velvet, laced with gold. Here was one unexpected! Since when was the head of the great house of Howard
friendly to the Bear and Ragged Staff of Dudley? "Good even,
m'lord Duke! Good even, Sir Nicholas!" To the pages coming
swiftly behind him, as he bowed the visitors into the great hall, he
was quick with his orders. "His Grace of Norfolk's cloak! My Lord
Pembroke's cloak! Sir Nicholas Throckmorton's cloak!"

On the scented rushes their feet fell softly, no echo rising to the
high rafters of the great hall. Supper had first filled and then emptied
it, only a cluster of men sat at one of the long tables, watching two
of their number dice. My Lord Leicester's gentlemen—Gentlemen
of the Horse, Gentlemen of the Chamber, Secretaries and Clerks—
had ridden out to fill London's taverns, cock pits and bear gardens.
They were young, with many wild blades amongst them. What bold
and ambitious lad would not want to attach himself to the Earl of
Leicester? And there was no feminine society in this house, no dances
in the Long Gallery, to hold men of an evening. Lord Leicester had
no countess to preside over this great household, to have her retinue
of gentlewomen with their tiring-women and chambermaids. His
bold blades were no monks but they must find their sweethearts
under other roofs. From cellar to tiles, it was a solidly uncompromis-
ingly masculine household.

"His lordship is awaiting you," said the usher, conducting the
guests to the great staircase. Their passage was marked through the
hall, the dicers stopped their game and turned their heads, two in
particular giving each other significant glances. But there was no time
for comments. The hospitality of Leicester House was famous, it had
to reflect its lord's magnificent heedless generosity. There were some
of Norfolk's and Pembroke's gentlemen standing in the hall. Richard
Verney pushed away the dice and rose to his feet, to bid them welcome, calling for sack and muscadell. He was like a quick, smooth
fox with his narrow dark-red head; rumour whispered, as swift and
pitiless a killer as a fox when he had a rapier in his hand.

The long gangling lad who had been watching the dicers and then
had gaped at the noblemen ascending the stairs, felt that he was
now in the very centre of the world. Young Christopher Blount,
belonging to that useful and skilful tribe, distant kinsmen and faithful followers to Leicester, had not long ridden from his country
manor to join the Earl's household. Now, seeing so many great men

pass in, he felt that he too was part of these activities which seemed to be steadily gathering momentum, till he also would be borne up on the crest of the wave. He looked at Digby putting away the dice in their leather bottle, pretty-boy Digby, with his soft dark eyes and wet red lips, in his graceful suit of dove-grey satin, slashed with silver and tied with crimson points, Digby, who was nearly as dangerous with a rapier as Verney, men said. He was smiling his rather secretive smile; soon he was to ride out into the night on confidential business for his lord. Verney knew what it was, young Christopher did not.

The guests were drawn to the table and the goblets filled. Christopher sat down again beyond Tom Underhill, the clerk whose task was to catalogue his lordship's belongings, a task which constantly ran away from him, for how could he keep up with that golden stream, gifts from her Majesty, gifts from great nobles, wealthy merchants and plain squires who wanted his lordship's favour, presentations from Corporations and plunder from the Spanish Main? And as swiftly the golden stream poured out in his lordship's magnificent spendthriftness.

The wine went down and jests came merrily. The group began to coalesce, hosts and guests. They were talking of the seized bullion, borrowed by King Philip of Spain from his Genoese bankers to pay his troops under Alva in the Netherlands, which storm and channel pirates had driven for shelter into English harbours.

"And cold harbour the Genoese ships found it!" cried a fellow of Pembroke's, tugging at his yellow beard.

"Why," said smooth Verney, "the Genoese agent in London told her Gracious Majesty that the bullion was not the King of Spain's till it was handed over to Alva in Antwerp."

"So her Gracious Majesty, with one of her choice oaths, declared that she'd borrow it, instead of her brother-in-law, and save him the cost of repayment!" cried one of the Howard men.

They laughed loudly, contemplating her red-headed Majesty appropriating the gold, the astounded fury and indignation of his Majesty of Spain, the rage and need of the Duke of Alva his Viceroy, the spluttering menaces of Don Guerau de Spes, the new Spanish Ambassador. In the middle of the laughter, Digby, who had been eyeing the hall clock, got quietly up, muffled himself in his cloak and slipped out to the stables. It was always merry to hear of foreigners being caught out but—— Some began to think of the consequences.

Zenith

"That old badger Cecil is burrowing against Spain," said a Norfolk man. "He'll call the tune but we'll pay the piper!"

The shadow of the world's mightiest power fell upon them. How could they withstand Spain? What was Cecil trying to do, persuading her Majesty into perilous courses? There was no love for Mr. Secretary Cecil in Leicester House. Its bold fellows were convinced of one thing; if it were not for the secretary with his cold grey eyes and his cold grey brain, they would have followed their lord in a splendid procession—as splendid as the Coronation ten years ago— to Westminster Abbey to see him joined in holy wedlock to her Gracious Majesty herself—and let no man put asunder! Then up they would go, up the golden ladder after his lordship, King's men!

Upstairs, at a door on the first-floor landing, the usher announced: "The noble gentlemen, m'lord!"

Robert came forward eagerly, embraced Pembroke, that faithful friend, extended a hand to the Duke of Norfolk—"My lord Duke, this is a happy day!"—"Happy for me, my Lord Leicester!"—and then clasped Nicholas Throckmorton's.

"It's a cold night! What say you to some hippocras?"

It came, steaming and spicy, in silver-gilt tankards, engraved with the Bear and Ragged Staff. A fire was leaping in the chimney, making the silver fire-dogs glow as if they were molten, throwing tongues of light and shade on the great tapestry of the "Story of Samson" which sprawled across the whole of one wall. Robert watched his guests sipping their hippocras, and thought what a long way he had come, how much water had flowed under London Bridge since those early days when the only duke in England had led the opposition against him as a greedy upstart too high in her Majesty's favour. How often had Norfolk and he literally been at each other's throats, rapiers halfway out of scabbards? And there was that never-to-be-forgotten occasion after he had been playing tennis. He had won a hard-fought game, and then had come striding up to the spectators' gallery, saluting those therein who were giving him applause, the Queen in the midst of them, making him swagger under her tender appraisal. He knew he looked well—whether in his damascened tilting armour or in the finest silks and velvets cut by Master Whittell—or now, playing tennis in his thin cambric shirt, which was damp and sticking tightly to his strong body. (His wise sister Mary had once said, shaking her head: "You are far too handsome, Robin! That is why you

222

are so mightily spoilt!") He had paused triumphantly before the Queen, and then had taken the handkerchief she was holding, to wipe his face with it, pushing back the black forelock which was lying plastered on his wet brow. Norfolk had sprung forward, shouting: "You insolent hound!" and had struck him in the face. In a second, he had returned the blow, and they would have been fighting with their bare hands had not several men seized each, and Elizabeth had roared out her usual oath, declaring that she would have arrested any that brawled in her presence, be he duke, lord or esquire.

Those had been the early days, when they had been so much in love that it had been impossible to conceal the happy intimacy between them. The court had been perpetually scandalized. Well—five and twenty was different to five and thirty—or rather six and thirty! That excitement in each other, its passionate intensity, the novelty, the very danger had died down in ten years, to be replaced by a relationship which was quieter, calmer, deeper and stronger. How deep and strong it was, he hardly realized. Only the years themselves could prove it, but he did know that it was impossible to picture an existence apart from Elizabeth.

There were still factions against him at court, but Norfolk was not his direct opponent any more. Sussex had replaced him. And there was always an eternal jealousy and resentment in Robert because Elizabeth leaned so much on the counsel of Cecil. She would hardly ever take a step unless she had learned his opinion on it first—though as often as not, after hearing it, she would pursue a deliberately contrary course! "But", thought Robert, "I do believe, were it not for this man, she would have married me. . . ." This was the principal reason why he was joining that ambiguous scheme which had multiple ramifications and objectives, many of them shadowy. The Duke of Norfolk was to solve one of the hardest problems of the reign by wedding the Queen of Scots, and therefore why should not the Earl of Leicester wed the Queen of England? They would overthrow Cecil with his opposition to both marriages, and his dangerous policy of enmity to Spain which amongst other things would cripple England's trade. The north, the feudal, remote, Catholic north would also be pacified. The Earls of Northumberland and Westmorland were with them. (Robert was not too sure in his inmost heart of those same earls.) In the south besides Norfolk and Robert, there were the Earls of Pembroke and Arundel, Lord Lumley and now that eminent diplomat and former colleague of Cecil's, Sir Nicholas Throckmorton. Robert knew that he could count on his brother Warwick, Master of the Ordnance, his brothers-in-law, Sidney, Lord Deputy in Ireland, and the Earl of Huntingdon, himself remotely in the line of succession. They would have a majority in the Council. Elizabeth might be angry at first, she might even be alarmed, but that was when *he* would take charge of events, and she would be filled with gratitude and admiration. At least, that was what he hoped. . . .

Nicholas Throckmorton was talking of the Queen of Scots, his thin dark face eager. He who had been somewhat of a Puritan, a colleague of Cecil and Bacon, and had in his diplomatic capacity been enforced to carry angry messages between the two Queens—one would scarcely have expected him to be a partisan of the Queen of Scots. And yet he was talking of her with that eagerness, tenderness, and even devotion.

"She is a woman to love and be loved," he said. "And she has never yet found one worthy of her. The ivy needs an oak, a wall to cling to for support. She has never had anything but rotten oaks, crumbling walls." (Thought Robert: "Any countryman would tell you that ivy can in time kill the strongest oak, crumble the strongest wall. . . .") "Her first marriage! She was a child wedded to another child, a poor sickly one, and her innocent devotion to him and his to her was pathetic. You cannot conceive what an exquisite young creature she was in those days, in France. La Reinette, they called her, the little Queen, and Ronsard himself said that no verses of his could do her justice." ("Throckmorton is in love with her, too," thought Robert.) "Her second! Young Darnley may have had a fine appearance, the outward man might be well enough, but the inward! Weak, base, vicious. . . ."

"To bring in the murder pack to kill Riccio in her presence was dastardly," agreed Robert, but his thoughts were straying to that strange and dreadful letter which he had first read beside Elizabeth at Hampton Court. ("God knoweth that I am punished to have made my god of you." . . . Poor devil! Poor rat!)

"And Bothwell!" exclaimed Throckmorton. "That bloodstained ruffian! If ever she turned to him, it was only the groping of her defencelessness towards strength. Anything else is calumny of her enemies."

("And this", thought Robert, "is the same Throckmorton who

224

sent us a dispatch from Scotland when she was imprisoned in Loch-leven Castle, telling us that he had heard from Maitland of Lething-ton, that Mary had refused the lords' demand to divorce Bothwell and consent to his trial for the murder of Darnley, even though this meant her return to the throne. She had declared that she would give up her kingdom and all she possessed and follow Bothwell to the end of the world in her petticoat, and all she asked was to be put with him in a boat—and let it drift where it would! *That's* the mood and spirit of the woman who wrote the letters and the sonnets of the casket!")

Aloud, he said cautiously: "The letters showed a stronger feeling than that!"

"The letters", said Norfolk with finality, "are forgeries. Lething-ton himself told me. He said she had a hand easy to counterfeit, and that he himself had often copied it. For amusement, one must suppose!"

(Thought Robert: "The wily Lethington can be convincing at two different times in two different opinions! Yet—Elizabeth said it too. That she had a hand easy to counterfeit and her enemies had every opportunity for forgery—so absolute proof is impossible. But Elizabeth believes the letters are genuine—in her inmost heart.")

"And now", said Throckmorton, turning to the Duke, "she at last has a man worthy of her!"

"The Queen of Scots has done me the great honour of accepting my devotion," said Norfolk portentously. "As her husband, it will be my duty and my pride to clear her from all calumny and restore her to her rightful place."

"Which will be an excellent precedent for Leicester, here, to wed our Queen!" said Pembroke quickly.

"Certainly, certainly!"

("Confound his Howard pride!" thought Robert. "He acts as if he were King, giving his permission!")

"Then true friendship might be restored between the royal ladies," suggested Throckmorton hopefully.

"The Succession must be settled—upon the Queen of Scots," demanded Norfolk. "At the time of our respective marriages."

"The Succession can only come to the Queen of Scots", said Robert angrily, "provided *our* marriage is childless!"

"Of course, of course!"

They stared at each other, like two swordsmen about to cross blades. Robert thought: "Confound him! What does he know?" Pembroke tactfully changed the subject: "Who is William Cecil to oppose such a just and reasonable settlement? I recollect that in the reign of her Grace's father, the Minister, Thomas Cromwell, was seized at a meeting of the Privy Council, and charged by the other Councillors who had him put under arrest."

"That", said Norfolk, "is what *we* shall do! We can charge him with endangering the safety of the realm, by breaking the ancient friendship with Spain, by most unjustly causing her Majesty to hold in custody that noble lady the Queen of Scots to appease the ruling faction in Scotland——"

"By ruining England's trade!" broke in Throckmorton. "The bullion is seized and what then? Alva lays an embargo on our trade with the Netherlands and confiscates all English merchants' stocks. The Queen retorts by confiscating the goods of Spanish and Netherland merchants, and I admit on balance, we had the better of it! But what's to come in the future? Antwerp is our biggest market, the export of cloth the very basis of our trade, as the export of raw wool was in bygone years——"

They debated it. The cloth trade, the merchants of London who must support them, and another and very different supporter, Henry Percy, Earl of Northumberland, the woes of that wronged and fascinating lady the Queen of Scots, the iniquities of Cecil who would not see the fitness of Thomas, Duke of Norfolk, to wed that same Mary, Queen of Scots, any more than he would admit the fitness of Robert, Earl of Leicester, to wed Elizabeth, Queen of England. Robert sometimes wondered what the last-named lady might think of their speech. Norfolk might say: "After all the Queen's Grace is a woman and it is men's business to rule!" But the Queen's Grace was rather more than a woman, if at the same time she was rather less. If this marriage —striven for during ten years—was at last achieved, would her attitude change? The Book of Common Prayer contained in its Marriage Service, the pledge for wives "to love, honour and obey". But somehow he could not see Elizabeth honouring and obeying him. She was quite capable of altering the words of the service if she ever came to wed—she could be high-handed with the Church when she pleased. He remembered, with a sudden grin, her shout at an unhappy preacher in the middle of his sermon: "Leave that! The matter is now thread-bare!"

Zenith

He walked through the Great Hall with his departing guests, his arm thrown loosely round Pembroke's shoulders, and bade them farewell at the main door. Then hearing a clock strike above the sound of the clattering hoofs, he turned swiftly, crossed the hall again and ran up the stairs as lightly as a boy with something of a boy's eagerness. He had the strange feeling that he was going back into an earlier existence.

The young fellow who had been married to the now almost forgotten Amy, had wearied so quickly of her and their life on his country property. Whenever possible he had hurried to court, where his father had ruled England, and the court ladies had been only too glad to give their favours to his handsome son. . . . Those were the days when he had loved quickly and lightly and had ridden away easily from brief passions. Then Elizabeth had taken possession of the whole of his existence, both as woman and as Queen. For ten years he had been faithful to her, though he was, as he would one day write—"a man frail". But now the first flame of their ardour had burned out and with it the piquance of novelty; Elizabeth had been sick and harassed for this past troubled year since the Queen of Scots had landed in England. She did not want a passionate lover so much as a devoted, tender friend. The Marriage Service had other words of wisdom, this time for husbands, when it separated "to love" and "to cherish". The woman Elizabeth wanted cherishing, she wanted sympathy and deep kindness. That he could give, and sometimes he thought that the confidence between them as private individuals reminded him of that between such a devoted couple as the Sidneys. But when he came to their public lives, the great gulf yawned, a gulf which could only be bridged by their marriage. As Queen to one of her principal councillors, she would swear and storm at him, crush him if he attempted to oppose her, and keep him on his level far beneath her. "God's death, my lord! I will have here but one mistress and no masters!" It was, perhaps, a combination of these circumstances which had thrown him into the arms of Douglass Sheffield.

Women had run after him during that past ten years, an intense difficulty with his temperament and Elizabeth's almost frenzied jealousy. The newly widowed Douglass was an exquisite creature, with beauty, youth and high breeding. She seemed to understand that it was impossible for him to love openly, let alone marry; he did not dream that her adoration planned that he too would love her so much that he could not give her up. *He* had once fallen into this error; believing that Elizabeth loved him too much not to marry him. He never concerned himself with what went on in Douglass's mind; she did not belong to the important things in his life, his high ascent of the steep and dangerous ladder of power and his enduring but complicated relationship with the Queen. (If this latest plot was successful and at last he married the Queen, Douglass would have, immediately, to vanish from his life.) Douglass belonged to the moment, but the moment was sweet.

Digby must have brought her by now. He opened the door of his chamber which gave on to the corridor leading to the private stair. Yes! That must be her step, he thought with a breathless pleasure. She came, with that graceful smoothness which made him think of a beautiful animal which might suddenly flee wildly away, holding her taffeta riding-mask in her hand as if she had only just drawn it off. The light from the fire ran shimmering over the red silk of her dress. He caught her up suddenly and carried her in, to the great velvet chair where Norfolk had been sitting. The perfume from her hair filled his nostrils.

"Red rose!" he said, and then asked: "Did Digby attend to your comfort? I told him to take every care of you!"

"Oh, he did!" She held out her hands to him. ("But her hands are not so perfect as Elizabeth's," thought one part of his mind. Nevertheless he kissed them.) "As we were riding to the side door, Robert, I saw a company departing from the front. By the torches I recognized my cousin, Tom. All is well, he did not see me! I didn't know he was a friend of yours?"

"Norfolk?" he shrugged. "Why—we are both Privy Councillors. We have affairs of State to discuss!" He straddled his legs with a confident gesture. "Nothing to weary your lovely head with! Such matters as the cloth trade."

"But that's important, isn't it?"

He stooped down, enclosing her face between his hands. There was a strange little pride leaping in him. She, too, by birth, was a Howard and she saw the Head of her House coming to associate with him.

"Never you mind about the cloth trade, lovely one! Your cousin Tom and I—we'll settle it!"

When he was kissing her he thought of how, when he was making love to Elizabeth, she would sometimes say, her cheek still pressed to his: "Rob—that last report from Antwerp——"

That she and he put the same things in the same places, that her enormous absorption in her crown dominated her as much as his hunger for that crown dominated him—that all else was secondary—he did not see.

Chapter Eight

The Queen was playing on the virginals when Secretary Cecil was announced. Her long thin hands halted upon the keyboard; for a moment she was still as if lost in thought. Then she turned and contemplated him.

"Sir Spirit, you look pensive! You may be seated," pointing to a nearby stool. "What is upon your mind?"

"Your Grace, it is with the utmost reluctance that I feel compelled to place the resignation of my secretaryship in your Grace's hands."

He was looking at her Grace's actual hands as they lay, quite still now, in her black velvet lap. She had taken off all her rings to play except the Coronation ring from which she would never part. Her fingers were very slender, very white, he thought, and yet they looked strong—even menacing.

"Now," she said, "I would wish to hear the whole of the matter. When I disagree with you upon a point of importance, you either threaten resignation or you take to your bed for a while. . . . Then we arrive at a *modus vivendi*! No! Don't argue with me. We understand each other very well, as old friends should."

"Your Grace is very good! It is not of my wish, but I have encountered such opposition in your Grace's Council, such enmity—yes, I can say enmity to the point of threats—that it is impossible for me any longer to conduct affairs. I have been blamed for the present conditions in the Low Countries, and the Duke of Norfolk——"

"Ha!" she interrupted. "My cousin Norfolk is mightily concerned all of a sudden with the Antwerp trade! I have observed it. He is veritably flirting with those disgruntled merchants who do not believe in the proposed venture to Hamburg." She leaned forward suddenly —he thought with the swift stoop of a striking hawk—"You have communicated with Killigrew at Hamburg?"

230

"Your Grace, he has the matters in hand, and the Hanseatics are making a hopeful response."

"Good. We'll show them yet! As if *I* didn't care more for the cloth trade, for the whole city of London from its richest merchant to its youngest 'prentice boy, than the Duke of Norfolk! *And* he has a far more dangerous flirtation——"

"Your Grace knows?"

"I need to know. With the Queen of Scots! Plague take that woman. . . . Can you make no arrangement with the Earl of Moray?"

"The Earl of Moray is not at all anxious to have his sister return to Scotland, under any terms, your Grace."

"Nor do I blame him!"

"He did indicate, your Grace, that her marriage to a suitable Englishman might help matters forward."

"But to find a suitable Englishman! There's the rub. My cousin Norfolk fancies himself in the role. She'd spin him round, as children spin a top!"

"I have a record, your Grace, of his and the Queen of Scots' communications with the Spanish Ambassador."

"With the Spanish Ambassador? Aha—the Spanish Ambassador! He's worse than Quadra. And we can scarcely hope for another plague to relieve us of *him.* . . ."

"She is also in communication with the northern earls. I have a long file of my agents' reports, your Grace."

"I believe she is Eris, Goddess of Discord, in person!"

"And there is also a decided majority in the Council and support in the south. The Earls of Arundel and Pembroke, the Lord Lumley——" he paused. He knew that the Earl of Leicester was also deeply implicated but he considered that it was wiser not to allude to this at present. Her Grace was not wholly reasonable upon the subject of the Earl of Leicester. But her discernment was never sharper in other matters.

"And also," she said, "you believe yourself to be in some measure of danger?"

"Yes, your Grace. I have learned that the matter may come to a head at the next Council meeting."

"And what", she asked, "do they think *I* shall be doing?"

She had got to her feet and was pacing up and down, up and down. He thought there was a suspicion of a limp in her tense movements.

For the past few days she had not danced, he recollected. Her voice broke into his thoughts.

"*I* shall make a point of coming to the next Council meeting. We shall see! My Spirit—*I* don't abandon my friends!"

"Your Grace is very good." The words were conventional but neither of them mistook their deep sincerity. He added with concern: "Your Grace has injured your leg?"

" 'Tis no matter. There was a bruise above my ankle, I think I must have had a blow when riding a'hunting, and it seems somewhat inflamed now. But I tell you—it is no matter! It will pass."

But he believed her to be in considerable pain. He knew that when she was troubled in any way, it was her practice to play upon the virginals. It seemed to comfort her and distract her thoughts. She now returned to her instrument and the music rose softly beneath her long fingers, first the air for a solemn pavane moving with conscious dignity, and then breaking into a lighter frolicsome vein, as of a country dance. A chord rang out which was followed by silence. She had turned again.

"So that was what troubled you!" she said.

"Your Grace, it is often said that all misfortunes come together." But she had leaned forward and was taking both his hands in hers.

"Sir Spirit, you will tell me *all* your troubles. I think there is some personal matter too! That's what old friends are for. Do you recall that time I nearly wept upon your shoulder?"

"So your Grace remembers?"

"I forget nothing. . . . Now—what is this matter?"

"Your Grace, my son is a grievous disappointment to me. My eldest child, Thomas. No care, no advice, I may say no money, has been spared upon him. He has had the best tutors, the best examples. He has been sent abroad. But to no purpose. He has no depth—either of intellect or diligence. All he takes seriously is the game of tennis to the neglect of his classics. He brawls and roisters. He eats too much and drinks more. He has become a spending sot, fit only to keep a tennis court."

"Time may mend him," she said slowly. "And you have another son, Robert. I think he is a clever youth."

"He is, though perhaps I should not praise him. He is intelligent and studious. All I could ask in that respect. But he is misshapen."

"His back can't harm his brains."

Zenith

"Your Grace, it was perhaps foolishness on my part but I have always dreamt and planned that my son should succeed me as your Minister——"

"And you thought I would not take him because he is a hunchback! Spirit, you should know me better! I admit—I like a pretty fellow. Perhaps it is a weakness. . . . I know, whether the Earl of Leicester picks a rose, or launches his horse in a gallop in the lists—or merely crosses a room—he does it with such perfect grace that it is a pleasure to behold him." She sighed and then her tone changed, became quicker, harder. "But what has *that* to do with affairs of State? I can value a good brain—if your son Robert has one-quarter of your ability, I can do well with him!"

The secretary could only express the fullness of his heart by raising her hands to his lips. If her wilfulness, her obstinacy, her frequent inability to admit *his* arguments, her storms of rage, sometimes drove him distracted—such moments as these could make up for everything. Unwittingly he had to thrust a finger into her concealed wound.

"Your Grace is very kind in the matter of my children. I would you had children of your own. . . ."

Her hands in his stiffened. Then she said, with cynical harshness: "What are children but trouble?"

She got to her feet and with uneven stride had reached the window, leaning on the sill, with her back to him. Still unwitting, he went on probing.

"I have always felt that your Grace would be an excellent mother." Then something in the absolute rigidity of that figure made him pause. It was a little while before she answered him but her voice was calm, though it had a flicker of mocking amusement.

"I have four million children and a mighty trouble they are to me sometimes! For they think they know better than I do, what is good for them. But they do not!" Again she turned, and came swinging back to him with that long man's stride, checked a little by her limp. "You and I," she said. "*We* rule England, you and I!"

In the Council Chamber, the light fell in long shafts from the tall windows, framed in curtains like velvet columns, The Councillors stood about in small groups, like chessmen momentarily abandoned by the players. The Duke of Norfolk was alone, apart from all others, contemplating his own greatness. The Earl of Leicester had his legs a-straddle, his thumbs in his sword belt, his chin tilted defiantly. Behind him were his followers, the Earl of Pembroke, who was his shadow, and his brother and brother-in-law, the Earls of Warwick and Huntingdon. Norfolk had determined to open the proceedings against the secretary and Robert felt that *he* should have done so—to impress and reassure Elizabeth when she learned of it. He turned from Norfolk, who had the air of standing for his portrait, to another little group which was coalescing around the Earl of Arundel.

An usher came like a stone thrown suddenly into a pool of still water.

"The Queen's most excellent Majesty proposes to attend the Council."

Norfolk moved irresolutely, looked at Arundel, looked back at Robert, and found no reassurance from either. The pose fell away for the portrait of Thomas, by the grace of God, King-Consort of England, Scotland and Ireland.

"My Lord," he said to Robert. "This places a different complexion on the matter. Seeing that you have her Majesty's ear, it would perhaps be better if *you* opened the proceedings."

Robert was obdurate.

"I think we have just decided", he reminded him, "that you, my lord duke, were the most fitting man!"

It was not the Queen's custom to attend her Council except on occasions. Had she got wind of their intentions? Robert found himself smiling with a sort of appraisal, though he was utterly confounded. She was equal to anything—his dear, damnable, disconcerting love! No wonder that in all the taverns of London, there was a delighted roar at her caustic jests, her quips, her crashing oaths, her undefeated repartee! But at this moment, he wished himself anywhere else. . . .

She came in, walking with pride, "high and disposedly", although a limp marred her step. One hand rested on the shoulder of Sir William Cecil, but nobody imagined that she was seeking support. She was dressed with an almost fantastic gorgeousness in purple velvet and cloth of silver, sewn stiffly with seed pearls; ropes of pearls hung from her neck under the enormous fluted cartwheel ruff, others encircled her waist and banded her hair. Robert looked at her eyes and then looked swiftly away again. He had met such a glance when about to cross swords with an adversary; she stared at her councillors as if she were a swordsman about to engage. They bowed low and then turned to Norfolk. He began—but the wind was out of his sails. He had pictured himself swooping upon the overawed secretary, now standing demurely beside that glittering figure whose relentless eyes probed into his very brain. He retailed the woes of the city of London now that the Low Countries were closed to them by the Duke of Alva's embargo. He admitted to himself that the matter seemed out of his hands and he was no longer directing it.

"My dear cousin, I am most happy to see how deeply at heart you have the welfare of the city of London! I am sure that you will be happy to hear the excellent prospects of establishing the Hanseatic city of Hamburg as a depot in the place of Antwerp. All the merchandise which should have been despatched to Antwerp in this past year is to be shortly sent to Hamburg."

But at last Norfolk had his cue, something to counter.

"Your Grace, I have reason to believe that the Duke of Alva might even intercept the merchant fleet. And there is great peril from privateers."

"So also thought I! I have ordered Admiral Winter to convoy the merchant fleet with his strongest squadron. I do not think either the Duke of Alva or any privateers will venture."

(Thought Robert Leicester: "Why did *I* not think of that? She is superb. .... I've often cursed her delays, her dilatoriness, her caution —but when the need comes, she can strike!")

The rest of the Council meeting went according to the Queen's plan, not that of her Councillors. Anyone who spoke to the contrary was stared out of countenance. When she swept from the Council Chamber, Cecil following her, they looked at one another.

"Someone must approach her Grace personally," declared Norfolk. He turned hopefully to Robert.

"A committee," responded Robert, but no volunteers came forward for a committee.

"The south of England, especially London, is so devoted to her Grace that we cannot attempt to impose our will upon her," said the Earl of Arundel.

"And I told Don Guerau to inform the Duke of Alva that Cecil would soon be overthrown!" said Norfolk, moodily.

"The less we have of foreign interference", said Robert, "the better!" He knew now, in his heart, that he had abandoned the conspiracy.

But Norfolk, thinking of the tenderly insistent letters of the Queen of Scots, the assurances given and received by the Duke of Alva and the urging of the leaders of the north—already embattled for the ancient religion and ancient ways—felt that he was a leaf caught up in furious gusts of wind, to be swirled here and there, contrary to his volition.

As the Queen and Cecil walked down the long corridor, the secretary said: "Your Grace was superb!" He was not greatly given to praising her to her face. She laughed.

"It was not so much. There was no *man* amongst them. Except my Lord of Leicester, and his heart is not in the matter!"

Cecil was relieved that she had observed Lord Leicester's part without his having to tell her.

"Yes, your Grace!"

"I'll draw it all out of Lord Leicester. Wait and see!"

That evening as Lord Leicester knelt beside her chair and her long fingers caressingly moved the hair from his brow, he told her the greater part of what he knew. He did not, of course, tell her that they had proposed to seize her Secretary of State and charge him with treason to the realm, nor did he tell her that he saw himself sweeping away all opposition and emerging in the role of conqueror when she would see him as her rightful lord. He told her of the opposition and discontent in the country, in the feudal north and the merchant city, of the belief that Cecil must go; he told her that Norfolk wished to marry the Queen of Scots. She said very little; those fingers seemed to have a life of their own as when they played upon the virginals. He felt that her brain was working furiously, but he knew little of its processes. Rather apprehensively, he asked her what she thought of the marriage.

"Why does he not tell me of it?" was all that she said. Her fingers strayed lightly across Robert's brow. Finally she spoke again in that same quiet voice.

"He is a conduit—a pipe to carry the ideas of others. But the conduit pipe does not know from whence the waters flow, nor where to."

Robert was with her at Greenwich, the day she saw her ships go down river to the new venture. A high wind was blowing, whistling alike in the bare branches of the trees of the palace garden, and in the rigging of the ships; cracking like great whips in the tugging, bellying canvas of the sails, painted and emblazoned in rich colours and heraldic devices. More and more sails ran up, their scarlets, blues and yellows swelling, as the ships came farther down river and the wind grew stronger. Some which had not yet unfurled their full spread of bright canvas, were towed by rowboats; there were small boats all about them, like darting water insects, hailing and speeding their departure. The river's banks were black with people to cheer the city's attempt to defy the Duke of Alva and his master, Spain. The tall carracks were heavy with piled merchandise, carrying the prayers and the very lifeblood of London, and around them like dogs guarding a flock, were the lower, narrower ships of Winter's squadron, with their broadside grin of black cannon mouths. As each vessel passed the Royal Standard at Greenwich, it fired a salute and white plumes of smoke coiled above the wind-ruffled steel-coloured water. Some of the ships had bands on deck, trumpets, fifes and drums, and the wind seemed to whirl up snatches of music and fling them to the watchers on the river banks. They were cheering—watchers and sailors—and the wind threw about the roar of their voices, too. The last small boats were falling back now, as under their full spread of canvas the ships made for the estuary and the open sea beyond.

Elizabeth was gazing after them, her body poised and taut, her head thrown back. Her cloak was slipping off her shoulders, and fearing the keen wind for her, Robert drew it on, close about her. She did not seem to notice.

"Are you seeing visions?" he asked her, and had to repeat his remark before she answered.

"Yes," she said. "Yes and no. I was seeing my ships sailing out to the ends of the earth. . . . And I was trying to calculate the forthcoming profits of the Hamburg trade!"

"You are the most extraordinary woman that ever lived!"

"That might be." But she was turning to him with an eager smile: "Ah—Robin! What comes over the men of this country when they get aboard ship? They shape indifferently as soldiers, but let them get a deck beneath their feet in place of dry land and they fight with the fury and skill of devils! And they fear nothing. . . . Nothing! Neither edicts of the Pope, nor the might of Spain, nor the floating mountains of ice from the frozen north, nor seas as high as their mastheads, nor all the unknown perils of the yet unknown globe! Philip—or his heirs—will curse the day he forbade them to trade with the New World. If they can't do honest trade, they'll plunder his plate ships. And Alva will lift the trade embargo or ruin the Low Countries! I tell you—nothing will stop those ships!

"Don Guerau curses Hawkins and his fellows, and I tell him that *I* can't stop the seamen of Devon and Cornwall. . . . Stop them? They play my game and they don't ask me to own them, if it's for the safety of this country. Pirates, Don Guerau calls them! Saucy sea cocks—devil's darlings! God bless them—nothing will ever stop them!" She laughed heartily, her eyes sparkling. "Many's the profit I've made from investing in their ventures—like you do."

"I love the brave fellows!" declared Robert.

"And so do I! Though I'm all horror, very properly, for Philip's Ambassador. They let the golden blood out of the veins of Philip's empire. . . . Norfolk and his party may want me to grovel to Spain, but I tell you there's a far larger number in this country that would have me hoist the banner of the Reformed Religion and assail the greatest King on earth—to aid their most bloodily oppressed co-religionists in the Low Countries. Of such is my Ambassador in France, Walsingham—that Italianate Puritan with his deep, cunning, painstaking mind and his burning fanaticism. Of such is my city of London from its richest merchant to its most truculent 'prentice. But they want their profits too!"

"And what do you want?" he asked her. The answer he got was more blunt and direct than he had ever expected.

"To keep this country out of the Continent's wars. Just that, Robin. . . . When I said to the Ambassador: '*Point de guerre! Point de guerre!*' I never meant words more!" She laid her hand on his arm and turned back towards the palace. Encouraging the sea raiders and seizing the bullion so Alva's troops mutiny for lack of pay—that I'll do. But no more!" She looked sideways at him. "And *I* like my profits as well as any!"

It was an uneasy summer, with tyranny crushing rebellion bloodily in the Low Countries, and strange deadly whispers in the North of England. Men began to realize that Elizabeth had given them ten years of quietness and safety, though when she had come to the throne the only future seemed to be turmoil and ruin. But in spite of these disquieting portents, in spite of her own bad health—for the infection in her leg had become an ulcer—the Queen went on Progress as usual. Robert, venturing to remonstrate with her against going on both these counts, had a furious remark slashed at him—God's death! If he didn't want to come, he might stay away! She also added if he were weary of being Master of the Horse, she might appoint her cousin, Hunsdon. There were also the young but violent Earl of Oxford and Christopher Hatton. . . . Robert, knowing her better in these days, did not argue. Later in the day, when she was standing in a window embrasure, apparently gazing out, she beckoned him over to her.

"Are you still asking for permission to withdraw from court?"

"I never would ask that! I would never leave you except at your command." He was kissing her hands, and heard her sigh. Then she said: "I should not be happy if you did not come on Progress." This he knew was a concession from her, the nearest her imperious nature could come to asking pardon, and it moved him.

When Douglass Sheffield heard, she wept.

"Oh, Robin, how long will you have to be away?"

"Two or three months," he said. "As usual." He was thinking how prettily Douglass cried. She did not screw up her face or storm, or let her nose become scarlet, but the tears rolled gently down from the soft darkness of her eyes.

"Come! It's not so long."

"Why must you go on every Progress?"

"Well—I am not only one of her Majesty's Privy Councillors, I am Master of the Horse——" He was hearing Elizabeth's voice: "I should not be happy if you did not come," and winced. Could one love two women at the same time? Apparently—when the feelings he had for each were so different.

"Her Majesty—always her Majesty! She devours you!"

He said in a cold angry voice she had never heard before: "I will not have you speak of the Queen like that! I told you before—I will not discuss her with you."

Douglass wept heartbrokenly. It was probably the wisest thing she could have done, but she was too unhappy to be wise. Robert gathered her closely to him. He was feeling—amongst other things—an irrational anger against Elizabeth. "If she had married me, this situation would never have occurred. . . ." he thought.

"Don't, sweeting!" he said aloud. "I'll see what I can do. Perhaps later on we could go to Kenilworth. I'd like to show it to you."

"I should like to see it! But I don't mind where I go as long as you are there!"

"I'll arrange something!" he murmured.

"Oh, Robin, will you miss me?"

"Of course I'll miss you!"

"My sister Frances will be there all the time you're on Progress."

"Well, what of it? I hardly speak to the Maids of Honour."

"She's in love with you!"

"Come, sweet! That's nonsense!"

"It isn't nonsense. And I've seen you pay attention to her. Much attention to her!"

"That *is* nonsense! If I ever seem to notice her—it's because she is like you. She's not so pretty but she *is* like you!"

"Robin, do you swear that's the truth?"

"I swear it!"

When the long, royal cavalcade rode out of London he did sometimes think of Douglass and her tears, but he thought more of the look of pain in Elizabeth's eyes. She ought not to be riding at all! If only she would obey him. . . . At the end of the first day she said: "Ride your quietest horse to-morrow, Rob, and take me pillion."

"More than gladly!"

If the Queen wished to ride pillion it was the duty of the Master of Horse to carry her. As they were riding through wooded uplands, he reminded her of a more unofficial occasion.

"Dear heart, do you remember when we went to Greenwich Fair?"

That had been an exploit of those early days of their first love. They had put on the plainest clothes which they possessed, and then, she on the pillion behind him, had ridden off to the fair without any attendants. At first they had attracted no attention. There were plenty of young fellows, court hangers-on, merchants' sons, country squires in for the day, with wives or sweethearts on pillion behind them. They had ridden around to see the various entertainments, the ever-popular but savage bear baiting with a tormented black monster chained to a stake and mangling the attacking mastiffs, jugglers in skin-tight, gaudy clothes, half-stripped brawny wrestlers, an actor on a high-raised booth with long black beard and tinsel crown, ranting: "I be Herod!" One could buy anything one fancied from the innumerable booths or wandering pedlar, including food and drink, both consumed enormously. And all around had milled that tight-packed crowd of people, the tight-packed smell of humanity, of horses, of bears, of new paint on the booths, freshly cooking food, spiced ale, and trodden, bruised earth and dust, while shouts rose from the dull roar of the crowd, advertising barbers, soothsayers, tooth-drawers, quacks to cure every ailment under the sun, fortune tellers, ballad singers, tumblers and dancers. He could remember the young Elizabeth laughing with an eager happiness, clasping him tightly round the waist as she rested her chin on his shoulder.

"I'm happy, Rob! I love people! Just ordinary people doing their day's work, or amusing themselves."

She had laughed and joked with the passers-by who had not at first recognized her, making Robert remember her father's popularity with the London crowds, how ready they had been to shout for "good old Harry!" She had got that easy friendliness from him with her red hair, her enormous, arrogant, ruthless will and her lusty enjoyment of life. Then they had reined in at a booth which sold gilded gingerbread and marchpane hearts pierced with tinsel darts.

"Buy your sweetheart a fairing, kind sir!"

"A heart, I beg you, Robin!"

The stallkeeper had looked from the dark, handsome gallant feeling in his pouch for coins, to his lively red-headed lady—and had suddenly recognized her. The Queen's most blessed Majesty! They had been mobbed, and surrounded perilously, amidst enthusiastic shouts. Almost desperate, he had struck out with his riding-whip, right and left—"Way there!"

"No, Robin! Don't hit them!" But a little later she had admitted reluctantly: "You must—if we're to get out!"

"Do you remember?" he asked her now. He felt her arms holding him tighten.

"I remember very well," she said. A little while later, she remarked with a disconcerting suddenness.

"This matter of Norfolk and the Queen of Scots! Do you think she seriously intends to wed him?"

"*He* is convinced of it!" Robert told her. "He's exceeding pleased with her letters. Apparently they express devotion. . . . *I* was thinking of her other letters."

"So they express devotion, do they? Would you be surprised to hear that, at the same time, she is writing smuggled letters to Bothwell?"

"That's a monstrous thing!"

"Yes—it's monstrous if a woman deceives a man. If a man deceives a woman—why, it's nothing!" Robert stared straight ahead, at his horse's ears and did not reply directly to this. Finally he said: "I wish we were rid of her! Perhaps if the Scots had executed her, it would have saved much sorrow."

"But it would be a dangerous and abominable precedent."

"Yes. But if she were guilty—proved——"

"I tell you I will not be her judge—except in one thing!"

"What?"

"It comes in one of her sonnets——

> *Entre ses mains et en son plein pouvoir*
> *Ie metz mon filz, mon honneur et ma vie,*
> *Mon pais, mes subjects, mon âme assubiectie*
> *Est toute à luy....*"[1]

"Her country!" she said. "Her subjects! Surely there I can both judge and condemn her!" The vehemence died out of her voice and for a moment she rested her head against his shoulder as if in weariness. Then she said, with quiet bitterness: "I think *I* am entitled to do that."

"You believe that the country and subjects always must come first?"

"Is not a king anointed with holy oil like a bishop?" she asked. "Such great responsibility must be consecrated. A sovereign rules by heaven's mandate. To God he must render account for the trust laid upon him. That I believe I must do one day. I took an oath before the High Altar at Westminster that I would put the welfare of my people above all else on earth. I will never break that oath, God help me! Even if it should break me."

Chapter Nine

The Earl of Leicester was fishing. The willows cast lacy shadows on the still waters of the river, now rather muddied by the recent rain. All was quiet; he could hear the soft plop of a rising fish or the dull hoof-beat of some grazing cow in the water meadows across the river, if a gadfly stirred her to sudden movement. Richmond Palace was out of sight behind a dark mass of tall trees, and there was no sign of humanity except for his page, Christopher Blount, sitting on a tree stump, and staring at the river. Robert felt a tug at his line and a light flick of his wrists showed him the fish was hooked and he might safely draw in. As the glistening body swung in the air, Blount came forward with the basket.

"It's somewhat small," said Robert. "This rain has not brought out the big fellows as I hoped."

"I think there's a monster, m'lord, down by the tree roots. I have been watching him."

"What bait will bring him out, lad?"

"Would a spider be better than a worm, m'lord?" suggested Blount. He picked up the pot of bait and then suddenly stared over Robert's shoulder.

"M'lord! There are two gentlemen coming across the meadows, and I think the foremost is his Grace of Norfolk!"

"Norfolk!" repeated Robert. He turned and straightened up. "It *is* the Duke. Take my rod, Kit, and I wish you better luck than I have had! And there is no need to speak of this meeting to any. . . ."

There was a strangely distraught look about the Duke of Norfolk. He came up to Robert with a disjointed step as if he were desperately trying not to run; his rich clothes were tumbled on carelessly as if he did not heed them enough to adjust his cloak or tighten his belt, but

243

his eyes held the most uncertainty. They wandered, refused to meet Robert's, and finally seemed to be staring at something beyond him. He did not answer Robert's greeting but burst out abruptly: "The Queen—how much does she know?"

"The Queen", said Robert, "has a habit of knowing more than is credited."

Norfolk caught at his elbow and walked him jerkily along the river bank away from young Blount and his own Gentleman of Horse.

"They told me that you were fishing," he said. "Fishing! You have an untroubled mind!"

Robert shrugged.

"This morning's rain made me hope the fish would rise," he said lightly. Norfolk pshawed.

"Fish!" he exclaimed and then added: "And William Cecil tells me that *he* approves my marriage to the Queen of Scots!"

"So much the simpler for you!"

"But——"

"We'll not get rid of Cecil. The Queen will never part with him. I may believe that if it were not for him, I should now be the Queen's husband—and yet——"

"And yet?" repeated Norfolk, his face twitching into a nervous frown. "You, yourself told me that the Queen wishes to marry you."

"As woman—yes," said Robert. At this moment it seemed that he had come strangely to understand Elizabeth's viewpoint. "As Queen —no. I think she perhaps may never wed."

"But man! Think of what you have said!"

"I still hope to marry her," Robert told him. But as he spoke, he seemed to hear an inward voice saying: "But I never shall. . . ." Nor did he believe that it was only Cecil. Cecil and he must accept each other and suppress their mutual disapproval finally; Cecil would always dread the Queen's emotional dependence on Robert just as Robert would resent the dependence of her reason on her chief minister. It seemed to Robert, walking on the river bank by the distracted Duke, that he was seeing a strangely clear vision of the future. That golden dream of a crown as Elizabeth's consort, it was fading as their first headlong passion faded, leaving a much deeper-rooted love, a love he had scarcely imagined before, though it did not prevent the need or possibility of such adventures as with Douglass. And the belief he might yet be supreme power in the State was almost gone too ; he was one of the greatest of her Majesty's servants and councillors, no more and no less. But, looking at the man beside him, he said abruptly: "You must tell the Queen! Everything! I beseech you for your own sake!"

"I cannot——" He was staring, as if he saw a dreadful phantom appearing over Robert's shoulder, in the peaceful water meadows.

"You must. Tell her of your proposal to wed the Queen of Scots, and the support you have. And promise her your loyalty when once you become King Consort of Scotland!"

"I—I——"

"You must! Come, now. The Queen was in the palace gardens when I went forth to fish. I dare swear she has remained there. The inflammation of her sore leg has somewhat subsided since she has been persuaded to rest it, but she is not likely to ride or walk far."

Norfolk followed him dumbly, but there seemed no confidence in him. Elizabeth was in the gardens with her ladies, walking slowly up a long avenue of pleached limes, the sunlight glancing softly on jewels and bright silks. Norfolk fell on his knees before her but seemed unable to speak. The Queen's eyes narrowed, but her thin lips curled into a smile.

"Well, cousin! So you are from London?"

"Yes, your Grace!"

"It seems I have been long buried in my rustic solitude." Her eyes twinkled and her lips curled more. "What news is there abroad?"

"Why—none!" muttered the Duke.

"None? You come from London, sweet cousin, and have no news of a marriage?"

"N—no—that is——"

But there was an interruption, a lad had come to present the Queen with a bouquet, and Norfolk stepped back. Robert saw him moistening his lips with his tongue. Leaning forward, he whispered: "Courage!" But Norfolk's eyes were haunted, and he could not manage to speak out even when the Queen in passing gave him a poke with her finger: "Look to your pillow, cousin! You seem strangely tongue-tied by my soul!"

"I was stricken with an ague," he murmured. "I think I am not recovered."

"I am sorry to hear it. I will have speech with you later."

But there was to be no "later". The Duke of Norfolk and his retinue were shortly seen, galloping like a whirlwind from Richmond Palace in the direction of London.

"For an ague-stricken man he spurs hard!" observed Robert.

"He is stricken with worse than ague," Elizabeth said. "He is stricken with a bad conscience."

"What did you mean when you told him 'to look to his pillow'?"

"Last year I taxed him with desiring to wed the Queen of Scots, and he answered that how could the husband of so wicked a woman sleep easily on his pillow?"

"When you suggested many years ago that *I* should wed her," said Robert, "you were proposing a post of danger!"

"I think there would have been no danger for you!"

"Why?"

She had turned away from him and he could not see her face as she spoke.

"She would have loved you. Women love you too easily, Robin! Do you think I don't know that half my ladies are sighing for you? That little fool, Frances Howard, goes crimson to the roots of her hair when you speak to her."

"Oh, come!" he muttered awkwardly. "They are not so foolish as you think!"

"Are they not? And I the biggest fool of them all!" She put her hand to his cheek and smiled sadly.

That day she was closeted long with some of her most trusted councillors, headed by Cecil. Those who called her dilatory and pusil-lanimous might well gasp. The ports were immediately closed and spies and couriers were suddenly cut off from the Continent. Pem-broke—deeper in the conspiracy than his friend Leicester—Arundel, Lumley and Throckmorton were placed under guard in private houses. The Spanish Ambassador, despite his furious protests, was placed under house-arrest in his own Embassy. The Queen of Scots was removed from Wingfield where she resided as the honoured guest of the Earl of Shrewsbury, to the security of Tutbury Castle under the guardianship of Robert's brother-in-law, the Earl of Hunting-don, who had, himself, a distant claim to the Succession, and there-fore was not likely to support Mary's. The Earl of Sussex, as Lord President of the Council in the north, was bidden to summon the Earls of Northumberland and Westmorland to court. They refused

246

and the trained bands were called out and men levied for the army; the Earl of Warwick as Master of the Ordnance commanding the southern forces, and the Earl of Sussex, the northern.

The Duke of Norfolk was bidden on his allegiance to return to court, but his London house was found empty. He had fled to his estates in the country.

"Your Grace, it would be well to temporize with the Duke," said Cecil. "He has much power."

"The time", she said, "for temporizing is past. . . ."

But the unhappy Duke had sown dragon's teeth and stood aghast at the harvest. He had dreamt of marrying the Queen of Scots and reigning with her as Consort in Scotland, they being the recognized heirs of Elizabeth, with the overwhelming but peaceful support of the whole of England. Now he found himself the appointed leader of a rebellion against his Queen's authority, with the north alone rising, and determined upon war. Receiving the Queen's summons, he began slowly to return towards the court. Whether he would have reached it of his own volition is problematical. Elizabeth sent Sir Francis Knollys, with a small force, to seize him and convey him—to his horrified astonishment—as prisoner to the Tower.

But the North—truly called "inly working"—arose. Here the spirit of the Middle Ages lived on, remote from the iconoclastic Tudor despots at Westminster with their new church and their new servants who had waxed fat on the spoils of ancient church and ancient nobility alike. The hardy peasantry scarcely knew any prince but their feudal lords, Percy Neville and Dacres. The old faith was alive, secure from reformers. Now a Queen had come, who was declared rightful ruler of England by that faith, and she had cast her strange enchantment on the leaders of the north, so they gladly joined the many to die for her. . . . Men flocked to the banners depicting the Five Wounds of Christ, wearing red cross surcoats as their fathers had done in the Pilgrimage of Grace, when Henry VIII had first broken with Rome. Let Henry's daughter tremble! They swept forward, seeming irresistible, burning every copy of the Book of Common Prayer and the Bishops' Bible they could obtain, celebrating a solemn Mass in Durham Cathedral. Sussex could not trust his levies, the brothers and cousins of the men advancing against him. Did not the garrison of Barnard Castle go over to the rebels? He fell back, though York was held securely for Elizabeth and the rebels did not venture to attack it. But they seized Hartlepool, a convenient port for the promised troops from Alva to land, and they came dangerously close to Mary at Tutbury. Again she was removed, far south, to Coventry. And in the south, Warwick's army was marching steadily on, over the miry tracks, an army which believed in the new ways, in the reformed faith, and shouted lustily for the last Tudor.

She sat late with her councillors, reading reports, her eyes narrowed and keen, checking every word, weighing and balancing it. After her burst of furious energy, when her couriers spurred desperately with her orders and the different forces moved, she was still. She waited and listened. Sometimes her passivity might deceive, but then she would thrust a sudden question to the heart of the matter. If fear or anger or sorrow tore at her, her Council did not see it.

After such a meeting on a November night Robert accompanied her to the privacy of her Withdrawing Chambers. Since the crisis he had moved from Leicester House to his former apartments in Whitehall. At first she had seemed to take this move for granted, and then one day she had said quietly: "I am glad to have you near me, Robin. . . ." In the long tapestry-hung room, two or three of the Queen's ladies waited. By the light of the candles, they could be seen, stifling yawns as they waited for release. "But", thought Robert, "they have had the sense to make up a good fire against the night's cold!" He handed the Queen to a high-backed settle facing the great hearth, and then began to tuck cushions around her. She seemed silent and withdrawn as if lost in thought, and when her hand chanced to touch his in the arrangement of the cushions, he was struck by its clammy coldness.

"Shall I bid them bring mulled wine?" he asked her.

"For yourself, if you will, Robin."

"If *you* will take it! You are weary and cold."

"Very well."

He knelt beside her, earnestly studying her face in the leaping tawny light from the blazing logs. It had the parchment hue of extreme exhaustion, and its bones, the bridge of her high nose, the point of her chin, the slant of her cheekbones above the hollow cheeks, seemed carved with a tense sharpness pressing against the taut skin. Then her half-closed lids lifted.

"Well, my 'Eyes'!" she said, using a favourite nickname for him. "What are you seeing?"

"That you are wearying yourself for your ungrateful people!"
She shrugged and then gave a half smile.

"Not so ungrateful!"

"Are you sorrowful?" he asked. He did not venture to say "afraid".

"How can I be other?"

"You put too much trust in Sussex!" he said with a sudden impatience. "If you replaced him by my brother!"

"I trust him. And your brother also."

"He seeks to poison your mind against me!"

"As you do—against him! Listen. I do not heed what he says of you. Neither do I heed what you say of him."

"If you trust Sussex," he said with sulky determination, "you might look with pity on Pembroke!"

"I shall release Pembroke."

"Dear heart, you make me very happy!"

"Ah! He is a good friend to you. Perhaps had he not been, he had not entered so deeply into this conspiracy."

Robert stared at her.

"When Norfolk was to be King Consort of Scotland, you were to be King Consort of this realm, I think! If I were wholly wise, I might have imprisoned you with Pembroke." She looked into his eyes and then laughed, a little. "But I am not wholly wise, dear love. . . ."

He said: "Surely you know that to save you from any hurt, I would give the last drop of my blood?"

She had taken his face between her hands.

"If I needed a champion, where else would I seek? And yet the world is not so simple. Norfolk in the beginning did not seek treason. He was be-dazzled. Where may not a weak man be led? If he had succeeded, four months from his wedding with the Queen of Scots, I should be in the Tower once more."

"And I also."

"Surely, dear heart. And this time we would not win out!"

There was a step behind them, and a young voice: "The mulled wine, your Grace!"

"I beg you to drink!" Robert said, rising to his feet. There was the Maid of Honour, Frances Howard, looking at him from Douglass's face, more soft and rounded by early youth. He smiled swiftly at her, but his attention was for the Queen, filling a silver goblet for her, and pressing her to drink. The thought of Douglass caused him a flicker of uneasiness. There had been tears and bitterness at their last meeting, and he abhorred scenes. Surely by every law and duty he must now cleave to the Queen? She was alike his sovereign and the love of his youth.

Elizabeth moved and spoke with the suddenness of a snake striking: "Set it down, Frances, and cease from your gaping at my Lord here! You have seen him often enough before!"

The girl had withdrawn with a sudden rustle of silk. He knew better than to intervene for her. (And Douglass fretted him: "You dally with my sister, I believe!" "I tell you, I do not!") Elizabeth was tapping the settle beside her. "Sit here, Rob, and you also drink this wine! We'll make it a loving cup."

He sought to reassure her, after his fashion.

"Whatever Sussex does, when my brother's army gets up to the rebels, you'll have no further need to fear."

"I have no fear of the final victory. Sussex has my cousin Hunsdon with him! I know my good staunch Harry. No bolder mastiff ever hung on a bear unheeding its claws, as he will hang on the foe!" But a frown passed over her face. "It is the aftermath I dread! For I must be harsh and make examples—of those poor fools who must learn most bitterly and bloodily to forget what they were once taught. And my heart will bleed for their blood. . . . But the world is watching me. Moray has called up his men to guard the frontier for me. If he thinks me a weak ally he will turn against me. And Mary's partisans in Scotland will seek to rise. France is watching, that heartless calculating Italian woman, and the Guises and the Huguenots. Alva watches me and he is Philip's greatest captain. The Dutch he persecutes, watch me. And behind them all, is Philip and the huge power of Spain which is turning against me. I dread Spain!"

The last words were hardly more than a whisper, but he saw in her eyes the expression he had not seen for seventeen years since they were in the Tower together. It was as if she had looked on the ultimate terror, and was forcing herself to meet it calmly. He made an incoherent sound and pulled her into his arms, vowing he would guard her from the whole world with his life. She seemed to relax instinctively as if she felt safe but her voice was impatient: "Not for myself! For the country. Do you think I want it served like the Netherlands?"

He thought: "Always the country!"

Zenith

Her thin lips tightened momentarily and she winced, seeing the harshness which would be forced on her, to spare it from the savagery of foreign repression. "Spare the rod and spoil the child!" She must take the rod to her unruly children so that they would be prevented from defying her to their own harm. The north was so remote that it was hard to control by subtler means. She felt ringed about by the merciless eyes watching her, watching her without any pity, waiting for her to make a mistake. But she would not make a mistake. She would show, implacably, who ruled her realm, printing her lesson with block and gallows, and then she could be merciful, to the satisfaction of heart and brain alike. But the strain of months seemed to be driving weariness deeper and deeper into her flesh. She turned with an instinctive thankfulness to the comfort which Robert alone could give her. Neither as councillor nor as lover could he solve her problems, but he could give her strength to face them.

Now she smiled. She could hear the faint rhythmical snores of the middle-aged lady-in-waiting, fallen asleep at last with her full chin digging into her ruff. She could imagine the girl Frances sitting, wide awake and tense, envying her, hating her. That lovely face had availed Frances no more at this moment than her twenty years' advantage. But this moment might not come again; Time imperilled it. She was not the girl who had walked in the prison garden, she was not the young woman newly crowned. In the early days she had only feared one rival, her cousin Lettice Essex, recognizing her own passionate determination in her. But now there were such exquisite creatures as Frances Howard with the terrible weapon of their youth. She would always be the centre of Robert's ambition, the sun in his firmament; there would be the shared memories and the habit of long companionship, but for how much longer would she be the woman he desired? She must seize such moments as these and hold them with all her strength.

As she had sat at supper with her ladies, that day, her young musicians, the Children of the Chapel Royal, had come to sing to her, their high silver boys' voices contrasting strangely with the words they sang, of love's ardours and age's sorrows.

> "I have loved her all my youth,
> But now am old, as you see:
> Love likes not the falling fruit,
> Nor the withered tree.

Zenith

Know that Love is a careless child,
And forgets promise past:
He is blind, he is deaf when he list,
And in faith never fast.

His desire is a dureless content,
And a trustless joy;
He is won with a world of despair
And is lost with a toy."

Her mind repeated: "A dureless content. . . . A trustless joy. . . .'
She thought: "Joy has wings swifter than a swallow's, to fly like a
swallow when autumn comes." She rose to her feet abruptly, and
heard the rustling and creaking of the awaking ladies, stifling their
yawns, and saw beside them, Frances, as slim and pliant as a willow
wand. To her she gave a crooked bitter smile of brief triumph. "Your
time is not yet. . . ." she thought, as she walked to the great bedchamber and the deft hands of her women. Soon he would come to
her, through the door behind the arras which Blanche Parry had
unlocked. The "world of despair" might fall back and be forgotten;
even if it were dureless and trustless, it was still joy.

The next day when the Queen was with her Council, Frances
Howard was called from the other Maids of Honour. Her sister, my
Lady Sheffield, had come to visit her. Douglass was standing as taut
as a bowstring, in a furred riding-dress of crimson velvet, bending her
riding-switch with nervous hands. There was a high colour in her
cheeks. Frances ran to her, threw her arms about her and kissed her,
feeling that quivering tautness.

"I must speak to you. Where can we be private?"

"In my room. Neither Mary nor Alice who share it with me are
likely to come now."

Douglass followed her in silence, and still in silence, watched
Frances trying to blow some life into the dying fire as she piled it with
faggots from the basket. Then she threw her steeple-crowned hat
with its heron's plume and her pearl-sewn gauntlets on to the bed
with a gesture of despair.

"I must have news of him!" she burst out. "Of Lord Leicester!"

"Of Lord Leicester?" Frances repeated. "It is well that the Queen
does not know why you have come!"

"The Queen! She's not a woman, she's a monster!"

"Douglass, have a care! Supposing someone overheard you. . . . Truly—curse not the King even in thy bedchamber!"

"I have not seen him since he took up his residence at court," Douglass said swiftly, as if she had not heard her sister's words. "I send to him and he will not answer. Then Digby—one of his Gentlemen of Horse—brings me a jewel and a message. 'My Lord is grieved but he cannot come to you. He is held by affairs of State.' Such a message—and a jewel!"

They stared at each other across the bed with a strange defiant apprehension.

"It is true," said Frances in a hesitant voice. "He *is* held by affairs of State. The Council meets—many days in the week. Sometimes they sit till late at night and the Queen with them. And when he is not engaged on such weighty matters, he is very lovingly attentive to the Queen and scarcely ever leaves her."

Douglass threw herself face downwards on her sister's bed. Her voice came, half strangled with sobs.

"There was never anyone so wretched as I! Or so ill used!"

"I don't understand," said Frances in a frightened voice. She put her hand on her sister's shoulder. "Douglass—what is he to you?"

Douglass Sheffield raised her tear-distorted face.

"He's been my lover for the past year! That is what he is to me! She threw herself down again. "And I love him to desperation. . . ."

"Oh-h." It was a small, hurt sound. Douglass misunderstood it. Defiance and bitterness now entered her wild mood.

"You are going to play the prude, are you? What do I care? I care for nothing but him! Nothing, do you understand? Let Charles say that people are talking of me—let them talk!" Charles was their brother, Lord Howard of Effingham.

"I love him, too," said Frances at last. Tears were close to her also. "And I think the Queen knows it—else she would not use me so harshly!"

"Love him!" said Douglass bitterly. "What does a child like you know of love? Or has he taught you?" She caught her younger sister by the arms. "So you are trying to take him away from me?"

"I have no chance. . . ." She thought: "He seemed to notice me more than the others. He would smile at me and stop to talk if the Queen were not by—and all because I am like Douglass! I thought it was for myself. . . . I was only a mirror for him, to hold her reflection!"

"But the Queen! Tell me the truth about him and the Queen!" cried Douglass miserably.

"The truth? Who knows except perhaps Mistress Parry and she is an oyster. . . . Yet I think he loves the Queen in his way."

"You say that to torment me! He does it for ambition. . . . How could he love her? She's nigh on forty—well, thirty-seven! What does her face look like in the early morning before she paints it? She dyes her hair, they say. . . . And she has an unhealed sore on her leg!"

"Yet in spite of these things, I do not think it is all ambition. They've shared so much in the past. If you saw them laughing, joking, teasing—in their way. And last night as she sat by the fire, he was on his knees with his arms around her waist, and she was holding his face in her hands. . . . She told me not to gape at him as I had seen him often enough before! Those are the kind of things she says. But this morning, she awoke in a wonderful good temper for her."

"She'll neither take him nor let him go!" cried Douglass. "Oh, I hate her!"

"So do I," said Frances slowly. "And I am terrified of her. And yet——"

"And yet?" repeated Douglass impatiently.

"She's so—tremendous. . . . So much more than one ordinary human being. The only time when she is like an ordinary mortal is when she is with him. Whether she's clapping his cheek and chaffing him—or gazing into his eyes as she did last night."

"I have felt it—that bond between them—that chain which holds him!" murmured Douglass. She got up jerkily. "I must attend to my face. . . . Where are your paints?" She sat down before Frances's mirror.

"And that is the only time when I pity her," said Frances softly. "Because she loves him too—very greatly. . . ."

Douglass made a savagely impatient sound.

"Tell him——" she said at last. "No—tell him nothing. . . . I must go. I think if I were to see him with her—I should run mad! Ah, it's finely lunatic! You—and I—and the Queen's Majesty!"

"And", thought Frances, "we all suffer."

She suffered much, having to watch the Queen and the Earl of Leicester, and knowing that the fancy which she had once cherished was only caused by her likeness to her sister. And at this time of tension the Queen turned more and more to the Earl's companionship. Rumour whispered daily that Alva's men had landed, and the walkers in the aisles of that strangely secular cathedral, St. Paul's, where a man might make bargains or assignations or fill his ears with the gossip of the town, heard the occupants of "Papist's Corner" gleefully declare that Mass would be said here and soon, when Alva paid his troops with the loot of Cheapside. . . . The story came to court and Frances heard the Queen laugh harshly as she said: "They do well to dispose of the skin before they have caught their quarry!" and saw her long fingers tighten as she spoke, on Leicester's brocade sleeve.

But no men landed from Alva, and the heart went out of the northern rebels so that they melted away without battle before the Queen's steadily advancing host. Of their leaders, Northumberland was ignominiously hanged and Westmorland fled to perpetual exile. Leonard Dacres, the third man in the north, held out a little longer, but Hunsdon went zealously after him, and with only half his opponent's troops, forced the crossing of the River Gelt, and with valiant determination, crushed out the last resistance. The Queen was overjoyed with her cousin's success, and to the official dispatch, added this postscript in her own hand.

"I doubt much, my Harry, whether that the victory were given me more joyed me, or that you were by God appointed the instrument of my glory; and I assure you that for my country's good the first might suffice, but for my heart's contentation, the second more pleased me. . . . And that you may not think you have done nothing for your profit, though you have done much for honour, I intend to make this journey somewhat to increase your livelihood. . . ."

She signed herself: "Your loving kinswoman, Elizabeth R."

To Robert she said: "Aha, my bold, staunch Harry! Is he not a trusty mastiff? Now they must teach that lesson to those poor fools in their own blood, so that the world may see who rules England! And then perchance, I may happily bind up the wounds. . . ."

Ship, Rumour whispered daily that Alva's men had landed, and the
walkers in the aisles of that strangely secular Cathedral, St. Paul's,
where a man might make bargains or assignations or fill his ears with
the gossip of the town about the crowded stones of "Papist's Corner,"
gleefully declare that Mass would be said here and soon, when Alva
paid his troops with the loot of Cheapside . . . The story came to
Paul and Frances, heard them both laugh sharply as she said:
"They do well to despair . . . . they have caught their
quarry!" and saw her long fingers tighten as she spoke, on Leicester's
brocade sleeve.

Chapter Ten

All the time the bells sang their brazen song. It was a steady
background to the trampling and thudding in the lists and
the sudden angry clang of steel as the jousters came furiously together. To the listeners at Whitehall, the bells of
Westminster clashed the loudest, distinct against the vibrating peal
from the city of London's one hundred bell towers, merged in an
undivided sound. It was twelve years ago this day that Elizabeth had
ascended the Throne, and her people were celebrating in thankfulness for dangers passed. All over the country the bells were ringing
and bonfires burned in London's streets; everywhere there was
junketing and merry-making. The courtiers displayed their skill and
strength before the Queen and the tiltyard was filled with gaily hued
trappings and fantastic blazonry. Rhyming couplets in French, Latin
and English were engraved on shields in place of ancient armorial
bearings, armour was painted, inlaid and damascened; the myth and
colour of High Renaissance pageants and masques overlaid the
chivalrous exercise of the Middle Ages.

The Queen sat in the centre of the gallery surrounded by her ladies.
A fur-lined cloak rose from her shoulders in winged stiffness, framing
her, rather than protecting her from the November air. Painted and
gilded gauze veils trailed cloudlike from the coif so heavily jewelled
that it resembled a crown on that flaming hair, whose hot colour
seemed to belong as little to nature as the careful pink and white of
the narrow oval face below. She was a figure for the baroque fantasy
of the scene, with countless yards of lustrous black velvet spread over
the huge hoop in a gown open down the middle to reveal another
below in cloth of gold, powdered with seed pearls like the great ballooning sleeves. This brilliant image serenely received the acclama-
tions of its worshippers; when the Earl of Leicester, the Lord Huns-

don and Master Hatton bore their opponents from their saddles, the crimsoned lips curled into a smile. But when the Earl of Leicester made his huge Almain grey caracole in triumph down the lists, as he waved his splintered lance butt, a tenderness crept into that smile and gave her face a sudden warming humanity.

Trumpets blared forth challenges, esquires and foot soldiers in bright attire paraded the lists, the warm pungent smell of sweating horses arose. Frances Howard, sitting amongst the other Maids of Honour, could see her sister Douglass in the side gallery, resting her chin on her clenched knuckles, her eyes darkly intent when the crimson and silver trappings with the Bear and Ragged Staff passed triumphantly below. Frances raised her hand to her brother, unhelmed in his tilting armour, standing beside Douglass and his wife, before he went down to mount his charger, held by an esquire. Gravely he saluted her, but Douglass never turned her head. She saw one being only in that great throng. But Frances's glance strayed from jousters to spectators. Many that had been imprisoned were now there; the Earls of Pembroke and Arundel were amongst the challengers, bestriding their snorting Great Horses in the lists. Sir Nicholas Throckmorton watched, wrapped in a heavy velvet cloak. Then came a stir amongst the onlookers, and Frances saw her brother Charles, as he descended the steps to the lists, greeting a tall figure. It was their cousin Thomas, Duke of Norfolk. In August he had been released from the Tower and permitted to return to his own house, on swearing on his allegiance to have no further dealings with the Queen of Scots.

The Queen saw him come in, and her lips tightened. Cecil had shaken his head at so much clemency. "Your Grace will take more harm by mercy than by justice." Hunsdon had put it more bluntly. "God's wounds, Cousin Bess! You'll be merciful one day too often!" She had answered both: "I will not rule by fear." The gallows tree had borne too much fruit already after the Rebellion. But the fervour of adoration which her people in London and the south had shown, after the collapse of the northern defiance, had brought the tears to her eyes. That fervour seemed to find its own tongue in the bells today. Yet, when she heard the confident talk of trouble being passed, she sighed. She thought: "Trouble is just beginning."

The menacing storm clouds on the world's horizon were taking definite shape, a shape which grew more sinister. In Madrid sat the most powerful monarch in Europe; Spain, the Netherlands and Milan were his, the Italian city states looked to him as overlord, he was the well-beloved of the Holy Father in Rome; in Vienna, his cousin was Holy Roman Emperor. The fabulous wealth of the equally fabulous New World beyond the ocean was his also. And every day he seemed to be turning further towards enmity. His ambassador had joined the plotters against her, his viceroy in the Netherlands, after placing an embargo on trade with England, had threatened to send troops to assist those same plotters. She remembered the brother-in-law of fifteen years ago who had pursued her with a cold but steady greed, regardless of his wife's unhappy devotion. He was slow, her brother-in-law Philip, and perhaps not bellicose, but she knew once his heart was set on an object, nothing could turn him from his ponderous but implacable way.

His religious fanaticism made her shiver, it was one with her sister's frenzied persecutions, and the shrill voice of John Knox calling for heaven's vengeance on his enemies. She had said once to William Cecil in quiet bitterness: "Truly not peace but a sword! Can there never be toleration in religious matters?" Seeing his astonishment she had added, with a harsh laugh. "If that were ever achieved—then worse might occur!" She knew she was fulminated against, for her strange attitude, by Catholic and Puritan alike, and accused of the sin of Laodicea. A weariness possessed her spirit, God was far away and the angry cries and smoke of war from the embattled factions, obscured Him. She could debate nice points of theology with ingenuity and force, giving chapter and verse to the best of her critics —but all that belonged to man. Robert was the most dear and close to her of all human beings—the only one close to her—but she got little satisfaction there. Robert's religious feelings were mainly a superstitious dread of divine vengeance. He would always seek to placate an earthly monarch, much more a heavenly one! Now he was getting older, his thoughts were turning uneasily to placation. It sometimes drove him into unexpected company with the Puritans. He had spoken with admiration of her Ambassador to France, Walsingham. "Yes!" she had said with impatience. "Francis Walsingham is a man of great ability. A skilled diplomatist, with great knowledge of foreign men and lands, a tireless worker. But he sees the world as a conflict between Christ and Belial. It is not so simple as that. . . . He would urge a religious war on me, in support of the

Huguenots and the Dutch." She grimaced. "Where should I find the money? I told him—the Lord will *not* provide!"

But Robert's eyes had kindled at the thought of a religious war. Give him the command and send him to the Low Countries—he'd gain glory for her!

"And save your own soul at the same time!" she snapped, her nerves jangled. "These are not the simple ages of the Crusades."

"Young Philip is restless at Oxford," he told her. "He wants to go and strike a blow for the Dutch. Wrote to tell me of some youngsters who have left Oxford to fight. He spoke of a Devonshire lad called Walter Raleigh."

"Ah!" she said, the name striking a chord. "That must be Humphrey Gilbert's young half-brother. Gilbert was a connection of my old Kate Ashley's, and was once in my household. Before I was Queen. He was a valiant fellow, quick to fight in private or public quarrel. I know he has served with Coligny and the Huguenots. So his half-brother is following his example? But we must not have Philip casting himself away in such foolish errantry."

"He's a romantic lad," said his uncle. "And somewhat innocent."

The remembered conversation whirled up in her uneasy thoughts. Hoofs thundered below, and the young Earl of Oxford, in armour of gilt inlay, sent his opponent clanging from his saddle. Amidst the shouts of acclamation, men slipped into the lists, caught the riderless horse, and helped the dismounted man to his feet. His helmet was off and she saw his round, red, sweating face. It was Tom Cecil, whom his father had apostrophized as "a spending sot fit only to keep a tennis court". Her thoughts went unhappily back to religion.

"Now", she thought, "religious persecution will be forced on *me*."

That May an unseen hand had nailed the Bull of her Excommunication on the door of the palace of the Bishop of London. Robert had been surprised at the little gasp of pain which had broken from her at the news.

"But," he said, "but—what do you care for the Pope in Rome?"

"I care this much!" she declared through clenched teeth. "Don't you see what it means? After struggling for years to hold back the Puritans from persecuting the Catholic recusants, arguing with Cecil, overlooking this and that? *I* don't want to interfere with my subjects' religious beliefs so long as they are loyal. Now— an' they are devout they are absolved from all loyalty! *That* I owe to Mary of Scotland —she's the rightful Queen now in their eyes!"

"Let Knox and his fellows kill her!"

"Merciful God—no!!!"

That had been one of the happenings of the year 1570. Another had been the assassination of Moray. He had been strong and coldly wise; if she had not always shared Cecil's high opinion of him, she knew he was her best hope of peace as ruler in Scotland. His death had caused Mary's faction to gain strength. They joined dangerously with her northern rebels who had fled across the border. She had been forced to send Sussex and his victorious army over the frontier to teach them a salutary lesson. The balance had been restored but she was making a final effort to come to an arrangement with the new men reigning in the name of the little King, to take Mary back on terms which would provide for England's safety. But Mary and her former subjects were proving equally intransigent. Cecil, a most reluctant envoy to the Queen of Scots and loudly asking God to guide him, repeated an insult which she had offered to Elizabeth. When told that she must renounce her claims to the throne of England in favour of Elizabeth and her issue, she had demanded that the word "lawful" be inserted before the word "issue".

"God's precious soul!" Elizabeth swore. "It comes well from her!"

"What's her meaning?" Robert demanded.

"Robin—surely you know that rumour has credited us not with one child, but two! Perhaps it is three by now. . . . Cecil has not recently given me agents' reports on the matter. . . ."

"What in the devil's name is supposed to have happened to these children? Do I eat them?"

"That has not yet been suggested. . . . Sometimes they are smuggled out of the country, sometimes strangled at birth." The bitter coolness in her voice was studied. It began to break as she murmured, turning her head away: "It is a cruel jest. . . ."

He had taken her by the arms and drawn her gently to him.

"Listen, sweet. One of my tenants at Kenilworth has been wed for twenty years without any children. And now his wife has given him a son."

Her face was pressed against his shoulder so that he could hardly catch her words.

"I would not ask for a miracle. . . . Is it a normal child?"

"A fine, lusty boy! I saw the brat myself." He heard her sigh and his hold tightened. "Why should we not wed—now?"

She was silent, seeming to cling to him. He thought dizzily: "She is going to agree!" She thought: "When he is gentle like this—if I might dare say 'yes'. . . . Then I might keep him against all the younger women!" If she could only hold this moment! But she raised her head, and her voice was cool and collected.

"Because I have told Francis Walsingham to do a thing which his diplomacy must applaud and his religious feelings deplore! To open negotiations with the young King of France, and one more important, his mother, for my match with his younger brother the Duc d'Anjou."

"God's blood!" he swore. "Have you a heart in your body? Anjou is nineteen—you are thirty-seven! He's a painted, vicious little boy! He delights to dress up as a woman—he——" Robert choked. "And his mother is that Italian Jezebel——"

"Who has no principles but expedience," she said swiftly. "I can bargain with her!"

They were apart now, staring at each other.

"Am I to believe you serious?" he demanded.

"In needing a French alliance? We need desperately an alliance. And I believe that Catherine de Medici is also viewing Spain with fear. Reports say she is turning to the Huguenots against the Guises, and is proposing a marriage between her daughter and the young King of Navarre."

"But your marriage!" he persisted.

"Leave it, Robin, leave it!" she had said wearily. She thought: "He can still be enraged at the thought of my marrying. I must be thankful for that. . . ."

Listening to the bells' song, she thought: "The troubles are beginning!" As her painted lips were smiling at the armoured figures in the lists, she was praying silently and inwardly.

"God be merciful and send peace! That is all I crave. Before I asked for glory, for a name which would resound through future chronicles, for a victory with the enemy's banners laid at my feet. My own triumph and glory is such a small matter after all. . . . Let my reign be even held inglorious, let my name be soon forgotten—but send my people peace. . . ."

Zenith

Peace was a mirage, clear enough to view in its loveliness but utterly intangible. She strove for it, debating with Catherine de Medici for the French alliance, with the Scots Commissioners and their deposed Queen, for whose return they showed an ever-increasing reluctance. If Mary could leave England with safety to herself and others! What solution could there be to this unhappy and dangerous problem? The Queen of Scots varied her wilful unreason with touches of childish pathos. She sent to Elizabeth as a gift the inkstand engraved with the cipher which had been used between them in the earlier and happier days of their correspondence. Elizabeth looked sadly at the Bishop of Ross, when he presented it. "Would God, my Lord of Ross," she said, "that all things were in the same state they were in, when this cipher was made betwixt us." Later that same day she said to Robert: "She is one part a child who believes it must be always forgiven, another the Siren in the old Greek legend who sang the mariners to their doom, and yet another the enchanted princess of faery laid under a strange spell." Her voice had been thoughtfully sad, but now, a flash of irritation crossed her face and her voice became harsh: "The whole adds up to the most damnation nuisance which ever plagued the life from anyone!"

But the French courtship progressed favourably despite the petulant declaration of the nineteen-year-old bridegroom that "he did not want to marry the old hag!" He might complain to his retinue of loose women, painted boys and curled and perfumed lap dogs, but his mother, however much she spoiled her darling in other ways, drove him on inexorably. She wanted the alliance as much as Elizabeth, who took a malicious pleasure in disconcerting the French Ambassador by repeating to him Anjou's worst observations. The unfortunate de la Mothe Fénélon thought the Queen of England must have her spies everywhere! To Robert, she made a great assumption of coyness and declared that to judge by his portraits, the young French prince was a very pretty lad. If she had not been the Lord's Anointed, Robert believed he would have shaken her. . . .

At this point he found himself promising to wed the tearful Douglass—"if her Grace wed the Duc d'Anjou". He gave her a diamond ring to seal his pledge, and rapturously happy, she forgot the saving clause. She considered herself solemnly contracted to him, and later she believed, virtually married. But even at the time he felt a stirring of misgiving. Douglass was an exquisite creature for dalliance but at other times he found her a trifle tedious. Also, she was developing an alarming capacity for making scenes. He reflected gloomily that Amy (who had not possessed a tittle of Douglass's beauty, grace and high breeding) had started with the same blind adoration, and had ended by making scenes of ever-increasing violence, until that last ghastly one, when she had clung hysterically about his knees, screaming that she would kill herself if he did not return to her, till he had thrust her away brutally, declaring: "Well—kill yourself! D'you think I would care?" He was apt to consider himself ill-used by women.

But while Elizabeth wrangled with the Scots Commissioners, endeavouring to make them take back their Queen and give her the shadow of her crown, if not the substance, Mary coveted and plotted for far more.

The plot of 1571, known as the Ridolfi Plot, from its principal agent, the Florentine banker, Roberto Ridolfi, was laid bare by the relentless secret service built by Cecil, and later perfected by Walsingham. It showed that as soon as an assassin had disposed of "that servant of all iniquity, Elizabeth, pretended Queen of England", as the Papal Bull called her, Mary and her future consort, the once pardoned Norfolk, were to be elevated to the throne by Alva and his invading army.

And a great shout of rage seemed to go up from the people of England. The London mob surged furiously through the streets, crying for vengeance on the "monstrous and huge dragon" the Queen of Scots, and the "roaring lion" the Duke of Norfolk. London was not ringing the bells, it was lighting the bonfires and feeding them with images and fittings from plundered Catholic chapels. Woe betide foreigners and papists then! This great surge of anger sprang from their love for their Queen; her recent peril had been like a lightning flash to show them their own feelings with unbearable sharpness. She knew it, and there was the ache of unshed tears in her throat. Once she put out her hands gropingly in the empty air, as if she would hold and press something even dearer than Robert. But she might not cling to this precious devotion. She must even oppose the wishes of those beings who only wanted to show their love for her, and their fidelity to the system which she had created for them.

She was tired and there was a pain behind her eyeballs, a pain which outlined the bones of her skull. She could still hear the argumentative voices echoing and re-echoing, and farther off, as chorus, the roar of the angry London mob.

Zenith

The Duke of Norfolk had been curtailed of his power after his first imprisonment, he had brought little the second time but treachery. . . . Elizabeth had forgiven him once, and she wanted to forgive him again. He was her cousin and she had pity for him, even affection. After his Peers had condemned him to death for high treason, she had hesitated to sign the warrant. Once signed, she had roused Cecil up in the small hours of the morning to have it revoked. But if she shrank from his death, how much more she shrank from the death of one who was ten-fold more responsible!

She had written a jingle of angry verse containing one strong line which surely summed Mary up for all time.

"The Daughter of Debate that eke Discord doth sow."

She had furiously broken off negotiating with the Scots Commissioners for Mary's restoration—how could she restore one who had been twice plotting against her own life and throne? When the King and Queen Mother of France, rather to preserve the dignity of their house than from any affection, had bade their ambassador intercede for the Queen of Scots, Elizabeth had shrieked out at him that no one had ever had so much to endure as she had at the hands of the Queen of Scots. She had shrieked so loudly that the retreating ambassador had believed her voice could be heard outside the palace. But she was fighting for the life of the Queen of Scots, against—so it seemed—all the forces in her kingdom. . . .

Those voices seemed to echo and re-echo inside the bony walls of her skull, sending the darts of pain flying. First came Cecil—whom she had recently created Lord Burghley—on whose judgment she relied more than on anyone else's. Skilfully he built up the arguments which she could not displace. Twice within so many years the Queen of Scots had plotted against Elizabeth's throne and her life, so that she was a perpetual peril to the realm. What peace and security could there be so long as she lived?

"What peace or security have I ever known—even before I was born?"

"It is not only your Grace's personal security. It is the security, peace and happiness of your Grace's subjects—who love you. . . ."

"And when have I failed them?"

"Your Grace has never failed them yet."

"But how can I have her executed? An anointed Queen?"

264

"She is also a guilty woman. Queens have died on the scaffold before."

She stared at him, her hands clenched.

"My mother...."

He had never heard her say those two words before. What a pall of silence had fallen on Anne Boleyn's name!

"Your Grace will forgive me. And there was also the Queen Katherine Howard."

"Howard—Howard! Too many Howards have died at the hands of my family. *He* is my cousin, and *she* also."

"Does your Grace put family affection before the welfare of your realm?"

"My Spirit, you know I have put nothing before the welfare of my realm. You know that I have set aside something dearer than family affection."

He read to her from a letter of John Knox. She had spoken angry words against this man for he had insulted her and he had insulted kingship, and she had gibed at him with Robert. Now she thought he spoke like a prophet of old calling down the anger of the Lord upon the head of kings.

"If ye strike not at the root, the branches that appear to be broken will bud again, and that more quickly than men can believe...."

Representatives of a milder religion than that of Knox added their pleas. Her bishops came to her from Convocation, declaring that "the Scottish Queen hath heaped up together all the sins of the licentious sons of David". Her Peers came in a deputation headed by Robert and besought her on their knees to the same effect. When they had gone, the lover remained behind and added his private pleading. "Dear love, if you will not think of your own peril, think of your subjects! That woman must die! Or there is no safety...."

"Rob, I cannot do such a thing...."

"You would not marry me for the sake of the country. But you would save her to your own peril and the country's."

Finally her Commons came to her, the most furious of all, forgetting their awe of her in their love and anxiety for her. Angry voices beating at her temples, the Puritan brothers Wentworth heaping epithets on Mary which would have delighted Knox, cold reason, hot anger, deep devotion—all storming at her and giving her no rest. In the middle of her arguments—patient because she recognized that devotion—words suddenly slid into her mind with strange force. She had hated Mary; she had envied and despised her at once, and yet she had had this burning pity for her. Now it seemed that this pity had crystallized into words.

She stared before her so that the faces became a whitish blur broken by the darkness of eyes and open mouths, and heard still the echo of those angry insistent voices. Then she opened her hands which had been clenched.

"I cannot put to death the bird that has flown to me for succour from the hawk."

Remembering her words, she covered her face with her hands. She had retreated as far as she might, soon a decision would be forced on her. It was forced on her now, in the quiet voice of an usher: "The Lord Burghley craves to see the Queen's Majesty."

She stared at her most trusted counsellor.

"Well?"

"Your Grace has ever been sensible of the people's will."

"I have."

"Your Grace, for love of you, for fear of losing you, of losing their religion and ancient laws, the people are in such a temper that they will brook little opposition. Your Grace is still resolved in refusing to bring the Queen of Scots to trial?"

"I am resolved."

"Then the Duke of Norfolk can no longer be spared."

"So the people cry for a victim? They cry for blood?"

"He is not an innocent victim, your Grace. He is a traitor twice over. Doubly treacherous to your first clemency."

"Will not imprisonment suffice?"

"Your Grace knows it will not."

"Then—his head or Mary's?"

"Put thus sharply—yes, your Grace. If your Grace is resolved to save her. . . ."

"I have denied her very much, I think—but I will not deny her life. Well! Prepare the warrant for Norfolk——"

"I have it here, your Grace."

After she had signed it, and he had gone, she sat on alone, hearing the voices echoing and re-echoing in her aching head.

Yet peace came, and the dark clouds in that sullen, mottled sky, drifted apart to show the clear blue. Peace, Elizabeth thought, must be weighed and balanced as on a usurer's scales, it must be sought as stealthily and greedily as a usurer seeks his gold. War starts with magnificence, the trumpets blowing, steel clanging, bright banners flying—but it leaves drying blood, crumbling ashes and an emptiness which aches. . . . She got her treaty with France, signed in 1572 at Blois, which was in effect a defensive alliance against Spain. She and Catherine de Medici both needed the treaty, and when the Duke of Anjou's religious scruples were given as an excuse for breaking off the marriage suit, she grinned mockingly. "It saves me from developing religious scruples myself," she said to Robert.

"Then you never meant to wed this boy?"

"My sweet Robin! Never!"

"You deceived everyone mightily!"

"Such was my intention. . . ."

The treaty of Blois bore fruit. The next year her brother-in-law, King Philip, wrote to her with more friendliness than for years past. He was sending her a new ambassador to replace Don Guerau, deported for his share in the Ridolfi Plot. He had also instructed his viceroy, Alva, to lift the trade embargo between England and the Netherlands. As the Hamburg venture had been a success, her merchants now had two strings to their bow. . . . Yet that precious treaty of Blois was nearly wrecked by the massacre of the Huguenots gathered in Paris for the wedding of their titular leader, the young King of Navarre to Catherine's youngest daughter, the Princess Margot. Elizabeth was sickened by the senseless slaughter of St. Bartholomew, but she held grimly to the treaty. She bade her Council recall young Philip Sidney, then gaining a final polish by being a Gentleman of the Bedchamber to the King of France.

But the Privy Council's summons came too late to prevent Philip setting forth on his wonderful journey. When it arrived at the English Embassy, he had already gone, saddened and sickened by the slaughter of St. Bartholomew, riding across France to the ancient cities of the Rhineland where the famous scholar, Languet, was to act as his mentor, showing him the historic universities and the new printing presses—in those days when printers were men of deep learning, who wrote many of the books they printed in the tradition of Thomas Caxton and Wynkyn de Worde—to pass to the Emperor's court in Vienna. Here was his third court, and one utterly different from that of England, where all the living forces in the country, all energy and enterprise whether good or bad, everything which pulsed with life turned to the glittering figure of the Queen at its apex. Different, too, was Vienna from the second court he had known, that of the Valois-Medici, where the rich extravagance of the High Renaissance, that fantastic scene glittering as if jewelled and enamelled, was cracking into decadence and he had seen the demons and furies of the tapestries and paintings suddenly spring to malign life and go ravening for blood through the streets of Paris. The Hapsburg court at Vienna moved with a sombre gorgeous ritual, as formal and ordered as the exercises of the Spanish Riding School where he studied the apotheosis of the manège. Yet he went on farther, down the broad Danube to Hungary, to the very borders of the realms of the Grand Turk, and returned homewards through the cities of north Italy, where the first magic of the Renaissance had blossomed, having his portrait painted by Veronese in Venice, and then passing northwards to the Low Countries where he was to be shown friendship by the two most remarkable men in Europe, Don John of Austria, illegitimate half-brother of Philip of Spain, victor of Lepanto and paladin of the legends, and one who was a paladin of the verities, at once the symbol and inspiration of a people's resistance, William the Silent, Prince of Orange.

The years of that decade which Elizabeth snatched from the jaws of war, ticked like the deep-throated palace clocks, ticked away the blood of St. Bartholomew's Eve, ticked in the new uneasy friendship with Spain, while Englishmen under such leaders as Sir Humphrey Gilbert crossed to fight for the Low Countries against Spain, and the Dutch Seamen—"the Beggars of the Sea"—sheltered in English ports. She felt the peace was a breathing space, running out before her eyes like sand in an hour glass. John Hawkins was often at her elbow now, that merchant-adventurer with the deep, soft Devonshire voice, and closeted long with her ministers, the ageing Burghley—her trusted 'Spirit'—now Lord Treasurer, and Francis Walsingham, the new Secretary of State, he whom she called an "Italianate Puritan", who built up a consummate secret service which, it was whispered, knew the very thoughts of foreign potentates in their remote palaces, to prepare for the coming struggle which he saw as a war against Antichrist, all the fanatic devotion of the crusader being mingled in this man with the Machiavellian cunning of the Renaissance. To these, Hawkins urged the building of more ships, ships that were to be longer and lower, swifter in the water and closer to the wind than anything yet launched. He despised alike towering superstructures and armoured soldiers in men-o'-war, he urged heavier guns which could tear out their opponents' sides and topple their spars. Finally, in the year 1577, Elizabeth made Hawkins Treasurer of the Navy. She devised names for the ships which were launched under his direction such as *Dreadnought* and *Swiftsure*.

To Robert, life did not pass as a ticking clock, ticking the years away, or as sand slowly but steadily trickling through an hour glass. Life was a collection of rich fruits for which he must strive and seize; when the rinds were empty he would cast them away. In the year 1574, when Douglass Sheffield bore him a son, he suddenly realized that all was ended between them. It was as if an enchantment had ended, as if he had awoken from a dream. There was no more excitement and desire aroused by her, by her huge, softly lustrous eyes, by those quick, smooth movements which he had once compared to a hind or some graceful wild beast, by her docile abandon to passion. That beautiful face had become a mask in procession of beautiful faces which might have stepped from the tapestries in Leicester House.

He had realized it one afternoon, when visiting her in her lodgings in a house beyond the straggling confines of Westminster. She was sitting in a cushioned window-seat before an open casement, and the reflection of the sun on the waters of the river beyond, filled the air with a sparkling brightness. She had been listless when he came in but now she turned to him, with a strange feverish intensity. Her words seemed to have the inconsequence and unreasonability of a dream. She was saying that now their son was born, that son who was his heir, he must acknowledge him, he must acknowledge their secret contract of marriage.

"Of marriage!" he repeated harshly. "Has madness taken you?"

"When you gave me that ring in token of marriage and solemnly declared before Sir Edward Horsey—your Italian physician Julio was there too——"

"You know I did but jest. I was recalling the old words of the ballad:

"I will you bring; and with a ring,
By way of marriage——"

He trolled the words out merrily in his rich baritone. "I wed!" he exclaimed. "It would be as much as my life was worth with her Majesty—as well you know! From the first time I came to you, you understood that our love must be secret."

"But you swore that you would marry me when the Duke of Anjou was seeking the Queen's hand."

"I said *if* the Queen wed Anjou! But she did not. Nor will! She will marry no one—unless she marries me!"

He could only just catch her words, uttered as if she had no breath —"So the child and I mean nothing to you?"

"No, sweet, never that! I'll provide for you both—'tis an ambiguous situation for you and I have felt it on your behalf——"

"You're mighty kind!"

"Come, sweetheart! I'll settle rents to the value of seven hundred pounds a year upon you—but there must be no more reckless talk of marriage. What would it serve you to ruin me? I am bound—you are free! Sir Edward Stafford is so desperate in love with you that I never saw a man more!"

"Edward Stafford!" she repeated and then turned to him. "I think you are a devil incarnate!" Her wide open eyes were as blank and dark, he thought, as two pits. Her mouth, open as she shrieked at him, was another pit. . . . "A devil without heart or conscience who has climbed to fame and power by selling himself to that monster in Whitehall, that demon who is neither man nor woman—that——"

"Be silent!"

"I will not be silent! For her you murdered your first wife—you had Julio to poison her——"

"She died from a fall from the stairs as well you know!"

"After Julio had poisoned her, you had Verney cast her body over the stairs! It is well known that those two do your killing for you! I think you killed John—my husband——"

"You're a case for Bedlam! You don't know what you're saying!"

"Bedlam, is it? And now you are trying to kill me, your rightful second wife! Why did you send Julio to attend on me?"

"Because he is so skilful a fellow and you did not make a good recovery from the birth——" he wiped his brow with his silk sleeve. "You are beside yourself! I'll call your women. Then, later, when you can talk reasonably, I'll have the settlements made——"

"Settlements! You'll have that Italian poisoner settle me in my grave! Oh, you devil, doing it for a worse devil—her Gracious Majesty——"

"I'll stand no more!" he shouted. As the door clattered to, behind him, he heard her scream: "Robin! Robin! Come back to me——" but he was down the stairs and out of the house, vaulting on to his horse before young Blount could hold his stirrup, seeing his men's astonished gaze about him, as they hurriedly mounted, in a scramble and flurry as he spurred out of the gate at a round canter.

It was a nightmare, he thought later in the day, when closeted with the Queen, his head lying on her lap, caressed by her long fingers. Did she instinctively realize he needed comfort? She was a strange woman. Every movement of her slender hands held soothing, but she was laughing as she told him of her retort that morning to that blue-blooded Grandee of Spain, Mendoza the Ambassador, when he declared to her that she was responsible for the depredations committed by her seamen on the treasure galleons of the King, his master.

"I said: 'I am as responsible for them, as my good brother of Spain is for the rigours of the Inquisition. . . .' He had no parry for that!"

"Someone should compile your retorts to the ambassadors of mighty Spain. I swear the one which delighted me was what you said to Don Guerau, about the Netherlanders: 'Why will not my brother Philip let his subjects go to the devil their own way?' "

"My best retort was when I was but a month a Queen—to Feria, and he told me to be careful of religious matters. There was a most perilous gulf yawning before me and I was so young!"

"Young and beautiful!"

"Robin, I was never beautiful. But I had the reputation of it, in those days. When I was young I was handsome, perhaps, or comely. . . ."

"You are still beautiful!"

"My dearest, you are the most valiant and unconquerable liar!"

"You like it from other men!"

"You are not 'other men'! You are my other self. . . . I'm past forty, Robin! Over twenty years since we were imprisoned in the Tower."

"It is my eternal regret that I did not rescue you from that same Tower——"

"A most pleasant fancy! To bear me off in front of your lily-white steed! Christopher Hatton would spin such fantasies."

"He is a good fellow, but he is a grand Romantic!"

"He is more. He is a Fantastic. These idylls of the Queen of Faery, of Gloriana, of Belphoebe—they are reality to him. He bears his adoration for the Queen—not for the woman, she is no mere woman in his eyes!—as reverently as if it were one of those finely blown, gold fretted bubbles of Murano glass. And as fragile."

She laughed. "My poor Sheep! It is a shame to mock him. Because I call you my 'Eyes', he says he must be my 'Lids', but I think him my Sheep, my Mutton. But I trust his fidelity. When Cousin Frank became too old for office, I made my trusty Sheep, Captain of the Guard. And a Wolf in Sheep's clothing he'll prove to my enemies!"

"God grant it, sweet."

He thought: "She's more desperately alive than ten other women! She may be forty, dye her hair fantastically and paint her face so thickly—and yet she can dim all these lovely fools——"

"Dear love," he said, "I wish you would honour and delight me by coming on Progress to Kenilworth. 'Tis nearly ten years since you visited me there. I wish to devise such an entertainment for you!"

"Next summer, I'll come, Rob."

He thought: "It shall be an entertainment which will make the world gasp. It will show me to be the greatest man of her realm. I might yet persuade her to marry me. There is no need for any foreign courtship now."

Aloud he said: "I love you."

"To how many have you said that?"

"Before you, sweet, I confess, alas, to many. I spoke then in ignorance."

She sighed and did not answer. She thought: "Do I dare to ask—'and to how many after'? All those pretty fools amongst my ladies—gaping at him! To-day he was troubled. Is it some woman! Is it his debts? But he comes to me for comfort, as I turn to him when I need it. . . ."

"Come," she said, "we may stroll half an hour in the Privy Garden, before I must read the secret dispatches from the Netherlands."

Chapter Eleven

The "princely pleasures" of Kenilworth in the year 1575 were to be remembered throughout the centuries. The July sun poured down on a scene of splendour, on a succession of elaborate and fantastic masques, pageants and plays, devised by the poet George Gascoigne, which followed each other with a recurrent richness that surely seemed to belong to a dream rather than real life. Such formally designed entertainments were varied by vigorous outdoor sports, hunting, hawking and jousting. Besides all the officials of the court, a vast number of the nobility had accompanied the Queen on her visit to one of the greatest of their order. However much jealousy might be hidden by admiration, the day was past for whispers about "Dudley upstarts". The Earl of Leicester was known, not only in England, by the nicknames of "the Great Lord" and "Dominus Factotum". He was almost a Prince of the Blood. . . . His entertainment for his royal guest was on a royal scale. Humbler persons came from far and near to gaze at the stupendous displays, and gasped at the thought of the astronomical cost to his lordship. A young couple came all the way from Stratford-on-Avon to see the sights. Their name was Shakespeare and they brought with them their little son, Will. . . .

The slanting shadows were beginning to fall, long and purple, on the trampled turf of the great gardens. The hot, still air seemed filled with the memory, alike of the sun's fiery violence and the sound of thousands of lusty voices. But now evening had brought a pause; the vigour of the summer's day was all but done, and there was a breathing space in the exertion of man's ingenuity. Soon the soft darkness of the summer's night would come, to provide an admirable background for the glare of torches and the flash and sparkle of fireworks, shining alike on the tinsel of the players and the jewels of the mighty. Till then entertainers and entertained might rest and relax.

In a comfortable, panelled room, its casements wide open, a copper tub of cold water stood on the floor, to cool the wine bottles, being leisurely drunk by the three high officers of his lordship's household. There was Thomas Blount, chatelain of Kenilworth Castle, his hair greying now above his weatherbeaten leathery face; Richard Verney with his narrow dark-red fox's head, his lordship's principal Gentleman of the Horse—"Master of Horse to her Majesty's Master of Horse" he liked to call himself—and the elegant Digby who carried out so many dark and delicate intrigues for his lordship.

"God's soul!" said Verney, "it's good to stretch one's legs for a moment! Up and down, up and down for a week, turning here, going there, sleeping like a horse on my feet, snatching food when I may. Body o' me! Here's my Lordship of Sussex's Gentleman to complain of this and that for his lordship's beasts, and are our stables to be shown in a bad light to him? Here's one of the French Ambassador's Gentlemen wanting to see my lord's grey goshawk. Here's the Head Yeoman with a list of complaints longer than his arm, of the guests' Gentlemen of the Horse demanding all things, their grooms brawling, the extra men, taken on, pilfering—one knave caught with two silver-plated bits in his pocket—all the grooms getting most incontinently drunk.... And you, Tom—you've had worse on your hands!"

Blount carefully filled his own and his companions' silver goblets from a newly opened bottle of wine.

"I confess I never thought this castle small", he said, "till I tried to fit these guests into it! It has shrunk to a hovel ... you have horses and men to contend with, my sweet Dick, but I have the fairer sex—their ladyships, their gentlewomen and their serving-wenches—into the bargain!"

"I assure you they hang about the stables—high and low degree alike!"

"Thus proving", said Digby with a sweet smile, "that the female is a mighty hunter! The gentlewomen come after the gallants, and the wenches for the grooms. 'Where the treasure is there will the heart be.' Verily!"

"And I have no time for 'em now, plague take it!" said Verney with a laugh. "Neither has his lordship—bless him! Except for the crown of her sex, for whom this is all devised."

Zenith

"And d'you know what it costs him?" demanded Tom Blount. "I was checking through the accounts with Underhill and the other secretaries—one thousand pounds per day!"

"God's blood!" swore Verney.

"For a throne—perhaps not so much. . . ." said Digby.

They looked at each other.

"It's his last throw," said Verney at length. "He's shown her—and the world besides—that he's the greatest man of her realm. He is showing her that he stints no trouble, no treasure, to pour out for her. Women like it. Kitchenmaid or Queen—they like a fellow to be ready to ruin himself for them. Which shows there's no prudence in 'em."

"*She's* prudent!" declared Blount. "She'll count every groat. But she likes her subjects to pour out the gold for her! Yet—when I look back twenty years—all this——" he made a sweeping gesture with one hand—"the power and riches and greatness of his lordship—it all comes from her. She denies him nothing—but a share in her crown."

"You remember the early days, Tom? When she was first on the throne——"

"I remember! They were a handsome pair and as hot in love as you please! They set the tongues wagging from Council Chamber to tavern. . . . The way he looked at her—the way she looked at him! And she could scarce keep her hands off him."

"She can't keep her hands off any pretty fellow. See her with one and you don't forget she's Nan Bullen's daughter. But let him go too far and he'll find she's Old Harry's daughter as well! There's a chance for any likely lad with a pleasing face, a good leg and a bold tongue, if he has the fancy and the spirit to fondle a tigress. He might scramble up a few rungs of the ladder. Digby, my gay peacock, I wonder you haven't ventured. You're about his lordship when he's at court, and you're as exquisite a fop as ever stepped. I wonder those long hands of hers haven't taken hold of you!"

"I keep in my station," said Digby with a curl of lip. "One of his lordship's poor Gentlemen! Aha, those beautiful hands of hers! What a wealth of cruelty, what a wealth of tenderness in those long fingers! And they never let go. . . . But d'you think any of her pretty fellows occupy her for more than an hour's flirtation? I trow not. Else his lordship would not take it so calmly. He's sure of her heart—if he may never have her crown!"

"Will he ever?"

"Well for us if he does! No men ever served a more loyal and generous master. She's pleased enough with this entertainment. D'you remember that great shout of laughter from her last night, at the water pageant, when that drunken knave pulled off his mask and bawled out, instead of his set speech, that he was no Triton, not he, but honest Harry Goldingham, very glad to drink her Majesty's health—and he had been drinking it all the evening! If she hadn't laughed so loud and so long, Goldingham u'd tasted the whip. . . ."

"She likes to laugh! God bless her Majesty and long may she do it. . . . She's got red blood in her veins."

"And a head as red as your own, Dick Verney!"

"It's a wig," said Digby.

"He knows too much of women! His lordship had better set him to do the wooing."

"Spare my modesty! If ever she weds, I believe it would only be he. She loves him! I've seen her by his bedside when he was grievously ill."

"Well!" said Verney. "Here's a toast. To the end of her Majesty's official virginity!"

The three silver goblets clinked together. Through the still hot air, from another window wide open, there floated the notes of a lute accompanying a tenor voice.

> "Disdain me not that am your own,
> Refuse me not that am so true,
> Mistrust me not till all be known,
> Forsake me not now for no new.
> Disdain me not!"

"A good song", said Verney, "for his lordship to sing now!"

"He's true in his fashion," said Digby thoughtfully. "For all the pretty Sheffields. . . . The Queen has that of him no other ever will."

Blount opened another bottle of wine.

"Digby is right. If she ever takes a husband it will be our lordship. The long memories of youth they share—their common danger in the Tower—their early passion—— And the good companionship of years together, fitting like a hand in a glove. Long kindness and present laughter——"

"Aye—laughter!" said Verney. "The last time they were hawking together, I was close behind when they reined in on the down, to watch his lordship's new ger-falcon strike. He puts his hand on her knee, and tells her a merry bawdy tale—'twould have had the Rose Tavern in a roar, he's a merry wag, our lordship—and she! Laughs as loud as she did last night at Goldingham, laughs till she cracks the paint on her face. Then she takes him by the beard and looks at him as if she would eat him. "Fie, Robin!" says she, "you should not be let loose with modest maidens! By God's soul! I'll tell the Bishop that one!" Says our lordship: "He'll never see the point, my sweet, unless you explain it." And she shakes her head and makes to be sorrowful. 'Bishops', says she, 'are not what they were!' That's how they are together. And that fine gentleman, Captain Christopher Hatton and the other courtiers, they must address her as if she were the Goddess of Love and Beauty, and rhyme it if they can! But she never wants that from *him*. They have their memories as you say, Tom, and their jokes. And let his lordship be sick and she's at his bedside as calm and as tender as any man could ask."

"There's only one thing to prevent their marriage. Which has prevented it since the hubbub over Dame Amy's death died down," said Blount. "She's a ruler and she'll never be ruled. And what does the world think of a man who's ruled by his wife?"

"You have it, Tom!" said Digby. "And she knows it! She knows he can be her darling and her delight but never her lord and master!"

Down one of the long pleached avenues in the gardens, a woman wandered with a strange drifting aimlessness. The red light from the sinking sun ran over the shimmering silk of her dress, but her large dark eyes seemed blank and lightless. It was Douglass Sheffield. Her brother and his wife, Lord and Lady Howard of Effingham, had made a determined attempt to draw her from the strange, dazed melancholy which had seemed to fall on her in the past year. It was deplorable her unfortunate entanglement with the Earl of Leicester, but it need not be utterly disastrous. Hardly anyone knew of the child she had borne him, and mercifully, the Queen had no idea of the whole matter. She must be resolute and turn her back on the past, she was only thirty and still lovely, and here was Sir Edward Stafford, who had been promised the Embassy in France, so madly in love with her that everyone commented on it. What a solution it would be, thought her brother, Lord Howard, if only his unhappy sister could be persuaded to marry Stafford! He knew about her affair with Leicester and about the child, but nothing, it seemed, could check his ardour and devotion. They had told her that she must come to the great gathering at Kenilworth, it would be most noticeable if she stayed away, everyone would talk. Let her show Leicester that she did not care! With a sort of limp heedlessness she agreed. The Howards brought her with them, and Edward Stafford came too. He was like her shadow.

She had not gone far down the pleached avenue when he came swiftly up behind her. She looked at him neither with pleasure nor annoyance, but, he thought, perhaps with acceptance.

"Where would you go—my dearest?" he sank his voice on the last two words. She shrugged.

"Nowhere," she said. "I thought it would be cooler out of doors."

She let him take her arm and they wandered off. On some rising ground they paused and stared back at the castle.

"One has some idea of the size from here," he said.

"But it's not real, Ned!" She had turned to him with a strange bewilderment in her eyes. "That was where I was so foolish. I thought I would be its mistress. How could I? Of a castle raised like Jack's beanstalk by magic and when the spell is ended—it will vanish!"

"Aye!" said Stafford through his teeth, fury swelling up in him. "It is magic, that such a vile scoundrel could be so raised up by one who is otherwise a very great Queen——"

"She's a witch, like her mother," said Douglass with a strange flat conviction in her voice. "I used to blame him but he can't help himself. She has laid this spell on him and who can break it? She uses him. He has no life but from her."

"He!" exclaimed Stafford. "By God! If I had him here, with my sword in my hand and he, his—nothing could save him! I would spit him through——" His face was convulsed. She looked at him with the same bewilderment but when she spoke it was with the patience one uses to a stupid child.

"But it wouldn't be any good, Ned. You blame him and I blame *her*. But nothing can be undone, *now*. If you had killed him ten years ago before I ever met him, then you would have saved me. It's too late now. What has been done cannot be undone."

"Yes it can!" he said. He had caught her by the shoulders and she stood looking at him with the same patient, dazed bewilderment. "If you marry me, Douglass, I can take you away. To France, where you need never see him again, nor the Queen either. Then you'll forget! Take the boy——" he could not bring himself to say the child's name, 'Robert', but he added: "I'll be good to him!"

"You are all goodness," she said. "Poor Ned. But I am a body without a heart—without a soul! What could that be to you? But if you want such a being—take her!"

Stafford drew in a long, shuddering breath. He raised both her hands to his lips, and kissed their palms with a furious intensity.

"Then I may tell your brother?" he murmured.

"Oh, yes!" her voice had no life in it. "Poor Charles! He will be so happy. . . ."

In a corner room, rounded by the curve of one of the towers, two women sat by a deep-cut turret window, also open on to the gardens. The Countess of Essex was clad comfortably in a loose silk wrapper as she reclined, very much at her ease, on a couch at the foot of her bed, and the friend who had come to visit her, burdened with her own stiff ruff and heavy brocades, envied her in the heat. She was envious on another point.

"Lettice," she said, "how lucky you are that one day your daughter will be mistress of all this!"

"What use will that be to me?" said Lettice Essex, drawing her brows into a straight frown above her eyes which seemed to have the same sullen lustre as black velvet. "When I'm a bent old hag, and nothing is any good to me any more, you mean I may have a corner here when my son-in-law is Lord and Master? If he ever is!"

"But, Lettice!" said her astonished friend, "I believed you were delighted at the thought of your daughter, Penelope, marrying young Philip Sidney who is his uncle's heir."

Lettice shrugged and then pushed over a decorated porcelain casket of sugar comfits.

"I did not make the match," she said. "Walter—my husband—did, because he has such affection and esteem for Sir Henry Sidney."

"But everyone says that young Master Sidney is brilliant and has such prospects——"

"Has he?" said his prospective mother-in-law. "Everyone's tongue is wagging about him because he has travelled so far and been shown such favour by so many great people. One moment he is being saved from the massacre of St. Bartholomew, and the next being received in friendship by Don John of Austria. He has talked with all the scholars of Germany and learned the art of the Spanish manège in

Zenith

Vienna—I confess I am somewhat weary of the perfections of Master Philip Sidney! He is a charming youth, no doubt, but I could wish he had some solid property before he marries my daughter. Still—Penelope is only twelve. She cannot be wed for three years, and who knows what will happen by then?"

"But, my dear Lettice!" exclaimed her friend. "I cannot understand you! Solid property—isn't the young man heir to the Earl of Leicester—heir to this very castle and estate? Isn't he high in the Queen's favour?"

"The Queen's favour? Well—since his return, my royal cousin has made him her Cupbearer, she tweaks his hair and calls him 'my Philip'. For Penelope's sake, I would rather she gave him one of those convenient monopolies! As for being his uncle's heir—supposing my Lord of Leicester weds and gets a son? Where are Master Philip's pretensions then? And even if he does not—Lord Leicester is in the prime of life. Is he to take himself to the grave to further Philip?"

"But, Lettice!" said the friend once more, leaning forward so that her lips were close to the ear of Lady Essex. "We all know why Lord Leicester does not marry——"

"Because he dare not! And now he is making his last great effort to wed *her*. . . ."

The friend felt a delicious tremor.

"I wonder?" she breathed.

"The world's wondering!"

"They've left it rather late—for a Prince of Wales——" whispered the friend.

"There won't be a Prince of Wales!"

"They say—fifteen years ago—there *was* a child——"

"There was not!" declared Lettice with the same emphasis. "My mother was alive then and one of her principal ladies-in-waiting. My father was Captain of the Bodyguard. D'you think they would not know?"

"I did wonder if her Grace was being slandered——"

"Slandered? If there's no child—in or out of wedlock—it isn't for want of trying!" said Lettice with a sudden viciousness.

"La—Lettice!" Her friend gave a squeal of delighted horror.

"How d'you think he gained all he has?"

"Oh—I declare—well, really——" She filled her mouth with

sugared comfits, nearly as replete as her mind with delicious and dangerous scandal, and looked at the Countess of Essex. A strange bitterness had come into the voice of Lettice.

"Nowadays", she said, "he has grown heavy. He has put on flesh. But sixteen years ago—when she first got her claws into him—he was the most magnificent young man that ever walked the earth. . . . And God help any other woman who dared look at him!" Her full lip had curled back and showed her pointed teeth.

"You don't—like her Grace?" whispered the friend.

"As much as she likes me! My mother had an affection for her."

"If she does marry Lord Leicester after all—Philip will be the Queen's nephew——"

"Much good he'll get of it! I am the Queen's cousin by blood—and much good I've had of it. . . . And perhaps she won't take Lord Leicester, and perhaps one day he'll have the courage to break away from her, and have a wife and son of his own, and good-bye to Philip's hopes! He'll get nothing much from his father. Penshurst is a small property, and Sir Henry, like my husband serving under him, is ruined by Ireland. Ah, my royal cousin, she expects her faithful servants to pour out their blood and their treasure in her service. Sir Henry, her Lord Deputy, is not a rich man and he is expected to cast what he has into those accursed Irish bogs. Walter is ruining his estate and his health in those bogs. . . . And what's to come of me then and of the children? I want a rich husband for Penelope! Not one with only expectations!"

"Ireland is a most grievous place," sighed the friend.

"And Walter is a chivalrous fool!" said his wife bitterly. "Better be like Robert Leicester, even if he does have to dally with *her*—without her wig, her paint, or her gorgeous apparel—she pays well enough for her pleasures!"

"You hate her, Lettice, I do declare!"

"I do. But I can wait. It's in our blood. Hers and mine! My grandmother, poor fool, couldn't. The old King toyed with her and then thrust her off, and she must marry my grandfather, Carey, and sink into obscurity. But her younger sister, Anne, she set a higher price on herself—and she got it—even if she paid in the end with her own life! She waited and got her crown. And her daughter knew how to wait—and she has her crown, her throne, her power! And I, too, can wait for what I want. . . ."

Zenith

The Countess of Essex's prospective son-in-law was, at that moment, wandering on the outskirts of the park with his friend, Fulke Greville.

"It will be pleasant under one of those great trees," he said. The red light of the sunset was draining the fresh green from the landscape, turning it to soft greys and violets. Fulke had paused a moment to look back at the gardens.

"Some gentlewoman coming as if after us—she's waving—it's your sister."

Philip turned, and then began to hurry back towards the hastening figure in the shining white satin worn by the Queen's Maids of Honour. Fulke, following, smiled at the eager girl running towards the tall youth. They were so alike! With the same delicately carved features, the same dark grey eyes, and above all, that same ardent expression, that strangely intense spiritual vitality. Amongst the more mundane and unimaginative throng, they seemed like wild birds flown into a barnyard. "Their minds", thought Fulke, "have wings to raise them so far above the rest of us."

"And how", asked Philip, "have you escaped from her Majesty?"

"She sent me! I was looking from the window, and I saw you two walking towards the park, and suddenly there was the Queen behind me and had taken hold of my neck between her thumb and forefinger. 'Ha! What are you gazing at, miss?' And then she looks out herself and says: 'You can go and join your brother if you wish! I give you your liberty till the torchlight masque begins.' So I ran. Margaret Ferrers asked: 'Please, your Grace, I should also like to walk in the gardens, now the cool of evening has come on!' And her Grace snapped: 'Cool of evening, God's precious soul! Making love to gallants in the bushes!' She keeps us like vestals. . . ."

"She's not so far wrong!" said Philip. "So long as she is not malicious."

"Malicious is sometimes scarcely the word!" declared Mary. She and Philip were walking hand in hand, swinging their arms slightly in rhythm with their steps. So often Fulke had seen them walk like that, in childhood at Penshurst.

"But", she added, as if in compunction, "she's kind to me."

"This Mistress Margaret," said Fulke. "I must investigate her. Is she pretty?"

"Very pretty! And very enterprising. . . ."

282

"They can be too enterprising!" said Fulke with affected gloom. Mary made a face at him. Fulke was almost like another brother, certainly a member of the family since childhood days.

"You mustn't take him too seriously!" said Philip.

"I never did!"

Fulke struck an attitude.

"I wish people would take me seriously! And all because I say: 'It's better to laugh than to cry!' When you come to court—laugh, laugh, laugh! At yourself first of all. . . ."

"Laugh!" said Philip. Mary felt his fingers tighten suddenly on hers. "There are times I feel I can bear it no longer—I must get away —out into the countryside——"

Mary could feel the anguish flowing through him. She had seen by the very way he had walked, with his faithful shadow, Fulke, behind him, that he was unhappy. Had the Queen seen it too, from the window, and therefore had let her go? The Queen saw and understood so much more than anyone could believe. . . .

"We are getting away," said Fulke. "To the greenwood tree. This very minute!" And he began to sing.

"You and I and Amyas,
Amyas and you and I,
To the greenwood we must go—alas!
You and I, my life, and Amyas!"

Philip was looking back at the castle, black against the brilliant sky.

"It is still so hot," he said. "Because there is no movement in air. Look at the smoke from the chimneys of the kitchen wing! It pours straight upwards—as straight as the downward flow of water."

"It is too hot for the birds to sing," said Mary. "They are so quiet."

Philip had put his hand to the bark of a great oak. Then he took off his doublet of pale grey silk, slashed with deep rose, and spread it carefully on the ground. "Sit on that," he said, and when she had settled herself, her white satin skirts spread around her like the petals of a wide-open lily, he lay down, full length, his head on her lap, and his arms in the ballooning embroidered sleeves of his fine cambric shirt, close to his sides. Fulke rested on his elbow and flipped idly at the flies and midges with his free hand. Mary looked down at her brother's face and then put a hand each side of his head, lightly holding his temples.

"Your hands are so cool," he murmured.

But she was having that strange fear which came to her sometimes and which she had only confided to one living person—the feeling that some strange peril threatened Philip. Yet he had passed unscathed through St. Bartholomew's Eve, he had finished his long journeying, he was safe at home, here with her holding his head in her hands—and yet she was afraid. It was not so much a physical danger that she dreaded, as some bitter sorrow which might strike at his very spirit, and worst of all the fear that he, and all that was within him, would not come to fulfilment. She remembered that extraordinary night when for the first and last time she had talked with that unbelievable intimacy with the Queen, and she had cried out that it was not only for herself that it would be such a terrible thing if Philip were killed in the massacre in Paris—Philip had so much to give the whole world—it was like some cup holding a rare and precious wine being dashed to the ground, poured away and wasted. . . . She remembered the tiredness and the understanding of the voice answering her: "My child, we must all do what we can, with all we have, in the time allotted to us. No one can do more. We cannot always see our work in our lifetime, sometimes like the seed, it lies underground. We can only hope that posterity will see that for which we have striven." It had taken Mary away from her own terrors and sorrows for a moment to see a picture of the Queen other than the glittering bedecked figure greedily drinking in elaborate flattery as if she could not live without it, laughing and rating—a picture of the Queen patiently building for the prosperity and safety of her country. She must tell Philip—he had seemed so disillusioned since he had come home and been given a small post at court. The heartless fortune seeking, the insincerity and the intrigues behind the glitter had disgusted him. She had felt too that he was disappointed in the Queen.

He was talking now.

"If I might be out of it all! No longer dancing like a performing monkey on my string. . . . Since I cannot go and fight by the side of that most noble and gallant gentleman, the Prince of Orange, I wish I could sail over the seas, to discover those new worlds beyond the ocean. I wish I might sail with Francis Drake. It is his hope, his dream, to sail the first English ship in that vast ocean which the Spaniards call the Pacifico, whose waters he saw from a tall tree in the isthmus of Panama!"

"I also!" said Fulke. "D'you remember Dick Hakluyt and the visit he paid to his cousin, Master Richard Hakluyt of the Middle Temple, and saw such maps that they fired his imagination for ever after?"

"This Dick Hakluyt, wasn't he at Christ Church with you?" asked Mary.

"Yes, he was at Christ Church with us," said her brother. "He told us how his cousin had begun to show him all the maps of the known world, and the great uncharted spaces—and then took out his Bible and read from the 117th Psalm—'that they which go down to the sea in ships and occupy by the great waters, they see the works of the Lord and His wonders in the deep'."

"Yes!" said Fulke, with echoing eagerness, "and besides voyaging through the Straits of Magellan into the Mar del Pacifico, to the Spice Islands, the believed Terra Australis and far Cathay beyond, there is this talk of a North-West Passage and a North-East Passage."

"There is one Master Michael Lok," said Philip, "a merchant of London whom I visited. You must come with me, next time, Fulke. It is his desire to fit out an expedition to be led by Captain Martin Frobisher—a great burly Yorkshireman—who they say is the most skilful sea captain after John Hawkins and Francis Drake, to find the mouth of that North-West Passage, in the frozen lands to the north of the New Found Land which Cabot discovered for her Grace's grandfather. There, it is believed, is the mouth of a wide channel which leads from the frozen lands, swiftly to the warm waters, and most shortly to Cathay. If only I might go on that voyage! But the Queen will not let me go!"

"Yet she too is interested in exploration," said Fulke. "That strange man, Dr. Dee, talks to her of the unknown lands."

"Truly a strange man! The ignorant say he is a great wizard—but if he really dealt in necromancy, would the Queen have him so often about her? When I was in Paris, all whispered that the Queen Mother of France practised the Black Arts. But to read the stars and riddle the future in a search for the ends of knowledge, need not mean devilish magic. . . . It was only the other day when the Queen had me in to lift maps and globes. Uncle Robin was there with her and Dr. Dee who had brought an Italian edition of the work of the Arabian geographer, Abulfeda. They were talking this time of the North-East Passage, and Dee held by the opinion of Abulfeda which is supported in part by the chart of the White Sea of Muscovy drawn by Master William Borough, that it would be possible to sail round by the north of Norway and past the coast of the Muscovites or as some call them, the Russes, to where, at a Cape called Tabin, the coast of Asia is believed to slant away south-eastwards, so bringing one swiftly to Cathay. I was so eager that the Queen laughed at me and clapped my cheek, saying: "But we'll keep you hooded, my brave peregrine, however much you tug at the jesses! You shan't fly free!"

"She'll not part with you!" said Fulke.

"She keeps me for this mumming and masquing!" cried Philip with impatience, "and will not let me do aught worth while for her. Ah! Sometimes I think she cares for nothing but idle displays and compliments! Once I thought she had such rare understanding—and that she would lead this nation to such glory——"

"Oh, Philip, I wish you had heard her when she talked of doing good by stealth and laying foundations on which others would build walls, and one's work lying like a seed in the ground. . . ."

"When did she say this?"

"It was when we thought you were lost in Bartholomew. . . . I did not know she could be so kind. She's harsh to her ladies—and none of the Maids of Honour likes her. She was never actually harsh to me, but she ignored me. Well—that night we got the first rumours—Mistress Parry was ill. She usually sleeps in the Queen's chamber, and only if she cannot, does the Queen choose someone else. And hardly ever one of the younger girls. You can imagine my astonishment when she chose me! I should have been afraid—if I hadn't been so troubled for you, I could hardly think of anything else.

At last I was alone with the Queen, on the pallet bed at the foot of hers. She read for a time by her candle. I lay quite still, hardly daring to breathe, and then she put the candle out, and I thought perhaps she would soon be asleep. I couldn't sleep. . . . Then she spoke to me: 'Mary—you are still awake!' So I begged her pardon if I had disturbed her and she said: 'Your thoughts disturbed me. Come here!' I went and knelt by the side of her bed, and she had lighted her candle again, and was looking at me, very keenly the way she does. And she said: 'You are grieving for your brother Philip?' I had never heard her voice so kind before, and what with having bottled myself up all day—I started to cry—and I found myself clutching one of her hands and pressing it to my face. She put the other hand on my head and said: 'Come, now!' And told me all sorts of things, how she had bidden her ambassador, Sir Francis Walsingham, have especial care of you, and how, she was certain, that the King of France would protect you, because he had made such a favourite of you before. *I* said that the King of France was a wicked man and his mother was worse, and then she laughed a little, and asked me if I had read Foxe's *Book of Martyrs*, and did he not depict her sister, the Queen Mary, as a most cruel monster? I scarcely knew what to answer and she said that when she read Foxe, she thought of her sister being kind to her as a little child with the toothache. 'Ah!' she said. 'There's none so bad that they have no good in them, and none so good that they have no bad in them!' Then she told me how Mistress Parry had read your hand when you were a schoolboy, and had foretold many things which had come true—that you were to travel far and have the favour of princes—and a great danger would come near you when you were abroad, but it would pass you by. She believed in Mistress Parry's fortune-telling."

"Some of it has come true. . . ."

"Oh, she was so kind to me that night! And talked to me about many things, till I felt less afraid. She seemed so sure that you were safe—I wonder whether she really thought so or was only trying to help me? I have never seen her like that before or since. In the end she took my face in her hands, and put her cheek for a moment against my head, before she bade me go back to bed again. It was when I told her that I felt you would do so much if you were spared, that she said no one could do more than strive with all he had, in his allotted time. . . ."

Philip was silent for a while.

"She is a very great lady," he said at last. "I wish she would always speak like that and not waste herself with trivial things. . . . I'm not the wonderful fellow you think me, Mary. Far from it! I only ask that I may do all I can, in my allotted time. . . ."

While his niece and nephew were so engaged under one of the great trees of his park, the master of Kenilworth, having completed his toilet, contemplated himself in one of the long mirrors which he had had imported especially from Venice. The golden embroidery and ornamentation were so thickly encrusted that the white satin, slashed with black velvet, of his doublet and trunk hose, was all but hidden. Around his neck was a golden collar, heavily gemmed and suspending the "George" of the Order of the Garter, the actual garter being buckled below his knee over his tight, white silk stocking. By his side hung a rapier with a jewelled hilt, and in his hands were his black velvet cap, its white plume fastened with a large diamond, and his white leather perfumed gloves, sewn stiffly with seed pearls and golden thread. Lettice Essex had not spoken from malice when she had said that he was putting on weight; like many ageing athletes, his muscle was turning to fat, but he was still a powerful and impressive figure to carry off his gorgeous attire. His once thick black hair was retreating from his brow at the same time as it was greying at the temples, but his fine dark eyes had their bold and yet thoughtful glance which had pierced so many female hearts. He considered himself carefully, and was not displeased with the effect.

A little later, one of the Maids of Honour came curtsying to the Queen, who was sitting reading on the day-bed by the window in her great bedchamber, to say that the Earl of Leicester craved to see her Majesty.

"I will come, tell his lordship, in a few moments."

As she moved with a slow dignity down the Long Gallery, a glittering and fantastic figure, with her jewelled head rising from the great cartwheel ruff, her natural outline lost in the huge swollen sleeves and the wide farthingale, his memory went back twenty-two years to the girl who had walked into the prison garden. The fashions of that age had been simpler, and she had been dressed very plainly in a gown of dark blue-green, but it had shown up her pale skin and red hair. There had been no ruffs in those days and the low, square-cut neck of the gown had set off her slender throat and white shoulders.

As he straightened up after bowing over her hand, he told her of these memories, and saw her thin, reddened lips smiling. This evening she had little paint on her face, and it was as pale as the remembered girl's had been. She laid her hand on his arm and they began to walk up and down the Long Gallery.

"You always moved so proudly and so gracefully," he said. "Even then you walked like a Queen."

"I tried to be as dignified as I could, so they would not see how desperately afraid I was." She made an odd little sound, half laugh, half sigh. "I shall never forget landing at the Traitor's Gate, on that

288

wet Palm Sunday morning. For years afterwards the sound of water lapping against stone steps turned me sick. . . . They only let me have one of my own servants, a lad to carry my valise, and he was blubbering and crying. I remember sitting on a stone and refusing to enter the building at first—I thought of being thrust into some dungeon or vile place—but I was not so badly lodged in the Bell Tower. The turnkey's wife—the mother of those two children—was quite polite and attentive. I remember her lighting a fire for me because it seemed so damp, and one of the children wandered in, and stared at me with her finger in her mouth, and I coaxed her to talk to me and finally picked her up on my lap—because I wanted to look at one face which was not a certain enemy set to spy on me! I think it pleased the mother for she said, after the manner of her kind: 'Oh, you do look ill, my Lady!' And I said: 'I have been grievously ill. Will they let me have a physician?' But she answered: 'I couldn't say, my Lady. You'll have to ask the Lieutenant in the morning. But if there's anything I can do for you, I will.' Afterwards my sister sent women to wait on me. Spies, of course, but civil. And I had my good loyal Harington."

"But you were so alone," he said. "We were four brothers together."

"Alone, yes. Always alone. . . . That first night I never slept a wink. I tried to imagine the questions they would ask me and prepare answers. I thought—of Thomas Seymour and my cousin Jane." She added in a voice so low he could hardly catch it: "I thought of my mother."

She never spoke of her mother, he reflected, she seemed to have a superstitious dread of her name.

"Do you remember her—at all?" he asked, greatly daring.

"I will tell you all that I remember. . . ." But they had walked to the end of the gallery and turned back again before she continued: "I must have been about two. Perhaps a month or so more. I can remember being dressed in my best after being washed and brushed till I was nearly desperate—and being slapped for sucking a string of pearls round my neck!"

"What child doesn't have such memories? I recollect being put into a suit of crimson satin fresh from the tailor and walking into a duckpond, dragging Guildford in with me! And my mother alternately smacked and kissed us when we were brought out. I think I was five!"

T   289

"You had a loving mother!" she said bitterly. "Well, I can remember the bustle and all the fuss Lady Bryan, the Mistress of the Household, made. Then my next memory is sitting on a strange woman's lap. I can't recall her face. Only her voice. . . . I have heard the echo of that bitterness in my own voice! She said: 'Jesu mercy! Why isn't she a boy? And so like her father too!' That is all."

"But people told you of her?"

"Very little. They whispered her name as if in dread. And Mary—she sometimes flashed out in mad hatred. She believed that *my* mother murdered *her* mother—by poison!"

"Sweet, don't dwell on these old unhappy things. You have come out of the shadows now." Her eyes were momentarily closed and he felt her weight on his arm. Then she opened them wide.

"Rob," she said. "Just as the only happiness I had in imprisonment was in meeting you in that little garden—the only happiness I have had as a woman, has come from you."

"Oh, my dear, I wish I could give you more."

"You have given me all that I dare have."

"No," he said with determination. "In those early days when your throne was not yet secure, when the world's tongue wagged over the death of my wife, it was not possible for us to wed. I understand it now. When I was young and my blood was so hot—I had no patience. I understand too that it was necessary for you to appear to welcome the courtships of foreign princes. But now we have that peace for which you crave——"

"For how long?" she interrupted.

"You are a most rightly beloved sovereign. All the old unhappy things—Amy's death amongst them—are forgotten. There is no reason why we should not marry now. I don't ask for the title of King. . . . Perhaps my father's Dukedom. What you will. . . ."

He heard her sigh before she spoke.

"Robin, if it were possible for us to marry, do you think I should have waited till I was forty-two?"

"But—once you believed it might be possible——"

"As you say, in youth the blood is hot and there is no patience. Perhaps your wife's death was a strangely disguised blessing. Our marriage is impossible!"

"I do not see it! It is not impossible. . . . Not now."

"Yes, Rob, my dear!" She was turning the Coronation ring on

her hand. "England is my husband. The Queen is dedicated to her people and she must rule alone. But the woman behind the Queen, who has had nearly everything taken from her—the woman who was once that lonely child surrounded by hatreds—she has had one happiness. Your love."

The shadows were falling heavily as the Countess of Essex, now dressed in shimmering satins, came out into the gardens. She gazed up at the very tall young man, his lordship's youngest Gentleman of the Horse, Christopher Blount, and a smile of appreciation played on her lips. Really he was an exceptionally handsome lad!

"Was that Lord Leicester gone into the little walled garden?"

"Er—yes, my Lady."

"How fortunate! I had wished for a private word with him—about his nephew Master Sidney who is betrothed to my daughter. Will you take me to him? Master Blount, is it not?"

So this lovely lady actually knew his name! Christopher stared at her in unconcealed adoration as he offered her his arm to conduct her. A little secret smile touched for a moment her face. She had seen the angry thwarted glance of Lord Leicester as he had strode headlong. She thought: "I've waited a long time. Perhaps it has not been in vain. . . ."

Chapter Twelve

The great Privy Chamber had subsided like a sea after the wind had whirled its waters into confusion. The Queen had led the throng in and out again, her hand resting on the shoulder of the small brown-faced man, whose dark eyes had the same metallic flash as his dangling earrings. The long jewelled fingers held him tightly, as from her extended arm, the tasselled and gold-fringed outer draperies swept the ground. Fantastic was her apparel of scarlet and gold, fantastic the circumference of farthingale and ruff, giving her the semblance of some glittering Oriental idol. The ladies were paler and quieter copies of their royal mistress, the young Maids of Honour gleaming in white satin; the gentlemen striding beside them, wore the same enormous ruffs and sparkling earrings, their beards were dyed vermilion, and the grotesque padding of their great bombasted breeches rivalled the farthingales in width. This retinue billowed after the two leading figures, but it seemed to break up in the Privy Chamber; only a privileged few followed the Queen and her special guest into the fastness of the Withdrawing Chambers beyond. The movement, the swirl of colour and the gleam of precious metals and jewels seemed to be quietening. The Privy Chamber fell back to its former expectancy.

Philip Sidney leant against the arras-covered wall, frowning a little as he thought of the Queen and the object of her attention. Beside him, as ever, was Fulke, and another dear friend, Edward Dyer, a slender youth with a quick hectic colour which came and went in his cheeks, adding to the simulation of his swooning adoration of the Queen. ("Boy," said his Uncle Robert, "you would do well to copy Ned Dyer, and have the Queen think you are dying for love of her." "But," Philip had persisted, "she is old enough to be my mother— and Ned's." "You are a damnation fool!" declared his uncle.)

Zenith

Both Fulke and Edward Dyer had accompanied him on his diplomatic mission to the Protestant princes of Germany, a mission on which he had set out with such high pride and hope. At last it seemed that he was to be given a post as worth while as it was important, and yet it had come to nothing, or to very little, and here he was, back again, kicking his heels at court. The Protestant princes had been weak and divided amongst themselves, and although the Queen had commended him after her searching cross-examination, there had been no more missions for him. He had been refused angrily when he had implored permission to sail with Drake two years ago in 1577. He remembered seeing that sturdy little figure, with the keen eyes in the deeply tanned face, swagger away down the Long Gallery of the palace, and how he had hastened in the opposite direction till finally he burst into the innermost sanctum, greatly daring, to find the Queen with his uncle, where they had just received Captain Drake and given him his momentous orders. The Queen had been out of breath, her bosom rising and falling, but there had been a light in her eyes which had made her look younger—almost as young, he thought bitterly, as she pretended to be.

"Rob," she had said. "If the King of Spain, if my Spirit, should get wind of it——"

"A fig for them both!" Uncle Robert had cried, and had thrown his arm round her waist and kissed her boldly. She had thrust him from her, but gently, declaring: "La—Rob! Not before this modest youth, your nephew! You'll abash him. . . ." But Philip, on his knees before her, had been begging and imploring her to let him go with Captain Drake. He had scarcely time to notice the by-play of these middle-aged lovers.

"You are ungallant," she had said, "wanting to hurry away from me so soon again." She had found the rebellious lock at the back of his head and tweaked it.

"Your Grace, it isn't that!" he had cried clumsily. " 'Tis that I want to do something for you!"

"Well—what about that masque you have promised to write for me?"

A masque! A later plea on a more formal occasion had awoken a cold anger—"God's death, sir! When I say 'no', it is to be taken as 'no'! D'you think to bandy words with me?" So he had written the masque and it had been acted before her when she had come to Uncle Robert's house at Wanstead the previous summer. That had been the last time, he thought, when there had been happiness, the last time before Uncle Robert had taken the step which was to have such a disastrous effect on Philip's own future, and might have an incalculable effect on the Queen.

Wanstead had not the spacious magnificence of Kenilworth, but every year it seemed that his uncle grew more fond of it and added to its perfections—Kenilworth might be a palace, he said, as splendid as any of her Majesty's, but Wanstead was a *home*. When he had made his final attempt, four years ago, to gain her Majesty's hand, would it have been wiser to set it in the intimate charm of Wanstead, rather than the splendours of Kenilworth, Philip wondered? The Queen had come last year with a very small retinue, several of whom had been members of his family, his Uncle and Aunt Warwick, his sister Mary, now married to Uncle Robert's closest friend the Earl of Pembroke, and his friends Fulke and Edward Dyer. Instead of the elaborate pageants of Kenilworth, they had acted Philip's *Lady of the May* and the Queen had laughed heartily at his comic character, Rhombus the village schoolmaster with his fantastic misquotations from Virgil, as well as commending his verse. He remembered the guests sitting on the terrace in the summer twilight, while the musicians played and sang to entertain them, and the air was heavy with the scent of flowers. The twilight had been gentle with the Queen and his uncle, softening the lines of her face as no paint could do, and shading his ever-increasing girth and baldness. Her hand had rested on Robert's shoulder then, but she had had affectionate attention for his nephew sitting at her feet. When the musicians sang some verses of his:

> "My true love hath my heart and I have his
> By just exchange for one another given
> I hold his dear, and mine he cannot miss,
> There never was a better bargain driven.
> My true love hath my heart and I have his."

She had touched Philip's cheek with a quick caress, murmuring: "Rob, what a gifted child this is!" His uncle had answered: "*I* never had that gift for making sweet verse. I often wished for it." "My dear, you had others. . . . And haven't you given me this lad to be my songbird?" Happy evening! So far removed from the ugly present. . . .

How different from yesterday in Leicester House.

"No—Philip! You mustn't kiss me! Mother will be furious. . . ."

"But why? Since we are betrothed——"

"Mother says she'll not have our betrothal. . . ."

"But——" No words, no breath to fight this agony.

"She's angry. She said: "Love and kisses are one matter. Marriage is another. What settlements will your sweet Philip make on you? What are you both proposing to live on? His father's debts? His father's hopes of recovering his expenses from our royal miser?"

Fulke was touching his sleeve, bringing him back to the present.

"Your uncle has just entered."

"He is beckoning to you," added Dyer.

Philip looked up, saw Leicester with Sir Christopher Hatton beside him, and saw the unmistakable gesture. Yet it was with a curious reluctance that he crossed the great chamber to his uncle's side.

"I had hoped to find you, Boy. You've heard the news?"

"What news, sir?"

"I thought her Majesty passed through the Privy Chamber?"

"She did. I was not chosen to accompany her."

"With that damned Frenchman?" asked Hatton.

"Yes, Sir Christopher."

"Let her!" said Leicester impatiently. "Let her chuck her dear 'Monkey' under the chin and enjoy his prancings! The point is—his master, Anjou, is to be summoned by her—to England!"

"He—— The former Duc d'Alençon——?"

"The younger brother of her former suitor, once also Duke of Anjou and now King Henry of France," said Hatton.

"Old Catherine's youngest whelp!" muttered Leicester. "It would make anyone think she was serious at last. We cannot have him here——"

"He's not fit to speak to any decent woman," said Philip with that fury which comes from horror. "I would not have my sister—or Penelope—in the same room as he! Some courage he has—unlike his brother. That I'll give him but——"

"Tchah!" Leicester had another fury. "I'm not concerned with his virtue or lack of it!"

"You", Hatton told him, "are the only man who can persuade the Queen."

"I'll do my best. Spy out the land for me and try to draw off the Monkey!"

Zenith

When Hatton had gone, Leicester beckoned his nephew into a deep window recess.

"Poor Christopher! He was one of the first of her pretty lads. Now, in middle age, he's a Knight of the Garter and Vice Chamberlain as well as Captain of the Bodyguard—so he can't complain! But understand her—never! She must have her procession of pretty lads or less pretty ones who can make her laugh. When I was a youngster, not much older than you, and he was the latest fancy, I was desperately jealous, I'll admit. I didn't know her so well as I do now, didn't know that there was nothing serious in her amusements. And I was hot in love with her, too, and ready to kill Heneage and Hatton. . . . Let her pet her 'Monkey'—but if Anjou comes over, it will be an awkward situation for her to wriggle out of without infuriating France. She might caper with Anjou as she capers with his envoy——"

"It isn't worthy of so great a Queen!"

"You're too damnation squeamish! I know what she's driving at— yet she has always had that incalculable streak. . . . Just on ten years ago she plucked peace out of the very jaws of impossibility, but she knows herself that she can't repeat it. Parma is the best general the King of Spain ever sent to the Netherlands—and I don't except Don John—and when they are crushed, our turn will come!"

"As I said, if her Majesty had only thrown our full strength on the side of the Prince of Orange, he would never have lost the battle of Gemblours——"

"I know you said it! And got your ears boxed for your pains. I've said it—Walsingham has said it. But with more tact. You know nothing of women! It's a pity you didn't learn something at that fine gay deboshed court which produced Jehan de Simier, Baron de St. Marc—her Majesty's Monkey! You had the chance!"

"Rather than learn in such a school—I'd know nothing!"

"It doesn't do, to be too good for this world while you are in it! It's not a mistake *she* ever makes. She'll do anything—cruel, unscrupulous, cunning—for the good of her country. When Anjou led his troops into the Low Countries against the Spaniard, Walsingham hurried to tell her that France as master there would be as dangerous to us as Spain. Says she: 'As if I did not know it! But if Monsieur d'Anjou will conquer the Spaniard for me—what then?' So naturally we asked why should he do that? Says she: 'If he were my husband or promised husband!' God's wounds, Walsingham's face! As a theory it would delight Machiavelli. Alone with me she says: 'Desperate diseases need desperate remedies!' And it is a desperate situation.... I say—fight! But she has this horror of war...."

"It would be a war against the forces of evil!"

"It would be a damned near thing too.... I've seen the Spaniard fight. They have the best infantry in the world. She says: 'We would be beaten out of existence if we fought Spain—unless we fought them at sea.' But Anjou coming over here! None of her previous suitors, the Archduke, the elder Anjou, the King of Sweden—none of them came. I must cajole her, make love to her—though she was never a woman to be kissed quiet——"

"You'd not do that now——!"

"You're too damned nice, Boy! There's no time for it."

When Philip rejoined his friends he saw their anxious expressions. Was his face such a tell-tale? He felt a sickness rising in him like a memory of the hideousness of St. Bartholomew's Eve. That ugliness, that bestial cruelty was lurking behind the gay pageantry.

"This court is a masque of Circe."

Fulke had him by the arm, Fulke was drawing him down to the settle beside them.

"Steady, Philip! Let's play a hand of primero. If you gaze about in such a mood we'll have a clash with Oxford or some of his bullies of the pro-French faction."

"I'd like a tangible opponent at my sword's end!"

"He's not worth it!" declared Dyer. "And he's a killer!"

"I know! Skewered a poor devil of a scullion, and then managed to evade the just reckoning! I know he's worth nothing. A highly bred swaggering lump of brutality.... But he would be something I could strike at!"

"He fences after the Italian school."

"Damnation, Fulke! I too can fence after the Italian school. It's just—it's——"

"I know. And you must do nothing."

"Your Uncle Robert", said Dyer, "is the one man who can handle the Queen. Leave it to him. Oxford's beneath your notice."

"Listen!" said Philip, with his eyes ablaze. "Can good ever come out of evil? Is doing evil so that good comes of it, ever justified?"

" 'Tis a nice philosophical point," said Dyer.

"All contained in the good old proverb!" suggested Fulke. "You need a long spoon to sup with the devil. Her Majesty has a long spoon, I think!"

Philip looked at them. In the middle of this creeping coldness, here was one warmth, in the middle of this shamefulness, something of honour—these men, his friends. He smiled, eager with affection for them.

"Forgive my foul humour! Have you the cards, Ned? We'll play a hand."

Dinner was over, when Simier kneeled at the Queen's feet in one of her withdrawing chambers.

"Well, Monkey?" she said. She looked at the darkly sunburnt mobile face, the dark flashing eyes, the golden earrings bright like the yellow slashing of his black suit.

"Madame, you have desolated your poor Monkey! What has this unhappy beast done?"

She took his chin between her thumb and forefinger.

"Nought. I've reflected. Women change their minds. Your Duke must wait after all."

"Madame does not realize what she does!"

"I do."

He seized her hands and began to kiss them, a lover's kisses, her palms, her fingers separately, the inside of her wrists. His mind was concentrating furiously on the angry suggestion thrown out by the Earl of Oxford—"You have Leicester to thank for this!"

"Madame," he said, "a beautiful woman never knows what pain she inflicts. Would you be so swayed by your Council—you who rule alone like the sun in the heavens? To be ordered by Milord Leicester?"

"Have a care! God's death! No one has ever ordered me. Least of all Lord Leicester. He has—personal reasons."

"Madame, for a man so recently and so happily wed himself, he acts strangely in trying to keep marriage from his sovereign!"

"Wed? Lord Leicester's been a widower for twenty years!"

"Since yesterday, Madame? I had not heard of the so sudden death of his lady. But it is a tragedy. . . ."

"What are you saying?"

She had moved with that quickness of a snake about to strike, her body stiff and convulsed in its glittering clothes, her hands wrenched away from him and clutching the arms of her chair till it seemed the knuckles would start through the skin.

"But surely Madame knows that Milord Leicester has recently wedded the beautiful widowed Countess—Milady Essex?"

The convulsed body stayed still in the same position, as if it were stricken into stone, the mouth open and awry, the eyes black and seeming sightless. Then he heard her gasp as if she were struggling ineffectually for breath. Her voice came rattling as if she choked.

"Wed to Lettice Essex?"

"But certainly, Madame." Apprehension touched his face. Was she going to have a seizure? Had he played with fire—in a powder magazine? But some of that spasmodic rigidity had gone out of her body, it had fallen back in her chair, though her hands still clutched the arms. She shouted and her ladies and the usher came running.

"Sir Francis Knollys! I must have him at once!"

In the period of waiting she made one remark and one only to Simier, made it with a quiet controlled fury like acid biting into wood.

"You are the envoy of a great prince with whom I hope to contract an alliance. You are a diplomat with a diplomat's immunity. But I tell you, if I find you have lied to me, your head shall be set on a spike on London Bridge."

At last the white-haired old man was bowing stiffly before her.

"Cousin!" she said. "Your daughter Lettice? Is she—the Countess of Leicester?"

"She is, your Grace."

"Have you proof of it?"

"Certainly. When my daughter informed me that she had been married to the Earl of Leicester at Kenilworth, by his chaplain, I demanded proof. It did not seem adequate. I had another ceremony performed at Wanstead in my presence and I caused the witnesses to swear to the fact before a notary. I have their sworn depositions."

"By God, you have an exact judgment of my Lord of Leicester!"

"Your Grace, I will not deny to you, that my opinion of Lord Leicester's private character is very low. *I* consider him a man debauched and unprincipled where women are concerned. It was far from my wish that my daughter should marry him. Having done so, it was my duty to see her honour safeguarded."

"Her honour!" Her body was twisting in the great chair, and her voice was steadily becoming shriller with rising hysteria. "I did not

299

know she had any—any more than her new husband! But you're a careful father, poor Frank! Careful of her honour—the honour of the Bullen women!!!"

Her commands were screamed in a strident voice. Her councillors came, Burghley and Sussex, an alarmed Hatton was told to bring a company of the guard to the ante-chamber, and finally—Robert, Earl of Leicester. But the figures of delirium were around her, memories became nightmares. What did she see? The young fellow picking roses for her in the Tower, his arms round her for the first time at Hatfield—"I love you!"—the weight of his head flung down in her lap when he had told her of his wife's strange death, the cold stillness of the sleeping palace as she had moved swiftly through the corridors driven by that desperate longing, and the belief that it was at last appeased, the belief that love had built a secret wall about her to shield her from all mortal hurt, that first time she had held him, sleeping, in her arms. The memories swirled about her, combating those actual masks, mouthing words she could not hear. One face for a moment held her fevered attention, a young face, white and strained with horrified eyes—his nephew, the lad who had written those verses with a ripple of joy running through them, verses sung to her so recently in a summer twilight.

"My true love hath my heart and I have his——"

The words echoed and re-echoed with savage mockery. Had it all been a lie from the beginning? Lettice with him in a corridor of Whitehall, her full red lips parted to show her gleaming teeth, Lettice, looking up at him with her sullen passionate eyes, Lettice leaning against him with a sudden abandon as he caught her horse—all the time had it been Lettice slinking greedily after him? Bitch—she-wolf! She was seeing *his* face now, not the face of her remembered young lover, but one coarser, fuller with age, and staring at her with a sort of despairing boldness, a face shut against her by anger and fear. Her voice came to her, uneven, cracking with rage.

"My Lord! Is it true—that you wed my cousin—that she-wolf?"

"Yes, it is true.... Last autumn...."

She sprang from her chair and struck that hateful face with all the strength in her, feeling her rings cut his cheek. She could hear her own voice, screaming, raving, searching for every abusive epithet, till voice and imagination alike choked. Then from depths unknown, she plucked her self-control. Her voice had the deadly coldness of a searching dagger.

"Sir Christopher! You will place the Earl of Leicester under arrest. Bring in your men. You will hold him till I have decided what I will have done with him. By God's wounds! He shall go to the Tower. . . . As other traitors do, before they die a traitor's death. . . . Take him out, Sir Christopher. Out of my sight." She was turning to Simier, who was watching her with an avid intensity.

"Monsieur, the passports for your Master, the Duc d'Anjou, will be made out immediately. My Lord Burghley, you will have it seen to. . . . In the meanwhile, Monsieur, you will write to the Duke, and tell him that it is my desire that he comes to England immediately."

The room was emptying. She leaned back in her chair, limp with a sudden exhaustion, her eyes closed. She could hear the feet clattering on the polished boards. She opened her eyes and saw Burghley and Sussex, one on each side of her, leaning slightly over her.

"Your Grace feels faint?" asked Burghley.

"I don't know—what I feel. . . ." Had not she heard from soldiers that when a man first receives a bullet wound, he feels no pain, only the shock? She added: "Make arrangements for Anjou's coming."

"Of course, your Grace."

"How long does your Grace intend to detain Lord Leicester?" It was Sussex speaking, Sussex who was Robert's enemy.

"Till he follows his father and grandfather to Tower Hill."

"Your Grace," said Sussex, speaking in a level, determined voice. "You cannot condemn a man to a traitor's death, for marrying and for concealing his marriage, however despicable the personal circumstances may be."

"And you are Leicester's enemy!"

"Always, your Grace, to his person and his policy. But I hope I am a man of honour."

The ghost of a laugh came from her dry throat.

"Honour, m'lord? It is a word I seem to have heard in the last hour. When one is as young as—Philip Sidney, one believes in honour. You and I, my lords, we should have outgrown these innocent beliefs. . . . They tell me that I am young and beautiful, that I have commanded Time to cease—my poets are continually telling me. Yet I am forty-five, and though when I have opportunity to contrive sundry disguises it may seem I have cheated Time somewhat, I do

not doubt **that** at this moment, I look my years—and more."
Burghley had taken one of her hands in his two swollen, gouty ones,
and was pressing it gently. She continued in the same weary voice:
"Lord Leicester may be released to-morrow. Twenty-four hours of
reflection can do him no harm. But he must keep out of my sight.
That must be seen to."

"I will see to it, in person, your Grace," said Sussex.

"Thank you."

When he had gone, she rose wearily to her feet.

"Spirit, give me your arm. I must lie down and rest, so I can appear
this evening and dance—as if nothing had happened."

"I commend your intention, your Grace."

"Spirit—do you remember twenty years ago? When that man's
—first wife died? My cousin Lettice won't fall down any staircases.
She's not the sort!" She stopped for a moment by a mirror, withdrew
her arm from his, and carefully adjusted her red wig, the pearl and
golden ornaments upon it, her ruff and heavy necklaces. "When Time
takes so much away, it might take away certain feelings. How old is
that young Anjou? Twenty-four? But of course, he is not wedding me,
he is wedding—my property."

"Your Grace is still a handsome woman."

"You are a good friend. And you have forborne from taxing me
with my mistake. My mistake of twenty years."

"We all make mistakes. But you do not make mistakes—for your
country."

"That is the kindest epitaph on my youth—now it is dead."

Some half an hour later, as she lay on her bed in the darkened
chamber, divested of all her finery, the red wig replaced by a compress of herbs, the pains of her body—aching head and eyes, cold
sick exhaustion, violent throbbing in the chronic sore on her leg—
were steadily being replaced by the far worse agonies of mind. "Now
I know", she thought, "what my father's first wife felt when she was
cast off for my mother! Now I know what my stepmother—that good
woman who was always kind to me—felt when she saw her husband,
Tom Seymour, kiss me. . . . Now I know why Robin's first wife killed
herself. . . . 'Love likes not the falling fruit nor the withered tree.' "
Wearily she wondered how long he had deceived her. During these
past eleven months since he had married Lettice, she had seen no
difference in him. He had been, as for twenty years, her dearest and

closest companion, who understood and shared everything. In that seeming serene understanding, passion had played a decreasing part, and yet he had been her lover on several occasions. This very summer he had been ill at court, and she had tended him night after night (when he was as demanding as a spoilt child), despite her own weariness, burdened with the business of State in the day time. The war clouds had rolled up once more, darkening the sky with menace. She had taken a chance, a gambler's risk when she had given Drake his secret commission to raid the coast of Peru—"the backside of Nova Hispania"—on his ostensible mission to discover the believed continent of Terra Australis. It had to be kept from Burghley who was becoming increasingly cautious in his old age. For once she had cast off caution and let her mind leap to Robert's daring. She wanted all the treasure she might lay her hands on to build more and more of those swift-sailing, hard-hitting ships of war under the direction of Hawkins. Then it seemed she and Robert had acted as one mind in their enterprise. But a long silence had fallen on Drake and the menace in the Low Countries grew blacker and blacker. To weaken Spain and not to strengthen France—those had been the thoughts tearing at her, as she had leaned against Robert's carved bedpost in a stiff aching doze in the small hours. Robert and the country both needing her—but there had been a happiness in giving to them. Piling blankets and wraps on him in the cold fit of the ague and setting a hot brick in flannel to his feet, while she debated in her mind the arguments of her council; sponging him in the hot fit and turning his pillows, changing his shirt when he sweated, and half her mind thinking of Walsingham's latest collection of secret reports. He had taken her hand to play with it childishly as he had murmured: "What a good wife you are!" She had thought at the time: "To you and to England." She had said aloud: "I do my best, dear heart." All the time he had been Lettice's husband. Of course one could not imagine Lettice cherishing a sick man, and no doubt, however infatuated, he had realized it. He always took great care of his comforts. . . .

Worse even than the memory of lying in his arms for the last time, was that memory of Robin playing with her fingers and drowsily murmuring what a good wife she was. Oh, Judas, Judas! And this very afternoon, when he had come to beg her not to invite Anjou to the country.

"My dearest," she had said, "at my coronation I promised to shed my blood if need be for my people. You know how desperate the situation is!"

"I know if you marry that little Frenchman it will kill me!"

"I think it might kill me too, Rob. . . ."

Perhaps he had discussed it all with Lettice, and they had roared with laughter. If his heartlessness was a whip, Lettice's contempt was a scorpion. Was there nothing left now her inmost citadel had become a whitewashed sepulchre? By God, she would marry Anjou if it were the last thing she did. . . . But could anything, ever, deaden the points of these darts of memory, piercing her?

> "Know that Love is a careless child,
> And forgets promise past:
> He is blind, he is deaf when he list,
> And in faith never fast. . . ."

Chapter Thirteen

Philip Sidney rode through the city of London on his way to Leicester House from Greenwich Palace. The crowds and the noise of the narrow, overhung cobbled streets distracted his mind momentarily from the meeting which he both longed for and dreaded. It was like a high rock piercing sullen waters, those muddy waters of dull misery which had covered his existence. From every booth, flat-capped 'prentices were bawling "what d'you lack?" as carts ground over the cobblestones, hoofs clattering, and a ballad singer in the doorway of a tavern, was singing at the top of a vigorous voice:

> "We be Soldiers three!
> God ha' mercy on such as we!
> Come forth from the Low Countree,
> With never a pennie of monie!"

The Low Country! If he might be there, doing a man's work, striking a tangible wickedness which could be slain and overthrown! Only what then would happen to his love—who had been his betrothed and was so, no longer—the Lady Penelope Devereux, the daughter of Uncle Robert's wife—his 'Stella'? Another ballad singer was challenging the first, two doors down.

> ". . . that this our Queen anointed,
> May vanquish all her foes;
> And as by Thee appointed,
> Let her lay sword on those!"

Did they know yet, those sturdy citizens of London, were they talking in their houses and their taverns of the downfall of the mighty Earl of Leicester? The noises swelled, vendors challenging ballad singers: "Cherry ripe! Cherry ripe! Ripe, ripe, I cry!" "What d'you lack, good sir, what d'you lack, sweet madam?" "Ha' ye any mice and rats? Vermin that creep up and down?" "Ha' ye any wood to cleave?" What rumours were circulating inside those tall houses which had each story projecting farther over the lower one, their gables and casements fretted and carved, their fronts striped with wooden beams against white plaster and tawny brick?

Seeing a gap in the pushing crowds, he touched his horse with his heels, and thrust on, past the looming gothic bulk of "Paul's", with its truncated steeple, never yet repaired after being struck by lightning early in the Queen's reign. The Papists had blamed the wickedness of the Protestants, and the Protestants, the wickedness of the Papists. Like enough, thought Philip, the Lord was weary of His creation of all creeds. Out of the city at last, and spurring through Fleet Street over the malodorous waters of the Fleet Ditch, to gain the wider expanse of the Strand, where the great town palaces of the nobility and the foreign embassies lay. Here passed to and fro serving-men in their blue liveries, their lords' silver cognizances on their arms or breasts; at high arched gateways lounged young gallants with hawk on wrist, Gentlemen of the Horse or Gentlemen of the Chamber to their various lordships. Philip trotted on, hardly looking to the right or left of him.

A message had come to him from Sir Christopher Hatton. His uncle, newly released from detention in the Fort at Greenwich Palace, had gone to Leicester House to collect his family before retreating to the rural fastness of Wanstead. He would like to see his nephew. Fulke and Ned, seeing his gloom, had tried to persuade Philip to come with them to the Paris Garden to see the bear-baiting. "Come, sweet Phil!" Ned Dyer had urged him. "Put off your melancholic humour and see blood and death and desperate violence! 'Tis a paradox, where blood flows, there is life!" Fulke had joined him: "Stake your last ryal[1] on Harry Hunks[2]!"

"My head's a bear pit!" Philip had answered. "And I am Hunks, and my thoughts the mastiffs. Besides I must go to my uncle."

"Alas, your uncle!" deplored Dyer. " 'Tis sometimes easier to handle Hunks and the mastiffs combined than our sweet, beloved Queen!"

---

[1] Ryal. Gold Elizabethan coin roughly equal to sovereign.
[2] Nickname for the baited bear.

"It takes as much courage—or more!" declared Fulke.

"I had occasion to advise Sir Christopher himself," said Ned Dyer, "when he was so grievously upset with her Majesty for the great mockery she made of those fantastic gold buttons on his doublet! I told him that although she does descend in her sex and is a very woman of caprice, yet she is our sovereign and must be treated so. Nor would she bear with his rugged dealings—though they may have diverted her once! Poor Sir Christopher, he was so desperate wrathful about those buttons!"

"This is rather more than buttons!" said Philip.

"Last night," said Fulke, "I thought she would eat the 'Monkey'. If the master doesn't soon come, she'll take the man!"

"All my gods, all my hopes," Philip thought, "have come tumbling down!" The Queen, whom he had almost worshipped from childhood, ready to wed a prince of the House of Valois which had caused the Bartholomew massacre, who had let his own father ruin himself after a lifetime of devoted service to her in Ireland, while she pranced and capered like a tavern drab with a mincing Frenchman—that gorgeously adorned figure raving and screaming at his Uncle Robert. . . . And his uncle, a demi-god of childhood's days, gay, magnificent, splendidly generous, once believed a paladin, but now surely hardly more than a lecher, a cheat, a grasper. . . . And Philip was no longer his uncle's heir.

He had been brought up to believe that one day he would be the Earl of Leicester and inheritor of all his uncle's vast property. The great world—and his creditors—had regarded him as the heir which had made things easier for him, although he had been cursed with a lack of ready money. He would only take the smallest sum possible from his father, knowing Sir Henry Sidney's financial difficulties, and the purely nominal salary of his court post barely supported his body-servant, Randal Calcott. The Queen had not allowed him to go on those overseas ventures which brought their participants golden gain as well as glory. He had lost the small sum which was all he had been able to venture in the scheme for finding the North-West Passage, when the Company of Cathay and its unlucky founder, Michael Lok, went bankrupt. His younger brother, Robert, had got deeply into debt, and Philip had committed himself to the hilt, trying to help him. Uncle Robert had occasional bursts of the former generosity, but he spent his money as it came, and now the greedy hands of Lettice held the purse strings. He doted on her, seeming helplessly infatuated. And she obviously hoped to give him a son. In the meanwhile she had no intention of letting her daughter marry his penniless, disinherited nephew.

Philip rode into the great stable yard of Leicester House which seemed a scene of the wildest confusion and bustle. Horses were being led from their stalls, often in peril of colliding with the lines of carts being loaded with trunks and boxes carried from the house by serving-men. Grooms, leading the saddle horses, swore savagely at the grooms leading the carts, and there was mutual swearing between all grooms and the house servants carrying the boxes. Hounds surged about, like newly released waters, yelping and baying. Gentlemen and Yeomen of the Horse volleyed orders; standing high on a horse block, Verney surveyed the scene, and now and again, cracked out a brief direction which reduced the chaos. Philip dismounted, avoided a collision with a pack horse bearing a "cadge" carrying hooded and leashed hawks, and bestowed his horse in the nearest empty stall. As he went to the steps leading to the door of the house, a woman's figure appeared at the top. She wore an open gown of heavy black silk over another of white tissue worked with silver and seed pearls; heavy ropes of pearls hung from her neck to her jewelled girdle, big pear-shaped ones dangled from her ears and others lay as ornaments on her thick, frizzed-out tawny-gold hair. It was his Aunt Lettice, Countess of Leicester. Her voice rang out, sweet and imperious.

"Kit! Kit!"

Young Blount came hastening out of the crowd.

"My sweet lady?"

"Kit, unless you see to certain matters for me, they will be forgot. Master Verney does not heed *me*. I want the bright bay, 'Nonpareil' —and see that he is saddled with the Spanish leather saddle."

"You know you have only to tell me——"

But she interrupted him abruptly, seeing Philip approach.

"Well, Nephew!" she said, holding out her hand, over which Philip bowed formally. "You'll find your uncle in the library. He seems to want to see you. He is anxious to hear if our royal tigress has stopped screaming for his blood, or whether she has happily consoled herself with the Frenchman!"

"I will go to him," said Philip briefly.

In the great hall, the rush-strewn floor seemed to stretch in a vast expanse with all the trestle tables taken down. More serving-men were carrying boxes under the direction of a steward, himself directed by one of the Countess's gentlewomen. As Philip came to the bottom of the stairway, he heard a pattering footfall, and there *she* was, running to meet him, her huge dark eyes aglow beneath that cloud of bright hair, more golden than her mother's, her lips in that red rosebud mouth just apart with eagerness. Lettice's eldest child, the Lady Penelope Devereux, was just seventeen. Their hands met, clasped and held, he murmured his own name for her: "Stella—Oh, my Stella!" But she was quicker to appreciate the situation.

"Come! I know where we won't be disturbed. There is no one in your uncle's room at the top of the stairs. They have taken from it all the things which are to be moved and no one will interrupt us."

Hand in hand they went up the stairs and in the gallery at the top, Penelope called to her younger sister, Dorothy.

"Doll—keep watch! In case Mother comes."

"Mother won't come!" said Lady Dorothy Devereux. "I last saw her in full cry after Kit Blount and I don't doubt she's run him to earth by now!"

Philip winced. He could not get accustomed to the way the young Devereuxes talked of their mother.

"You never know," said Penelope. "She seems to be everywhere to-day. There's a dear! Keep watch."

They went into that very room where the Duke of Norfolk and Sir Nicholas Throckmorton had discussed the germination of the Northern Rebellion with Robert, ten years ago, the same room into which Robert had once carried Douglass Sheffield. The huge silver fire-dogs had been taken away, but the tapestry of "the story of Samson" still covered the walls, Samson's rolling muscles still menaced the Philistines. But Philip, able at last to hold his Stella, and press his lips on hers, did not notice his surroundings. So much seemed to be shut out, all the ugliness of the past days at court, all the sick humours in his brain healed.

"Stella!" he said at last. "Your mother cannot be so inhumanly cruel as to break our betrothal now!"

"She can do anything. And don't hope for any help from your uncle. He would never dare to oppose her. Mother has him under her thumb. I am sorry for him! People talk about the 'wicked earl', they say he has seduced so many women—but it seems to me that he has always been dominated by women. First the Queen and now Mother. They are both so much stronger than he."

"But surely", he persisted, "your mother would not break an arrangement made by your father. It was his especial wish."

"Philip, she never cared about his wishes when he was alive, and she cares less about them now he's dead. She told me that she hopes she will have a son now. "Poor Robin!" she said. "Denied a wife and child all these years!" She only wanted you as a son-in-law if you were his heir. . . . She says I must marry someone with a fortune. . . .'

"No, Stella, no!"

She looked at him, at his face whitening under its tan, and suddenly felt that it was she who was eight years older, she who knew the world as it really was. She could not tell him all that her mother had said, she could not tell him the name of her suitor, she could not hurt him so much. Whatever this dreadful proposed marriage might do to her, it would even be a worse agony for Philip.

She had said to her mother : "But I love Philip!"

"Well—love him! That I'll not mind. . . . He's a handsome lad, though too much of a saint for my taste. Still—perhaps he'll learn. . . . But marry him, you cannot! He has scarcely two angels to rub against each other. All he had was the expectation of being his uncle's heir, and soon, I hope, you will have a baby brother to be that! Who knows what your step-father's future may be now, since the old hag has found out that he dared to marry without her leave? I will not have him squander another penny on any of the Sidneys. We'll need everything he has, and you must make a good marriage. I have had an offer for you. From Robert Lord Rich."

"Mother! That lout, that—— When he was last at dinner here, he was so drunk he fell from his chair——"

"What does that matter? D'you know what they call him? The 'rich Lord Rich'. You will marry him. Never mind if he is too fond of the bottle. He'll bestow his attention on it—not on you. And you will be able to spend his money. You know you like money—you enjoyed poverty no more than I did! Give him an heir—it will safeguard your own position—and then make him leave you alone. He has his bottle! And then you can enjoy your sweet Philip!"

"Philip—is not like that!"

"More fool—he! Don't you be a fool!" She had turned and caught her daughter by the shoulders. "Listen to me, Penelope. You must learn what the world is really like. . . . It is not one of those charming pastorals in your Philip's verses. When I was your age, I was in love with your stepfather. You see him now as a middle-aged man with a paunch, a red face, a head going bald. But twenty years ago, a more splendid young man never walked the earth! And he knew how to make women love him. . . . If I had been allowed to marry him then, I might have gone on believing in true love till death us do part and all that charming nonsense! I might have been as romantic a goose as you are now. . . . But, oh no! I had to be married off quickly—to your father whom I despised. He—Robert Dudley—was designed for the Royal Virgin's kept man. And very well he has done by it! And I found—my compensations."

("Yes," thought Penelope, "you've always had gallants since I was a tiny child. And each year they get younger. Christopher Blount is the youngest yet, as well as the tallest and the best-looking and the most blindly adoring. It was only yesterday I found him with his head in your lap. . . .")

"Don't be a fool, child. Learn to wait. We all have to learn."

But, remembering these words, Penelope thought: "Not Philip. He will never learn. He's not like that. . . ." Suddenly, but gently, she took his head in her hands, under her chin and rocked him as if he had been a child. "Oh, my darling, my darling!" she thought. "What is this hideous world going to do to you? I am *her* daughter, I'm stronger, harder, less scrupulous. Perhaps it's the Boleyn blood that Grandfather talks about. But you—my Philip—what will happen to you?"

Looking up at her, he said: "And I was such a blind fool to begin with! When we were first betrothed, you were a child and I hardly more. I agreed because I knew my father wanted it so much. But I never realized—till I came back from Germany—blind idiot! All the time, I was riding from Greenwich to-day, lines were running in my head. I'll make a sonnet of them, when I have time to write them down."

"Philip, what are they?"

He began to recite.

"Not at first sight, nor with a dribbed shot,
  Love gave the wound which while I breathe, will bleed——"

There was a quick rapping on the door and Dorothy Devereux's voice: "Mother has just entered the hall, with Kit Blount gaping after her. She's looking everywhere about her!"

"Thank you!" said Penelope. "We're just coming—separately. Go on watching!"

She turned to her young lover.

"Philip—I want you to know this—whatever happens! They may separate us—they may force me to marry someone else. Perhaps you will get your heart's desire and sail away like Drake to the ends of the earth—and not come back. . . . But whatever it is—even if I wait till I am Mother's age, even if I love again in a different, lighter way —there'll never be anything like this. Like this between you and me. . . . And I'll never forget——"

But his arms were round her now, crushing her, not a boy's arms any more, but a man's, and his mouth was crushing hers, crushing all thoughts but of his enfolding nearness, and there was no more time. Then time returned, and they stood apart, and she was whispering: "*She* mustn't know we were together. Go down the stairs at the back, the little stairs—they say that your uncle's lovely ladies used to be smuggled in that way by Digby—and go to your uncle in the library. Go quickly!"

"Stella!" he said once and then went swiftly, running light-footed.

His uncle was sitting at the table with the green velvet tasselled cloth. He had a limp dejected look, Philip thought, like some great hulk cast up on the strand. The light fell slanting on the ribbed and serried rows of books lining the room, silent minds which did not speak. Underhill, the secretary, had got to his feet with papers in his hand. Philip entering heard his uncle say: "That'll be all, Tom." Then he turned and stretched out his hand.

"Dear lad!"

Philip, clasping it with both his, made a strange discovery. The splendour had been roughly stripped off Uncle Robin, the glamour of childhood's days had gone—and yet Philip cared for him as much as ever—in a different way.

"I had your message, sir, from Sir Christopher and I came at once. He thinks you are wise to go to Wanstead."

"Aye! A cave in a corner of oblivion. . . . That is all that remains to me. Twenty years I have given to her, the best twenty years of my life. Served her in slavish fidelity and now to be cast off like a stray cur, because I dare to want a wife I can acknowledge before the world and a child of my own!" Philip writhed inwardly at these complaints. They were not worthy. "Empty words, grinning scoffs, watching nights, fawning days—all a court favourite's life! Gave up my liberty, competed with the sovereigns of Europe for her hand, staked all I had. Listen, Phil, boy! If she had taken me four years ago, at Kenilworth, she could not have bestowed less on me than my father's—your grandfather's—dukedom. I would then have asked her to give you my earldom. . . ."

Thought Philip: "If I had been an earl—and the Queen's nephew —how Lettice would have encouraged my wedding to Stella!" Aloud he said: "Oh, sir, don't dwell on it, now! I ask for nothing."

"But I would have done better for you. . . . How is she? What is she doing?"

"She?"

"The Queen! Is it all the Frenchman now with her?"

"Yes. He has her entire attention. . . ."

Leicester made an indescribable sound of disgust.

"Despite everything!" he muttered. "I can't endure the thought she should wed——" He broke off suddenly. Lettice was coming into the room. With a swift movement she had enfolded her arms about him, laying her cheek against his head, and gently caressing the purplish bruise and cut on his cheek where the Queen had struck him.

"Dearest Robin. . . ." Her black eyes looked coldly at Philip over her husband's head.

"My lovely one!" said her husband.

His hands came up and covered hers, he was smiling fondly.

"And what news has Philip brought?"

"Very little—Aunt. All her Majesty's attention is for Simier. One supposes her marriage to the Duc d'Anjou is a foregone conclusion."

"What a lovely pair they'll be. That little prince with his pockmarks, and that nose which they say looks like two noses clapped together! And she with——"

"Leave it, leave it!" murmured her husband uneasily. He turned to his nephew.

"How does the Queen behave to you?"

"She does not appear to notice me."

"Pembroke will watch my interests as well as he can. . . . He'll keep an eye on you. And so will your Uncle Ambrose. But there's little hope of present favour for any of my blood!"

"I wish I had permission to leave court and fight in the Low Countries!"

"You would attach yourself to the Queen's—future husband?" asked Lettice.

"Never! Rather than have the very generalship of his Horse, I would trail a pike for that gallant honourable gentleman, William, Prince of Orange!"

"No, no, lad. Don't leave court, unless the Queen should send you away. She had an affection for you. . . . You can stay with Pembroke at Barnard's Castle, now this house will be closed, if you are not at court."

"Yes, sir. Or at Sir Francis Walsingham's place at Barn Elms. He has very kindly told me that I am regarded as a member of his family."

"Yes, he once said to me he has looked on you as a son ever since you stayed in the Embassy over St. Bartholomew's Eve. . . ."

"I think I will go there to-night."

"Give my greetings to Sir Francis and tell him there is no more I can do in this sorry business of the French marriage!"

Jogging on his tired horse down to Barn Elms, Philip had a yearning for the quietness of this other house. To stop thinking of the Queen and his Aunt Lettice like two hawks, striking against each other for their prey—and the poor figure cut by the prey! Yet it was better even to dwell on this ugliness, or the sordid necessity of his debts, than the agony of losing Stella. At Barn Elms there would be peace like his own home of Penshurst. Sir Francis was the deepest diplomatist of his age, the master of an unexampled secret service, a Puritan of a fanatical fervour who saw the approaching conflict between his country and Spain as the war between Christ and Belial. But at Barn Elms he was a gravely affectionate husband and father and an understanding friend to Philip, who needed the contrast to his Uncle Robert and *his* household.

As he dismounted in the shade of three tall trees, a little figure came running round the house, holding up her long taffeta skirts, nearly as full as a grown woman's, Walsingham's eleven-year-old daughter, Frances, whom Philip had first seen as a four-year-old child on her mother's lap on that never-forgotten dreadful night in Paris when the whole Embassy had sat up, the men prepared to defend the house till the King's Guard came clanking through the bloodstained streets to assume its protection. She came eagerly to Philip, and then hesitated with a moment's shyness.

"Well, sweetheart!" he said, stooping to kiss her. "Do you think I may come to supper and stay the night?"

"I'm sure. . . . I'll tell Father and Mother you are here!"

While he handed his horse over to a groom, Frances had run to her parents, and bobbing a quick curtsy, had told them, with the same eagerness, of their visitor. Then she paused, and her dark eyes were very serious. "Father—Philip looks so unhappy!"

"Then we must try to make him less unhappy!"

How well they had succeeded for the time being, Philip realized later, as he sat by the open casement of his room, before going to bed. The Walsingham family life had temporarily banished the vision of his Aunt Lettice, but could anything ever deaden the loss of her daughter? Wild thoughts of eloping with Stella, of taking her to Penshurst where they could be married by his father's chaplain, or to Wilton, country seat of his brother-in-law, the Earl of Pembroke, where Mary would surely help them—had to be abandoned with the bitter reflection that he had not the very money to pay for their journeying. The Queen's Grace and Lettice Leicester in their battle over Robert, had shattered the hopes of these two young creatures. A weariness came on Philip. If he could sleep and so escape from the very intolerability of life! Words slid into his mind and began to form lines, giving him an echo of that ease only to be found in Stella's arms and sleep itself. He started to write.

> "Come Sleep, O Sleep, the certain knot of peace,
> The baiting place of wits, the balm of woe,
> The poor man's wealth, the prisoner's release,
> The indifferent judge between the high and low——"

How different it was next day, back again at court, back to the pomp and colourful turmoil, the whispers and rumours, and Randal, his man, telling him how several tradesmen had pressed their bills on the previous day, tailors, jewellers, saddlers. The city of London now knew that the Earl of Leicester was married and Master Sidney might no longer be his heir, knew too that no one related to the Earl was likely to enjoy her Grace's favour. But here was Fulke, throwing his arm round Philip's shoulders. "Come and play tennis!"

But they were scarcely on the court, taking up their positions, when the clattering of feet in the gallery announced the arrival of a large number of spectators. Fulke spoke out of the corner of his mouth.

"Oxford and a good collection of his bully swordsmen. And Monsieur de Simier! Pay no attention to them, Phil. Oxford wants to pick a quarrel with you. Ned heard him say yesterday that he'd like to clean the court of Dudleys and their followers."

"I am not afraid of him. . . ."

But steps clattered on to the court behind the players, and a high-pitched voice cried: "I have now engaged the court."

Philip swung round. The Earl of Oxford stood, with his hands on his hips, his handsome florid face thrown back. Behind him, like expectant hounds, Philip saw the ring of hard, thrusting eyes.

"My Lord," he said. "I happen to be playing now."

"You? Get off the court—you damned puppy!"

Fulke saw his friend stiffen, and breathed the word "steady", but Philip's voice was as cold as steel.

"I should be glad to know whom your lordship is addressing. 'Puppy' is a word used for the offspring of dogs. . . ."

"I am addressing you, you Dudley whelp! And if you don't get off the court, I'll kick you from it!"

The dark flush had spread over Oxford's face and he showed the bloodshot whites of his eyes like a vicious horse. His bold handsomeness was replaced by such a mask as if he were playing Rage in one of the popular symbolical pageants of the time. Philip pressed his clenched hands against his sides to prevent himself striking that purplish mask.

"Your lordship has carefully picked the odds to favour yourself."

"God damme! D'you think I'm afraid of you?"

"I shall endeavour to find out. You will hear from me, my lord, after the proper manner."

Then they were walking past that ring of menacing eyes, and the quizzical, flashing ones of Monsieur de Simier, the Queen's 'Monkey'. Outside the court, Fulke suddenly threw his arms round Philip.

"Thank God, you're away from them without harm! There were you stripped to your shirt, no weapon but your racket in your hand, and he with a sword at his side! He's a killer. . . . He's drawn on an unarmed man before and murdered him. If he were not de Vere, Earl of Oxford, he would have swung for it! He would draw on an opponent and run him through, before the other had time to unsheathe. . . ."

"He'll draw on an armed man, next time!"

Nothing would turn Philip from his purpose. He sent his cartel to the Earl of Oxford and it was accepted. Neither the stern admonitions of members of the Council nor the pleas of friends could move Philip. Oxford had become in some sort a symbol of the ugliness of the world which was choking him, he would oppose it with his sword and all his strength. Finally Sir Christopher Hatton—who had an affection for him—added his expostulations. Oxford was a dangerous man and a powerful noble; as the leader of the faction which supported the French marriage he was high in the Queen's favour, and Philip as Leicester's nephew had best try to avoid her displeasure. But Philip, consumed by a cold fury, sat down to write to Sir Christopher.

"As for the matter depending between the Earl of Oxford and me, certainly, sir, howsoever I might have forgiven him, I should never have forgiven myself if I had lain under so proud an injury as he would have laid upon me. . . ."

The letter was hardly sent, when an usher came to his room. The Queen's Majesty demanded the presence of Master Sidney immediately!

She received him in a small chamber to which he had never penetrated before. Its high ceiling was carved with the gilded heads of angels, the whole of one wall seemed taken up with a great rectangular window of leaded glass while the others were hung with tapestries of dark, glowing red as if the room were wreathed in fires. The usher said: "Master Sidney, your Majesty!" and fell back, ladies-in-waiting with a soft rustle of silk seemed to eddy away, and Philip was alone, face to face with the Queen in her chair. He dropped on his knees. She was in plain black unrelieved except for the rich lace at her throat and wrists, edging her fluted ruff. Against the darkness, her jewels blazed. He had never seen so many jewels on her before, ropes of pearls set with rubies and emeralds hanging from her neck to her girdle which was a gemmed galaxy, her hands in her lap stiff with rings, huge-pear-shaped pearls dangling from her ears to her ruff, and that blazing red wig banded with so many stones, milk-white pearls, emeralds, diamonds and sapphires, that it seemed like a small crown. From the high forehead to the sharply pointed chin her face was painted a completely unnatural pink and white, the thin curving lips crimson. Her eyes were so dark, that he thought he could not tell the colour nor scarcely distinguish the pupils. Her voice was cold and dry and yet shaking as if some great wind of anger was blowing near by.

"So, Master Sidney! What is this I hear of you? You are proposing to brawl and fight in the very precincts of my palace?"

"Your Majesty, the Earl of Oxford put such an insult upon me that I needs must challenge him to a duel."

"Needs must, God's death! Who are you that you must avenge every insult? Are not greater than you insulted? Is not your Queen insulted?"

Philip was silent.

"And he—he is an Earl—de Vere of Oxford—a great nobleman! Are esquires to bandy insults with such and challenge them? I think you must have the Dudley insolence!"

Her hands shot out, gripped his shoulders and jerked him.

"Two generations attainted traitors and yet your uncle dared———" Her cracking voice broke short. She swallowed and continued in a quieter voice: "I notice you do not say—'what my uncle does is naught to do with me'!"

"If your Grace will forgive my saying so, whatever I may personally think of my uncle's actions, I will defend them in the face of the world!"

"You're mighty bold!" She leaned forward, her voice taking an extraordinary concentration. "Listen to me, Philip! I have had my Lord Oxford here, and I have told him that if he persists in this duel with you, if he gives another insult or challenge, if he so much as draws his sword halfway from its sheath—I'll have him in Tower! And I say the same to you! If I hear of either of you persisting in this duel, it shall be rigorous imprisonment. By God's son—I—and I alone!—rule here!"

Her hands came up from his shoulders to his hair, and caught the rebellious lock at the back. He thought dizzily that they had ceased to be the talons of a Fury and had suddenly become marvellously gentle.

" 'Twas always unruly. . . . I'll not have him fight you!"

Then she was pressing Philip's face against her knee, and her voice was again choked, this time with unshed tears.

"My little Philip—I'll not have him hurt you. . . ."

But he raised his head and looked straight at her dark eyes.

Zenith

"Your Grace is very good! But such as he—could do me no hurt that matters."

Her voice was sad, tired and reflective.

"You would quote Holy Writ, my Philip? 'Fear not they that slay the body but only they that slay the soul'? Oxford could not hurt your soul. But he might grievously hurt your body. Call it, if you will, the caprice of a selfish old woman."

"Not selfish—nor old—your Grace!"

A smile came on her face for the first time with a sudden glowing tenderness.

"And you are no courtier—no liar! But old enough to be your mother, if God had seen fit—to make me any man's mother. . . . Now go! And keep your tongue and your blade still!"

He kissed her hand fervently, bowed very low, and backed out of her presence. She was resting her chin on her hand and her eyes were inscrutable.

Chapter Fourteen

He came, he saw—and some said he conquered. The court at Greenwich awoke one morning to find that the heir to the Throne of France had arrived, with a mere handful of followers at the water-gate in the small hours, when his forerunner and "wooing ambassador", Simier, receiving him, had difficulty in preventing his ardent master from rushing straight to the bedchamber of his "Perfect Goddess" to wake her like the Sleeping Beauty. Simier recorded all this in a note, which she read, at her normal hour of awakening, which told her of the Duke's fervour and with what difficulty the "Monkey" had at last got him to bed, adding: "Would God, it was by your side." The majority of the courtiers who learned of it, considered it all of a piece with his previous behaviour which showed "his licentious foreign impudence". Since the dramatic announcement of the Leicester marriage, her Majesty's familiarities with her beloved "Monkey" had outraged even the supporters of the French marriage. Her attention, her speech, her laughter were all for the "Monkey", now gazing ardently into her eyes, devouring her hands with kisses, whispering quick jokes and quips into her ear, or sitting on the floor at her feet, caressing her ankles. If so much was allowed the man, what of the master?

She, who had always kept her fingers on the public pulse, who had ultimately bowed her arrogant will to the feelings of her beloved people, seemed blind to the storm of rage rising in the country. The massacre of St. Bartholomew's Eve was a fresh memory. Was their Queen, whom they loved more each year, with a fervent devotion blended with a chuckling appreciation of her as a ripe "character", to marry the son of the "murdering Italian Jezebel"? The ever-growing Puritan faction blazed up, and their forceful preachers thundered from the pulpits. Those close about the Queen saw she was too deeply

occupied with the great wound dealt her to heed much else; most believed that the wound was to her immense and palpable vanity.
Whether she had a heart was debated as keenly as her virtue—or lack
of it—by contemporaries and later opinions alike.

Afterwards she saw it like the delirious whirl of a nightmare.
Strange hatreds and stranger desires tore at her like harpies. For
the past decade there had been a golden serenity in her relationship
with Robert, a happy intimacy of mind which had seemed to grow
deeper as the fires of passion burned down. Simier's announcement
had cast oil on those fires, but this resurgence was bitter as that early
passion had never been. Circumstance had driven their love underground when they were young, it had been muffled in deceit, but in
itself it had been a joyful thing, a source of happiness and strength to
sustain her in her public life. Now, when remembrance was a fantastic procession of evil, a masque of all the lies and lusts grinning at her,
devil-faced, and Robert and Lettice the worst masks of all, she was
tormented with a sick desire for him, though at the same time she
could have gladly caused both his death and Lettice's, or their supreme humiliation, to pay for hers. All the old wounds had broken
open and bled; the very foundations of the past were cut away at a
time when she was turning this way and that in a frenzy to escape
seeing the empty loneliness of the future. That dark face with the
flashing eyes, that quick tongue with its outrageous compliments,
those caresses which were a challenge—her "Monkey" had brought
her some assuagement—and now his personality seemed strangely
merged in his master's, and his face superseded by that odd, ugly
little face, pin-pricked all over by smallpox, made grotesque by the
huge distorted nose, and partly redeemed by the intense vivacity of
the sparkling black eyes. And he was a Prince of a most ancient
House, the son of a King who might one day be a King himself, and
subtly and boldly, he pressed his royalty and hers with a vision of the
two of them on their eminence together, with the rest of the world far
below, at their feet.

One of those days which were poisoned and feverish with that sick
longing for Robert, she was driven beyond all discretion. Perhaps an
intercepted glance of distaste from young Philip Sidney for her fondling of the ugly princeling—who was *he* to venture such criticism of
her?—perhaps a memory of the other great wound dealt to her private
emotional life—the birth of Mary of Scotland's son when her only

comfort had been in Robert's arms—goaded her now. Robert's marriage, like the birth of Mary's son, had shown the emotional bankruptcy of the woman behind the resplendent crowned figure. The "barren stock" who had not been able to hold her lover's love. . . . The triumphs of her crown could not heal *that*. She looked at the lively, ugly young man at her side. He too had his nickname now. Taking one of his stumpy, short-fingered hands in her long ones, she had said: "Frog's paws!" He had not been disconcerted. "Élisabeth, chérie, do not all your countrymen call mine 'frogs'?" "Mon p'tit Grenouille!" she had said.

Now, when memory and disapproving present eyes were spurs to the frenzy seizing her brain, she gave him a swift flashing smile. "Mon Grenouille, did I not promise to show you that miniature of your grandfather, painted for my father at the Field of the Cloth of Gold, when they were the two most splendid young sovereigns in Europe? Come!"

Taking that squat stumpy hand she led him into her great bed-chamber. Let all think the worst! Let their tongues clack! They had called her loose woman long enough. . . . Let someone tell Robert! Her "Frog" reacted even quicker than she expected. He clapped his hands. "Brava! You cannot conceive with what desperation I have wished to be alone with you!" She made no resistance when he pulled her down to the cushion-filled couch, a spark of cynical amusement telling her that being shorter than she, he would find it difficult to kiss her competently when standing on his feet. But now he could—and did —kiss her very competently . . . murmuring the while that he adored her wildly and that as a lover he was *formidable*! "Lies, lies!" she thought, "but it is always lies! Robert lied and lied. . . . Let me shut out the memory of his lies with these!" All her torment was in the desperation with which she clung to him. He was a man, he was young, he desired her—or gave a good imitation. . . . There were a few moments of madness in his arms, madness to blind that hateful vision of Robert with Lettice. Perhaps there was a thwarted hunger in both, the young man with his secret feelings of inferiority for his small size and ugly face; the woman dreading the onset of age and all it brought. But though moments of madness could banish Lettice, they could not finally banish Robert—the splendid young Robert of twenty years ago. Yielding to this ugly youth could never obliterate that memory. She put him from her with a sudden firmness, and tried to collect her whirling thoughts. Anjou had enough experience and shrewdness not to press his advantage. Ma foi! She is not cold, that one! So much the better. . . . But she thought: "If I was the light woman they say, it would be so simple! Robin, Robin, why am I faithful against my will?"

Yet there was to be a day when she felt a burst of honest affection for her Frog. They were side by side, high above the lists, under her emblazoned canopy. Beneath them, the jousters in damascened armour and gaily hued trappings, clashed boldly upon each other. The stumpy hands were closing on hers.

"Élisabeth, adorée—I would like to break a lance to show how much I love you!"

"An old woman like me?" she said cynically.

"Listen to me, Adorée! Shall we waste time in sadness because I was born too late and missed your youth? It is not profitable! Any more than to weep because I am not so tall that you must look up at me—or that I have not a face like Adonis? Why weep for my face or my size—or your youth? Do you not know that after a while lovely young girls become dull?"

The small, sparkling eyes were looking intently at her.

"And do you not know that lovely young girls are dull beside you? Do you know why—I like you? Because you are more alive than twenty other women!"

"I like you, too, François, mon p'tit," she said with a candour which matched. "And for the same reason!"

"Yes! Me—I am alive. . . . In my whole family, only I and my sister Margot—she who married Navarre—we are the only ones. My brothers—bah! They did not live before they died, and my brother, Henri—when he has dressed the part, he makes a charming girl in appearance! That is the kindest thing one can say about him. . . . Now all there is of me—it is a man! I do everything with a vigour you cannot believe! You and I together, Élisabeth, cherie, what shall stop us? What shall we not do? Your England, my France and the Low Countries together—we shall be the greatest power on earth!"

"France is not yours yet. And your brother may have an heir."

"France will be mine! Do you then expect the Bon Dieu to perform a miracle and cause Henri to become a mother?"

She chuckled with appreciation.

"No, mon Grenouille, I never expect miracles. Most miracles, I find, are the result of very hard work. . . ."

"And that, perhaps, would be too hard!" The short fingers tightened on hers. "Adorée—marry me! You will not regret it!"

She paused a moment, seeing before her the abyss of loneliness. Yes, he was *alive*, this little fellow, he was gay, amusing and intelligent. He could make her laugh and there was the memory of those conflicting emotions in his arms. . . . No, perhaps, she would not regret it.

"Yes," she said at last. "I'll marry you, François! But understand! On *my* terms, as drawn up in consultation with my Council. . . . I don't share my crown. And you must know this. That my country has always meant more to me than anything else. There is no glory of my own that could ever cause me to consent to its slightest harm."

"But Adorée, allied with France and the Low Countries it will be so strong!"

"You must first drive Parma from the Low Countries!"

"I will do it. Have no fear! But I need money. To pay my troops and to engage more. You will give me money, Élisabeth, adorée?"

"Some," she said reluctantly. "I must consult my Council. . . . When I think of the subsidies I have already given the Dutch—and so little achieved!"

"I will achieve! But it will need money, and my brother, and Madame, my mother, they are more ready with their blessings than gold."

"And I have little. It is King Philip who has the gold mines of the New World—not I!"

"We will have them yet, too. When the might of England and France are together, and you possess such sea captains! Look at your Drake, whom the Spaniards call El Draque—the Dragon. In Paris there are rumours from the Spanish Embassy of the tremendous havoc he has wrought in Nova Hispania."

"He?" she said coolly, "I do not know where he is!" But her hands tightened on the arms of her chair. "What do they say he has done?"

"That he has sailed into the Mar del Pacifico, the first foreign ship ever there, and taken the richest carrack of Peru, loaded with gold and jewels!"

"God's soul! I am not responsible for everything done by those unruly sea cocks." Her lips were compressed.

"We understand each other, Adorée. . . ."

"Do we?" she demanded and laughed. "The agreement for the marriage, it must be put to the Council. And the question of granting you a subsidy for your troops in the meanwhile—a *very small* subsidy. . . ."

"How I long for our marriage!" His eyes were sparkling even more brightly. "We will not weary one another."

She laughed again. "No, François, mon petit Grenouille, whatever else we do—we will not weary each other!"

She thought: "He is a small flame at which I can warm my cold hands. And perhaps he can make me stop thinking of Robin."

And there seemed for a short time that perhaps this strange marriage might make an impossibility come true. Burghley had summoned the Queen's physicians to give their opinion on the highly important and delicate matter of the Queen's prospects of bearing children. She would be forty-six next month, and Walsingham and his party in the Council had roundly declared that a first child at that age would be the death of her. But the physicians had assured Burghley that such a birth would not be fraught with especial perils. She herself had taken this pronouncement in absolute silence.

Huic—who had once told her that she would never bear children—was long dead. His successor was a strange man, Lopez the Jew, driven by the Inquisition from his native Portugal. She had found him inscrutable, always seeming to hold something in reserve, and yet skilled beyond all his English colleagues. She had him summoned to her bedchamber, and presently he stood before her in his long black velvet gown, his head bowed slightly as if in submission, but his dark liquid eyes surveying her with a sidelong shrewdness.

"Your Majesty's leg is troubling you?"

"Not unduly. Considering how long I danced yesterday, it is better than of late. I was curious to have your opinion, Dr. Lopez, on a case which chanced to interest me. It is of a woman—who has been blamed for childlessness. She was married—for twenty years without children. Yet her husband had none by his previous marriage, and he had a brother who was also childless. Is it conceivable that the fault is not in the woman, and if she wedded again, she might yet bear a child?"

"Your Majesty will understand that with persons completely unknown to me, I cannot make any pronouncement. Yet on the facts given—it seems within the range of possibility that this woman might bear a child." For a moment he raised his head a fraction, and under their heavy lids, his eyes seemed to glint. Then head and eyes submissively dropped again. She thought: "He knows quite well what I mean. . . . But we will maintain the fiction!"

"Thank you!" she said. "It interested me for the moment. Now for a matter of importance—quite important since it is delaying my signature to State documents. I have the most curious pain in my right thumb!"

After he had dealt with the thumb, she sat on alone in her bedchamber, thinking. Supposing it was possible after all these years to have a child! Robert had had no child by his first wife, that Robsart woman, nor had she heard of any bastard, and his brother Ambrose was also childless. Supposing Huic was wrong. . . . Now everything between Robert and her was ended, what did it matter who her child's father would be? It would be *her* child, and she put out her hands with a nervous groping movement as if she could imagine touching it. Then she raised them and covered her face with them. "But", she thought, "I am old, old, old! Whatever Burghley has persuaded the doctors to say, or whatever they have persuaded themselves, I would surely die! And I do not want to die! Half my work is not done, and only I can do it." Her thoughts swung her this way and that. For so long, since the death of Robert's first wife, she had seen the perils of marriage. The Queen's husband who was not a king, who must not be a king! There had seemed everything against her marriage—unless she could give the country an heir. During the early years, she had been filled with a strange mixture of hope and dread that she would find herself with child by Robert. How much she had wanted to be the mother of Robert's son no one but herself would ever know. But against that desperate longing, had been the dread that the hurried marriage this would entail might shake her from the throne. And even if this were not so, she knew from the very hour that Robert's ring was on her finger, he would never stop striving to be king and ruler—her master. And loving him as she did, how could she fight him adequately? She had only managed to control him by cutting her life in two. The Crown remained supreme, and he like all the others must bow down to it. But in a marriage where love did not tie her hands, she could fight for and obtain mastery. She thought she could prevent the young Anjou from having any say in the rule of her kingdom. He would have the Low Countries, and perhaps France one day, and those might surely sustain his ambition? Now at last, at the time

when she had lost Robert, it seemed that not only was it safe for her
to marry, it was even better for the welfare of her country to marry
this especial candidate. And there was the possibility of a child,
something she could love openly before the world, something that
would secure the succession. She could let Mary Stuart go, and be
free of that burden.

"But I am too old. . . . I would surely die!" An icy hand had been
laid on her heart. "Such a lonely death with no one now who would
care. . . . And the country, what would happen to the country?"
Against this came the thoughts of a baby who would become a little
boy, something that would run to her and hold her, a love that need
not be concealed, a mind developing in her hand. To teach him Latin
—to teach him life—how to weigh and measure when to dare and
when to draw back—how to understand—and rule!

She summoned her Council to debate marriage agreements, and
became aware at last of the rage her proposed marriage was exciting
in the country. In her present mood it awoke a return of the rage in
her. But before the Council met, a printer in Creed Lane in the City
was turning out copies of one of the most inflammatory pamphlets
ever written—*The Discovery of a Gaping Gulf whereinto England is
like to be plunged by the French Marriage, if the Lord forbid not the
banns by letting her Majesty see the Sin and Punishment thereof*. And
as this pamphlet was coming off the press, a number of horsemen
were making their way to the town house of the Earl of Pembroke,
that frowning pile overhanging the Thames, Barnard's Castle.

Philip Sidney had been advised by Sir Francis Walsingham that
his presence would be required at "a meeting of a few of her Majesty's
councillors at this unprecedented time". He had ridden through the
summer's dusk in the narrow, stinking, overhung lanes of the City,
beside the Secretary of State, but few words passed between them. As
they drew up before the massive door of his brother-in-law's residence, four horsemen came in after them, and with some surprise,
Philip saw his uncle, Leicester, dressed very quietly for one used to
such sumptuous apparel, and only attended by Digby and a couple of
grooms. He was out of his saddle and at his uncle's stirrup before
anyone else could come forward. Leicester, dismounting, embraced
him with all the old affection, and kept an arm round his shoulders.

"Ah, Sir Francis! We need this lad!"

Walsingham's dark, swarthy face—which had made the Queen

nickname him her "Moor"—had a look which mingled doubt and concern.

"I agree with your suggestion, my Lord. It is a possibility. I only hope it will not be the cause of any trouble to Philip."

"D'you think I would cause trouble to Philip?" declared Leicester with over-effusiveness. Philip, somewhat mystified, followed his elders in. When they were finally gathered into an upper room, its heavy velvet curtains drawn, the wax candles showed him many of her Majesty's councillors had come to his brother-in-law. Besides his uncle and Sir Francis who had arrived with him, there was his own father, Sir Henry Sidney, a man prematurely worn and aged, his Uncle Ambrose, Earl of Warwick, Sir Christopher Hatton and the new Lord Chancellor, Sir Thomas Bromley, a pronounced Puritan. Sitting quietly by his father's side, Philip listened to the debate which was soon dominated by his Uncle Robert. He was evidently talking of a forthcoming pamphlet—the very "Gaping Gulf".

" 'Pon my soul, I had no need to urge the fellow, after I had been seeking one with a fiery pen! He would have written without any assistance or commendation from me—held it a mission from the Lord. A most zealous Puritan, this John Stubbes! I think his 'Gaping Gulf' will whip up a crescendo of fury."

"It will be most potent fuel for flames already burning," agreed Walsingham. "Surely her Majesty will then realize the opposition in the country."

"But it is most inflammatory!" protested Hatton. "It will enrage her sweet Majesty. . . ."

Leicester gave a short bitter laugh.

"I would not be in her royal presence when she reads it! But! I have a more subtle and tactful remedy. A letter to her Majesty from one for whom she has a true affection and trust." He laid his hand suddenly on Philip's shoulder. "You, my lad! When you told me how her Majesty had received you to stop your duello with Oxford, I could well see that for all her rebukes to esquires challenging great noblemen, her genuine affection for you was at the back of it."

"Her Majesty was very good——" murmured Philip.

"She has always cared for you. The last time I spoke with her——" A frown flickered over his face. "She said you were the only man at court with a conscience. If she gets a letter from you, she'll know well enough it will not come from any urging of mine."

Zenith

"Nevertheless, my Lord," said the Chancellor, with his precise lawyer's mind. "You are urging him. We all are."

"The Queen is a damnation shrewd judge of men!" retorted Leicester. "She knows well enough, Sir Thomas, if you and I and the whole of the Privy Council were to urge young Philip here, he would not disobey his own conscience. Come rack, come rope—he would stand to his conscience."

"But you understand, Philip," said Walsingham, "that such a letter from you might cause, at least, the temporary loss of her Majesty's favour."

"I have had rather kindness than favour from her Majesty," said Philip slowly. "And I would repay it by doing all in my power to further her Majesty's good. And the good of the country. I am persuaded they are the same. If her Majesty will be displeased with me, I am sorry but my own consideration would not check me."

"Dearest boy," said his father, speaking for the first time. "You must be sure that you know what you are venturing."

"For myself, I care nothing of the consequences, if I may serve the Queen. If you think, sirs, that any words of mine would move her——"

"Listen, Philip!" said Leicester, leaning forward and speaking to him as if they two were alone. "We have chosen you to write as the Queen trusts you. We are—grown old in the ways of courts. We have all played the politician too long. The Queen will mistrust our motives. But however angry she will be, she will not mistrust yours. You are acknowledge to be the leader of the younger men—that is why Oxford and the other swaggerers are jealous of you. Your merits have been noted outside this country—did not Orange himself say there was no other man to whom he would sooner give his own sister in marriage? The Queen knows that—as well as she knows your conscience!"

"Sirs," said Philip again, "if you think that the Queen would heed any words of mine against this abominable marriage alliance, I will very gladly write. . . ."

It was dark when Philip took leave of his uncle. As he drew on his perfumed pearl-embroidered gauntlets, Leicester remarked: "The country is most hot against Anjou! D'you know what they were singing in the hostelry where we stopped to bait our horses?

"Good people of Flanders, pray do not suppose
That 'tis monstrous this Frenchman should double his nose:

Zenith

Dame Nature her favours but rarely misplaces
She has given two noses to match his two faces!"

"He has courage and some enterprise unlike the rest of his family,"
said Philip. "But he is as treacherous as any other Valois." He paused
and then added with some hesitation: "Uncle Robin, how is—
Mistress Penelope?"

"Well enough! Still writing her sonnets? That's a way to please
women, you young dog. Still. . . . I would have asked you down to
Wanstead, but her mother thinks you distract her. . . . I miss you,
dear lad, but I would not oppose your aunt in any way just now.
She is expecting a child!"

Philip could not keep the bitterness out of his voice. "I would not
force myself on you!"

Leicester's hand on his shoulder tightened.

"Lad, I'm sorry. . . . She's a pretty little wench, my stepdaughter,
but we must get you an heiress. A rich widow for choice! I'll do my
best to advance you when this hubbub has boiled down!"

"I would not have you think me ungrateful! But there is some
advancement for which I could never pay the price!"

The palace clocks were chiming the early hours of morning and his
candles had burned low in their sockets, before he had completed the
copy of the letter in his fine Italian hand. He had hesitated at first
after writing the commencement—"*Most feared and beloved, most
sweet and gracious Sovereign*"—but he had gradually warmed to his
task and that single-minded passion which illumined his sonnets
sprang to his phrases.

"*Howsoever fine wits may find further dealings or painted excuses,
the very common people well know this; that he is a son of a Jezebel of
our age; that his brother made an oblation of his own sister's marriage,
the easier to make massacres. . . . Even at first sight, gives occasion to
. . . diminish much of the hopeful love they have long held to you. . . .*

"*Now the agent party which is Monsieur . . . taught to love greatness
any way gotten; and having for motioners and ministers of the mind,
only such young men as have showed they think evil contentment a
ground of any rebellion; who have no commonwealth but in faction, and
divers of which have defiled their hands in odious murders. With such
fancies and such favourites, what is to be hoped for?*

Zenith

"Against contempt, if there be any which I will never believe, let your excellent virtues of piety, justice and liberality, daily if it be possible, more and more shine. . . . Lastly doing as you do, you shall be as you be, the example of princes, the ornament of this age, and the most excellent fruit of your progenitors, and the perfect mirror of your posterity."

But the 'Gaping Gulf' which cried out the fury of a people had now come into Elizabeth's hands, and was answered by her own fury. It vilified Anjou and his House, it recalled Bartholomew in words of flame, it declared that her Majesty's expectation of death in child-birth was fearful. For the first time she was filled with bitterness against her own people. Had she not sacrificed her personal life abso-lutely for their benefit? Had they no gratitude that they were to deny her her last chance of marriage—deny her her last hope of a child? She gave orders that the author and printers of such a pamphlet were to be immediately sought for and arrested. Even in her rage and des-pair, the cool mechanical part of her brain recorded the danger of such an affront to France. But all her personal torment was in her fury when she had recalled a statute of her sister's made to protect her detested brother-in-law. The arrested Stubbes was to have his right hand struck off by the headsman—and let him be thankful it was not his head! But her councillors after sitting a week in continuous debate sent a deputation to her, led by Burghley—Burghley who had been urging her for twenty years to marry—to tell her that they did not see how this marriage could be.

The stone walls were closing around her now and she seemed to be beating against them like a captive bird. To be fighting for a man for whom she did not care, as she had never fought publicly to marry Robin! Was this not the summit of bitterness? She had forgotten now the very outline of her Frog Prince, forgotten the sick impulse which had sent her into his arms, forgotten the affectionate appreciation of his lively humour which had once sweetened the matter. She was struggling only for something to fill the great void in her life, strug-gling to keep that hope of a child a little longer yet. She stormed at them, but it was with a despair different to the fury vented on Stubbes. Did they then wish the line of Henry VIII to become extinct? Was she to be denied the comfort of children in her old age? Was she to be denied what her meanest subject might have? Her councillors left her in an unyielding silence, and presently a letter was brought to her, the letter from Philip Sidney. She read it through slowly and carefully and the words—"diminish the hopeful love they have long held to you"—bit into her brain. The cold, sick exhaustion of absolute despair had seized her now; there was no more rage or frenzy left. She felt drained as if she had given the blood she had once promised to shed if need be for her country and people. She had surely shed more than her blood. . . . She covered her face with her hands and wept— wept for her lonely frightened childhood, for her danger-shadowed youth, for her early love which had been forced into secret ways and finally destroyed by treachery, for her last chance of a son—and her ladies were afraid and left her alone.

When Philip was finally summoned to the Queen's presence, he was past caring for any consequence of his letter. He had just learned of the forthcoming marriage of his Stella to the Lord Rich. The smooth line of sonnets had left him, his mood was summed up in the agony of a dirge-like litany:

> "Ring out your bells, let mourning shows be spread
> For Love is dead:
> All Love is dead, infected
> With plague of deep disdain:
> Worth as naught-worth rejected,
> And Faith fair Scorn doth gain.
> From so ungrateful fancy
> From such a female frenzy
> From them that use men thus,
> Good Lord, deliver us!"

That the Queen could have understood the mood of his verse, he did not know. As he knelt before her, he was aware with some little surprise of the parchment greyness of her unpainted face under the flaming wig and brilliant jewels.

"Well!" she said. "So here is another that would rule his Queen! Who would deny her a husband and child such as her poorest subject might have—any ordinary woman!"

"But your Grace is so much more than an ordinary woman!"

"And—so much less. . . . If there was any presumption, Philip, I forgive you because it was honest. But you are not a courtier."

"I would not wish to be one, your Grace. I am your servant till death. I only ask you to try me. I wish you would send me to the Low Countries to strike a blow for you against our most dangerous enemy."

"I will not have you imperil your young life. Though you can leave court if you so wish. But I thought you were betrothed, and no longer wishing to ride away on knight-errantry."

"I am no longer betrothed, your Grace."

"Why?"

"Because her mother—my aunt—does not hold me to be of enough substance to wed her daughter now I am no longer my uncle's heir."

"So that she-wolf made that—that weak coward disinherit you?"

"My uncle would never disinherit me, but now his wife, my aunt, is with child——"

He started, shocked beyond his own trouble, by the animal sound of pain which broke from the Queen's throat.

"Get away! Get out of my sight. . . ."

He got away, to the green peace of Wilton for a few months, to the beloved sister who understood him better than anyone else. It was ostensibly to divert her during the last months of her first pregnancy, but surely as much to divert his own sore, tired mind, that he wrote *The Arcadia.*

But there was no Wilton, no Arcadia, to furnish escape for the Queen. Her final courtship dragged on its farcical way for two more years, though she knew she would never marry her "Frog". Her last hopes and illusions were gone—Anjou was even a military failure suspected of duplicity—but she knew she bought time with him, time to prepare and arm for the inevitable struggle bearing down on her which she had so long dreaded. He had never been anything more than an illusion, her Frog Prince, but she made him serve her turn. There were more prancings and posturings, public kisses and ex- change of rings, subsidies to maintain the armies he so inadequately led. The country had calmed from the fury of the "Gaping Gulf" to another mood expressed in a resuscitated folk-rhyme, which had a rollicking tune and a rollicking chorus. Soon everyone was singing it loudly. It swept the country.

> "A Frog he would a wooing go!
> Whether his mother would let him, or no!"

In 1581, there was a moment of glory when Drake returned from

Zenith

his triumphal and incredible circumnavigation of the globe, with his *Golden Hind* weighed low in the water with captured Spanish treasure. It was a triumph for her who with the eager support of Walsingham and Robert had given him a secret commission against the caution of Burghley and his supporters. Nowadays Robert was no longer her love, no longer even her companion, but he was still perforce her councillor, and slowly and with bitter reluctance, she began to approach his view that Spain must be opposed openly. The treasure Drake had brought her and the prudent management of Hawkins in her shipyards, could build her more ships. So she knighted Drake on board the *Golden Hind*, and defied the protests of the Spanish Ambassador, conscious that her people were with her again and the Frog interlude forgotten.

Yet, when Anjou died of a fever in 1584, her apparent grief was not all false. He had been young, eager and lively. She could weep—a little—for youth and vigour and excited hope finally quenched, for that small flame at which she had once hoped to warm her cold hands, extinguished.

Chapter Fifteen

I t seemed natural to her that at this moment of crisis her thoughts should turn to Robert. Five years may hide twenty, but they cannot destroy them. That closeness of mind and body for twenty years was so deep planted that she felt it now, as she sat in the little pavilion, with her pointed chin resting on one jewelled hand. Before her eyes, the Privy Garden spread its geometrical shape; its neat beds edged with trim box, the whole enclosed by walls of the same mellow brick as the Palace of Richmond, against which fruit was slowly ripening. In the centre one tall yew cast an almost purple shadow. Overhead, in a sky whose blue was dimmed by a milky haze, a kite hovered like a dark fleck of mud spotting the shining curve of the heavens. She could hear, far off, the jolly cries of a boating party on the river. The summer's peace was all around, a sleepy ease drawing its fertility from the blessing of the sun warming the moist soil, but there was no peace upon earth nor in her mind. She had walked up and down with her long stride, around that formally designed garden, her ladies dutifully following her, and then had abruptly waved them away from her, to sit in the little pavilion.

All her life, she thought, had been spent in struggling with and postponing the inevitable. When it came she faced it with a flat, cold courage which surprised herself more than others. She alone knew the immense nervous tension which had ravaged her and for so long. When she had come to the throne twenty-six years ago, it had seemed that her country—and she with it—would soon be overwhelmed by immense perils. Slowly and with an infinite patience and complete lack of scruple, she had started to rebuild the ruins. She had drawn upon the best brains of the country to serve her, balancing the impetuosity of Robert against the caution of Burghley. No lie or subterfuge was too dark or tortuous, no wound to her own personality too agonizing, to be employed for the country's welfare. The great powers of Europe had loomed like armoured giants above her exhausted and impoverished little country. She had bought it time to regain strength by any means which came to her hand. When she sent money secretly to the "Lords of the Congregation" in Scotland and denied it in open council, when she denied her own heart's longing to marry Robert and show her love to the world, when she sent her seamen into the jealously guarded waters of the New World and bade them deny her commission if needs be, when she coquetted brazenly with the Duke of Anjou—all these denials had one positive end in view. That she was achieving it, every Progress showed her. In that quarter-century prosperity and confidence had grown beyond her wildest hopes. She belonged to the New Age which was turning its back on the old ways, the New Age born of the miraculous New Learning which had made men reach out to the farthest horizons, challenging all long accepted beliefs from religious to geographical. Not for her the simple faith of the medievalist, there was nothing of simplicity in her nature, except at its very depths. But no medieval fanatic could have shown a more single-minded devotion than she did to the welfare and safety of her beloved people.

The news of the assassination of the Prince of Orange had just been brought to her and she knew that she must either give open aid to the Netherlands or see them go down. To give open aid would almost certainly bring the dreaded weight of Spain upon her country, at the very least it would be hideously wasteful of blood and money. Her own age and succeeding ones have freely accused her of being stingy with money; most of them seem to forget she was far more stingy with the blood of her subjects. But neither morally nor materially could she face the crushing of the Netherlands. So long the war party —that curious blend of zealous Puritans and daring young adventurers, who had accepted Robert as their leader—had urged her to send forces to the Netherlands. It was the war against Anti-Christ (as Philip of Spain saw it in reverse) and at the same time they believed to crush the Spanish forces therein would save their own country. So they urged her to step forth as the Protestant Champion, a role for which she had no desire. She was the champion of the English people to save them from material harm; their souls they must save for themselves. In an age which knew it not, she inclined towards religious toleration. But at every increasing move made against her by the Papacy, her Puritan extremists clamoured louder and louder for Catholic blood. In 1580, the Papal Secretary replied to an inquiry made by certain English Jesuits.

"Since that guilty woman of England rules over two such noble kingdoms of Christendom and is the cause of so much injury to the Catholic faith and the loss of so many million souls, there is no doubt that whosoever sends her out of the world with pious intention of doing God service, not only does not sin, but gains merit."

The guilty woman's Parliament immediately passed further repressive laws against the Catholics in reprisal which the guilty woman herself viewed with weary distaste. Sometimes she swore at Walsingham, calling him "protector of heretics" and gibingly asked him if he found Jesuits under the bed? It was the age of plot and counter-plot, plots of madmen and fools, plots of deep cunning contrived with the aid of Spain and the Papacy, plots which only existed in the brain of Walsingham. Elizabeth knew well the cause of these plots whether innocent or guilty, but at this moment she would not consider the problem of Mary of Scotland. "Sufficient unto the day is the evil thereof." Now she wanted Robert's encouragement and reassurance to strengthen her to face the ugly future. Robert had believed in the policy of fighting Spain in the Low Countries. She had respected William of Orange; he loved his Netherlanders as she loved her English, but she would not peril her English except for their own advantage.

She turned to the little group of her ladies waiting patiently beyond the garden pavilion.

"Anne," she said. "Where is your brother-in-law Robert?"

The Countess of Warwick came forward.

"He is at Kenilworth. You know that his little son, the Lord Denbigh, is dying? He was summoned there because the child has not many hours to live."

"I did not know!" said the Queen harshly. She stared at the shimmering sky and saw nothing. Robert's son, Robert's heir, Robert's only legitimate child, the prize for which Robert had struck her that deadly wound. She was well aware of Robert's longing for an heir, and it was not only in self-comfort that she had realized a son was at least as powerful a reason for the marriage as his enslavement to Lettice's voluptuous body and ruthless mind. She could remember the bitter rage which had filled her when she had heard of Lettice triumphantly giving birth to Robert's son. Now that rage had grown dim and faded.

"I did not know!" she repeated. "No one told me."

"It will be a terrible blow to Robert, your Grace."

"Yes. . . . He loved children—and was beloved by them. Anne, when you have the definite news of the child's death, tell me, so that I can send to him."

Send to him she did, so that Robert was to write in answer to a letter of condolence from Sir Christopher Hatton:

"Her Majesty . . . whom on my knees I most humbly thank for her most gracious visitation by Killigrew. She shall never comfort a more true and faithful man to her, for I have lived and so will die only hers. . . ."

When Hatton brought this letter to show to her (as no doubt, its writer had intended) she raised one ironic eyebrow. He was simple at heart, her "good Mutton", in spite of his years swimming in the whirlpool of court. She thought: "If I had to love, why did I not choose this man who adores me, to whom this fantastic—and useful —love-game, which has grown up about me, is real? *He* would not betray me. But I have nothing more for him than affection and appreciation." No! It was the man who had written the letter, who had written *"for I have lived and so will die only hers"* and had utterly betrayed her, whom she loved and would love so long as there was breath in her body. . . . Fool, fool, fool!

They had been hard, those five years. She herself had made so much of Robert Dudley, raised him so high as well as drawing out and training those qualities in him which he had once scarcely known that he possessed. He was one of the greatest of her councillors and she could transact no business of State without his being there; when she took her place at the Council table, she must encounter that cool yet penetrating glance of his dark eyes. He was her Master of Horse, who always rode behind her in every State procession, the second most splendid figure therein. She could escape his presence as little as she could escape the memory of their joint past. And all around her poisoned tongues whispered how the Earl of Leicester doted upon and adored his wife. . . . That learned court put it wittily into a Latin tag—"aliquando mulierosus, demum supra modum uxorious . . .".

Truly he had been given to women—that accomplished rake who

had possessed so many including his Queen. . . . And now he was to dote above all measure upon his wife—upon Lettice, her cousin and enemy—that "she-wolf"! When he left Elizabeth's presence, when he went from the Council board or the State procession, she knew he would go to Lettice, to be enfolded in the happiness of their own private world, walled about impenetrably with walls against which she could dash herself in despair. . . . Yet sometimes force of long habit imagined a door between them.

When he had returned from escorting her "Frog-Prince" on his final departure, he reported to her in a solemn voice which was belied by the twinkle in his eyes, that he had "left Monsieur high and dry on a sandbank". She had caught the twinkle and chuckled in spite of herself. There had been a humorous note in her retort: "I wish I had my little Frog swimming in the Thames again!" It was so easy to joke with Robert. . . . But what badinage could pierce the great barrier?

Now at last he was kneeling before her in that withdrawing chamber to which he had not penetrated for five years. Anne Warwick had drawn away her ladies with her usual tact.

"You have been very good to me—at this time!" he said.

Feeling his lips on her palm, she shivered. Caresses were false coinage—when they two had been young, such touch of lip or hand had had golden value—now its worth was nominal. She put her hand to his cheek in the old manner and thought in bitter defiance: "I do this for my own pleasure!" But that he suffered, she could tell by his eyes. She knew him so well—"for better, for worse; for richer, for poorer; in sickness and in health"—and though she often desired to punish him, she would have no other hand strike him, not even that of God.

"If there were any comfort I might give you——" she began.

"Who but you could comfort me?"

That, she thought, is true. Perhaps he intended it for flattery but he recognizes that ultimate fact. . . . We have been too long bound to one another, all the waters of the sea cannot drown that—no, nor all the lusts of the flesh! Perhaps there will never be joy again in our belonging to each other, but we will always belong to each other in sorrow. She looked hard into his eyes, made a grimace and then sighed. My false true love, we cannot escape each other so easily, you and I. . . .

She beckoned abruptly to him to take his seat in a chair beside hers.

"This matter of aid to the Low Countries!" she said. "I would con-

sult you upon it. . . . We must determine many things privily before
it comes to open Council." Thank God for the Crown of England
and the duties appertaining thereto! So often a burden, but so often
her only support. Who said that work well done is its own reward?
But his smile was warming and there was a comfort in taking up that
long-accustomed friendship. Their minds fitted, like a hand in a
glove, and the thorny problem of aid to the Low Countries was a
beginning of many other consultations. The Court marvelled and
whispered and her latest favourite, a gifted young Devonian, Walter
Raleigh, sulked.

But she took a quiet, illusion-free happiness in this resumption of
companionship with Robert. She might say with a dry bitterness: "I
do it for my own pleasure!" But she admitted: "We cannot escape
each other, he and I, and so long as he recognizes it also. . . ."

But soon after this, she was to find herself his furious champion.
Printed in Antwerp, many copies of a small green-covered book were
smuggled into England where they sold with rapidity. The original
title was *The Copye of a Letter wryten by a Master of Arts at Cambridge* but it was soon nicknamed "Father Parsons' Green Coat"—
under the belief that it had been written by the famous Jesuit, Father
Robert Parsons or Persons, who had a lurid notoriety in England—
or else the title under which it was to pass to posterity, *Leycester's*[1]
Commonwealth. Its object was simple, the fantastic vilification of the
Earl of Leicester to whom all crimes possible and impossible were
attributed, and the pressing of the belief that he was the true ruler
of the State owing to the unholy infatuation the Queen had for him.
Starting with his believed relations with the Queen, every scandal of
the past quarter-century was rehearsed, as was every scandal relating
to the death of his first wife. But Pelion was piled upon Ossa, scarcely
any person of note had died in the past twenty years but they had
been murdered by Robert. The whole was told with a vivid racy style
which piled salacity upon sensation. It outrivalled the infamous
"Detection" of George Buchanan, written, it is said, by order of the
Regent Moray to blacken the character of his half-sister the Queen of
Scots, with the Casket Letters appended.

When it came to Elizabeth's hands, she did not think of the abuse
and the slanders heaped upon herself, she saw only the attack upon
the being who was to her still the dearest on earth. When she sum-

---

[1] "Leycester" was the spelling of the period.

moned him to her presence and was at last alone with him, she said briefly, but in a voice which shook from anger: "I will have this monstrous vile filth banned by order of the Privy Council!"

His voice sounded dazed: "I knew I had enemies, but I never dreamed of such hatred. . . . It makes my head reel!"

"I'll rest your head!"

It was on her lap again after so many years, no longer covered with that thick black hair which had now thinned to baldness and become grey. She passed her long hands lightly over his brow and temples as if she might caress away his troubles.

"But worse than any attack on me", he said, "is that on you. . . ."

"No matter, Rob! I think I am inured to scandal now. *I* am not accused of these murders, only of loving you too well—which I do—and of giving you too much power—which I never have. I have only given you such power as I believe you deserve. Never mind the attack on me."

"But I do mind it. And after it—a long way after—the attack on my fellows! To accuse Dick Verney of having any hand in Amy's death!"

"That is your Master of Horse?"

"Was. He died last year of a fever. Kit Blount has his place now. . . . God rest poor Dick, he had a loyal soul. He was an uncommon rare hand with a rapier too. I won't say he hasn't run through a few inconvenient rascals for me—but in fair fight! No—if any man had a hand in Amy's death, it was Tony Forster! And he's dead now, too."

"Robin," she said slowly, "the last time you saw your first wife, you believed that if you left her—abandoned her—she would either kill herself, or the man Forster would kill her——"

"Are you too accusing me?"

"No more than I accuse myself. When you asked me for permission to go to Cumnor, I did not believe that the reason was the worsening of her illness. No, my dear! Such blame as lies on you, I will share with you equally. We are old, Robin, now. Two and fifty. Let us speak of this once and for all."

"Well then! I did believe she would kill herself or Forster would kill her! And I did naught to prevent it! I wanted to marry you—the woman as well as the crown!" His hand came up and caught hers.

"Elizabeth—that wasn't a tear?"

"They're not all dry yet. . . . I could still weep for that girl I once was who hoped so much! After such a childhood, such a girlhood it was a wonder that any hope was left in her. And yet if that woman had not died the way she had—I would have made the great mistake of marrying you. I loved you more than my own soul—but never more than my country. . . ." She was silent for a long time and then she said: "So it was for the welfare of England and not the welfare of Robert Dudley—that she was driven to death!"

"Can you not leave her? Why delve in these ancient charnel houses? Let the dead sleep!"

"Do they sleep? Her blood be on my head. . . . Yet you are right. Speaking does no good. But these other lies—I will oppose them with all my power!"

"Aye—they're foul lies! That I should murder my own friend Nicholas Throckmorton! I suppose such a mind would think it likely I killed Essex and Sheffield——"

"Is it true then—about that woman Douglass Sheffield?"

"Yes—that's true. . . . Poor Douglass. . . . She was a lovely creature, but I think she became crazed. Half this farrago about poisoning—she screamed it at me one day. She was raving!"

"When was that?"

"Before you came to Kenilworth—ten years ago. I had promised to settle money on her and the child and she raved like a maniac——"

"When you cast her off! Ah, Robin! Why this melodrama of poisoning and stabbing? You can kill by omission. These women who loved you and you cast them off. . . . So your wife Amy dashed herself over the stairway, and Douglass Sheffield raved and now—they say —is half the time in melancholic fits. I was stronger than either——"

"You——"

"Yes, I! And I had something I loved more than you. The country. But I am strong—I am sometimes amazed at my own strength. And so is that damnation she-wolf you married, Rob! Be careful with her —she's stronger than you."

"I'll not have her abused!"

"God's death, I'll say what I will!" He could feel the hands on his head stiffen like claws. It was back again, the barrier, she thought. The other women, the other infidelities, they were chaff. But Lettice had one-half of him. . . .

"I wanted a wife, a son!" he said. "Don't you understand?"

"Understand! Didn't *I* want—you for my husband and a son?" She began to laugh bitterly.

"You were my true love," he said. "But you wouldn't marry me. And in some ways—she's like you!"

"God's precious soul! Is that a compliment? And to which? Of course—there's a likeness. There's the same blood and what blood! Aye! All those years ago when young Tom Bullen came to court with his fortune from Cheapside and wedded a duke's daughter—what a breed he sired!"

"Young Tom Bullen?"

"Sir Thomas Boleyn, later Earl of Wiltshire. My grandfather. *Her* great-grandfather. About the same time that Tom Bullen started to come up in the world, so did Edmund Dudley. . . ."

But his mind was off, on to another subject.

"And that ruffian dares impute me base blood! Young Philip— bless the lad!—is writing a 'Defence', and he says his 'chiefest pride is to be a Dudley!' "

"Philip is very loyal!" she said, but a sad little smile flickered on her lips. The sneers at his origin seemed to rankle more than the accusation of crimes. But she could ease that sting.

"Rob, if they sneered at your birth, it was from bitter jealousy. Because there was never a man who looked more kingly than you!"

He said: "I love you. Do you believe it?"

"Yes, I believe it." But she added in her mind: "After your fashion!"

"Very well!" his voice was jubilant. "Then kiss me properly—as you haven't done for so long a time."

"And whose fault is that?"

"Mine! I confess it."

"We are too old for these games."

"No, we are not!"

He had turned so he could stretch out an arm and draw her face down to his. Later he said with a curious note of satisfaction: "If you had married that damned little Frenchman, I should have wrung his damned Frog's neck. I would have taught that Frog a wooing to go! Why—what the devil are you laughing at?"

"Oh, Rob, Rob! You are incorrigible. You may have as many wives and mistresses as the Grand Turk—but I must have never a one but you! Oh, Robin, Robin. . . ."

Chapter Sixteen

Leicester House had bitter memories for Philip Sidney. There had been that summer of 1581 when he had returned to London from the green peacefulness of Wilton, to find that the young Lady Rich left her sottish husband as often and as long as possible, and stayed with her mother and stepfather. Lettice, having once ruthlessly separated Philip from his Stella, now the wealthy marriage was safely achieved, did her utmost to push them into each other's arms again. Her daughter had been a good, sensible child in wedding the odious but "rich Lord Rich", now she deserved some pleasure. But to Philip, it had been the tortures of Tantalus. There she was, his Stella, with an ever-ripening loveliness.

> "She comes, and straight therewith her shining twins do move
> Their rays to me, who in their tedious absence lay
> Benighted in cold woe; but now appears my day,
> The only light of joy, the only warmth of love. . . .
> My heart cries, oh it burns, mine eyes now dazzled be:
> No wind, no shade can cool: what help then in my case?"

No help, truly, for him. His hours apart from her were passed in wild dreams and were poured into his sonnets. He must write and yet:

> "Come let me write. And to what end? To ease
> A burthened heart. How can words ease, which are
> The glasses of thy daily-vexing care?"

If his love and he might take ship and sail into those unknown waters he had yearned to explore and there perhaps find a better world—but though his thoughts had wings and could move swifter than wind-filled sails, his body was earthbound. Around him was the glittering labyrinth of the court, the dark intrigues and gay panorama of the Anjou courtship, and his uncle was back in power though not in favour so that Leicester House was filled with the opposers of the marriage, arguments and plots beating the air about Stella. . . . The great tournament at Whitehall which combined all the elaboration of a court masque with knightly exercise, when he had been one of the four challengers, "The Children of Desire" in gorgeous panoply, and Stella's face in the gallery looking down on him. Strange contrast to the aching loneliness of the sleepless night.

> "With how sad steps, O Moon thou climbst the skies!
> How silently, and with how wan a face!"

Then Stella at last again in his arms, in the little garden pavilion by the river, and it seemed that the whole meaning of life was contained in that brief ecstasy. "Oh love come quickly, let us go together— away from all this, never to be separated!" Let the world be lost, let its wrath and censure be defied.

> "Only Joy, now here you are,
> Fit to hear and ease my care.
> Let my whispering voice obtain
> Sweet reward for sharpest pain:
> Take me to thee, and thee to me!
> '*No, no, no, no, my dear, let be. . . .*' "

She had been afraid. Or had her fear shown a better knowledge of him, than he himself had then known? Waiting in the dark, in the crowded streets, with the flaring lights of the link-boys' torches, the shouting of revellers, the clatter of hoofs and the rattle of wheels on the cobblestones—and then missing Stella's coach, seeing it whirl past him unheeding, and the delirium which drove him to the very threshold of her hated husband's house, staring hungrily at the few lights left in the windows, wondering which was hers. . . .

> " 'Who is it that this dark night
> Underneath my window plaineth?'
> 'It is one who from thy sight
> Being, ah, exiled disdaineth
> Every other vulgar light.' "

And the cold hopeless dawn which had brought reality mercilessly to face him. Was this the end to all that he had dreamed and vowed?

The clear light of his religious faith, his knightly ideals, his devotion to his country and his longings to strike a blow against the great tyranny—were all these to be forgotten? So many had believed in him, he thought with a sudden shame, so many had expected great things from him. His parents who were now old and weary, his dear sister Mary who had always shared his imaginings, the noble old scholar Languet who had first shown him the great world, William of Orange his hero, and all the young men who gathered about him, taking him for their leader—was he to shame these with his failure? Had all hope ended in this—that Philip Sidney desired his neighbour's wife? However despicable that neighbour, however luckless his love and he had been, what else was it? And what was there for him except one of the typical intrigues of the court gallant, a fashionable adultery? His uncle had been hero or villain of many such. . . . Had love lifted Stella beyond her ordinary nature so that she comprehended him better than he himself? Was it love's gift to her, that understanding how such an intrigue could only be an agony to him, a desecration of all in which he believed? After their final parting in the riverside gardens of Leicester House, he had put her words into verse.

> " 'Astrophel,' said she, 'my love,
> Cease in these effects to prove;
> Now be still, yet still believe me,
> Thy grief more than death would grieve me. . . .' "

But there had been years of despairing pain before he had come to that acceptance, when he had written in torment the last of the "Astrophel to Stella" sonnets—"Desire, desire I have too dearly bought!" Leicester House had held too many bitter memories of Stella, and he turned against it as a symbol of that worldly philosophy which had caused bitter pain. At this time he drew closer to Walsingham and the older man showed the best of his complex nature to Philip. Both believed in the same end, to strike down the great military tyranny of Spain. Through all the ages there have been those ardent natures who believe that they have found the great conflict, and that the forces of evil have materialized in a concrete shape. In the early Middle Ages these idealists poured to the crusades beside the mercenaries and power-greedy monarchs; in the twentieth century passionate young men fought and died in the Civil War in Spain.

Zenith

For Philip and his age, it was the struggle of the Netherlands against the King of Spain. Both his simple idealism and the fanatic depth of the Secretary of State believed also that they might ensure the safety of their own country by striking Spain in the Netherlands before Spain could strike them. The years at last brought a post which was at least congenial to Philip, to be deputy to his ageing uncle the Earl of Warwick, Master of the Ordnance, where he could supervise the arsenals in preparation for the struggle which he believed must come. The Queen conferred a knighthood on "her Philip" though she was inclined to gibe at him for "falling amongst Puritans" and she was not at first pleased when he married Walsingham's daughter, Frances, at the age of fifteen, though later she relented and became godmother to their baby girl. A successful courtier he would never make, though he had more gifts and graces than any of the other young men of the court, but many from high and low were beginning to look to him as a leader in the great struggle looming ahead. He was happier now, living in his father-in-law's house at Barn Elms, giving his very young wife a tender devotion far different from that earlier storm of love, writing the "Apologie for Poetrie" and inspecting arsenals and foundries. . . .

But as he spurred now for Leicester House, easing reluctantly to a trot through the crowded city, but going at a round hand-gallop down the Strand, his hopes were dashed. They had been high—at last the Queen was doing what he had hoped and expected of her, sending aid to the Netherlands, a thousand horse and five thousand foot under the command of his Uncle Robert, and he himself was to sail with a garrison of eight hundred in a few days' time for Flushing, one of the two towns given by the Dutch in pledge. Now his father-in-law was sending him to his uncle, ostensibly to give the Queen's orders that all preparations for the expedition were to be held up, but in reality to implore his uncle to come and persuade her Majesty. If he could not, no man could! So thought Philip, hurrying through the crowded great hall of Leicester House, packed with men, swashbuckling captains from Ireland and the Low Countries, boot and saddle boys from many a campaign swaggering beside sleek city purveyors and brawny armourers, preceded by an usher yelling: "Sir Philip Sidney to see his Lordship!"

His Lordship of Leicester was in the great library, lying on a couch with three dignified beings beside him, city merchants by their dress, their manners solemn and their eyes rapacious. There was Underhill, the secretary, with one of his clerks, with their quills, ink horns and sheets of crackling parchment all ready. As Philip hesitated in the doorway, he heard one of the city gentlemen say: "Now, my Lord, in the matter of the proposed mortgage on the Manor of Wanstead——" Leicester saw his nephew, and waved to him, cutting the man short.

"Philip, dearest lad! You see her Majesty's Captain-General laid low. My new charger threw me in the manège yesterday. Still—as I am leading a charge on Lombard Street with the aid of these good gentlemen, my bankers, this couch will serve as a steed!" But his eyes read Philip's face shrewdly. "You have news of some moment?"

"Yes sir. From my father-in-law."

"I must hear Mr. Secretary's message. Tom! Take these gentlemen to your room and let them see the rent roll of the Denbigh property and the half-yearly statement of the Cloth Monopoly. . . ."

The bankers having been bowed out and Leicester and his nephew now alone, he said: "Bad news by your face, Philip!"

"The worst. The Queen says hold up all preparations. My father-in-law is nigh distracted——"

"We can't hold up—now. I must go to her."

"My father-in-law begs you to, sir. One moment her Majesty talks of halving the forces promised, the next, she says that you cannot go—— And she is enraged with my father-in-law—swears at him that he is leaving England unprotected with our best forces going overseas and there will be a Spanish invasion. Yesterday, she was arguing with him when she heard the guns of a ship, saluting the Royal Standard as it came up river. She asked where it hailed from, and as luck would have it, it was Lisbon and Cadiz. Nothing would content her but the master be brought to her presence, and do you think a poor ship's master would waste such an opportunity? All the King of Spain's harbours, said he, are filled with shipping fitting out for the proposed 'Enterprise' against England. Dockside gossip and Spanish brag—but her Majesty took it for Gospel, and flew at my poor father-in-law in such a rage that she pulled off her shoe and threw it at his head!"

Leicester's lips were quivering suspiciously but he answered in all sobriety: "Poor Sir Francis! But he cannot handle her. . . . Now, old Burghley can. I must go to her. I'll take my barge rather than my coach since I ache in every bone. I'll need your arm, yours and that of my dreamy rakehell of a stepson's, if he's here. You can both be my crutches!"

But before he could go, the Countess of Leicester swept in, followed by a long slender auburn-haired youth with dark, glowing eyes.

"Robin—you are not fit to go forth!"

"My love, I must. I have to see her Majesty on urgent business."

"It's always urgent when she wants dalliance! Or perhaps she only wants you to pledge your last spoon for the privilege of paying for her glory. She'll keep those claws of her's on the last tester——¹".

"Mother!" said the young man reproachfully. "They aren't claws! They are the most divinely lovely hands I have ever seen."

"Wait till they box your ears, then! Still, if you talk that nonsense to her—you may get some advantage for it!"

But young Essex only smiled and caught hold of Philip.

"It's good to see you!" he said. "Are you from the court?"

"I'll need you, too," said his stepfather. "You and Philip must be my crutches else I cannot move."

"Three proper men to dance attendance on my royal cousin—that'll please her!"

"I'll come gladly. Unlike you, Mother, I adore the Queen!"

Lettice smacked her son's face with a sudden fury, but he continued to smile. The Gentlemen of the Chamber were busy attending the Earl of Leicester, tightening his points, bringing his boots, his cloak and his black velvet bonnet corded with pearls and adorned with a drooping plume which he set on his head at a dashing angle. Its bold cock and the glance of his fine dark eyes which no woman from the Queen to the chamber-maid had been able to resist, made the onlookers forget the ageing heaviness of his face and the greyness of such hair as he had left. He still had the manner of what once he had been—the apotheosis of gallantry. As he crossed the great hall, leaning heavily on the two young men, he said to his stepson:

"Boy—don't praise the Queen to your mother!"

"But I adore the Queen, sir. She's a wonderful woman!"

"Of course she's a wonderful woman! But don't say so to your mother!"

In his great barge, its lusty oarsmen pulling hard so that the brown water of the Thames ran chuckling under the stern, he said to his nephew: "Phil, dear lad, I am like to leave you an encumbered heri-

¹ Tester = Sixpence.

tage! You know how hard it is to get subsidies from your fellow Members of the Commons. . . . And with her Majesty's caution in things financial, and the commercial shrewdness of the Dutch—'tis necessary for me to raise every penny I can to help with the Expedition. But it's hard on you."

"Uncle Robin," said Philip reddening. "Never think of me. In such a cause—one would give everything gladly—to one's own life. . . ." How unimportant this second heirship to his uncle seemed! He had a strange dedicated feeling that at last he was stepping forward into a new life, better than anything of which he had ever dreamed. Orange, his hero, was dead, foully assassinated but, at last he was being allowed to fight *his* fight, and those two figures who had towered over his childhood—two whom he really loved though they had hurt his idealism—the Queen and his uncle were at last championing the beloved cause. The gravity of his face was lost in the sudden warmth of the smile he gave his uncle.

"That is my true picture of you—giving everything!"

"So you call me spendthrift—like the Queen does!"

"Not spendthrift! A princely generosity which does not count the cost. . . ."

"You're a plaguey odd lad!" But he put his hand on Philip's shoulder and kept it there for some time.

At Greenwich Palace, the Earl of Leicester was conducted as swiftly as his painful steps could carry him into her Majesty's presence, where she sat in the Withdrawing Chamber overlooking the Thames, tangled with ships' masts. There, amongst her cushions in a deep window-seat was that brocaded, jewelled and painted figure, with the unreality of a gorgeous image. But her voice was human enough.

"Robin—what's come to you?"

"My sweet Lady, a trifling fall in the manège. But I must use these lads as crutches else I might not have the happiness of standing before you."

"Proper crutches!" she said, and the thin painted lips smiled. "I was about to send for you and you anticipate my thoughts. . . . Come! In my little music chamber there is a day-bed on which you can lie while I talk with you. Crutches! Do your office."

They had settled him, she busying herself as well as the young men, putting a cushion behind his shoulders with a practical air. Young

Essex knelt at her feet, saying: "I would gladly suffer a thousand falls if those divine hands might tend me."

She caught the boy's chin, tilted up his face and stared at him.

"Would you?" she said and a strange glowing tenderness charged the next words. "Would you—Cousin?"

"Ten thousand!" But she was looking over his head at Philip.

"*You* are glad enough to leave me, Philip!"

"I am glad to do your Majesty true service. . . ."

"True service which rids my court of its brightest jewel! Yes, that is what you could be if you would! Well—I will speak with both of you later. Now I have matters of importance to discuss with my Lord here."

But when Robert and she were alone, she said: "That boy! Rob, is he your son?"

"Sweet, I don't know what you mean! He is Devereux's boy, my stepson."

She sat down at the virginals and played a high, delicate air.

"Rob—do you remember? The air they played to me on the recorders when I rode into Kenilworth?" She got up and walked jerkily across to his couch. "Rob—if we had had a son—did you ever wonder what he would be like?"

"Never seriously. . . . Why——" But he had caught one of her hands. "My dearest heart, you are so troubled!"

"Troubled? Beyond anything you can imagine. I've hardly slept this week. What have I done? Committed my country irrevocably—to engage the world's greatest power. . . ."

It came flowing out, as if she were at the end of her tether. Slowly, painfully, he raised himself, put his arm around her and drew her against him. Her courage, pride and arrogance were thrown aside, she was sobbing against his shoulder, her terrors for the country, and at last her fears for herself. She felt more ill than anyone knew, she would die and he would be far from her. . . . He was later to write to the anxious Walsingham: "*She used very pitiful words, begging me not leave her. I did comfort her as well as I could, only I did let her know how far I had gone in preparation. . . .*" He had comforted her for nearly thirty years, helping her to maintain the imperious façade for the rest of the world.

"Trust me!" he urged. "I'll bring you glory and strike Spain a mighty blow!"

"Trust you?" she repeated. "I never trusted your ambition, Rob, even when I loved you most. . . . Hark to me! The first moment we can get fair terms for the Dutch, the fighting stops! I would not waste the blood of one pikeman, the gold of one ryal. . . . I will not be the sovereign of the Low Countries. Again, and again, I have told the envoys. . . . It is not for one prince to set the subjects of another against him, but Philip has played the tyrant so monstrously, that I will support them in their struggle to win fair terms from him. But neither I nor my General must annex the Low Countries to my Crown!"

"But why, Sweet?"

" 'Twould be an abyss of peril. To be bound irrevocably to the Continent, to have land to defend beyond our moat! No! If we want to win territory, let it be far overseas in the New World. Young Raleigh and your nephew, Philip, are right there, and my wise old John Dee."

Robert had dreamed of himself as Viceroy of the Low Countries but he was too wise to press that view now. He promised to do all that she asked, and added glory to his promises. He would return to her as fast as ship and horse could carry him, if she needed him. He calmed her, and she said in a weary voice: "Now—what a sight I must look! My face will have run. . . ." She covered it with her hands. "When one's young, and one's hair and complexion is one's own ——!" He looked at that piled mass of flaming false hair seeming frosted over with diamonds and pearls and thought of her own coppery hair in a rippling mass on the pillow twenty-five years ago, and whispered this memory into her ear.

"I don't mind your seeing me so, Rob, because once you saw the best of me. But now—I must keep up appearances! I can still hold the young men, Raleigh and your stepson, my cousin Essex. . . ."

"Of course you can!" She was brightening, and he must encourage the mood. "What is this tale I hear of you? Did you really throw your shoe at Sir Francis?"

"And hit his solemn head with it—a lesson to him!"

"You *are* a devil!" he said, with admiration, and they both began to shake with laughter.

"Oh, Rob, I wish you'd seen it!"

All was well, he tightened his arm round her waist.

"Give me one of your garters as you did Anjou, and I'll carry it to more glory than he did."

352

"Not glory, to safety! 'Twas not my intention to give the garter—the plaguey thing slipped down when I was on board Drake's ship and the French Ambassador must seize it as a prize for his master! I said, yes, he might have it later, if he would return it then—as I'd nothing to hold my stocking up!"

"That damned Frenchman was privileged to see you put it on!"

"Well—I still have a passable leg. . . ."

"Better than any of your Maids of Honour."

"Devil fly away with you, Robin! How do you know about *them*?"

"Hearsay. I was jealous then. You never gave *me* a garter!"

"I gave you—rather more."

"Everything worth having!" He had raised her hand to his lips. She looked at his downbent head. "And Lettice?" asked her mind. But he could both soothe her—and make her laugh. Yet the cold fingers of fear still touched her.

"Remember!" she said. "What I told you concerning the Low Countries."

He went—at the head of a gorgeous retinue of knights-at-arms, esquires and five hundred mailed troopers from his own estates—and was received by the Dutch as if he were a cross between an emperor and an archangel. He wrote back rapturously describing how loud the shouts had been—"God save Queen Elizabeth!" They could not have been louder in Cheapside amongst her own loyal people. He declared that he "liked this matter twenty times better than he had in England". All the notorious Dudley ambition soared in him. At last it had proper meat on which to feed. He was away from his imperious love, who even in her first passion for him, had shouted at him—"I will have here but one Mistress and no Master!"—now here was a Master and no Mistress. He was doing it for her of course, winning glory for her as a true knight should, but he was doing it his own way, and plenty of the glory would stick to him. . . . She watched him with misgiving.

She had known that soaring ambition in him from the day she had ascended the throne. The woman in her was enraptured by it. Had she been no more than the Countess of Leicester, how she would have fed it and fought for it! But the Queen hated and dreaded it. It was the undeclared reason why she had not married him. He had been difficult enough to handle sometimes without marriage. And now here was his full-flown ambition coinciding with her open challenge to Spain. She did not like an open challenge; she preferred to send her sea raiders to harry the Spanish plate fleets ostensibly on their own account, and let English volunteers pour across to the Low Countries under such captains as Gilbert, Willoughby and Norris. An ambiguous situation which could be turned this way or that and might be finally evaded altogether suited her. She never wished to pledge herself finally to anything—except to her country. And she had an honest hatred of bloodshed.

Then the bombshell burst. The Dutch had offered him the virtual sovereignty of their country, Governor-General and Stadholder, the title borne by the late Prince of Orange. Robert—yearning for a throne and balked so long—accepted with rapture and some secret misgiving. On 25th January 1586, he took the oath of office at The Hague. He had written, of course, a coaxing letter to Elizabeth, explaining the (doubtful) advantages to her of this step, but by ill luck she heard first from the Dutch Estates-General, seeming that he had thrown over her authority without even acquainting her. Worse was to follow. Lettice was in a frenzy of jubilation and gave her tongue free rein, so that her enemies and the Queen's—and both had many —carried her remarks to court. Lettice could play the queen as well as her Great-Aunt Nan's daughter! She was preparing to come over "with such a train of ladies and gentlewomen, and such rich coaches, litters and side-saddles, as her Majesty had none such, and there should be such a court as should far surpass her Majesty's court here. . . ." Ill-wishers bore this, gloatingly, to Elizabeth.

It seemed at last that Lettice had triumphantly won the long, grim and completely unscrupulous warfare between the two cousins for the person of Robert, which had been carried on, openly and in secret, from that day in 1559 when the young Queen had found her favourite dallying with her still younger Maid of Honour. And that madness began to boil and bubble in Elizabeth's brain, oversetting her usual shrewd judgment. This was the cruellest blow he had dealt her apart from the announcement of his marriage. The woman suppressed so long and harshly by the Queen, had burst out at last, and seemed likely to wreck the Queen. And the Queen had sufficient cause for agitation apart from the woman. Her ambitious favourite to have such dangerous power, to have flown against her express commands not to assume sovereignty in her name or his, which would have committed her irrevocably against Spain, dishonouring her royal honour which had been solemnly and openly pledged that she had no design on the allegiance of the Netherlands.

Robert received a letter whose fury astounded him.

"How contemptuously We conceive Ourself to have been used by you, you shall by this bearer, understand. . . . We could never have imagined, had We not seen it fall out in experience, that a man raised up by Ourself, and extraordinarily favoured by Us above any other subject of this land, would have in so contemptible a sort have broken Our commandment. . . ."

He must publicly renounce the absolute government he had taken upon himself. He had hurt her so much, both by defying her and by seeming to show that he belonged solely to Lettice, that she must hurt and humiliate him, regardless of the consequences. Her reason was overthrown, and could not tell her that it was to her own injury and her country's, that her Lieutenant-General should be so humiliated, and lose his consequence and authority in the eyes of the Dutch ally. Even his former adversaries such as Burghley, hastened to point this out, and beg the Queen to reconsider the decision made in fury. A long and essentially sordid wrangle followed, frantic messages from Robert coinciding with angry ones from the Queen. Burghley brought her towards reason by threatening to resign, and gradually her brain retook the control from her emotions. But harm was done irrevocably by the time he received another letter which addressed him as "trusty and well-beloved" and stated: *"It is always thought in the opinion of the world, a hard bargain, when both parties are losers, and so doth it fall out in the case of us two. . . ."*

Her pen had stopped when she had written that line and she covered her face with her hands. Always, always, had it been a hard bargain between Robert and herself—always had they both been losers! The woman had at last revenged herself upon the Queen, and had hurt them both. And she had hurt Robert. Nothing he could do would ever stop her loving him. She should have known this better by now, after she had forgiven him for his secret marriage. In the middle of her anger, when Hatton had told her that Robert was sick, she had hurriedly sent her own physician over to him. . . . In time she had consented to receive his imploring letters and had carried them away to read in private, knowing they would bring tears. (She had taken to keeping his letters in a little chest beside her bed together with that miniature of him as a splendid young man which had been long ago shown to the Scottish Ambassador, wrapped in paper on which she had written "My lord's portrait".) It seemed now as she tried to look at the matter coolly, that he had been showing off to impress her as much, if not more, than for the sake of the detested Lettice. And now his hurt and hers, was to be joined by hurt to her country's cause, by her withholding authority and supplies to the army he commanded. No glory for him—poor Robert—his command in the Low Countries was a fiasco. Blood and gold were squandered and to no purpose. Later she was to write to him a personal letter which began:

"Rob, I am afraid that you will suppose by my wandering writings that a midsummer moon hath taken large possession of my brains this month, but you must needs take things as they come in my head, though order be left behind me. . . ."

In it, she begged for her troops (which she felt her own anger had made her fail).

"And for Norris and other captains that voluntarily and without commandment have many years ventured their lives and won our nation honour and themselves fame, let them be not discouraged by any means. . . . It frets me not a little that the poor soldier that hourly ventures life, should want their due, that well deserve rather reward. . . ."

With it she sent money with an injunction to punish any unjust official who was withholding the troops' pay. She finished it:

"Now will I end that do imagine I talk still with you, and therefore loathly say farewell [here a drawing of two eyes, his nickname], *though ever I pray God to bless you from all harm and save you from all foes, with my million and legion of thanks for all your pains and cares.*
"As you know, ever the same. E.R."

Ever the same, she would love him and in the end forgive him. They had had their last quarrel, had they but known it, and had harmed many besides themselves. But there was still another bitter blow in store for Robert. There was to come that sorrowful day when he sat in his tent outside the besieged city of Zutphen, writing to Sir Thomas Heneage, long ago a rival, but now a well-tried friend, describing the result of a furious attack on a Spanish attempt to force supplies into the city.

"Many of our horses were hurt and killed, among which was my nephew's own. He went and changed to another, and would needs to the charge again; and once passed those musketeers, where he received a sore wound upon his thigh, three fingers above his knee, the bone broke quite in pieces; but for which chance, God did send such a day as I think was never many years seen, so few against so many. . . ."

He continued writing, praising the exploits of other gallant young men, saying: *"But I can hardly praise one more than another, they all did so well."*

Sadly he returned to the fate of his beloved nephew, so sorely and desperately wounded.

"Albeit I must say it, it was too much loss for me; for this young man, he was my greatest comfort next to her Majesty of all the world; and if I could buy his life with all I have, to my shirt I would give it. How God will dispose of him I know not; but fear I must needs, greatly the worse; the blow in so dangerous a place and so great; yet did I never hear of any man that did abide the dressing and setting of his bones better than he did; and he was carried afterwards in my barge to Arnhem; and I hear this day, he is still of good heart and comforteth all about him as much as maybe. God of His mercy grant me his life! Which I cannot but doubt of, greatly. . . ."

England mourned Philip Sidney as a national hero. He had become a symbol of selfless gallantry, this young man of great promise. The achievements foretold for him, and the worldly success had not come. His success had been more intangible; everyone who had known him, prince, statesman, philosopher, soldier or 'prentice boy, had loved him. His kingdom had been the hearts of others. The Queen received the news with great sorrow and for two days put aside the business of State. He had gone away from her in these later years, he would not be the brightest jewel in her court and contribute to her entertainment, and she had held him back wilfully from the exploits he had longed to engage upon. He did not understand the necessities of statecraft and had seemed to judge her hardly, but he had died in her service. She had prevented him from the hazards of sailing with

Drake and saved him from Oxford's dangerous blade, but she could not prevent the fate which Blanche Parry had read from his hand twenty years ago. Now she ordered him a funeral as magnificent as any monarch's, which was followed by the highest and the lowest in the land.

And that unhappy year, 1586, brought Robert back to her. When at last, they were alone together, she looked at him with a strange dismay. His face had become purple, mottled and heavy, he looked old, unhealthy and exhausted. She made him sit, and kept his hands in hers while he talked to her of Philip, as if at last he was sure that someone would understand him.

He said: "I would have given every possession I had to have saved him. . . . There was never anyone so patient in his end. He suffered tortures, but his courage and cheerfulness to those around him, especially to his poor wife who was nursing him, was a thing to be marvelled at. They came, great Dutch officials, Pensionaries and Councillors, learned ministers with whom he would discuss theology, ordinary men and women, that leader of the German mercenaries, Count Hohenlo whom our fellows call Hollock—and a plaguey quarrelsome, arrogant swaggerer he is, yet he too loved Philip—and all our lads who held him as a demi-god. . . . They would come, begging to see him, waiting for hours for the chance of a word with him. He had the deathbed of a saint for he thought all the time of saving trouble for others. Truly a minister of religion said: " 'Tis *I* that can learn of *him*.' To try and make his wife smile he made some jesting verses on his missing cuisse which had caused the desperate seriousness of his wound—and had them set to music and sung beside his bed so she would think him better than he was. Aye! Whatever agony he was in, he would smile at her and tell her he was better. He had no cuisses in the attack because a friend of his had set forth without any and Philip must needs give up his!

"Such a deed is typical of him, but even more is that one which they are rightly commemorating in the broadsheet with his portrait and the words: 'Thy necessity is yet greater than mine.' After he was wounded he rode a mile and a half on horseback till he collapsed from pain and loss of blood. Our fellows were around him, and he was parched with thirst, craving water. At last a half-empty bottle was found for him on the field, but then he saw a dying pikeman lying on the ground beside him, and must give the water to him, saying: 'Thy necessity is yet greater than mine!' In that gesture—you have the whole of Philip!"

"May he long be remembered as an example," she said. "We need such in this sorry world."

"He was good," said his uncle, "and so perhaps beyond my understanding, but I know that after you, he was the dearest thing on earth to me. . . . That poor child, Frances, his wife! She was very brave so long as he lived, but after his death, she collapsed and miscarried of her second child. Being not well enough to travel when I left, young Essex has promised to bring her home later."

"Poor child!" repeated Elizabeth. "But what of his love—your stepdaughter? Ah! The unhappy women who can make no open claim!"

"That was ended long ago. But I went to her just now, and she cried out: 'Philip was too good for this vile world! So he must be taken!' Such bitter despair, and the look in those dark, glowing eyes of hers—they are like yours, Sweet."

"The Bullen eyes!" she said. "But mine were always far narrower. . . . But you say it was ended—between them?"

"Yes. After her mother made that marriage, I tried to help them. It was my fault! I should have settled property on Philip so he might have married her. He was bred up to be my heir, poor lad! I admit my fault to those poor young creatures—though he had another sort of happiness with his Frances. . . . Well, I tell you one evening they were down in the garden pavilion by the river, and I hoped they were happy making love to each other. It's been the best happiness I ever knew—loving my love, when she loved me!" He felt the hands he was holding tighten. "Then I saw him come away, with his face as white as death, and Penelope shut herself up for twenty-four hours, and that was the end between them." He heaved a great sigh before he continued: "Mary, his sister, is collecting all his verses and writings. She wants to edit them and have them published. They shared everything, those two. And young Fulke Greville is going to write his Life. They are setting to work to keep his memory alight. Mary gave me his last sonnet. I think you would wish to see it."

Silently she took it from him and read:

"Leave me, O love which reachest but to dust,
  And thou, my mind, aspire to higher things.

Grow rich in that which never taketh rust:
Whatever fades but fading pleasure brings.
Draw in thy beams, and humble all thy might
To that sweet yoke where lasting freedoms be;
Which breaks the clouds and opens forth the light
That doth both shine and give us sight to see.
O take fast hold; let that light be thy guide
In this small course which birth draws out to death,
And think how evil becometh him to slide
Who seeketh heaven and comes of heavenly breath.
Then farewell, world! Thy uttermost I see:
Eternal Love, maintain thy life in me."

She said very slowly: "It was if he knew he would die."

"That is what I thought."

"But it is the best thing he ever wrote, Rob. . . ."

"I never understood him," Robert repeated. "But I loved him. Yes, I loved him!" She looked at Robert and saw that the tears were running openly down his cheeks. Who would have recognized the magnificent, the sinister Earl of Leicester in that broken, grief-stricken old man? But now he was to say the words which were finally to heal the breach between them. He had had a loyalty to his wife, he would never say a word against her to Elizabeth, and they had avoided her name when speaking together. She had always feared—the origin of her late fury—that however much his past was hers, Lettice truly held his present. But now he said: "Lettice never cared aught for him. She can't understand what he meant to me!"

"I understand!" she said. She had got her arms round him now, and was holding him as she had done when they were young. This was the end to that long battle and she had won the unseen victory, not Lettice. Now he and she were old and tired, it was to her he brought his sorrow. She thought: "I do grieve for Philip—but how much more I grieve for your grief, my love!"

Chapter Seventeen

T he Queen had ridden to Hampton Court from Whitehall in that bitter winter of 1584. She had declared that she would be frozen in her great barge and so would prefer to ride. Heavy skies, the colour of pewter, were low and crushing, drawing the life from the landscape, dimming the sparkle of the frost but keeping its bite. Purple-nosed horsemen drew their furred velvet cloaks tightly around them; even the movement and merry jingle of a round trot did not bring warmth. There were heavy sables over the Queen's shoulders but they could not prevent her fingers in their perfumed gauntlets nor her feet in their Spanish leather boots from gradually losing all feeling. She did not complain, but rode on, her hawk's profile staring straight in front of her like the figurehead of a galleon. And the men around her, handsome Raleigh and his followers, knew better than to speak to her, when she looked like that. It seemed that she was lost in thought, but she saw well enough the dark figures lining her route, though she had no time for the gay ones about her. People always crowded round her when she rode out, a-hunting or on Progress, informally or in ceremonious procession; they had shouted for her since she was a young girl and her sister had been bitterly jealous—there was nothing new in *that*. But there *was* something new about these silent crowds which had an air of waiting from time immemorial, of waiting as long as the trees, as long as the houses. They were all kinds, ragged beggars, pert 'prentices from London, small tradesmen, farmers, country squires and their gentlewomen.

When the retinue came in sight, with the unmistakable figure of the Queen following the advance guard, they fell on their knees on the frozen ground. She heard their cries. "God save your Majesty!" "God save our Queen and shield her from her enemies!" "God protect your Grace!" And at the back, like the far-off muttering of a thunderstorm, like the far-off cry of a hunting wolf-pack, she could hear the angry sound: "Death to your enemies!" "Death to the Papists!" "Death to Spain and all foreign tyrants!" Then came one shrill cry in a boy's breaking voice: "Death to the Queen of Scots!"

There it was, the cry which she had evaded for sixteen years, asked by the one voice she would never deny, the voice of those she loved beyond all things in heaven or earth—her ordinary English people. She had tried to stifle that voice after the Northern Rebellion and the Ridolfi Plot, but it had echoed and re-echoed through the feverish years of the 'eighties as plot succeeded plot, plots futile like that of the imbecilic young man who had set off pistol in hand to shoot the Queen and "set her head upon a pole for she is a Serpent and a Viper", to plots as dangerous as the one just disclosed which was to pass to history as the Throckmorton Plot. Its prime mover, a nephew of Sir Nicholas Throckmorton, had worked hand-in-glove with Mendoza the Spanish Ambassador. Lists of Catholic noblemen and gentlemen believed ready to rise, and havens where foreign troops might safely land were captured in his house and the rack—that accepted part of sixteenth-century judicial procedure—discovered others. Mendoza accused before the Council had answered with defiant bluster. "If the Queen did not like the sound of words, he would try to satisfy her with cannon." Everyone had marvelled at the quietness of the voice in which she had answered him, as calm and as cool as to a partner in the dance. "If you speak to me in that way, I will have you flung into a dungeon." Now he had gone, the last of those Spanish diplomats who had sheltered behind their diplomatic privileges to plot against the Queen and country to which they were accredited, and it was with the fresh memory of this last exchange, that she rode from Whitehall to Hampton Court.

She would never forget those kneeling crowds lining the way in the bitter, gloomy weather, or their fervent cries for her protection, she would never forget their deep rage against her adversaries, and that shrill cry: "Death to the Queen of Scots!" It remained with her for the rest of that poignant year, 1584, when the Prince of Orange was foully murdered and she at last pledged herself to open support of the Dutch, when the death of his little son and the publication of *Leycester's Commonwealth* brought a partial reconciliation between herself and Robert.

She was to remember it, when Burghley had a private audience with her, his hunchbacked son carrying his papers. He was telling her of the "Bond of Association", a direct consequence of the Throckmorton Plot. She looked down at the old man, sitting as was his custom on a stool by her high, carved chair.

"This Bond, then," she said, "pledges all its signatories in the event of my death——"

"In the deplorable event of your Grace's *murder!*" he corrected her. His grey eyes were implacably calm and steadfast.

"Well, in the event of my murder, to take the law into their own hands, and kill without any trial, anyone whose claim to my throne, was advanced thereby. Naturally that means the Queen of Scots, though they don't say so!"

"Naturally, your Grace. I think you perhaps forget that all our authority is derived from you, and in such a terrible event, authority would be authorityless. Lawless murder cannot shelter behind the Law."

She rested her chin on one hand and asked abruptly: "Are they signing this Bond?"

"Robert," said the old man, "give her Grace the figures."

The hunchback smiled. He had a smile which was both sweet and patient, as deliberately pleasant as his gentle voice.

"In Yorkshire alone, your Majesty," he said, "seven thousand signatures have been made and so many more are expected that it is believed they will fill a large trunk. The city of Coventry has formed an association and is sending a Loyal Address with two hundred and one signatures and seals upon it. And, of course, the support in the House of Commons is practically unanimous."

"The House of Commons!"

"Yes, your Grace," said Burghley and there was a determination in his voice which she had not often heard. "It is to be the first business of the Session."

"But——" she said hesitantly. "I would not have anyone suffer for another's fault. Even though the plots may benefit her, she must first be proved guilty of conspiring——"

"Your Grace knows well whether that woman is innocent or not. Your faithful Commons only reflect the country's desire to protect your Grace since you will not protect yourself. Does your Grace realize your people's fear and despair at the thought of losing you?"

She saw those crowds kneeling by the roadside under the winter's skies.

"Yes," she said. "I realize." She looked at the man whose judgment she trusted more than any other mortal's. "I wish", she continued, "that my negotiations with the young King of Scots had borne fruit. If he had received his mother and stood her guarantor. . . ."

"Would an angel be able to stand guarantor for the Queen of Scots, your Grace?"

"It was worth trying. Scotland allied with us and France, and *her* menace withdrawn—then Spain must retreat without warfare!"

"Yes, your Grace. It was worth trying and you tried it, till this vile plot was discovered and you learned that while she appeared to be negotiating with you and her son, she was more truly negotiating with the King of Spain, the Pope and her cousin Guise, to bring foreign armies to overthrow you."

She had the feeling so well known to her, of being edged into a corner, one way of retreat after the other being closed. But why should she care about Mary? She hated Mary surely—an unending trouble to her and the realm, like an old wound, like a sore—like that ulcer on her leg which had tormented her for so many years. She had stubbornly averted her attention as much as possible from both Mary and the ulcer, trying to pretend that neither existed. And now the ulcer seemed to be healing at long last. But the problem of Mary would not heal. . . .

"My hopeful godson, the King of Scots," she said, slightly to change the subject, "is very cautious, for his years."

"I have heard him described as 'an old young man', your Grace. Robert! Tell her Grace the last report we have had on him." (How he was always bringing that son of his forward!)

"Your Majesty, the King of Scots was so described by an eye-witness. 'Awkward in his movements but scholarly in his brain, shrewd to the point of slyness, timid but patient, loving money but having little of his own, and like the king described in Holy Writ, walking delicately—amongst his turbulent nobility.' "

She looked at him, thinking: "Have you at the same time, described yourself? 'Awkward, scholarly, shrewd, sly, timid, patient, loving money, walking delicately?' " She was trying to read Robert Cecil. That sweet smile, that soft, charming voice, he put them on like his elegant suit of black velvet, the jewelled gold chain about his

364

neck, the finely starched ruff and the cloak carefully arranged to screen his deformity. What did he *feel*? Then she was to get a strange flicker from his inner mind.

"And your Majesty, again to quote from the Bible, he has his eyes on the Promised Land—the hope of being appointed your Majesty's successor——"

She broke in harshly: "Let him hope! Children dream of apples, and waking to find they have none—weep!"

Colder, crueller, keener than any danger from any plot was the thought that young men of Robert Cecil's generation, like the young King of Scots, were looking forward to the day when someone must succeed her. . . .

She forced some alteration on the Bond of Association before it was passed by Parliament, insisting on a tribunal to try "any believed guilty of compassing her death", but she could not mistake the temper of the country. Mary was removed from the custody of the Earl of Shrewsbury who was believed to be too easy-going, and given a more stern custodian, a Puritanical ex-ambassador, Sir Amyas Paulet. She was also sent to Tutbury Castle, but as she complained of its discomforts, she was subsequently removed to Chartley, a moated manor house belonging to the young Earl of Essex. And then came that unhappy year, 1586, which was to see the Queen's anger against Leicester in the Low Countries. In that year also she could no longer evade the problem of Mary.

She was closeted with another of her ministers, not the wise old Burghley but the sombre, fanatical Walsingham, and he was telling her that he had discovered—his chief agent being a renegade priest, George Gifford—how Mary had established a secret post out of Chartley.

"Your Majesty, it is effected in this way. The letters she sends are concealed in the bung-holes of the casks of beer supplied to Chartley. The brewer is heavily bribed by her, but since he is also in my pay— and a very honest man—he hands the letters over to me."

"A very *honest* man indeed!" said she, raising her narrow brows.

"Needless to say, these letters are in cipher, your Majesty. But I have an excellent fellow, Thomas Phelippes, who, I believe, can read any cipher. He makes a copy of them and the originals are passed on—to the French Ambassador and many other persons."

"Passed on?"

"Your **Maj**esty need have no apprehension. I am watching everything most carefully! But it is necessary to discover all the persons implicated."

She thought: "Of course. He is not seeking 'all the persons'. He is waiting till Mary commits herself finally, till she writes one letter which will convict her. He is giving her the rope with which to hang herself." She shivered a little before that dark, burning gaze. Here was the same relentless fanaticism which tormented human flesh to the Glory of God, that fanaticism which had been in her sister Mary and her husband, Philip of Spain. There was no room for pity—when man took upon himself to interpret the Will of God. Mary would be allowed to go on, till the tally was complete, and then he would strike. This time Elizabeth could not save her cousin. Why should she? And then memory rushed upon her, that first strange vision of Mary as the enchanted princess who might cast enchantments upon others, but could never escape from her own spell.

When she was nineteen and at her zenith, beautiful, beloved, sung by poets, stirring men's ambition and imagination, the crowns of France and Scotland on her brow, she had said strangely: "Peradventure that casualty might be better for me than to live. . . ." Once during her brief unhappy reign in Scotland she had been sick to death in the border town of Jedburgh so that they had opened the windows for her soul. Spies reported her saying in her long years of captivity: "Would God I had died at Jedburgh!" Elizabeth thought: "Would God she *had* died! That casualty would have been better for me. . . ." She remembered words in the letter Mary had sent her when she fled to England—"Next to God, I have no hope but in your goodness."

Had she been good to Mary? She had saved Mary from the sullen fury of her own people, and for a weary time from the anger of the people of England. But she had taken liberty from that creature who was so strangely wild and free. There was comfort and dignity in that cage which had cost Elizabeth fifty-two pounds a week for eighteen years—bitter to her financial caution—but it was still a cage. Her untamed wings must tame themselves against its bars. Could that ever be forgiven? And Mary would not understand the reason. She could not understand. The safety, the welfare, the glory of the people of Scotland had never been important to Mary. She had always been too deep in her own intense passionate life. She could not conceive another intensity and passion, Elizabeth's feelings for England and its people. That was why the fear of death crept closer every year to Elizabeth, chilling her with a desperate horror. She could not bear to think of leaving her country and her people, of ceasing her undeviating struggle for them, of no longer drawing the warmth of life itself from their love. Heaven could give her nothing to replace that; hell nothing worse than its deprivation.

She could never meet Mary face to face. How could she say: "Cousin, I had to do it. . . ." Cousin! That was what she had called the young Essex that day when he had come in, supporting the limping Robert, and she had suddenly seen him as the longed-for son, incarnate. (Robert in the early days had laughingly spoken of "a red-headed lad" and "Harry, Prince of Wales" but when taxed by her query, had admitted that he had never given any serious thought to the appearance or character of any imagined offspring.) But she swung her mind away with a shudder from any bracketing of the adored lovely boy with Mary and her strange aura of doom. The voice of England had cried for Mary's death. But she would make one last effort to save Mary. Walsingham had spoken of the French Ambassador as receiving and sending many of the packets of the secret post, although the "Enterprise" was directed by Spain. France, if sometimes uncertain, was, on the whole, a friend, but her ambassador might help a Queen Dowager of France in small matters. Could she convey a warning to Mary through him?

She drew that courtly and distinguished gentleman to her, at her next great reception, and brought their conversation to the Queen of Scots.

"Monsieur," said she, "you have much secret communication with the Queen of Scotland, but, believe me, I know all that goes on in my kingdom! I myself was a prisoner in the days of the Queen, my sister, and am aware of the artifices that prisoners use to win over servants and obtain secret intelligence." Staring with a strange intensity at his embarrassed face, at his quick deprecation, she thought: "Tell her, you fool! Tell her, warn her. . . . Warn her to stop setting the rope about her own neck!" She had done all she could. For the sake of her people she could not do more.

But if Mary received a warning from the French Ambassador, she did not act upon it. And the evidence piled up in the patient hands of Walsingham, waiting in something like ecstasy. They were foolish and mainly inefficient, the young men who plotted. There was a touch of fantasy and a touch of pathos in them. Anthony Babington and his five comrades who were to carry out "the tragical execution" of the Queen of England had their portrait painted, together, in commemoration. Adoration of the Queen of Scots was strangely blended with their religious faith in an adolescent fervour. It would have been simple enough to gather them in before they could begin to be dangerous; such was not Walsingham's purpose. He had a faith and fervour which matched theirs in intensity and it had neither pathos nor inefficiency nor yet fantasy. The spearhead of the Devil, the 'bosom serpent' must be convicted finally and beyond hope of reprieve. The Queen's illogical weakness must be overcome, her fear and her indignation must be aroused. He had more hope of the latter than the former; she lacked the ecstatic courage of the martyr but she was no coward. This plot took advantage of her trust in her people and her liking for a presentable young man. Two of her Gentlemen Pensioners wavered on the outskirts of the conspiracy and it was notoriously easy for any handsome lad to gain access to her presence. She would not take precautions, saying proudly that she would not believe anything worse of her people than a loving mother would believe of her children. Then an action of the conspirators again played into Walsingham's hands.

On a hot summer's afternoon, when the shadows sloped long and purple on the green turf, Elizabeth became aware that she was walking with Death. Around her were the familiar sights and sounds, the rustle of her ladies' silk skirts and the murmur of their conversation, tall trees silhouetted against a sky like shining turquoise enamel, casting dappling shadows, here and there the sun winking on a jewel, the scent of grasses ripening blended with the musky perfumes used by all the women, including herself, the faint tick of the watch in the golden ball hanging by a chain from her girdle, which Robert had once given her, pricking its slight sound through the dullness of footfalls on the turf, and above all the sound of her own heart beating with a sickening pounding heaviness against her whalebone encased ribs. For Death was very near and was steadily coming nearer, in the shape of a tall young Irishman, George Barnewell, whose face she knew quite well from his haunting of the Presence Chamber, and whom Walsingham had recently told her was one of Babington's closest associates.

Much farther away from her was the only other man, young Fulke

Greville, walking beside a lady, a spray of fern in his hand as if he intended to fan his companion with it, and no sword at his side. All the rest were her defenceless women, and beside the long well-shaped legs of Barnewell swung the scabbard of his rapier, balanced by a heavy poniard. She remembered how often she had thought, half in jest and half in earnest, that she would like to die on her feet. Now it seemed that she was to get her wish with Barnewell's blade through her. She could feel in anticipation the cold flame of that piercing pain as darkness would close the summer day. She was acutely aware of physical life about her, the feeling of her brocade skirts under her damp hands, the swift weaving flight of a bumble-bee, the warmth of the sun on her face. All sensations were magnified when their moments were numbered. She jerked her head up and stared straight at Barnewell.

His eyes wavered, would not meet hers, his feet ceased to approach her. Warmth and purpose came into her body which had been frozen by horror, she could fight—as she had fought all her life—again. Her eyes were her sword, thrusting a furious concentrated glance at Barnewell. He could not meet them, *his* eyes wavered, his cheeks reddened and his mouth twitched. She felt that she was holding him back, and now the first chill of physical fear was past, she knew how much more she was defending than her own person. She saw Barnewell give an obeisance with his head, back, turn swiftly and make off in the other direction. Surely the others could hear the beating of her heart!

She relieved her feelings afterwards by declaring in a voice of strident bitterness how ill-guarded she was, and how none of her gentlemen had worn swords that day. There was bustle and confusion, Greville, kneeling at her feet and swearing to die for her, drawing a toy dagger, his only weapon, Gentlemen Pensioners and Yeomen hastily summoned, running here and there with bare blades and brandished halberds. On their return to the palace, a Maid of Honour immediately had noisy hysterics.

"You fool—girl!" Elizabeth snapped at her. "No harm was intended to you!"

She was only too aware that she was on the edge of such screaming laughter herself, and on the return walk, heaving waves of darkness had threatened to drown her. She held back faintness and hysteria, as she had held back the would-be assassin—by sheer will power.

Zenith

"Take that girl out—and pour cold water over her!"

It was that quiet, sensible woman, the Countess of Warwick, who, bringing her mistress a goblet of wine with her own hands, mentioned the name of the one person in whose presence she could relax.

"Robert will be distracted when he knows, your Grace."

"I wish he was here now," she said flatly.

She sipped the wine, wrapping her long fingers round the twisted stem of the goblet. Yes, her frightened body wanted keenly Robert to put his arms round it and comfort it, but he was in those accursed Low Countries. She said in a harsh voice: "God's death! What a hero it was, that could not face an unarmed woman's eyes!"

Walsingham perhaps permitted himself one sigh at the thought of her peril. Unlike Burghley, he had no personal affection for her. She would not take up the sword against the Anti-Christ in Rome whose secular arm was the mighty King of Spain and drive forward into the great apocalyptic war of which he dreamed. The campaign in the Netherlands was draining away to slow, squalid disaster. If she could make peace with Spain (and therefore with the Devil) she would do it. She was not firm in the Faith and he had the uneasy feeling that if the Pope had not excommunicated her, and pronounced her deposition, and if the Jesuit Mission had not commenced its work, she might have left the Papists alone. But even such as she was, he admitted her death would be a disaster. Yet the risk was worth running if it might inflame her against the Queen of Scots. Those about her said she was shaken. And at last he had in his hands the evidence for which he had longed and prayed.

Babington had written a lengthy letter to the Queen of Scots, describing how he and five comrades would slay the Queen of England, while others would hasten to rescue Mary from Chartley, ready to meet the promised foreign armies. At last she answered him with a letter of warm approval—her principal anxiety being for her own safety while they carried out their plans. Walsingham felt some compunction for his own Queen, and had Phelippes add a forged postscript asking the names of the six would-be assassins. He did not want a repetition of the Barnewell incident!

He brought the proofs to Elizabeth, and saw her lips compress till they became a reddened slit. She could no longer evade the demand. He had snared both Queens, one to her death and the other to its consent. And he had delivered his country from lurking danger.

Zenith

Yes, Elizabeth thought, the trap has closed on Mary, she has rushed into it with the madness which takes hunted beasts and he has finally shut the door. But what he does not see—what no one sees—*I* am shut in with her. . . .

Legal processes succeeded and became agony and death, formal phrasing was translated into rack and gibbet, quartering knife and cleaver. The young men who had wrapped up the stark fact of murder with nebulous romanticism went to a grim death. They had been tools to her whom they served, tools to those who entrapped her. And now her turn was coming.

The Privy Council demanded that she be sent to the Tower before her trial, but Elizabeth had cried out at that. The Tower was too keen a memory. The strong walls of Fotheringay Castle would serve instead. On 11th October 1586, her trial opened there. From the moment of the plot's open discovery Mary's gestures had been superb. In the mirror of history she would stand with splendour; perhaps she knew it. At her trial and at her death could have been uttered those words for her grandson whose end echoed hers. "She nothing common did or mean, upon that memorable scene. . . ." The verdict at her trial was a foregone conclusion, but she defended herself with courage and intelligence, gallantry and wit. The world's eyes were upon her and she would not falter. Let the evasions, the desperate struggle, the twisting, the writhing of conscience belong to Elizabeth. She too was as surely condemned. Mary saw it if others did not.

The Queen had driven all away from her as she crouched on her cushions spread on the floor, all except Robert, kneeling beside her. He had brought to her his failure in the Low Countries, his humiliated ambition and his bitter grief for Philip, and the woman had comforted him for the wounds which the Queen had dealt. Now in her torment, she could only turn to him.

She said: "You were very patient with me, Robin, when *her* son was born. . . . But this is even a worse thing she has done to me. To make me guilty of her death!"

One of her hands was spread out on the floor. He laid his on it, and began to rub it with his thumb.

"You are not guilty——"

"More guilty than the hangman. I can't do it. . . . I can't sign the warrant!"

"You will do it. For your people you can do anything."

371

"You have cause to know. . . . Oh, God! What next will be asked of me? They all crowd around me. Burghley, Walsingham. Now Walsingham is ill, his deputy, Davison. All the councillors. Deputations from both Houses of Parliament. I begged them to bear with me in 'greater conflict with myself than ever in my life'. Then the others come—the advocati diaboli. The Ambassador of France. The Ambassador of Scotland. Yes, she is the devil. . . . But not for the reason Walsingham thinks. Ah! It would be a judgment on all my Council— on Parliament—if the young King of Scots allied himself with Spain——"

"He'll never do that. You are paying him four thousand good English pounds every year by the new treaty and you hold up to him the hopes of the Succession. I had a letter from him—he says: '*How fond and inconstant I were if I should prefer my mother to the title, let all men judge.*'"

"If he is vile, does it help me to be vile?"

"You are not vile, dear heart. Nor is it vile to have her executed. It is the Queen's duty—but the woman shrinks from it!"

"And so much! But to order her death, neither Queen nor woman will come well out of it. . . ." She struck the floor with her fist and he could hear her rings rap on the boards. "Oh—the unfairness of it! For I am better than she——" She drew in a long shuddering breath, before continuing. "I do not mean as woman to woman. God alone can judge. But as *Queen*. I have been Queen before everything else."

"And so you will continue."

"But that is why I hate her! Because she dared what I did not dare. Because after her husband's murder, she did what I longed to do— after your wife's death!"

"Not back to that!"

"Yes, Rob. It is so strangely the same. And she took her lover openly before the world——"

"To the grievous and desperate harm of her country and people. You did better."

"Then", she said, "you do love me. Or you would not tell me that."

"There is a simpler way than open execution. I had word with her son's ambassador——"

"With the Master of Gray?" She gave an odd convulsive little jerk. He could not see her face in the gathering dusk, only the flash of the whites of her eyes. "He comes to me, too, the smooth, glib, handsome fellow, that pleasing devil's advocate, with his open formal protests and pleadings, and his secret insinuations. And from France—from King Henri and his mother, Catherine! All these black hints—to save the prestige of a crown, to save the prestige of the Royal Houses of France and Scotland, to save the conscience of King James—the Queen Mother of France pretends to no such hypocrisy—to make away with her privily."

He said, after a pause: "It would be easier for *her*—than the scaffold, the block, the axe——"

"Would it be easier for *me*?"

"Let them write another chapter to *Leycester's Commonwealth*! I will take it upon myself, for your sake. Let it be blamed on me. I will write to Paulet."

"No, Robin. Not on you."

She had covered her face with her hands and sat silent so long that all the light faded and the window's long rectangle was just visible against the darkness. Then she whispered so softly that he could only just hear.

"I wanted to save her. . . ."

But her hands were not strong enough to hold back the weight of doom. The rumour of another plot sponsored by the French Ambassador threw the country into a panic. And the day came when the warrant for Mary's execution lay before her and a newly trimmed quill was in her hand. Waiting beside her was Davison, Deputy for Walsingham and acting for him during his illness. He was looking at her with a curious expectancy—like a dog at a hole, she thought with a shudder. Here was the end of the long strange twisted bitter story of Mary and herself, a scroll of formally lettered parchment and a newly trimmed goose quill which would write the huge elaborate ELIZABETH R. with its loops and flourishes. To write that name was death for Mary and yet it was condemnation of herself. But sign it she must; she could find no alley of escape. Her brain twisted a little, picked up a loose end—if the news of the signing was brought to Mary, it might shatter her defiance. She might break down, confess the guilt she had so strenuously denied, beg for mercy. "And then I might save her," Elizabeth thought. "Because *I* should have won the duel—the duel of years! She would not be dangerous then. . . ."

She wrote, slowly and deliberately, under Davison's avid eyes. He should surely have a slavering tongue and panting jaws. . . . The

373

quarry was so near. . . . She swung round on him and Hell looked out of her eyes. Her voice crackled with biting savage sarcasm.

"Go, tell Sir Francis Walsingham! The grief thereof will kill him outright!"

Silence came after the signing. She heard nothing of the preparations made to execute one who had been a reigning anointed Queen in her own right, and the wife of a great monarch, a princess allied to the oldest and noblest reigning Houses of Europe. Surely a dreadful pomp and panoply must be prepared for such an execution? But there was only this frozen silence as if life itself held its breath. There was an end to angry clamour, to deputations from this great body and that, from angry voices imploring, threatening, cajoling, insinuating —a quiet emptiness which still seemed to hold the echo of those voices. Certainly there was no message of capitulation from Mary. . . . Her ministers avoided her. Surely before they could execute their warrant, the matter must come before her again, they would ask her advice on formal points, and she could revoke it as she had once revoked Norfolk's, fifteen years ago. . . . Then she remembered Robert and his wife's death, how he must have left the frenzied young woman, knowing that she would kill herself unless that sinister figure of Forster killed her first. He had washed his hands of the matter, gone away and waited, technically innocent but guilty in spirit—as she was doing now. . . .

She was riding back to Richmond Palace at the end of the winter's afternoon, when she heard the clang and jangle of church bells. Her high hawk's nose twitched, the air was acrid with the scent of burning, and the early twilight was filling with the murky red glow of bonfires lighted in street after street. Discordant voices rose, clashing with the bells, roaring cries of savage triumph. In the courtyard, stiff in her saddle, she demanded the reason.

"The people are rejoicing over the execution of the Queen of Scots, your Majesty!"

"God's death!" she said. "And I am told nothing. . . . Where is that lying knave Davison, who so exceeded his instructions? Where is my Lord of Burghley?"

Her councillors came, not without fear. She was poised like a snake about to strike, waiting tensely, holding back fury while she flung quick, probing questions at them, till the picture of that last scene at Fotheringay was held vividly before her. Then she turned upon them.

"By God's soul!" she swore. "I never intended nor wished for her death. I signed her warrant—I did not tell you to hurry her to execution!"

Then she cursed them from her presence with a rage which recalled her father in his later days. None knew whether she was acting, or playing from her heart. None knew if she believed her own words. She scarcely knew herself. The Truth-in-a-Lie or the Lie-in-Truth had robbed the abstract of its values. True it was that she did not wish or intend Mary's death; true that she gave no instructions for the execution. But she had signed the warrant, and she knew it was possible for her councillors to put it in effect without further preamble.

She would neither eat nor sleep, but sat on the day-bed at the foot of her gigantic four-poster, resting her chin on her hands. Outside the night was made garish with bonfires and noisy rejoicings. England was awaking from a nightmare; the inner danger to all they loved and valued had been removed with one sure stroke. But nightmare had enfolded the Queen who was left alive. It was with some relief that the frightened whispering group of her women admitted the Earl of Leicester. They withdrew thankfully into the ante-room.

He knelt down beside her, took her wrists gently but firmly and drew them away from her face.

He said: "Dear heart, it had to be."

"Yes. . . . It had to be that I was defeated and dishonoured and she triumphed."

He sought for comfort. Just as Elizabeth had changed him from handsome, swaggering gallant to great potentate and administrator, she alone could sound depths in him which he did not know he possessed. What had made him say those words which were contrary to his own belief—that she had been right in refusing to marry him? That had stilled her bitter secret envy of Mary's reckless marriage to Bothwell.

"Years ago," he said, "when we were both young, you told me that your own honour, your own good name, counted for nothing against the safety of the country. By her death you have bought safety."

"Yes, I have done that. But her death is her victory. . . ."

"She died well," he admitted grudgingly. He could gladly have wrung Mary's neck with his own hands. His nature was not complicated, it could not follow Elizabeth's through all the dark labyrinthine turns. He did not comprehend the strange spiritual conflict between her and Mary, but he would have done anything to help her. He was a strange mixture of a deep instinctive tenderness and an amoral lack of scruple—a mixture which had proved the undoing of so many women who had loved him. He had no conscience in the matter of the Queen of Scots, he only wanted to ease Elizabeth. He got stiffly from his knees, and sitting beside her on the day-bed, put his arm round her waist. She was skin and bone! he thought. She worries herself to death. . . . The girl he had once held had been slim but this seemed like a skeleton beneath the jewel-sewn brocade.

"Died well!" she murmured. "So she might, knowing how she struck me down! Well she might say to her weeping servants: 'Weep not! For to-day you will see Mary Stuart free from all her cares.' *I* will not say that. Death will not come easily to me."

"You will live", he told her, "for long years, to the happiness of your people."

She leaned against him in a stiff exhaustion. Her eyes were closed but he knew she did not sleep. Her thoughts were going round and round on that wheel. Sometimes he could tell their mood by the words she spoke.

"I must tell so many lies now, but I will never find one to help myself."

And again: "She must have hated me so much! If she had had any mercy, she would have asked *me* for mercy. . . ."

And finally: "She was like a sleep-walker going to the edge of the precipice and only my hand could save her. I knew it, I knew it!"

"You did save her, from Carberry Hill till yesterday. For twenty years."

"But it will be forgotten. It will only be remembered that I was her death."

Dawn found them so, its cold grey light turning the candle glow yellow and feverish.

Chapter Eighteen

The portentous year had come, 1588, the year of dread and marvel dawning in a red apocalyptic glow, the "Grande Climactericke Yeere of the Worlde" for which astrologers, prophets and soothsayers had forecast "marvellous and fearful and horrible alterations" set forth in the ancient Latin verses beginning:

> "Post mille expletos a partu virginis annos
> Et post quingentos rursus ab orbe datus
> Octogesimus octavus mirabilis annus
> Ingruet, in secum tristia fata feret. . . ."

Perhaps the time of the prophecy might not have been so exact had it not been for Sir Francis Drake. Philip of Spain, after a quarter-century of provocation, had determined to crush his wicked sister-in-law and her godless unruly kingdom in the preceding year; he had prepared a vast fleet optimistically christened "The Invincible Armada" which was to be crammed with his armoured veterans. But at the beginning of 1587, Drake had swooped upon it as it lay at anchor in Cadiz harbour, and made the skies scarlet with its burning. "El Draque" had sold his soul to the devil who had given him a magic mirror in which he could watch all the movements of his enemies' shipping and gauge their exact position. So said the Spaniards. Drake told his Queen that he had "singed the King of Spain's beard", and she permitted herself a smile. She enjoyed Sir Francis's choice of a phrase. She herself had produced a remarkable saying whose ringing defiance enormously cheered her people—"By God's death! I would send my fleet to disperse the Armada even if it were in the interior of Spain!" Certainly both his admiring fellow-countrymen and dismayed enemies credited Drake with magical powers. . . .

Her saying and Drake's were repeated to a chorus of clinking pewter pots in numberless taverns. Ah! She was a one, she was! And didn't care a snap of her long fingers for the Pope, the King of Spain and the Devil himself. . . . That was the way to talk to *them*, and those who had seen her—few sovereigns had ever been so well known by sight thanks to her Progresses—could well imagine the defiant toss she would give to her head crowned with one of those bejewelled flaming wigs, "of a colour never made by nature", and the ringing note of defiance in her voice. As for Frankie Drake, after his double exploit, first smashing the Spaniard in the Caribbean and then in his own home waters, no doubt he and his seamen could chase the Dons to the very gates of hell. But these pot-valiant heroes had no idea that their embattled heroine was still trying, with a cool desperation, to negotiate peace through the Prince of Parma, before the greatest King on earth let loose his forces on her kingdom. . . .

For the general public such magnificent swaggering gestures, for her councillors the shrewdness of a diamond-hard, diamond-bright brain—and something of her inmost feelings only escaped into a few phrases of the prayer she composed to be read in the churches at this time. The Earl of Leicester, who had come to her in her writing-room, bearing some of the Council's decisions for her approval, stood for a moment, reading them over her shoulder. Forty years ago, Ascham's pupil had had an exquisite formal Italian hand like a professional calligrapher's. There was only a shadow of that perfection now, lingering in the elaborate flourishes of the capitals, and ordered formality had become a weary and yet determined scrawl. She had covered so many miles of parchment since then including endless signatures, and nowadays her arm and her right thumb often ached unbearably—"though the gout it could not, it *dare* not be!" Robert read aloud those words which had suddenly struck him as coming from the very depths of her heart.

"O let Thine enemies know that Thou hast received England . . . into Thine own protection. Set a wall about it, O Lord, and evermore mightily defend it."

Then he said with a sort of simplicity: "You're asking their prayers for the country—not for yourself!"

"I pray—and ask others—for that which matters!"

"God's soul! You matter! You are the most precious thing to

your people—the very symbol and inspiration of their resistance!"

She said nothing but her fingers moved on the table as if she were playing on the virginals.

"And if they knew the especial peril threatening you now—a shout of rage would go up from the whole country!"

"Have Walsingham's agents discovered a new plot? 'Twould be sensible to murder me as soon as the Armada is sighted."

"A damnation sight worse than murder!"

"I do not grasp your meaning, Robin."

"The latest report that Walsingham has from his spies, is that of a command to the Spanish forces—to take the Queen of England alive!"

"Well?" she said coolly, raising her narrow brows. The dark flush of anger was turning his face purple.

"Whether it is the device of those viperous Jesuits or he who calls himself Allen Cardinal of England and already has spewed out snakish venom, who have so persuaded King Philip, or whether he sees himself as an Oriental despot, a heathen Emperor like Tamburlaine——"

"I can scarcely see Philip play Tamburlaine." That play by the young Cambridge graduate Marlowe had been the sensation of London the year before. Thousands had flocked to see Alleyn in the title role, "threatening the world in high astounding terms" in Marlowe's tremendous blank verse. "Well," she continued. "What does this Spanish Tamburlaine of yours intend to do with me?"

His voice was choking, shaking with fury.

"Is it then a civilized Christian monarch? He would send the Queen of England in chains across the Alps, to be led barefoot through the streets of Rome in triumph—— God's soul, as long as I have a hand to draw a sword——"

The only reaction which she showed was to narrow her eyes and then interrupt him with a fierce eagerness: "Body o' me, you are right, Robin! If the people of this country did know, there *would* be a shout of rage! They must know! 'Twould marvellously stimulate recruiting—and the raising of money.... I have it! We'll have bulletins printed, telling the people of the fate the Spaniard intends for us all. That will steel their resolution. And we'll put in any news of good cheer to hearten them. Is the Council still sitting? If not, they must be summoned. I would have this put in hand at once."

Leaning on his arm, she passed along high vaulted galleries, by dully glowing tapestries, and tall windows whose stained glass shone like jewels with the sunlight behind it, and laid pools of reflected colour on the polished boards.

"You know," he murmured, gently pressing her arm, "if the worst came and all was overthrown—I would most surely get you away to some safety!" He could feel the shiver go through her.

"Rob! my dear! But then—nothing would matter. . . ." She had closed her eyes for a moment and her body had become taut. Then she began in a low insistent voice: "I don't think of it. I will not let myself think of it! I was hardly more than a child when I had to learn how to keep my thoughts from the unbearable. . . . But it's there, Robin, there all the time. Like a footfall in the next room. . . ."

But she was marvellously vigorous and cheerful with the Council, pressing her idea of a news bulletin to be published during the time of crisis. Mercury was the messenger of the gods—let it be called the *English Mercury.* When Lord Treasurer Burghley cautiously agreed that an excellent effect might be produced for little cost, she broke out: "It need cost nothing. It must be for sale. Aye! The booksellers of Paul's Churchyard and Paternoster Row will do a roaring trade. I know my English! They'll value—and believe it more if they pay for it!" So the first English newspaper was conceived and born. And only Leicester guessed what went on behind the resolute façade, when she considered the possibility of defeat, of the Navy beaten back, and those inhumanly cruel, inhumanly efficient mailed veterans pouring ashore to rend England like the Low Countries, to drown it in blood and fire and torture without mercy. The thought had been a shadow between her and the summer's sunlight, a bitterness in the wine she drank, a despairing discord sounding through the sweet music played for her. As the days lengthened from spring to summer, and she sat till late with her Council, calculating, arguing and planning, seeking to stretch the Exchequer as if it were elastic, reading dispatches from Drake at sea and Hawkins at the Navy Board, scanning muster rolls, and the reports of Walsingham's secret agents on the Continent, she heard that "footfall in the next room", that footfall of doom which might one day cross the threshold. . . . But at this time of barely endurable stress, she had happiness in her personal life.

On a May afternoon, the Queen walked slowly up and down the terrace overlooking the river at Greenwich, and she leaned on the Earl of Leicester's arm. From the Palace of Placentia to the Bridge with its double row of houses, that broadly coiling strip of Thames was known as London River, and a forest of lacy ships' spars rose from its cold, bright waters, till they clustered most thickly in the Pool, between the Tower and the Bridge. But there were not so many ships to-day in London River; when the Lord Mayor and the Common Council had been asked for five ships and five thousand men to man them as their contribution against the Armada, they had begged to consider the matter for a few days, and then had returned answer that they would give ten ships and ten thousand men, and there were a further twenty thousand men ready to fight for her Gracious Majesty, over and above the trained bands, the best militia in the kingdom. The Queen was gazing upstream, past the remaining masts to where, guarded by the defiant outline of the Tower, London began, a dark mass of buildings, vast and of undefinable shape, quivering a little in the smoky haze which rose from its chimneys whose cooking-fires were burning for the five o'clock supper. Two Maids of Honour in her retinue, a discreet distance behind her, whispered together.

"The Wicked Earl! He now has the air of a faithful husband, devotedly attending his Lady of thirty years' standing."

"They *have* a most married look, truly...." She giggled and added: "And it is thirty years since——"

"Since *what*?"

"Since H.M. came to the Throne and *he* became Master of the Horse. Oh, Lord—years and years before we were born! He must have been handsome then!" She added with unconscious cruelty: "Perhaps *she* really was handsome then too."

"Sh-sh! If anyone should hear you!"

The court noticed that the Queen and the Earl had not been so inseparable since the melodramatic announcement of his secret marriage nine years ago. To older courtiers, it recalled the young Queen saying, laughing: "Lord Robert has become my little dog! Where he is, they say, I cannot be far off!" Then they had been so palpably in love that their hot blood had not paid decorum's dues; now they gave the impression to onlookers of a devoted elderly couple. The enormous pressure of work alone had been enough for the Earl's being in his apartments at court, and not at Leicester House, and perhaps that was why he did not appear to realize all that was going on there.... High Society was consumed with malicious delight at the picture of

the Wicked Earl—who had deceived so many husbands in his day—
himself as a deceived husband. There was gleeful chuckling at his
Lady's shocking behaviour with handsome young Blount—Sir
Christopher since the campaign in the Low Countries—which was
setting all tongues and ears agog. Leicester who was believed to be
the Queen's lover, to have murdered his first wife and two inconvenient husbands, my Lords Sheffield and Essex, to have driven the
unhappy Douglass melancholy-mad—this accomplished profligate
was now wearing the horns for his erstwhile page and present Gentleman of the Horse. It was much better than any play! But one glance at
him showed that his lady-killing days were over; he looked a sick
and weary old man, his body which had once been so lithe and
strong, fat and ponderous, his face heavy and of an alarming purplish
colour. He had never been the same since his return from the Low
Countries when the Queen had been so infuriated with him, and yet
—here she was turning to him now more than ever. She seemed to
have forgotten all her young favourites, except one. When that splendid youth, his stepson Essex, was with them you might have thought
the three a happy family.

"And now," she thought, "at this time of the greatest stress in my
life, I am allowed the illusion of having a husband—and a son." And
here was Robin, comfortably close in body and spirit, smiling at her,
and his eyes and smile could always recall the young man of thirty
years ago.

"I'll swear your thoughts are worth more than a penny? What are
they?"

She paused a moment before she answered: "Rob, do you remember when I came to the Throne?"

"Shall I ever forget? It was a radiant creature who rode into cheering London. You were in purple velvet with a scarf about your
neck, and I rode next to you——"

"But was the country radiant? Do you remember that? The people
were impoverished and divided amongst themselves, my unhappy
sister had blown upon the fires of persecution, the treasury was empty,
the currency so debased that the money market at Antwerp jeered at
creditless English gold! Add to that a loathed and unsuccessful war
at the side of a treacherous and disliked ally—and religious and
political factions ready to fly at each other like ravening wolves! The
Ambassador, Feria, told me I might only hold my throne through the

favour of his master, Philip of Spain. *I* told him that I held it by the Grace of God and the love of my people——"

"And so you have! No sovereign was ever so loved. And despite foreign plots, the Jesuits, and the followers of the Queen of Scots, having all done their worst, you are leading a united country against the Spaniard. A prosperous country, a country of men who will dare anything, who have drained the golden blood from the veins of Philip's New World, men who have carried your flag into endless seas—where are the waters in which your ships have not sailed?"

"And to turn to the sober and prosaic—to the cloth trade! Which has far surpassed the old trade of the raw wool of the Staple. Besides the adventurers sailing in the so-called Spanish Main, there are hundreds of ships carrying English cloth to Europe, building up that prosperity which has made English money and credit the highest on the Continent."

"And it is your achievement!"

"No. It is the achievement of the people of this country. I gave them their chance—that is all. You see, Robin, I always believed in them. I believed that were they given long years of peace to develop their resources, all was possible. For thirty years I've kept the peace—and I haven't cared by what means! The Continent has been torn asunder by wars and civil wars, but a generation has grown up here in peace, and I think it a generation bright with promise. They have sailed into uncharted seas—of knowledge as well as of a new world. And what songbirds—musicians and poets—your nephew Philip, his friend Spenser, Walter Raleigh who is so many things, the author of Tamburlaine—but the list is endless! And the shrewd merchants, and the men who build the ships and weave the cloth—they've all had their chance. By God's precious soul! I say now, it was worth it, the price I paid.

"That was why I didn't marry you, my dear. That was why I played at match-making with the greatest princes of Europe for my suitors. That's why I helped the Dutch and Huguenots—to weaken France and Spain—but I would never help them so much that I would endanger this country—that's why Mary of Scotland had to die. . . . Oh, I have lied and cheated and counted cunning with the Medici. Machiavelli wrote : '. . . when the entire safety of our country is at stake, no consideration of what is just or unjust, merciful or cruel, praiseworthy or shameful must intervene.' I'll not deny his doctrine. . . ."

"Your people are right to love you!"

"Ah, Robin!" she was smiling crookedly. "They love me for the wrong things. They love me when I openly challenge Spain—when I swear defiance like a tavern swashbuckler! Poor sweet fools, they love me when I imperil them far more than when I plot and struggle for their safety. . . ."

She sat down and he took up her fan of curled ostrich plumes set in a jewelled holder, and began to fan her with it.

"And your safety," he began, "which is so important to them. I wish you'd heed it! You could not be in a more dangerous place than Greenwich. Too near the estuary, the open sea, facing Parma's ports. Haven't I argued with those men of peace on your Council not to spread our forces along the South Coast? The Spaniard will not waste *his* soldiers landing between the Lizard and the Cinque Ports! If he does, it will be only a diversion. The west-countrymen don't have to be taught how to fight the Spaniard—give them powder for their muskets and some heavy artillery and they'll drive any such attacks back."

"Well—haven't I supported you, Robin? An't our main striking forces to be quartered at Tilbury to guard Thames estuary and London, and you are to have command? Hasn't Huntingdon as big an army in East Anglia as Norris and Raleigh have in the south west?"

"Yes, you saw it, if some of the others didn't! The Spaniard will try to break through in the Narrow Seas, and not land his men till he has made juncture with Parma and Parma's Army of the Netherlands, the best fighting troops of Spain! They can easily be ferried over in flat-bottomed barges under the cover of the Armada's guns to join its soldiers, and London, the heart of the country, lies before them. And here are you—*between* London and the most dangerous part of the sea coast! If aught happened to you, there would be no spirit left in the people. Sweet, you would do me so much honour and happiness if you would reside at Kenilworth till the danger is over. It is remote from all coasts being in the centre of the country, it can accommodate a large garrison and be defended if needs be——"

"God's death!" Her eyes, narrowed and glittering, and the curve of her nose made her look like a ger-falcon about to strike. "Do you propose to immure me under the same roof as your wife?"

"No!" With more haste than forethought, he added: "Lettice prefers Wanstead."

384

"God's wounds! So Kenilworth is good enough for me, but not good enough for my cousin——"

"My dear," he said patiently, "nothing I have is good enough for you, but I am so consumed with anxiety for your safety!"

The expected fury was cut short. He did not know she was thinking: "He looks so old . . . so sick . . . so tired. . . . That damnation she-wolf would neither notice nor care! And at this time, he cannot have the rest he needs."

"I know, Rob," she said, with a gentleness which made him stare. "But my place is with my soldiers. The Kings of England lead their men into battle."

"You are a woman——"

"I may have a woman's body—a feeble old woman's—but my heart"—she took his hand and suddenly pressed it to her brocaded bosom—"feel its beat! It's a man's heart. The heart of a King of England!"

"I wish your soldiers could hear you! But——"

"I'll have no 'buts', Robin!" Her eyes had that hard glitter again, and her voice was as sharp as steel. But she kept the hand she had pressed to her heart, in her fingers, lying on her lap.

There was a stir amongst her retinue, the Maids of Honour were suddenly smiling and their rounded cheeks were going pink. A tall young man was striding along the terrace, pulling his plumed hat from a head which shone in the sunlight like a newly peeled horse-chestnut. It was the young Earl of Essex, and he dropped on his knees before the Queen. How soft and young his lips felt against her hand! Like a child's mouth, this youth in his twentieth year, and it brought a sudden glowing tenderness to *her* eyes and lips.

"Well, you rascal!" said his stepfather. "Where've you sprung from?"

"I rode through Finsbury Fields, and saw the men drilling! I tell your Grace there's a splendid spirit in them! They're like hounds in leash, longing to be slipped at the Spaniard."

She cupped his face in her hands and said with gentle mockery: "And you to lead them! What a swashbuckler it is. . . ."

She had seen him that day, when he and Philip had been Robert's "crutches", as a vision of the son for whom she ached, the son by Robert. Her practical mind had made her ask—was he truly Robert's son? And a fantasy slipped in too—was it possible to conceive a soul?

Zenith

He seemed a symbol of that bright and lovely generation which had grown up in her thirty hard-bought years of peace at home. She thought: "Philip might have been that to me, but he grew up austere —he fell among Puritans and judged me hardly, and then his light was so harshly snuffed out!" But what was there in this young Essex, that he seemed to bring back her own youth, and make the lost years fall away?

Soon, she thought, smiling, she would be supping in a room where the river breeze would give imagined life to the figures in the tapestry hangings, and her only companions would be Robin—who had come back to her now that he was old and weary—and this lovely lad, and the music would play softly, lutes, viols and recorders. For an hour, she could be happy, and seal her mind against horror borne nearer in the galleons of the Armada.

Drake had implored permission to re-attempt his singeing of the King of Spain's beard. Let him once against destroy the Spanish Fleet in its home waters! But her voice was raised against it. The Spaniards would be prepared this time, and supposing the two battle fleets slipped past each other unseen on the wide expanse of sea, and while Drake sought them vainly, a Spanish army was landing unopposed? The fleet was her prayer and her reliance, that it would prevent the enemy ever landing. She thought of the thousands, drilling with clumsy enthusiasm in London's fields and on every village green, being sent against Parma's veterans. The fleet was the only certain hope. The bulk of it was concentrated at Plymouth, under the command of the Lord Admiral, her cousin (and Douglass Sheffield's brother), Lord Howard of Effingham, whom she called "noblest of the Howards". He was a great gentleman with unbounded enthusiasms for the west country sea captains and their strategy, enough the grand noble and diplomat to rule and compose disagreements between those turbulent and fiercely individual seamen, Drake his Vice-Admiral, John Hawkins who had gained release from the Navy Board where he had forged his mighty weapon, big rough-tongued Martin Frobisher, Davies the great navigator, Hawkins's son, Richard, Fenner of the "seven Portugals", Amadas and Barton who had prospected for Raleigh and found Wingandacoa renamed Virginia, and many more like them—no easy team to drive. And Howard had sufficient greatness of spirit to leave the direction of strategy to his Vice-Admiral. Besides this, the main battle fleet, there

386

were forty ships under Lord Henry Seymour and Sir William Winter blockading Parma, and the fleet of the Dutch ally was ready. James of Scotland had promised any help in his power, and though Elizabeth had little faith in him, she knew he would sell his soul for the Succession to the English Throne. It had come, now, the hour when all she had built was to be tested, and she faced it with a deliberate outward calm. There was no trace of the woman who had clung to Robert and "used very pitiful words" before he had sailed for the Low Countries, but then she had never whole-heartedly believed in that expedition to the Low Countries. . . . She could recognize the inevitable when it came.

The hour of testing had come too for Robert. In the Low Countries he had thought of his own high-sounding glory; he would prove himself the greatest general of the age, a great ruler—a king! He would show Elizabeth, who said he was her "creature" and that she would "have here but one mistress and no master", who had denied him that share in her crown—he would show her that he could be her equal. . . . But now he did not stop to consider the portrait of himself which would, one day, be painted on history's canvas, he did not stop to wonder how he was impressing his contemporaries; he thought only of the urgent danger before him and how best to grapple with it. He was closer in spirit to Elizabeth than ever before, as he worked himself to the point of exhaustion.

Greedy he was for power and authority, but only so as to carry out his designs unhampered. Desperately he struggled with the overpowering matter of supply for the armies and the fleet, preventing contractors and middlemen from coining and cheating in their country's necessity, forcing officials to disentangle themselves from red tape. He inspected eager untrained recruits equipped with nothing but courage and sent them back till at least they had pikes in their hands which they knew how to use. He drove away those land sharks who proposed to sell food and drink at exorbitant prices to his troops at Tilbury. There were conferences with other generals, with all those experienced mercenaries of the Low Countries and Huguenot Wars, led by Sir John Norris, eldest of five famous brothers known as the "Chickens of Mars", who was probably the most competent handler of troops in the field which England possessed at that time. But even Norris had to be converted from the belief that the Spaniards would try to land on the south coast. There was the Queen to argue with, because she resolutely refused to go to safety at Kenilworth or on the Welsh border, she would be with her troops when the invasion came. With difficulty he persuaded her to withdraw from Greenwich; she considered the Tower for a moment, rejecting its strong walls because "in summer it stinks of plague!" and finally—by what effort on his part Robert hardly knew—he persuaded her to compromise by going to her Palace of St. James, to the north-west of Westminster. The Council could meet there, she was close to the capital, not too remotely in communication with his headquarters at Tilbury—and, he thought, at least London lay between her and the danger. Around the palace, in those green fields which were one day to be called St. James's Park, was encamped the Army of Reserve which also was her bodyguard, commanded by her aged cousin, Lord Hunsdon. Her "good Harry" was a greybeard now, with limbs as stiff as his armour, but he had the same spirit which had once forced the passage of the Gelt, to hang on the foe like a bulldog, till one or other was choked out of life. He, of all men, might be trusted to resist the Queen for her own good.

"Aye, if she swears at me, I can swear at her!" he said to Robert. "And if she tries to ride to battle, I'll take her bridle-rein tho' she takes her finger nails to my face!"

She had to be dealt with and the long meetings of the Privy Councillors, for was not Robert the greatest of these after Burghley and Walsingham? There was no rest for him, for body or for mind, and his body was failing him. Once it had been a magnificent young athlete's, now it was fat and heavy, sometimes racked with rheumatisms and agues, dragging with exhaustion as the days passed. There were other times, even more alarming, when the blood thundered so loudly in his temples, that he could hardly hear the voices around him and the whole world swayed before his aching eyeballs. His longings were now drained of all ambition—the danger to pass and then to be able to relax at his beloved Wanstead in forgotten peace. But while his thoughts strayed to this, they did not paint a picture of Lettice in the quiet of his favourite home. Lettice was in the midst of a whirl of energy at Leicester House, surrounded by her children, young Essex and Penelope Rich, with their friends and contemporaries, headed by Christopher Blount. Lettice was no cherisher of sickbeds. She was a mate for a vigorous man. No—it was Elizabeth he wanted now, at Wanstead, to talk of the old days, her long fingers moving over the virginals, or caressing his head. But that was all a dream. Before him, as before the whole country, lay the great struggle. He wrote to Walsingham: "*They have put me to more travail than ever I was in, in my life. . . .*"

One summer's evening he came to the Long Gallery at Leicester House. The musicians were playing the gay and lively airs for the two most gay and lively dances, the coranto and the lavolta. Figures in bright silks stepped, sprang and whirled, and the coloured light ran shimmering over them from the tall windows emblazoned with coats of arms, the Bear and Ragged Staff, encircled by the Garter and crowned by an earl's coronet, alternating with the armorial bearings of his noble connections, Greys, de Lisles, Beauchamps and Talbots. Eyes flashed like the earrings which seemed to dance above wide fluted ruffs, white necks and bosoms whirled, beards, dyed the fashionable vermilion, bobbed gaily up and down. All that was gay and reckless gathered at Leicester House, and many a young captain snatched hours from Tilbury or St. James's, changing steel and leather for silk and satin. Not yet had the coast-long chain of beacons flamed the scarlet message of danger.

The master of the house stood watching them, his back turned to a vast spread of canvas showing the rash Actaeon pursuing the goddess and her nymphs, gold-tinted flesh whirling against a dark, shaded wood like the dancers whirling before him. He saw Lettice, his wife, springing lightly, hand-in-hand with a boy no older than her own son, and thought: "How young she looks!" He saw his stepdaughter, Penelope Rich, her tawny-gold cloud of hair adorned with clusters of great milky pearls as she cast a glance at the tall young man who handed her, which was at once abandoned and heedless as if she wanted to drown in the present moment. Then Lettice saw her husband, with one hand to his gorget of dark steel as if it pressed too tightly. Gracefully she disengaged herself from the dance and came towards him. The leader of the consort of viols was eyeing him with deprecation, but Leicester waved him to play on. It was at this moment that he realized that youth with its ardours and excitements had left him far behind. How bright, how lovely—how cruel it was! And Lettice seemed so young. . . .

"Don't let me stop your pleasure, my dear! I was looking for young Robin"—but his eyes could not distinguish his stepson amongst the dancers—"is he here?"

Lettice's smile had turned suddenly to temper.

"He—here! He is—as usual! With her gracious Majesty. She has him with her, evening after evening, playing chess, playing cards, playing the devil knows what—he comes home at cock crow." She added with an extremity of bitterness: "I never before credited Robin with such worldly good sense!"

"But it isn't worldly good sense, Mother!" Penelope Rich slipped out of the dance, her bosom rising and falling. "You know Robin couldn't be worldly if he tried. Any more than a bird which flies from bough to bough, from this cluster of fruit to that. When his excitement or his interest are aroused—off he goes! Just now, he is fascinated, absorbed—enchanted by the Queen."

"Why do you want him?" asked Lettice tersely. "Have you—news?"

"No, my dear. I am riding back to the camp, to meet an engineer from the Royal Dockyards to inspect a river block with which I am not satisfied. It would be instructive perhaps for him."

"He is apparently being instructed in court favour!" said his mother. Behind her, Blount towered like a sentinel. Reluctant duty was struggling on his face.

"Do you wish me to ride down with you, now, my lord?"

"No, no, Kit! I have Digby and two of my officers. . . ." His eyes were caught for the moment by an emerald pendant, burning with a slumbrous green fire against the black silk of Blount's doublet. Since when could he afford jewels like that, Robert wondered?

"So late?" queried Lettice, raising her plucked and trimmed brows. Penelope turned to her stepfather with a sudden warmth.

"But you are too tired!"

"No, child, I am not so tired. . . ." He stooped forward and kissed Lettice's faintly perfumed cheek. "I must be going, my dear. Needless to say, I'll not be back this night!"

As he went, he heard behind him, music rising and whirling like the dancers.

The city was quieter in the late summer dusk than he had ever known it, but then so many of its youngest and most eager men were out at Tilbury. Taverns hummed and murmured and splashed their crude yellow light on the shadowed cobbles, but the narrow, overhung lanes were strangely empty. In the hot, still air, the stench of summer London thickened, with neither wind nor rain to cleanse it.

Zenith

By the great dark bulk of the Cathedral, a knot of men eddied across the road. One looked up at the horsemen, stared and shouted: "God save your lordship!"

Popularity was a strange thing, especially with teeming London's mob. It had worshipped Elizabeth since she had been a captive princess, but there had been jealousy in its feelings towards the man she had obviously loved. They had accorded him a grudging admiration for his pomp, his strength, his magnificence, but they had fastened avidly on all the scandals and black rumours which had found form in *Leycester's Commonwealth*. "And yet", thought Robert, "they've never hated me so much as they hate Raleigh. They hate him as much as his west-countrymen love him! They made a hero of Philip, and now young Essex seems to be slipping into his shoes. He's the idol of the 'prentice boys!"

A ragged cheer rose in the gloom.

"Take us against Spain, m'lord! Throw 'em into the sea! Death to the Spaniards—to hell with the Pope!"

"I'll take you against Spain!" said Robert, rising in his stirrups. "An' they ever get so far, we'll make them swim home!"

Roars of exultant laughter drowned other sounds. The horsemen went on, and as they clattered down the Cheap, two rode ahead with flaring torches. Horn lanterns bobbed here and there like great glow-worms. Hearing the horses, a ballad singer turned from the door of a tavern, to troll out at the top of his voice:

> "What is Love? I prithee tell!
> It is the fountain and the well.
> It is perhaps the sanctus bell
> "Which tolls all into Heaven and Hell!"

"Heaven and Hell—veritable truth!" thought Robert. He felt in his pouch and cast a coin to the singer, who snatching it up and seeing by the light of the tavern door, that it was not the expected groat or tester, but an angel, began to bawl: "A thousand blessings on your Honour's Nobility!" The verse ran through Robert's head, as the horses' hoofs echoed and re-echoed through the now silent and empty galleries of the Royal Exchange. He was thinking of Elizabeth and the young Essex. Penelope was right—the boy was like a bird darting from branch to branch with his eager but ephemeral interest. A brilliant, gifted, lovable boy, but not reliable! And he was not like the run

391

of Elizabeth's "pretty lads". He was something more—and above all she thought of him as something more. Why did she say—"he's the son we might have had. He's the spirit of youth. When I'm with him, I'm young again . . ."—why? The eager boy and the middle-aged woman with her storied experience—what was linking them?

Now they were out of the city by Aldgate, through poor, huddled suburbs, haunts of every miserable and squalid vice, and into the open country by the Whitechapel Road, with the night air cool and sweet on their faces. There was a cold sweat on Robert's brow and on his steel-encased throat, a cold sweat like death's. It was part of the exhaustion which was slowly closing in on him, a patient exhaustion which said: "I bide my time. I will not take you finally—yet."

When they came at last to Tilbury, the darkness and starlight were alike fading in the cold grey light from the east. Robert found that he was reeling in the saddle, and it seemed that others noticed it for there was Digby at his stirrup, proffering a silver flask. "Sack laced with old brandy, m'lord!" He took a pull and it seemed to draw fire into his numbed vitals. A nebulous white mist was rising from the river and the river flats, coiling around them in wraithlike smoke, making everyone's face look drawn and ghastly—how did *his* face look? Digby had him by the arm now, as if he thought he might fall. But there was the engineer from the dockyard, in his heavy leather jerkin.

"You want me to inspect this block, m'lord?"

"Yes! Yesterday, I had them sink a lighter and set a great chain— 'twould hold light craft, sloops, pinnaces and barges. But I doubt me if it's strong enough for a heavy vessel. The Spaniards have these great ocean-going galleasses which might burst it asunder."

"I'll get them to row me out, m'lord. If it were strengthened with masts, 'twould tear any ship's timbers apart——"

"Aye! Row out! This must be sure. The Spaniards'll try the river gate on London."

The mist swallowed up the little boat, till only the creaking of its rowlocks could be heard. Digby, at his elbow, was speaking in a low insistent voice: "I'll make things ready in your pavilion, m'lord. You must get between blankets and sleep when you've had a hot drink!"

"Another pull from your flask, and a fresh horse, and I'm off to Gravesend! I want to see for myself if they've strengthened those gun platforms for the heavy culverins I ordered."

Zenith

He thought wearily: "If I had Philip! If only I had Philip now...."
But there was no one he could completely trust in this hour. He must
do it himself.

"M'lord, you're not fit! You're exhausted. At your age——"

He did not deny his age as he set his hand on his faithful follower's
shoulder.

"Digby, my good fellow! Before this tale is told, many a trim lad
will pay with all his blood. So the old ones must do somewhat...."

Chapter Nineteen

At four o'clock in the afternoon of 19th July 1588, the Duke of Medina Sidonia, Commander of the Spanish Armada, sighted the Lizard. In his flagship, the galleon *San Martin*, he was leading that vast crescent of ships spread for miles upon the sea, shimmering in the heat haze dancing on the waters, moving with the formal stateliness of a court measure, in such high pride and dignity as befitted Spain. Brightly flew their silken banners and emblazoned sails, the banners which had been consecrated in the churches of Spain, amid clouds of incense and solemn chanting. It was a crusade against an abominable race, alike pirates and heretics, who had defied God's Vicar in things spiritual, and the greatest king on earth, in things worldly. Now the grey line of their coast showed above the glittering tossing summer sea; their hour had come. Who could be more powerful crusaders than the sons of the men who had won the battles of Pavia and St. Quentin and had ever since dominated the continent of Europe? All of those one hundred and thirty ships were crowded with armoured soldiers; fifty-eight thousand tons of shipping filled with thirty thousand men, and two and twenty thousand of these were soldiers to a mere eight thousand seamen. Some fifty of these ships were first-line fighting galleons, higher in the water than the English craft, harder to manœuvre but more menacing in close-grappled fighting, when their mailed warriors could sweep down on the decks of lower vessels. But even bigger than these were the gigantic carracks, hulks and galleasses, gathered from every port in Spain and Portugal, from Naples, Genoa and Venice, loaded with men and armaments, their holds filled with cavalry chargers. Let them once be landed, the best army in Europe, and they would go over half-trained volunteers like a tidal wave!

And the wind was against the English fleet lying in harbour at

Zenith

Plymouth. Fate offered Medina Sidonia one great chance to bottle them up in miserable impotence, but he was not even aware of Fate's offer. He had his orders, the orders which Leicester had divined, to force the Narrow Seas, effect juncture with Parma, and land upon the north Kentish coast. In the Narrow Seas, he believed he would encounter the English battle fleet. The Armada sailed on, and as night fell the English ships were warping out of the Cattewater into the open Sound, to seize the weather gauge from the enemy, before he realized their presence. There they were, those "long, low ships, sweet to handle", carrying only half the crews of their adversary, but those crews trained seamen; better gunners at heavier guns; a professional navy to fight a professional seaborne army. And while they moved upon the darkened waters, the country behind them sprang to a scarlet glow as beacon flared after beacon, and horsemen thundered through that night when few slept. It was England's turn then to pray, to watch and to pray.

The news was brought to St. James's Palace in that coldest hour before the dawn begins. The Queen was still awake, resting her cheek on one long hand against her gold-tasselled pillows; sleep had not come easily to her since she had heard that the Armada had sailed from Spain. She knew what this sound of bustle must mean, thudding footsteps and hoarse voices in the corridors, before some of her women burst in, wrappers pulled hurriedly about them. She caught a flash of white eyeballs in the candlelight and heard frightened, excited voices: "The Spanish fleet's been sighted, your Majesty!"

"I will get up," she said, "and speak to the messenger myself."

Her dressing had never taken so short a time since girlhood's days, but her hand was quite steady as she applied the paints which a waiting-woman handed to her. A candle flickered uneasily on her dressing-table, it was burning sideways. A high nervous young voice exclaimed: "It's making a winding sheet!" Someone gasped audibly, they all knew how the Queen hated to hear allusions to man's mortality—how she had rebuked the young Lord Herbert for calling a pie a coffin! Now she said curtly: "Trim it—and don't babble!" She looked into the glass and steadily her eyes and lips looked back at her. They were as controlled as her hands. She had learned that control, over thirty-five years ago, in the Tower, waiting to be shown the warrant for her execution. She had collected herself in readiness for *that*, prepared herself to be calm, her hands and lips steady, determined never again to implore Mary for mercy, for a hearing—though there was an unheard screaming inside her head—determined to walk firmly and make that last speech.... The silent screaming was beating inside her skull again. She fought it down with unspoken words: "Set a wall about it. . . . O Lord and evermore mightily defend it!" She had never prayed for herself like that. . . .

There were other girls, gathered at the window, peeping round the heavy curtains, one declaring: "I can see the glow of the coast beacons!" "Oh, Anne, you could *not*! 'Tis a camp fire." Girls got more stupid and wanton, every year, the Queen thought. Had she ever been a girl like that? No! When had she been allowed a girlhood as others? Or marriage—or maternity? . . . But when she had got to the ante-chamber, she was given again that strange illusion of maternity—and of her youth being returned to her. There was young Essex, rubbing sleep from his eyes, his ruff awry, his points half trussed, but a gorgeously damascened cuirass buckled on. As he knelt before her, she set the ruff to rights. "Dear child!" she said, and he seemed a child then. But when he rose to his feet, to offer his arm with a courtly bow, he seemed tall and strong and the pressure of his arm warmly reassuring. Leaning slightly upon it, she swept out, hearing the whispering and rustling of her Maids of Honour behind. Those silly little wantons would like his arm round their waists! She pressed it with a sort of triumph. He was telling her with eagerness, that he thanked God that he was with her that night at the palace. He spent half his time in attendance on her person, and the other half at the camp at Tilbury, where he had raised and equipped a regiment at his own expense, dressing them in his orange colours.

"Naught can happen to-night, here," she said. "And yet—I am glad you are with me."

"I would never choose to be elsewhere!"

Still leaning on his arm, she heard the kneeling messenger telling of that great crescent of slow-sailing Spanish ships spread for miles upon the summer sea—"Aye wi' great flaming Popish banners flying!"—advancing upon her shores in a high and stately pavane, a pavane of death. Her body felt as if it were laid upon those threatened shores to receive the first thrusts in her own flesh.

"And the fleet?" she asked.

"Your Grace, the winds are against them. They're yet in Plymouth, but Spain goes on——"

Zenith

If the fleet were delayed, if the fleet were trapped!

"My Lord Howard and Sir Francis will do all mortal man can," she said.

"Yes, your Majesty! Sir Francis, he said, he'd warp them out, and get the weather o' the Dons again. Burning keen they are to get at the men of Spain, your Grace!"

The sun came up to find both fleets at sea, and England and its Queen waiting. She did not know till evening that her ships were free.

In the meanwhile she must wait. Her Council met daily but there was little they could do either, beyond attending to matters of supply. When Burghley, that man of peace, bewailed the astronomical cost of this, she agreed with him, caustically.

"An' we win this great battle, I think we will go bankrupt!"

"I am inclined to fear that your Grace is right. But if we do not——"

"Then it would scarcely matter. . . ."

He had been with her from the beginning, from *before* the beginning of her reign, he knew how empty the Treasury had been thirty years ago. "The spendthrift is loved", she thought, "as much as the parsimonious man is hated—but heaven knows what ruin might have come, had I not been careful!"

But she was in another mood when she spoke to her cousin Hunsdon.

"Harry, when we hear a landing has been effected, your army, which is the reserve, goes forward to support the troops on the spot. And I go with them."

"God's wounds, Cousin Bess, you don't go into danger while I can stay you!"

"God's wounds, Cousin Harry, neither you nor the King of Spain shall stay me!"

He sent privily to the Earl of Leicester, the only man who might possibly stay her, and told him of her resolve. To her other councillors, she was implacable. Her place was with her soldiers, while her fleet was fighting what was, perhaps, England's Salamis.

On 21st July the two fleets first made contact, and then commenced that great running fight of ten days up the Channel. By day and by night, doors and windows in the coastal towns shook and reverberated with the thunder of salvoes. The anxious watchers could see the shapes of embattled ships out on the tossing horizon, their sides wreathed with innocent-looking coils of white smoke. But at night there was no innocence in the smoke wreaths, they glowed red as if spewed out of hell-mouth. On swept the fleets, and at Dartmouth the Devon men cheered their Drake to the echo, for his prize, the first taken, came ashore with his prisoners, Rear-Admiral Don Pedro Valdez, his Castilian gallants and his steel-plated soldiery. Still on, past the boiling seas of Portland where Frobisher was hard beset, and another great galleon, that of Don Miguel D'Oquenda, was abandoned by her crew off Weymouth, and the Spaniard had no chance either to land or to employ his chosen tactics of close-grappled fighting, hand to hand. There was no end to the furious music of the guns, as one great Spanish ship after the other fell victim, but never an English ship. By the Isle of Wight the Spaniards made an attempt to land, remembering perhaps the transitory success of a French fleet there in Henry VIII's reign; but they were fought off, and Howard was desperately sending into Portsmouth every light craft he could spare, for powder. No one had anticipated this furious cannonade of days; the Spaniards themselves had expected but one day of furious fighting in the Narrow Seas. The existing system of supply could hardly deal with such a stupendous demand. Portsmouth sent out all the powder possessed, and the running fight went on, drawing close to its climax. For here were the Straits of Dover, and beyond them, the other side of the Narrow Sea, were the southern ports of the Low Countries where Parma's veterans waited. Here Spain must force a landing to thrust at England's vitals, or else fail for ever. They had lost ships and they had had to fight on their opponents' terms, but they were still a well-ordered fleet, handled with courage and coherence.

Of all this, no man was more aware than Robert, now Commander-in-Chief with the title of "Lieutenant and General of the Queen's Armies and Companies". His anticipations had been proved right, but there was no time for boasting, as he drove all under his command with the same iron resolution as he drove his own flagging body. Any moment his forces, many with only a month's training, might be locked in a death-grapple with the most powerful troops in the civilized world. Then came Hunsdon's message, reinforced by those of other councillors, that the Queen had determined to be with her armies when the invasion occurred.

The Spaniards were within sight of the Straits of Dover, and Seymour's squadrons were moving down to join Howard and Drake, when a barge, manned by relays of lusty rowers, swiftly bore the

Lieutenant-General from Tilbury, through London, to land at
Whitehall stairs. Leaning back, under the canopy, his body relaxing
in brief thankfulness for an end of vigorous movement afoot or in
the saddle, he reflected that this was probably the last day when it
would be safe to leave his main army. Now or never he must convince the Queen that if aught happened to her, the heart would go
out of her soldiers; she could hardly realize how she had become the
supreme symbol to them of all they were fighting for. And yet, and
yet, he thought, how a sight of her in her present mood would hearten
them! He rode swiftly to the secluded Palace of St. James, listened to
the expostulations of anxious councillors, the baffled anger of old
Hunsdon—"God damme, if she sets her heart on aught—she's my
Aunt Nan again! There was never such powerful obstinacy in woman-
kind before!"—and briefly nodded his head. He would do his best
with her Majesty, he said.

In the old-fashioned low-ceilinged rooms, her golden brocades
glowed against the dark panelling. He could feel the tenseness in the
still beautiful hand he kissed, and her voice was abrupt.

"You have news?"

"No more than you have. The enemy approaches the Straits of
Dover which he must force. The final hour is upon us."

"Yes. . . . Oh, Robin! They'd have me a craven. To hide my head
till the battle is over, to desert those fighting for me. God knows if
there is any help or comfort I might give to my soldiers, they should
have all of it."

"Help and comfort you shall give to them. Who better?" He could
see the smile suddenly lightening her face, and braced himself. "But
go into danger, you shall not!"

"Shall not! By God's Son—am I the Queen of England or the puppet of my councillors?"

She had jerked to her feet and walked up and down, like a captive
beast padding in its cage. He stood watching her, seeing the light from
the windows running over her wide farthingale, watching the tightness
of her crimsoned lips, the smouldering darkness of her eyes under
bent brows.

"You are the Queen of England and the most precious thing
therein. Too precious to be ventured near the hazards of the battlefield. As your Lieutenant-General, I would not answer for my troops
if they believed their sovereign mortally hurt. All courage would go

out of them. To fight the best troops of Spain which include Parma's veterans, they must be whole-hearted."

"Have I suggested that I must go aboard the *Ark Royal*, Howard's flagship? Or head a cavalry charge? No, all I ask—God's death, *ask*! All I *demand* is to be at the headquarters of my army."

"And that is yet too perilous."

She threw herself down with a gesture of fury.

"I have it! My most wise and valiant councillors who despise me in their hearts for being a woman—haven't I taught them yet what I am?—think me a creature to be coaxed and wheedled. For thirty years I have had a manifest affection for you—what King, what Emperor has no weakness?—and they would snare me by my weakness, my affection. Send my Lord of Leicester—he'll cajole her! Say they." She made a savage gesture with her hand. "Sit! I'll not have you towering over me so!"

He was level now with those angry eyes. The blood was thudding in his temples so that her face, white with rage under its paint, swayed up and down.

"So you think you can cajole me, my Lord?"

"Not cajole," he said. "Command!"

The words were scarcely uttered when dismay seized him. What had he done to throw away every chance of persuading her? At this affront, she might do anything, even to cancelling his commission. He could see movement quivering in her hands and anticipated a stinging blow in the face. But he persisted.

"To venture your person, I will not allow it!"

Her head dropped and her hands came up. But they did not strike him. They took his hand, with which he had hit his knee in hardly realized emphasis, and raised it to her lips. As if in a dream unbelievable, he heard her voice: "As my lord wills."

He stared at her, his mouth open with the completeness of his astonishment. Speech would not come to him. She was smiling.

"To think I could not say it for thirty years," she said. "Not till I am an old woman—in a wig. . . ."

"Did you want then to say it?" he asked.

"The woman wanted sometimes what the Queen could not have. . . . And I was Queen and will be, till there is no breath left in me."

"You will not now venture yourself to pleasure your subjects."

"And to pleasure you. I will not unsay it. It was a relief, Rob, you can't understand. To yield. To your strength."

He said: "I think of that night in Windsor when you first came to me with your green cloak around you——"

"I could—and did—give you the woman, but never the crown."

"It took me long years", he said with a crooked smile, "to learn that the crown is virgin."

"Truly virgin! Ungiven, unshared. Ringed with inviolable fires."

"That is part of your legend. The legend of the greatest sovereign this country has ever had."

"Only history can say that. But no sovereign ever loved his—or her —people more."

"And that too is part of the legend. And I'll venture on a prophecy. That the defeat of the Invincible Armada of the greatest king on earth will be one of the glories of that legend."

He saw the colour rise hotly in her cheeks and then go back.

"If——! If it is defeated it will be Howard and Drake and the sea captains. And you and the soldiers. Not I."

"Who inspired us and gave us our chance. And built up this nation so it might defy that same greatest king on earth?"

"Rob—are you then so hopeful of the outcome? No—in honesty? I can't sleep at nights. All that defeat would mean is on my pillow. And I can let no one know. I am all confidence for the world."

"Yes, in sobriety, I am confident. But it will be a most desperate struggle."

"Robin," she said more gently. "You are very tired!"

"Yes," he admitted, "I am tired. But not too tired to do all that your Lieutenant and General can and must. Afterwards, I'll rest. I think I shall have earned it!"

She looked at him for a long while, and put another fear away with those terrors held under lock and key, and never allowed to appear. Then she smiled quickly, and knew that he would not know that it was forced.

"I will pleasure my Lieutenant further," she said. "Before he returns to Tilbury, what would he wish to do in the hour before departure?"

"What would give him the most rare pleasure would be to hear his sovereign play upon the virginals."

Listening to the music flowing into the quiet air like drops of cool water, he thought of how she could pass from the Fury to this Being of serene calm.

He had long returned to Tilbury on the night of the 27th when the news was brought to her that the Armada had run for shelter off the French coast between Calais and Gravelines. There they hoped to brace themselves for the effort of forcing the Straits, and briefly to rest. Walter Raleigh was at her elbow now. He had been one of her principal commanders ashore in the west country, but the danger had long since swept past the coasts of Devon and Cornwall, and Raleigh had come post-haste to London, chafing with impatience to be in the fight. She enjoyed him, his dashing elegance and his brilliant original mind, and was glad, for the first time, that young Essex was at Tilbury. For he was beginning to show a wild and unreasoning jealousy towards all upon whom she bestowed especial favour, and his passion against Raleigh had something frenzied and unbalanced in it. But she had banished these apprehensions for the warming knowledge that such jealousy sprang from the boy's adoration for her.

Now she watched the scarce-concealed impatience of the tall figure in the gleaming cloth of silver which she knew he longed to change for armour. He never forgot to pour out passionately poetic sentiments to Belphœbe, his goddess, but behind she could feel the moment's straining eagerness—"The Spaniards must be driven from shelter and engaged!"

"Aye, but how?" She had narrowed her eyes, and watched him as keenly as a cat might watch a mouse-hole.

"Most beloved Queen if they were forced out in confusion——"

"Ah!" she said. "Would fireships effect it? I was thinking of Jenebelli at Antwerp."

Raleigh was on his knees before her, kissing her hands.

"Only you, most glorious and beloved Queen, could have thought of it!"

" 'Tis like enough Sir Francis has thought of it for himself. But I will have you despatched to the Lord Admiral."

She would not keep the most fascinating gallant by her side if she could achieve anything by his absence.

On the night of the 29th, nine flaring torches burst upon the unsuspecting Spaniards at anchor. Nine small fleet auxiliaries had been sacrificed, to blaze like tar barrels, reflecting in the dark skies and darker waters, their hideous scarlet brilliance. For the first time panic fell upon the brave men of Spain, as they tried with desperation to escape the fiery death. Out plunged the great galleons, each one for herself, fouling their anchor ropes, running aboard each other, heeding no plan or purpose in their headlong frenzy. So they came to battle with their relentless adversaries.

On the following day was fought the greatest sea-fight to date, the Battle of Gravelines. A Spanish veteran declared that the cannonade made Lepanto seem like child's play. That mighty cannonade crashed and reverberated from the white cliffs of Kent to the Flemish sand-dunes, and the echo came thudding to the ears of the Londoners, to the ears of the waiting Queen. But her wish was to be gratified, for Robert had written, asking her to come to Tilbury.

". . . You shall comfort not only these thousands, but many more that shall hear of it. And thus far, and no further can I consent to venture your person. And by the Grace of God, there can be no danger in this, though the enemy should pass by your fleet. . . ."

For the Spaniards were through the straits at last, but lacking many of their gallant company, gone down in smoke and fire off Gravelines, after having had "their feathers plucked little by little" in the running fight of ten days, and "there was not lost one cockboat of the English". Gravelines had beaten the heart and the spirit out of them, but those ashore did not know, as the Royal Barge ran down to Tilbury, greeted by a rolling salute from the guns of the Blockhouse. There Robert escorted his Queen in a gorgeously ornamented coach, with a guard of horse and foot, while the fifes cried shrilly above the rattle of drums and the pounding beat of hundreds of feet. The sky was heavy with the promise of thunder, but a small breeze was springing up from the Nore, making the bright flags strain at their staffs, harbingers of the changing weather at sea. . . .

There was still the threat of thunder the next day, with unearthly purple clouds piling up in a dazzling sky, as the Queen came to review her army. She had made her plans and had retailed them the evening before to her Lieutenant-General, who had applauded their mixture of the theatrical and the sincere, which she knew how to combine so well. She had a rough outline of her speech memorized, but she would improvise on it as the mood moved her. He knew she was a forceful *ex tempore* speaker and though the author of *Euphues* might gasp in envy at the elaboration of her metaphors when she felt so inclined, she could on other occasions speak that plain yet golden prose which was used to such mighty effect by the translators of the Bible. And she always knew how to say the right thing to her people, inspired by a mixture of strangely deep devotion and shrewd understanding. The proud and great might dread her shattering snubs, but how well she could address the humble and ordinary! Who but she, thought Robert with a spurt of tender amusement, would have reassured that little official, shaking with fright and almost speechless at having to receive Majesty, by pretending to be afraid of him and his brother civic dignitaries? "Come hither little Recorder, it was told me that you would be afraid to look upon me or to speak boldly; but you were not so afraid of me as I was of you; and I now thank you for putting me in mind of my duty. . . ." And there had been that anger of hers when she had struck her knee and exclaimed: "How *dare* Philip of Spain invade *my* realm?" which could not but hearten her soldiers.

She would put on armour, she said, and ride a Great Horse, and then had given Robert a sidelong smile and asked him if he remembered in the first year of her reign, how she had ridden out, accompanied by him and her cousin Hunsdon, to exercise with the trained bands? Yes, he remembered very well, that lithe, eager girl with a boy's plumed cap on her copper head, in a damascened cuirass, waving a naked sword as her fiery Neapolitan jennet curveted and sidestepped—and Hunsdon had called him "her knight". He knew she remembered that too by the way she smiled. But, she had added with irritation, she had tried on a helmet in London, and the weight of the plaguey thing would give her a splitting headache in a quarter of an hour! He suggested that a page should carry it.

"And don't let your women buckle you too tightly into your armour," he warned her. "You had best appoint me Esquire of the Body! Women never understand steel!"

"At our age, it scarce can cause a scandal, Robin, as it did long years ago when you brought in my clean shift!"

This memory set them both laughing. It must be eight and twenty years ago, he thought, when they were newly lovers and hating to be long separated, that he used to visit the Queen while she was breakfasting in bed, waited on by her Maids of Honour. As luck would chance it, one had come in, bearing the Queen's clean shift, and he must seize it and make a mock-solemn proffer of it, to the hysterical giggles of the Maids of Honour and the loud expostulations of Mistress Kate Ashley. "My lord—will you give over! 'Tis not seemly ——!" while he pretended to discover a new protocol which laid it down that while the King was on Progress the Master of the Horse had to hand him his clean shirt. "But my sweet Lady is no king. . . . My lord, will you have done!!!" And Elizabeth had thrown the chicken wing she had been nibbling (in that fork-less age) to the ground while she pealed with laughter at Robin's capering and Ashley's indignation. Only the Duke of Norfolk had learned of it, and had complained to the Privy Council. . . . "Robin," said she now, "let us be glad that we loved and laughed while we were young!"

She could laugh still, in spite of the months of slow, and days of acute, strain. As his men would say, setting their cocks at a main, she was a game 'un. She must be nearly as tired as he, and had confessed that she seemed to ache in every bone when she had time to think of it, but praise God! she hadn't often the time. That evening as she had sat in his pavilion, the candles flickering in the breeze, the hum of the great army encamped around them, she had jested readily, even rather broadly at Cardinal Allen's unbridled vituperation of her. 'Twas a compliment, she declared, to be credited with so many lovers, though if she had had one quarter of them, how would she find time for affairs of State? He had responded gallantly by declaring he was proud that the Cardinal had declared him to be chief of them, though the candles had suddenly swum and dipped before his eyes, as the blood began to thud in his temples, and she laid her hand lightly on his, whether for his remark or for the sick look on his face, he never knew. But a little later he had caught a strange look on *her* face, as she glanced at the young Essex taking a great night-moth from a nearby candle. He had never seen that look before, it was— unguarded. . . . He felt strangely that he must warn her. It might be months before they were together again, he felt so utterly exhausted and drained of strength. . . . Perhaps when his command had ended he would be laid for weeks on a sickbed. So when the Queen and her Lieutenant-General had drawn a little apart, he began—clumsily enough, he feared. The boy was a delightful and gifted creature, but he was unreliable. His strange volatile mind drifted without reasonable direction. And he was as proud as Lucifer and would brook no guidance. . . . "He's a dreamy rakehell," he murmured. "Would seduce a girl and forget her face the next day!" Here the Queen interrupted with a cold fury. Her young cousin was no rakehell, he was too fine and rare. It was the shameless way the young women pursued him. Girls got more brazen and wanton every year, her Maids of Honour were the worst of the lot! He did not venture to contradict this tirade, but he thought that the young woman, who had once laughed at him teasing Ashley, had not always had this bitter fury against the loves of others. *That* had come to full bitterness after the announcement of his secret marriage. . . .

"Well, sweet," he had murmured at length, "I dare swear the gallants are as much to blame."

"Surely! Men would rather be seducers than husbands!"

But he had managed to turn her anger to laughter again.

"Do not look so hotly upon me! I do vow that *my* intentions to my true love, were most honourable! But *she* would not have me in the way of matrimony. . . ." And she had thrown back her head to laugh merrily. So it had ended, that strange evening, when memory had almost drowned the present. But after she had retired to the house where she and her attendants were to spend the night, he thought of the principal anxiety of the next day. She had insisted that she should ride alone, apart from her retinue, while she addressed the troops, so that all might see her. Burghley and the whole Council expostulated. What a target she would be for some spy or fanatic in the pay of Spain! The thought turned Robert sick, but he knew she must have her way. She had said: "I'd rather die than live to mistrust my people." He had answered her: "Tell them that!"

And now the day had come under that bright hectic sky. As far as the eye could see the trampled raw-looking earth was covered with men in martial order, the sun casting stabbing reflections from helmet, cuirass and pike head. Such a vast company of soldiers had not been seen in the country since old King Harry had been a young man, leading his armies to France. If much of their equipment was either improvised or lacking, as none knew better than their Commander, he also realized there was such a spirit in those scarcely trained men which was not often found. They might just have won an Agincourt, instead of waiting to face the world's most dangerous foe. They were bursting with cheerful defiance and would have gone headlong at any landing Spaniards. Most of the London Trained Bands were at Tilbury, and the Cockney militiamen had been cracking joke after joke, getting more irreverent and bawdy on subjects which might well have

406

caused them anguished fear; they were excruciatingly funny about the King of Spain, the Prince of Parma and the Pope. How close in spirit to them Elizabeth was, Robert thought suddenly, able to make danger into a joke. . . .

But a hush had fallen upon that great concourse, as horses' hoofs drummed on the turf. At the sight of the first magnificent figure, the Earl of Ormonde carrying the Sword of State, all the pikes and lances rattled to the ground in salute, the flags bowing. And then the silence was broken by an immense roar of cheers which rolled along the lines and kept on longer than one would have believed possible for mortal throats. Riding quite alone, came the Queen. She was on an Almain grey, seventeen hands high, caparisoned in scarlet and gold. No dainty barb or jennet for her now, but a destrier, a horse of strength, ready to carry a man in steel from top to toe. Her head was bare except for the jewelled band across that flaming wig whose almost vermilion hue could be seen across the river. . . . Over a dress of scarlet brocade embroidered with gold and silver, she wore a steel cuirass polished till it glinted, and damascened in gold. She had the collar and pendant George of the Garter round her neck as men wore it, and the actual Garter buckled on her right arm; a sword hung by her side, and in her hand was a carved ivory truncheon. Half a length behind came the two earls, Leicester and Essex, in full armour, but bareheaded, and after them a staff of gorgeously accoutred officers. Walking behind the Queen's charger came a page in the royal livery emblazoned with the Tudor Rose, carrying her plumed helmet.

On went that brilliant figure past those roaring lines of men. Robert thought he had never heard such a mighty greeting, it made one dizzy, and all the time he had his terror of an assassin, some bedevilled fanatic who would dare the certainty of being torn limb from limb. . . . Everyone could see her, such a blaze of bright, hot colour and brighter polished steel, no marksman could miss. . . . He wondered if she realized this, but presently he thought she was almost intoxicated with the fervour of the cheering. And so they went on till she reached a small eminence in the middle of the camp, and reined in with her great Standard behind her, the Plantagenet Leopards quartered with the Lilies of France, tugging at its staff in that breeze which grew stronger and stronger as the livid clouds began to pile up in that dazzling sky. Out at sea it was already blowing up to a gale. . . .

Zenith

The heralds about her, and the officers in the long lines tried to silence their yelling men but it seemed almost impossible. Then she raised her ivory truncheon, and the silence at last fell heavily, so heavily that one might hear the proud creaking of the tugging silken standard. Then she began to speak, and her voice had a strident ring which carried well. Only a part of her soldiers could hear of course, but they all seemed to be hanging on her lips, thought Robert.

As she had ridden out, she had debated in her mind whether to begin with "My good people" or "My faithful people", but these adjectives seemed pale and weak for such tremendous love and devotion which had been roared at her. She drew a breath, swallowed and then began, and it seemed that her spirit was flowing incarnate from her mouth.

"My *loving* people, we have been persuaded by some that are careful of our safety, to take heed how we commit ourselves to armed multitudes, for fear of treachery." She paused, and then a sudden passion filled her voice as it changed from the royal "we" to "I". "But I assure you I do not desire to live to distrust my faithful and loving people——" but here such a roar came from the multitude before her that her words were drowned. They surged forward as if on a single impulse, waving their morions, and yelling till it seemed their throats must crack. It was quite a while before she could continue and tell them that though tyrants could fear, under God she had placed her chief strength and safeguard in the loyal hearts of her subjects. ("When she speaks from her own heart", thought Robert, "her words are golden.")

"—and therefore I am come amongst you, as you see, at this time, not for my recreation and disport, but being resolved, in the midst and heat of the battle, to live and die amongst you all, to lay down for my God and for my kingdom, and my people, my honour and my blood, even in the dust. . . ." When the applause for this died away, she made a sweeping gesture with her ivory baton and shouted back at them: "I know I have the body of a weak and feeble woman, but I have the heart and stomach of a king, and of a King of England too, and think foul scorn that Parma or Spain, or any prince of Europe should dare to invade the borders of my realm; to which rather than any dishonour shall grow by me, I myself will take up arms, I myself will be your general! . . ." And then, after that recurring storm of cheering had reached an incredible crescendo, unbelievable even after what had gone before, she ended by praising Robert—"this my General"—than whom no sovereign had ever had a more noble and worthy subject, and promising by the word of a prince that they should be paid as they deserved. Soldiers' pay in the sixteenth century was even more uncertain than the hazards of the battlefield. . . .

When at long last Robert came to assist her to dismount at the Commander's Pavilion, he noticed that tears had ploughed their furrows down the paint on her cheeks. (She had made her face as red and white as any player on the Bankside boards, but that and her incredible wig had made her easy to see.) But all she could say with some irritation was that she did not know how men bore their armour, and when he suggested she should disarm for dinner, she snapped with still more irritation, a fine general she would be to do that!

"Fine general you are. You have so inflamed their hearts that they would face the whole army of Spain!"

The tears had come again to her eyes. She said in a breathless voice: "God bless them!" and pressed his hand hard, before throwing back her head, and striding in. And in the early evening, as the great camp hummed like a beehive around them, and the Queen leaned against her cushions in her high-backed chair, sometimes sipping a little wine and water and sometimes playing with her sword which she had kept by her (though her armour was now laid aside), messengers came spurring urgently, demanding her Majesty's presence. They carried dispatches from the Lord Admiral and Drake, and the soldiers must find breath again to cheer, for the danger was past.

After their crippling losses at Gravelines, the Spaniards did not dare to turn again and fight their terrible adversaries, not even to force their return through the straits; they could not attempt to make juncture with Parma. They went on—in headlong flight. Before them lay the unknown perils of the northern seas as they sought to flee home by a route of terror, round the north-western coasts of Scotland and Ireland, jagged by storms. But to them there was no terror so great as the English broadsides, even though a gale had sprung up furiously to beat upon their already battered remnant. Wrote Vice-Admiral Sir Francis Drake: *"There was never anything that pleased me better than seeing the enemy flying with a southerly wind to the northward. . . ."*

When the dispatch had been read aloud to the Queen and those about her, Elizabeth cried in a high cracking voice: "God blew with His winds and they were scattered. . . ." and then about an octave lower and so softly that only those near her could hear: "God is very merciful . . . to me and mine. . . ." and covered her face with her hands, her shoulders shaking.

She was overwrought, Robert thought. Accompanying her in her coach on the way from the camp to her residence, he heard her talk with a sort of hysteria of how it would now be possible to disband the troops, pay them off and save the drain on the Treasury. He ventured to expostulate. The Spaniards might find their courage again and turn, Parma might yet essay somewhat on his own.

"No, they won't. The heart is out of them!" She added on a light-headed note: " 'Twould be a fine celebration of victory to go bankrupt and pawn the Crown Jewels!" Then that flaming wig was on his shoulder for a moment and she was whispering: "Robin, I am so tired, and I ache in every bone. . . ."

But the next day, when he came to take leave of her on her return to London, she was very calm and collected, and all solicitous for him. Indeed as they looked at each other, each thought the other weary to death.

"Robin, you are ill! My Dr. Goodrowse cured you in the Netherlands. I must have him here."

"I should be glad of his medicine again, dear love."

"I'll have it sent you. What shall you do—when your command ends?"

"Go by easy stages to Kenilworth. By Maidenhead, Rycott and Cornbury. Then when I've rested somewhat I'll take the waters at Buxton."

"You must be well when we celebrate the Victory on Accession Day! I must have my Lieutenant-General at my side. Promise me, Robin!"

"I'll do my best."

"And Robin—thank you for what you have done. For me. For the country."

"I count myself happy to have served either." He had taken her hands. "Your people have justified your belief in them. And remember this. Forever after—they will believe in themselves."

"Robin," she said. "I want you to kiss me."

Zenith

Very gravely he put his hands on her shoulders and kissed her, before giving her his arm to lead her out, past the bowing throng which lined the way to her coach.

She sent the medicine after him on his journey towards Kenilworth with a small personal gift. At Rycott, he wrote in reply, telling her that it did him more good than anything else, and wanting *"to know how my gracious lady doeth and what ease of her late pain she finds, being the chiefest thing in this world I do pray for, for her to have good health and long life. . . ."* She would have wished to rest now; the lifting of the strain had shown how unbearable it had been, but the people wanted to see her on every possible occasion and shout their joy. The land forces were being speedily paid off as the fleet came home in triumph, and she grumbled comfortably with Burghley over the state of the Treasury, but the country's finances were as strong as its men to meet the challenge. And while England rejoiced, the unhappy Armada pursued its terrible homeward path, its Calvary of death and shipwreck, as galleon after galleon, torn apart by great storms, went crashing to doom against those grinding northern rocks. At long last Medina Sidonia and a shattered handful bore the news of disaster to a Spain which had been utterly confident of victory. It made a proud people hang their heads in shame and mourning. Philip the King shut himself up in the gloomy fastnesses of the Escurial, and spoke to no one but his confessor.

A medal was struck to commemorate the great victory, and bore the words: "Flavit Deus et dissipati sunt." God blew with His winds and they were scattered—the most humble and arrogant words ever spoken.

The day before her fifty-fifth birthday, the Queen awoke from an afternoon's doze to find a strange hush amongst her women. She stared; and none would deliberately meet her eye. Then she saw the Countess of Warwick coming forward.

"Anne," she said harshly. "Anne! What is wrong?"

"Your Grace, I have the grievous misfortune to bring you bad news."

"Not Spain—again——"

"Not Spain, your Majesty. My brother-in-law, Robert."

The blood drained out of the Queen's face, leaving the rouge blotchy on her cheeks. She had gripped the tapestry so tightly that her pointed nails tore it.

411

"Your Grace knows how sick and weary he was?"

"Yes! Yes. . . ." It was a hoarse whisper.

"Your Grace, at Cornbury he fell into a continual fever which no remedies could abate. He died on the fourth of this month."

She had sent them away from her for there was nothing that any-one in this world could do for her. She lay, face downwards on her great bed, her arms outspread, her hands clutching at the hangings, clutching at air, at the utter emptiness of existence. She was not weeping. "An old woman's tears are soon dry," she thought.

It was not even the immediate shock. Her whole life had been a succession of such cruel shocks and she had learned to withstand them, although each one took its toll of her. It was the thought of the future, of the aching agony of utter loneliness, of that wound which could never heal as long as she lived. And through that void, memory was reaching to stab her, a memory of a young man in the garden at Hatfield with his arms round her, telling her for the first time that he loved her. And she had said: "Say it. Say it again, Rob! Say all the foolish things lovers do. . . . I'll remember them. When I am alone. When I am old." How had she known? And he had answered: "You'll never be old. Nor alone as long as I am here."

She sat up, shivering although the day was warm.

"But you are not here, my dear love," she whispered. "And I am old. And alone for ever."

From the little chest by her bed, she took that letter he had writ-ten her from Rycott. She did not dare yet to re-read it though she knew it by heart, she—"the chiefest thing in the world" for which he had once prayed. She held it in her hands and then laid it against her cheek as if some of his life still remained in it. Her pens and paper were waiting. She had been going to answer him.

She took up her quill and wrote on it, with deliberation—"HIS LAST LETTER".

But she could not hide herself away with her grief. Her people were rejoicing and she must rejoice with them. November brought a day which recalled her Coronation with the unceasing clamour of the bells. Not for thirty years, not since they had first greeted their new Sovereign Lady, had they rung so. In every church tower in England, they pealed that day, so surely the air must have quivered and vibrated

412

above the entire land from the brazen joyful song, as relays of ringers, primed with good ale, tugged at their ropes. As she lay awake that early morning in Somerset House, at the very gates of London, she could hear the music from its one hundred bell towers, and the tremendous clang from the great cathedral.

> "Upon Paul's steeple stands a tree,
> As full of apples as may be. . . ."

Vast brazen apples swaying up and down! Thirty years ago, she had heard them as a young woman on the day before her coronation, the other side of London, from the Tower. Then they had seemed to celebrate her belief in herself, her five and twenty years' struggle to keep alive and come to the Throne, now they celebrated something infinitely more important, the success of her mission upon that Throne. All the time while her women were arraying her in robes of purple velvet and cloth of gold, the bell song continued. As she stepped out into the forecourt at the head of her retinue, she could hear the undercurrent of human shouting to the peal and clang.

In such a procession as again recalled Coronation Day, she travelled in a triumphal coach, so described by the ancient chronicler: "A chariot-throne made with foure pillars behind to have a canopie, on the toppe whereof was made a crowne imperiall, and two lower pillars before whereon stood a lyon and a dragon, supporters of the armes of England, drawne by two white horses. . . ." And as she travelled, the duel of sound continued between the bells and shouting human throats. At Temple Bar she paused for the traditional ceremony of the Lord Mayor offering her the City Sword and Sceptre, while the City Waits sang upon the ancient gateway, and then on into her capital city, the blue-hung balconies filled with the City Livery Companies, and the roadway packed with the ordinary citizens, so there was scarcely room for the colourful procession of notabilities on horseback, and the chariot-throne, with Gentlemen Pensioners and Yeomen Halberdiers walking on each side of it, to pass. And before the Queen's procession, in triumph were borne the captured banners of the enemy, on to the Cathedral of St. Paul where the Bishop of London, the Dean and fifty other clergy awaited her in copes and vestments of such richness as had not been seen since before the Reformation.

So lay the outward scene before her eyes but she was seeing many other things. The thin lips smiled though she was almost dizzy with sound, and once she had looked behind her when the memory of the coronation procession had become especially vivid, but it was not the young Robert Dudley riding after her but her new Master of the Horse, Essex, leading her caparisoned palfrey, and meeting her turned head with a sudden vivid smile. But human relationships must go back for this hour in a truce to her sorrow for Robert and to her affection for this young man, the last and only personal thing left for her to love. At this time she belonged only to her people, who through their efforts and hers were at long last safe from the dangers she had dreaded and struggled against. Not only that they had defeated, but knew they could defeat, the forces of the greatest king on earth.

Her chariot had halted before the Cathedral's West Doors, and as the young Essex handed her down, the roar of voices reached a final crescendo. She smiled at him and then went on alone towards the clergy in scarlet and gold, advancing to meet her. But her eyes were dimmed as if with tears and she seemed to see the High Altar at Westminster where she had taken her coronation vows. Before the West Doors, she fell upon her knees with her hands raised in prayer, and a sudden silence dropped on the great multitude.

Book Three

SUNSET

" . . . Within the hollow crown
That rounds the mortal temples of a king,
Keeps Death his court; and there the antick sits
Scoffing his state, and grinning at his pomp;
Allowing him a breath, a little scene,
To monarchize, be fear'd and kill with looks;
Infusing him with self and vain conceit—
As if this flesh which walls about our life,
Were brass impregnable, and humour'd thus
Comes at the last, and with a little pin,
Bores through his castle wall, and farewell—king!"

SHAKESPEARE, *Richard II*, Act III, Sc. 2

"Sad it is, that we cannot even keep
    That hour to sweeten life's last toil: but youth
Grasps all, and leaves us: and when we would weep
    We dare not let our tears fall, lest, in truth
They fall upon our work which must be done.
And so we bind up our torn hearts from breaking:
Our eyes from weeping, and our brows from aching:
And follow the long pathway all alone."

THE EARL OF LYTTON: *A Night in Italy*

"Singulariter sum ego donec transeam."

PSALM CXL

Chapter One

Her ears were straining for the whirring clang of steel upon steel, struggling to pierce the creaking and rattling of the unwieldy gilded wood which made up her springless coach, bouncing and straining over the rutted road which led to Marylebone Fields. It was not often that the coach of Penelope, Lady Rich, was out so early in the morning; the hedges were spread with dew-drenched spiders' webs, glistening in the light from the clear, almost white, sky, which had the cool wet gleam of water. The shadows of night had gone and the sun's passion and strength had not yet coloured it. A pale bright light, scarcely of this world, lay upon everything.

But Penelope's whole mind was strained to hear that sound which she already heard with the ears of her imagination. Her eyes looked up with bitter eagerness, past the stolid blue backs of John the coachman and Will the footman, and saw beyond them, as the road curved, the figure of a groom holding three horses under a branching tree. She shouted with impatience, prodding John's broad back.

"Stop! Stop here!"

"Here, m'lady?"

The coach creaked to a standstill, John was staring at her, and Will had sprung down to open the door.

"You will wait here till I come back."

"Come back, m'lady?"

"Yes! No, Will, I don't want you. Wait here, both of you. My brother would have it so!"

One impatient gesture had brought her out of the coach and past their gaping faces, to go through the gate which opened on to a field.

The grass appeared covered with the same white veil which lay on the hedges. As she plunged into it, she could see her feet make dark prints. Ahead of her lay a wood in which the night's blackness seemed to have retreated. Air and light, the faint moist smell of the awakening earth, and the high note of a bird had the same cool remote purity. It brought her back to childhood, and a dawn-early expedition with her brother and sister at Chartley. It was a long time since she had been out in the country so early as this! Last night in the Long Gallery, as the viols throbbed a lilting coranto which matched the hot, bright lights and hot, bright colours in air filled with the smell of candles burning low and heavy musky perfume, she had heard the whisper: "Lord Essex to fight a duel with Sir Charles Blount in Marylebone Fields to-morrow at dawn—a duel to the death!" That had been a world as removed from this unbreathed-upon freshness, as the girl who had once loved Philip was removed from the gay, the daring, the light Lady Rich. Yes! She had once loved Philip Sidney so much that she had believed her heart would break. Perhaps it had broken, and now she was contriving to live without it.

It would be hours before that sodden lump of flesh would awake inside his purple bed-hangings, that drink-sodden lump of human flesh who was her husband, Robert Lord Rich. "Whom God hath joined, let no man put asunder." God? His agents then were the Queen's Majesty, and Lettice her mother. Strange agents for the Deity. But Mother was right as she always was in things worldly. I see him seldom, and he scarcely ever touches me and I can spend his money in a dream of extravagance. . . . Yes, Mother was right. The Children of Mammon are wiser in their generation than the Children of Light. Philip was a Child of Light. . . . What am I? A Child of Mammon, of perdition—the last of the Bullen women?

Then she heard the expected sound, the eager clinking of rapier blades, and picking up the skirts which hung from the grotesquely wide, fashionable farthingale, she ran as she had not run for years. The darkness of the wood was about her and the smell of age-old rotting leaves; she pushed past small, whipping, tearing twigs in something close to panic. Her brother could fence, as he could tilt and ride, better than any man in the Queen's court. But if that strange mind of his should waver, should dart away from his antagonist, as it so often darted away from the bare essentials of life, what might not happen? A bird flying across that pale, bright sky, a jewel swinging from his opponent's ear, might be enough to distract his attention for those vital seconds.

Sunset

She broke out of the wood just as the sun seemed to ride flaming into that cold, innocent sky. Its glow drained all the colour from the world, turning it black, grey and white like a pencil sketch, but it made the shirts of the two men shine like those deadly streaks of steel whirring about them. She stood for a moment clenching her hands, not knowing what to do. Then the sun picked out a golden ornament hanging by a crimson ribbon round the neck of her brother's antagonist. Just as she noticed it so sharply she believed that her brother had suddenly noticed or re-noticed it; it was the distraction she had dreaded. Not that he forgot the fight; his blade swung in wild glinting arcs moved by a purposeless frenzy, all science gone. She realized that one of his horrified rages had burst upon him. Ah! What an opening he was giving. . . . She loved to watch men in the fencing yard, knew something of their art, the Spanish School so ordered and formal in which body and blade must make a geometrical pattern; the Italian School so quick and subtle, no ordered pattern but an infinitely swift adaptation of the opponent's thrust and parry. But Essex was leaving his body wide open and unguarded in his frenzy of attack. She drew her breath in as she saw the thrust coming. Here was a nightmare made real, a nightmare when doom suddenly upreared and one could do nothing. But she did not scream. She saw something else. A look like horror on the other swordsman's face and a desperate move of his wrist, spoiling the pattern of the lunge. His blade ripped the cambric of her brother's shirt and then was stopped from its deadly purpose, swerving down to plunge into the padding of the great bombasted breeches, piercing his thigh, not his side. Essex staggered and then went over like a felled tree.

She ran then as they all moved, and was down on her knees, holding up her brother's head, as the three men stooped over him. She saw Sir Charles Davers, one of her brother's most devoted followers, gaping at her, but her brother himself did not seem surprised. That was typical of Robin, to accept the unexpected serenely but to be astounded by the dull facts of everyday life. . . . But she had no time to think of his idiosyncrasies. As she looked at his leg in the white hose, darkened at the ankle by moisture from the wet grass, she saw the bright, sticky, scarlet flow begin, running down his thigh, past his knee. She pulled up the leg of the puffed trunks and the blood ran freely over her hands. Philip, she thought, Philip was wounded in the thigh. . . . Scarves and kerchiefs were being thrust upon her, she tied one about his thigh above the wound, twisted a sheathed poniard in it to stop the flow of blood, and did not realize that the poniard had been handed her by her brother's opponent.

The flow had become a trickle; she laid her own clean handkerchief folded into a pad over the small deep hole and began to bandage it swiftly and deftly with a long embroidered scarf. If that man had not made that last-moment wrist move deflecting his blade, her brother would now be dead. He was speaking in a voice of anguished eagerness.

"Before God, Essex! I would not have hurt you for all the profits of the Spice Islands!"

Her brother's smile was wide and embracing.

"Nor I, you, sweet lad!" (Thought Penelope: "At this moment he has forgotten the cause of their fight.")

She looked up at the eager handsome face hanging over her and her brother, at the cleanly cut profile and the velvet-soft brown eyes, which were filled with distress, genuine and unforced.

"I saw what you did," she said slowly, and the colour came and went in Charles Blount's face like a girl's. He was staring at her. Her steeple-crowned hat had fallen off and the sun was burnishing her hair like a newly minted ryal. She did not know that Charles Blount thought she looked like an angel in one of the paintings of the Italian School, one of those warm, passionate creatures in whom earthly qualities seem rather magnified than transcended.

Davers was talking of riding to fetch a coach.

"My coach is waiting in the lane," Penelope told them.

"Sweet, good Pen!" said her brother. He had no surprise that she —and her coach—had apparently dropped from the clouds. Getting him to it was difficult; he was tall and heavy and Davers and Blount had no easy task, half-carrying, half supporting him, while Penelope hovered in agony lest the wound should break out bleeding again. It was Blount, she noticed, that took command, arranging how Essex should be best bestowed in the coach, wrapping a velvet cloak about him which he took from his own second whose arms were burdened with doublets, cloaks and swords, peremptorily ordering John her coachman to stop at the first tavern to get a draught of aqua-vitae for his lordship. Then it seemed that they were rattling off, Penelope beside her brother and his late antagonist opposite to him, supporting his injured leg to protect it from sudden jolts. Yes, he was very good-looking, she thought, and obviously so concerned for Robin. He had not waited to put on his doublet and ruff but had loosely slung his crimson-lined blue cloak about his shoulders. She could see now the ornament which hung round his neck by a crimson ribbon. It was a golden chessman, a queen. His eyes followed her glance and he said quietly: "The most unhappy occasion of this our duel."

Essex began: "Pen, Sir Charles was victor at the tilt yesterday, and her most dear Majesty gave him the queen from her set of chess for a favour. I cannot endure others wearing her gifts and cried out: 'Now I see that every fool must have his favour!' 'Twas desperate unmannerly of me"—he held out his hand to Blount, who grasped it—"but I cannot bear to share her." His voice became violent like that of a man drunk or in fever. "I cannot! I cannot share her! She is mine utterly, as I am hers. I can't endure it. Any other between us!"

Penelope shuddered. It was raving. "So", she thought, "a boy might speak of his first love. And this is an old creature of sixty. Oh, it's horrible, horrible!" Blount was speaking calmly and reasonably.

"There can be no question of me or any other coming between her Majesty and you. But she is the centre of our universe and the sunlight falls on all. Likewise she is the source of all honour and award."

Whether Essex heard him was doubtful; his face had gone grey and his head lolled back limply against Penelope's shoulder, when his frenzied words had died away. She could see the dark stain spreading through the improvised bandages, and was thankful for the competence of Charles Blount when they stopped at a tavern, his voice crisp and soldierly, hurrying a drowsy tapster into bringing brandy. It revived Essex enough for him to give another wide smile to Blount, as if to assure him he had no personal antagonism against him, to the contrary! Only no one must dare come between him and the object of his strange adoration. As the coach creaked its burdensome way on to Essex House in the Strand, Penelope made nervous conversation.

"I think you are no relation to our stepfather, Sir Christopher Blount?"

("Fool that I am," she thought. "He is the younger son of Lord Mountjoy. He would consider Kit and his family very small beer.") But he replied calmly: " 'Tis a different family."

At the great doors of Essex House, bustle and turmoil received them. In the crowd of men, she could see her stepfather towering above the others as he and Sir Gilly Merrick, her brother's steward, pushed their way to the front. Essex was cheerful as he was lifted out.

"Am pinked in the thigh—no vital wound!"

"What is that?" Penelope could hear her mother's voice, a little shrill, as all fell back to make way for her. Lettice's figure, in a richly embroidered gown of orange-tawney, was full and several chins rested on her jewelled ruff, but her skin, where not covered with rouge, was smooth and white which set off her hair, bright and metallic with dye.

She was bending over her son, all solicitude and love. Her daughter looked at her with cynicism, her thoughts running somewhat after this fashion.

"Yes, it is true he was always her favourite child. Not that she really cared for any of us. She would never suffer us to discommode her. Since we were handsome children it sometimes pleased her to have us about, thinking we enhanced her charms, and of us all she would always choose Robin. Certainly he was the most lovable. I was very young when I saw through her as if she were a pane of glass, but he never did. Truly, he never does comprehend other people. . . . He forgets how, when our father died and we were left so desperately poor—he was the poorest earl in England—she took every penny for herself, to put on her back. She was starting to hunt down Leicester, while her son's tutor at Cambridge wrote to his guardian, Lord Burghley, asking for money as it was not seemly that his young lordship of Essex should go well-nigh ragged. But Robin has forgotten it. And now—perhaps it is not all play-acting. Since the Queen began to dote on him, *she* too has begun to dote!"

Essex was smiling up at his mother.

"I have lost no more blood than any barber-surgeon would take from a lusty customer!"

Men were carrying him shoulder-high towards the great carved stairway, as Penelope touched her mother's sleeve.

"He *has* lost much blood. A dangerous quantity!"

Lettice raised her eyebrows slightly at her daughter, hatless and dishevelled, with her hands and sleeves bloodstained, and yet managing to make such things negligible by that glowing loveliness. The admiration of the strange gallant, with his cloak slung over his shirt, was palpable. Lettice had not lost her eye for a pretty fellow; she smiled, thinking her daughter flaunted her indiscretions like a banner.

"The physician will be here in a matter of moments," she said.

Penelope paused at the half-open door of her brother's great bed-chamber. There was still a small crowd about him, his Gentlemen of the Chamber and pages trying to get him into bed, and Lettice presiding over all. Penelope could hear her voice.

"Nay! Do not jerk him lest you set the blood flowing again, cut the hose from him."

Yes! He would be safe in those plump capable hands whether she truly loved him or not, Penelope thought, as she leaned against the tapestried wall in sudden weariness. Her knees were shaking. Charles Blount was leaning towards her.

"I feel I have no right to be here," he said, "in the midst of his household. But I am so truly concerned to learn how he does."

"You have the right." She did not know what made her say: "Better a chivalrous antagonist than a false friend!"

"I would not be his enemy of all men living! I do bitterly regret this duel——"

"He insulted you! Though I am certain he had no personal animus against you. It is this most strange desperate adoration of her Majesty—which is beyond my understanding."

"Her Majesty is a marvellous woman—and even though she seems to thwart him at times, there can be no doubt of her devotion to him."

"Of the two, that is more comprehensible. . . ."

She seated herself in an "X" chair set against the wall of the galleried first-floor landing, and beckoning to a passing serving-man, told him to bring wine for them.

Blount was talking with eagerness.

"Your brother is the leader to whom all ardent spirits are looking. They say—I think truly—that the mantle of Sir Philip Sidney has fallen upon him."

She winced; that wound was still raw. She sipped her wine and then gained control of herself.

"I do not see the resemblance—between my brother—and Sir Philip——"

"That same chivalry surely, that high nobility of soul?"

"Yes," she admitted. "There is the same chivalry, the same horror at the baseness, treachery and greed of mankind, the same incapability of a low or mean action. But the rest of their approaches to life are utterly different."

(She thought: "Philip, for all the richness of his imagination, was disciplined. He had a strain of the austere. He seemed to embrace pain as he embraced his glorious—useless!—death. At such pain my brother would swerve, startled. His thoughts are undisciplined. He is borne by his impulses here and there. I once compared him with a bird. He is like that bird which flew into the hall at Chartley, and swooped here and there, dashing itself against the high walls, in its vain search for freedom.")

"The Great Armada is defeated. What then?" said Blount. "Our ships are paramount upon the seas. The country is more prosperous, more rich and comfortable than even in the early days of her Majesty's father, and yet there is a strange dissatisfaction in the land. With fullness and satiety has come a weariness of the spirit, a boastfulness, a greed, a venality. The old chivalric ways are forgotten."

"You would agree with that eminent Puritan divine who preached to the household here, two days ago. He compared England with Jeshurun who had waxed fat and wicked."

The latest in a procession of pulpit-thumping divines—they had always been in the midst of the most fervent of the Puritan party. Her grandfather Knollys had been a veritable pillar of that party which had so strangely combined with those eager and adventurous young men who had once taken her stepfather Leicester for their leader, united by their common desire for furious warfare upon Spain. Her mother had learned to dissemble her natural paganism before that stern old man, her own father, though she had at times startled and amused her children by imitating the forceful preachers afterwards. But she had once declared that she loved them for the sake of the mutual hatred obtaining between them and her royal cousin. Penelope would never forget that occasion when her mother's obvious rapture had excelled Leicester's embarrassment, at a preacher who was furiously condemning the Queen for not giving more help to the co-religionists in the Low Country, accusing her of the sin of Laodicea.

"I know thy words, that thou art neither cold nor hot. I would thou wert cold or hot. Therefore, because thou art lukewarm, it will come to pass I will spew thee out of my mouth!"

Always, thought Penelope, our lives have been entangled with the

Sunset

Queen's. My mother, my brother and myself, my first stepfather and Philip, his nephew and my love. Our existences have been bound and ordered by that woman, we could not break free from those chains of love and hate, riveted by her caprice. . . .

And here was Charles Blount, once again joining the Queen's name with her brother's.

"It is your brother who can lead the country back to nobler ways. The Queen is a wonderful woman but she is old. But when her favour and affection rest so strongly upon him, what might he not do?"

"He might do anything—truly. But not with the Queen. Not——"

She paused as Sir Gilly Merrick hurried by, one hand grasping the arm of the physician in his long black gown.

"But of natural course with the Queen! Is she not the centre of our universe, our veritable sun? And for the balance, set the wisdom of her age against the impetuosity of his youth, her caution and prudence against the nobility of his high endeavour and you shall have a wonderful compound——"

"Oil and water do not compound!" She looked up at him and knew that here was a beginning, not an end between her and this man.

"One day, I will tell you much, to explain—the dread of her Majesty which I have."

People were eddying out of the bedchamber now, past the tall figure of Sir Christopher Blount, standing like a sentinel. Lettice's voice could be heard speaking incisively to the physician. In the gallery, up the stairs and in the hall below, so many were waiting in apprehension.

("Yes," thought Penelope, "it is true, Robin is the leader that all the young men look to. What an immense household he has, how they flock to be his Gentlemen, of the Chamber, of the Horse—clerks in the Secretariat working upon the secret intelligences gathered by Anthony Bacon. All that is bold, adventurous, striving, hopeful, greedy—all that hold the ardour of life, come to him!")

She turned to Charles Blount.

"You will stay and dine? My brother would wish it. . . . I am certain of it."

"You are most good. But I am scarcely attired——" He looked down at his shirt as if he was aware of it for the first time. Penelope beckoned to one of her brother's Gentlemen of the Chamber.

Sunset

"Master Tracey! Will you take Sir Charles to a room and provide him with clothing and anything he may require?"

Blount's lips were pressed hard on her hand before he turned to go. She could hear her brother's voice, raised as if in echo to her present thoughts. ". . . a chivalrous knightly foe! A most gallant antagonist!" She walked in, to the Great Chamber. Essex was now bandaged and between the sheets in the huge bed whose four posts were silver cherubim, seeming to hover over him in protection. More prosaic and earthly, his mother and his physician stood, watching him with a different calculation. In the background, Gentlemen of the Chamber were taking away bloodstained clothing and bandages. Several of the household had pressed in after Penelope, past Sir Christopher still standing in the doorway like a soldier on duty. One was aware of the crowd beyond the door. It was like the levée of a monarch, with the great angel-pillared bed for a throne. Essex was talking with feverish excitement.

"I do not know whether she does such things to try my devotion! She can try it seven times in fire, seventy times seven. . . ."

Penelope could see her mother clenching her hands, driving her nails into the palms. But Lettice knew better now than to curse the Queen in front of her son. Essex went on.

"When she holds me back, bars me from gaining glory—for *her*! When she raged at me for sailing on the Lisbon expedition, when she prevented me going to aid the Huguenots—she said: "I'll not have you go like that inconsiderate fellow Sidney. His life was wasted, knocked on the head——" It was Penelope's turn to clench her angry hands. So that was how the Queen spoke of Philip! Did she know how *she* had wasted his life? "If she had given him one-half—no, one-quarter—of all she has lavished on that man Raleigh—that wretch as my brother calls him—Philip would be alive to-day, and I married to him. Oh, how I hate her! I blame her a hundredfold more than Mother. Mother did her best for me according to her lights. I understand her better now. And if such were her lights—it is the Queen's fault again!"

There seemed a stir in the crowd on the landing without. An usher came through, and hesitated on the threshold.

"The Lady Sidney craves news of his lordship. She would see his lordship——"

"And most glad I am to see her ladyship!" Essex cried.

426

Sunset

"This", thought Penelope, "is too much, that this woman also must fasten upon Robin. She who stole Philip—his 'sweet child' as he called her—demure, sly creature who took what should be mine! She may not have had his dreams, his passion, his verse—but she had *him*, all his tenderness. . . . And she took advantage of Robin's devoted admiration for Philip, of his knightly protection of his hero's widow when he escorted her back from Arnhem. . . ."

The slender figure came in, her blue-grey farthingale swaying. She dipped a half curtsy to Lettice, her sleek, dark head bowing. Then she went up to the great bed, and it seemed that she had banished all the others, and they two were alone.

"Robin, I am so grieved to find you wounded! Sir Charles Davers acquainted me of your hurt."

She had taken one of his hot hands in both her cool ones, as he murmured: "Dear Frances!" She addressed herself to the physician.

"Is not his lordship somewhat fevered?"

"Indeed yes, my Lady, but since he has lost so much blood, I hesitated to bleed him——"

"Of course! But should he not have complete peace and quiet?"

Scarcely understanding how it was done, the human tide found itself eddying back, out of the great bedchamber till Essex was left alone with Frances Sidney, the physician and one page. Outside Penelope turned furiously to her mother.

"She is right! But it is you or I who should have done it! That sly Puritaness! Setting her prim cap at Robin. . . . Must she always be wife to England's hero?"

Lettice raised her brows.

"You are overwrought. . . . Robin sees nothing but Gloriana, the Faerie Queen. Our sweet Cousin Jezebel!"

"See her! But he cannot see her as she really is——"

"He sees no one as he really is!"

"If he did! He talks of her as if he were her lover——"

" 'Tis a spiritual relationship, they are soul mates!" Lettice was grinning bitterly. "A novelty for her! But one day he shall see her as she is, see her cruelty, her greed, her vanities, her cheatings and lyings —to match her appearance, the painted old death's head, padded out in fantastic clothes, spangled with jewels—and hardly a hair left under that wig, her teeth black and rotten, for years a running sore on her leg—the Faerie Queen! And yet that poor weak fool, Leicester, crawled back to her at the end—when he was finished. As he lay dying, it was of her that he spoke! And he was scarcely cold when she swooped like a vulture upon me to recover all the money she had lent him—stripped me bare!"

Thought Penelope: "He was scarcely cold when you married Kit Blount and bedecked him with Leicester's jewels and finery!"

She asked: "Mother, was she ever beautiful? When she was young?"

"Only in her own thoughts!" With grudging, Lettice added: "But she was a clever wanton and could catch a man. She held Robert Leicester for ten years—no easy task! She was not ill-looking. . . . But always too thin." Lettice contemplated her own ample curves with satisfaction. "How delighted she'll be with to-day's work! Two young gallants fighting over her deathless beauty!"

Before the Queen went to dine in Whitehall Palace, the news was brought to her. She had demanded the whereabouts of the Earl of Essex.

"Your Majesty had flung him into the depths of despair and fury by giving a favour to Sir Charles Blount!" said a quick, smooth lady-in-waiting. "He could not endure to see your Majesty so much as smile on another man. This morning they fought most desperately in Marylebone Fields and he is wounded."

"Seriously?" The Queen's voice was sharp as she leaned forward in her chair, tightly grasping the arms.

"He was thrust in the thigh, your Majesty, but it is not dangerous."

The tense figure seemed to relax. She said harshly: "God's death! It was fit that someone or other should take him down and teach him better manners!"

Those about her thought that her most imperious Majesty was sometimes tyrannized over by her young cousin and favourite.

Chapter Two

The Lord Treasurer was going to see the Queen's Majesty. The Gentlemen and Ushers of the Privy Chamber bowed low and opened all doors, as the old, old man, leaning heavily on his stick and on the slight, deformed figure of his son, passed by. For thirty-five years he had been her chief minister and closest adviser, for thirty-five years they had held these intimate conferences when the two shrewdest minds in the land weighed and balanced the affairs of State behind closed doors. He came out seldom now, but when he did, immediate access to the Queen was his without asking; if the exercise of it was no longer palpable, his power was still immense. He was the last of his generation in power, the generation which remembered the uneasy England of forty years ago, the poverty, the uncertainty, the dangers which had overhung the young Queen at her Accession. The Earl of Leicester had gone, the most talked-of man in his day, his exact relationship to the Queen a perpetual question-mark, his brother, the Earl of Warwick, had died the following year, and next to follow had been the Secretary, Sir Francis Walsingham, that deep, clever and fanatical man, and Sir Christopher Hatton, who thirty years ago as a law student had stepped a galliard so elegantly, and died Lord Chancellor. All these had gone, also the Queen's first Lord Chancellor, Sir Nicholas Bacon, the brilliant Sir Nicholas Throckmorton, Sir Henry Sidney and his Lady, the Earl of Sussex, and Mistress Blanche Parry, principal Gentlewoman of the Privy Chamber. The grim chorus of the Scottish poet might have echoed through Whitehall in the ears of the Queen.

"Timor mortis conturbat me."

"You think, sir," murmured Robert Cecil in his father's ear, "that her Majesty will discuss with you the disposal of the vacant Attorney-Generalship?"

Sunset

"We will discuss it, I have no doubt. Dispose of it, yet, I know not."

Robert Cecil's pleasant smile did not alter but he was thinking: "The old woman's disposition to dally and procrastinate grows worse with the years. She seems to like to keep offices vacant, or at least not bestow them officially. Since Sir Francis Walsingham died *I* have virtually held his position as Principal Secretary, with the conduct of foreign affairs, but I am not given the name, nor the full power, nor the full emoluments, though I do the work. . . . It is possible that it is caused by her thrift—in giving power as well as in giving money." Her tendency to delay he might deplore but he could understand. He too could bide his time. In this noisy world where the strutting peacocking champions seized so much, if one was born with any disadvantage in the race for power, if one was a woman, or a cripple or deformed, one had to bide one's time till these magnificent virile heroes over-reached themselves, and then one reaped the benefits of a waiting game. Just as such men as Raleigh and the Earl of Essex despised—or pitied and despised—him for his hump-back, statesmen had once—long years ago—despised her Majesty for her sex. Had not his own father often told of how, in those early days, he had never believed that a young woman of twenty-five could comprehend the weighty business of State? Now of course, nothing could exceed his father's admiration for her Majesty's qualities of mind, which went with a genuine devotion to her. The devotion was not shared by his son. Her Majesty was an interesting study—no more.

"My cousin, Francis Bacon, has written to me, sir," he told his father. "In this same matter of the Attorney-Generalship. Asking my good offices."

"Francis", declared the Lord Treasurer, "lacks both the years and the legal practice for such a position. Now the Solicitorship—that is another matter. How answered you, Francis?"

"I assured him of my goodwill towards him but advised him to invoke the aid of the Earl of Essex. The Earl has already promised him the position."

"Promised him! Oh, temerarious, headlong and foolish young man to promise aught which lies within the Queen's will!"

"Certainly, sir, it may well make her Majesty go to the contrary."

"If she knows of it—and there is little she does not know—it will for a surety make her go to the contrary. . . ."

Sunset

A Gentleman Pensioner was lowering his gilt-headed battle-axe in salute at a door, as an usher proclaimed: "The Lord Treasurer, the Lord Burghley, craves to see her most gracious Majesty!" Maids of Honour in gleaming white satin dipped curtsies. Burghley smiled and patted the cheek of a granddaughter before he made his way towards an inner room and that unmistakable voice which said: "My Spirit! Come to me!"

Robert Cecil did not accompany his father to the inmost sanctum. He settled himself with his usual sweet patience in a highly carved chair, prepared to wait hours if need be. He knew he was of no interest to the elegant and well-bred young women who waited upon the Queen and so he paid them no more attention than politeness demanded. If he had been the Earl of Essex or Sir Walter Raleigh, they would have been round him like bees around a honey-pot, he knew well.

Sir Walter had, indeed, gone too far, to his own misfortune and the abrupt cessation of his climb to greatness. He had seduced one of the most attractive of the Maids of Honour, Elizabeth, daughter of Sir Nicholas Throckmorton. It was said that he, the Captain of the Guard, had climbed over a roof and entered the Maids of Honour's quarters by a window. There had not been such a scandal in the Coffer Chamber (as the Maids' Withdrawing Room at Whitehall was called) since that bold piece, Mistress Anne Vavasour, had given birth to an illegitimate child by the Earl of Oxford, therein. The Earl had been sent to the Tower, and so last year had Sir Walter, together with his partner in sin. Her Majesty had been incensed. The unchastity of the Maids reflected upon her and her court, and she had the disposal of their marriages. Moreover, Sir Walter had shown such adoration for her person that it had been believed that he would stay single for her sake like the late Lord Chancellor Hatton. But she was more than incensed when they persuaded the chaplain of the Tower to marry them. If her Majesty and the Lord Robert Dudley had really made love in those grim walls forty years ago, it had not made her sympathetic to other lovers therein. But then she and Lord Robert had never achieved matrimony. . . . Nothing enraged her more than a runaway love-match.

Cecil beckoned with a curved forefinger to his niece, the recent object of the grandfatherly pat. The Lady Elizabeth de Vere was the daughter of that Earl of Oxford who had once seduced Mistress

Vavasour; he had always been an atrocious husband to poor Anne
Cecil. Their daughter was now one of the youngest Maids of Honour.

"Well, my child!" said her uncle. "Has his Lordship of Essex been
with her Majesty this morning?"

"Not this morning. Late yesterday afternoon just as her Majesty
was going in to supper. Perhaps that is why her Majesty sent him
away so soon."

"Oh, so her Majesty sent him away? No doubt she did not wish to
be kept from her supper!"

"Perhaps. . . . He was shouting—the way he does—and her
Majesty said: 'Go to bed, Robin, go to bed! And awake in another
humour. . . .' Then when he was in the ante-room he stamped his
foot and threw open his arms like *that*—and declared: 'I'll not endure it! Human flesh cannot bear such!' " Elizabeth de Vere stopped
short. She was aware of the black glances of her companions for telling tales on the hero and darling of the Coffer Chamber. That lus-
cious beauty, Elizabeth Southwell, who adored his lordship so openly,
looked savage.

"His lordship is a little excitable," suggested Cecil sweetly, "and
it was provoking for her Majesty to be kept from her supper!"

A little excitable! Elizabeth de Vere thought her uncle as usual
had made an under-statement. Neither Edward Alleyn on the boards
of the Rose, nor Richard Burbage on those of the Globe, could rant
and storm and pour out high emotion as did his lordship. He had no
fear of shouting at her Majesty, of passionately upbraiding her, as no
one had dared in mortal memory. Sometimes on these occasions, a
devil would enter into her Majesty ("You mean her usual devil is
joined by seven others worse than the first, as in the parable," said
Elizabeth Southwell), and she would taunt and goad him into such a
frenzy that he would burst from her presence and run headlong forth.
At other times, these storms ended in sweet reconciliation, his lordship's handsome head on her Majesty's lap, while she brooded over
him like a maternal hawk. ("A vulture, you mean," said Elizabeth
Southwell.)

The doors of the inner room were closed. The Queen and the Lord
Treasurer were seated in high-backed chairs with a table between
them covered by a gold-fringed carpet-cloth. As time crept upon her,
she seemed to shrink and retreat into the serried gorgeousness of her
apparel. Farthingale and ruff became wider and wider, sleeves swelled

Sunset

beyond the circumference of the normal human body, her Majesty was lost within them, and it was impossible to calculate her form. Only the women who dressed her knew that she was a skeleton, still covered with skin but almost devoid of flesh. Between the flaming impossibility of the wig and the width of the cartwheel ruff, the world could only see a carefully painted skull, domineered over by that high, arrogant, hawk-like nose; but from their deeply sunken sockets, the dark, glowing eyes were disquietingly alive. One thing alone time had scarcely touched, her long, beautiful hands. Their skin was drier and the blue paths of their veins more distinct, that was all. But Burghley did not see her as she was now; his eyesight was dim and the picture of the vivid young woman of thirty-five years ago was perhaps more clear than the present. They had been together a long time, she and he, and she was not young any longer, but though in her sixty-first year he could not see her as old.

But she saw him more distinctly and a cold hand tightened on her heart. So much and so many had gone, she dreaded losing him. Her inquiry for his health had a deep earnestness. He was tormented by the gout, he told her, and often could neither walk nor use his fingers for writing. The waters of Buxton and Leamington now did him little good.

"Spirit, I am truly sorry."

"I am most sorry in that it prevents my serving your Grace as I would do. My only consolation is that I have trained my son Robert to do all that I possibly could in that same service."

That little deformed creature? She reflected upon him. Yes, he was wonderfully clever and carefully trained. He had evidently inherited that perfect efficiency which had brought order thirty-five years ago into the chaotic disorder of the State; which had disentangled issues financial and political in the light of cold reason and had always chosen and taught the right subordinates to carry out his policy. So she had always found William Cecil, Lord Burghley, and if he had been timid and over-cautious, there had been plenty of reckless spirits about her to set in the balance. But he had a heart, this old man, the years had given him an unfailing devotion to her. The son had skill in statecraft, but a heart? She doubted it.

"Though you have trained your son to be as like you as possible," she said, "you are to me in all things, Alpha and Omega."

"Your Grace is very good to me. . . ."

Sunset

"Then I but repay good with good."

She remembered the first time she had found that affection, when Amy Dudley's death had startled the world. She had nearly broken down completely to her councillor. He had put his hand on her shoulder. "There. . . ." he had said. "There. . . ." And evidently that kind hand had found her too thin, to judge by a remark he had made several days later. She burst out now with an impulsiveness which recalled that young woman she had once been.

"My Spirit, do you recall how once you told me that I should drink plenty of cream for the sake of my health?"

"Certainly, your Grace. Your Grace was very slender as a girl, but you were somewhat angered with me, and declared you had no wish to grow fat."

"I was considering my father in his later years," she explained. Would Robert Cecil ever tell her to drink cream? She doubted it very much. "But there is a cream of the spirit—shall we call it? Loving kindness, of which my life has had little. So what I have had, I recall."

"Your Grace had an unhappy childhood."

"Boethius tells us that the blows of misfortune strike us to a better shape and adversity is our best teacher. I am working on a translation of 'De Consolatione Philosophiae'. Since there seems not to be an adequate one, I am making one for myself."

"I should indeed be interested to see your Grace's translation. Unhappy is the man who cannot learn from adversity. But alas! There are many such in this age."

She thought : "He means Essex. Will he ever learn—or is he utterly unteachable?"

"There seems a strange venality of soul amongst the young men," he said after a pause. "When one considers the candidates for some post, one must often hesitate in the face of proved ability when it does not seem accompanied with true principle."

"My Spirit, I believe you are considering the Attorney-Generalship?"

"I think it should soon be filled, your Grace."

"But would it not be better to wait and be sure of finding the right man?"

"I could scarcely find myself in more agreement with your Grace."

"Nevertheless, I do not doubt you have a candidate in mind?"

Sunset

"Yes, your Grace. Your Grace's Solicitor-General, Edward Coke. He has a most profound knowledge of the law and is a forceful personality."

"You do not then support the candidature of your nephew, Francis Bacon?"

"I do not, your Grace. My nephew, Francis, is a man of theory and lacks legal practice. He also lacks years."

"So does Edward Coke."

"He is nine years the senior of Francis, your Grace."

"Your nephew, Francis, has considerable ability."

"Considerable, your Grace. But he was one of the young men to whom I referred. Those who show high ability without equally high principle."

"You think he lacks principle?"

"I believe at the very base of his being, there is a lack of principle. . . . A lack of true feeling."

She leaned her head on one hand. She thought: "I believe that also. And of your son, Robert! But you would never see it." Aloud she said: "You interest me. The Earl of Essex is extremely anxious for me to give the Attorney-Generalship to Francis Bacon."

"The Earl of Essex is a young man, lacking experience."

"And principle?"

"I would not say so, your Grace. I would I might say it of those around him."

"I also!"

"There are many wild, discontented, and greedily ambitious young men about him, your Grace. My nephew, Anthony Bacon, the elder brother of Francis, has established an information service from the Continent——"

"And the information is remarkably accurate. Lord Essex is well informed on foreign affairs. He speaks knowledgeably at the Council."

Burghley inclined his head.

"In that Secretariat, there are many dangerous intriguers. There is one Henry Cuffe, a man cynical, a born plotter, devoured by ambition. Then there are many young noblemen who have an attachment for the Lord Essex which they should reserve for their Sovereign. The Earl of Southampton——"

"Lord Essex's cousin."

"Then there is the young Lord Mountjoy who has just succeeded to the title."

"A gifted youth!"

"He has a liaison with the Lady Rich, your Grace."

"Those girls are as precious sluts as their mother before them!"

"The Lady Rich is held somewhat as a light woman, your Grace. And his lordship's mother——"

"Is a strumpet!" said Elizabeth fiercely. She added more quietly: "But Lord Essex has such a generous devotion to his family, he lets them exploit him. He lets many exploit him. These young nobles, these clever intriguers such as Cuffe——"

"And many wild and worse than wild young men, your Grace. In Essex House there are many disbanded captains from the Low Countries and Ireland—swordsmen and bullies. I think of veritable bravos who would sell their swords to the highest bidder and stop at nothing, men like Owen Salisbury and Thomas Lea."

"So you do not like the background of Essex House for your nephew Francis? Nor do I. I am not disposed to trust those within. The pity is that his lordship's very nobility of soul prevents him from seeing through his associates. And he is ever too generous."

Burghley knew better than to find fault with the Earl of Essex. She continued: "And I did not like that speech of Francis Bacon in the House of Commons. A man of his ability—and it was an able speech I'll not deny—must know that the subsidy is essential."

"It was a mischievous speech, your Grace."

"Truly mischievous! A bid for cheap popularity. First he exploits the general prejudice against taxation, second, with more subtlety, he exploits the pride of the Commons against the Lords' interference when the Lords proposed a conference on this same subsidy. 'Twas clever—and unprincipled!" Leaning forward on the table, she began to speak with a swift earnestness: "My Spirit, you know as well as I that the revenue of the Crown is not enough to maintain the burden of my government! Even if God in His mercy would grant us total peace, I doubt if it were enough. But now the House of Valois is extinct, can I let Henri of Navarre and his Huguenots be crushed by the Guises and Spain? An' I did, who would raise the loudest outcry? My faithful Commons and the men who voted for them! Then I must assist the Low Countries still, although never was anyone sent such a bottomless drain! I must maintain the fleet lest Philip send yet another Armada. I must keep order in Ireland. . . . Though it is my people who clamour most for a vigorous policy, I have sought to keep much of the burden of these wars from them—have I not sold Crown lands? Have I not sold my jewels? Even so I have needed the subsidies—and so I am called greedy and grasping! Because I have cut my expenses to the very bone, I am called parsimonious! The country is more rich and prosperous than ever it has been before, but its Queen scarcely knows where to turn for an extra angel! And yet the principle is—no direct taxation voted by Parliament save for exceptional times. Against a Spanish Armada, an Irish rising, a war overseas, they will vote a subsidy. Not otherwise. But the time will come, and must come soon! When the government of the country can only be maintained by regular taxation voted yearly by Parliament. And that will give both Houses the right to direct and shape policy."

"Which will be fraught with peril, your Grace."

"Verily! While I am yet here, I can handle my faithful Commons. For they *are* faithful in their hearts to me, and I think they love me a little. . . ."

"Perhaps they know somewhat of how I love them, and how I would spend my all for them. . . ." Her mood changed. She laughed. "And can I not play the diplomat? My worst struggle with the House was after the birth of the King of Scots, when they declared that unless I marry or appoint a successor, they would vote me no money that year, and I had sore need of it! The whole country was humming like an overturned beehive! I had arrested one of the most intransigent Members—and the wrath of the rest exceeded all things! But I gave way with grace, I released this Master Dalton; with my hand on my heart, I craved pardon for offending against their ancient privileges, and I declared I needed but two-thirds of the subsidy promised. Then all was done!" Her smile became wide and embracing. "I am not yet married, nor have I yet appointed my successor. . . ."

"It is true wisdom to know when to yield."

"But when I am no longer here, and another sits in my seat who neither loves nor understands these my people—then I have dread!"

"Your Grace must not talk as if you were old!"

She looked at him. She was surrounded by sycophants who told her that she had made a compact with Time and her beauty was ageless; she told herself: "I yet possess some quality which can dazzle them, hold them, make them forget my years. . . ." But this man spoke from his heart. She laid her hand on his swollen, gouty one.

"Your Grace will bear in mind the filling of the Attorney-Generalship?"

"I will constantly bear it in mind."

At that very moment, his lordship's candidate was dismounting at Essex House. Master Francis Bacon did not live therein like his brother Anthony, he dwelt in chambers at Gray's Inn with several retainers, half servant, half companion, beautiful dissipated young men, whose extravagance was adding to his mounting debts. His debts indeed had become desperate—if only Essex might clinch the matter of the Attorney-Generalship with her most capricious Majesty! He stood for a moment, after handing over his beast to a groom, surveying the scene with those delicate sparkling hazel eyes, which were somehow faintly reptilian. An enemy was one day to say that he had the clear, bright eye of a viper. The yard of Essex House was full of gallants, some watching horses or hounds being led up and down, others with hooded hawks on their wrists. It pullulated with vigorous young life, that vigorous young life which gathered around his lordship, those ruffling blades "knights of the Order of Essex". Her Majesty had been enraged at the number of knights he had made during the campaign in France. Master Bacon reflected that this had been perhaps the crowning mistake in a campaign filled with mistakes. Essex had at last persuaded her Majesty to let him lead the force she sent to the aid of Henri of Navarre. He arrived with a retinue adorned in full panoply of his colours of orange and gold so that the beholders gaped. In the friendly rivalry of athletic contests before Henri IV, Essex "did o'er leap them all". But while military affairs went from bad to worse, he risked his life, hawking behind the enemy's lines. At the siege of Rouen, he challenged the Governor to mortal combat, the winner to have the city. 'Twas a page from Froissart, reflected Francis Bacon. But the Governor was, deplorably, not a champion from Froissart; he declined the challenge.

As Bacon entered the house, several more gallants wrapped in cloaks that were brave with gold and silver lace, came thrusting out, their patrimonies on their backs, their futures mortgaged to the fortunes of the Earl of Essex. "As mine is," thought Bacon moodily. He knew what had barred his rise, the jealousy of his uncle Burghley who dreaded that his nephew's brilliance should overmatch his de-

Sunset

formed son's. No help had come from her Majesty's chief Minister for his nephews, two of the most gifted young men of an exceptionally gifted age.

An usher came forward—"His lordship is in the library, Master Bacon, I will conduct you thither"—and preceded him over the rush-strewn floor of the great hall. On one of its many tables, sat a young fellow, swinging his long legs in their carnation silk hose, as he strummed a lute in accompaniment to his song, the ballad of the moment. Other voices joined his for this verse or that, of the "Lamentable Ditty of Mr. Page's Wife", and the song was punctuated by the rattle of dice from another party at the far end of the table.

> "And Plymouth proud, I bid thee now farewell.
> Take heed you wives, let not your hands rebel;
> And farewell life, wherein such sorrow shows,
> And welcome death, that doth my corpse enclose."

Lusty young voices of men who lived for the moment, roared out "welcome death". However many gentlemen did Essex maintain? If her Majesty had not granted him a most profitable monopoly, the farm of the customs on the sweet wines, he would be bankrupt by now, thought Bacon. As he ascended the stairway, in the wake of the usher, he could hear the first singer alone, in a clear and true tenor.

> "And thou my dear, that for my fault must die,
> Be not afraid the sting of death to try:
> Like as we lived and loved together true,
> So both at once we'll bid the world adieu!"

In sweet melancholy, the notes floated away in the air. They titillated the ear of Francis Bacon, but his mind reflected: "Essex was to see *her* yesterday. If there had been good news, he would surely have sent!"

It was a family gathering in the huge library, shown by the light pouring in from the long window, in the middle of which was the shield of Devereux quartered with Bohun, Ferrers, Bourchier, Rivers and royal Plantagenet. The master of the house, leaning forward against a desk used to prop up great folios, had plunged his hands into the wild confusion of his dark auburn hair. He was not yet dressed but wearing a furred silk chamber gown. Beside him, her hands folded in her lap, her eyes dark pools of quietness that watched his every movement, was Frances his wife, who had been the widow of Philip Sidney. All the others were watching him; Anthony Bacon with a glance of sombre devotion, his gouty leg swathed in flannel and resting on a stool, Penelope his sister sitting in the window-seat, swinging one foot in her gold-buckled shoe with nervous irritation, Lettice his mother in a cushioned chair, rigid corseting struggling with her ample body. Over her hung the long figure of her third husband, Christopher Blount, a jewelled chain which had once belonged to the Earl of Leicester ablaze against his black satin doublet.

Essex looked up as Bacon entered, his large dark eyes tired and tormented as if they had gazed into the weary hours of a sleepless night.

"Francis," he said. "I have not yet done that matter for you! I have not *yet* persuaded her Majesty. Yesterday she began by arguing in sweet enough reason—you were too young, you lacked experience —and I declared that such a man as you scarce needed experience, you were born with such knowledge within the walls of your skull——"

"My poor Francis!" called Penelope Rich in a voice crackling with nervous exasperation. " 'Twas your speech in the Commons against the subsidy! When you said the gentry must sell their plate and the farmers their brass pots e'er it be paid."

Anthony Bacon looked sadly at his brother.

" 'Twas an excellent speech, and much commended in all parts of the House but——"

"But not commendable to her most Gracious Majesty," took up Lettice.

"It is Burghley," said Francis Bacon. He had expected it, but he had gone pale.

"The old fox!" said Anthony.

"The old vixen!" retorted Penelope. "Who can never make up her mind! Who never has, and is too old to learn now."

"You mistake yourself, my child!" declared Lettice. "An' she wants a thing, she makes her mind up swiftly enough! 'Tis when *others* want, that she hesitates! She plays with their desires, as a cat with a plump mouse between her paws. Oh, no! She'll not eat it yet, nor will she let it go!"

"No, Mother," said Essex. "No. . . ."

"But yes, my poor boy! She knows your hapless devotion, she

delights in goading you, in tantalizing you, you are the bear in the pit, the bull in the ring, for her to bait!"

Indeed as he raised his tousled head and stared about him, he did look like a tormented beast facing his persecutors.

"In the end she drove me from her in angry impatience——!"

"And laughed and laughed at the sport you gave her!" cried Lettice. Frances Essex made an almost imperceptible movement towards her husband. Her eyes stared levelly at her mother-in-law.

"No!" he said, but there was pleading in his voice.

"My Lord, you have been very good——" began Francis Bacon, pale-lipped and bitter. Essex tossed back his hair from his eyes.

"Good! And I have done naught for you. But I will!" He suddenly sprang to his feet, and threw his arm round Bacon's shoulders.

"Francis, dearest man! I will have it for you, I will! I pledge myself. Her Majesty will not deny me in the end—she is like the Lord, she chasteneth those she loveth——"

"She—loving!" cried Lettice.

"Her Majesty is devoted to Robin," said Frances Essex with a quiet hard emphasis, "but she may have the most excellent reasons for wishing to give the post to another candidate."

"None other so worthy!" cried Essex. "Francis, don't think I'll abandon you! I will struggle further. I would rather die than fail my friends. It shall be done."

He was smiling now, and his smile was like the sun coming out from a heavy cloud.

"My friends are so dear to me, I can only count it joy to struggle for them. My dear Anthony, my dear Francis—you are the two I would help above all others!"

He still had his arm round Francis, and was giving his other hand to Anthony. An enormous warmth and strength like sunlight itself seemed to be pouring from him. He was suddenly filled with energy and confidence. For a moment an unguarded look crept into his wife's still face, a look of agonized protective tenderness.

"You'll dine with us, Francis?" Essex next demanded.

"The dinner is wellnigh ready," said his wife. Essex seemed to realize for the first time that he was in his dressing-gown.

"I do apologize for this my attire!" He was making a bow to his wife, mother and sister, before he added with childish simplicity: "I was so troubled that I forgot."

Sunset

Penelope thought: "It's not because he has not yet grown a beard or that his hair is on end—I think it's something in his eyes—he does not look a day over seventeen and he is five and twenty!" She gave her sister-in-law a glance which was returned, of flat distaste.

"Why had Robin to marry her?" she thought. "To bring her here —to remind me of Philip, to drag open that wound, to see her child and Philip's playing in this house, to remember that Philip died in *her* arms. . . . I'll not look back—like Eve looking back at Eden! Why should I suffer? I want to lose the past in loving Charles. . . . That seeming unhappy duel brought my brother a devoted friend, and to me the only man I have loved except Philip. Surely I am entitled to some happiness!" Let her remember Charles Mountjoy telling her how he had loved her since the day of the duel, quoting Marlowe's line—"Who ever loved that loved not at first sight?" But a shadow fell on that memory cast by Frances Essex's cold eyes. "I know she says: 'How did Philip ever think he loved that wanton?' But he did. . . . And let her contrast the two men she married with the one forced upon me! That cold Puritanical judgment of hers has neither mercy nor understanding! But I will concede that she can give Robin rest—and peace. . . ."

Essex had gone out and a tension went with him. The room seemed suddenly quiet and flat.

Chapter Three

Twelfth Night at Whitehall. Viols and recorders pouring their sweet plaintive notes into the hot air, bright colours swirling, musky perfumes swirling; numberless wax lights burning, golden collars and jewels seeming to burn between the carved, fretted and gilded ceiling and the gigantic chessboard squares of black and white marble flooring. The long tables of the Presence Chamber had been cleared away under the reverent supervision of countless officials bearing white rods. The golden plate had been carried off from which the diners had eaten, the bubble fantasies of Venetian glass from which they had drunk, the immense salts, golden ships and towers and mythological deities which had dominated the tables. The entertainers had gone; tumblers in scarlet, whirling supple limbs, ballad singers pouring out in anguished delight the struggle of youth and love against death, rollicking mummers, the apotheosis of those to be found all over the kingdom, clattering their hobby horses and jingling their bells, the flapping dragon which the silver-clad Sir George must slay, puffing out fireworks, a strange contrast to the elaboration of the masque, whose performers in their rhyming couplets filled with a hundred classical allusions, praised Gloriana. The tables and the ceremonial panoply of dining having now gone and with them such entertainers, the court entertained itself with the dance.

On a high throne, beneath a gold-fringed baldachino, the Queen watched them. The poets had not lied when they proclaimed her ageless; she was neither young nor old, that glittering figure did not belong to time at all because it was completely unreal. She might have been an image borne high above a procession of enraptured worshippers. The only signs of humanity were those watching dark eyes and the long hands which tapped the rhythm of the measure on the

443

carved arms of her throne; sometimes a foot in a diamond-buckled golden brocade shoe joined them tapping. Music, the dance, these had always been two of her principal pleasures. Below her the great throng shifted and changed in the lovely flowing movements over the black and white squares of a giant's chessboard. Some of the dancers glancing up at the throne thought that the brilliant figure in black and gold looked like a fantastic chess queen; the Black Queen with the White King beside her. The Earl of Essex, standing by her, was in white from head to foot, broken only by his golden collar and the blue and gold Garter buckled below his knee.

"You should dance," she said, her eyes leaving the dancers for his tall figure.

"I would be here. Don't send me from you!"

Her thin lips smiled but she did not answer at once. The colourful figures were springing lightly up and down in the quick and merry rhythms of country dances, dargasons, jigs, almains and heys, the dances for the very young who were light of foot and of heart. And the tall youth beside her was begging her to dance with him!

"Or have I craved too much favour?"

"Yes!" She saw a startled look come into his eyes, like an affronted child's. She took his hand and laid it between both of hers.

"Not from me! From that figure who carries the scythe and hour-glass. . . . There was a time when I could have danced with you, danced away the hours till the sun came to mock the candles, but you were scarce born then!"

"But you have made a compact with that figure. The sand may run through his hour-glass countless times but his scythe cannot touch you."

The black moods, the rages, the wilfulness had left him. They had filled her with anger and a strange dread. How dare he storm at her, arrogant boy? She saw danger in any yielding to his imperious will, and danger, too, in giving posts of responsibility to any of his followers who had such blind perilous devotion to him. And yet how easy to understand that devotion—how easy to love him. . . .

She still danced, sometimes "six or seven galliards of a morning". But she danced in her Withdrawing Chambers with a few chosen associates; it was a long time since she had danced before a great audience, on such an occasion of high ceremonial. She had been one of the best dancers of her time, she could not bear to fail, to be slow, heavy or stiff. . . . And then to pay the price in aching exhaustion. . . . Not for her these frolicsome country dances, nor the Lavolta with its high springs or "volts", or a dance nearly as active, the Coranto, called the Dance of Love, for the gentleman must kiss his partner's cheek in the last figure. Memories here, of Hatton breathless and enraptured as if he were really saluting a deity, and Robert Leicester who would always kiss her lips instead of her cheek. And here was this young man of whom her reason sometimes wondered were he Robert's son, just as an errant imagination let her pretend that he was hers. Dance with him? Perhaps a galliard—her thin lips compressed—or a pavane, stateliest of all dances.

"An' they play a pavane, you may lead me."

He had gone down on one knee to kiss her hand in gratitude.

"Let me bid the musicians play one."

"When they have finished this set. I would watch. . . . Though they do not dance so well now. There is whirling and confusion, and they do not hold the true pattern and harmony of the dance. Ah! When I came to the throne, there was such dancing as is not seen now. Night after night here in Whitehall. . . . There was one Sir William Pickering, who was said to be the handsomest man in the realm and the best-loved of all the ladies. I would have him lead me sometimes and there grew up a foolish rumour that I wished to marry him." She laughed. "In his youth Lord Keeper[1] Hatton was the best dancer in England and then there was your stepfather, Lord Robert Dudley. . . . There are no such dancers left now!"

"Why was I not there then?"

"Better not," she said cryptically. But she would not answer the query in his eyes and tell him her thoughts. The young Elizabeth had found Robert Dudley hard enough to handle, how could she ever have handled this headlong passionate creature? But his thoughts had taken another of their birdlike swoops, he was speaking of music, of his cousin Lord Hunsdon (the son and successor of the old Lord) who had a musician John Dowland who had written a wonderful Pavane.

"My musicians play the music of Master Dowland. Your cousin— *our* cousin!—bestowed on me some of his compositions. Go, speak with the Leader of my musicians. Has it a name, this wondrous Pavane?"

[1] In contemporary talk the Lord Chancellor was usually called the Lord Keeper, i.e. Keeper of the Great Seal.

Sunset

"Most surely, dearest Lady. 'Tis the first of a series of seven, and Master Dowland calls them the Lachrymae Pavanes. . . ."

More than fifty years ago, Kate Ashley had told her that such a cold shiver as this meant that someone was walking over the place where one day your grave would lie. . . . Strange boy! The Pavane of Tears, why had he chosen it?

The music was pouring into the air, showing that sorrow has its own beauty, its own splendour of ritual. Essex was smiling at her, bowing as he asked: "Most dear Queen, will you bestow happiness by gracing me with this Pavane?" A hush fell on to the multitude as she gave him her hand and let him lead her on to the floor, and into the solemn and stately measure of the dance, that dance which was drawn from the proud pacing of peacocks.

Sir Robert Cecil, unobserved as he leaned against the tapestried wall, watched the two leading figures of the Pavane with misgiving. His father, the aged Lord Treasurer, had spoken to him, before leaving town for the peace of Theobalds, his country estate, telling him of her Majesty's decision on the vexed question of the Attorney-Generalship. It had become so much more than the problem of the merits or demerits of Francis Bacon and Edward Coke; it was the symbol of a vast conflict. After listening to his father, Robert Cecil had hugged himself in thought; his smile became sweeter than ever. But now as he watched the dance, he felt the chill of apprehension. The Queen after all was a woman, and women were romantically inclined; he liked them to be romantic, charming—and foolish. He was truly sorry for some of them, for Elizabeth Raleigh, née Throckmorton, who wrote so pleadingly to him to help her adored Walter. But there could be no question of pitying Elizabeth Tudor; one could only watch with apprehension. . . . She seemed yielded to the pleasure of being handed through the formal movements of the Pavane, to delight in the presence of her partner. She might give him anything. It would be woman's nature to do so. That storied, labyrinthine intelligence of hers could challenge any masculine one, but at this moment, suppose that she surrendered to a simple impulse?

A week later, he could smile at his own fears. As he stood in the doorway guarded by a gigantic Yeoman Halberdier, waiting for his coach to come, he saw the Earl of Essex striding with a furious indefiniteness over the smooth gravel. The main road ran through the vast, wandering Palace of Whitehall, a collection of buildings, some

446

beautiful, some ramshackle, which seemed to grow rather than be built. Like Hampton Court, Henry VIII had snatched it from his fallen minister, Wolsey, to replace the ancient royal palace of Westminster destroyed by fire, all except its great hall. Where the main road ran through the royal precincts it was laid with gravel and carefully and repeatedly rolled. But his Lordship of Essex was kicking up this smooth gravel. He was lost in thought, swung by emotions which tossed him about as his heavy white velvet cloak was tossed by the sudden gusts of the icy wind which whipped round corners. Cecil watched him narrowly, till he saw his own coach come rolling under the arch. Then he advanced, an all-embracing smile on his face, and touched the thought-lost Earl on the sleeve.

"Might I give your Lordship a seat in my coach? I am going to the Strand."

Essex stared at him for a moment, blankness succeeded by curiosity. Then this, too, faded.

"I thank you, Sir Robert."

As they entered the coach, Cecil reflected that doubtless some page or gentleman of his Lordship was even now anxiously seeking him, bearing his hat and gloves, and some Gentleman of the Horse waiting with his charger. The coach rolled on, under Holbein's famous arch and into the royal suburb of Westminster, with its venerable Abbey, the ruins of the old Palace of Westminster beyond, the Houses of Parliament, the Great Hall, and the riverside mansions of the nobility and diplomats. Cecil looked at Essex who was staring straight in front of him. A strange exultation filled him; he could not contain it. It rippled through the notes of his voice.

"The Attorney-Generalship is to be filled next week, at long last. I pray your Lordship to let me know whom you will favour?"

Essex turned, and his baffled glance might have been that of some beast brought to bay—a stag encircled by hounds.

"You are surely aware that I stand for Master Francis Bacon, your cousin?"

Cecil smiled, but his voice was at once surprised and sarcastic.

"Lord! I wonder your Lordship should be about to spend your strength in so unlikely or impossible a manner." The smile widened. "If your Lordship had spoken of the *Solicitorship*, that might be easier of digestion to her Majesty."

Essex cried out: "Digest me no digestions! For the Attorneyship for Francis is that I must have!" He struck his knee furiously, it was all he could do not to throw himself upon the smiling little man beside him. That deformed little creature—it would be like striking a woman. . . . His large, dark eyes seemed to grow larger and glow. They were extraordinary eyes, reflected Cecil, so dark that it was difficult to judge their colour, and yet strangely luminous. In the faces of his Lordship's mother and sister, these dark glowing eyes had cast enchantment. He realized with a start that the very same eyes—although narrower and now deeply sunken—looked from the face of her Majesty. . . . To trace their origin, you had only to contemplate a portrait of one who though she now lay in an unnamed grave in the Tower chapel, had once been Queen of England—Anne Boleyn.

But Essex was shouting at him in a great passion of hurt rage and indignation: "And in that I will spend all my power, might, authority, and amity, and with tooth and nail defend and procure the same for him against whomsoever!" His whole body was shaken with fury, he uttered threats against any other who should take the office. The rage, the indignation and the curious quality of boyish innocence came to a climax with these words: "And for your own part, Sir Robert, I think strange both of my Lord Treasurer and you that you can have the mind to seek the preference of a stranger before so near a kinsman!" Reproach drowned anger in those large, dark eyes. Sir Robert Cecil lowered his own; he made no reply to this outburst and a heavy silence succeeded in the coach. At Essex House, where the coach halted, the Earl said abruptly: "For this journey in your coach, Sir Robert, I thank you!" and then sprang out, striding headlong, his cloak drifting behind him, his bare head tousled. Cecil made an almost involuntary gesture of deprecation with his hands. This furious and unbalanced young man knew nothing of compromise or bargaining; a whirlwind could reason as well as he.

In the great hall of Essex House, the abrupt entrance of the Earl and his obvious state of distraction, caught the immediate attention of his followers. Lutes, dice and cards were thrust aside, and as the news spread into the yard and stables, horses, hounds and hawks were forgotten, as all the young men crowded about him, Sir Charles Davers at his side: "My dear Lord! What is wrong?" Essex rarely restrained his feelings. Whether in prayer to her Majesty or amongst his followers, he was accustomed to pour out his ideas and emotions.

"It's not to be borne!" he shouted. "Her Majesty assumes affection for me, and yet she intrigues against me behind my back with the Cecils!"

"The old fox and the young fox!" declared Davers, leading the chorus of angry voices cursing the Lord Treasurer and his son.

"To-day, I demanded from her a definite answer as to Master Bacon, and she evaded me, put me off, told me she was yet pondering the matter. But she had evidently settled it with the Cecils—with that little creature whose mind is more crooked than his body—him she confides in, not in me—who worships her!" His voice rose to a yell, overtopping all the other voices which were clashing as angrily as if they were brandishing the blades at their sides, demanding an end to the domination of her Majesty by the Cecils, to sweep away the counsels of the old, the dodderers, the traitors!

"But her Majesty is also old. . . ." said Henry Cuffe, who had left the library where he had been working, summoned by the uproar. It had brought Frances Essex out of her chamber, to gaze in dismay over the balustrade of the gallery. Robin in one of his frenzies and the others inciting him, heating his brain, stirring up his rage, when he needed calming, soothing, diverting. . . . Then she became aware of another leaning on the balustrade, looking down, and saw the slow smile spreading on her mother-in-law's plump, rouged face. There was the real enemy, who would soon, quietly and deftly, with that rich caressing voice of hers, pour acid into his wounds, and inflame him by a dozen insinuations against her Majesty. That terrible lasting hatred between these descendants of Mary and Anne Boleyn—lazy, sensual, easygoing Mary Boleyn who had lost a crown and kept her head, and her ruthless, ambition-devoured sister who had laid her crowned head on the block—had they once hated each other, those two, that the daughter of one and the grand-daughter of the other should be mortal enemies? Or was it that long battle over the Earl of Leicester? A man whom Frances's Puritanical young mind had once severely condemned as utterly worthless, till she too had fallen momentarily under the spell of his charm. When Philip had died at Arnhem, what wonderful tenderness he had shown her! "And yet," she thought, "and yet he would not even pay Philip's debts after his death, so his funeral was delayed till my father, who could ill spare the money, paid them!" Leicester, at once the most tender and most selfish of men, the most understanding and most heartless, yes, a woman *could* love him but she ran the risk of breaking her heart. That whispered mysterious tragedy of his first wife—either murdered or driven to suicide by cruel heartlessness—and the Lady Stafford, once Sheffield, who was now half melancholy-mad—women who had loved and trusted Robert Dudley and had had their hearts broken. Had the Queen and Lettice hearts to be broken? The Queen was inscrutable. But Lettice had no heart left or she would not endanger her only son by so driving him against her enemy. . . . She remembered Philip's serious young voice: "My Aunt Lettice is an abominable woman." But he would never say a word against the uncle who had failed him so often. His last letter from Holland to her father, contained the agonized sentence: *"My Lord of Leicester, you know I will not judge!"* Philip had loved his uncle, and in his strange manner his uncle had loved Philip. It was not hypocrisy, he had been heart-broken at Philip's death, though he had done so little for Philip in life. There had been that letter which had so enraged Lettice when she had learned of it. Essex had told Frances about it before their marriage. Leicester had written: *"This young man, he was my greatest comfort next to her Majesty of all the world——"* Leicester, that monument of infidelity, proving that he was faithful after his fashion. . . . The Queen and he, who would ever know the whole truth about them? She remembered overhearing her mother ask her father: "Was the Queen in her youth truly Lord Leicester's mistress?" And her father had answered: "God knoweth. . . ." But she must have loved him, thought Frances, else she would not have forgiven him in the end. He had betrayed her as he had so often betrayed Philip, those two for whom he had cared more deeply than for any others. Philip had always forgiven him, and she had, at long last, after years of estrangement and despairing fury. An idea came suddenly which Frances's sternly trained Calvinistic mind found alarming. If human beings could forgive Lord Leicester for his sins and treacheries, perhaps the Lord God could also forgive him. . . . But what a legacy of hatred he had left behind him!

She looked down with despair at her husband's face, pale and upturned as he cried out his anger against the Cecils, his grievance against her Majesty. The excited heads and faces bobbing around him were like rough waves amongst which he must drown. But he was drowning in those ancient passions, those old loves, those old hatreds, ghostly and yet bitter, as strong as death, floating around him. Once she had thought she could take him away from them, give him the peace he needed, but that dream was fading. He had this wild, boundless ambition which was perilous to any but a crowned head, which would never allow him the peace of obscurity. Add that to these legacies of ancient passion, to his fantastic devotion for the Queen which might swing round suddenly to a fantastic hatred, to the enigmatic character of the Queen, to the ambitions and greeds of all those eager, ruthless young men about him, and add it finally to the character of Lettice. . . .

He was coming up the stairs now, his face still pale and damp with sweat, Davers, Christopher Blount, Henry Cuffe and Merrick around him. Frances moved to meet him with a feeling of impotence. She could do nothing at this moment, but there was one who could . . . and would. Lettice was also moving towards him, saying: "Robin, my dearest boy!" How prevent a mother from sympathizing with her son?

By the evening his brain was boiling, as he lay tossing between the serene figures of the four silver cherubim at the corners of his bed. All his life, he had been subject to these strange attacks; let him have some mental shock, let his imperious will be thwarted, let someone he loved hurt him . . . and he was in high fever followed by complete collapse for days. They had done their worst, thought Frances, his mother and that bright-haired shameless creature his sister—whom Philip had once loved!—(and her own hatred for them frightened her, it was sinful to hate so much!)—Christopher Blount their echo, that bitter-tongued man, Henry Cuffe, and Davers and Merrick with their blind devotion for him, their anger if he did not get what he wanted. These had all heaped fuel on the fire.

At last they had all gone, leaving her alone with him. Night had silenced that turbulence under the roof of Essex House. He lay so heavily and profoundly asleep that he might be dead. She sat in the carved chair, by the fire banked with sea-coal, only one candle on the table by her elbow. The clock ticked, coal fell in the fireplace, once some draught shook the green tapestries. Time was passing so slowly away that it might be infinity. Moonlight was slanting through an ill-drawn curtain to fall in a pool of whiteness on the floor. The precision of her nature made her get up and draw it to; besides, people said that it was dangerous for moonlight to fall on the sick. She was standing with her back to the room when she heard him give a long shuddering sigh, and came swiftly over to the bed. His eyes were wide open; against the unnatural pallor of his face they looked black and enormous. This was surely not one of the best jousters in England, the young Paladin who had ridden to war in France. He was as weak and helpless as their baby son. . . .

"Robin?"

"I am thirsty. . . ."

She gave him milk to drink, and clasping his hand on the cup, found it as cold as ice and clammy.

"You are cold?"

"Yes."

She went to the next room, where Tracey slept in his chair, and gave him orders to transmit. Bricks must be heated to be wrapped in flannel and set to his Lordship's feet; a hot posset prepared. Back in the bedroom, she cast logs on to the glowing mass of coal, and they burned up suddenly with a crackling, leaping flame which cast a ruddy glow on the silver cherubim. She heard his voice saying: "I am cold to my heart. . . ." When the stir occasioned by the arrival of the hot bricks and the posset had died down, and he was sipping, he began to talk in a slow dreamy voice. Usually by the time he had passed to the cold collapse which succeeded the sudden fever, he was purged of the emotions which caused it. But now that burden still lay on his brain.

"The Queen," he said. "Can it be true as my mother thinks, that she enjoys tormenting me?"

"Remember", she told him, "that your mother hates the Queen very greatly and so cannot impute any good motive to her. Why does your sister also hate her Majesty so much?"

"Because she believes that the Queen prevented her marriage to Philip. If the Queen had given him some high office, my mother might have let her marry him."

Frances drove her nails into her palms in her effort to keep silent. "Thank God, Philip died before he could know how vile she is, shameless creature, living here in open sin with Mountjoy her lover!" went her furious thoughts.

"But I love the Queen," he said. "She has so rare and extraordinary a mind. She is the only person who understands me. In some way we belong to each other."

"You are related closely in blood."

Sunset

"Do you know what she once said to me? I was sitting on the floor, leaning my head against her knee and she asked me: "Would you wish to be my son?" And I answered: "Truly. . . ." She put her hand on my head and I could hear her sigh. Then suddenly she changed, she was harsh, bitter and mocking. "Of a verity, you would! To be Prince of Wales and heir to the throne! God's precious soul, you would!' I told her: 'Surely, Madam, any man would wish to be a king. But at that moment I was not thinking of the crown, I was thinking of you.' And she answered me: 'I wonder. Oh, I wonder!' "

"I believe her Majesty has a true affection for you. Remember that her position forces her to be suspicious of motives."

"But not of mine! If those incarnate devils poison her mind against me——" he was raising himself on his pillows, gasping. Gently she pressed him back against them.

"Robin, you must rest, you must not excite yourself!"

"I say to you if I found those who were separating her from me, I would kill them with my own hands!" Exhaustion seemed to seize him. "They must not hold us apart, she and I together what might we not accomplish?" It was a low intense whisper. Then he added with a strange sort of dismay: "But she is old. . . . It's true what Cuffe said! She's like some strange image that has gone on through the ages, smelling of musk and spices, the paint caked thick upon her face— no living, loving, warm flesh. . . . But her hands are still as young and beautiful as when Leicester loved her. . . ." His whisper died away, he lay limp, his forehead cold and wet. She started to rub his hands in anguish, and re-arranged the hot bricks. He began to murmur again: "Why will she not accept when I offer her the best brain in the land? Francis is the most rare man, it is true when he said he had taken all knowledge to be his province. . . . He is such a genius as is seldom seen!"

"My dearest," she said, "I can only counsel you this. Since the Attorneyship is likely to go to Coke, ask for his vacant Solicitorship. 'Tis my belief Lord Burghley would not oppose you. He might assist."

"Surrender? Grovel to those? I would rather die!"

"Not to them. To her Majesty, our sovereign. Which is of natural course. And you would help Francis."

"Help I shall! I will not have him suffer. I will give him my manor at Twickenham."

453

Sunset

"Submit to her Majesty, and strive for the Solicitorship. . . ."

"No!" His voice gradually died away and became indistinct. "The best . . . for Francis . . . only the best for her, for the kingdom . . . for her and for me!"

Chapter Four

The Maids of Honour were craning at the door of the ante-
chamber, their ears agog and straining, Mistress Elizabeth
Southwell going white and crimson by turns, and muttering such perilous things against her Majesty that the others
shushed her in agitation. The long, running battle between the Earl
of Essex and the Cecils over the Attorneyship had reached a new
climax in the matter of Dr. Lopez, the Queen's physician. He had
always been a strange, foreign, enigmatic figure, Ruy Lopez, the Jew
of Portugal, and now he was suspected of being in a Spanish plot
upon the Queen's life. He had got intimate with followers of the Pre-
tender to the throne of Portugal, Don Antonio, to whom her Majesty
afforded half-hearted succour, as he might be useful against Philip of
Spain who occupied his kingdom. Now it had been found that
some of these penniless followers of Don Antonio had been bought by
Philip of Spain, and looming behind the obvious plot to murder Don
Antonio, was the shadow of a conspiracy upon her Majesty's blessed
person. Spain, plots, murder, these words had been linked together
for years, and the names of the conspirators sounded satisfyingly
foreign and sinister—Ferreira da Gama, Tinoco, Gomez d'Avila,
Manoel Louys and Andrada—enough to conjure up menacing figures
slinking into this country, wrapped in deadly secrecy, emissaries of
the wicked King of Spain and the wicked Pope, perhaps even Jesuits
and certainly possessing horns and tails. . . . So the Maids of Honour
had whispered excitedly in corners, ever since it seemed that Dr.
Lopez was implicated. The Jews were a most extraordinary, sinister
and mysterious race, and nobody knew very much about them as they
had been driven out of England hundreds of years ago. Dr. Lopez of
course was officially converted to Christianity. . . . One girl whispered
that Jews practised the most terrible black magic in their religious

455

rites and sacrificed Christian babies, another that they were closely connected with the Jesuits, though she could only produce as proof of this, that both were children of the devil! But all these strange happenings had got mixed up with the feud between Essex and the Cecils so that the Maids of Honour were listening at the door behind which his Lordship shouted at her Majesty, and her Majesty shouted back at him, and Sir Robert Cecil watched in silence, and they could all imagine that smile which they could not see. . . . No doubt, he was sheltering behind her Majesty's huge farthingale from the fury of Essex!

For the plot had been discovered by the intelligence service of the Earl of Essex which was so ably directed by Master Anthony Bacon, and already had administered so many slaps in the face to the official intelligence service under the direction of Robert Cecil. Dr. Lopez had been arrested and Essex had exerted his right as a Privy Councillor to cross-examine the man himself. A preliminary examination by the old Lord Treasurer, his son and Essex had ended in disagreement. The father and son had not thought Lopez guilty of anything but undue familiarity with the conspirators who were, after all, his fellow-countrymen; Essex persisted in holding him guilty, and had carried off the doctor to Essex House to be further cross-examined by himself and those brilliant young men, the brothers Bacon. Now he had returned to Whitehall to storm at her Majesty. But her Majesty stormed back.

Did she not call him "rash and temerarious" and how dare he bring accusations against an innocent man which he could not prove? The listeners could hear the royal anger swelling till it drowned his lordship's. The Queen's voice had become harsh as it always did in one of her dreaded tempers. "God's death! 'Tis my honour that is at stake!"

"The hateful old hag!" muttered Elizabeth Southwell, "when he is striving for her safety!"

"Sh-sh-sh!" came the horrified chorus. Then came her Majesty's voice like the crack of a whip.

"Out! Out of my sight!"

The doors opened, and the Maids of Honour scattered. Lord Essex did not bounce out like a tennis ball as he sometimes did after a scene with her Majesty; he did not throw his arms up and shout, but came swiftly and in deadly silence, seeming to skim rather than walk in his rapid progress. His face was as white as the proverbial sheet and his eyes as black as coals. He was hardly out of sight when her Majesty marched out of the inner chamber. Perhaps she caught a flicker of defiance in the eyes of Elizabeth Southwell, perhaps she had even heard her remarks—one could never be sure what she overheard—for she slapped her face very deliberately, once on each cheek. Her Majesty always hit hard and as she wore so many rings it was not at all comfortable. Elizabeth de Vere who was timid, was very glad that she had so far managed to avoid her Majesty's wrathful slappings. She thought her uncle, Robert Cecil, looked exactly like a cat who has finished a bowl of cream. He was actually thinking that his father was over-anxious to anticipate any danger from Essex; give his lordship enough rope and he would hang himself in time. It was a marvel that her Majesty stood as much as she did.

Her Majesty thought that also, as she sat at dinner, crumbling a manchet of bread, and staring moodily at the nervous girls serving her. Her brain, her sense of sovereignty, her well-tried statecraft, were appalled by him. But she did not see how she could do without him, he was the only human being left to her for personal love; she knew her terrible need for love which had been so cruelly treated by life. A strange need in the Tudors—those ruthless, self-deified, arrogant creatures—they were devoured by that insatiable longing. Her father, whom she had known only as a bloated giant, tormenting and tormented, what misery he had caused his six wretched wives! And yet surely they had caused him even greater. . . . Her mother and her mother's cousin Katherine Howard, both of whom he had had beheaded, had hurt him as much as any living person can hurt another. She had known exactly how he had been hurt, on that ghastly day when Simier had revealed Robert's secret marriage. . . . Whispers came out of the nightmare shadows of childhood—the once gay and lovely Katherine saying before she laid her head on the block: "I die the Queen of England, but I would rather die the wife of Thomas Culpepper," and how the King had burst into tears before the horrified faces of his council when he had ordered her death—*her* own mother whose name he would not allow spoken after *her* death, but when he lay dying and all believed that life was extinct, he had suddenly heaved himself up against his pillows and cried out in an agony —of love, or hate, or a twisted mixture of both?—"Nan Bullen! Nan Bullen! Nan Bullen!" and spoke not again. And her unhappy sister with her unhappy love devouring her, dying broken hearted. If the Tudors were great sinners, they paid greatly. It was true that all these things came in earthly life, heaven, hell and purgatory, whether they did or did not fill the great void of death.

She had forgiven Robert Leicester because she needed him, and they had had a year or two of peace and comfort before he had died. He could always soothe her, for though he rarely knew her inmost thoughts, he always knew what she felt. But young Essex was the antithesis of soothing!

She glared at the girls about her and hated them very savagely because they were so young. Young love could suffer agonies but it could find such simple assuagement, as Robert and she had, thirty years and more ago. "There isn't one of my maids", she thought, "who wouldn't be in Essex's arms if he crooked his finger." But she who was not fanciful had to pretend either that she was young again, or that she was his mother. And now it seemed a devil had entered into him, against which her reason warned her. Why could he not be the gay charming boy with whom she had sat up till the small hours, playing cards in the sleepless nights before the Armada came? Or as he had been after Robert's death, when he had scarcely spoken any words of comfort, but had put his head in her lap as if he knew that terrible need for something to love? Or as he had been a few weeks ago on Twelfth Night, leading her out in the Pavane, making her feel that the years had all slipped away and she was five and twenty again? But a dreadful little inner voice demanded of her : "What can you and he ever be to each other? You are not his mother. . . . You cannot be his love!" She writhed away from it. She would not look at her face now in a mirror, she did not want to see what it had become. Why did her mind hold up mirrors which were so much worse? And now she felt so sick and weary and her head ached unbearably—when that impossible young man had deprived her of the best doctor she had ever had!

Later she was told that he had gone straight from her to his own chamber in Essex House, locked himself in and refused to see or speak to anyone for two days. She frowned ; made a sarcastic remark or two, and inwardly was deeply troubled.

Two days the Earl of Essex cut himself off from the rest of the world, even from the patient Frances, before he re-emerged, just as he was, in a chamber gown, unshaven, his hair not brushed, and joined

Sunset

Anthony and Francis Bacon, in their remorseless interrogation of the prisoner. They were both brilliant and ruthless cross-examiners, but they admitted that the Earl, this time, excelled them. He was inspired —by some strange dæmon—hurling piercing questions that seemed to thrust into the very soul of Lopez. That secret reserve was cracking, that superior little half-smile was no longer flickering on his lips, the dark eyes were no longer containing a hidden knowledge, they were the panic-wild eyes of a trapped beast. . . . Lopez began to stammer out an extraordinary story, of being a double spy, of being employed by the late Sir Francis Walsingham to deceive the Spaniards, of Spanish payments and a ring of ruby and diamond drawn from the finger of the King of Spain, of an affectionate embrace from that august and terrible personage. The brachygraphy writers—ancestor of modern shorthand—hastily scribbled down the unbelievable statements. Anthony Bacon looked from his brother to the Earl of Essex. This story of being secretly in Walsingham's pay was fantastic, and Walsingham being dead, could never be confirmed; but here was enough for a committal for trial—and trials for high treason led invariably to the scaffold. Lopez had confessed that the Spaniards had offered him large sums of money to poison her Majesty; he had confessed to receiving a priceless ring from the very finger of King Philip. . . .

Back in his great bedchamber, the Earl was being dressed by his Gentlemen, but he was filled with such excitement that they had a hard task trying to truss the points which secured his sleeves and great bombasted breeches to his doublet, as he threw about his arms and legs. How could one dress his hair or set his ruff when he jerked his head so repeatedly? He was crying out wildly that even now when he had this confession how could he convince those "devilish" Cecils, who would sacrifice her Majesty's precious life, to save their own faces and authority?

A look of tenderness came on the sombre face of Anthony Bacon, showing his devotion to this young man, for whom he worked without respite both his ailing body and brilliant mind.

"My Lord," he said. "As to my cousin, Robert Cecil, I think you speak truly, but my most worshipful uncle, the Lord Treasurer, is another matter. We know him—his cunning and greed for his ancient privileges and how he will cling to them——"

"The old fox!" interjected Francis.

"Aye! The old fox! Yet the old fox has a heart. Somewhere he has a true affection for her Majesty. Appeal to that, my Lord, and I believe he will heed her danger."

"If he supports you," said Francis Bacon, "then *her Majesty* must heed her danger...."

A clerk came in with a roll of parchment. The report in brachygraphy had been copied out in a fair Italian hand while his lordship dressed. Essex snatched it.

"I must go at once!"

He seized his cloak from a page and forgot the plumed hat being offered him at the same time; another page who was buckling on his Lordship's rapier was almost overturned, as he sprang forward, dropping his perfumed gauntlets on the floor. As he ran down the staircase, shouting for his black Andalusian mare, they noticed that he had forgotten his boots and was still in velvet slippers. When the mare was brought hurriedly round, he vaulted on to her back, and drove his spurless heels into her ribs. His Gentlemen of the Horse were now running about in the same agitation as his Gentlemen of the Chamber had been; shouting for their horses and their boots, tumbling into the saddle, and spurring raggedly after his Lordship, who was going down the Strand at an extended gallop, his white cloak fluttering from his shoulders.

When he burst in upon the Lord Treasurer and his son, the latter reflected that he had never seen his Lordship of Essex quite so dishevelled. His hair was often on end during one of his emotional scenes, but now his ruff sloped one way, and his cloak another, till it almost fell from his shoulders, one of his silken nether-stocks [stockings] was split above the ankle, doubtless by his stirrup iron, as all he had on his feet were mud-splashed velvet chamber slippers. He was waving a roll of parchment as he exclaimed: "My Lord, I beg you, whatever opposition there has been between us in the past, to take heed of this most deadly peril which has encompassed her dear and precious Majesty!" His face was white and shining and his eyes were filled with tears. Burghley was inevitably moved.

"I beg that your Lordship will explain! Anything which touches her Majesty's welfare or safety, is as important to me as it is to the entire realm. You believe her to be in great danger?"

"In such danger as she has not been since Anthony Babington his devilish conspiracy! I will go further. I think this more perilous than the plots of Babington, Throckmorton, Parry or any other. For there was always some difficulty for an assassin to gain access to her presence, though her most princely courage and trust in her people has always made her take risks——"

"Indeed!" said Burghley, kindling, "It would be the most grievous thing if her love and trust for her people was ever abused!"

"Here it would be abused in truth and by an assassin in most close and confidential attendance upon her, possessing her absolute trust— a veritable snake in her bosom! I beg you read the account of this latest interrogation of Ruy Lopez!"

When the Lord Treasurer and his son had read the report from beginning to end, they did not question it, or argue. Burghley indeed was moved by the thought of the Queen's peril, Anthony Bacon had guessed rightly. Robert Cecil thought: "He has struck my father in his most tender place, his devotion for the Queen. . . . Is it by chance or was he so advised? After these disclosures, we must proceed, it would be too risky to oppose the prosecution now. But how unfortunate! The influence of Essex will be trebled!"

"My Lord," said Burghley, "we must at once to her Majesty."

The court was astounded by the spectacle of the aged Lord Treasurer arm in arm with the Earl of Essex who was hurrying him at a pace which his old and gouty feet found uncomfortable, and following them closely came Sir Robert Cecil. Something truly portentous must have occurred.

Elizabeth always knew the inevitable though her supreme art was perhaps postponing it. If her faithful old Spirit with his years of wisdom, and his sharp, shrewd son, who was so opposed to Essex, now both agreed with him, she would not resist them to her own peril. She did not exactly have an affection for Lopez; she was used to him, she appreciated his skill, she would always try to prevent an obvious injustice, though none knew better than she that life was not fair. It never had been and never would be, either for the sovereign's majesty on the throne, or the ploughboy. She had known *that* since she was a child. She had had many good and bad things in her sixty-two years; triumphs, glories and vast power to balance the dangers, the miseries, the emotional frustrations, but perhaps the only true justice she had received, either in reward or retribution, was that the bulk of her people returned the great love she had for them.

She did not absolutely reject the story that Lopez had been employed by Walsingham. Her ministers rejected it and she herself thought it unlikely, but it was always possible with that mind which was even more tortuous than her own. . . . She remembered retorting to Leicester's observation that Walsingham's right hand never knew what his left hand did—"Rob, I swear to you that his thumb does not know what his forefinger does!" Another memory came to her, making her smile in retrospect. The year before the Armada sailed, when her enemies were pouring out an immense stream of propaganda against her private character, the King of Spain was supposed to have received a young man calling himself Arthur Dudley and declaring that he was the Queen of England's bastard. While Leicester had been filled with anger at "this latest trick of Spain's", she had chuckled. "Softly, Rob! I am not so sure. . . . Perhaps the only begettor—father and mother—of this 'our' child, is my Secretary of State!" "But, sweet—I beg you expound!" "An' Walsingham could find a young man of suitable appearance—red hair and a high nose, they say!—school him till he is word-perfect in answer to all the questions which would be put to him, and let him creep into the confidence of King Philip—what a priceless agent he would be! But me no buts, Robin. I would I had thought of it myself."

"But surely", she thought, "Walsingham would never have ventured to tamper with the royal physician, even if he once had done so with the royal honour! For myself, he cared not a jot or tittle, but he cared everything for the Reformed Religion, and if I died, it would have been sorely imperilled!"

For the first minutes her mind did not pass to her own danger. It was not until Burghley and his son had withdrawn, and Essex, yet remaining, was pouring out impassioned words.

"You called me 'rash', 'temerarious', 'unjust' and 'arrogant' when it was your danger I was struggling against! Can you not see? Here is a man trusted by you for years, in the closest attendance on you, admitted to your bedchamber if you are sick, with none but a few of your ladies by you, mixing and compounding drugs and potions for you! How simple for him gradually to instil a slow and subtle poison, in small but repeated doses so none might guess. You would not die suddenly so that any would be suspected, but slowly you would become more and more ill, till none could save you. . . ."

She saw. She remembered the inscrutability of Dr. Lopez, the half-flicker of a smile on his lips, the watchful, veiled eyes. She put her

Sunset

hand to her brow. Truly this had been a greater danger than an assassin from outside with pistol or dagger.

"Oh, my God!" she whispered. "My times are in your hand. . . ."

Essex flung himself upon his knees before her chair, throwing his arms round her waist till she thought he would crush her with the fury of his emotions.

"If he had killed you, it would be like plucking the sun out of the heavens! We should all be in the dark and cold. . . . I could not endure it——" He was sobbing as he buried his face in her lap.

The strangest feelings were running through her. Here was a triumphant answer to that deadly inner voice which asked her: "What can you ever be to him, or he to you?" He had been brought to an extremity by the thought of her danger, every gesture was of adoration. It seemed to shine from his large, dark eyes as he raised his head. Just where his auburn hair grew off his brow, there was a narrow line of milk-white skin where the tan ended. Moved more than she had believed possible, she bent forward and touched it with her lips. She had not kissed a single human being since Leicester died. . . .

Then to steady herself, to let the moment's emotion pass, she began to tease him about his disarranged clothes. So often she had to adjust the angle of his ruff and now she began to retie and tighten the points of his sleeves. "Child, your points are not trussed properly! What are your Chamber Gentlemen at, that they let you come forth so dressed?" His clothes were as gorgeous as Leicester's had once been, but he always put them on so badly.

"I scarce gave them time. I was in so desperate a hurry to convince the Lord Burghley."

She shook her head but her smile was tender.

"I could think of nothing but your peril! Since I last parted with you, I have scarcely eaten or drunk, and I have not slept." He added with a complete lack of self-consciousness: "I am very tired."

"Well—sleep then!"

She pushed a couple of her cushions on to the floor for him, and pressed his head against her knee. He fell asleep so soon that it astonished her; his emotions had exhausted him. Her own were doing the oddest things to her. She believed that she had been in great danger and he had saved her from it, and yet at this moment, she felt that *she* had saved *him* from a danger vast and undefined, and was

463

still protecting him. So long as he slept here, his head and shoulders a-sprawl on her lap (and the weight of him would soon give her rheumatic cramps!) no harm could touch him, and he was away from those evil influences, from Lettice the arch-enemy, from that bold girl his sister and that sly little Puritan his wife, from that dangerous crew at Essex House, the ruffling gallants and cunning intriguers devoured by their ambitions and greeds. Hushed too were the strange influences within him which sometimes sprang up so dangerously, the furies and the wild perilous ambition. He could be as brilliant as he was wayward, but she never felt she had any sure control over him—except at this moment. At a time when she could remember too uncomfortably the violent force of his arms which had clutched her, and could see the powerful width of his shoulders, she saw also how much of him was a child as yet, would always remain a child as long as he lived, and did not know that the woman whom she brushed impatiently aside as a "sly little Puritan" was the only one who would have agreed with her. His sleeping face was a boy's. How old was he now? Twenty-five or twenty-six, the age at which she had taken up the burden of the crown. But his face asleep looked as if it were at least ten years younger.

He slept on and the early winter twilight shadowed the room. Once the Countess of Warwick looked in, raised her eyebrows a trifle, and curtsied out. Elizabeth was cramped but she did not waken him. She wanted to hold this peace; something told her that it might never come again. The room was in soft darkness except for the pale oblong of the window, and lights were twinkling beyond the door, and in other windows. There were sounds outside, some horseman clattering by with a rollicking song, and he stirred. There was just enough light for her to see the entranced dreamy smile on his face which he gave her.

"Do you know where you are?" she asked a little sharply.

"Not fully," he said simply. "I knew that you were here and that I was happy—and safe. . . ."

Safe! She started. Why should he think her thoughts? And where *had* they been? In what strange enchantment, magic idyll out of this very hard and relentless world, had they drifted? But he was waking fully, and craving her pardon for so presuming.

"Presuming to save my life? Give me your arm, dear Cousin." He helped her to her feet, and they were back in the ordinary world again. But some of the dreamy happiness was still remaining. While he supped with her and her ladies, she teased him a little about his velvet chamber slippers, but her teasing was without malice. There was no malice either in her mock reproof of his habitual extravagance. Even the monopoly of the sweet wines could not cover the expenditure of the "poorest Earl in England".

"So you are in debt, you rogue? You keep too many rascals!"

"Most sweet Lady, I am in debt. . . . But I cannot fail these my dear friends—not rascals truly but most gallant gentlemen!"

"Gallant spendthrifts! But I will do somewhat for you to ease your embarrassments."

"Somewhat" was a draft for four thousand pounds. She had given him money often before but never so much as this. He was affectionately grateful but hardly surprised—any more than a much-loved son would be. But in her present mood this pleased her. She was to have, however, a moment of dismay.

"After all this, most dear Queen, I still beg for something further. . . ."

She clenched her hands. Was this the Solicitorship for Francis Bacon? Even Burghley had somewhat tepidly pressed his nephew's claims to that office, and she was quite aware of Bacon's ability. Nevertheless—she did not wholly trust him. Nor did she trust Essex. She had realized this while he slept, she could give him all the honour and pleasure she might, but it was to her own peril, if she increased his power. If her government were to be packed with his men, whose first allegiance might be to him, so strange a fascination did he cast over his followers, she would have no safety. He was as incalculable as a tempest. She loved him, needed him, must have him by her to sweeten her life; but she could only do this if she kept a firm hand on her own authority.

But he was asking for a favour for the great tournament next week! She had been angry with him, so he had not dared to ask her before! Smiling, she gave him a pearl-embroidered glove for his helmet— what other had a better claim? When he jealously demanded that she should not give a favour to any other, she laughed aloud and cuffed his cheek.

"To none other, my champion!"

When he had gone, she smiled a little, but the smile soon faded. There was her problem which she could never escape. Even a weightier one than Robert Leicester had been in her youth. She had always feared *his* pride and ambition, but they were little things compared with the unbalanced strain in Essex. And however often the man in Robert might have betrayed the woman in her, and even how often his ambition had seemed to affront her crown, she did not doubt his ultimate loyalty. He had entered into the beginning of the Northern Conspiracy because he had believed that to overthrow Cecil might lead to their marriage, but as soon as he had caught the first whisper of foreign intervention and her personal danger, he had gone back to her. But Essex was different. . . .

Oh, yes, she loved him! Though she scarcely comprehended it. She would give him all she could—except power. . . .

Chapter Five

He was returning in triumph. The world was agape with his exploit; and his own countrymen acclaimed the great deed of '96 as the true retort to the Armada of '88. Drake and Hawkins might lie dead beneath the waters of the Caribbean, but England still had Essex to lead her to victory! Ballad mongers poured out their effusions to be chorused in the taverns, and had not Master Edmund Spenser, author of the *Faerie Queene*, friend of Sidney and Raleigh, and hailed in his own age as its greatest poet, brought out these rolling stanzas?

> "the noble Peer,
> Great England's glory and the world's wide wonder,
> Whose dreadful name late through all Spain did thunder,
> And Hercules' two pillars standing near
> Did make to quake and fear.
> Fair branch of Honour, flower of Chivalry,
> That fillest England with thy triumph's fame,
> Joy have thou of thy noble victory!"

There had been much that the Queen had dreaded and disliked at the whole idea of the expedition, but her heart had leapt when the first tales had come ringing through the cloud of rumour. Essex entering the harbour of Cadiz, tossing his hat in the air so that it fell in the water as he shouted: "Entramos! Entramos!" while Raleigh ordered a fanfare of trumpets to sound in proud defiance after each salvo of Spanish artillery. All ships crowding to the van in the naval action, just as the men poured up the scaling ladders to take the fortifications, with the rivalry and chivalry of gallant boys, and truest chivalry of all, Essex's noble insistence that the inhabitants of the town should be treated with honour and generosity. Spain's mightiest port had lain helpless in the hands of *her* forces, which Philip's great Armada had not been able to achieve with one yard of English soil. It was, in all truth, a stroke which would thunder through Spain and receive the world's wonder. . . .

It was needed at a time when her two greatest sea captains had died in failure off Nombre Dios, when four Spanish galleys had made a tip-and-run raid on the Cornish coast, when Ireland was once again torching up in rebellion, aided by Spanish arms, Spanish gold, and Spanish promises, when Henri of Navarre was fighting hard-pressed for the crown of France against an army of Guises and Spaniards, and draining more gold from her (to say nothing of men) than even the Low Countries! Philip, her brother-in-law, who had once desired her so greedily, now hated her and hers with a cold implacability. Though he was rotting alive with a multiplicity of dreadful diseases, in his vast Escurial in the fastnesses of the Guadarrama Mountains, where day and night prayers and chants ascended in clouds of incense which dimmed the candle-glitter on the altars, he would still strive to avenge the humiliation of defeat which she and her country had put upon him.

Such a victory as Cadiz was also needed after three bad years at home. The year 1593 had been a terrible year of plague, with London's bells tolling and the doors of London's houses painted, one after the other—"Lord have mercy upon us!" Rain had destroyed the crops, there had been bad harvests for these three autumns, and Want stalked in the wake of Pestilence. She knew well enough that the country was still, in the main, more prosperous than it had been in mortal memory, but the highest and lowest in the land did not share in the prosperity. The Queen's Majesty must strive to carry the burden of Government with inadequate revenues, and a Parliament which firmly held to the notion that taxation to run the realm could only be called for in exceptional circumstances; she wrung her subsidies from the House of Commons with a mixture of cajolery and brow-beating. And at the other end of the scale, the landless men, dependent on their wages, were hard hit. In famine years, prices needs must soar, and they had been generally rising through the past half-century through the inflation caused by the vast influx of gold and silver from the mines of the New World. This she would fight; her government must struggle to keep down prices and insist that the magistrates fixed minimum rates for wages. From the beginning of her reign, she and her ministers had drawn up successive enactments which had created the first Poor Law. She was never sentimental but she had a warm-hearted shrewdness. The old remedy for "all masterless men and sturdy beggars"—the unemployed—was to whip them through the town at the cart's tail; this she held was crass foolishness. Work must be found for them; it was the duty of the magistrates in each town and parish to strive to do this and see that they were paid an adequate wage. Likewise the helpless— the aged and the sick—could not be left to the casual charity, either of the Church or the wealthy. Charity covereth a multitude of sins, she quoted wryly, but I want responsibility! The State must enforce that man is responsible for his unfortunate brother—there must be a poor-rate levied. But these last three years had sorely tried such arrangements.

Resounding victories filled no bellies; none knew better than she. And yet—man being an irrational animal—they did hearten and encourage the facing of all difficulties. Her friends in France and the Low Countries would be heartened also, and her enemies in Spain and her rebels in Ireland dismayed. This all was achieved and Essex was safe. . . . So she would rejoice. . . .

She would try to forget so much. Her hatred of war and its necessities, her dread of sending the fleet away when the Spaniards had made that brief attack upon Penzance, her equal dread of the cost of expeditions only partly lulled by promises of vast plunder, and the greatest unconfessed dread of giving Essex too much power at the same time as endangering his young life.

But she could not keep her gallant hawk hooded upon her wrist; he must sometimes range free. The passing years had made him more difficult. He had not learned discretion and he was losing some of his engaging boyishness as his ambition hardened. But with what a fine burst of generosity, he had set sail! Reconciling himself with his enemies, showing all friendliness to the Cecils, and greeting Walter Raleigh, his sworn personal foe, as brother-in-arms how could she do other than rejoice at such reconciliation? But even upon that, had a shadow fallen already. Howard of Effingham, the Lord Admiral, had been in command of the fleet with Raleigh (now pardoned and back at court) as his rear-admiral; Essex had been the General in command of the land forces. The first dispatch she had received had a piece of paper slashed out of it above the signature of Howard.

Sunset

She soon learned the reason. Essex had insisted on his earldom's precedence, to sign his name above his superior officer's. Howard, incensed, had cut out the signature. She shook her head and frowned; so they were quarrelling already! Howard had proved himself a tactful commander of the fleet against the Armada, she had little doubt with whom the principal fault would lie.

During the absence of Essex, she had taken the opportunity to give Robert Cecil the official appointment as Principal Secretary, whose duties he had so long filled. Now he had the name, the prestige and the full emoluments. Essex in spite of his failure to obtain either the Attorneyship or the Solicitorship for Francis Bacon, did not cease from pressing his candidates for office. Before his departure, he had been urging that she appoint as Principal Secretary, the scholarly diplomat, Sir Thomas Bodley. He would have been infuriated at the confirmation of Cecil's claim. She was not afraid of him—oh, no! He was her subject, her creature, as all other men were, even he to whom she had once given all her youth's passion. She, who was hailed as a goddess by her court, could crush that reckless young man to a proper subservience. But by doing so, might she not lose that strange adoration? After each stormy scene, it became more difficult to resume their old relationship. And—it was not only the hated mirrors which told her she was old—these dreadful scenes exhausted her. Not for nearly forty years had anyone dared to shout and rave at her, and attempt to brush aside her decisions.

It had been so comfortable and easy to appoint Cecil in the absence of Essex! The power was slowly passing from the gouty old hands of his father, to his; he had a perfect efficiency, this deformed little man with the seraphic smile and the gentle charming manner. But one day, not long after Essex's departure with the Fleet, he had planted a barb which rankled, and she could not be sure whether it was intentional or not. He had continued his father's custom, of bringing to her all matters about to be laid before the Council, to discuss them first confidentially. One such meeting had been concluded when he added, with an angelic smile: "Lord Essex and his forces were given such a mighty send-off by the City! Was not your Majesty impressed?"

"These foreign expeditions are always popular—the Lord God alone knoweth why!"

"And Lord Essex is so popular, your Majesty!"

470

Sunset

"All youth looks to him—ruffling gallants and 'prentice boys alike!"

"Ah, yes, your Majesty, the 'prentice boys! I expect we shall soon hear from angry masters and angry fathers, of indentures broken and lads run away to sea. But it is not only the young. I thought, and so did others, that it sounded in Cheapside as if your Majesty had been riding through the city. No one has ever been so cheered before except your Majesty. . . ."

The barb festered. Essex was a subject, a creature of hers, for all the foolish fancies of a moment which depicted a gallant young Prince of Wales riding forth to war! It was dangerous for a subject to have such popularity—it was intolerable that the people could love any other as much as they loved her. . . . How hungry she was for that love, how she sustained herself upon it, ever since that day, three and forty years ago, when she had been released from the Tower, though still a prisoner under the custody of Sir Thomas Bedingfield! As the barge had been rowed up river, she had been cheered to the echo from the crowded wharves, despite fears of the Queen's anger. She could still remember herself so plainly as a thin, pale girl of twenty, sitting in the stern, clenching the hands which lay in her lap, and not venturing to wave back to the shouting throngs, to respond to that warmth which was thawing her heart frozen by fear and misery. The troubled frown of Bedingfield at the spontaneity of the demonstration had warned her against any gesture, but it could not prevent that leap of her spirit. "Oh, loyal hearts—I'll never forget— and if I ever come into my own, I will repay!" She would never forget and she had repaid. But to see that love given to another, was unendurable! For a few moments she found herself hating Essex. . . .

Yes, that memory had festered, and the mutilated dispatch had agitated, two dark shadows on his bright glory.

Yet when his triumphant procession had surged through the narrow streets of London to Whitehall, and the clamour had stilled when he was on his knees before her, she was only aware of happiness.

"I thank you for myself and for the whole country."

"Happy am I to have served you!"

His face was older. It was leaner and harder, and his fresh boyish complexion had the sallowness of fading sunburn. He had grown a beard at last, not one of the once-fashionable tapering pointed beards,

471

but one growing straight down with rounded edges. In the succeeding weeks every young court gallant, indeed every young man aspiring to fashion, endeavoured to trim his to the same shape. The "spade beard" was the last word in manly elegance. But it was a mere outward form of his putting boyish things aside; his whole manner was more definite and assured. His previous furies and assertions had appeared a frantic rebuttal of his own self-doubts. Now he seemed to realize himself and his power. Had he learned balance and proportion?

She took his face between her hands and stared down at him as if she would draw out his very soul. "If you were my son, how glad I were to see this day. . . ." she thought.

That day was all happiness, Whitehall aglow with a thousand candles shining on the dancing throng in the Presence Chamber, as he led her out for the first galliard, and she was young again and the years were lost, deep beneath the waters of the Thames which lay beyond the glittering palace like some great black mirror. All his gallant followers, with their sunburn and their scars, had changed their steel and leather for velvet and satin, and the court ladies were gazing at them with tender, reckless eyes. In the city and the Bankside, the taverns would be doing a roaring trade with soldiers and sailors throwing down their golden prize money on the wine-stained tables, stringing bright gems about the necks of the eager drabs. Yes! It was a night to forget the recent horrors of plague and the price of bread, a night when even a queen could forget her burdens for an hour or two, a night to dance and sing and find no realities but candle flames and red lips and wine a-sparkle. A night for the young to love, like that girl, the sister of Essex, in that dress of white and scarlet, as white as her slender throat, as scarlet as her painted lips, standing by the Lord Mountjoy, her fingers still interlaced with his, not caring how many saw how she looked at him. "If I could be young again," the Queen thought, "for one hour with Robert. . . ."

A voice came into her fancies, the voice of Essex.

"Beloved Queen, will you grant me a favour?"

"What is it?"

"Promise me before you hear it!"

"Boy!" she exclaimed with a harsh note creeping into her voice. "I dare not that. You might want my crown—my sceptre!"

"I swear to you on my knightly honour that it concerns neither

472

your royal crown nor anything else which belongs to your sovereignty. . . ."

"Nevertheless, tell me!"

"I ask you to receive my mother at court."

She was suddenly cold from head to foot.

"No!"

"Why? She is your cousin——"

With a swift furious intensity she answered him: "So was the Queen of Scots my cousin! So was the Duke of Norfolk. . . . The King of Spain, whose realm you have struck so mightily, is my brother-in-law. God save me from my family! Except you. . . ."

He was very calm but determined.

"To-night, you have feasted and honoured your commander beyond his deserts. And yet his mother may not be present! Further, if I am of such little importance, reflect that she is the widow of one who, when he lived, was the greatest man of your realm."

"No!!" She had raised her hand as if to strike him, and her breath escaped with a gasp.

("If you cannot understand, how can I find words to tell you, to tell anyone, of the hurt and humiliation that woman, that she-wolf —once put upon me! Now when the memory of Robert is so near, that I feel I must be able to touch him if I put out my hand.")

Essex had gone white; he was bowing low and backing out of her presence. She was alone, though the musicians and dancers were still there, though the lights still burned and the music still played. But she had been alone since Robert died! Why had Essex to remind her of the years when she had been alone in Robert's lifetime, when gloating tongues had whispered how the Earl of Leicester doted on his wife? One last picture before the night ended. That Maid of Honour, Elizabeth Southwell, silhouetted against the pale oblong of a window, her lustrous white satin shining but her face in shadow, as she threw back her head in a sudden abandon and a man's hand came to her chin to raise her lips to his, and his dark silhouette looked like Essex. Everywhere young love to taunt her now she was old and alone, and remembering that she had had once to share the man she had loved so passionately with her mortal enemy!

Daylight brought bitter realities, to replace bitter fancies; anxieties for the Queen instead of for the woman. Howard's report to the Council, Raleigh's report; a picture less golden than the first bright vision of triumph. A Spanish fleet in the inner harbour with a cargo valued at twelve million ducats had gone up in flames, set alight by the despairing orders of the Governor. Spain had lost the value, but so had her yawning exchequer. His Lordship of Essex had pressed ahead so recklessly against the fortifications, that he had taken no precautions to protect the captive fleet. But there must be, in spite of this, vast plunder taken? Vast plunder rather squandered, for his Lordship of Essex had bidden his followers help themselves in recompense for their gallantry. Hardly anything for her exchequer—and yet it was demanded that she should pay wages to the men engaged, especially the seamen who had not had such opportunities for loot as the soldiery. She sent for Essex.

"God's wounds! You malapert, ruffling swaggerer! Who gave you leave to dip your greedy fingers into your Queen's treasure?"

"God's soul, Madam, my fingers are clean of the touch of one ducat! I gave their due to the men who have gained deathless glory for you, and for the whole country."

She could imagine him against a background of burning ships, burning fortifications, the air reeking of smoke, the land of blood, casting away treasure with insane nonchalance.

"God's wounds, when did deathless glory pay any bills? That treasure was mine—or rather the country's—not loot for a pack of whoreson braggarts, of thieving coystrels, of bully swordsmen, of Bankside rufflers, of——"

"Men who accounted it glory to die for you!" They were both shouting now as loudly as they could.

"Die for me? Rob me! And you too, you——" She choked. "And now you demand that I pay these men——"

"Would you have them starve? The men aboard the ships could not take so much as the soldiers——"

"Starve—God's death! When London town has held high revel since your fleet came in—and every day is Bartholomew Fair! Every leather jack and fustian doublet reeking of musk and ambergris, every tarry rogue who never aspired higher than a pot of ale now swilling Rhenish, Muscadell, Sack and Canary till he vomits, every Bankside whore with her pearl necklace, and the high-born ones about my court with their diamonds—and you say they starve! Mayhap empty bellies will teach empty brains discretion!"

"So 'tis true what is said of you. That you care for naught but

474

money—for stinking gold—which in your scales weighs more than brave men's blood——"

"More's the pity your brave men thought not the same! Your cut-purse cavalieros! God's blood! Is this country run on a handful of groats? You prancing young fool—for nigh on forty years I've struggled to save what you call stinking gold—and cast away as if it truly stank! Save it so England won't starve!"

Her fury had died down, leaving only the grey ashes of exhaustion.

"Essex, Essex! You may grieve and watch over your brave men for an hour. I've watched over and grieved for the whole nation—and for eight and thirty years!" Her head was whirling giddily.

"I would have had treasure for you!" he said. "They would not listen to me—Howard and Raleigh! An' we had waited, as I urged, off the coasts of Portugal, we might have taken the West Indian fleet, the Treasure Fleet worth twenty million ducats. But no! The fleet needed provisioning, we were low in powder, low in victuals, and the fainthearts would sail for home!"

"So!" she said bitterly. "Much glory, little gain!"

She had sunk into a low chair and Essex was on his knees before her. She put her hand on his head.

"Is all to be weighed against gold?" he asked bitterly.

" 'Tis the measure of this our age. I made it not! God send you as much wit and discretion as He has bestowed on you high-leaping courage. Then I were well served indeed."

Elizabeth Southwell was waiting when the Earl of Essex came forth from her Majesty. "Last night!" she thought. "Last night. . . ." But he walked past her as if he did not see her, his face shadowed with melancholy.

In Essex House, he found his family gathered in the Great Chamber. Frances, his wife, was at her embroidery, in—out! in—out!—flew her needle as if to mark the calm rhythm of her thoughts. His stepfather, Sir Christopher Blount, was reconstructing the harbour and fortifications of Cadiz on the table before him. A book, his step-daughter's fan, his wife's golden thimble, his own sheathed poniard, a carved curio box, an empty tankard which had once held his draught of sack, all these represented different objects. From time to time, he would look up and demand of Mountjoy: "Hey, Charles! Am I not right?" Mountjoy was in the deep window-seat, his arm round Penelope's waist, her head on his shoulder, openly exulting in him, smiling triumphantly at her sister-in-law, whose swift needle seemed to say as each time it went in and out—"shameless—shameless!" Lettice hung over her so much younger husband.

"Lord, Kit, you have me marvelled! How can you remember it all so, when you saw it only in the heat of battle, with the cannon in your ears?" Her plump hand came caressingly on his shoulder. Her daughter thought, with a curl of mocking laughter in her mind: "Mother despised both her first and second husbands, she plundered them and betrayed them with any gallant that took her fancy! Now she dotes on her third. . . . She would give him her last ha'pence even if she starved!"

Essex came in and threw himself heavily into a chair.

"Robin—what ails you?" His sister's voice had a note of anxiety.

"I tell you I am as much distasted with the glorious greatness of a favourite as I was before with the supposed happiness of a courtier. . . . The wisest man who ever lived, said when speaking of man's works: 'Vanity of vanities, all is vanity!' "

"Come, Robin! Leave such preachifying to Master Abdy Ashton o' Sundays." Penelope wondered whether her remarks would sting her sister-in-law by such reference to her favourite Puritan divine, now chaplain of Essex House. "You, the glorious commander of a victorious army, have no need for such melancholy."

"My poor, sweet boy!" Lettice chimed in. " 'Tis the sour green jealousy of that ancient Vanity in Whitehall, who grudges you her subjects' love and praise!"

"True enough!" said Penelope. "All the old women—whether in farthingales or hose—are jealous of you."

"Dear lad," began his stepfather, "the whole country is looking to you, as its rightful leader! To have a woman—an old woman—at the head of affairs is clean contrary to nature. For our valiant fellows of Cadiz to be under petticoat government—it's an outrage! The female sex"—here he looked lovingly at Lettice—"is to be adored—but it is not to rule!"

Penelope giggled. She was thinking: "You dear fool, Kit! From the first day you came gaping after Mother like a mooncalf, she's ruled you as completely as possible. Petticoat government! You live under it, and seem not to know it. . . ." She tossed her head back with its cloud of golden hair.

Sunset

"Long live King Robin the First!" she cried. Her sister-in-law spoke now, for the first time, and her voice was as cold as ice.

"Penelope, such heedless remarks can only endanger your brother!"

"If Robin can't trust us all here, then he were truly sunk—without trace!"

Frances Essex went on sewing. She did not reply.

"I cannot bear it!" burst out Essex. "The vile ungrateful abuse she heaped on those men who faced hot iron and cold steel for her—ran into a storm of shot with her name on their lips—planted her flag upon the ramparts of her mightiest foe! To rate gold higher than they!"

"Gold—she worships it!" cried Lettice. "I tell you even in those days when she was most hot for Leicester, she would have sold him gladly for his weight in gold! And often I told him that. . . ."

"If Howard and Raleigh had not prevented you, you would have had the treasure fleet," declared Mountjoy. "Howard's a fool—and Raleigh's a knave! It is your enemies who poison her mind against you. These small, jealous souls. Every man of spirit looks to you. She was a great Queen, but she's past her zenith. . . . She must now put some of the burden of governing on other shoulders. They should be yours, but that hunchback, Black Raleigh and the rest of the crew, struggled against you!"

"Yes," said Essex musingly, "she is past her zenith. I had forgotten how old she is! One does not think of her as old. . . . But she is!"

"Old and crabbed and sour—the country looks to you!" proclaimed Christopher Blount. "You must go forward!"

"God helping me—I will!"

Frances Essex's needle flew in and out, in and out; her lips were tightly pressed together.

Chapter Six

Cadiz had no successor; the "Islands Voyage", the expedition against the Azores, had been a failure. Essex had demanded and received the sole command, but the only man to achieve any fame or success had been his second-in-command, Walter Raleigh, who, so Essex declared, had disobeyed his orders. The quarrel between them had flared up with a new deadliness. While it raged, the treasure fleet carrying the annual golden tribute from the New World slipped safely past to Spain. Even worse happened; while the English commanders wrangled and delayed, yet another Armada set sail for England's shores, which were saved by a miracle. In sight of the Scillies, storm winds sprang up and with them, a deadly fear arose in the hearts of the Spaniards. What memories of the first Armada and its hideous ending had chilled the courage of a brave nation? Without an English sail sighted, let alone a shot fired, the Spanish galleons fled abjectly home, to cast the dying Philip into despair.

Elizabeth received her commander with such anger that he withdrew to Wanstead and vowed never to come again into her presence. He was impossible! And yet—and yet what a bitter loneliness he left behind him. . . . She remembered her agony of soul when the fleet had first been believed wrecked in a tempest, her joy when she heard it was back in port refitting, and Essex was safe! To have lost him— but again was it not possible to lose a person completely while they yet lived? Those dreadful years when Robert had ridden behind her as her Master of Horse, had sat at the table as one of the greatest of her Privy Councillors, while razor-tongued rumour whispered how enraptured he was of his wife, how he adored and doted upon the creature!

But if Essex barred himself away from her, he was not barred away from others. All restless, eager and bitter young spirits rode down to

Sunset

Wanstead. The young Earl of Southampton (who was beginning to outbid Philip Sidney's sister and her son, the still younger Earl of Pembroke, as a patron of poets and the drama), the Lords Sandys, Monteagle and Cromwell, and of course Lord Mountjoy his devoted lieutenant in each of his military enterprises, all the men who had followed him to the wars in France, to Cadiz and to the last disastrous expedition, fine gallants with all their younger son's portions on their backs, or hardened captains, flotsam of the wars in the Low Countries and Ireland, the discontented, the ambitious, the hopeful and the hopeless. They would not be ruled by a capricious old woman who had for her principal advisers an ancient man doddering on the edge of the grave, and his puny hunchback son! They filled the air with their angry complaints, protestations of devotion to Essex, and rollicking songs; the stables were filled with their horses. With them came gay gentlewomen, proud slender necks rising from jewelled ruffs, scarlet painted smiling lips, bright bold eyes; some attired in wide farthingales of the latest fashion, others boldly dressed as pages, in boys' doublets and hose. They were angry and thwarted but they could love and laugh and dance till the sun rose. And in the midst of this whirling seething household, the urgent joys and more urgent rages, Frances Essex moved calm and unruffled, ordering her servants and her kitchens, seeing to the welfare of her husband and children, looking with cold distaste at her husband's mother and sister and the gay gentlewomen about them, but never opening her lips in disapproval. There were still times when Robin needed her and her only, when he clung to her as if for protection, when he prayed with her, or with that sombrely devout man, the Reverend Abdy Ashton. She could wish that he would listen to Charles Mountjoy—whom she preferred of the young gallants about him despite his shamelessly open liaison with Penelope—or to the brothers Bacon. Mountjoy and the Bacons were all for his sweeping away such opposition as that of Cecil and Raleigh, but they did not subscribe to the perilous creed of abuse against her Majesty. If only Anthony Bacon were not so sick a man! But each month he seemed to withdraw more and more, leaving the work of the Secretariat and the overseas intelligence to Henry Cuffe, who was as clever as he was unscrupulous and hated her Majesty as much as Sir Gilly Merrick, Steward of the Household. These two, and even more than they, Sir Christopher Blount, never ceased from trying to inflame the mind of Essex to hatred. Frances did not doubt who was behind the utterances of Blount, who barbed his thrusts and gave them biting subtlety. Openly, Lettice was all maternal sweetness and soothing, as she had never been in his neglected childhood. Her poor, beloved boy, her darling son, she could cherish him ten times better than the old harridan at Whitehall! That he needed such cherishing, no one knew better than Frances. Rake, dreamer, leader of men, lost child, he was all these by turn, and it seemed that the extraordinary woman who ruled the realm, could understand the last; if Lettice understood it, she only exploited her knowledge.

Francis Bacon, who had been consoled with the Earl's manor of Twickenham just as Bodley had been consoled by a priceless library captured from a Portuguese bishop on the Cadiz voyage, gave Essex excellent advice. She could hear his calm reasonable voice in her memory: "My dear Lord, this is how her Majesty must think—'A man of a nature not to be ruled; that hath the advantage of my affection and knoweth it; of an estate not grounded to his greatness, of a popular reputation; of a military dependence." Above all he must eschew the popular reputation and the military dependence which could only disquiet her Majesty, he must refuse military offices and make discreet speeches against popularity, he must seek to emulate the late Lord Leicester and Sir Christopher Hatton who had given way to her Majesty in all things. In fact, thought Frances bitterly, he must change his whole nature. . . .

She walked on, her housekeeping keys swinging from a narrow golden chain depending from her girdle. Voices were arising, the voices of young men, singing in the hall below.

> "Th' ape loves to meddle
> When he finds a man idle,
> Else he is a-flirting
> Where his mark is a-courting;
> When women grow true
> Come teach me to sue——"

A roar of laughter and then: "Heard you this?"

> "Raleigh doth time bestride
> He sits twixt wind and tide,
> Yet up hills he cannot ride,
> For all his bloody pride!"

More roars of laughter and the banging of silver tankards against the tables. So many eating and drinking at Robin's expense! she thought. She turned for a moment to look from the gallery window to the gardens of Wanstead which Leicester had had once laid out in such formal elegance. But their green peace was broken by strolling figures, by chattering grooms holding several horses before the house, cracking jokes with the falconer waiting with the hooded birds. Would Robin ride out? This morning John Harington—the Queen's godson and "Boy Jack"—had come down. He was a merry little fellow, with a doggish devotion to Essex which excused him somewhat in the eyes of Frances, for his liking for lewd jokes. Had he not created a slight scandal at court by translating a saucy impropriety from Ariosto, describing the search of two young men for one perfectly virtuous woman—which they found not. . . . It was said that the Queen had laughed heartily first but then had fetched Harington a box on the ear and had made him translate the rest of the work (which was somewhat ponderous and not enlivened by any more spicy interludes) as a penance. "If they had searched amongst the women in this house!" thought Frances, "they might well have had such an end to their quest!" She had just seen her husband's mother and sister, the leaders of these women.

Lettice was voluminous in a silk wrapper; her increasing fatness made it a relief for her to leave off her stays. Beside her, Penelope Rich, in a riding-habit of Lincoln green, heavily laced with silver, looked as slender and pliant as a young tree. She carried her steeple-crowned hat and heavy hawking gauntlets in her hands. Lettice cocked a merrily malicious eye at her daughter-in-law, and said: "So Jack says our Royal Virgin is a-moping for Robin!"

"Virgin!" said Penelope. "Why must she be called 'virgin'?"

"Lord, my sweet goose! To hide her barrenness. . . . Why, a Troop of Horse and a Company of Pikemen couldn't get her with child!"

Frances averted her eyes with distaste and swept past, hearing Penelope's laughter which had a hysterical note.

"You've frightened Mistress Prim away, Mother!"

Lettice chuckled bawdily.

"I wonder if it's true what little Bess said when she visited us?" she remarked. "Little Bess" was the first cousin of Essex, Elizabeth Vernon, one of her Majesty's Maids of Honour.

"That Robin is enamoured of the pretty Southwell?" asked Penelope.

Sunset

"Bess says Robin's boarded her and she's sunk! Lord! 'Twill do him all the good in the world!"

"You're a bad woman, aren't you, Mother?" said Penelope, but she smiled.

"Why so ungrateful? I like to see the young enjoy themselves! Haven't I helped you with your sweet Charles? Didn't I choose you a husband who's your banker now and no more? Though your pretty little lad is the living split of Charles, Rich is too drowned in strong waters to take it in!"

"Rich", said his wife, "has cognac, not blood in his veins!"

Lettice roared with laughter.

"Lord, Lord! Then some tapster will set a spigot in him!"

"He can for all I care. . . . Anyone else would have died of that amount of strong drink!"

"Alcohol is a wondrous preservative they say. Was it Francis Bacon who showed me a two-headed duckling preserved in a bottle of spirits? Rich is in no bottle but he's fairly pickled—an' he does die, you'll scarce need to bury him!" She laughed further at her own wit.

"Bess is making eyes at Harry Southampton, and he at her!" Penelope told her, not sorry to change the subject.

"Again 'tis excellent. Harry thinks too much of the playhouse, of the verse that player fellow of his writes for him. What's the man's name?"

"Shakespeare. Will Shakespeare."

" 'Tis no matter. The man or his verses."

"It's excellent good verse, Mother. I applaud Harry's taste."

"Likely enough, but verse and drama are only life at second-hand. You want to live your own life for yourself and not read about other people living it!"

Two children were coming along the gallery, a slender thirteen-year-old, Elizabeth Sidney, leading her little half-brother. Lettice began to coo at her grandson.

"My sweet chuck, my little lamb! Where is my comfit box?"

"If you please, Madam," said Elizabeth Sidney, "Mother does not like Robbie to eat sweets between meals."

"That's too hard! Come now!" She was pressing sugared comfits on the little boy. Penelope thought: "She was always like that with us. But if we troubled her—'Take those spoilt brats out of my sight!' "

Sunset

She glanced down and started violently. Philip's grey eyes were looking gravely at her out of Philip's daughter's face. When the children had gone on, Lettice peered at her daughter, noticed that her bosom was rising and falling, and her cheeks were white under their rouge.

"Have you seen a ghost, Pen?"

That was just what she had done. . . . Lettice stared further and then chuckled. She had always marked the likeness.

"You are not still dwelling on your erstwhile sweet Philip?"

"I'll not have his name on your lips!"

Penelope's voice had a shrill, hysterical note in it, and tears were starting from her eyes. She had always avoided that child as much as she could, but never before had she seen the likeness so plainly. It pierced her, through all the barricades she had built, her headlong gaieties and the luxuries she bought with Rich's money, her reckless ambition for her brother and even her passion for Mountjoy. "Oh, once!" she thought. "I was different. . . . If I had been allowed to marry Philip, I should not be what I am."

"Your father was a sentimental fool—and you're the same at bottom. You don't get it from me!" Lettice told her. "Come now! You're not proposing eternal fidelity to his memory? Even his widow re-wed!"

Penelope had control of herself again.

"No, Madam!" she said bitterly. "I am your daughter as well, am I not? That would be asking too much!"

Footsteps were clattering on the stairs, she heard one particular voice, and turned and ran, straight into the arms of Mountjoy.

"Charles, Charles! Where have you been? I want to ride out, whether we hawk or not! To get away—away!"

"Sweet, we can't—at least I can't." He clasped her tightly as if to soften his words. "I'm for Whitehall with Robin. Jack Harington says the Queen is pining for him, is turning against Raleigh and his pack! We must strike when the iron is hot."

She reached up, grasping his small "pie-dish" ruff which he wore inside the gold-embroidered collar of his riding-doublet.

"No, Charles, no! What's the good of it? Of trying anything with the Queen?"

"My darling sweet, you're overwrought. 'Tis essential to do everything to heal this fatal breach between the Queen and Robin."

"No! Oh, believe me, Charles, if you ever loved me! The Queen

—she's a terrible creature, she'll destroy Robin. . . . He should be kept out of her claws. She destroyed Philip—gave him crumbs for a living and sent him to die in the Low Countries. She hates love and life and youth! I used to wonder whether she or my mother were the worst, but Mother's at least human, she doesn't hate life——"

"You are overwrought!" he said firmly. "Have you quarrelled with your mother? I thought you and she were good friends."

"Oh, yes, we are friends now she has made me like herself——"
She was sobbing wildly against his shoulder. Mountjoy rested his cheek against her head.

"I'll be back so soon! What shall I bring you from Goldsmiths' Row?"

Frances Essex found her husband in their chamber. A page was drawing on his long boots while Tracey clasped a cloak about his shoulders.

"Robin?" she said.

"I am going to the Queen!"

She did not answer and he continued rapidly : "Harington tells me that she is rejecting the poisoned counsel of those that hate me. I would not wish her other punishment for her cruelties than this, to know the faith of him she has cast away and the baseness of those she kept. I will go to her, and kiss her lovely hands. . . . They shall heal, not smite. . . . Yes, she's old, and her mind is a labyrinth and yet, and yet—— The emptiness of a world without her! It aches. . . . I must go."

"Go," said Frances, "in God's name."

Before the house was the whirl of departure, Tracey holding the Earl's stirrup, men mounting, bright-eyed little Harington beside Sir Charles Davers, Mountjoy leaning from his saddle to take Penelope's chin in his hand and kiss her passionately, the swashbuckling swordsman, Tom Lea, commanding the escort. As the hoofs drummed away, Lettice cried out with a sudden bitterness : "He's going back to her! Poor weak fool, back to the hand that strikes him! Why do they go back to her—her, that old hag? Leicester went back. The old doting fool, he crawled back to her—to his 'sweet Elizabeth'——"

"Mother," said Penelope who was now calm. "You did not want Leicester then!"

"I did not want him to go back to *her*! Can you not understand?"

"Such a hatred? Yes!"

Sunset

Frances Essex did not speak but gazed as if her soul were in her eyes.

In a couple of days he was back again like a whirlwind, springing from his horse and running into the hall, like a boy from school.

"All is well between the Queen and me. She has created me Earl Marshal so I now outrank Howard!"

Frances thought: "The military office against which Bacon warned him! No more gallant man ever led soldiers into battle but he's no general, no strategist——"

"For once she shows good sense!" cried Christopher Blount, clapping him on the back. "Her most gallant captain!"

"Oh, Robin, tell us!" This was Penelope and her mother pressed forward: "My sweet lad!"

"I told her how she grieved me by favouring my enemies while I was fighting for her in the Islands. I come back to find sly Cecil Chancellor of the Duchy of Lancaster as well as Principal Secretary —she promotes him always in my absence—and she's made Howard of Effingham, Earl of Nottingham! We are both earls but as he is Lord Admiral, he outranked me. The Earl Marshal is the equal of the Lord Admiral, and as my peerage is the older creation—I now outrank him. Oh, and yet another thing. Mother—the Queen has consented to receive you. I told her I could not endure it if she did not. . . ."

"Lord a'mercy!" exclaimed Lettice, going first red and then white. "I must have new attire from top to toe—new jewels——"

"Anything—everything!" said her son in haste. He had turned to his wife: "Frances, you say nothing!"

"Oh, my dear! If you are happy I ask for nothing else."

He had asked, Elizabeth thought, for the hardest gift in her power to bestow. "No," she had said. "No, Robin!" and her voice had been pleading not angry. But to have him back again—the sweetness of it! She promised . . . but she did not implement her promise.

Time after time, the former Countess of Leicester went to the court, was taken to the Privy Gallery to wait for her Majesty to pass out that way. But her Majesty did not come, either she remained within the fastnesses of her Withdrawing Chambers, or she went forth by another way. Then Essex would go and storm and sob at the Queen, in one of his frenzies, and she would give him her word . . . and break it again. Sometimes he fell into one of his fevers, and would lie in the great bed at Essex House between the four silver cherubim. Once he wrote some lines when lying there in the cold exhaustion which filled him when the feverish fit had burned down.

> "Happy were he could finish forth his fate
> In some unhaunted desert, where, obscure
> From all society, from love and hate
> Of worldly folk, there should he sleep secure. . . ."

Happy were he! But his desert was haunted and by love and hate; the worldly folk would give him no rest. Sometimes he spoke of the Queen with a simple boyish affection. "She's a wonderful woman," he said to Frances, and told her how the Queen had routed the Polish Ambassador, who, to the astonishment of the entire court, had addressed a most expostulatory monologue when presented to her. In solemn, sonorous Latin he had actually rebuked her Majesty for interfering with the commerce of Poland and told her that his King would bear with it no longer. It was unprecedented and the ministers and courtiers had all gasped; astonishment made their Latin desert them momentarily, the only language in which they could converse with the Ambassador. Not so the Queen. She had sprung to her feet and poured out a torrent of Latin, vigorous, vituperative, sarcastic and utterly quelling, an *ex tempore* flood, as forceful and eloquent as it was unrehearsed. All the educated could, of course, read and write some Latin and it was the language of learned scholars; but it had long ceased to be the tongue of everyday usage, warm with the breath of life which she had suddenly breathed back into it. Those around her were amazed and delighted, the Ambassador crushed. Turning to the men by her throne, she had said with a smile which seemed to glow from her deeply sunken but still brilliant eyes as much as from her thin painted lips: "God's death, my lords! I have this day been enforced to scour up my old Latin which has lain long rusting!"

Essex had repeated this story to Frances with that deep and tender satisfaction which the triumph of someone very near and precious to one can always evoke. But later, recalling her last rejection of his mother, he would mutter into his pillows: "She's a devil, a devil!"

Nor did his frustrated and tormented emotions always drive him into fever. Sometimes they drove him into the arms of the court beauties, only too ready to receive him. The sensation of the moment, eclipsing the bets and wagers on whether her Majesty would ever receive the widow of Leicester, was the discovery that the lovely Maid of Honour, Elizabeth Southwell, was with child. She did not deny that it was Essex. Packed home in disgrace, she adopted an attitude of ecstatic martyrdom. While the court was reverberating, and her Majesty's fury reverberating most of all, it was reported that the Earl of Essex had gone to St. Paul's Cathedral, that extraordinary church, the greatest exchange in the city of London for all things from legitimate business ventures to criminal exploits, where the fashionable rubbed elbows with rogues of every sort, the "coney catchers" out to pluck the guileless, where men went to learn the latest scandal or the latest news from abroad, to make an assignation or to seek for employment. But the Earl did not join the worldly, the secular walkers. He was on his knees before a side altar, for several hours, seeming lost in a trance of prayer. "The bird which flew into the hall and could not find its way out again," thought his sister, Penelope. But if that old monstrosity at Whitehall were gone, their "Cousin Jezebel", he would find his way. . . .

Elizabeth Southwell disappeared, but apparently she had her successors. There were rumours that the Earl was now paying court to two more Maids of Honour, Mistress Brydges and Mistress Russell, her great friend. They were all christened "Elizabeth" which was most confusing, quite two-thirds of the Maids had the Queen's name. Then it was reported that her Majesty had come upon these two, evidently waiting for Essex in some place of assignation—one to dally with his lordship while her faithful friend kept watch—and had fallen upon them in an outburst of rage, striking them and slapping them till they fled, so stricken with panic that they stayed at the house of a sympathetic friend and did not dare to return to court for several days.

Then the Lady Mary Howard, another Maid of Honour, provided a sensation. This was a proud siren with eyes as deep as bottomless pools; already she had a reputation as a breaker of hearts. One night she appeared in a superb gown of velvet with a deep border of cloth of gold, stiffly sewn with pearls, such a dress as might have been worn by a Princess of the Blood. And Essex had led her out in the first galliard and did not ask her Majesty if it were *her* pleasure to dance! The next day her Majesty thunderstruck her Maids by appearing attired in Lady Mary's gown. The effect was grotesque for her Majesty was taller than Lady Mary and the gown revealed somewhat more than her Majesty's ankles. Savagely she swooped upon the unlucky Lady Mary.

"What think *you*, my Lady, of my new gown? Is it not too short and ill-becoming?"

"Y—yes." They could hardly hear Mary Howard's voice.

"Then if it becomes me not for being too short, it becomes *you* not for being too fine!"

Mary Howard never wore that dress at court again. She was, momentarily, as crushed as the Polish Ambassador. But the discerning could observe that few were more wretched than the nerve-tormented Queen.

Lettice chuckled bawdily over her son's amours. Illicit coupling delighted her, and this hurt and enraged her royal cousin most excellently! She did not like her daughter-in-law, and was disappointed that "Mistress Prim the Puritan" did not show herself disconcerted. Penelope stared at her sister-in-law in astonishment. Had that woman no feeling? She seemed as outwardly unruffled as ever, moving serenely and competently about the arranging of the vast household, caring devotedly for the welfare of her husband and children. If one saw a troubled crease between her brows, it was only when she had been checking through the household accounts with Sir Gilly Merrick the Steward. The hangers-on of Essex House consumed so much food and drink! Apparently she did not address a single word of reproach to her husband. When he was ill, she nursed him with the same patient care. "She cannot love Robin or she would feel something, show something!" thought Penelope with a longing to smash that unnatural calm, a longing which was hysterical.

It seemed that her Majesty could never bring herself to receive the former Countess of Leicester. Lady Chandos, a friend of the Essex family, offered her assistance. She would give a great banquet for the Queen at which Lettice could be present. The Queen agreed, but as the royal coach was waiting at the main door, one of the Gentlemen of the Privy Chamber came running down with a message to take it back to the stables; her Majesty would not go forth that day. Lady Chandos's banquet was cancelled at the last moment; Lettice's comments on her royal cousin were of a lurid indecency. Essex had been ill again with an attack of fever, but when he heard the news, he got up and flung on his velvet dressing-gown. "I'll go to the Queen now. Have my coach ordered instantly!" Frances had caught at his arms.

Sunset

"No, no! You will take cold, you still have fever——" But seeing the violence of the impulse she stopped. This was her rule; not to fight, or resist or protest, only to accept. . . . She wrapped his thickest cloak about him, and told young Tracey to see he was covered in the coach; the boy was devoted to Robin. When he had gone, she knelt down in prayer.

At Whitehall the Earl of Essex, obviously risen from a sickbed and only in his dressing-gown, demanding to see her Majesty on a matter of urgency, was admitted by the back stairs leading directly to the Withdrawing Chambers. He threw his cloak to young Tracey and then strode after the usher.

Her Majesty was sitting in the smallest Withdrawing Chamber with the Countess of Warwick. She was dressed in a robe of silver brocade embroidered with strange patterns. Human eyes seemed to peep from her wide skirts among the flashing gems. She leaned her chin on her hand and was staring at a space in front of her, her own eyes half hooded. Lady Warwick watched her, but when she saw Essex she turned her glance from the Queen.

"Robin, you are ill!" she exclaimed, astonishment and anxiety breaking her habitual serenity. She had always been friendly with Essex and his sisters ever since Lettice, their mother, had married her brother-in-law, Leicester. He made a sweeping gesture with his hands. The Queen seemed to pretend not to see him till he knelt before her. Then she spoke in a harsh voice.

"It appears you want your death, to come now, so!"

"I think that *you* desire my death, Madam!"

"No, no. . . ." she said wearily. Her accustomed fight was not in her, and as she listened to his impassioned reproaches, she did not make the excuses she had used earlier on, that her head ached and that young Cecil had told her that he thought a courier with important messages might arrive from Ireland that night, and she wished to learn them as soon as the man came. She had thrown these aside. She put her hand to Essex's head, touched his feverish temples, and sighed.

"They must accommodate you here to-night," she said. "You are very ill. I will have Dr. Goodrowse sent for. You cannot go back to Essex House, and you should be in bed immediately."

"I will not go to bed! It were better for me to die, since you delight to wound me so! You promised to receive my mother——"

"Later, later. . . ."

"You have promised me so often, and each time you have broken your word!"

She closed her eyes and the strength, and the last illusions of youth went out of her face. It was a skull covered with parchment.

"Boy, you don't know what you ask. . . . Bring her. In four days' time if you are recovered."

"But how do I know if you will keep your word?"

She did not upbraid him. She touched the Coronation Ring which never left her finger day and night.

"I promise you on this that I will receive her the first day you are well enough to bring her. Now will you return to your own house or go to bed here?"

He went back to Essex House and fell into an exhausted sleep and heavy sweat. By the next day he was free of all fever, though limp and as powerless as a small child.

"He does not know, he cannot know!" Elizabeth thought, "what I have done for him!"

Those were the thoughts which filled her when she saw Lettice at last advancing towards her, across the Withdrawing Chamber. The scene had a nightmarish unreality. The actual figure of Lettice seemed less important than the concession she had made to Lettice's son. Lettice was curtsying, her wide skirts sweeping around her with a rustle of silk, and giving her eyes a half-upward roll as she had always done, sly and demure at once. Lettice stepping away from Robert in a corridor of this very Palace of Whitehall, to drop the most demure of curtsies belied by her sly, yet sullen eyes. . . . A feeling as if of acute physical pain began to bite upon Elizabeth. If memory started unrolling its scrolls she must run mad! Lettice was kissing her hand. . . . But she had given a royal promise and she must keep it—royally.

She put her arms round Lettice and raised her up.

"Cousin!" she said. She touched Lettice's cheek with her lips for one second. "Cousin!"

Lettice gasped. She had not expected this reception. She dabbed a kiss which landed somewhere on her Majesty's shoulder. Her voice was a squeaky echo: "Cousin!" Then they looked at each other, and both thought: "How *old* she is!" and Elizabeth: "How fat she is!" and then Lettice: "She's a skeleton!" and again both thought: "What would Robert think of her now?"

Sunset

The Queen motioned Lettice to a chair and seated herself. The Countess of Warwick drew near as if to be of assistance. The Maids of Honour, waiting in a bevy in their gleaming white satin at the end of the chamber, held their breath. Bess Brydges said afterwards that she expected an explosion any minute. As for Essex, his smile was radiant. He flung himself on his knees before the Queen and his mother. Elizabeth threw him a cushion, and sitting on his heels before them, he first kissed the Queen's hand and then Lettice's. But the affection he was showing to both seemed to twist in Elizabeth's heart like a knife blade. Always, always she had had to share the beloved object with Lettice! Lettice who had been Rob's wife and Essex's mother. . . . Oh, it was too much! Because she would not, dare not share her power, could not give or share her crown, in her life as woman only, she could never be sole possessor but could only share! Even in her secret stolen life with Robert—she remembered the first time she had gone to his chamber in the dead of night, with her green cloak hiding her face, and Robert's body-servant had believed that she was the Countess of Essex! And she would never know whether to believe his protestations that Lettice had not also come, stealthily by night. . . . Never, never could she completely trust.

They talked uneasily, Lettice being apt to gabble from nervousness. Elizabeth thought: "The only thing I could wish to ask her, is the one thing I cannot utter. To ask her about Rob's last illness. . . . But like enough she scarce heeded him! She would be dallying with that Blount of hers!" The two of them together, it was a cruel grotesque. She thought light-headedly: "I should have invited the Lady Stafford. . . . Is the ghost of his first wife hovering near?" All the women whom Rob had loved—or pretended to love—all those poor fools who had believed themselves happy for an hour in that illusion. Had Lettice shared those very same tendernesses, little jokes, protestations of undying love, those same caresses? But she must not let her thoughts drift so or she would indeed run mad! She looked at Essex and lightly cuffed his cheek.

"You have your own way, Master Robin!"

"He always must!" Lettice told her. "Ever since he was a small child. Else he becomes ill!"

"Since he was a child?"

"I do assure you! His nurse spoilt him. She would always say: 'I beg you, my Lady, don't thwart the boy! Or he'll fall into a fever.'

491

Oh, he's been a trial to me! But he's a very good, loving son at heart."

"A—good, loving—son?"

"Worth six of the daughters. Daughters have not half the natural affection."

"I'll take your word for it, Cousin, though I know nothing of daughters. . . . The girls of this age are mainly worthless!"

"Lord, Cousin! They are only young!"

"One doesn't appreciate one's youth—till one's lost it. . . ." She thought: "When I was five and twenty and you were sixteen, I got him away from you. But when I was five and forty and you were thirty-six, you took him from me, and flaunted your conquest before the whole world! Then when he was old and sick and tired, that last year of his life, it was me that he wanted again. I loved him—ten times more than you ever could. And yet I loved this country more. Was he hurt at it, or only angry?"

Lettice was saying: "I appreciated my youth. I enjoyed it!"

"I am glad to hear it," said Elizabeth acidly. "There was little to enjoy in mine." Lettice gave her a sly inquisitive glance but said with treacly hypocrisy: "I vow your Grace's sister was a monster of cruelty to you! I remember my parents, how they grieved over it!"

"Your parents were my good loyal friends and kinsfolk."

So they talked, or tried to talk, and Essex and Lady Warwick joined in. Lettice and her son dined privately with the Queen and her ladies before departing. When they had both gone, the Queen turned to Lady Warwick, with a note in her voice like a too taut lute-string which might suddenly snap.

"Anne, did you see the fantastic colour that creature dyes her hair?"

Lady Mary Howard begged to be excused and another maid, Mary Fitton, went with her. Safely out of earshot, they pealed with laughter, they giggled, clutching at each other, they rocked.

"Heaven's mercy, what about the colour of her own wigs?"

"Lady Lettice's hair is her own—you can see the grey at the roots."

"What would Leicester think of them now?"

"I saw him once when I was a child and he was a fat old man with a red face! Yet they say he was the greatest ladykiller in England."

"Truly ladykiller! Didn't he murder his first wife?"

"It didn't stop the others falling in love with him! But do you think they really remember, her Majesty and Lettice, now they are both so old?"

Chapter Seven

Her Majesty was debating the grievous situation in Ireland with three of her chief councillors; the Earl of Essex, the Earl of Nottingham (who had been Lord Howard of Effingham) and Sir Robert Cecil. The news could not be worse; the Lord Deputy, Lord Borough, had suddenly died at the time when the Irish were rising in greater force than ever before. An army of theirs was strongly besieging the principal English forts on the River Blackwater; if they gained this position the Viceregal City of Dublin lay open to them. At last they had a leader who could both unite the wild clansmen and show a decisive strategy, Hugh O'Neill, Earl of Tyrone. And Spanish aid, men, munitions, skilled captains and skilled counsel, was pouring to him by a hundred devious ways, urged by the last flickers of energy in the moribund Philip. Indeed, reflected Robert Cecil, matters had never been worse there in her Majesty's reign of forty years. It was imperative to appoint a new Lord Deputy who would take a firm grasp of the situation, but Lord Essex—as usual!—held matters up by fiercely disputing the choice.

Her Majesty had chosen one of her Privy Councillors, Sir William Knollys, elder brother of Lettice and so uncle to Essex, a quiet but competent man who exercised a slightly restraining influence on his nephew. On general grounds, Knollys was as good a choice as could be made, Cecil thought, and one would presume that he would have the support of Essex and his very dangerous faction, all those turbulent young men. But Essex would not hear of it! Fiercely he insisted on Sir Peter Carew, who was no friend of his. It looked, thought Cecil, as if he wished Sir Peter to fail, regardless of the country's danger.

493

Sunset

They were all standing, a tense little group by the head of the Council table, in front of the Queen's chair which had been pushed back. She had her hands clenched, her narrowed eyes were glittering with rage as she confronted the equally furious Essex. Neither seemed to see anything else. Cecil and Nottingham hovered, in inevitable silence, unable to get a word into the conflict of those two angry voices. At the table, Windebank, Clerk of the Signet, rustled some documents in sheer nervousness.

The Queen's voice had become a harsh scream.

"By God's son, I say Knollys shall go! I say it! And it is upon my word!"

"Tchah!" Essex made a sound of frenzied disgust, and swung round on his heel, deliberately turning his back on his sovereign. Cecil drew in his breath and her Majesty moved, with a swiftness of fury surprising in one who was old. She caught Essex a resounding box on the ear, which sent the crimson flooding up to the roots of his hair.

"Go and be hanged!" she shouted at him, and struck him on the other ear. For one second he stood still, and the blood drained from his face leaving it deathly white. Then with his eyes starting from his head, he yelled at the Queen: "This is an outrage that I will not put up with! I would not take it from your father's hands—no, not from the greatest king on earth!" And as he spoke he came wildly at her Majesty, half drawing his sword from its scabbard, as if he would strike her down. . . .

It was one of those seconds which have the depth of eternity, when movement seems frozen into a tableau. Not that Elizabeth moved; she was absolutely still before the violent menace of the young man. Cecil felt the cold sweat starting inside his ruff, in another moment— if time could ever move—— Time did move, and Nottingham seized Essex by the shoulders, spinning him round, away from the Queen. But she yet stood still, as if she had been stricken into stone. Cecil felt his knees shaking, he put up his hand and cautiously wiped the moisture from his neck. Essex's long body looked as if it were being held up by the strong hands of Nottingham; his eyes were not sane. For another agonized moment he seemed to hang in the air, and then he moved again, wrenched himself from Nottingham's grasp, and fled headlong from the room, slamming the door furiously behind him. As the bang reverberated, a little sound joined it when a piece of gilded plaster fell from the doorway to the ground, broken by the force of the slamming. They could hear the racing clatter of Essex's feet gradually dying away in the corridor beyond.

He had recovered the powers of movement but they seemed still frozen. Nottingham was swearing, very pungently, very softly, under his breath. Cecil looked at the Queen. She had gone a strange colour, that of wood-ash in a dead fire. Against it, against the harsh outlines of her cheekbones, the rouge stood in two dabs of unnatural red. Never before had her flaming wig seemed to have such garish unreality. She looked, thought Cecil, like a corpse which can yet remain upon its feet. . . . Would she fall, would she faint? Yet he hardly dared to approach her. Then she turned, took one step and seated herself in her high chair, clasping its arms. But the knuckles of her thin, beautiful hands looked like polished ivory. Then she spoke, calmly, a trifle flatly.

"Master Windebank, I wish to have again the report of Sir Henry Bagenal. . . ."

Silence fell upon that last outburst of violence and fury. The Earl fled to Wanstead as he so often had done, and his discontented followers poured after him. *That* was nothing new. But what would her Majesty do to revenge this unparalleled and dangerous affront? If she had ordered him to be flung into a dungeon of the Tower, no one would have been surprised. The whole court conjectured the Earl's future punishment. But her Majesty did nothing. . . . She sat late with her Council, she read and re-read reports from Ireland which daily grew more alarming, she checked muster rolls, and accounts from the Exchequer and the Ordnance. She did not mention the name of the Earl of Essex.

But she thought about him, without rest or peace. She thought: "After all, he hates me. . . ." She remembered his mad eyes as he came raging at her. He had not touched her bodily, but he had touched something in her soul. Her strange love for him was still there, but her mind had no illusions. He was a danger to the realm, the focus alike for discontented youth, and the money-loving, Spaniard-hating city of London. No other subject in her reign had such perilous popularity. It was so easy to love him! Punish him? She shrank from it. Perhaps he would come back, and put his head on her lap again and ask for reconciliation. But dare she ever give way to him? And if she did, could she ever trust him, would she not always think of that concealed hatred which had so suddenly flamed up? Leicester had betrayed her with other women, they had often quarrelled, but there had never been this terrible hatred like a blade between them. But they could love as man and woman, and passion is a great healer. What could she be to Essex or he to her? An old woman's darling! He is the son of Lettice, he is not your son. . . .

He was not completely in silence at Wanstead. He wrote to her. She seized upon the letter with an unconcealed eagerness, but it contained no apology. It began with a conventional courtier's phrasing.

". . . *I have preferred your beauty above all things, and received no pleasure in life but by the increase of your favour towards me. . . .*"

She grimaced. Her beauty! It was not very likely. . . . With paints, with false hair, with ever-increasing richness of attire, she believed she yet made an impressive figure—but not beauty! Still men had so addressed her for nigh on fifty years. She had once said to Robert: "I was never beautiful but I had the reputation of it as a girl. . . ." a remark she was to repeat in her old age to a sympathetic French Ambassador. But her stepfather's greedy advances to her at the age of fourteen had first taught her that she was a woman desirable to men, very desirable. . . . If she were five and twenty instead of five and sixty, she did not doubt she might have plucked Essex from the arms of his Southwell and the other little sluts. What would he be like as a lover? A whirlwind. . . . Utterly unmanageable, who would never have accepted her compromise as Robert did. But why let her thoughts stray so dangerously? She was more than old enough to be his mother and yet she was not his mother. . . . She had never been wife or mother, only secret lover, and it had left an unappeased ache in her heart. She read on. The next sentence had a bitter sincerity.

". . . *by the intolerable wrong you have done me and yourself, not only broken all laws of affection, but against the honour of your sex. . . .*"

And again: "*And now since my destiny is no better, my despair shall be, as my love was, without repentance.*"

He signed himself with proud humility: "*Your Majesty's most humble servant, R. Essex.*" But there was no humbleness whatsoever in that letter. He did not give an apology, he demanded one.

Other letters passed between Wanstead and the outer world. The Lord Keeper Egerton wrote to him urging him to apologize and make his peace with the Queen. He received a most fiery and intransigent answer. The sentences in it crackled with a thunderous passion.

"*When the vilest of indignities are done unto me, doth religion enforce me to sue? Doth God require it? Is it impiety not to do it? What, cannot princes err? Cannot subjects receive wrong? Is an earthly power or authority infinite? Pardon me, pardon me, my good Lord, I can never subscribe to these principles!*"

So he would challenge the very authority of her Crown? That she might never abate for all the love in the world, he, like so many others, must learn that to touch her royal sceptre was to touch a burning flame. . . . She sent him a caustic verbal message.

"Tell the Earl that *I* value *my*self at as great a price as *he* values *him*self."

But a cloud of melancholy descended on her. The news was disquieting from Ireland. Sir Henry Bagenal had marched to the relief of the Blackwater forts; he was killed and his army defeated, Tyrone was across the Blackwater, advancing upon Dublin. There was personally disquieting news from Wanstead. Essex was reported to have made perilously rebellious remarks, full of "dangerous discontentment". It was said that his chief confidant, always at his elbow, was his stepfather (who was only some ten years older than he), Sir Christopher Blount. Christopher Blount! She knew well enough who was behind Blount, that woman whom she had kissed and called "Cousin" to please "that woman's" son. . . . And behind *him* were all his rakehells, his disbanded captains and discontented younger sons, above all the head of his extensive secretariat (now that Anthony Bacon's health was failing), that unscrupulous intriguer, Cuffe, never hesitating to inflame the mind of Essex. Further, so many young men of promise, young nobles about her court, were flying moth-like to this most dangerous candle. The young Earl of Southampton—she was enraged with Southampton! He had followed the example of Essex and had got another Maid of Honour with child, Essex's first cousin, Elizabeth Vernon. A secret marriage followed without the Queen's permission which was required before any Maid of Honour could marry. It was said that young Southampton, who had been on the Continent busily gambling away his inheritance, had been fetched home and hurriedly married to Mistress Vernon, owing to the exertions of the Countess of Essex, who had done her best for her husband's orphaned cousin. The angry Queen had sent the pair to meditate upon their sins in the best apartments in the Fleet Prison, for a while.

"I think I shall recruit my maids from the harlots of the Bankside," she remarked to the Countess of Warwick, with some acidity. " 'Tis conceivable that they would be more virtuous! Anne! What is wrong with the young people of this modern age?"

"Youth is dangerously discontented," agreed Lady Warwick.

"Yet it is a better, a safer age than ours," mused the Queen.

"Safer, your Grace, but perhaps not better. In the more perilous world of our youth, there were great things to strive for, and great deeds to achieve."

"Truly! Drake sailing his *Golden Hind* round the world—and those countless emulators of his who dared so greatly. . . . They knew how to live, *and* they knew how to die! Humphrey Gilbert when his ship, went down in a tempest, with a Bible in his hand, calling out to reassure his crew: "We are as close to God on sea as on land," and Philip giving away the goblet of water to the other wounded man. . . . We were then a small country, Anne, which might be crushed beneath mighty antagonists, but none of them flagged or failed! Those were the men who defeated the Armada. But now when we have become one of Europe's great powers, paramount at sea, rich, prosperous and strong, there is nothing but greed, treachery, wantonness and irresponsibility. 'Tis a generation without faith! We believed in something—I believed——" she stopped short, and thought how sympathetic Anne Warwick's eyes were. "*I*", she continued, "did not fail in my faith to this my country."

Then came the most poignant reminder that the old days had truly gone. The Lord Treasurer, Burghley, was dying at Theobalds. It was impossible that he could recover. She rode straight away to visit him. She had been his guest so often and so long that he had built greatly on to Theobalds to accommodate her suitably, but now she only came with a handful of attendants, so small a retinue that the elder son, Sir Thomas Cecil, his red face solemn now, could hardly believe that it was the Queen's Majesty. Hastily she put aside any suggestion of pomp, or of formal entertainment; she did not wish to discommode them, she only wanted to see her dear friend.

One of his Gentlemen of the Chamber, who was conducting her, hesitated a moment at the low and narrow doorway leading into the

Sunset

Lord Burghley's bedchamber, and regarded her Majesty with some embarrassment. One could scarcely ask *her* to stoop her head! But he looked at the high jewelled ornaments rising from the towering red wig, and had an unspeakable vision of its being knocked off by the lowness of the arch. "If your Majesty would not mind—if your Grace would consent to stoop——!" But there was something like a twinkle in her eyes, he noticed with reassurance.

"For the King of Spain, I will never stoop—but for your Master's sake, I will, with gladness!"

With that she ducked her bedizened head, and came through the low doorway, to pause gently beside the great bed, in which he lay against his pillows.

"Your Grace," said that very feeble voice, "this is indeed a great honour for me!"

"Since you cannot come to me, I must come to you." She sat down in the chair which his gentleman pushed forward, and very lightly touched one of the swollen tormented powerless hands which lay so limply on his embroidered counterpane. She had clung to that hand once when she had said: "I love Lord Robert, I love him dearly— but as God is my witness, nothing improper has ever passed between us. . . ." How long ago that had been! How very long it had been since those days when she had waited at Hatfield while her sister's life flickered out, and this grave-eyed man had first come to her side, unobtrusively vigilant, a fund of quiet counsel. But when she spoke again with a sudden anguished eagerness, he recalled that red-headed young woman of twenty-five.

"I cannot do without my Spirit! God alone knoweth what you have done for me and mine . . . what mistakes you have prevented my making!"

"I do not think—even in the early days—your Grace would have made many mistakes."

"I do not know what I might have done without you!" She was remembering the time that so many of the Council had opposed him when the Northern Rebellion had begun to smoulder—in men's minds if not yet in their deeds—and she had said to him: "*We* rule England, you and I!" She said now with a sudden passion which came from her depths.

"I would not wish to live longer than I had you with me!"

There were tears in the old man's eyes, and it was some minutes before he began to talk, expostulating with her, telling that she must not speak as if she were old (!) and that as long as he lived, he lived only to serve her, but if it were God's will that he should die—and he was in his seventy-ninth year—he hoped in heaven to be a servitor for her and God's Church.

She sat very still. She knew he would die, that even now he was slowly going away from her, away from the country he had helped her to rule and to guard, away from all the problems which still lay heaped up before her, like so many mountains which she must climb. For such long years she had depended upon him as she had never depended upon anyone else, and she ached with a quiet but unappeasable sorrow. She could have wept—both for him and for herself—but it was very bad to agitate so weak a man, worn out with the years as well as with pain, and she dreaded the effect of tears on the elaborate façade of paint she built up upon her face nowadays. She remembered the early days, how neither had at first altogether trusted the other on personal grounds. She had thought him dry and heartless and he must have thought her too gay, too flippant and too self-willed. He had been coldly baffled by her shafts of mockery when she teased him. Then—at the first crisis caused by the strange death of Robert's wife—she had discovered that he had an affection for her. He had never understood her passion for Robert; at first he had been utterly horrified by it, but he had always sympathized with the distress it caused her. The young Elizabeth had once asked him, half in gaiety, half in bitterness: "Sir Spirit, were you ever in love?" He had considered the matter gravely; perhaps when he was a youth at Cambridge, but later on—no! But she must not think he did not have the deepest affection and esteem for his wife. . . . It was not long after her discovery of his fondness for her that she discovered an equal one for him—and to what strength it had grown!

Now she asked him if he had minded her teasing, and he smiled, and told her, in that weak voice, that he had come to enjoy it, something which she had long suspected.

"Then I was not utterly unbearable, my Spirit?"

"Your Grace! Your intelligence was always beautiful—astonishing at first in so young a woman. . . . It ever had a rarity unbelievable, though its workings often showed most curiously."

She chuckled with appreciation but he was continuing: "What I always most deeply admired in your Grace, was your ability to

choose the right course for your country, however much personal
pain it cost you."

"It wasn't possible—ever—for me to have married Lord Robert?"

"I wish for your Grace's sake, it had been. . . ."

"And the Queen of Scots," she said wearily. "She had to die, didn't
she? But I struggled so long against it!"

Frail against his pillows, he yet had a ghost of his old implacability.

"Your Grace, there could be neither peace nor safety while she
lived."

A sudden foreboding fear touched her. She thought: "Will I be
asked for a third thing so hard?" Speaking quickly to drown this
thought, she said: "But the diplomatic duels with France, with Spain,
with the Scots—I had enjoyment from them. They were often marvellously stimulating!"

It soothed her sorrow to be talking thus familiarly with him. For
forty years they had discussed the problems of her reign, quietly,
shrewdly and painstakingly, for forty years vast decisions had been
arrived at by these quiet discussions. But now she must ask him how
he felt; it seemed he had little pain except in those gout-tortured
hands. He was so weak, so tired—that was all. He complained only
of one thing. As he had lost the use of his hands, he could no longer
feed himself and he was weary of the broths spooned down his throat.
His son Robert had sent him partridges for which he had a partiality,
but when he had made an effort to feed himself he had found it quite
beyond him.

"Sir Spirit, I will feed you!" And ordered at once that a partridge
should be placed on a spit. She was so pleased when it came and she
could do something for him, thinking: "We can only comfort ourselves for the sufferings of others by actively striving on their behalf."
With great care and the aid of that new-fangled invention from Italy,
the fork, she managed to give him tasty titbits. His relations realized
suddenly that her Gracious Majesty had put aside every vestige of her
accustomed pomp and seemed to become a member of the family.
She fed him, put liniments and dressings on his swollen fingers,
arranged his pillows and moved him in bed if necessary, doing all this
with a gentle competence which astonished them. There was no doubt
that he enjoyed her ministrations, and to have her quietly conversing
at his bedside. Her sickroom manner was admirable.

Sunset

Strolling in the grounds with the Countess of Warwick, hearing a little wind rustling the leaves and grasses dried by the August sun, she said with a strange fervour: "No prince ever had a more wise and loyal counsellor! No woman ever had a better friend!" And then added: "Anne, is my face running?" But when the news of his death was brought to her after her return to Richmond, she wept bitterly and unrestrainedly. . . .

"Such deaths", she thought, "seem to knock holes in the walls of our existence which let through the biting winds. . . . And nothing can close them!" She had lost her love, now she had lost her best friend. Yet another death was to impinge upon her life. A month after the funeral of Burghley at Westminster Abbey, there died her brother-in-law and eternal antagonist, Philip of Spain. Her lover, her counsellor and her enemy—they were all gone now and her world was breaking up fast. Who was left of her generation? Her cousin Nottingham, the Lord Admiral, that quiet woman, Anne Countess of Warwick—and Lettice. Lines of verse swept into her mind from the masque "Summer's Last Will and Testament" which seemed to paint the falling leaves of autumn.

"Falingtado, Falingtado, to wear the black and yellow,
Falingtado, Falingtado, my mates have gone, I'll follow!"

Then she was reminded that the young and vigorous can die, when news came from Wanstead that Essex was gravely ill, and physicians were being called in consultation. She sent one of her own, immediately. But Essex recovered, and in due course she received a letter of thanks from him for the doctor's attentions and her inquiries; affectionate and grateful, but not one word to refer to the dreadful scene in the Council Chamber. He came back to court when he was well enough, as if nothing had happened, but that scene lay between them, though neither spoke of it. It was an abyss at whose edge each halted, knowing well where it lay, avoiding its depths with meticulous care, but pretending that it did not exist.

But the problem of Ireland could not be left; and at the next Council meeting she pressed the claims of Mountjoy. Increasing rumour whispered that he had been as successful in the land attack at Cadiz as Raleigh with the sea; they had been responsible for that resounding victory, not Essex, a figurehead, if a gallant one in the forefront of the battle. He was young, but youth must be served, it

502

Sunset

clamoured to take the lead and reject the halting counsels of age. Mountjoy was a gifted young man. He might go far if he were detached from his present dangerous company at Essex House, from the fascination of Essex himself, and from the arms of Essex's sister. Would Essex oppose his friend as he had once opposed his uncle? He did.

"It is too much for Mountjoy!"

The soft, smooth voice of Robert Cecil: "My Lord, would you then take this most onerous task upon yourself?"

Then she saw it. It was only for a second, and she believed that her eyes alone recognized it, the flash of blind, panic fear, as of a stag cornered and brought to bay by the hounds. She forgot the abyss, she forgot all considerations, and the words trembled on her tongue. "No, Robin, no! You must not go! Or you are undone!" But they were never spoken. The look of fear faded; he threw back his shoulders and declared that, God helping him, he *would* take the task upon himself. . . . A tide of arrogant self-confidence seemed to sweep him forward, he delivered a slashing criticism of the previous Lord Deputies and their policies. He was utterly sure.

After the Council, she drew him apart.

"It will look different the other side of the St. George's Channel. It is a country of disillusion, where clear-cut decisions are nigh impossible, a slow, heart-breaking bewildering terrain to fight over——"

She could see the smile on his lips, mocking and pitying, and imagine his thoughts—"an old woman's fussing!" She turned aside with a shrug. But Robert Cecil smiled, that smile like a seraph's.

If the Earl of Essex settled the Irish matter, well and good. If not —then the Irish matter would settle the Earl of Essex. . . .

Chapter Eight

Ireland, said the Venetian Ambassador, is the grave of Englishmen. Truly, reflected Robert Cecil, and the grave of their reputations, even that of the Victor of Cadiz. The sunlight of triumph did not shine upon his banners. That strange green land seemed able to avenge her children upon their oppressors. The Earl of Essex had sworn to drive out Tyrone, now virtually in command of the whole of Ulster, but he delayed . . . inexplicably. He rode with his army into Leinster, he rode into Munster, he hunted and was feasted, he dubbed knights which he had been expressly forbidden to do, he locked up his armies in garrisons (a fault he had rated in others) and he lost many men by disease. But he did not engage the enemy. The angry Queen, as usual at her wits' end to find money, declared that by God's death, she was not paying him a thousand pounds a day to ride on Progress! His Lordship of Essex, thought Robert Cecil, had been given a great length of rope and he was hanging himself as fast as he could with it.

His cousin, Francis Bacon, agreed with him. Francis Bacon was showing great attention to his cousin, Robert, these days, who reflected that one must not be so vulgar or so brutal as to refer to rats leaving sinking ships. Yet there was no doubt that such popular sayings, though quite deplorable, were very apt; Francis certainly knew on which side his bread was buttered. . . . He had really done his best to advise the Earl to abate his dangerous courses, but one might as well advise the gales to stop blowing. Master Bacon now trimmed *his* sails to more promising breezes and was rewarded by being appointed one of her Majesty's Learned Counsel, to be employed alike as interrogator and prosecutor in Crown cases. Robert Cecil never underestimated the scintillating intelligence of his cousin; he had no doubt that Francis could be of even more use to him, than *he* to Francis in

Sunset

the hopes of the latter. Although her Majesty had refused to advance Master Bacon while he was under the ægis of the Earl of Essex, and did not appear to have much warmth for him, she always enjoyed his witty and profoundly intellectual conversation. He had tried without much avail to divert her suspicions from a most suspicious book.

This was John Hayward's *Henry IV* which described in detail how a bold and resolute man, coming from Ireland with a devoted army at his back, had overthrown the Anointed Sovereign. It was dedicated to the Earl of Essex. . . . Bacon was summoned to her Majesty as one of her Learned Counsel (and the one whose conversation she preferred) to advise her upon the possibility of prosecuting Master Hayward for High Treason. Master Bacon's delicately sparkling eyes surveyed her Majesty's obvious rage and anxiety. She was badly shaken. He murmured with a deprecating gesture that he doubted whether Hayward could be prosecuted for so dangerous and prodigious a crime as High Treason, but undoubtedly the man was a rogue and should be prosecuted for felony. . . . For felony! What did he mean? He shrugged elegantly. It was a shameful case of plagiarization from other authors. The rogue had lifted whole passages of Tacitus! But her Gracious Majesty—like another great queen centuries later—was not amused. . . .

Afterwards he admitted to the Principal Secretary that he was astounded at the Earl's reckless folly in permitting such a dedication.

"Are you really, cousin!" said Robert Cecil. "I must confess nowadays that nothing his lordship would do, could surprise me any longer!"

His lordship had even commenced the campaign in the most foolish and high-handed manner possible. To take the question of his appointments alone! To make Southampton General of Horse was insane. That gay and irresponsible young lecher had had no experience in the field; far worse, he was heavily under her Majesty's displeasure for his seduction of Mistress Vernon and their secret marriage, and had only shortly come out of the Fleet Prison. Next Essex appointed his stepfather, Sir Christopher Blount—a man odious to Elizabeth—as his Marshal of the Army. She had not liked it but she had borne with it. Blount was known to have a sturdy competence as a soldier in the field. But when his stepson proposed to make him a member of the Irish Privy Council in addition, she had flared up and told him that such positions were not in his gift. Essex sulked, raged and protested, but all noticed that he kept both men by him and it was strongly believed that they held the posts *de facto* which her Majesty had refused them *de jure*.

Such a beginning could surely only have one end. . . . Still his lordship seemed unable to force a decisive action upon the enemy. Then came a most disquieting rumour. Tom Lea, that gentlemanly cutthroat—considered the most desperate character in Essex House, no mean distinction!—was sent as messenger to the rebel Tyrone to arrange a parley. The parley actually took place with the two Commanders meeting at a river ford, midstream. Southampton, lingering on the bank, had been instructed to see that there were no eavesdroppers, but it was whispered that one or two had concealed themselves in the bushes. Certainly the most terrible and ominous rumours began to float over to England, that the two sworn enemies had proposed an alliance, the one to become King of England and the other King of Ireland. . . .

Then his Lordship of Essex, accompanied by a large number of his adherents, suddenly left his command in Ireland for a hasty return to England, against her Majesty's express command. . . .

The little group in the great library at Essex House had an air of imminent arrival or departure. They were still muffled in their cloaks and booted to the thigh, splashed with mud and dishevelled with hard riding. An air of furious decision hung over them, and it was shared by Penelope Rich in her scarlet brocades and Henry Cuffe in his sober suit of black. Sir Christopher Blount's voice was ringing out in a spirited harangue.

"Now is our hour! We must make sure of the Court at Nonsuch, and the only question is whether to strike at once with all our gallant fellows here—mount a couple of hundred and spur right away—or pause to raise the city—call out the Trained Bands——"

"Yes!" cried Penelope. "Robin, if you rode out now, the city would rise for you like one man! There isn't a 'prentice who would not throw down his work to follow you! With them, all young and vigorous, as many of the Trained Bands as possible, with your captains from Ireland, your veteran soldiers to lead and stiffen them, you'd have such an army that none could withstand you!"

She caught her brother by the arms and shook him with a nervous savagery. His face was grey with fatigue and the shadows beneath his eyes looked like bruises; his whole manner was slightly dazed. He hardly appeared to notice Penelope's assault upon him, her furious hands and insistent voice which seemed to tone with her bright hair and the brilliant colours of her dress. But none of these things impinged on the consciousness of Essex, and his dark eyes stared over her head with a dreamy intent on the unseen. "Robin!" she jerked him wildly. "Raise the city, Robin! Ride out like a king!"

Cuffe's voice thrust in with a quick hissing insistence.

"I don't agree with your Ladyship, though I'll not doubt the eventual success. . . . The time to strike is now. Now! If his Lordship rides, seizes the court at Nonsuch, all the rats in their holes, Cecil—Raleigh—Cobham—all the rats in a trap——" his hate nearly choked him—"catch that old—her most Gracious Majesty—get *her*——"

Only the words "her Gracious Majesty" made contact with Essex's drifting mind.

"Yes," he said as if he had made up that mind at last. "Her Majesty. I must get to her at once. Now!"

"Make a cavalry charge of it!" cried Blount. "In two hours—no, in one! I'll have them in the saddle for you, ready to follow you anywhere!"

"Men? I only want half a dozen to ride with me. And I go this minute."

"Robin!" screamed his sister. "You have run mad! Venture into their power? Cecil the Toad and Black Raleigh! You must ride as a conqueror! Show them, show that old woman who is called Queen —show them all who reigns in the people's hearts, and who will soon reign in verity——"

"Peace—let me be!" He had disengaged her shaking hands. His eyes seemed to open wider. "You are all pride and anger. . . ."

Then he had made one of his headlong exits, shouting: "Davers! Davers! To me! St. Lawrence! Tracey! Lea!"

The Lord Grey of Wilton, a friend and adherent of Robert Cecil, was riding to the court at Nonsuch, the country palace in Surrey, about ten miles to the south of London. His horse was fresh and he began rapidly to gain on a party of six horsemen, flogging their weary beasts. In view of the prevailing rumours, he was rather more than surprised to see the Earl of Essex only accompanied by six followers, and all of them obviously striving to make as good pace to the court as possible. He whipped up his own horse; he could not delay a minute with the news.

As he cantered past, he was shouted at, and one horseman, using whip and spurs, came thudding after him. It was Sir Thomas Gerard, one of the many knights created by Essex.

"My Lord! My Lord! Will you draw rein? I beg you will speak with the Earl."

"No," said Grey in truth. "I have business at court. . . ."

"Then I pray you, let my Lord of Essex ride before, that he may bring the first news of his return himself."

"Does he desire it?" asked Grey, looking at the red, angry face.

"No! Nor I think will desire anything at your hands!"

Grey drove his spurs in and his horse galloped away headlong. The others had reached Gerard and were questioning him excitedly. Sir Christopher St. Lawrence, another "knight of the order of Essex", drew his sword with a flourish.

"By God's heart! I'll have at him and spit him through—as I will his master, Cecil! I'll kill them both, so help me God!"

"He's out of reach and on a fresh horse," said Gerard.

"I have a dag," said Tom Lea, unslinging it.

"Peace!" said Essex. "It would be assassination! I must get to her Majesty! I must!" And they pressed on, their horses almost galloped to a standstill.

Grey poured out his story in something like a frenzy when he reached Nonsuch and Robert Cecil, who was the minister in attendance on her Majesty.

"London is packed with his men from Ireland, all his rakehell captains! They say he means to appeal to the city. There isn't a 'prentice who wouldn't up and follow him!"

"With their clubs as in a ward riot?"

"With pikes and muskets! 'Tis nothing to smile at! Half of them are Trained Bandsmen—and Sheriff Smith who is principal commander of the London Trained Bands is the Earl's, body and soul they say. He'll raise the city, militia, apprentices, rabble and his own followers who have left Ireland a'plenty! 'Tis the most desperate perilous sedition since '69!"

"But his Lordship is not raising the city and mustering an army. He is galloping for her Majesty with only six followers."

"He must surely have an army following him. He——"

"But not very close. And in the meanwhile he will arrive first, with only those same six followers."

Sunset

"Then—then you mean he will be in *our* hands?"

"My most excellent friend, you have reached that point somewhat slowly. . . ."

"But what are you going to do?"

"Nothing at present. Everything is being done. By his Lordship of Essex!"

The Queen was at her dressing-table, wrapped in her Chamber gown. A Maid of Honour had knelt to put on her Majesty's diamond-buckled shoes, having just put on her Majesty's silken stockings. Another was fetching a selection of wigs for her Majesty's choice, still more were directing the tiring women bringing out different articles of clothing. Looking at the Queen, at her few wisps of grey hair, at the wrinkled parchment covering the bones of her skull, the Lady Mary Howard thought: "She might be a hundred. . . ." Then vitality awoke in those deep-set eyes, vitality, the dregs of youth and a sudden intent eagerness. Feet were clattering noisily on the boards and the door burst open.

One of the women screamed and they all gasped. For anyone beyond her Majesty's immediate attendants, for a man, a young one, and the Earl of Essex at that—to see her Gracious Majesty before that unbelievable façade was erected upon the ruins. . . . She sat absolutely still, seemingly without breath, as he came running, threw himself on his knees, clutching at her as he laid his head on her lap. The force of him, the painful strength of his arms, his weight pressing—these recalled memories of other times when he had burst in upon her, and of one time when, exhausted by his own emotions, he had fallen asleep with his head on her lap. He had come to her often enough dishevelled, but now, though his clothes were on properly, he might have ridden straight from the campaign. He was spattered profusely with mud, his boots reeked of horse's sweat, he was unshaven with his hair and beard tangled, a heavy sword swung at his side and clanged against his spurs as he knelt, and beneath his leather jack, she could see the steel of a gorget or breastplate with its bluish gleam. And what was he thinking of her, bereft of her defences against time? How did he see her? Or was he seeing anything at all but the fantasies of his own brain? She had said once to another man: "I don't mind your seeing the worst of me now, Rob, as once you saw the best," but this young Essex had never seen her at her prime, let alone her youth! "If he were my son——" her thoughts began, but the stark truth was—that he might be her enemy. . . .

He was pouring out a confusion of words, of his thankfulness at reaching her, though the whole world had combined to separate them. She picked out phrases and protestations. He declared that she had surrounded herself with his enemies and let them poison her mind against him, but he would have them swept away. His army was ready! He had been advised to ride in force, but he could not wait! It was for her safety. . . . She had worse enemies than Tyrone. He would explain simply enough the situation as regards Tyrone, he had not dared to trust it to a letter which might be misinterpreted, altered by enemies. Enemies, enemies! The word ran through his excited speech, hers and his, they together must sweep them all away, he had his army—— She put her hand very gently on his chestnut head. Perhaps she was already in his power, perhaps his hare-brained and vicious followers had overpowered her guards, seized her ministers and courtiers. . . . She might be in mortal peril, when all the ugly forces behind him showed themselves openly. Then he raised his head and asked her simply: "You are glad that I have come?"

"I am always glad to have you with me!"

Yes, that was true, but it was one of those truths which seem a lie, in which she had so often traded. If only she did not have to use one against *him*, to guard herself with that verbal fencing, to deceive him with the serpent's wisdom of fifty years! Because it *was* true, she *was* glad to have him with her now and always, even if such gladness was also a wound. She thought: "My child—my dear child! If only I might have you quietly to myself, away from all your moral cut-throats, away from my burdens of State, and try to read your riddle, free your brain from such maggots. . . ." But that was impossible. She always knew the impossible.

She moved her hand, gently and caressingly on his head, gently she appeared to agree with his excited remarks. Yes, she was sure he could explain everything to her. ("And to my Council! An' it still functions!") Then she chaffed him lightly, clapping him on the cheek. What a way to come into a lady's bedroom, in his reeking boots! But when he began to murmur apologies, she laughed them away. It was no matter! Only he must go and attire himself suitably and give her a chance to dress. He kissed both her hands with fervour and went.

She told her ladies to get her ready as quickly as possible, not missing the rapt look in the eyes of Mary Howard. Before he had left for Ireland, *that* had been the most notorious and flamboyant of all his amours, and nothing could quench the languorous defiance of the beautiful girl. She had even disobeyed her Majesty point blank, had refused to carry the royal mantle in the garden because she wanted to day-dream of Essex when she was not with him. . . . She seemed to proclaim that nothing said or done to her could take this rapture from her, this rapture of being Essex's loved woman. Elizabeth had once felt an immense rage with the Lady Mary die away under the pressure of a greater weariness. She had told her, with a tired, bitter sarcasm: "Remain in virgin state—as much as may be!" She was quite certain now that the Lady Mary would steal away to him at the first opportunity. Let her—let them! She had other things of which to think. As soon as she was attired in her full panoply—"as soon", she thought bitterly, "as Ezekiel's miracle of the dry bones is well-nigh repeated, a daily miracle!"—she despatched the least scatter-brained Maid of Honour (in her opinion which was very low as regards her maids) to bring Sir Robert Cecil to her instantly. She would then know the extent of her peril and the position of Essex. . . .

Sir Robert Cecil was told how the Earl had burst into her Majesty's bedroom before she had her wig on or so much as a dab of paint. . . . He smiled, stroked his chin and observed: "Well, well! What a discomposing personality, his Lordship!" Still smiling, he went off to reassure her Majesty.

A few days later, stunning news was brought to Essex House. His Lordship was to be detained as a prisoner during her Majesty's pleasure, and confined at York House, the residence of the Lord Chancellor, Egerton. Her Majesty had appeared to receive his Lordship with every show of pleasure, the first messenger had told. There had been no need to send Christopher Blount's two hundred horsemen down to intimidate Nonsuch. His Lordship was to make his report to the Council; that was only natural. It had seemed that once again he had succeeded, once again he was bestriding the crest of the wave. Then the incredible, the appalling news!

Christopher Blount was pacing up and down the Great Chamber at Essex House.

"Did I not tell him?" he demanded. "To go alone so! Folly and worse than folly! Insensate madness. . . . Now, they hold him as a hostage. . ."

Sunset

"Cecil the toad and Raleigh the rat! And Cobham the scavenger kite!" cried Penelope.

"An' we had been with him!" said young Southampton, tossing his red locks.

"But you were not allowed, Harry! Poor Robin, he trusted our sweet Jezebel. . . ." Penelope's voice rasped with bitterness. She turned furiously to her sister-in-law, as usual stitching busily at her embroidery.

"Of which are you most jealous, Frances? The Lady Mary Howard or her Gracious Majesty? Upon my soul, I think you have most cause to fear the latter!"

The Lady Essex did not rise to this taunt. Raising her head from its attention on her work, she replied calmly: "You seem to forget that Robin's best hope in his peril, is her Majesty's favour."

Penelope brushed this aside. "How did she do it? Is it witchcraft? There goes Robin, as a'hungry for her as if she were his dearest love, throwing his head on her lap, pouring out his soul, and she persuades him that his return is all her delight, that she has no such happiness in the world as to have him with her—so that our most innocent Robin declares afterwards to all and sundry that he thanked God after so many storms abroad, he found a sweet calm at home—then when it is too late for us to do aught, she pounces! Like a cat who has let the mouse think that it strays safely beyond the reach of her paws. . . . How did she so beguile him? Why—when he came to her she was not yet dressed, she was without her wig, her paint——"

"You can't conceive how she looks!" said the young Countess of Southampton, the former Maid of Honour. She laid her hand on her husband's jewelled sleeve, and giggled.

"Yet she tricked him better than any great beauty!" burst out Penelope.

" 'Tis witchcraft and why not?" demanded Lettice. "Her mother was a notorious witch!"

"Our own blood, Madam!" said Penelope.

"Tchah! What of it? Didn't the old king say he was beguiled into marrying her by witchcraft? The devil taught beguilement to Great Aunt Nan *and* to her daughter! But one thing for which we may be thankful, his eyes are open at last. Didn't he say—'her mind, her conditions are as crooked as her carcass!' " Lettice shook with an odd passionate angry laughter. "He said: 'I am deceived. . . .' "

512

Sunset

"Aye, he did!" cried Southampton. "He cannot understand her base trickery! His nature is too noble——"

"Too simple!" said his sister bitterly. "But what are we doing?"

"Patience, sweet girl!" expostulated her stepfather. "Now we are doing all. Cuffe has the pamphlets ready for distribution far and wide, and let them follow upon the fiery indignant talk of all our gallant fellows in every tavern, 'twill keep the heart of London inflamed. You see they dare not speak of a trial, they dare not put him in the Tower, they can only detain him with the Lord Keeper who is his sworn friend."

"Yes, that is so," declared Southampton. "We agree that so long as he is only detained, in all honour, with the Lord Keeper or with his uncle, Sir William Knollys, we will not resort to any violence, lest it jeopardize our rightful cause."

"D'you think Jezebel and the Toad did not know that?" Penelope cried furiously.

"Come, now!" said Blount. "Is not your Charles in close touch with his Majesty of Scotland who looks to receive his crown at Robin's hands? His Scots Majesty will let no harm come to Robin. Robin shall out-rival him who was called the Kingmaker in the last century!"

"And how ended the Kingmaker, the Earl of Warwick?" asked Frances. "Was not King Edward IV deeply resentful that he received his crown from Warwick?"

"Caw! Caw! Caw! Need you croak so?" cried Penelope. "Must you croak like the crows that sit upon the gallows to pick out the dead man's eyes?"

"It will not help anyone, least of all your brother, Penelope, if you become hysterical," Frances said coldly.

"I have a heart!"

"So do others. But they do not wear them on their sleeves."

And one thought: "Philip loved *that*!" and the other: "Philip married *that*!"

"All will be well!" young Southampton declared. "They cannot stand against us, against all that we command!"

"The doting old fool will want Robin back!" sneered Lettice.

"Will she?" queried Southampton. "She seems well enough. At that foolery of Compton's in the tiltyard, she laughed till she near burst her laces. When he came on after the jousters, dressed as a fisherman, with half a dozen of his fellows bearing a great net with a blown-out representation of a frog therein. 'Twas another vile dig at our Essex. Compton, Cobham and Grey, they are the foul kites that swoop at any piece of filth left behind by Raleigh and Cecil! And yet she laughed!"

"She didn't laugh at Jack Harington! Did you ever see a man so frightened? She caught him by his girdle and nigh shook the life from him, swearing: 'By God's son, I am! no Queen! That man is above me!' That's how she speaks of Robin!" declared Penelope.

"So he should be above her!" cried Christopher Blount. "She is afraid of him.'. . ."

"Not she! She was so angered that she shook all spirit from poor Jack!" said Lettice. "But she watches the way the wind blows. Why, they scrawl vilenesses on the very walls of the Palace, abuse of Cecil, of Raleigh and of their vermin pack, worse than to be found in any Bankside lane—and she stomachs it. She must! But the old snake is not yet broken. 'Tis anger more than fear. And mayhap she will start to dote again even if she laughs at the buffooneries of Robin's enemies. She's like her mother, she'd laugh on the scaffold, laugh in hell!"

But Sir Robert Cecil did not indulge in anything so vigorous as a laugh. Only his smile never wavered, even when the scrawlers of obscenities wrote on his own door: 'Here Lieth The Toad.' The situation had been very delicate, very ticklish, but one's enemies made such incredible mistakes. If one waited long enough, and when events started moving, gently and almost imperceptibly manipulated them in a different direction to their original. . . . That after all had been her Gracious Majesty's policy for forty years. For the first time Robert Cecil began to share his father's appreciation of her Majesty's abilities. How much more was achieved than by those blustering methods of going into action with a flourish of trumpets! Yes, the old woman had forgotten more than most of his generation had ever or could ever learn! She was nearly finished now, of course, and torn by a perverse deep-rooted affection for that impossible and dangerous young man, but what a brain it was! He thought he had diagnosed the situation as regards Essex. He remembered how she had declared angrily: "If he were my son, I should imprison him in the highest tower in England for deserting his command!" Her voice had broken a little on the words "my son". *That* was how she saw Essex. But that also was being delicately attended to. His cousin, Francis Bacon, was really doing very well, and had displayed a serpentine ingenuity in running with the hare and hunting with the hounds. Now, however, it seemed rather perilous to adhere too closely to the hare. . . . He had made an admirable suggestion to her Majesty, planting a barb in the very heart of her affection.

She had discussed with her Learned Counsel the ways and means of bringing Essex to trial before the Star Chamber, for so grossly mishandling the Irish campaign, treasonable intercourse with Tyrone, and finally deserting his command against her Majesty's express orders. Quite an unpleasant tally! But Bacon had advised her Majesty that it might not be possible to press the charges home. The Earl was too popular! To alter slightly a phrase of that popular dramatist, who was patronized by the Earl of Southampton, if it were a sin to covet popularity, her Majesty was the most offending soul alive! And Francis had told her in effect that her own popularity was not strong enough to outface that of Essex in a public arena, and the "matter had best be wrapped up privily"! Not, thought Robert Cecil, that *that* was altogether true. It would be interesting—but dangerous— to set the people's love for her Majesty squarely against their love for Essex. The tavern orators and wall-scrawlers did not abuse her Majesty. Oh no! They believed she was misled by Cecil himself and the others against whom their abuse was directed. Now the vilifications and scrawls were blaring against Francis Bacon. He did not like it. He came to his cousin, his voice shrill with indignation, declaring that he "had the privy-coat of a good conscience!" Cecil's smile became angelic. He was quite sure, whatever people said, that his cousin had no evil intention against that unhappy gentleman, the Earl of Essex. . . . (But he had just managed to instil the most deadly and subtle poison against the Earl of Essex into her Majesty's mind!) He added: "For my part, I am merely passive and not active in this action; and I follow the Queen and that heavily, and I lead her not. . . ." In fact, though he did not say so, he was dealing with the entire situation and with her Majesty's self, after her Majesty's manner of waiting upon events. Other people could not understand, they were peculiarly irritated by that smile of his. Walter Raleigh— now his firmest ally against Essex—wrote him a furious energetic letter. Clamorous phrases assaulted his brain.

Sunset

"I am not wise enough to give you advice; but if you take it for a good counsel to relent towards this tyrant, you will repent it when it shall be too late."

And again:

"And if her Majesty's favour fail him, he will again decline to a common person. . . . Lose not your advantage; if you do, I rede your destiny!"

"No," thought Cecil. "I do not think Sir Walter is wise enough to give me advice! Such precipitation. . . ."

So the summer months of the first year of the seventeenth century drew away with Essex still a captive in the Lord Keeper's house. There was much angry buzzing in the taverns which obviously originated from Essex House, but the bees did not sting. . . . And then in the late autumn Essex fell gravely ill.

On the 28th of November 1600, when the early twilight was drawing in, the Queen arose suddenly in her Withdrawing Chamber and gave orders. Her great barge must be prepared for she was going to the Lord Keeper's, York House in the Strand. She beckoned the Countess of Warwick to her. "Anne, I would have you come with me. No other lady. . . . Which of my lords and gentlemen are now waiting in the Privy Chamber?" A Maid of Honour was despatched and then an usher. The Earl of Worcester was there, the Lords Grey of Wilton and Compton, Sir Walter Raleigh and Master Fulke Greville. Her Majesty asked them to summon the Earl of Worcester as she would have him attend her in her barge. No, she would take no others. . . .

Dusk was coming thick as they went down to the royal stairs. A heavy white mist was rising up from the steely bosom of the Thames to join the winter's murky air. The great barge, which in summer, with its canopy of cloth of gold, its many banners, and its attendants in scarlet braided with gold, would run down river with a Venetian pomp, now seemed to be nosing its way into darksome fantasies, as the mist coiled about it. Presently lights sprang out on the bank from the great houses of the Strand, making the darkness opaque. On the other shore, a reeking vapour, white and ghastly, was steaming up from Lambeth marshes. The Countess of Warwick looked at the Queen, huddled closely in her heavily furred mantle. It was too dark for her to see Elizabeth's face, but she could observe the tense still-

516

ness of that figure sitting so close beside her. And there was no gesture that one could make to try and pierce that dreadful loneliness.

Lord Worcester, sitting facing them, observed: "Winter comes on apace now, your Grace."

The Queen said: "Winter always comes. One cannot escape it."

"But spring follows hard after," said Anne Warwick.

"Spring does not come for everyone!"

At the landing stage there was a great stir, torches streaming in the dank air, the Lord Keeper himself falling on his knees as her Majesty came ashore on Lord Worcester's arm. She bade him rise and then asked curtly: "Essex—what of him?"

"Your Majesty—he now seems in a sort of stupor. The physicians saw him at two o'clock, and they will be returning later in the evening. For days he was in high fever, high raving fever which naught could abate. Then after your Majesty's most clement permission for his Lady to come to him, the fever seemed to fall, yet he is dazed and scarcely knows anyone. . . . The physicians are much disquieted."

"I will go to him."

They were walking through the Lord Keeper's formal garden, their way lined with torches, the resinous smell of their burning in the air, their flames flaring and wavering in the breezes, showing the spectral shapes of leafless trees. The Queen continued to speak.

"Sir Robert Cecil persuaded me that there could be no harm in letting his wife come to him if the rest of his family were barred."

"Indeed, yes, your Majesty. She will give him no evil counsel. She is a good woman. Which is more than I can say for his mother or sister."

Upstairs a black-gowned apothecary was mixing drugs at a table in an ante-chamber. Here the Lord Keeper and the Earl of Worcester halted. The Queen went on, and Lady Warwick waited at the door. Elizabeth saw the figures of tapestry hangings sway and dip in the light of a banked sea-coal fire, she saw the four posts of the bed, and then with a rustle of silk, the young woman sank to the floor in a deep curtsy. In a curt whisper the Queen asked her: "Well—how is he? Good—or bad?"

"It is good, your Grace, that the high fever has left him. It is bad that he is so weak and exhausted and his brain is so confused that he hardly knows anyone. He will not know your Grace. . . ."

The Queen went to the bed and stood looking down. He was lying on his back, his head moving restlessly on the pillow, as if he were in an evil dream. Sometimes he muttered but his voice was so faint she could hear nothing of what he said. She stooped and touched his temple. It was wet and cold. He moved a little at her touch and his eyes opened, but she knew he did not see her. He stared past her, through her, as if she were a window, as if she were not there at all. . . . Wherever he was, she was not; there was no longer any bridge between them. She could hear Frances Essex's tense breathing and knew that both she and Anne Warwick were watching her intently. She thought with an emptiness of despair: "If I were his mother, I would know what to do. . . ." Then he moved again, so that his cheek was against her hand, and she felt her eyes burn and smart with unshed tears. "But still he does not know me, and *I* shall never know truly whether he hates or loves me."

She did not know how long she stood there, leaning forward, her hand against his cheek. Then she turned and Frances Essex was curtsying low before her once more and whispering gratitude for being allowed to come to him.

"You are very forgiving, Madam!" Elizabeth said.

"Forgiving, your Majesty?"

"He has been a mightily unfaithful husband to you."

"But I love him, your Grace."

The ante-chamber was empty; the apothecary had been summoned out to speak to the Lord Keeper in the corridor. Elizabeth looked at the Countess of Warwick. When she spoke it was in a low, bitter voice.

"Very forgiving!" she repeated.

"It should not be so hard for your Grace to understand. You also —forgave much."

She stared. "I? Anne—did you then know about Robert and myself?"

"Yes," said Anne Warwick placidly.

The widow of Robert's devoted and only long-surviving brother —perhaps it was inevitable that she should know.

"Ha! Perhaps then you hold yourself my sister-in-law?"

"I would not presume so."

"No, you would not. But you are my friend, I know. . . ."

"Yes."

She put her hand on Anne Warwick's arm.

Sunset

"It seems so long since Rob died. I have lived too long, I think."

"The people would never agree to that."

"Would they not? They are always ready to shout for something new, I believe."

"But they need you."

"Their devotion is all that is left to me now."

"It seems so long since Rob died, I have lived too long, I think."

"The people would never agree to that."

"Would they not? They are always ready to shout for something new, I believe."

"But they need you."

"Their devotion is all that is left to me now."

Chapter Nine

The cold clear light rose from the river, burnished by the harsh white gleam of the winter sun. It showed the yard at Essex House, filled with horses standing saddled, like some military camp. Penelope Rich leaning from a window, seeing everything illumined in that harsh, yet passionless light, felt a surge of exultation. "Now!" she thought. "Now at last! Action!" Action to burst that steel net which had seemed to be binding them to a bitter impotence, strangling their hopes, action against a tangible foe, now a more deadly but intangible one—the strange adoration of Essex for the Queen—was overthrown.

A year ago he had been released from the Lord Keeper's house, and sent back to his own, after most of his followers had been ordered out of it. He had been admonished by the Star Chamber, not brought to trial. Francis Bacon had said the Queen dare not bring him to trial, he the people's darling. But Francis was a rat and deserter who had sold himself body and soul to the Cecil faction. . . . The Countess of Essex had said that she believed there was still enough of her Majesty's old affection for him left, for her to dread punishing him. Penelope had snorted with contempt at her sister-in-law's view. Then finally he had been released from all restraint, allowed to reassemble his household and go anywhere he would, except to the court, except to have any access to her Majesty. She had refused to answer any of his pleading, imploring letters, she had refused to renew the sweet wines monopoly. "Because she is a miser herself, she sees everything in terms of gold, and believes if she reduces him to destitution, she has finished him!" thought Penelope. At last Robin had seen that she was his enemy, after his mother and stepfather, his sister and all his adherents had been dinning it into his ears for so long. They had no need to do so any longer. Sometimes he cried out and raved against

520

her Majesty so that a few of his supporters had been scared away, such as Jack Harington, who had received his knighthood at the hands of Essex. But that gay rattlepate had a genuine affection for his royal godmother and had left Essex's house never to return, murmuring: "His speeches of the Queen becometh no man who hath *mens sana in corpore sano!*"

But others clustered to him. He had only to ride through the city, go to the Paris Garden to see the bear-baiting or appear in any of the theatres, to be mobbed by an enthusiastic crowd. The young and restless had always crowded to him, now it was said that every man who had a grievance went to Essex House. With them came those whom Elizabeth had called "moral cut-throats", who profited by fishing in troubled waters. Essex House hummed and pullulated with those who believed that society could only be improved if the whole structure was pulled down in ruins. And one of the most fervent of these was Penelope. Together with their stepfather, Blount, she urged her brother towards violent action. He must seize the court and imprison his enemies as he had failed to do on his immediate return from Ireland, he must force his will upon the Queen and make himself virtual ruler of the land. Penelope's fervour had become hysterical on the defection of her lover, Mountjoy. He had been one of the inner circle around Essex, comprising Christopher Blount, the Earl of Southampton, Sir Charles Davers and Henry Cuffe; he had been the intermediary with the King of Scots. But he had become Lord Deputy in Ireland in place of Essex, and he was succeeding where Essex had failed; slowly but relentlessly he was driving Tyrone back and back. Was it possible, thought Penelope in anguish, that he had cherished a secret grudge against Robin, for originally opposing his appointment? She could not believe that of Charles and yet—— The blow had fallen. He had been asked point-blank to bring over part of his army from Ireland to assist in the rebellion and he had refused.

"To satisfy my Lord of Essex's private ambition, he would not enter into an enterprise of that nature."

He had written privately to Penelope begging her to persuade her brother to withdraw from such a perilous enterprise and "recover her Majesty's favour by ordinary means". He entreated Penelope not to endanger herself. In mounting hysteria, she had desperately pursued an opposite course. Behind her she seemed to feel the warmth of hatred for the Queen which had burned in her mother's heart for forty years. Lettice was saying very little these days. The momentum she had released was going forward at a terrible pace; her husband and her daughter were urging her son on, while behind him surged his followers like a pack of hungry hounds. Nothing could hold them back now.

And yet, and yet—— Their plans lacked a vital coherence. Essex might rave at the Queen, and yet there were times when he fell into his unhappy dreams of wanting her, needing her, as if she alone could unlock a door which would allow him to escape from his troubles and confusions. Then he shrank from action; not for any fear of danger, for he had a curious unawareness of physical danger, but for fear of hurting or angering her. He agreed that her government must be swept away and all her Privy Council brought to the block except his uncle, Knollys and the Lord Keeper, but he could not bear to contemplate any harm coming to her. He seemed lost in that dream of they two together, supreme and hand-in-hand as when they had danced the Pavane of Tears on Twelfth Night. Truly the measure which the Queen had stepped with Robert Devereux, Earl of Essex, belonged to the tears of life, *lachrimae rerum*.

But action had been forced on him. The day before, Secretary Herbert had come, summoning him to appear before the Privy Council.

"They seek your death! The Queen seeks your death!" Lettice cried at her son, as he stood very still against the heavy window curtains, the window's light shining on his white doublet.

"You'll never get to court alive!" declared Christopher Blount. "You'll be set upon and poniarded! Raleigh'll have you murdered. Ferdinando Gorges (another follower of Essex) has pretended to be in friendly intercourse with him to gain information, and there is no doubt your life is encompassed. You must strike now!"

"Yes, now!" cried Penelope and Southampton echoed her.

"Yes, now!" he agreed, but his eyes stared past them, as if seeking that which was yet unseen. Only half his mind seemed with them as they sat till late, making plans, drawing up the details of the morrow's action. Christopher Blount was to command the assault on the gates of Whitehall. The Earl of Southampton, the Lords Mounteagle and Sandys, the little Earl of Rutland who had just been married to the fifteen-year-old stepdaughter of Essex, Sir Charles Davers and Henry

Sunset

Cuffe, they all sat around the table in the library, debating and arguing, and Penelope Rich was the only woman there. Sir Gilly Merrick, Steward of the household who hated her Majesty most hotly, went out at the head of a turbulent company of the gentlemen of Essex House. To the Globe Theatre they went, and Sir Gilly took the manager aside to demand the performance of a certain play, one written by my Lord of Southampton's Master Shakespeare. It was the first of the plays he drew from the historical chronicles, *Richard II*.

The manager had demurred when Sir Gilly insisted. Everyone knew that such a play dealing with the overthrow and murder of an anointed sovereign was held to be seditious. He pleaded it was old-fashioned, no longer in demand. Sir Gilly hurled money down on the table.

"Put it on, I say! There is forty shillings extra!"

The manager had complied. The house was packed with Merrick's ruffling blades, and supposing, as so many whispered, that the Earl of Essex was about to return to power? That evening, Sir Gilly, with a sword in one hand and a goblet of sack in the other, had cried loudly that he had shown them the sort of leader England needed, another Bolingbroke! Neither a weak doting King nor a doting old woman for a Queen!

Now morning had come, as cold and sharp and bright as steel, and that river of furious energy was ready to burst its banks. "Action at last!" thought Penelope with some of the same rapture with which she had thrown herself into the arms of Mountjoy. There was a stir in the great hall below, a murmur like the sea moving over a bed of shingle. Voices drew individually from the press of sound, she heard Tom Lea shouting: "Throw them out! Throw the Great Seal out of the window!" She leaned over the gallery, staring at the small company passing through those angry human waves. She could see the face of the Lord Keeper Egerton and that of her uncle, William Knollys, close behind him. With them was the Earl of Worcester. Those of her Majesty's councillors who were friendly towards Robin! The old hag is setting her trap well, but we know better! She found she was clenching her hands, longing to join in the shouting: "Throw them out! Shop them up! Shop them up! Throw the Great Seal out of the window!" The Lord Keeper was trying to speak. He had come in the Queen's name, to ask the occasion of this great assembly and bid them disperse peacefully; if any had just and lawful cause of complaint it should be investigated. The chorus was let loose again, headed by the voices of Tom Lea and Owen Salisbury. "Kill them! Kill them! Throw them out!" Penelope saw her brother striding towards the head of the stairs, and as he raised his arm, the furious mob fell back from the councillors who began to ascend.

"My Lords," he said. "It is too late for me to speak with you now."

They pressed on towards him, and the mob followed them, but one gesture from Essex had stayed their violence. Others were clustering to him, Christopher Blount and Lettice, Southampton, and the boy Rutland, Sir Gilly Merrick. In a doorway, Cuffe hesitated.

"Essex!" cried the Lord Keeper. "Listen to the voice of reason before it is too late. . . ."

"Robin—I beseech you!" began his uncle, Knollys.

Essex made a strange gesture.

"It *is* too late," he said. Owen Salisbury—considered second worst desperado after Lea—had pushed forward to his side.

"Salisbury, you will conduct their Lordships to the library and you will guard the door. You will not suffer a hair of their heads to be harmed but you will not let them go forth till I bid you. On your allegiance, I charge you!"

"I obey, my Lord!"

"Essex!" the Lord Keeper finally cried out. But he and the others were shepherded forward, Salisbury with his bare blade between them and the mob. The library door clattered to, and Christopher Blount shouted: "Now! Now!" There was more shouting in the hall below as a man struggled to make his way through. He was calling: "My Lord! My Lord!" It was Sir Charles Davers.

"Yes?" said Essex. "What is it?"

"My Lord, the guards at Whitehall are doubled! They are prepared! We'll never carry the place by surprise assault!" His speech was punctuated by his panting breaths. "Never—my Lord—you must fly—to Wales—or to Ireland!"

"It is too late," said Essex and he smiled a strange unearthly smile. Davers was beside him, his chest heaving.

"My Lord, they are prepared! Cecil knows! He has everything ready. He, his brother Burghley, Raleigh, the Lord Admiral, Lord Cumberland——"

Sunset

"Go to the city, Robin!" shrieked Penelope. "The Trained Bands! Sheriff Smith promised you!"

"Yes, he promised me a thousand men."

"We must forward now!" said Blount. "We cannot delay an instant. With a thousand of the city's soldiers and our own followers we can carry Whitehall. Forward!"

They were all about the tall, irresolute figure of Essex. Southampton was demanding: "It's that or our lives! Don't you see——? Your enemies, Cecil and the rest, they'll have your life! Cecil who would sell the country to Spain——!"

"I must get to her Majesty!" said Essex desperately.

"Do you think you'd be allowed? Your enemies will kill you, sell the country—— You'll come to her Majesty at the head of your victorious army, trampling over the bodies of your enemies!"

Essex was staring, his eyes brilliant, his forehead glistening with sweat. His lips were moving and Penelope wondered if it were prayer. But it seemed to be lines from the ubiquitous Master Shakespeare:

"If it be now, 'tis not to come; if it be not to come, it will be now; if it be not now, yet it will come: the readiness is all!"

He raised his voice and echoed Blount with a mighty shout.

"Now! We'll raise the city, and we'll take Whitehall! I will carve my way to her most dear Majesty's side through the blood of traitors!" His voice dropped. He murmured: "I remember so well how once I pressed my way to her side, drove back the Cecils, convinced *her*—whose mind had been bewildered and befogged by my enemies —triumphed though not by action of the flesh—and at last when she and I were reunited, I laid my head on her lap and slept. . . . I cannot sleep again, I think, there are clouds of angry dreams about me, till she disperse them! Oh, when I have driven them all back, the pride, the anger, the lies and the malice, the shouting of hatred, then I will sleep again. . . ."

He was running down the stairs, shouting joyfully: "To arms! An Essex! An Essex! To arms! A plot is laid for my life—for all our lives! To her Majesty!"

Lettice was clinging to her husband frenziedly, froth on her lips.

"Kit, if you ever loved me, you must kill the Queen! Oh, swear to me you'll kill that devil, that accursed witch—Kit, my darling, my dearest love! If once she turns her eyes upon Robin, he is sunk, sunk under baleful enchantment! Kill her, Kit! You need a silver bullet for

525

a witch. . . . Run your sword into her, stab her, kill her! Oh, Kit, an'
you ever loved me, do this for heaven's pity!"

Blount was breathing as shortly as if he had been running.

"Come, sweetheart! I'll not fail Robin. . . . An' it needs be—I'll
draw blood even from the Queen's Majesty!"

Then he too was running, and Southampton, young Rutland,
Mounteagle, Davers and Merrick, pressing close to his Lordship,
heading that crowd which surged forward like a pack of hounds for
their meat, like flood waters hungry for dry land. Penelope was drawn
after them, as they poured out into the Strand.

They did not stop to fetch their horses, they did not fall into
ordered lines as soldiers, they had no muskets, no defensive armour,
only a pistol or two and their swords. They were not an army, they
were a mob, as they streamed down the Strand after Essex, half
running, half walking, shouting: "To arms! To arms! Cecil has sold
the country to Spain! There is a plot laid for my life! To arms!"
Beside him, looking strangely elongated in black from head to foot,
gesticulating fiercely and yelling strange rallying cries: "Saw! Saw!
Saw! Tray! Tray! Tray!" was Christopher Blount. On they went, with
incoherent fury towards Ludgate.

Penelope stopped, and put her hand to the gatepost. She felt weak
as if she had lost blood. Beside her, her mother was staring after the
retreating mob. Her face was purple under its pink paint. Frances
Essex came forward, *her* face as still as if it were carved in stone. With
a cold anger beyond description, she stared at her husband's mother,
at her husband's sister. Behind her was her daughter, the little Countess of Rutland, her eyes round with childish terror.

With a soft but terrible intensity, Frances said: "Do you not know
that you will answer for what you have done, before God?"

She outstared them both, Penelope and old Lettice.

"You will answer before God!" she repeated.

Essex House was an empty shell, echoing with quietness. Penelope
lay back on a day-bed, unable to combat that sudden drained exhaustion. She wanted peace, she wanted darkness, she wanted
Charles's arms round her to blot out the world's jangle, she wanted to
bury herself under the oblivion of sleep. But she could not rest. She
heard her sister-in-law's implacable voice, while her whole being
seemed strained towards the city, into which her brother had led his
men, that frantic rabble. The day became timeless, passed into an

aching emptiness, through which every sound seemed to travel with strange foreboding.

She did not know what hour it was when her sister-in-law came and said in that same relentless voice: "Owen Salisbury has obeyed me, and let out the imprisoned councillors. Ferdinando Gorges has taken them back to Whitehall." Penelope stared at her, her brain unable to make sense—"Owen Salisbury has obeyed me. . . . Ferdinando Gorges has taken them back to Whitehall. . . ." Whitehall! she screamed the word.

"They are proclaiming Robin a traitor all over the city. The heralds are proclaiming him," said his wife in that same icy voice.

"Heralds! In the city? But has he not seized it? Are not the Trained Bands mustering for him?"

Frances shrugged and turned away. Lettice came padding up, suddenly seeming old and flabby, her voice whimpering.

"Pen, Pen! What's happening! Has no one any news?"

Penelope took her hand gently.

"Frances has heard . . . of heralds. . . ."

"Sir Ferdinando Gorges informed me. He is going to Whitehall, to make the best terms for himself. He says it is the time for everyone to try and make their own terms. I did not attempt to stay him."

"I wonder you did not accompany him?" shrieked Penelope.

"I thank God, now and eternally, that Philip never knew what you truly are."

"No. I spared him that. . . . I let him keep his dreams whatever they cost me. I hurt myself not to hurt him. But how could you understand human feelings, you block of marble?"

"Feelings! The feelings you boast of are petty lusts, petty ambitions, petty prides——" she stopped abruptly. Her daughter was there, the little Countess of Rutland, all her married dignity of a month cast to the winds, no more than a terrified child grieving for that other child whom she had married.

"Mother, Mother! Where were you? I searched everywhere. . . . What is happening? What will happen to Roger?"

Frances put her hand on her and seemed to quieten her by touch.

Henry Cuffe suddenly appeared, biting his nails, his eyes shifting this way and that, as if he expected an enemy to appear.

"My Lady. Had I not better burn the papers? The dangerous papers?"

"You must do as you think fit, Master Cuffe," said Frances.

He took his fingers from his mouth and muttered.

"But his Lordship has the most important letter of all, from the King of Scots, in a black bag hanging round his neck. . . ."

"I know. We can do nothing about that."

"But what is happening?" Penelope was shaken by the shrillness of her own voice. Cuffe darted a sidelong glance at her.

"They're surrounded, my Lady. Shut into the city. There's a guard at every gate."

"A guard! A guard of what?"

"Soldiers, my Lady, the Queen's men. They say that all the Trained Bands of the surrounding counties have been called up, and the Tower garrison. The Lord Admiral is there with men from the Fleet. The Bishop of London, the Earl of Cumberland, Sir John Leveson—they are all commanding troops."

"But the London Trained Bands? The best in the country!"

"I haven't heard anything of what they're doing, my Lady. . . ."

"But Sheriff Smith promised!" cried old Lettice.

"Yes, my Lady. The last news I had before the city was closed was that his Lordship had gone to the Sheriff's house."

"Then all will be well——"

"No, my Lady. When his Lordship entered, the Sheriff went out, by the back door, to the Lord Mayor. The Lord Mayor they say was with her Majesty's men when his Lordship was proclaimed a traitor."

Lettice was choking with terrified fury.

"That filthy, cringing knave, Smith! That whoreson traitor——"

"A traitor to Robin, Mother," said Penelope. "Not to her most gracious Majesty!"

"I must go and burn the papers if your Ladyships will excuse me."

Elizabeth Rutland was sobbing helplessly.

"Mother, Mother, what will happen? What will they do to Roger?"

Penelope felt as if she gathered herself together. She leaned forward, looking straight at her dead love's child, taking that cold hand with young Rutland's wedding ring on it.

"Listen, Elizabeth!" she said in a quietly determined voice. "Whatever happens—even if the worst happens—no serious harm will come to Roger. He is too young! He will not be held responsible."

She and her sister-in-law exchanged glances like sworn enemies at a truce to perform some action of mercy such as bringing in the wounded. Elizabeth Rutland was leaning her cheek against her mother's shoulder, as she faced Penelope. She looked at her with a sort of imploring gratitude. Penelope got to her feet.

"I'll have a horse saddled and ride out to try to gain news."

"No, no, Pen!" cried her mother. " 'Twould be dangerous."

The setting sun was splashing orange on the western skies, when there was bustle at the water gate. Men were landing from wherries and barges. Essex stood, tall and aloof, in the middle of the bustling throng getting ashore, making fast, and lifting two limp bodies on to the landing stage. One stirred, raised a head in rough bloodstained bandages, it was Christopher Blount. The other lay quite still, covered by a blue velvet cloak.

"My sweet Kit!" shrilled Lettice. Frances had taken her husband's hands and was gazing up at him. "His eyes see spectres," thought Penelope. "He looks as he did as a child with the nightmare." He was pointing to the covered body.

"Tracey is killed," he said in a flat voice. "He was killed for me. He stepped in front of me to take the bullet. We tried to force our way through Ludgate, but we could not. They killed Tracey and we killed one of theirs I think—and Kit was wounded. So we got down to the river before they could prevent us."

Thought Penelope: "Very few have come back with him, though. And those that have—all the spirit's out of them. Only Tom Lea has his swagger. He would swagger in hell. . . ." She turned eagerly to Southampton. "Harry! What has happened?"

He pushed back his long red locks. "Oh, my God!" he said. "It was terrible. Terrible! Not a soul rose for us. The city gaped, and did nothing. Smith turned traitor. And Pickering, the armourer of Cheapside who had promised Robin everything, refused to give him arms. Robin said: "Not for *me*, Pickering?" And her Majesty has raised the strongest forces since the Armada. The city will do nothing for us."

"Oh, those vile, cringing, mercenary city scoundrels——!"

Her brother was swinging round, turning upon her.

"You proud and angry woman! Do you never think of your sins? Mine so hang over me that they encompass the whole of my being. . . ."

The two young Rutlands were clinging to each other. His round face, innocent yet of the razor, was horror-stricken. "I don't under-

stand!" he said. "They turned from us as if we had the plague. . . ."
In the morning he had run gaily off on his first adventure, waving his
sword and shouting. "Oh, the poor babies!" thought Penelope. She
could hear her mother, who had suddenly turned into an old woman
this day, whimpering: "My sweet Kit, my sweet and lovely lad!"

They were in the hall now, and she thrust a cup of wine at Southampton who looked at the end of his tether. He was talking of the
impossibility of getting a message through to his wife, in his town
residence, Drury House, in Holborn. "Bess won't know if I am alive.
. . ." Then he repeated: "Oh, my God, it was terrible! Walking, walking, calling them to rise, our own men drifting away, and those stony
faces staring, giving us no emotion but greedy curiosity. . . . And
Robin looking as if he were cast alive into hell!" That, Penelope
agreed, was how he looked still. . . . She could hear men bustling
about, blockading the gates under the direction of Sir Charles Davers
and Sir Gilly Merrick. She supposed their enemies would soon come
after them. She was not mistaken, and it was not long before the
house was surrounded by soldiers.

A white flag was hoisted in demand for a parley and Essex went up
on the roof to speak. The opposing forces were commanded by that
resolute old man, the Lord Admiral. In a stentorian voice, he bade
Essex surrender to the Queen's justice.

"I will never surrender. I will die sword in hand and my body can
be buried beneath the ruins of this house."

"Have at you then, i' God's name!"

Musketry began to spit against the walls. Men came running down
the stairs.

"Captain Salisbury's been mortally wounded!"

"Owen Salisbury?"

"Yes! He would stand at a window, endangering himself, saying
that his life was already forfeit, having imprisoned the councillors
and affronted the Great Seal! The second volley hit him."

One of the Countess of Essex's gentlewomen had hysterics.
Frances bustled them, the children and most of the servants to the
river side of the house, where no shots might come through the
windows. Penelope preferred to stay with her brother and his companions in the great hall. Presently she heard a voice which made her
start violently. It sounded like Philip Sidney's, but it was his younger
brother, Robert, who had come unarmed to the postern.

Sunset

"Essex, Essex!" he cried. "Listen to me. I bear a message from the Lord Admiral. He says if your Lady and all other gentlewomen, yes and the women servants, would wish to leave the house he will permit it. They may have an hour to get ready and then they may leave by the river."

"Tell the Lord Admiral, I am deeply grateful for this his most generous offer. I will ask my wife to go and take all the women and children."

"I will tell him. But Essex, for pity's sake surrender! He has sent for artillery from the Tower and for culverins from ships in the Pool. He'll blast the house about your ears. . . ." But Essex did not answer. Penelope thought: "I won't go with the other women. I won't!" Tom Lea looked at all the whitening faces around him and laughed. He picked up a lute which someone had left on a table, struck a chord and began to sing from the popular ballad.

> "Like as we lived and loved together true,
>   So both at once we'll bid the world adieu!"

"Not that song, Captain Lea!" cried Penelope.

"Why, Lady Pen? 'Tis mightily appropriate."

"Damnably appropriate. They will make such ballads for us!"

"I'll warrant! They'll sing us the length of the Kingdom!"

"And we will not hear for our ears will be stopped with earth!"

"Never earth! They will be filled with the four winds of heaven. Above London Bridge, with our heads on spikes!"

When the sounds of the artillery being moved started, grinding and clattering on the roadway outside Essex House, he sang in gay defiance, as if to challenge the heavy engines of death.

> "Hey nonny no!
>   Men are fools that wish to die!
>   Is't not fine to dance and sing
>   When the bells of death do ring?
>   Is't not fine to swim in wine,
>   And turn upon the toe
>   And sing hey nonny no,
>   When the winds blow and the seas flow?
>   Hey nonny no!"

The barge ran down river, away from the doomed house. Frances

531

Sunset

Essex held her little son against her knees. Her daughter, Elizabeth Rutland, pressed close to her, holding a piece of her skirt as if for reassurance. Frances was thinking of her son. How much will he always remember? How will this shape him? He was staring with fright at his grandmother, her tears making a puddle of the rouge on her cheeks. Lettice was wailing: "Oh, my poor, sweet Kit—to leave him behind so sorely hurt! And Penelope alone with all those men, and Robin——"

"They are in God's hands, Madam," said Frances.

"Oh, Mother, will I ever see Roger? He'll be killed!"

"Roger is in God's hands. We all are. Every hour of our lives."

"But they aren't in God's hands!" screamed Lettice. "They are in the hands of that devil, my cousin, Elizabeth. . . ." She began to babble of "my poor, sweet Kit", "my poor, pretty Penelope", and "Robin—my boy!" Frances looked at her in sorrow.

"We can only pray," she said softly.

"Prayers won't move Elizabeth!" She looked wildly around her, from one bank of the river to the other. Then in a dreadful whisper she asked: "What have I done?" Her voice rose to a frenzied shrillness. "What have I *done*?"

Essex had gone up on the roof again. Night had fallen but the tossing flames of torches showed him the wicked muzzles of culverins.

"Nottingham! My Lord Admiral!" he called.

"I am here!"

"To save the lives of all in this house, I surrender. . . ."

Lea had caught Penelope's wrist.

"Listen, Lady Pen! I'll not be taken. I'll get away, and make one final throw for him!"

The great gates were unbarred and thrown back. Essex was coming forth in the torch light, into the cold night air. He held his sword by the blade. Solemnly, he proffered the hilt to the Lord Admiral.

Chapter Ten

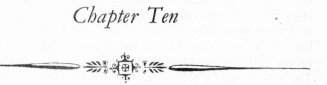

Sir Robert Cecil had every reason to feel pleased with himself. He had known now for a long time that there could be no peace while the great problem of the Earl of Essex remained unhealed. Now it should be healed by the sharpest of all medicines, and he and his chosen associates could progress in their task of administering the realm, consolidating the gains of that remarkable half-century, and preparing for the future. Her most gracious Majesty was approaching the allotted span of three score years and ten, and such events as the Essex rising were scarcely conducive to its lengthening. She was a wonderful woman, or rather had been one, but her day was past. The obvious successor was the King of Scots, and though Cecil understood well enough her Majesty's objection to naming her successor in the past, there was no reason left now—except in the mind of her Majesty. No doubt she saw the King of Scots as a *memento mori*, it was perhaps only human. But one important factor had already been extracted from the traitor, Cuffe, that his Lordship of Essex had been in touch with the King of Scots, who was sending the Earl of Mar, one of his closest friends, to London that very summer. Only now, the Earl of Mar would not meet the Earl of Essex—who by that time would be past meeting any one on earth—he would meet Sir Robert Cecil, who would take pains to assure him that if his Scottish Majesty would only leave everything to him, Cecil, make no moves, support no such adventurers as Essex, he could solemnly promise that when God saw fit to take her Majesty unto Himself, the crown of England should pass as surely and peaceably to the King of Scots as if he had been Queen Elizabeth's eldest son. For that reason all the treasonable correspondence of Essex with the King of Scots would be carefully suppressed in the Trial for Treason. One did not wish to cause any unpleasantness for one's future monarch. . . . He had suggested this suppression to her Majesty, without, of course, stating the reason. But she knew it, he could see, as the bitter smile curled her lips. She had made an uncomfortable remark, seemingly apropos of nothing, of how little faith there was left in Israel. . . . He was far from being without feeling, and he was sorry for her. But he was looking forward into the future, when James VI of Scotland should be James I of England. Then one would be able to make peace with Spain. England needed it, Spain needed it. But the main obstacle was the old Queen herself, not that she did not desire peace, but she had become a symbol of their humiliation to the Spaniards. It was odd really, because she was the most unwarlike of mortals, apt to be cynical about glory, and perpetually filled with a shrewd anxiety over finance. Paradoxically, she who had shrunk from war and from all perilous glories, had become the symbol of adventure in the Grand Manner, of Drake's great circumnavigation and of all Drake's gallant imitators, of the resounding defeat of the Armada and the splendid seizure of Cadiz, just as she was acclaimed as the shield and buckler of the Low Countries and the Huguenots. (And how she complained of lending money to these her Protestant—and improvident—allies!) Add to these trumpet calls of Fame, the more sober and solid advances in prosperity and culture, and he would not really be surprised if in the future, men would speak of an Elizabethan Age, and say that the last Tudor was the greatest. . . . But the Age was ending, and being succeeded by one which heeded rather practical money-making considerations than high-sounding exploits. He could imagine a future which would regard the West Country seamen's preying upon the plate fleets of Spain as scarcely better than piracy, and would regard with horror her Majesty's habit of jobbing out ships of the Royal Navy on these highly speculative and piratical ventures. Yes! The Age was ending, but he could spare a sigh for its splendours. The sixteenth century had been miraculous with its wonderful florescence of the New Learning, when mankind had challenged all the accepted beliefs and the horizons had fallen back. The seventeenth century would be very different. Perhaps *its* symbol would be the Puritan merchant, the Bible Christian who was also a shrewd man of business, who laid up for himself treasure in heaven and on earth. Had Essex been the epitome of the follies, the wild reckless extravagances of that Age which had lived so magnificently and heedlessly in the moment? Essex flinging the treasure to the men who had taken Cadiz was another symbol and one which must perish. But the splendours of the Age had gilded him too. When the Queen signed his death warrant, perhaps she was also signing the death warrant of the Elizabethan Age.

Cecil readily admitted that she had risen magnificently to the occasion. When she had heard of Essex in the city, she had wanted to ride out at the head of her troops, "to see what any rebel of them durst do against her". He, his brother Burghley and her Majesty's own cousin, the Lord Admiral, had had the greatest difficulty in staying her. The only satisfaction she must have got out of the sorry business was the people's loyalty to her. Essex might be their darling and their hero, but when they realized his purpose was treason, they refused to rise. She had stressed the point when the French Ambassador had hastened to visit her to commiserate and congratulate. The perfidious vanity of those foolish ingrates who sought to set themselves against the Crown! She began to describe contemptuously how the vainglorious young men had marched through the city calling upon it to rise, and the city had gaped at them for madmen. She jeered at them —but her laughter was hysterical. She was near breaking point, Cecil could only hope that she would endure till Essex had made final expiation on the scaffold. Somehow, he believed she would. She never failed her country, and it was the necessity of her country's peace and well-being, that Essex should die.

She had been calm and reasonable when he had visited her to discuss the preliminaries for the trial, but he had been struck by her appearance. To begin with, she had not the vestige of paint upon her face and her skin was like worn parchment. Her wig looked garish and ill kempt. Most noticeable, she had not changed her dress—one of black taffeta with broad golden bands—since the rising and it was sadly crumpled. He noticed a wine stain on the golden brocade at the wrist as if her hand had shaken when drinking. She needed a fresh ruff. It was obvious that one of the vainest women who had ever lived, who had always paid the most meticulous attention to her appearance, was completely unaware of how she looked.

He began to press for his cousin Francis Bacon to be appointed as second Counsel for the Crown in the trial, after the Attorney-General.

"Would he?" she asked flatly. "The Earl was his patron."

"He knows his true allegiance, your Majesty!"

"He wants money, I expect."

"Indeed, he does, your Majesty. He was seized for debt the other day and I had to get him released."

"Well—use him. 'Tis a wondrous intelligence. Most subtle."

"Most, your Majesty! Sir Edward Coke is very able but his manner is sometimes unfortunate. Violent—even brutal—and it is apt to create a prejudice in favour of the prisoner——"

"Who is, already, of a most dangerous popularity. . . . Well, Sir Robert! What does Master Bacon require—as his thirty pieces of silver?" Cecil gave a discreet giggle. "A thousand pounds?" she asked abruptly.

"Well, rather more than that, your Majesty. . . ."

"Certainly. To betray such a man as his Lordship of Essex is surely worth more than a paltry thousand! Two thousand, then?"

"Oh, no, your Majesty, not so much as that! Francis would be deeply content with fifteen hundred pounds."

She laughed. It was a horrid sound. He went on to discuss all the traitors except their principal.

"There are four very dangerous men, your Grace, who must be convicted. Henry Cuffe the chief secretary, who was the brains of the enterprise, and Sir Christopher Blount who was the chief advocate of this abominable violence."

"Blount by all means!" Her lips curled back in a snarl to show the blackened stumps of her teeth.

Blount was his name and blunt his nature, thought Cecil. He had most stupidly let a very dangerous cat out of the bag. . . . Whereas Essex with a species of crazy sincerity, and most of his followers with terrified emphasis, had declared that they meant no harm to her Majesty, Blount had roundly declared that if needs be they would have "drawn blood from her Majesty's self". There was little doubt that his wife was behind that. Lettice's furious hatred for her royal cousin had surely signed the death warrant for her "sweet Kit".

"Then there are Sir Charles Davers who has been Essex's right-hand man in all enterprises, and Sir Gilly Merrick——"

"He who ordered the playing of *Richard II*? By all means! See to it that they are all four convicted."

Sunset

"They will be, your Majesty. But one could recommend clemency in other cases, some of the young nobles, for example. One might even show mercy to Southampton."

"He is an emptiness, a nothing. Yet he is so deeply incriminated I do not see how he could escape the verdict in all fairness."

"Not the verdict, your Majesty. Your Majesty's prerogative of mercy——"

"Ah, my prerogative of mercy? It is a strange thing, Mr. Secretary, but I have never been able to exercise it for myself. . . . I will consider the case of the Earl of Southampton.

"Then there is the young Earl of Rutland and Lord Mounteagle."

"A child and another emptiness. . . . They will have had the sorest fright of their lives. Let them go with a fine!"

"I commend your Majesty's decision. Then there is the Lady Rich, and although there is no doubt she was a most active instigator of the rebellion, and as she persisted in remaining in Essex House when the other women were allowed to depart, was taken to the Tower, I could advise your Majesty to show her some mercy——"

"Let her out. Now."

"Without any further penalty?"

"Yes. She has been interrogated, I take it. Let her go. I know she is guilty—but Philip Sidney loved her once."

"I believe he did, your Majesty. They say she was the 'Stella' of his sonnets. . . . (How the old dwelt on the past!) But there is a more pregnant conclusion of the present day. No doubt your Majesty is aware that she is the mistress of Lord Mountjoy who is doing so exceedingly well in Ireland——"

"Yes, yes!" she brushed aside the present. "Let her go. She is the last of the 'Bullen women'. As wanton—and as unhappy as them all. . . ."

"Then, your Majesty, I will discuss their briefs with Sir Edward Coke and Francis, my cousin."

"Yes. Those four you named, condemned. Perhaps Southampton. . . . And——" She seemed to shrink into herself, writhing back in her chair as if in agony. Her eyes were closed. She could not say the name "Essex". Cecil bowed low and departed.

Behind their conversation had hovered the shadow of an unnamed figure—Lettice. Have you found me, O my enemy? "So long", she thought, "there has been that deadly struggle between us. It has ended now, and neither of us has won. We have both been most miserably defeated. . . ."

That evening she sat at supper with her ladies. She could eat little. Only some soup and a manchet of bread, with which she played, rather than ate. It was very quiet; her Majesty had refused her musicians and would not talk. Then suddenly sound came, from behind the door which gave on to the passage leading to the kitchen quarters. Feet clattered eagerly.

For one wild second she thought it was Essex. . . . So often he had burst in on her, unheralded, by back ways; he had risen from a bed of sickness to come and plead with her in his dressing-gown. . . . She clasped her hands together. "Oh, my child, my child, if you have indeed broken away—from my prison and from your vile friends— and come back to me, I'll save you! They shan't touch a hair of your head. . . . I'll keep you by me so long as I live. . . ." she thought. With the swiftness of thought, three of her Gentlemen Pensioners raced across the supper room with their drawn swords in their hands, and flung themselves through the door whence the sound came. Other sounds had succeeded those eager feet, a clank, a thud, an oath— "God damme!"—drowned by a gruff voice (belonging, she thought, to a senior Yeoman of the Guard): "Ah, would you?" and a scuffling sound which died away. She rose to her feet, snatching at the sword she had kept by her since the news of the rebellion. It was rusty, and came raspingly and unevenly from its scabbard. It was a sword Robert had given her, forty-two years ago, laid away as lumber for an immemorial time. . . . Here was Raleigh, Captain of her Guard, his chest heaving under his silver cuirass.

"Most dear and beloved Queen, thank God you're safe! The vile scoundrel Essex——"

"He's here? You've taken him?"

"Not he, your Majesty! He's under lock and key in the Tower, he'll never get out. . . . But the worst of his rogues, the desperado Lea, got into the kitchens, stole up by the scullions' stair, meaning to seize your Majesty and hold you at point of death till you signed a free pardon for Essex——"

She said deliriously: "So one was yet loyal to him?"

She was back in her larger Withdrawing Chamber with her agitated ladies about her when the full irony of the situation struck upon her. She had let herself believe that somehow he had come back to her, that any moment he would appear, throw his head on to her lap, wipe out this hideous nightmare—but it had only been a creature of his come to threaten her life. . . . He hated her! Hate was round her, a ring of demon faces grinning. Surely the tapestries moved, there was another lurking assassin behind. . . . She struck wildly, her blade piercing the hangings and jarring on the plaster behind. Again and again, she struck at the billowing hangings in a frenzy, scarcely aware of the agitated cries from her ladies, seeming to see Lettice's face grinning at her from the tapestry.

"Oh, your Grace—your Majesty—shall I call the Guard?—Oh, your Majesty, Madam!"

She swung round on them.

"Get out—you silly strumpets!"

She waved the sword at them and they fled headlong. Only the Countess of Warwick waited in the doorway. But she was past wanting Anne Warwick's sympathy.

"Go, I say! It isn't fit for the quick—to watch the sufferings of the damned in hell!"

"Hell, your Grace?"

"Aye, hell! Know you not 'Dr. Faustus'? '. . . for where we are is hell, and where hell is, there ever we must be. . . .' Leave me!!!"

Anne Warwick was gone. Elizabeth looked about her, at the flickering candle flames showing the ripped hangings. The sword fell out of her hand, to rattle on the floor. Oh, let them kill her if it would end this! She threw herself into a chair, her head on her arms murmuring the name of her dead love which was also the name of the man whom she had pretended was her son. . . . "Robert, Robert! Rob—come back to me!" But she was walled in by a huge silence.

It continued. Essex made no appeal to the day of his trial, when he and Southampton were charged before their Peers in Westminster Hall, with Sir Edward Coke and Francis Bacon as principal prosecutors for the Crown. The patient crowds waited for hours before the hearing, both within and without the walls; the Queen waited in Whitehall.

He would not beg his life from her, he would maintain this barrier of hatred and defiance. And yet, she felt a flicker of illogical pride in him that he would not cringe before his accusers, that he met them with the same superb swagger as he had assaulted Cadiz. The clouds and confusion had lifted from his brain when he was face to face with his enemies. The stag was at bay! When Walter Raleigh was brough to be sworn, he jogged the frightened Southampton with his elbow, declaring so half the Hall heard: "What boots it to swear the fox?" Contrasted with the obvious mortal terror of Southampton who palpably begged for his life, and assailed by the blunderous malevolence of Coke, sympathy mounted to that proud courage. "I am indifferent how I speed," he said. "I owe God a death. . . ." Coke was doing badly from sheer brutality. Cecil consulted behind the scenes and Francis Bacon was put on. "Now the serpent is the most subtle of the beasts of the field. . . ." Slowly but deftly he encompassed Essex in his toils. He gathered up all the loose ends and tied them into a noose. He built up the evidence, adding all its twos together to make a row of the fours of damnation, for a man to whom two and two had never made a simple four, for a man who had struggled for Bacon's advancement, even to the danger of losing her Majesty's favour, a man who had given to him so greatly and generously. It was done exquisitely, thought Robert Cecil, by a virtuoso whose instrument was the human intellect and its ingenuity. Only to the ordinary man, it stank to the heavens. . . .

The dark eyes of Essex were fixed on the prosecuting counsel with a strange intensity. "I call forth Master Bacon against Master Bacon," he said. Bacon brushed aside so pitiful a digression, what did it matter if once he had served the Earl?

The end was inevitable; conviction of high treason and the sentence of a traitor's death with its ghastly details of dismembering. It was the Victor of Cadiz who threw back his head and proudly answered: "I think it fitting that my poor quarters, which have done her Majesty true service in divers parts of the world, should now at the last be sacrificed and disposed of at her Majesty's pleasure. . . ."

He was cheered as he left the Hall to walk back to the Tower with the edge of the axe turned towards him, and his judges and the opposing Counsel had to be protected by soldiers. The situation, thought Cecil, was yet filled with peril. Supposing her Majesty delayed in signing the death warrant? One must remember her horror and the repeated cancellations of the warrant for the Duke of Norfolk, thirty years ago; the whole business of the death of the Queen of Scots!

But when the warrant was brought to her, she did not delay making the enormous ELIZABETH R. with all its loops and flourishes, on the crackling parchment. She could hear her own voice, young and eager as she rode through the city on the way to her Coronation.

"And persuade yourselves that for the safety and quietness of you all, I will not spare, if need be, to spend my blood."

How much more she had been asked to spend than her blood for the "safety and quietness of them all"! She had sacrificed her private happiness when she had not married Robert Dudley; she had sacrificed her peace of mind when she had consented to the death of the Queen of Scots; and now she was asked to sacrifice the blood of the dearest creature on earth. She could not be asked for yet another sacrifice, for there was not another to make. She had not broken her solemn pledge to her people; it was breaking her.

He made no plea for mercy. Was he still obdurate in hatred and defiance, or was he seeking to spare her? For if he had pleaded his life in the old terms of affection—— She shivered. She was spared that last anguish. But was he still filled with hate towards her? She did not know till just before the end.

He had made one request, for his chaplain, the Rev. Abdy Ashton, that most devout Puritan whom the Countess of Essex held in such esteem and affection. Ashton was permitted to go to him, and the day before he was to die, he asked for Cecil and three other councillors to come to him, and to them he said: "I am most bound unto her Majesty that it has pleased her to let me have this little man, Mr. Ashton, with me for my soul . . . in a few hours he has made me know my sins unto her Majesty and unto my God. . . ." Then he fell into the last and most terrible of all his frenzies, crying out upon all those who had driven him against her Majesty. His guilt was great, but so was theirs. With the fury of despair he cursed his stepfather, his followers such as Charles Davers, and Henry Cuffe to his face; even Penelope his sister was not spared. "Let her be looked to," he cried, "for she has a proud spirit!" The Lord Admiral, for one of his audience, was disgusted, declaring: "Who would have thought this weakness and unnaturalness in this man?"

But Elizabeth understood. He had made his last gesture to tell her that he had finally turned from Lettice and all her works, that he rejected in horror and despair those poisoned counsels which had separated them. At the end, he told her that in his strange way he was still hers, but he would spare her and his own honour, a plea for mercy. The next morning, standing on the scaffold on Tower Green (where Elizabeth had once expected to die) in his scarlet shirt, he again acknowledged his sins and confessed that he was "justly spewed out of the realm".

She heard the Maids of Honour whispering.

"My dear, the people at the back of the church started to murmur —like a rushing wind—as soon as the preacher commenced with his 'Ne pereat Israel; pereat Absolon!' "

"Out!" she cried upon them. "Out and do your foolish prattle beyond my hearing." They fled. Her Majesty was like a wild beast these days!

But she could not shut out that voice which assaulted her bruised heart. She sank into a chair and covered her face with her hands, feeling her tears burn as if they had become vitriol. That voice would not spare her, because it was the echo of her own soul. Israel must not perish: Absalom must perish. . . .

"And the king was much moved, and went up to the chamber over the gate, and wept; and as he went thus he said:

" 'O my son Absalom, my son, my son Absalom! Would God I had died for thee, O Absalom, my son, my son!' "

Chapter Eleven

The mechanism, being yet wound, continued to run. . . .
She felt this as the months succeeded each other. A great
stillness seemed to have fallen; it was only broken by
angry lampoons upon Cecil and his Colleagues:

> "Little Cecil trips up and down
> He rules both Court and Crown."

—and mournful ballads of the lost hero:

> "Sweet England's pride is gone!
> Welladay! Welladay!"

When she rode out at first, after the execution of Essex, she was received in a horrified silence. She thought: "They cannot see how I
had the strength to kill him! I did not know that I possessed it myself. . . ." But the mechanism still ran; she worked with her councillors, appreciated the perfect efficiency of "little Cecil" and rejoiced soberly over Mountjoy's success in Ireland. Sometimes she,
who had always enjoyed the society of boys and young men, shrank
from seeing any, especially those who had been companions or
associates of Essex. When her godson, Harington, for whom she had
had an amused affection since his childhood, came to court, she sent
him an angry message: "Go, tell that witty fellow, my Godson, that
it is no season to fool it here!" But later she relented and saw him.
The conversation drifted towards Tyrone, whom Mountjoy was
steadily driving back. Harington began eagerly to describe the Irish
leader in the hopes of diverting his godmother; he had been with
Essex during the treasonable meetings which had led to the truce. At
first she did seem interested in his description of Tyrone, his two

young sons and his wild Irish followers, but suddenly recollection smote her.

"Ah, that reminds me! You saw this man—elsewhere. . . ."

"Elsewhere" had been at the side of Essex; her eyes filled with tears to the distress of Harington.

They came to her, asking for her instructions to have the banner of Essex removed from the Chapel of the Order of the Garter at Windsor.

"Leave it hanging there."

"Leave it?"

"He served me well—once. . . . For the sake of his young son and his widow, I would not have that forgotten. I would have them know that I remember——"

Again she was to do more. Cecil came to her with great deprecation and patient persistence. He was building up a vast reputation for mercy. Southampton's death sentence had been commuted to one of imprisonment for life. ("My life," thought the Queen, "not his. My successor will set him free!") Besides Essex, only his stepfather Blount, Davers, Merrick, Cuffe and Lea were executed. Many escaped with a fine—and a fright. Now Cecil was cautiously making a plea on behalf of the widowed Countess. She was suffering from the persecution of a blackmailer and in despair had appealed to Cecil.

"Though her late husband was a condemned traitor, your Majesty, it is nevertheless a most unjust and abominable case, and it would create a most excellent impression if your Majesty——"

She waved aside the "excellent impression" and impatiently asked for the facts. On the sudden return of Essex from Ireland, his wife had sent certain letters out of Essex House, fearing lest it be searched, to be kept by a follower of his, one John Daniell. The letters were doubtless unfortunate—perhaps even treasonable. Cecil made a movement with his hands. Certainly they were dangerous, but it hardly excused the abominable conduct of Daniell who demanded three thousand pounds before he would return the letters. Otherwise he threatened to hand them over to the Council. The Countess of Essex was in straitened circumstances and could only raise a little more than half the sum demanded. The scoundrel sent her forged copies and then renewed his blackmail. In utter despair she had confided the case to Cecil. Although the letters were no doubt treasonable, he could recommend that her Majesty——

544

Sunset

"The carrion crow! Have him brought before the Star Chamber and prosecuted with the most extreme rigour possible!"

"I am happy to find your Majesty in such merciful agreement! Blackmailers are frequently pilloried and condemned to lose their ears——"

"Would he could lose his tongue too, vile carrion crow! The utmost rigour, remember! And, as no doubt the Star Chamber will order a heavy fine, at least two-thirds of it must be paid to the Countess."

Daniell did have his ears sliced off in the pillory, and was compelled to pay two thousand pounds to the Countess of Essex, who wrote a grateful letter to Cecil. Then she and her children seemed to sink once more beneath Elizabeth's horizon, living as they did in rural retirement. Another figure—one of baffled impotent hatred—had also disappeared from Elizabeth's sight, the figure of Lettice. Elizabeth thought: "She and I have now done each other all the harm possible in our two lives." Elizabeth had passed into a strange void beyond love and hate, a void beyond life itself.

Sometimes she seemed to be watching life as if from far-off windows, and such a melancholy seized her, that it appeared she had plumbed the depths of despair. At other times life was nearer, as if only a pane of glass separated her. Then the heavy atmosphere of the court would lift and all was "frolick" there. She would sit, her fingers eagerly tapping out the rhythm on the arms of her chair, as her courtiers and ladies stepped the dance before her. No Pavane of Tears, no solemn measure, but the light and joyful movements of country dances were what she wanted to see. The music—gay, lilting, and young—could disperse all melancholy, letting her spirit cast down its burdens and spring too. But she could rarely dance herself, and suddenly she would realize that the dancers and their happy youth were cut off from her, that there was no one waiting by her chair except that deformed little man with the charming manners who could make a witty comment as deftly as he handled the reins of government. Then another sort of melancholy seized her, a desperate hunger for the youth and gaiety forever lost, a longing for life itself at its most ardent. Why should she want her youth again? It had been shadowed and bitter, from the age of fifteen a relentless battlefield! Did she want a second chance—to try and gain what she had now lost?

That was when she felt that life was slipping so quickly through her fingers, and she snatched at it in terror. She had won her outward battles, the glories had piled up for her Crown—but what was left to her but this strange stillness holding the echoes of the past? She had enjoyed some of that upward climb, the triumphs, the won battles. She had gloried in her Crown and had taken pride in her conception of sovereignty as a sacred office. This she would never deny. But now she seemed to have gained the top of a high mountain and she was tired—and completely alone.

Since she had come to the throne over forty years ago, she had only leaned in affairs of State on the reason and shrewd kindliness of Burghley. Since he had died, she knew she must face all decisions alone. She might—and did—have a good opinion of his son's efficiency and intelligence but how much more she knew than any of these young men, how much more she had forgotten than perhaps they would ever learn! But in her private life she had been aloof from everyone except Robert. Only to him, had she ever dared to give way, to tell him of her fears, pains and anxieties. But he was dead. They were all dead. Her lover, her friend—and the son of her imagination. To whom might she turn?

She had never been a "woman's woman". Anne Warwick and she knew each other very well, but they did not talk of their knowledge. She preferred to have Anne by her, but she could not see herself pouring out agonized confidences in her ear. The only woman close to her had been Ashley, dead thirty-six years ago. She could still hear that fat comfortable voice saying "my dearest child!" But even then, even on that night in the Charterhouse when she had come to London at the beginning of her reign, she had said: "No one else but you says it. You won't say it much longer. . . ."

But sometimes she had to talk and given vent to her thoughts and memories, seeming to choose people who only moved casually into her orbit, as if she had run out into the streets and laid her hand on a passer-by. The French Ambassador, de Maisse, found she would talk incessantly, on all subjects except those his diplomacy desired to broach. She showed strange sides to her nature, strange and unexpected. He had always heard of her as one of the vainest women in the world, surrounded by a web spun from golden dazzling flatteries. Now she said: "I was never beautiful. Oh, no! But I had the reputation of it in my youth." And she had laughed happily as if at some memory.

Sunset

She also confided in him the agonies of soul she had undergone when waiting for death in the Tower at the age of twenty. She still dreamed of it she told him, but she did not tell him that nowadays in that dream, it was Essex kneeling on the scaffold, and she would wake out of it with a violent start, to light her candles and stare with defiant horror at the darkness. Yes, the nights were not easy. . . . With an indescribable sadness she told de Maisse, that she herself was partly to blame for the fall of Essex; she had made too much of him. If it had been possible to spare his life without danger to the State she would have done it, for all his ingratitude to her.

Another day, Anne Warwick came to her and told her that the Keeper of the Records of the Tower, the learned Antiquary, William Lambarde, had made a book of his researches and desired to present it to her Majesty. He had asked the Countess of Warwick to give it to the Queen.

"Let him bring it himself, if he so wills!"

When the old scholar was brought to her presence, she greeted him with the warmest smile.

"Good Master Lambarde, you intended to present this book unto me, by the Countess of Warwick," she said, "but I will none of that, for if any subject of mine do me a service, I will thankfully accept it from his own hands."

She took the book from him and began to read it aloud, pausing to ask the delighted Lambarde the meaning of different technical phrases, saying with a smile that she would be a scholar in her old age and thought it no scorn to learn.

"I am", she said, "of the mind of that philosopher who in his last years began with the Greek alphabet."

But she had come to that part of the book which dealt with the unhappy reign of Richard II and her face darkened.

"I am Richard II," she said, "know you not?"

"It was the wicked imagination of a most unkind gentleman!" declared Lambarde with uneasy fervour. "The most adorned creature that ever your Majesty made!" He was horrified to see the tears fill her eyes.

"He that will forget God", she said slowly, "will also forget his benefactor. . . ."

But her love for her people still burned like an undying flame. To them she would give all that was left. She was having less difficulty this last year or so with the House of Commons. In the previous Parliament, she had been voted a triple subsidy, and now when the news was received of a Spanish army landing at Kinsale to support and encourage the faltering Tyrone, she was voted a fourfold subsidy. But as she had foretold, the more money her "Faithful Commons" voted for the costs of government, the more responsibility they would demand in administration. The session had not long commenced, when a member arose to attack the system of monopolies, which was part of the Royal Prerogative, and a most unpopular one.

A monopoly was a royal grant for the sole right to make or sell certain articles. To a sovereign perpetually short of ready money it was the only way of rewarding either faithful service or personal favourites. Leicester's fortune had been built up upon such grants. As they were farmed out several times through a series of middlemen, each of whom tried to squeeze out more money, the system was riddled with abuses. And now the House of Commons demanded that this system must either be reformed out of recognition—or go! Tempers rose to boiling point in the House despite the efforts of her Majesty's councillors. One angry Member declared that bread would soon become a monopoly. Cecil went to the Queen and told her that he had never seen the Commons in such a frenzy. She smiled.

"Little man, little man! When you have lived as long as I, and have had as many years' experience of the faithful Commons, you will understand their frenzies." She added: "Their day is coming and coming fast. It will be stayed only so long as I live."

Cecil frowned. She did not seem to understand that something must be done immediately. She was so old! She seemed to be failing physically faster every day. When she had opened this very Parliament, and had risen to make her speech from the Throne, in her resplendent robes and crown, she had suddenly staggered as if overcome, and it seemed that if certain gentlemen had not hastened to support her she would have fallen. Had she addressed her last Parliament? He gave her a shrewd searching glance which was countered by that level comprehension which seemed to hold the ghost of mockery.

"These abuses must be remedied," she said. "And at once. Tell the House that I will issue a Proclamation promising immediate reform."

When he came again to her, he was in a different mood.

"Your Majesty, the hearts of the Members are so full that some of them wept, and they prayed aloud for your Majesty's preservation. Mr. Speaker entreats that he may lead a deputation to give thanks to your Majesty."

"When the Proclamation has been issued I will gladly receive their loves and their thanks."

Cecil looked at her. She had done it again—the incredible old woman! Her yielding, as his father had once said, was a sign of strength. There was a sparkle in those deeply sunken eyes and her lips were curling into something approaching a grin.

"Little man! I dealt with the House of Commons before you were breeched!" But she patted his cheek.

When the Speaker was choosing his delegation, there were repeated shouts of "All! All!" and he sent to ask whether her Gracious and Beloved Majesty would receive the entire one hundred and forty Members? To which she replied that the accommodation was limited but they were all very welcome.

As her "Faithful Commons" knelt before her in the Presence Chamber at Whitehall, while their Speaker made his oration, she realized that this was her last Parliament, that in all probability she would never have a chance again to address her people through these, their chosen representatives. She must speak to them of all that was in her heart; she must testify to her faith in her sacred office of sovereignty and her devotion to her people; she must try while the time yet remained to her, for time buried all things and the years would lie like fallen leaves upon her work. She began:

"Mr. Speaker, we perceive your coming is to present thanks to us. Know I accept them with no less joy than your loves can have desire to offer such a present, and do more esteem it than any treasure or riches. . . ." She was speaking to them, as she had once spoken at Tilbury, but with a fervour which came from the knowledge of time's passing. "And though God hath raised me high, yet this I account the glory of my crown, that I have reigned with your loves. . . ." She must make her testament of kingship—"my heart was never set upon any worldly goods, but only for my subjects' good. What you do bestow on me, I will not hoard up, but receive it to bestow on you again, yea my own properties I account yours, to be expended for your good, and your eyes shall see the bestowing of it for your welfare."

Leaning forward, she beckoned the kneeling men to rise and stand for she would yet speak longer. They had come to thank her, but she told them that she would rather thank them for bringing such grievances and abuses to her knowledge; she spoke to them awhile of the burdens and duties of a crown, likening them to the drugs prescribed for a sick man, pills gilded over to hide their bitterness, as the outward glories of a crown concealed its cares and troubles. And when she came to end this, which posterity would call her Golden Speech, the passion which rang in her voice performed a miracle, for it became as young and fervent again as the voice of that girl of twenty-five who had ridden through London on her way to be crowned.

"And though you have had, and may have, many mightier and wiser princes sitting in this seat, yet you never had, nor shall have any that will love you better."

And so she made her farewell, asking the Speaker in a voice that had suddenly become old and weary again, to bring these gentlemen to kiss her hand before they left. They kissed it, the one hundred and forty of her faithful, though troublesome Commons, and then to the sound of trumpets, she left the Presence Chamber.

That evening, as she rested against her pillows (for she was weary beyond description) the Countess of Warwick came to her.

"Your Grace, Sir Robert Cecil asked me to tell you of the dispatches from Ireland."

"To-morrow I will see them. I am—too tired, now."

"Sir Robert would not think to weary you with them now. He only wishes you to hear the good news. Lord Mountjoy has defeated the Spanish army in a pitched battle and it has unconditionally capitulated."

The Christmas of 1602 passed with the accustomed twelve days of feasting and junketing at Whitehall. Then when the New Year came she decided to go to the Palace of Richmond. It would be, she said, a "warm winter box" for her old age. She expressed the wish to make the journey in the saddle and not by coach although it was a bitter, freezing day. Her cousin, the Lord Admiral, expostulated bluntly with her. It was not for one of her years to ride on such a day. With a flash of her old spirit, she exclaimed: "My years! Maids! Get to your horses." And when she was mounted, she went at so round a pace that her retinue was hard put to keep up with her.

"Body o' me!" gasped Mary Fitton to Bess Brydges. "If I can gallop like that when *I*'m seventy!"

Sunset

She had ridden her horse to a standstill by the time they reached Richmond. "Whether her Majesty was weary or not", said Robert Cecil, "I leave to your censure...." But it was the last time she ever went on horseback, for at Richmond, that February 1603, a strange lassitude and exhaustion fell upon her. She scarcely complained of any symptoms except an inflammation of the throat which gave her fever, but her strength seemed to be draining from her. Impatiently she waved away her physicians. She knew her own constitution better than they did, she said. But she felt as if she had fallen into an abyss between life and death.

Once a human being tried to reach out across that gulf of despair. Her godson, John Harington, was kneeling beside her, as she sat on a pile of cushions on the floor. He was trying to make her smile, trying to divert that black cloud of melancholy, reading her some of his humorous verses which always used to make her laugh. Laugh.... How she had once laughed, she and Robert when they were young—bantering and mocking the solemn, teasing and joking each other! Memory swirled giddily, of herself on her cushions like this, with Robert's arm round her waist and his voice was whispering in her ear: "Listen, sweet! There was once the thinnest tapster in the world and he served in an ale house near the Paris Garden. A drab came to order a pot of March ale and she was as fat as he was thin and she said . . ." But she could not remember what the fat drab said to the thin tapster, all now left was the dregs of memory, of two ghosts, an eager red-headed girl laughing with her handsome lover. . . . They were as real as Jack Harington reading his verse—or rather as unreal—for all things about her were phantoms. She made the movements of her face which should create a smile and said: "Boy Jack, when you feel creeping Time at your gate, these fooleries will please you less. I am past my relish for such matters." He turned quickly away but not before she saw the tears suddenly start in his horrified eyes. That evening he wrote sadly to his wife in the country:

"Our dear Queen doth now bear the show of human infirmity; too fast for that evil which we shall get by her death, and too slow for that good that she shall get by her releasement from pains and misery...."

She had pain; one of her fingers was hurting her intolerably. She stared at it, and saw that her Coronation Ring which she had not taken off for forty-four years had grown into the flesh. It was the

symbol of her marriage to the realm, and that marriage would so soon
be dissolved. . . . She offered no resistance when her ladies were for
fetching a goldsmith to file it off. She put out her hand for the man,
thinking that Time which had defaced so much, had left some of the
beauty of her hands, had distorted them but very little as if in
mockery. The ring was filed in two halves and she picked it up. Well!
Yet another thing had ended.

That night she was tormented by a feverish confusion of nightmare, when faces bobbed up and down like the masks of devils
against a world which was being fast drowned by smoke and flame,
and she saw Essex on the scaffold and tried to save him but a voice
cried: "He is dying for the deaths of Amy Dudley and Mary Stuart
your cousin!" and Robert was staring at her with that dreadful shut
defiance which had been on his face the day she had discovered he
had married Lettice. And finally there was Lettice, jeering like a
demon: "You are a barren stock, you have nothing, nothing! They
are both mine!" Then she was alone in a ring of flames which had
destroyed the world, licking up all the kindness, all the tenderness
and goodness, so that she was alone, alone, alone!

She awoke and demanded to get up. She could stay no longer in
her bed. Her ladies would not wish to stay in their beds if they saw
such things in them as she did! After that she remained on a low chair
or on a pile of cushions on the floor, refusing food and drink and
medical attention. Her brain fought the phantoms. If only there was
one person left who cared for her and not for her Crown! Anne
Warwick had been away from her for the past week or two, by
reason of illness. All the others were peering with agitation and heartless curiosity, their thoughts towards the rising sun in Scotland. Yes,
he would come soon, that son of Mary Stuart! She had once said to
Robert: "The King of England was born in Edinburgh——" How
would he deal with her beloved people? He would never understand
them but he was the best choice possible, he would have that clever
little man Cecil—she was certain that Cecil was in close touch with
him as Cecil's father had once been with her when her sister lay
dying. . . . James was shrewd and had picked his way carefully between the violence of his nobles and the domination of the Kirk.

Unlovely and unlovable though he was, his very vices of cowardice
and avarice would keep him from wars and perilous adventures. She
had given her people the chance to stand on their own feet, and the

days of absolute monarchy were ending. Her "Faithful Commons" were greedy for power. And James's two eldest children were beautiful young creatures, full of hope for the future. He had given them royal English names which the Tudors in their turn had taken from the great Plantagenets. Henry and Elizabeth. There was a third child, a boy, a sickly baby called Charles, but he was not expected to live long. She need not concern herself with Charles! Young Henry Stuart was a lovely lad, filled with promise. A little ease crept into her mind, but her women were fussing at her. No! She would not go to bed! She wished to rise to her feet and stand but she could not raise herself from the low chair. Peremptorily she ordered her women to draw her up. She would meet this thing called Death on her feet!

Standing up at last, she braced her muscles for a final effort. Come, Death! Make an end! Why tarry so? What had she now to live for? Her courage had come back, but Death did not come. Hours passed without number; the candles dipped and swayed as she heard agitated whispering about her; clocks chimed and struck. She clenched her fists and leaned back against the wall. Would the end never come? Ah, yes! The scaffold was more merciful than this!

At last—after fifteen hours, her terrified women whispered—her aching muscles gave way and she sank to the cushions on the floor. Yet she lived and her release did not come. More people were beside her, asking her if she desired her chaplains, or the Archbishop of Canterbury who was waiting. "No!" she muttered. Since life remained to her, she would still hold a little longer to the things of this world. Would she have her musicians? She inclined her head. The cool fluting of the recorders seemed to soothe her.

But still one more person was kneeling by her, and his voice was so insistent that she could not escape it. It was Robert Cecil.

"Your Majesty, to content the people you *must* go to bed!"

So he thought he could impose his will on hers? She raised herself as much as she could on one elbow, and summoned her last strength.

"Little man, little man! The word 'must' is not used to princes!" Bitterly she whispered: "If your father had lived, you durst not have said so much, but you know I must die and that makes you presumptuous!"

He had gone now, and the women were arranging the cushions under her head. But Cecil came back and there was another with him, a face which looked at her with genuine affection and pity, her cousin the Lord Admiral. He had been away from court as his wife had just died. He took her hands and she realized for the first time how cold and stiff they were in contrast to his warm strength. He was talking urgently, telling her to go to bed and let her physicians come to her. She must make a fight of it, and she would recover yet! Where was her wonted courage?

"The case", she said, "is altered with me. . . ."

He had his arm round her shoulders now to raise her, and began to spoon some hot liquid into her mouth. She thought it was broth but she could hardly taste; yet she did not resist this last kindness. Then he laid down the spoon and she saw him make a sign with his hand. His other arm tightened round her shoulders; he was lifting her and other people were taking her legs to carry her. Well, she would not resist this. . . .

She was lying in her bed at last, and her councillors were gathered at the foot. When before had she seen that look of cold calculation on the face of Robert Cecil? She could not remember. He was asking her to appoint her Successor.

"The King of France?" he tried her, as a test of sanity.

A frown flickered over her face. Did he think her mad? He asked her other names. Her cousin, Lady Arabella Stuart, or the descendants of another cousin, Catherine Grey, by her marriage with the Earl of Hertford, a marriage she had held as illegal. She whispered angrily: "I'll have no rascal's son——!"

"The King of Scots?"

She tried to say: "A king shall sit in my seat which has been the seat of kings," but she did not know whether her voice was audible. She moved her hands, and the watchers saw her make a strange gesture as if she had lifted an invisible crown from her head.

They had left her now; she had performed her last royal duty. Cecil sat at his desk, smiling gently. How long that old woman took to die! How much strength there had been in her. . . . But he had sent a draft of the Proclamation of James as King of England all the way to Edinburgh where it must make glorious reading together with his news that the Queen could only live a day or so longer. Yes! All his plans were coming to fruition and he might soon go forward into the New Age. The Garter, an earldom, what might not the grateful James do for him? And he would be the supreme power in the State. There was no rival left. He had dreaded Raleigh, but now he had settled *that* too. A word or two of warning of Raleigh's ambition and vanity to the King of Scots, more vigorous words from his trusty follower, Lord Henry Howard, and the thing was done. King James would never trust Raleigh. If God had made him small and crooked, He had given him a tenfold better brain than these strong, straight, handsome men. . . .

She had finally done with the things of this world, and her Archbishop of Canterbury, John Whitgift, one of the strongest and most zealous men who had built her new Church, was kneeling by her bed. He was praising her, telling her all she had done for the Reformed Faith.

"My Lord," she whispered, "the crown I have borne so long has given enough of vanity in my time. I beseech you not to augment it in this hour when I am so near my death."

Perhaps she had neglected things spiritual in her struggle to maintain her trust to her people. She believed she might account in all honesty to God that she had done her best for them, however much it had cost her. She had been a grievous sinner in many other things without doubt, but there she had been faithful unto death. She had tried to build a Church which would shelter all; a hope of youth perhaps, but it had sheltered many. Again she had done her best; if she had erred, perchance she had thought more of her people than of her God. And now she was losing her people. They would be looking northwards, they would forget. Over seventy-five years ago, a man who had adored her enchanting, wayward, wanton, unhappy mother, had written her a poem.

> "Forget not yet the tried intent,
> Of such a truth as I have meant,
> My great travail so gladly spent.
> Forget not yet!"

The beloved object, man, woman or country forgot so soon! But her travail for her country had been gladly spent. She would not count its cost. She tried to fix her fading thoughts on Whitgift's prayers. Surely she needed mercy! There had been the death of Robert's wife. She had paid for that, again and again, but she would not evade moral responsibility. Then there had been the death of Mary Stuart, Queen of Scots. She had let Walsingham hunt her and trap her to her death. . . . Perhaps she had even been innocent, perhaps that letter had been forged. . . . But Mary's death had given England peace and security. . . .

The dying woman knew she should be praying for herself, but she was praying still for her country. Let James deal gently with it, let it be strong, peaceful and happy! If she had done much which was wrong for it, let her be the one to pay, not the country! Set a wall about it O Lord and evermore mightily defend it. . . . She would be scapegoat gladly, now and in eternity if the country might escape suffering!

But the burden seemed to be slipping from her, and the prayers of the old man were fading from her ears. She thought that she walked again in the gardens at Hatfield and Robert had his arms around her and was saying: "I love you!" and she knew it was the truth. But time had ceased to be a river flowing on, its waters were mingled, for the sky was filled with the brightness of the captured banners of the Spanish Armada borne in triumph before her, and behind her rode Essex, and he was twenty again, unshadowed and hopeful. Then these too faded, for the things of this world were with her no longer.

Epilogue

There was a strange figure in Whitehall, waddling and unlovely in its padded and quilted suit, strange beside the memory of that once eager and graceful young woman with the copper-bright hair. James, King of Scotland and England by the Grace of God, had arrived to take up his new inheritance. His wife, that floridly pretty Danish woman, who was already beginning to drown her distaste for her husband in strong waters, and his two beautiful children to whom the English looked in such hope, were exclaiming rapturously at the new possessions. Queen Anne could not get over the old Queen's three thousand dresses and eighty wigs!

"James, have you ever seen such things?"

"Wheesht woman! I maun ha' an inventory made o' her jewellery. 'Tis mair to the point. There are my mither's ain pear-rls which the Pope Clement gaed to his niece Catherine de Medici and she gaed them to my mither. And they were sold to Queen Elizabeth for a guid sum, aye—a ver-ry guid sum! And noo' I ha' them again!"

But now he was questioning that admirable man, Sir Robert Cecil.

"Weel, Sir Robert! Soon to be my Lor-rd, eh? Bearing in mind the words o' the blessed Scriptures—'where the treasure is, there will the heart be also'—I am desirous of opening the wee kist by her late Majesty's bedside."

"The little pearwood chest, your Majesty?" hazarded Cecil.

"Aye! The wee pearwood kist. . . . Maybe 'twill be mair jewellery."

But he was disappointed. It only contained a few sheets of paper with faded writing upon them. He took one up and read: "*How my gracious lady doeth and what ease of her late pain she finds, it being the chiefest thing in the world I do pray for. . . .*" He turned it over. He

557

could recognize the Queen's strong writing on the outside. "HIS LAST LETTER." But Robert Cecil had recognized both hands.

"Your Majesty, it is a letter from the late Earl of Leicester to her late Majesty!"

"Oh, aye!" James was reflecting. He was remembering those dreadful letters in the silver casket which his mother was supposed to have written. He had burned them; perhaps the most honest thing he had ever done for his mother. But he would do more for her now; he would have her body brought from Peterborough and buried in the chapel of her ancestor, Henry VII, at Westminster Abbey, where he would so soon be crowned. He would bury his mother one side of the chapel, and Queen Elizabeth the other, so that the two cousins who had been opponents in life, would lie near to each other in death. And he would erect a fine marble monument over each. Perhaps it was the least as well as the last thing he could do for either. . . .

"Aye!" he said again. "I'm thinking. Was there no' a fearfu' lot of talk o' her late Majesty and the Air-rl o' Leicester?"

"Well, yes, your Majesty. A long time ago."

"A long time ago. True." He added piously: "De mortuis nil nisi bonum. . . ."

"Your Majesty's gracious humanity is only equalled by your scholarship!"

On 28th April 1603, Queen Elizabeth came again to Westminster Abbey, to lie for the rest of time near the altar where she had sworn her oath to her beloved people. Stow, the chronicler, described her funeral procession thus:

"At which time the City of Westminster was surcharged with multitudes of all sorts of people, in the streets, houses, windows, leads and gutters to see the obsequy. And when they beheld her statue and effigy, lying on the coffin, set forth in royal robes, having a crown on the head thereof, and a ball and sceptre in either hand, there was such a general sighing, groaning and weeping as the like hath not been seen or known in the memory of man; neither does history mention any people, time or state, to make like lamentation for the death of their sovereign. . . ."

29th July 1948

Apple Tree Cottage,
Rowledge.